£1

Belmundus

by
Edward C. Patterson

Belmundus
Book One of the Farn Triology
by
Edward C. Patterson

Dancaster Creative
www.dancaster.com
edwpat@att.net

First Kindle Original Edition, March 2013
Copyright 2013 by Edward C. Patterson

Other Works by Edward C. Patterson
No Irish Need Apply **ISBN 1434893952**
Cutting the Cheese **ISBN 1434893847**
Bobby's Trace **ISBN 1434893960**
The Closet Clandestine: a queer steps out **ISBN 1438220502**
Come, Wewoka & Diary of Medicine Flower **ISBN 1438227639**
Surviving an American Gulag **ISBN 1438247230**
Turning Idolater **ISBN 1440422109**
Look Away Silence **ISBN 1448651921**
The Road to Grafenwöhr **ISBN 1460973860**
Are You Still Submitting Your Work to a Traditional Publisher? **ISBN 1441407383**
A Reader's Guide to Author's Jargon and Other Ravings from the Blogosphere **ISBN 1468071432**
Oh Dainty Triolet **ISBN 1451535376**

Farn Trilogy
Belmundus – The Farn Trilogy – Book I
Boots of Montjoy – The Farn Trilogy – Book II
The Adumbration of Zin – The Farn Trilogy – Book III

Southern Swallow Series
The Academician - Southern Swallow Book I, **ISBN 144149975X**
The Nan Tu - Southern Swallow Book II, **ISBN 1449994202**
Swan Cloud – Southern Swallow Book III **ISBN 1466499591**
The House of Green Waters — Southern Swallow Book IV
Vagrants Hollow — Southern Swallow Book V

The Jade Owl Legacy Series
The Jade Owl **ISBN 1440447977**
The Third Peregrination **ISBN 1441456724**
The Dragon's Pool **ISBN 1442170999**
The People's Treasure **ISBN 1453850813**
*In the Shadow of Her Hem — **ISBN 1478203064***

Coming Attractions

Green Folly
Nicholas Firestone – China Hand series
Pacific Crimson — Forget Me Not
Dearest Flower of My Heart — Mail Call from Two Generations
Plum Flower Journey

For further information contact *edwpat@att.net*
or visit Dancaster Creative at www.dancaster.com

To the Living Legacy of the Cherokee People

And to my Native American Great Grandmother

Lillian Devereaux Patterson

(Dawes Roll #8721 — M2139

Acknowledgements

The creation of this work has spanned many years — my entire creative life, in fact, born in my noggin as I walked back and forth to school in the late-1950s and riding the subway in the mid-1960s, realized in many forms — an epic poem, an opera libretto and finally a novella called *Adrift in Eternity*. I suppose the inspiration came from Voltaire's *Candide*. I was not up to completing it in then. Another imaginative strand hit to me in the early 1970s with the completion of an unpublished novel on Native American themes called *The Nioche*. Both ideas lay fallow but on fertile soil until 2003, when I married them to the protagonist — a young A-list actor who, like Gulliver or Alice, manages to get wedged in a strange world — *Farn*, a canvas for recurring themes immersed in my Cherokee family heritage and culture. My love of words has engaged me in ways that I scarcely understand, but I have allowed Father Tolkien to lead me into that light. So I offer my readers a passport into this world, born in my imagination.

I would like to thank my friend, Margaret Stevens (Peg) for her constant support and word wizardry. Peg has stuck with me as an adviser and reader through my entire published career. I would also like to thank Sharon Schroeder, who first glimpsed an early draft as a beta-reader back in 2003 and encouraged me to forge on to completion.

I have dedicated this work to a woman I have never met — Lillian Devereaux Patterson, my great-grandmother, who's presence on the Cherokee rolls has inspired my study of native customs and the *Tsalagi* language. Despite this, *Belmundus* is an epic fantasy, meant to engage and entertain my readers. It is not designed as a history lesson or a critical indictment of one people against another. On the other hand, any idea rattling around an author's head for fifty-five years should be provocative, so be prepared for a jolt.

Adadooski.
Arkmo.

Edward C. Patterson
March 2, 2013

"Nine Houses Has Farn
Nine houses rule the world of Farn
Balanced in perpetuum
About Primordius Centrum —
Volcanum holds the firebrands,
Aquilium has the waters' keep,
In Aolium's realm the air depends,
While Terrastrium mines the earthen halls.
Montjoy lifts the orb of art,
Protractus totes and measures all.
And Magus weilds the wands of time
While Pontifrax chants the holy rites
To draw the portals twain aligned
Into Zin and Zacker's care,
Beyond the darkest brightest lair."

from The Book of Farn — The Realms

To each Elector three branches made
Deigned as sons and daughters born,
Renowned Sceptas and Seneschals
But as towers apart shall grow,
Never fruitful within their bounds,
So to the outlands they must go,
To gather succor into dough —
The life force must they always hoe.
But each may draw a double mate,
And thus may sow and populate,
A harvest to serve and ease their shade —
A scattered horde as duty paid,
Smiling kin for the alliance trade,
But as mules these Thirdlings be,
Until there comes the mending free.
Then a fourth shall bloom in Farn
Uniting houses — the outlands darn
'til suns and moons reflect no more
And Zin and Zacker close the door.

from The Book of Farn — The Promise and Prophecy

"Dsulasi dona owaynasa,
Ulushoo ita ha yeeyasa,
Awaydeesga akali
Ustigunana digaswosdi"

"My feet go far from home,
I fall because I roam,
I tote my people's load,
Along the weeping road."

from a Cetrone Folk Song — the Weeping Road

Amaykwohi

Waydeelagu

Yuganavra

Yuyutla

Ayelli

MONTJOY CITY

Kalugu

Forling

Farn

Table of Contents

Part I: The Audition

Part II: Exploring the Part

Part III: Takes and Retakes

Part I

The Audition

Chapter One

Astral Beauties

1

"I'm a star," he whispered to the young man in the mirror. "A star," and then chuckled as he thought about a giant gas ball, ignorantly fixing planets in orbit for no other reason but gravity.

Harris Cartwright, born nineteen years earlier and christened Humphrey Kopfstutter, smiled dimly in the mirror. Dimly, because the hotel room shone amber with its upscale ambience — flattering light designed to be so. Still, in any light, this *star* of stage and screen was a Narcissus; although his reflection sometimes tamed him.

Harris moistened his bottom lip with his upper, and then winked. He shrugged, and then preened, coming closer to his reflection, nearly kissing the glass. Pucker he did; then laughed. His grin exposed a brilliant smile, a gap between his two front teeth — a chasm his mother meant to have corrected when he had landed his first role as a wee urchin in a Dickens remake. However, the gap and his alluring eyes kept the roles coming until . . . well, until the adolescent leaped the gulf between child actor and teen idol; done with ease and without scandal, drugs or an arrest record. Now Harris leaped the second gulf — youthful high school parts to the dashing hero. Still, he could hide his secrets safely from public view — although the public pried.

He winked again, and then turned around on the stool, which faced the dressing table. The hotel was accommodating — equipped for a range of actors from A-list to C, now that the Tribeca Film Festival had rolled in this town. The SoHo Grand, the classiest bed roll in this lower Manhattan neighborhood, had no vacancies this weekend.

Harris stood and stretched. He had slept the day away and, now as evening hugged the New York skyline, he was up for nocturnal festivities — a sneak preview of his new film *The Magic Planet* to be followed by a Q&A panel and light refreshments. Who knew what would come beyond that? These junkets were regulated to a point, but burst like fireworks when the rockets spent. Harris might take an evening romp with his co-star. The prospects loomed, so

Harris stretched, chucked his underwear, and then headed for the shower.

2

The hotel room was small by luxury standards, but the Grand had arisen like morning cream. The warm rooms shimmered with golden walls and amber lighting. All that wasn't silk, was satin. When not occupied by a nineteen-year old, the king size bed wore an olive satin spread, seagreen silk sheets, a princely counterpane and stately pillows. Now the bedding was tossed asunder as if cats had fought in the sack. Clothes were strewn on the floor in a trail from dresser to bed, from bed to shower. Books and scripts kiltered in piles on the dressing table, and the telephone directory sprawled beside a tray with last night's room service caking in partnership with this morning's breakfast. No lunch — evidently.

The shower room opened directly into the boudoir, a glass panel separating it from the minibar. To Harris, the steaming water would be his wake-up call. He wasn't sure what time it was (and he didn't worry, because Tony watched those details). However, a schedule would kick in eventually. It always did on publicity junkets. Soon, a flock of studio bullies, who, as well-meaning as they pretended to be, would erase his freedom. They were the paycheck, after all, and who was he?

"I'm a star," he gurgled, spitting out a mouthful of amber water. He laughed again, the stream plastering his curly hair into black slick. He shook the cascades from his eyes and laughed again, and then ran a soapy cloth over his newfound biceps. His last flick demanded his body beef up from a teenage lanky noodle to a swashbuckling space pirate. He was unaccustomed to the added musculature, although the chicks dug it.

At the thought of *chicks,* Harris smiled, leaning against the glass wall and letting the shower permeate every pore — every crevice. He felt giddy, his hormones having run the gamut of sexual urges and experiences lately. Still, he refused to declare a preference in public. He couldn't even admit his affinities in the shower stall, because he wasn't sure he had a preference — a weather vane at times; at other times, as sure as the partner who shared his bed. One thing was positive. He hadn't time to ponder the issue now or do more than scrub his groin in this shower-call.

"Maybe later," he mused, and then hastened to finish, turning the taps and waiting for the steam to clear.

Harris reached for a towel — a preliminary dry, beginning with face and hair, and then creating a silly turban, which didn't squat well on his noggin. He grabbed a second towel for his nether parts, marrying this more ample terry around his waist into something akin to Pharaoh's kilt.

"A star," he said again, and then slid open the glass door.

The room's chill met him and he noticed something queer. On the shower door, written in the condensation, were letters. He squinted, thinking he might have accidentally etched these sigils, but he hadn't. These *were* letters — clear and definite.

C U L8R C M J

"What the fuck?" he said, pawing the initials. "See you later — CMJ?"

He turned, looking for uninvited company.

"Tony?" he called. "Are you here?"

Harris inspected the room, walking over his debris, pushing linen with his feet and picking up his clothes as he went. Opening the closet door cautiously, he expected to encounter Anthony Bentley-Jones, his co-star and best friend. A joke, perhaps. However, the closet, devoid of actors, contained only tonight's wardrobe.

Harris threw off the turban, and then returned to the shower door, hunkering for another inspection before the initials faded. But they were still clear. He rubbed them. They remained. He pushed back, landing on his ass.

"They're inside. Whoever wrote this was in the fucking shower with me."

He crabbed back to the bed, took the room in again, and then laughed.

"You're nuts, Humphrey. Scared by a little soap scum?"

He shook his damp hair, and then sought the dryer.

3

Again the mirror loomed while Harris dried his hair. He inspected his cheeks for blemishes and his chin for the scar remnant — a nick from a sword accident on the last film. It healed nicely — nothing makeup couldn't hide, and was more pronounced two weeks ago, when he had walked the red carpet in L. A. Tony fussed over the scar so much, Harris thought Mom had tagged along. Mom wasn't the stage door kind, but she had rules — good rules, which worked well for a child actor transitioning through this Thespian world. Mom's rules guided Harris to regard acting as a job rather than a privilege. A good thing, because he loved his job. He hated these junkets and the crowd's rush. The red carpet was his least favorite thing, although he was gracious to his fans and never withheld his autograph.

He mused on his last prance on the red carpet. Unlike tonight, a public preview at a festival, two weeks ago the event was an invitation-only première. He was tuxedoed and spotlighted — the press in full attendance — interviewers great and small, each with frivolous questions like *did you find the battle scenes hard? Did you perform your own stunts? We hear talk about you and Romey* (Romaine Rowan — the heroine). *Any truth to it?*

Drone. Drone. Drone.

Harris danced around these questions. He hugged Romaine and Tony and the director, McCann Phillips. He stood with them and posed and preened and bathed in a shower of flashbulbs and strobes behind the usual studio spoiler backdrop. It was a whirl until he saw . . . saw *her*.

She, a fan, cocked her head and grinned. *She,* dressed in black denim and a leather cap, was unlike other fans, who stretched arms forward, pens in one hand, books in the other — this girl in black denim stood patiently, smiling confidently, and then . . . winked.

"Do you see her?" Harris whispered to Tony.

"What ya talkin' about, mate," Tony replied. "All I see is a sea of screamin' Mimis, and you know not one of 'em's me type."

"I didn't mean that," Harris said. "I mean, focus your ass and look at that one over there — the one that's casing me."

"They're all casing you. I mean, who wouldn't, you damn cutie?"

"Stop it."

But Tony wasn't in the mood for sightseeing. The whirl distracted him. *They* were the attraction. The stars. The fans, white noise.

White noise.

Except that *one*, there. That *one* in black stillness. Then Harris, compelled to speak with her, broke ranks, despite the push to enter the theater.

"Where ya goin', mate?"

"Nowhere," Harris muttered, his eyes drifting to that wink in the crowd.

He went to the sidelines, suddenly accosted by hundreds of arms and pens and books and screaming women. They broke his reverie. He grasped one book, and then another, and yet another, signing and scribbling on demand. When he looked up, *she* was gone.

"Gone," he said, now into the mirror, and then pouted.

But he had seen *her* again; last week near his mother's house in Santa Monica. While heading to the Yatzy Club with his little sister, Harris wore his usual public disguise (thick glasses and a false nose). He encountered a gaggle of fans. Sarah, his sister, always a good shepherdess, tugged him across Santa Monica Boulevard to avoid detection. There were times for adulation, and times for anonymity. Harris liked the Yatzy Club because the DJ, although recognizing him, would never blow his cover.

Normality.

Crossing the boulevard, he spotted a lone wolf coming in the opposite direction.

"It's *her*," he muttered.

"*Her* who?" Sarah asked.

"I don't know," he said, loosing himself from his sister's arm.

The lady wore black denim — the same outfit she had at the première. She strolled with swagger, her head down, but she looked up when she passed him. She winked, her chalk-white skin amplifying her crimson lips. She had a green beauty mark on her right cheek. Harris gasped — his chest hitching. But even as he turned to follow her, she hastened to the curb.

"Wait," he called.

She didn't. She raised a departing hand — an alluring fist wrapped in a black fingerless glove — on her finger, a captivating jade ring. Then, as if the night had swallowed her, she disappeared. Harris reached the curb.

"Do you know her?" Sarah asked. "You look . . ."

"No." he replied. "She's . . . How *do* I look?"

"Smitten, Humph. Let me fix your nose."

They had neared the gaggle of club girls. One latex slip and Harris would be a rooster fending for his life in the henhouse. He let his sister repair his nose and straighten his thick glasses. Still, he meant to pursue the phantom lady, only . . . *where did she go?*

"She's a dream now," he said into the mirror, the hairdryer aimed at emptiness.

The lady in black denim — the evasive girl of the night, no longer remained in reality. She stalked Harris' dreams this last week. He spent the afternoon trying to escape her clutches. But she lingered — on the red carpet and at the curb, winking and waving, and then coming close to his ear, her crimson lips and chalky cheeks an arabesque to his quaking soul. These were good dreams, but fell short of *The Magic Planet.* Harris had spent so much time on bizarre sets, this shade had to be a remnant hallucination from a cut scene — a scripted snippet chastised by better reason, never to be seen in the projector's flicker.

"You're spoiling me," he muttered, shutting the dryer and nodding his head before his image.

A knock at the door interrupted this reverie.

"It's open," he shouted.

"What d'ya mean, it's open, mate?" came a voice from the hall. "'ow can it be open?"

Harris set the dryer down and let the towel fall. He let his co-star in.

"Well, don't cover your nuts for me," Tony said, bouncing in as if it were his room. "And what d'ya mean, it's open?"

"I was testing you," Harris replied. "And you didn't mind me butt naked last week."

"Well, we've no time for that sort of thing now. We're late, and King McCann'll have those balls if there's a repeat of . . ."

"Hush up," Harris said, without malice.

"Is your minibar stocked?" Tony announced, aiming directly for it. "Or should I ask? You sip only fizzy drinks and water, unless there's a bloody 'eifer up 'ere filling jugs with chocky milk."

"You know we have to pay for that shit."

"You're payin', thank ye. Me cooler's gone empty some'ow." He shrugged and grinned. "Get dressed and . . ." Tony raised his hand toward the bed. "What a toss we 'ave 'ere? Did you 'ave some birds in? I'm green with envy."

"No. Nothing like that," Harris said, pulling on his briefs and heading for the closet. "I slept, mostly."

"Looks like you wrestled the queen 'ere."

"No, you weren't anywhere around," Harris replied, chuckling. "Get your drink. I'll be ready in a shake."

Anthony Bentley-Jones, the draw of the East end and many a rear end, bowed first to the bed, and then the minibar. He was a *good egg*, as they said across the pond. He was four years older than Harris, but in the *biz* longer, having made his first cereal commercial at age two, his Mummy hell-bent on keeping herself in gin and marijuana. The Bentley-Jones franchise (which began as the Koslowsky enterprise) was not as smooth and carefree as the Cartwright-Kopfstutter dynasty. Little Antonin's Mummy drove him from stage door to audition to rock video to TV commercial to rascal roles until, by age ten (just over a decade earlier) he was a bundle of talented nerves and molested by a string of equally talented directors. He still landed plum roles, but his decadence factor overshadowed many jaded actors three times his age. However, he had his good looks and came out of the closet three years ago, with much aplomb. The rumors that he had slept with every one of his co-stars (male and female) were true, or so he told the press.

They don't call me Bentley-Jones for nothin', dearies.

Tony pulled the minibar door ajar and perused the choice of little bottles.

"I see the munchies 'ave gone missin'." He glanced at the floor. "Your aim is bleedin' off. I 'ope you made it to the loo better'an you did the dustbin." He rattled through the shot bottles, putting a few in his jacket pocket. "And what'll grace your glorious body tonight?"

"Something simple."

Harris alluded snidely to Tony's *over-the-top* outfit — very Dorsetshire — a flowery shirt beneath a blue blazer, a pink hankie mushrooming from where the yacht insignia should have been — a fedora (duck feathered – green) and, of course, an Ascot.

"Simple? Jeans and shitekickers?" Tony drawled like a Dallas native just short of Yorkshire. He turned, and then glanced over his tinted glasses at the young American. "Now that's bloody fetchin'. Turn 'bout and let your Auntie Antonia assess."

Harris had donned a green silk shirt and a white jacket with matching pants. He was stunning. He knew it, but dummied down this wardrobe choice. He was more comfortable in, as Tony had stated, *jeans and shitekickers*. He refused to do a runway twirl for *Auntie Antonia*, although he had seen the runway on many a fashion week.

"Listen," he said sternly. "I told you the judge is still out on me and the coming-out ball."

"I 'ate when a man can't make up 'is own mind," Tony said, pouting. He held a gin sample in one hand and a Post-it in the other. "You just want the best of both worlds — and I guarantee that you'll never get anything better'an me."

"Stop it." Harris squinted. "What's that?"

Tony lifted the bottle.

"Gin."

"No . . . that?"

"Oh. This was stuck inside ya minibar. Maybe a note from the mice that you ate their munchies. Stole their splif too, I bet." He looked at the Post-it, and then frowned. "Not the mice. It's from a secret admirer. It says," he adjusted his glasses. "It says — I C U *and* C U 18r, CMJ."

Harris shuddered. He rushed to Tony's side, swiping the note, and then stared hard.

"You did 'ave a bird up 'ere in this cage today," Tony said, fretfully. "You needn't 'ave lied. I mean, we're not a couple or anything like that."

"Nothing like that, and I didn't have . . . *a bird in this cage* today."

Tony shook his head knowingly.

"Ah, you said the door was open. So that's 'ow it's done. You know in some cat 'ouses an open door is a signal for . . ."

"Stop it. I had no one here. At least, no one that . . . Anyone could have stuck this in the fridge."

Tony pocketed the gin and shut the minibar door with his foot.

"Keep your little secrets. Let's just get a move on, mate. The limos'll be lining the curb and we mustn't keep a Rolls-Royce waitin'."

Harris Cartwright, star of stage and screen, sighed. He glanced about his home away from home and wondered about the journey.

This was the only life he knew, and now he must move along a professional course.

"You're right," he said. "We're stars — giant balls of gas. Let's go fill the galaxy with our stink."

"Why, what's crawled up your arse, mate?"

Harris grinned. He was the master of the moment in his green shirt and white duds. He had a Q&A to give and flashbulbs to embrace. It was illusion, but he knew no other life.

Chapter Two

Pursuit

1

Harris peered out the limousine window at the passing New York City lights — lights like none other on the planet. The Manhattan skyline fascinated him. He had lived here for a brief spell when he made his crime drama *Bad Boys in the City*. He had invested time exploring the museums, the clubs (those that let him in as a courtesy and not by proof of age), and the hustle-bustle of Greenwich Village at night. His destination tonight was the Village 7 Theater, a Tribeca Festival venue. The ride was short.

"There she be," Tony said, pointing through the traffic. "Small, but at your service."

"Are you shit canning your accent tonight?" Harris asked.

"What accent, mate?"

Harris laughed. Tony could slather the Yorkshire when he wanted the audience to lean forward and listen attentively. *Gets their undivided attention, it does,* Tony would say. However, he played Captain Joseph Baneworthy in *The Magic Planet*, a character as American as American could be — not a hint of the Yorkish tongue. He could have been cornbread Des Moines. Mr. Bentley-Jones was an actor, after all — a star and, as gas giants went, as seamless as the sky.

"Get ready for the crush," Harris warned.

"This is a wee preview, laddie," Tony replied, tipping his head backwards to empty a minibar special.

"You'll need a breath mint," Harris said, fishing in his pocket.

"Nothin' doin'. I'm 'ard drinkin' Joe Baneworthy, the Commander of *The Galaxy 12*. The public should expect 'ooch on me kisser." He laughed. "Besides, a preview crowd's shy of the première crowd with 'alf the paparazzi."

"I know. Still, the world's watching us."

"Not without a ticket, mate." Tony yawned. "I could use a noddy 'fore I get too pissed."

"You can't sleep through your own performance."

"Why not? I was sleepwalkin' on the set. I could 'ardly watch the rushes. I mean, when we do the legitimate gig, we're not in the audience enjoyin' us. It's bloody work, you know. We've no right to sit back and look in the looking glass."

The looking glass. Harris knew the looking *glass*. Sometimes he winced at his own performances. In the beginning, it was fun, but he was a kid. Now, whenever he was in the audience, he was a critic. Always something — a misplaced inflection or a facial twitch. Directors were the ultimate critics, and if satisfied, actors could be happy. Still, Harris couldn't imagine sleeping at either a première or a preview. Fun flickered seeing himself twenty-feet high, luminous in the dark and delivering art to a crowd of adoring strangers chomping popcorn and silencing cell phones.

"You don't want to know if they liked your performance?" he asked Tony, who leaned forward preparing to exit onto the red carpet.

"I can tell without watchin'. I listen to the chairs."

"The chairs?"

"Aye, me laddie. Silent chairs mean I've earned it. Creaky chairs means the lions are restless and owed a refund."

Harris laughed, not because it was funny (which it was), but true.

"You're not that rich," he replied.

"But you are, mate."

The limo door opened and the flashing commenced.

2

The crowd, large for the space — Eleventh Street being narrow, the red carpet had been shortened between a few silver stanchions. A modest festival security detail pressed the fans to the curb.

Harris popped a grin, radiating his famous tooth gap. Shouts of *Harris* cut the night air, with here and there an *Anthony* and a *Romaine* and an *Audra* and a *Max* and a *Milton*. The entire cast arrived in mixed fashion and different length limousines. There were some calls for *McCann*, but directors usually weren't regaled from curbside. However, this was a prestigious festival, and a fan or three were here to admire the McCann Phillips' screen craft. Generally known for television work and three romantic screen comedies, *The Magic Planet* was his first foray into epic fantasy. His chops rode on its success.

Flashes pumped like fireworks and interviewers massed at the theater's glass doors, microphones at the ready. There, Harris groped for Tony, as the cast coagulated into a lineup — posing for the world. Harris trotted out his latent humility to assure the paying public their icon was human and, like the rest of the species, flushed the toilet.

Harris waved at the fan blur. If the cordons fell, the crowd would charge him like bulls at Pamplona, skewering him with adoration. But his mother had coached him well:

Humph, she had told him, never look upon their love as real. They have lives beyond you and when you're bigger and older, they will embrace the image fixed within your work and not the one hidden from their view — the true you.

Mother Kopfstetter was right, of course. Harris was wise enough to keep his work life separated from his personal life. But Mama never said to ignore the sweet aroma when the two overlapped naturally.

Scanning the face blurs and following the interviewers with their lollipop mikes accosting Romaine with questions about a recent tumble she took over her pet poodle, Harris spotted one clear face in the crowd. He shook his head, because he didn't trust what he saw.

"Tony," he whispered. "Is she here again?"

Tony placed his chin on Harris' shoulder to capture his sight line.

"That's 'er, all right, mate. You got yourself a class-A stalker."

"No," Harris replied. "I don't think she's stalking me. I think she wants to talk."

"*C U l8tr*, mate and all that."

Suddenly, Harris was beside himself. Could she be his mysterious scribbler? Only one way to find out. He broke ranks and retread the red carpet, Tony at his heels.

"You can't do this, mate. Trust me. McCann'll 'ave your balls."

"I don't care. He's not God."

"Maybe not, but 'e can blackball you all the same."

Harris reached where the lady in black denim had stood. Again, gone. *Fled.* Immediately, the crowd crushed in, trying to tear off a souvenir — his white jacket perhaps. Perhaps his ear. A security guard pushed the fans back.

"Mr. Cartwright," he said. "Mr. Bentley-Jones. It's best you both go back to the press queue."

"Listen to 'im, mate."

Harris ignored them. He saw his target on the other side of the street, and in motion, heading south on Third Avenue. He glanced at the guard, assuming command.

"I need to leave," he snapped. "If you don't want my body in a bag, you'll corral these fans and clear a path."

The guard blinked, but then waved two other guards to follow the order. When a gas giant speaks, who disobeyed? They pushed the adoring fans to form a narrow path.

"'arris," Tony shouted. "This'll be on the Internet in less than an 'our."

"I don't care. Enjoy your sleep."

Harris didn't wait. He scurried between outstretched arms and dashed along Third Avenue into the night.

3

Harris had lost the lady in black denim at once. But he felt her presence — a pheromone trail. He couldn't tell why. He was like a lion stalking an antelope. But who stalked whom, and was Tony's suggestion true? Could the lady be a stalker? Could she have planted those mysterious messages in his hotel room? Even so, why was she at a festival on the East Coast, when she was a West Coast denizen? Many questions more interesting to the police than a working actor loomed. But Harris didn't need answers. He needed her and he couldn't tell why.

The magnetic draw entranced him until the neighborhood changed. After marching through Cooper Square and passing Cooper Union, he now tramped in *the Bowery*, the homeless haven. In the past, these *down on their luck* indigents were called *bums*. Drunks and foul-smelling society weeds huddled in doorways, strewn to the curbside and confronting Harris. One staggered to a car stopped at a traffic signal and cleaned its windshield with a dirty rag. This returned Harris to reality. He stood at the corner of Second Street and the Bowery. He hung a right, not because he knew where he was going, but it felt correct.

His pace quickened. As he progressed, he had second thoughts. Tony could be right. By bolting from the Tribeca Festival's press queue, Harris would be broadcasted on *YouTube*. The world would wonder *what's up with Harris Cartwright?* Had this good conduct paragon finally tapped the drug fairy? Had he a secret longing to squeegee stalled cars in the dead of night? *What's up, mate?* What would Mom think about her squeaky-clean little boy?

Then he heard the click of high heels — stilettos. Had he entered the realm of prostitutes and street-walkers? This was the East Village, after all — a neighborhood that never closed its doors to business. But no. Ahead he spotted his target and thought to run. But even in Santa Monica on that fateful night with his sister, the dark lady vanished when he stormed her. So, he too followed with caution when he crossed Second Avenue and then, a block later, First.

She turned left and crossed the street, halting in front of a landmark — one Harris knew, although he had never been inside. *Happy Pings.* A Chinese restaurant with a twist, because all the waitresses were drag queens — a vision of gay China. The fact this lady stopped here gave Harris pause — a pang of wonder. She didn't enter, so Harris darted into an alleyway and peeked over the garbage cans.

He peered long and hard, but when a rat distracted him (or perhaps a cat prowling deep in the nightshades), it shook his focus. When he refocused on *Happy Pings*, the lady was gone.

"Shit."

She probably entered the restaurant. He slipped along the concrete wall, the cold bricks marring his white jacket. He heard the vermin stir again before sensing a presence behind him. He turned and, from the darkness, a shadow emerged.

"Fuck," he yelped. "You scared the shit out of me."

"You should be scared," she said. "I do not take well to stalkers."

"Stalker? Me, a stalker? I'm not the one who shows up everywhere *I* show up."

She laughed. When he thought about it, he laughed too.

"So here you are again," she said. "And you showed up just where you showed up."

"It's stupid, but you know what I mean."

"Do I?"

He got a good look at her face. Bleach white — unnatural — a canvas for face paint. Her lips were crimson, and she still had a green beauty mark on her right cheek. She smelled of roses — a whole damned floral shop's worth.

"I'm sorry if I've jumped to conclusions," he said. "It's just, I thought . . . I thought, since I keep seeing you, you might have . . . might have . . ."

"Been looking for *you*?"

"Well, you've crossed my path more than once — here and in L.A. What am I to think?"

She lit a cigarette, took one draw, puffed out smoke, and then crushed the butt on the alley's foul pavement.

"At least you could buy me a drink."

Harris regarded this change to *Mae West* with suspicion. Caution raised its head.

"Sure," he said, affably. "You were heading into . . ."

"Happy Pings. Do you know Happy Pings?"

He clicked his tongue, scuffing his feet.

"Not personally," he replied, and then decided on full disclosure. "Damron gives *Happy Pings one-and-half* to *two stars* for Szechuan cuisine and . . . drag queen waitresses — a gay hoot."

"Good. It is *one-off . . .* like me."

Red flag. Harris smelled a practical joke — a Bentley-Jones practical joke. Revenge. Harris pulled one on Tony on *The Magic Planet* set. Good, clean fun, but not taken in the spirit intended. McCann Phillip's assistant, Pam, slipped script changes under the actors' trailer doors — line alterations for the next day's shoot. Harris jiggered these with devilishly inappropriate dialogue for his co-star. Tony dutifully memorized them and came swaggering onto his starship's deck delivering (in his best American accent) the bogus lines.

Last night's prawn makes me ill today. Who's got the cuttlefish to cure me?

Everyone roared — Harris doubled-over. However, McCann was furious, and not at Harris, but at Tony, who flew off the handle in his best Yorkish — a word shower of *fookin' arse 'oles* and *bloody mudder 'umpers*. He didn't talk to 'arris for a week.

Harris thought now: *This is revenge.* Hire a drag queen to allure him at the première, and then have her show up in New York (with mysterious Tony-planted messages). Then, when the sexually ambivalent Mr. Cartwright came to it in the end, he'd be up on *YouTube* in the arms of a *dick-and-balls* Amazon (shy the black denim). Kinky and mean. With these thoughts, he paused.

"Are you coming?" she asked, beckoning with her eyes. "Or are you afraid to be seen in public with me?"

"I'm coming. I'm surprised you'd want the drink at . . ."

"Oh, I get it." She pressed him against the alley's wall, smothering him in floral iniquity. "Go ahead. Explore if you must. Satisfy your curiosity."

Her aroma overcame him, his heart beating wildly. But the invitation to feel her up would dispel doubt. He decided to accept, feeling her firm breasts as they engulfed him. If these were falsies, they were good falsies. They terrified him at first. As attractive as she was, Harris wasn't into the bizarre.

Was this the answer to the prank script?

His hand crept down to her skirt buttons. Nervously, he explored, cautiously travelling toward her crotch. No bulge, thank God. Not Bruce in Black Knickers.

"Satisfied?" she asked, her eyebrows raised.

He withdrew his hand like the Dutch boy from the dike. She gave him a wet kiss, and then drew back, continuing her course toward the restaurant. He galloped after her.

"I'm sorry I doubted you," he said. "I'm not a prig. I'm open to almost anything. But I think of you as a woman and if you turned out to be a man, I wouldn't get violent or anything, but . . . but when I look for blueberry pie and discover steak tartar, it's a letdown."

She lit another cigarette, took a deep drag and blew smoke over his head.

"Shut up."

He noticed that brilliant jade ring on her right hand — incised with a funny emblem — a shepherd's crook or something like it. His eyes followed the ring as she smoked.

"You like my ring?"

"It's bait to wear it on First Avenue. I've expensive bling, but I wouldn't sport it in this neighborhood."

"No. You are just sporting a completely white outfit, walking the streets like a lighthouse in a storm." She turned him around. "Nice brown brick mark on the back."

Harris slipped off his jacket and stared at the stain — brown as if he had changed a diaper on his new, Indochino dinner jacket. This outfit had been earmarked for fashion week. Now it was earmarked for the dumpster.

"I'll leave it off."

"You will not," she snapped. "You look like the Green Hornet with it off."

"Do I?" he laughed. "The Green Hornet?"

"I did not mean to flatter you."

She tossed the cigarette aside, not bothering to stomp it. She grabbed the jacket, holding it high. Her black fingernails, the most prominent items free of her fingerless gloves, raked the stain. She turned the coat around, and then presented it back to him. Clean as the day it was bought, only two days ago.

"How did you do that?"

"Magic is my hobby. My daddy is a magician."

Harris grinned, and then donned the jacket.

"You could open a dry-cleaning business."

She didn't seem amused. Instead, she retrieved her still-burning cigarette from the pavement, and took another drag, before extinguishing it on the restaurant's stoop. Harris wondered if she just lit it up for effect. At any rate, he never would pick up anything from the pavement and shove it between his lips.

Yuck.

"So are you up for me?"

Harris chuckled. He was *up* and hoped he could keep his self-control in the restaurant, especially one served by flaming Chinese drag queens.

"I've come this far," he said.

She gave him her arm. He escorted her beneath the chintz lanterns into *Happy Pings.*

Chapter Three

Happy Pings

1

Happy Pings bustled — a glitter palace for every bad choice in Chinese décor — paper lanterns, dragon tinsel, lucky characters and, of course, six drag queen waitresses running the gamut from Suzie Wong to Mei-lin Schwartz (outsized in a tight dress like a squid overhanging its cuttle bone). The *Maitre D'* (a Mandarin named Jose) popped two menus from a gigantic red fan-shaped rack, and then bowed. Harris expected Fu Manchu to roll by in a rickshaw.

"How many, *prease?*"

"We're here for drinks only," Harris said.

The man raised an eyebrow and returned the menus to the bin.

"You can feed me, while you are at it," the lady chirped. "I am far from home and could stand a meal."

"Of course," Harris said, grinning. "Then it'll be two for dinner."

The *Maitre* D' snatched the menus again, bowed (again), and then pointed the way — a short flight to the mezzanine, which had a fine view of First Avenue. Suddenly, he halted, turned and looked Harris over.

"Wait," he said. "Aren't you . . ."

"No," Harris snapped. "I know what you're about to say. People often mistake me for him, but I'm *not* him."

Jose, or whatever his name was, grinned, registering disbelief.

"The customer is *arways light*," he said, in his best (or worst) imitation Charlie Chan. He strode toward the table, pushing aside a beaded chandelier. He waved the menus at a few gawking diners. "No," he said. "It's not *leary* him. Just a *rook-a-rike*."

Harris tried to hide his face. He was in no mood to hold court. Only one person held his attention and not for autographs. (Jose) stopped at a window-side table — a perfect view of First Avenue.

"Bo Peep will be your server," (Jose) said, dramatically presenting the menus. "Enjoy your happy meal at *Happy Pings*."

He drifted back to his station, whispering to anyone who would listen:

That man over there is Hallis Cartlight, but no one ret on.

Harris shifted his face to the shadows. He fumbled the menu, perusing an unusual blend of Chinese-Jewish entrees.

"What looks good?" he said to the lady.

She reached across the table and pushed the menu flat.

"I do."

Harris smiled, his gap most fetching.

"I won't argue with that, although . . ."

"I am different from your usual fare."

"Just like this menu. But how d'ye know that?" He paused. "Ah, yes. You've been . . . you've been watching me." He wanted to say *stalking*, but feared renewing that discussion.

"You have been watched before."

"By whom?"

"Millions."

"That's not what I meant. Millions don't know me. They certainly don't know my dating habits. I'm careful. It's hard to see how you've figured it out."

"Regard this as an audition."

Cheeky comment. Perhaps the lady went too far. Still, as she said audition, she smiled for the first time, her ivory whites beaming between those luscious, crimson lips. Harris chuckled, and then lifted the menu.

"Are *you* on the menu tonight?" he asked, a good opening line.

"That depends."

"It certainly does." He laid the menu flat again, and then stared into her eyes, trying not to be sucked in. "I generally don't date fans."

"Generally or never? *Am* I a fan? Is this a date? I do not recall being asked out, and for that matter, accepting. Who is the pickup here?"

"Is this a pickup?*"*

She didn't answer, but raised her menu, blocking eye contact. This released Harris from a dozen other questions. Drowning a first encounter in a rhetorical sea was always unwise. Was this the Q&A he had bolted from at the Tribeca? Then, at the menu's edges, he spotted the ring — that jade ring with its curious sigil. *Fascinating*. It unsettled him. He heard it hum, so compellingly he looked out the window at First Avenue. But in that glance he saw the reflection of a woman draped in robes, a shimmering tiara crowning her head. He gasped before realizing it was their server's reflection — the ever-fetching Bo Peep.

"Do you need a few minutes, hon?" Bo Peep asked in a raspy stevedore's voice.

The server was poured into a costume — one-part Japanese, one-part Chinese, one-part Thai and the balance in Bangladesh — a Cook's tour of Asia from crown to toe. She sported a lampshade hat crowned with red tassels and a swirl of golden spikes. With a five o'clock shadow at midnight, dim light was Bo Peep's friend. Since no one replied at once, Bo Peep tapped pencil on pad.

"I guess you lovebirds need more time."

Bo Peep's retreat unplugged the interrupted conversation. The lady fanned herself with the menu and batted her lashes.

"I *am* a fan, Harris Cartwright," she said emphasizing his name.

He shot a look toward the other guests, hoping this announcement wouldn't trigger an autograph stampede.

"Glad to know it," he whispered. "I usually don't announce my name when I'm out."

"Trust me, they know who you are and will try nabbing you the first chance they get. But they cannot."

"You're sure about that?"

"Yes. I shall prevent them. If hounded, I shall ring you with fire and singe their eyelashes. I will bite their fingers and devour their passions."

He laughed.

"Hungry, eh?"

"You do not know how hungry," she said. "My appetite brooks all passion."

Brooks all passion? Harris thought. She must be in the Berkeley crowd.

Suddenly, Harris felt passionate from his little toe to his groin — less hungry now. More horny. The lady continued to fan and preen like Theda Bara in Silent Film Classics Class 1.0.

"I *am* a fan," she murmured. "Your biggest fan. You will never know one as ardent as I." He flinched. "Does it scare you?"

Harris recalled police cases — fans latching onto the objects of their devotion and never letting go until they hacked their obsession to bits.

"It scares me a little."

"You *should* be scared," she said, as she had in the alley. "I get what I want. Do you know what I want?"

"Egg Foo Young?" He chuckled nervously, and dived for the menu. "We ought to look this thing over before Miss Bo Peep tackles us."

"Such talk endears you to me. I have always enjoyed it when you talk like that."

Odd comment? Harris blushed, and then tried to escape her eyes, but the ring caught him. He gawped, the jade mesmerizing him.

"That ring dances," he muttered.

"So it does. My prized possession — a captivator, like you."

"I'm at a disadvantage," he stammered.

"No ring of your own?"

"No. You know who I am and evidently did your homework; the fan sites on the Internet, I guess. There's a trove of info about me. I hear they have my jock size listed."

"But you do not wear a jock."

He tensed, trying to decide which was stronger — the hormonal dance or the urge to run. The hotel was only two blocks away. Its proximity could serve either purpose.

"You know everything about me, but I don't even know your name."

The lady lowered her eyes — an overall diminution of her luster.

"I assumed you knew," she said.

"How would I know your name?"

"I should be insulted."

Harris grasped her hands across the table, gazing into her eyes.

"Why should you be insulted? How could I know it? If you sent me fan mail, understand that I get so much I read only one in a thousand. And I answer one in five thousand. It might sound cruel, but that's reality."

"No," she said. "No fan mail."

He released her hands.

Perhaps a Post-it or a shower stall scribble?

He winced.

"I'm at a complete loss."

"Perhaps my expectations are high," she said, looking away. "We should order. Miss East Asia comes again."

Bo Peep returned. Pencil tap. Suggestions? *Surprise us* (as if we're not already surprised). Ah! Two orders of *Happy Pings'* Mu Shu Pork Wraps with a side of Potato Latkes. *Wunderbar!*

2

"Charminus," she exclaimed, offhandedly.

"Excuse me?"

"My name is Charminus Montjoy."

She announced this with aristocratic punch, contradicting her Goth-girl appearance. Harris decided she was a fellow actor — perhaps a distressed one, out of work and seeking a part in a future film. This wouldn't be the first time he'd been tapped.

"Charminus Montjoy?" he mimicked, condescendingly matching her tone. "Sounds stagy. Are you in the business?"

"What business?"

"Acting. I mean, you know me through my films. You're a fan. But with a sweet name like Charminus Montjoy, I could see it on the boards. Is that why you expected me to know you?"

She watched him spread his fingers, spotlighting an imaginary marquee.

"Enough, Mr. Cartwright," she snapped, the aristocrat retreating. "Is Harris your real name?"

"You know better, knowing as you do. It's Humphrey, as in Humphrey Bogart . . ."

"Or Master Humphrey's Clock — tick tock." She grinned. "I like Harris better, for now. We shall see."

"I suspect you'll call me something else later."

"I do not know. Is there a later, Mr. Kopfstutter?"

"Now that's a name that had to go," he said, rolling his eyes. "My mother saw to that at once. Cartwright's her maiden name."

"And Harris?"

"That she snatched from thin air, I suppose."

"You could have been Harrison or Harry or Horse's Ass."

"Some people think I'm a horse's ass."

"But not enough horse to need a jockstrap."

He laughed so loud, neighboring diner's attentions were drawn to the window table. Even Bo Peep peeped.

"You have a sense of humor," she said, flashing the ring. "You are as precious as my captivator. Where I come from you would be the village clown."

"And from where do you hail?"

Charminus Montjoy fell silent. The ring flickered as if attempting to shake the subject.

"Really, Miss Montjoy," Harris said, pressing. "Where do they name their children so regally?"

"Brooklyn," she announced.

"Brooklyn?" he howled.

She was not amused. She pushed the ring into his face. Harris gawped at the jade. He suddenly thought he saw a different face — the face of an older woman — an aged version of the lady in black denim — a fleeting image, but it sobered him. He glanced out the window where he saw Bo Peep's linebacker reflection approaching with the meal.

The *Mu Shu* and the *Latkes* came with a *pu-pu* platter — assorted fried crunchies — tasty and on the house for the *rook-a-rike* and his date. Accompanying the trays, pink cocktails fizzed, a concoction decorated with diminutive paper umbrellas, spiking maraschino cherries. Harris raised his glass.

"To Charminus Montjoy," he said as happily as Ping.

The lady winked, raised her glass and sucked the cherry from its spike. Her tongue beckoned. Harris knew. He didn't care whether she stalked him, was a nutty actress trying to break into the business or the lost Czarina of Russia. He had to have her, and soon. He couldn't devour the *pu-pu* platter fast enough. His chest heaved and he reached for her hand. She might be a one-night stand or she might lock him in his room like the lady who kidnapped the novelist in the popular tale. He didn't care. The mind ruled not, and neither did the heart. When he touched the ring, a hot wave flooded his soul. He felt faint.

"Charminus," he whispered.

"CMJ," said she.

He didn't heed.

"Charminus. My hotel's a hop, skip and a jump from here."

"I know."

"I would very much like it if . . ."

"I do not hop nor do I skip, and jumping is far beneath me. However, a brisk walk to your bed sheets might prove better than dessert."

He grinned.

"Dessert?" croaked Bo Peep.

"Not now and not here," Harris snapped at the server. "Just give me the check."

He left a good tip.

Chapter Four

An Invitation

1

Harris snuggled on the bed's edge, his face mashed into the pillow, his ass tangled in green satin. His eyes flashed opened, but his head didn't move. Sunshine reflected the wall's gold like a firebrand, causing him to wince. Painfully, he turned over, his legs stiff and his back in a vise.

"Holy crap," he muttered, and then looked to the opposite pillow remembering someone had been in bed with him — at least when he dropped off to sleep. She wasn't now — not surprising, but disappointing.

"Holy, holy crap," he chanted, rubbing his eyes, and then grinning with recall.

Between the pain and the rude sunlight, thoughts of her enmeshed him — a vision of the lady without her black denim. Charminus rocked him like the sea rolling onto jetties. She took him to the rodeo. He tried to sit up. *Difficult.* He looked for her. Perhaps she lingered.

"Holy crap," he said again, this time like a choirboy avoiding the bishop.

The room was trashed. The mirror kiltered off the wall. The pictures were at fun house angles. The desk chair was upended, and his clothes were scattered from the couch to the windowsill to the minibar. His green shirt hung on the otherwise shadeless lamp.

"Holy crap," he said, jumping to his feet — aching feet, bucking him to the wardrobe.

Harris groped for his pants. Finding them under the nightstand, he fished through his back pocket expecting his wallet to be missing. Not much in it, but it might highlight his bed partner's reason to flee. However, his wallet was there and intact — seventeen dollars, credit cards and a California license and registration. He drew a deep breath through his nose, and then sat in the debris, grinning again.

Satisfied resignation.

"Charminus Montjoy," he murmured, recalling the experience, but not entirely.

Odd. He remembered the thrust, burying his face in her chest. He recalled her bosom swelling, and her clamped legs around him. Then he rode her and she rode him and his heart stopped. Literally, it had stopped, or at least he turned numb with paralysis.

"I was dead," he said, suddenly demure.

The world ceased in those dark hours. No breath — a sudden gasping for life. Like, rebirth. Yet there it was a cold act — a ferrous pain, striving to extinguish him, body and soul. He closed his eyes now and tried to recall coming back from the brink. He couldn't. Nor could he recall his climax. This saddened him.

Much effort for a forgotten moment.

"But where'd she go?" he stammered. "How can I find her again?"

Suddenly, Tony loomed over him.

"What the 'ell 'appened in 'ere, mate, like I don't 'ave eyes to see for meself?"

"How did you get in?" Harris snorted, trying his best to get up.

"Door's ajar. Bleedin' open to the world. Do you need to go to 'ospital?"

"Give me a hand, will ya. I'm just sore."

Tony bent and helped him. Harris staggered to the bed, breathless and a tad depressed.

"So, was she worth it?" Tony asked. "I assume you shagged 'er before you turned the room on its 'ead."

"It was like nothing else I've ever felt."

"Does that mean you liked it, or are you 'aving second thoughts?"

"I scarcely remember it. I bet I'm in deep shit with McCann and company."

"Not really, mate." Tony sat on the bed, bouncing. "I told 'im you took queer — some oysters at luncheon. Everyone knows that feelin'. Told 'im you've been bloody glued in the loo for the last six 'ours and's best to give you a wide berth."

"Thanks for that."

"Well, with you out of sight, the rest of us 'ad a better shot at the limelight. Ol' King McCann seemed pleased to step into *the numero uno* spot at the Q&A. But if I'd known you'd be doin' the dirty with craven zeal, I'd 'ave told a different tale, I would 'ave. Would 'ave said you were 'omesick for Mum and went back to the 'otel to pine."

Harris grinned, but then winced. Tender neck.

"Are you sure you don't need *el medico*?"

"I'll be okay." He raised his arms, showing a bruise on his elbow. "I wish I knew where this came from."

"Black and blue all over? That's a slam-dunk contusion ripe and proper. Are you sure you weren't dwarf wrestlin' last night?"

Harris reached for his briefs, but couldn't quite make it. Tony scooped them up, twirling them.

"I don't make a point of explorin' wide fronts after the fact, but I think you need a dresser."

Harris grabbed the briefs.

"I can manage."

"Can you manage breakfast?"

"I thought I'd have something sent up, but I'm not hungry."

"Spoken like a true sex 'ound. I think you need to find your kit in this shite and forget the baps and join me in some bangers."

"I'll pass."

"Well, I'm not a child-minder."

"If you put it that way . . ."

Tony grinned, and then hopped to the minibar.

"Did you leave any squirt in the reefer?"

"You're welcome to whatever's there."

Tony opened the minibar's door and laughed.

"The mice 'ave been and gone again."

He popped out a Post-it, waving it. Harris leaped for it, despite the pain. He read it before Tony had a chance to grab it back.

"It's from 'er, I bet. A nice shag, but I'm all buggered out note."

"Nothing like that," Harris mumbled.

It was an address:

> *13-13 McDonald Avenue – Mortis House —*
> *Brooklyn*
> *Take the F Train to Bay Parkway.*

Harris' heart burst. She had left a trail — an invitation — *take the F Train.* He didn't know Brooklyn well, but he knew where to hop a subway. He meant to do it.

"So, what's she say?"

Harris folded the note, and then winked.

"Private."

"Ah, she loved your wankie so much, she's promised to wreck another 'otel room."

"Something like that."

"Well, need I remind you we 'ave an engagement uptown at MTV at two on the 'our. Your chum with oysters won't cut rum into King McCann's fairy cake this time."

"Don't get your panties in a twist. I'll be there."

But he knew he wouldn't be going.

"Well, put your Jimmy-'at away and come down and nosh."

Harris limped to the floor piles and harvested his wardrobe.

"Don't wait on me," he said. "I'll be down in a few. Just order me something light."

"'ow's about *Wavos Rancheros* with a side of biscuits and tea?"

"Coffee, and the rest sounds perfect."

Tony hesitated as if seeing through the ruse, but what could he do? He had lied for Master Cartwright and would do so again.

"Right 'o," he said. "Don't rodger me."

"I wouldn't think of it."

Tony shuffled out, closing the door gingerly. Harris ceased dressing. He went cautiously to the door, assuring Tony was gone. One quick open did the trick. Then, he put his pain aside, reread the note and quickly assembled his jeans and *shitekickers*. He would get the jump on Tony, slip past the restaurant's door, the *concierge* and the doorman. He needed to move fast and had no time for his disguise. Swift and focused, overcoming bruises stiffness. He was heading to Brooklyn.

Taking the F Train, he thought, chuckling. The fucking F train . . . again.

2

Harris had been in Brooklyn once on a location shoot for *Bad Boys in the City* — a scene on the Red Hook docks. He little recalled the place. Now, as the subway emerged from a tunnel, scaling a high bridge over those same Red Hook docks, he saw them for the first time. He couldn't imagine living in such squalor. He pressed his face to the window, his breath fogging the pane. He kept his profile low, fearing recognition. In these Internet days several stalker networks would happily post a celebrity sighting and map it for the universe to follow.

Twice he thought he might have been recognized. A Chinese woman leaned forward and stared at him as if registering his face to the top twenty *Most Wanted* photos. She squinted in constipated recall, but then, at Canal Street, she picked up her truck and detrained. Harris held his breath until the train pulled away, leaving her bemused on the platform. He imagined when she reached home, she'd smack her head and shout: *that was Hallis Cartlight.*

Now recognition loomed again as he disengaged from the window. A teenage girl sat opposite him, smacking on a wad of Juicy Fruit. Suddenly, her jaw slacked and she stared at him like Svengali striking Trilby. Harris squirmed, averting his eyes. He knew that stare — a prelude to hysteria. He whistled.

"Do I know you?" she asked, her mouth recommencing to chew.

He shrugged. *Did anyone ever know anybody?* He expected a pounce — a seized opportunity and an enlightened announcement to the other passengers, who otherwise read or slept. Harris thought to avert her by confessing and begging her silence under the circumstances. *What circumstances?* However, the teen cocked her head, wavering. To encourage her doubts, Harris took a cue from the other passengers, closed his eyes, and feigned sleep.

The train lurched into a station. The doors whooshed.

Bing bong. Bing bong. Smith and Ninth Street. Stand clear of the doors. Bing bong.

When Harris opened his eyes, the girl was gone — Juicy Fruit and all.

Relief.

Harris kept his eyes shut for the trip's remainder. The train had plunged into the earth — tunneled again. Harris listened intently for the mechanical voice.

Bing bong. Bing bong. Church Avenue. Stand clear of the doors. Bing bong.

He opened his eyes. Church Avenue was a major stop, because the sleeping and reading passengers hurriedly detrained. When the doors closed, Harris was alone. The car rattled briskly now, lurching, and then rising once more into sunlight — aloft again, this time on an *El.*

The neighborhood hugged the old elevated line. The houses were quaint. Harris ratcheted to his feet and, holding tightly to the overhead bar, gazed at the passing rooftops — flat with exhaust fan kiosks and pigeon coops nurturing the flying rats of the city. The film *On the* Waterfront came to mind, and he sighed. *I could have been a contender.*

Harris broke his reverie to consult a route map. If he stayed on this line — the F Train, he'd be in Coney Island. That fabled place engendered thoughts of a time past. If he hadn't been on this mission of dire passion, he'd be happy to detour to the beach.

The train slowed, screeching into a lonely station. A sign slid into view.

Bay Parkway.

"This is it," he said, hesitating, but then took a stance before the doors.

Bing bong. Bing bong. Avenue I – Bay Parkway. Next stop Kings Highway. Stand clear of the doors. Bing bong.

Harris confirmed the stop on the Post-it. When the doors slid open, he stepped onto the platform. A chilly breeze blew through his hair. He looked both ways, unsure how to proceed.

Bing bong. Bing bong. Next stop Kings Highway. Stand clear of the doors. Bing bong.

The train pulled out, revealing a canyon between the inbound and outbound platforms. Harris twisted one way, and then another before deciding on his exit plan. Right was probably the way, but he chose left and couldn't tell why.

He hastened, chasing the rear of the train, but it out raced him, leaving him in its wake. He could see the next stop along the steel road in the distance — *Kings Highway*. He reached a metal staircase, and then a catwalk, which descended to a ticketing area in the *El*'s belly.

I could ask directions, he thought. However, the booth seemed deserted. Perhaps going right would have been best.

A bus passed on the street below, so Harris decided to hit the pavement and ask a passerby. But when he reached the staircase's end, no one passed on the street. The road beneath the *El* had a street sign which read:

McDonald Ave.

A cross street angled beneath the *El*. Its sign read:

Bay Parkway.

Harris hopped off the curb and crossed at the light in search of the Post-it address:

13-13 McDonald Ave — Mortis House.

When he reached the opposite side, he had no problem finding it. Only one house on the block and it stood in the middle of . . . a cemetery.

3

A cemetery. A Jewish cemetery, if Harris knew his history, and he knew Jewish history, because he had played a child in a concentration camp in an early gig. He recalled the symbols and signs on the set. It had not been an uplifting experience, but it left an indelible impression. His mother cautioned him when taking the role, which exposed him to horror, striking a nerve perhaps no child should experience. However, after soul searching and dialogue, Doris Kopfstutter guided her son through it. She, always on the set, stood at the ready to console him after the horrific scenes. These memories didn't encourage Harris, considering Charminus' lusty invitation.

He reached a rusty iron fence. Should he hop back on the train and take that excursion to Coney. Suddenly, his pain, which had subsided in expectation's cloud, returned like a hammer.

Another train roared by overhead, its *bing bong* announcement muffled while it discharged passengers, and then rattled back toward Church Avenue and its dark tunnel. Harris felt rattled back into that dark tunnel. He stood at death's broad plain — a tombstone prairie, which susurrated a quiet message over the wrought-iron fence. His heart sunk.

She's suckered me, he thought.

"She's suckered me," he muttered.

He kicked the fence and faced the *El*.

"She's suckered me," he shouted.

Then he heard a different rattle — the sound of a metal gate shaken by the wind. He turned and stared. The gate wasn't inviting. It hadn't opened for him. As far as he knew, it was locked.

How do people get in? He was suddenly amused.

"They kick the bucket, that's how."

Why would Charminus lure him to this forsaken spot where the departed rested for eternity? And what building stood on the grounds? From this distance, it *looked* like a house. Perhaps for the groundskeeper — an undertaker's haven.

Of course, the gravedigger would be an old hunchback with a game leg, who carried a spooky rake and spade.

Harris shuffled along the fence until he reached the gate. Locked. He kicked it and . . .

. . . it opened.

He stepped back, staring at the line of graves. He didn't know these people when they were . . . people. Nothing to recollect, except harrowing ash plumes. Perhaps he *did* know them.

He stepped under the wrought-iron arch, which proclaimed this place to be:

Washington Cemetery.

It could have read:

Arbeit Mach Frei.

He sauntered toward the house respectfully, passing headstones — granite and unadorned except for shrouded urns and smooth prayer stones set on each as markers, evidence of people visiting their beloved dead. He read the names.

"Goldstein — Samuels — Piepschnik — Vernick — Rothberg — Zuckerburg — Rolnick."

He halted.

"Montjoy!"

He shook his head. No, it read:

Mortis.

He rubbed his eyes, and then sighed.

"No. It's Finckelstein. I must be going nuts." He halted. "I gotta get outta here."

As he turned from the house, he saw the gate had closed. He started toward it, but halted again, the house whispering to him. He turned and faced it. It had transformed into an old Victorian. *Odd.* It had been nearly a shack, but now it had two-stories with Gothic trim in seven shades of gray.

"Well, I've come this far," he muttered, leaving the grave path. He drew up before the black stoop and cobwebby porch. The front door was shut, but the house number beside the lintel read:

13-13 — Mortis House

"This is it, but . . ."

His *but* hung in the air, as *buts* often do — the signature of the noncommittal. He had forgotten his drive — his need to be consumed again in Charminus' fire. The lady in black denim's vision had faded. A whisper engulfed him — a beckoning, which he didn't comprehend — a mysterious language. He imagined the jade ring and its sigil, the image riveting him to the spot. His feet might have turned and his body may have fled to the gate, climbing over it; bounding up the metal *El* stairs and waiting for the annoying *bing bong*. But he melted to the spot. He focused on the closed door and the foreign whispers and the jade ring. He daydreamed. Must be. Whether he would wake or not, remained an unanswered question.

Suddenly, the breeze kicked him hard, shaking him from this reverie. The door opened slowly, creaking like a corny script call in a B movie. He almost laughed. But it made him uneasy. *Mortis House's* front door opened wide. No one greeted him — not even a hunchbacked gravedigger. No shrouded urns or the shades of Goldstein or Vernick or Zuckerburg. No. Only hollow darkness and a whispering, which he understood now.

I am waiting.

Harris Cartwright, born Humphrey Kopfstutter, against reason, climbed the stairs and entered the darkness of *Mortis House.*

Chapter Five

Mortis House

1

In dark and musty *Mortis House*, a filigree of light streamed from a hallway window, imprinting the staircase — an old wooden easement tacked with faded carpeting. *Uninviting.* Harris edged his way across the foyer until he reached the banister. He grasped it like an anchor in the doldrums, and then glanced back at the door. Slowly it closed, latching shut. He didn't panic, but noted he might be trapped. But how? Wasn't this *13-13 McDonald Avenue* — the place Charminus had on her mysterious invitation? Wouldn't she be here expecting him? He gazed up the staircase.

"Charminus," he called, not loudly, but gutturally — just above a whisper. "Charminus, are you there?"

No answer.

As his eyes adjusted to the dark, he observed the banister — serpentine — a species of dragon, gnarly headed and now under his paw. He inspected his hand before cautiously returning it to the creature's spine. He took a first step, the tread creaking — naturally to any haunted house, or so he thought. An aroma struck him — a wisteria and hyacinth blend — strong and medicinal. It drew him to the landing, the steps continuing their rise to a broad balcony. An array of shut doors lined the hallway — not inviting, but the aroma had to come from somewhere. He heard a noise — a susurrating rustle of silk perhaps, and then crystals rattling. He cocked his head to listen before calling again.

"Charminus, is that you?"

Still no answer. Suddenly, someone floated passed him — a woman in a leathery tan gown, toting a tray. He concluded she was the sound's source. She had long black tresses and wore a purple band around her forehead, a crystal ornament dangling from its center. She moved ghost-like, her feet not touching the floor and, when she reached the door, she passed through without opening it.

"Hey," Harris called. "Who are you?" He reached the top. The question wasn't *who are you*, but *where am I?* "What's this place?"

The floral scent strengthened, wrapping his chest. It turned him back to the staircase. In that turn, he espied a shape emerging from the shadows. He thought it might be the ghost lady returning to answer his questions, but it was Charminus.

"Thank God, it's you," he said.

"Who else would it be?" He pointed to the closed door. "Ignore it. That is my Trone. Take no notice. I certainly do not."

"Your Trone?"

Charminus spread her arms. No longer clad in black denim, she wore deep purple — a velvet robe, cinched by a golden waist chain. A jade-jeweled skullcap restrained her hair. She flashed her jade ring, snapping Harris away from his questions. Entranced, he bowed to her like a servant in the halls of love.

"I knew you would come," she said, "and on your own accord."

"You invited me," he said, caught in her orbit.

"I left you a trail — a test for your passions. You *do* have passions, Harris, and I have pleasures to spare."

"Funny thing that," he said, nervously as she embraced him. "I don't recall much from our roll in the hay."

"Perhaps," she replied, raking her hand through his hair. "Perhaps, that is best. Recall compels the soul to drift, leaving the imagination nothing but wisps of ardor spent."

"I don't understand."

"Yes, you do." She kissed him. "You do, or would not have come."

Suddenly, the door opened, bright light chasing the darkness. Harris saw the other woman — the servant or, as Charminus called her, *the Trone*. Her flowing tresses flew when she turned to greet her mistress, bowing. Charminus didn't acknowledge the homage, so the servant removed the empty tray, leaving two glasses and a flask beside the bed — for there was a bed of considerable proportions here. Harris had never encountered a hayloft like this one in his life, designed for an orgy of ten.

I'm screwed, he thought, although it didn't deter him. Perhaps this time he'd recall the pleasure and a different room trashed rather than one which would show up on his American Express bill.

She led him in. He noticed her voice had changed — deeper and more resonant, like a cave about to swallow him. He felt unmanned.

"Perhaps we're moving too fast," he stammered.

"You should have thought about that before last night."

"I might have been hasty," he said, with little conviction. His heart raced. "Maybe I should put on the brakes."

"Men like you can't tame your wild instincts. That is why I chose you."

Chose you? Was he on the auction block? Unsettling, but he was ruled by an unexplained compulsion. Whatever his mind said, his groin would contradict it.

She released him. He didn't try to leave. He didn't think he could. Instead, he toured the room, looking for the mysterious light source, because the room was windowless. He almost asked her about it — small talk before foreplay, but she embraced him again, her robe opened now, revealing a sheer shift. Her breasts grew exactly as they had at the first encounter.

"Perhaps we should have a drink," he said.

He grasped for the flask, an acrobatic endeavor from within her arms, but managed to get free. He poured the bloodred liquor into the goblets, and then offered her one. She received it, panting as she winked above the rim. The wine changed to deep purple as Harris drank. He knew it wasn't wine. No grape aroma, but a sharp intoxicant, perhaps in the formaldehyde class. He hesitated, but she upended his vessel, forcing a mouthful to overspill his lips. He spit some out, but swallowed the rest. Suddenly, he was breathless.

"What is this stuff?"

"*Corzanthe*," she replied. "A local vintage."

"They distill wine in Brooklyn?"

"Hush. You were not recalcitrant when you stalked me at *Happy Pings*. Why this coyness, Harris Cartwright?"

He blinked, setting the goblet on the bed stand. He felt giddy.

"I don't know," he muttered. "I'm in Brooklyn, in a strange house, in the middle of a fucking Jewish cemetery, in a bright lampless room without windows, drinking Corzan . . . whatever it is the floating woman you called a Trone brought in here. I can't think of a reason I would be . . . coy."

She laughed, and then downed her *Corzanthe*.

"You are somewhere, Harris Cartwright," she announced. "Dear, dear, Harris Cartwright. How I hate that name. But you are a keeper."

"A what?"

"Never mind. We are here in my bedroom — a special place for me, and . . . for you. Few men are invited to it. Most long to languish here, but succumb to the enticements before reaching my favor."

What was she babbling?

"I feel funny."

Drunk, he supposed. *From one sip of wine?* But it wasn't wine. A local vintage designed to heat his blood hotter than molten lead — to put iron in his pencil and motion in his hips. He didn't feel bad. He recalled the Valium he had in the hospital when he had a boil lanced on his butt. He floated now. Perhaps he was becoming . . . her *Trone*.

"I'm not into psychedelic drugs," he murmured, fuzzier as the moments fled.

She stopped his inquiries with a kiss.

Dizzy.

He spun onto the bed, caught between her legs, a vise giving both pleasure and pain. He gasped for air, descending into a deep well filled with jade light.

Dizzy.

His head ached as much as his groin. The floral aromas overcame him.

Was this death? He had the same sensation in his first go around with Charminus — his heart stopping as if on life support. He had never associated sex and death; yet it must be, because he dropped into oblivion, losing his control to this charmer — this succubus, who drew his life force from his pith.

He tried to pull away — to wiggle from her clamping — to roll off the bed, as if it had a ledge. But he was trapped. When would they destroy the furniture? It was useless to resist. He had no thoughts as he exploded.

"No," he cried.

"Yes," she wailed. "Forever it will be so, Harris Cartwright. You have come to it willingly and . . ."

". . . on my own accord." He went limp and, finding her vise loosened, rolled to the space beside her. "On my own accord," he gasped, the room spinning. "But it's too much."

"Can you have too much, Harris Cartwright?"

She tried for a second go around, but he pushed himself up and crawled to the bed's edge.

"I'm spent," he murmured.

Then he discovered he was still fully clothed — not one garment removed. He was as dry as a desert. He rolled off the bed, but failed to stand. He saw Charminus' heaving breasts above the blanket line. The light overcame him. He crept along the carpeted floor.

Shag, he thought and didn't know why he noticed, except he grabbed its nap, and pulled hard, which slammed him to the floor. He promptly fell asleep, thanks to the local vintage.

2

Bing bong. Bing bong.

Harris opened his eyes in a flash. He felt the ground move — a gentle sway. He monitored for the sound heralding the next station. But he wasn't in a runaway subway car. He was plastered on Charminus' bedroom floor. The *bing bong* was his imagination. The room's brightness had faded. The walls reflected silvery motion, obscuring movement outside the house. Had *Mortis House* been swept off by a tornado? Was he heading for Oz?

He was moving, or at least *Mortis House* was in motion. He sat up and peeped over the blanket mound to see his passionate captor, but the bed was empty. He hoisted himself up. He was still fully clothed. Perhaps all this was the aftermath of the bad Potato Latkes. Or . . .

He glanced to the bed stand. Two empty goblets set there, a testament to *the Corzanthe*. The flask was gone. Had he glugged down more of the stuff? Was the motion a Corzanthe hangover? He ruled out nothing. He ached and felt bruises beneath his shirt. He searched the room for his seducer, when he remembered he had somewhere to go.

"MTV," he muttered.

He staggered to the door, which he expected to be locked. But he twisted the knob freely, and escaped to . . . to where?

The hallway, once downright Edgar Allan Poe, had transformed into something more appropriate for the Starship Enterprise — a steel corridor drifting into infinite. He couldn't see the end. He was on a balcony still, but the staircase had become a spiraled ramp, something from Frank Lloyd Wright's drawing board. The serpentine banister was still draconian, but had turned white with gold stripes punctuating the scaly segments.

"I should have brought my skateboard," he mused. He scratched his head. "That wine was pretty potent." He took a cautious step. "I think I've fallen down the rabbit hole."

Perhaps the local vintage should have come with a *Drink Me* tag. Harris' grounding in children's fairy tales and *The Magic Planet* sets kept panic at bay. Any other mortal would have raised their hands in terror, screamed like the proverbial painting and ran to the edge of . . . of where? *Infinite? Eternity?*

"There must be a better explanation than booze," he muttered, grasping the dragon's back and continuing his descent. "Booze and a subway ride," he said. "That's all it is."

He didn't believe it, but, like his audience, he had mastered suspending disbelief. It was all illusion, after all. It was the only life he knew.

Suddenly, two eyes stared up at him from the downstairs foyer. It was . . . *the Trone*, that lovely being with the long tresses, the purple band and the ability to float like a feather. She appeared startled when their eyes met. She diverted hers, bowed, and then withdrew.

"No, wait," he called, hastening down the ramp. "I need your help."

That burst illusion's bubble. Fear crept into his noggin. Denial fled to the rafters, if rafters there be. Still, he pursued the evasive woman to the dragon's head, but she was gone.

"Wait," he said.

Suddenly, he jolted. The house halted, throwing him into the walls. The light changed from muted green to surreal yellow. He heard exotic music — no, not music, but rain. No. Not rain, but water flowing. Had this house the sonority to lull the senses as much as the wine had? What a strange place. It wasn't the place he had entered before his hop in Charminus' monstrous bed. Still, he was here.

"I know that sound," he mused, his eyes widening, drawing up his lip corners. "The sea."

He went to the door and touched the knob, now an exotic latch. Upon his touch, it made a familiar sound.

Bing bong. Bing bong.

The door slid open, revealing the bluest of blue skies. The old *El* had vanished and, with it, the tombstones and the gray porch. Instead, a stone ramp cascaded from a pink veranda onto a beach — and beyond the strand, as broad as the world is round, rolled a turquoise sea.

Chapter Six

Plageris on the Bottleblue Sea

1

"I'm not in Kansas anymore," Harris muttered as he descended the causeway.

A warm breeze caught his cheek and he smiled. A blend of anxiety and peace filled his heart with — a tug which kept his eyes fixed to the glorious seascape — a seascape slightly off the beam.

"Not Coney Island," he said.

How could it be with a pristine strand and tropical sea? He tasted brine in the wind, which beckoned him to take a dip. But restraint ruled him. Was he daydreaming or on an unexplainable trip to Bermuda? He walked backwards, keeping an eye on *Mortis House*, the Victorian monstrosity, which had been transformed to match the setting, its foundations buried in pink sand. A veranda, smooth and brightly stucco, blanched under a steeply-peaked roof — a modern pyramid, defying time reference. The gables swept into the dune wall like a cornucopia sprouting cascading blossoms and creeping vines.

"Must be a dream," he said, waiting for his dead Uncle Andy to show up and offer him a job as a chorus girl.

Such were the composition of dreams — Caribbean visions raised on the shingles of a caretaker's shack, now devoid of tombstones and rusty gate and clattering *El* line. It had all the ingredients of undigested bits from *Happy Pings*.

"No, not Coney Island nor Kansas," he muttered. "Maybe *peyote* buttons in the bottom of *the Corzanthe* bottle."

He shook his head and shrugged, resigned to the dream's entrapment. He turned, continuing his progress toward the sea. *Pleasant.* It could be worse. He could be dodging lava flows on Kona. He strutted across the sand, heat pulsating through his *shitekickers*. Soon his socks would be foot warmers. However, shucking his boots could mean their loss. In this dream, they might turn into fuzzy slippers. No time for impulse. He had to get a grip.

Harris had been on beaches before, but never a deserted one. The place didn't feel real, but he wondered how real felt? This world was one-off. *One-off what?* He reached the water's edge, the tide slicking beneath the sky's luster. He shaded his eyes, glancing skyward.

"Holy crap."

He staggered, his jaw held in suspense. Above blazed two suns, near to each other like twin firebrands, except one was smaller than the other, as if the larger gave birth to the smaller. Harris longed for sunglasses. His vision danced; eyes playing tricks only to be compounded by the sighting of three faint moons, He spun around looking for more oddities, if anything could top these. The moons, sizes and shades, were pastel impressions — artifacts in the day sky where they couldn't compete with the two gas balls.

"Not possible," he snapped.

He scratched his head, laughing to himself, continually gazing up, hoping the sight would change. If he saw nine suns or a three cows jumping over the moons, it would at least confirm this as a dream, but the double stars held fast and the satellites lumbered faintly in their wake. He kicked the slick and moved back to the sand, marching toward the edifice which once had been *Mortis House.* Suddenly, he halted. He detected movement on the periphery.

"What the fuck is that?"

Birds hopped along the shoreline; at least they looked like birds. Gulls, but not quite. These were smaller and blue, with red eyes, one leg and spiked crests, which could have been antennae — not like any gull he had ever seen before — even on *the Discovery Channel.* Cautiously, he approached, observing as these blue gulls pecked through the mud, dining on what Harris supposed were worms. These bugs slithered like lumps in gravy on the water's margin. The birds whipped their antennae about, snapping and swallowing a wiggling wriggling meal.

One blue gull turned its attention away from the pecking and plucking. It studied Harris, and then hopped on its single leg toward him.

"Shoo," he said. The bird was determined, hopping closer. "Shoo! Fly away. Whatever the fuck you are, I'll kick your ass if you come closer."

The bird didn't understand English. It sprang forward, landing near Harris' right foot and proceeded to attack his *shitekickers.* While this appeared to be a fruitless mission on the bird's part, its beak couldn't be underestimated. It had a thrust, breaking the instep's shell.

"Shithead," Harris barked. "Go 'way, or I'll stomp you good."

The bird ignored him and pecked again. Harris saw interest rising from the flock. He had to stand his ground or he'd lose a toe at a minimum and who knows what if the blue-feathered gang went berzerk.

Harris raised his hands like a crane (a move he recalled from *The Karate Kid*) and squawked. The gull froze and squawked in reply, perhaps incited the flock. Harris danced about, stomping and contorting his face like a teenage zombie, a part he played a few years back in music video for *The Underground SOBs*. The bird attacked again.

"Aggressive little bastard."

The other hoppers bounced toward him, so Harris converted the squawk to a *Peter Pan* howl, and then spun about like a lunatic loose from the asylum. It did the trick. The idiot bird sprang away like a blue feather ball on a pogo stick. The remaining flock arose, protesting in unison, but Harris continued his corny dance. If anyone saw him now, they would have called for the white jacket brigade. The one-legged wonders whooshed off over the sea. Harris whooped and yelped, mocking them, flapping his arms and cantering down to the slick. Then he took one final run at them, forgetting the creepy bugs slithering in the tide. His boot hit them, sending him flying like a novice ice skater flat to his ass.

"Fuck!"

His hands met the worms and the creepy crawlers and the pincer earwiggy things. He moaned, and then pushed up, slipping again, sliding until he reached purchase in the sand. He scrambled backwards, all the while flicking hideous creatures from his pants and boots. One got as far as his face.

"Fuck! Get off 'a me!"

He flipped it off and slapped his cheeks a few times, breathless. One final check to confirm he was critter free.

"Stupid bugs." He gazed over the waves at the retreating gulls. "Idiot birds."

And two fucking suns and two extra moons. He panted.

Dream or not, he wanted out. He didn't recall any dream that physically attacked him. Well, he did, but he woke up in a sweat before anything harmed him. Now he just had the sweat. He began to realize there was no waking up, because this wasn't a dream.

"And where's Charminus?" he muttered. "Why isn't she down here doing the bunny hop with me? I'm a star, after all."

Then he regarded the double star — two gas balls, dancing the hokey pokey for all he knew with a suite of phantom moons hanging like lanterns on a back lot over a marmalade beach with CGI birds. Harris Cartwright didn't feel like a star now. He felt in trouble. Then another flock caught his attention.

2

These birds flew over the sea in a V-formation.

"Pelicans."

He was sure. He had seen pelicans at Fort Lauderdale during Spring break. But these pelicans were odd — larger than their Floridian cousins. As they came nearer, they cast massive shadows over the waves. Their bills were double-pouched. *Fascinating.* However, as Harris observed them amble across the sky, he noticed they headed his way, aiming for the beach. An idiot gull flock swirled beneath them like dive bombers.

"Shit," Harris croaked, backing toward the house.

It might be prudent to get in out of the way of . . . of what? An attack of killer pelicans, lumbering like B-52's on a bombing raid. The lead beast squawked and flapped its wings on a beeline to Harris. He was glued to the spot, oddly, his mouth agape — heart racing. He was transfixed to the hot pink sand.

Perhaps this is my purpose. Bird food.

Then, from the sea's depths, a massive jaw arose, clamping the point pelican, snapping it from the sky. The bird screeched, its companions winging away. The jaw's long teeth viciously ripped its victim apart, the pelican squawks ceasing. By its length, this creature must be a sea serpent. Mottled brown, it cut the waves like a torpedo, its tail swiping the idiot gulls that hovered for morsels of the beast's quarry. Harris had seen a creature like this one in a painting — in a coffee table book on prehistoric critters. Dumbfounded, he sat on the sand, ignoring the bugs.

"*A mosasaur*," he muttered, remembering the monsters name. "But how?"

The giant crashed through the sea, its hump displacing the waves. Pelican blood tinted the foam to pink. The flock turned from shore and the idiot birds scattered, the feast having concluded.

Harris shook his head. Flabbergasted, he had enough for one day. He'd get his bearings, get in the house and find Charminus or perhaps the lovely floating being — the Trone. He'd thank everyone for funny wine and the strange sex. He'd insist on a hitch back to the *El* and the *bing bong* and the gum-chewing inquisition in the world he knew.

He managed to stand, watching the sea dragon jumping the waves — a leviathan, noble in its way, but not a great attraction for a seaside resort. This certainly wasn't Coney Island. Slowly, he screwed his courage and walked toward the incoming tide, this time staying clear of the creepy crawlers. As he watched *the mosasaur*, he felt strange — as if being watched. He thought about Charminus. He turned quickly, expecting to see her on the veranda, but was surprised again. Watching him was a man with blonde curls and sideburns. He wore an emerald green cloak and a kilt.

"I would not venture too close to the waves," the man said.

"Who are you?"

"A friend," he replied. "I thought you were venturing too close to the drink, my boy. That would never do. This strand is nasty, but nastier if you venture into the water. Never into the water."

Harris cocked his head. *Unbelievable*. Who was this fool? Where did he come from? The house? Nothing surprised him now, because he stood in a place with two suns, three moons, blue gulls, carnivorous pelicans, creepy crawlers and a sea serpent. There was bound to be other wayfarers on the path. But this stranger, despite the ludicrous garb, was British — and not your Tony Bentley-Jones Eastender, but someone posh — a Kenneth Branaugh knock-off.

"Excuse me," Harris said, marching toward the intruder. "I'm not that stupid."

"I did not say you were, dear boy."

"Why are you calling me *dear boy*? I'm not a boy and there's nothing endearing about me. I'm fucking pissed off."

"And who can blame you? Certainly, not I."

The man raised his hands in a welcoming gesture. He might have been ten years older than Harris. Behind him sat a strange contraption — a round canister platform. Harris wasn't in the mood to ask, but the friendship offer couldn't be ignored, regardless of form.

"A friend, you say," Harris snapped. "If you were my friend, you'd get me the fuck out of here. I don't know much about the effects of drugs — especially that *Corzanthe* shit, but I do know when it wears off, you and everything else in the loony world will be gone and I'll wake up in a back alley with my pants wrapped around my head."

"Now that is a fallacy, dear . . . Well, a deep fallacy." The man frowned, but then cocked his head. "Despite your inclination to the contrary, this place is a reality. True, it is different from *our* realm, but you shall acclimatize to it. Eventually."

Harris didn't receive this news in the spirit intended. He shook his fists.

"I don't buy it." He pointed to the sky. "And why am I seeing double — triple even. What happened to the old ramshackle house that stood there? And what was that thing in the water, and . . . and . . . who are you?" He trembled. "And where's . . . the . . . exit . . . out of this dream?"

His shout resounded to the sky, scaring the blue gulls. They matched his yelp with yelps of their own. The man shrugged, and then approached cautiously, probably to comfort Harris.

"Firstly," he explained. "You are not seeing double, unless you consider the double-star of this realm unusual. But, of course, you would. I did when I first was drawn here."

"Drawn?"

"I shall tell you in a bit. Not all at once. Preliminaries are necessary. As to the creature in the waves, it is *a misancorpus*, although I heard you call it *a mosasaur*, and that is close enough to understand it if that is your reference. I know no such reference, but I assume time has marched on and such things are discovered daily. *Misancorpus* grow to over one-hundred and forty stone, they do. I must say, they are not bad eating — at least the few times I have had the pleasure. As for *Mortis House*, it is still there — changed, no doubt. But take cheer, it shall change again."

"That doesn't cheer me one bit."

"I thought it would not, but you must know such buildings are barely buildings — more like vessels or conduits to the outlands."

Harris pondered this, deciding it made no sense. This man's *yakkity-yak* raced too easily, relegating truth to the sidelines. The man might be a magician or perhaps *the Wizard of Oz* — a humbug, after all.

"You said you were *drawn*," Harris said. "What does that mean? Is it like abduction? Have I been kidnapped?"

"No. In fact, you have been saved."

"Saved?"

"To be drawn here is to be spared."

Spared?

"I'm lost, not saved."

"It is a difficult concept to grasp. Perhaps you need more time to ponder things. As for myself, I was drawn from *your* world — from a different time and another land."

Harris sighed, and then turned back to the sea. He wasn't getting a straight answer. He looked over the waves trying to spot the beast again — this thing called *the misancorpus.*

"You're British?" he muttered.

The man came close to his ear.

"An Englishman, sir. The British business came later." He grasped Harris' shoulders and turned him. Then, he bowed as if receiving an audience's adulation. "I am Sir John Briarcliff, the principle player at Her Majesty's Theatre Royal — everything from Hamlet to Caliban."

"You're an actor?"

"A Thespian, to be sure. Now I grace a different stage — a different role — part of being drawn and . . . saved. I am called now Arquebus, the second consort to the Scepta Soffira, the youngest daughter of the Elector of Montjoy."

Harris was dumbfounded. Although he perked up at the name Montjoy, it was the only word he recognized, but brought him no consolation.

"Whoever you were and whatever you are," Harris snapped, "I want none of it. I want out of here . . . now. I've a life and it ain't here."

"I am afraid there are no options available other than the one they afford us, Mr. Cartwright."

Harris whirled out of Sir John's grasp.

"Mr. Cartwright? How do you know my name? What happened to *dear boy?*"

"Be calm, sir," Arquebus replied. "Just as I was drawn by the Scepta Soffira, you were drawn by the Scepta Charminus." He bowed again. "I have been sent to be your compass — to help your transition."

Harris' eyes bulged. He spit, turning abruptly and marching back to the tidal sweep.

"Not too close, now," Arquebus shouted. "Beware *the misancorpus.*"

Jabberwocky, Harris thought.

He didn't care if the beast wallowed ashore and swallowed him for dessert.

3

Harris prowled the shore, sobbing and flagging his arms. He thought about his mother and sister and California and red carpets and Tony. Misery engulfed him. Tears burst their dikes, coating his cheeks as surely as the bugs slathered the water's margin. He couldn't digest any of this. All he had wanted was . . . well, a roll in the hay with a sexy and mysterious lady. But he still didn't recall the *sex* part. The exhaustion was there, but never the fireworks moment. Was it worth this trip into *the Twilight Zone?* Now he was supposed to swallow a crock about being drawn to serve *the Queen of the Night* who snatched him away in a drug-induced hallucination. He didn't really believe that this Arquebus — Sir John Briarcliff, actor from a different century, actually existed beyond imagination. Still, it felt real. Gulls and serpent and bugs and double-suns . . . and an actor bowing for applause.

Suddenly, he felt humming — from the sand.

"What new devilment is this?"

He laughed, because it was a line from *The Magic Planet.* He halted and turned quickly to see what followed him. Arquebus did, now in an open-air contraption — the platform cylinder, which Harris recognized as a hovercraft, humming along on a hush of green mush emitted from its bottom.

"What?" he asked.

"You must not stray," Arquebus called.

"I don't give a fuck."

"For an actor, you certainly have mastered the red light district's vernacular."

"As I said, I don't give a fuck. Why not leave me alone, Sir John?"

"It is no use, my boy."

Harris raised his eyebrows.

"You can call me Harris."

"How Dickensian," Arquebus said. "I *knew* Boz. I performed the best Fagin to his recollection. Standing ovation from a full house. Do you know the stage's pulse?"

"I've been there," Harris quipped.

"I am so glad, because unlike Scepta Soffira, who prefers stage Thespians, Scepta Charminus leans towards the Magic Lantern stars."

"They collect actors?"

"I am not sure the word *collect* is the most appropriate one; but if you see fit to regard it as such, you had better keep it to yourself. As for the third sister, Scepta Miracola, she has two consorts from the Asian theater."

"Are you telling me I'll be surrounded by . . ."

"Men of the trade," Arquebus beamed.

He landed the hovercraft, and then stepped out.

"What is that thing?"

"An advantage, my dear . . . Harris. We call it *a Cabriolin*."

"*We* call it that?"

"The people of Farn."

"Farn?"

Sir John came close now. He looked into Harris' face, and then placed an arm about his shoulders.

"You have fight within you, which is commendable, especially for a consort of Scepta Charminus. You shall need it. *My* mistress is the gentle sort. Still, Farn is your new home."

"Not so," Harris said. "I won't stay here."

"*This* is not Farn. *This* is Plageris on the Bottleblue Sea — a stopping point on your journey. It would have been best if you had stayed in *Mortis House* until we reached *the Ayelli* overlooking Montjoy City. But you emerged and saw and . . . well, you are here now and what else could I do but begin your indoctrination?"

"Farn?" Harris snapped. "And where is Charminus?"

"You never ask that question. She will find you when she seeks you."

Harris looked for the first time at this so-called *friend.* He saw a face — classic and stage worthy. It may have been drawn from the Victorian age, but it was lithe and elastic.

"If you met Charles Dickens, you must be ancient."

"Yes, as you shall be to your co-consort, who was drawn from an age beyond you."

"What?"

"The days go friendly upon us here. We are not immortal like the Electors and many other denizens in Farn, but we do enjoy the aging process' cessation. There are many much older than I who might look like my younger brother."

Harris trembled now. He thought about his many glances in the mirror, tracking his face as it matured. It was by no means old, but he knew one day he'd look there and see the epitome of King Lear or Prospero and without the benefit of makeup. But the Farn plan was not compensation for losing all he knew and loved and wanted — his dreams, his fans, his friends, his sister, his . . . mother. That thought convulsed him to tears again.

"I must leave here," he sobbed.

Then the trumpets sounded.

Chapter Seven

Kuriakis the Great

1

The horns belched — sharp trumpeting followed by drum beats and kazoo tunes. Harris shaded his eyes, watching the distant sand roll toward him.

"What is it, Sir John?"

"Kuriakis comes with the Pod."

A line of strange hover crafts — *Cabriolins*, emerged from the dust devil. The drivers wore wind-swept capes — a colorful lot — silver, gold, purple, morning-glory and marigold. Some shook rattles. Others struck tom-toms, floating beside the trumpeters, bleating black ram horns. At the procession's center, a giant sat astride what might have been a horse, except the jet-black beast stood twelve feet at the withers. It had horns and red eyes that flashed at the marauding idiot birds swarming around the crew like gnats. The ebony creature rocketed, its hooves not touching the sand, like *the Cabriolin* brigade. The runners floated above the strand, green fire wreathing their feet.

"What a spectacle," Harris muttered.

The horse rider, draped in silver, his helmet squared to his cheeks, carried a long ivory staff, which danced with blue lightning. He raised it, shooting a bolt toward the sky. Then, dropping without warning, a large bird dipped to the dust line.

"Hunters," Harris muttered.

The Pod were hunters and the bird, the prize. The prize was losing this contest, especially after three *Cabriolins* ascended the heights and ran beside it. The bird snapped and swerved and dipped, but *the Cabriolins* kept up.

"We best lie low," Arquebus said to Harris. "We must not interfere with my lord's sport."

Harris shook his head and stepped forward, prominently, despite the warning. The prize became clearer now. At first, Harris thought it be might another variety of strange pelican, but as it drew closer, he saw a flying reptile.

"*Pterodactyl*," he muttered.

"*Terrerbyrd*, my friend," Arquebus said, tugging Harris back. "It will surely spear us if we remain here. If luck prevails and *the byrd* spares us, my brothers will run us over. If *the Cabriolins* miss us, our lord's steed, *Nightmare*, will surely mow us down."

"I guess we're fucked," Harris said, unheeding.

He snapped free of Arquebus' hold and marched toward the Pod, his neck craning up to view *the terrerbyrd.* He calculated that *the Cabriolins* were high and would miss him, but the runners might give him a slam. Then he saw the horse — *Nightmare*. It shape shifted between raging bull and irate stallion. It snorted red steam — steam as red as its eyes. The rider appeared fierce also, his eyes no longer set upon the prize, but on Harris.

What fool is this? came a voice.

The voice rattled in Harris' brain. He wished he could answer it, but he wasn't telepathic, although he heard the question as if he were. He banished fear. Finished with it, he was. What more could they do to him? The rider was distinctly the authority here. Sir John could babble about the *whys* and *wherefores*, but he didn't hold the key to the exit. So this rider — the voice in Harris' head, was the man of the hour — if he were a man. Harris couldn't tell. He could be the devil himself.

"Hey," Harris shouted, shaking his fists. Arquebus moaned warnings. "Hey! I'm no fool."

Laughter rattled around his head. But perhaps the rider was right. Arquebus yelled, but the racket drowned his voice. *The terrerbyrd* swooped. No pigeon, this, but as big as a Piper Cub, gliding directly at Harris, its long snout open to clip him, but more likely preparing to cut him in two.

"Sir John," Harris called, his fear suddenly returning.

Too late to enlist help. Running wouldn't serve in the short course, so Harris slammed to the ground, lying flat. A gust blew above him and a jaw snapped. He rolled sideways when *the byrd* tried to catch him. He peered into its dead, hate-filled eyes. This set Harris' adrenaline flowing — the last push needed. Everything in this world had been against him. Time to fight back.

When *the terrerbyrd* finished its pass, Harris stood.

"Get down, Harris," Arquebus shouted.

Harris turned. The Pod approached frantically, *Nightmare* galloping on a green cloud.

Fool, came the voice again.

"I'm no fool," Harris shouted, and then proceeded to prove the voice correct.

When Harris turned back toward *Mortis House, the terrerbyrd* had landed, its claws scratching the strand angrily. Its towering wings folded like laundry and it clumsily hopped toward Harris with intent. Harris ignored the collective warning shouts from Arquebus and the Pod. He even ignored the voice in his head.

"You son of a bitch," he shouted at *the byrd*. "You think you're hot shit and can take a chunk outta me."

Harris hobbled as he walked, loosening his right *shitekicker*. It was tight, but his swelling anger helped him rip through the laces and yank the boot off. He swung it over his head.

"Get the fuck out of here, you escapee from *Jurassic Park*," he screamed, and let the boot fly.

It hit *the terrerbyrd* on the snout, dazing it. The creature kiltered left and right like a windmill attacked by a lance. It raised its snout and cawed to the wind. The Pod moved forward, and *the byrd* hopped toward the waves, and then took flight.

"You sorry son of a bitch," Harris shouted. "Go home to your Mama and leave me the fuck alone."

Harris turned, facing the Pod. The voice in his head was now a roaring laugh. It embraced him like a champion.

2

Arquebus pulled Harris to his knees, Harris resisting. He hadn't given in to *the terrerbyrd*. Why should he give an inch to something infinitely smaller? Although *Nightmare* and its rider, might be fiercer.

"Respect, Harris," Arquebus muttered. "You must bow before our lord."

"I'm sorry, Sir John. You might have forgotten you're a Brit and should only bow to Queen Lizzie, but I'm red, white and blue and standing tall."

Six Pod members pursued *the terrerbyrd*, jetting over Harris' head. Others remained, including four dressed similar to Arquebus. They surveyed Harris with disturbing interest as if trying to find his true measure through his skin. Harris locked his gaze on each in turn — an attempt to shake off their stares.

"Harris, you must observe protocol," Arquebus snapped.

"Let him stand," the rider said, removing his helmet, handing it to the waiting runner.

Harris assessed these runners as servants. The others remained a mystery, but he noticed the group that pursued *the terrerbyrd* was younger, sporting a different garb — crimson tunics, silver breastplates and short leather caps like old-fashioned football helmets.

"If you wish it, father," Arquebus replied, and then bowed.

Harris cocked his head. His own father had died when he was three, so he never accorded any man the paternal honors. He didn't think he'd start now.

"Why is he unfettered?" the rider asked Arquebus.

"He awoke prematurely and decided to explore. He is inquisitive, beyond fettering . . . in my opinion."

"Fettering?" Harris muttered, frowning.

"A term to describe the confinement imposed until we have reached our destination," Arquebus explained. "You were never scheduled to visit Plageris until you knew more about your situation."

"No harm done," the rider said. He laughed again.

The four men in *the Cabriolins* laughed on cue. Arquebus nervously joined them, but Harris recognized this as protocol.

The rider dismounted aided by two runners. A giant, he was commanding by virtue of size. His ivory staff flashed when striking the ground. Harris felt every vibration. The rider wasn't old, but mature — craggy even; yet refined. Emeralds speckled his braided gray beard. On his right hand shone a colossal jade ring. Harris recognized the shepherd's crook sigil as a twin to the one on Charminus' ring.

"So you are the new one," boomed the man.

"New one?" Harris replied.

"Do not speak unless you know what you are about," the man chided. "You may think you know, but you stand before me bootless under *Solus* and *Dodecadatamus*, wondering about things beyond your ken." The man grinned. "But be of good cheer. Your confusion will be short-lived. Plageris is foreign even to the people of Farn. When you are settled, the mysteries shall fall by the wayside."

"I have begun his clarification," Arquebus said.

"To no avail, I presume."

The man raised his hand — the right one, extending the ring toward Harris.

"Kiss it," Arquebus whispered.

"Is he the pope?" Harris snapped. "I'm not Catholic."

"It does not matter, Harris. Do not be prickly in this."

"Prickly?" He gazed into the rider's eyes. "You know I'm a stranger in this land. I don't mean to stay here. I'm depending on you to show me the way out."

"The way out?" carped one of the *Cabriolin* drivers. "This may seem like theater, but be assured, there is no *way out*."

This man, in a bright-yellow cloak, left his *Cabriolin*, bounding toward Harris.

"Do not meddle, Tappiolus," Arquebus said. "A time might come to strike your Lucifers, but this is not it."

"Why not?" asked the man, sweeping his cloak over one shoulder. He inspected Harris like a drill sergeant. "You might think you are a hot potato, sir, but I have seen your work. Flash in the pan."

Harris frowned. *Who the hell was this guy?* He had a perceptible Italian accent, which befit his pencil-thin mustache.

"How could you know my work?" Harris snapped.

"I know it," Tappiolus said, showboating for the others. "In film school we studied your filmography. Not inspiring. Examples for avoidance."

Harris twitched, but Arquebus held him back. The other three men laughed. However, the giant — that stately being called Kuriakis, kept his hand extended, waiting for Harris' lips to grace knuckles in homage. Harris brushed Arquebus' away, and then turned. This stirred the others to rebuke — a chorus of indignant growls.

"How dare you turn your back on the Elector," Tappiolus snapped. "You are unworthy of us, sir."

"Perhaps, you are correct, Tappiolus," Kuriakis said, disappointment in his voice.

Harris gazed along the strand. *The terrerbyrd* still gave a merry chase, its wings flapping its pursuers away. Then Harris saw his enchantress on *Mortis House's* veranda.

"Charminus," he murmured.

"Ah, yes," Kuriakis said. "My daughter." Then to Tappiolus. "Whether this new consort is worthy, he is still only second to you in her eyes. Take consolation in that and accept it, Tappiolus."

Harris turned. He recalled Arquebus' talk of a co-consort, a film actor drawn from the future.

So that's how he knows my work.

Verified, the insult stung more now.

"You're an actor too," Harris said to Tappiolus.

"We are all actors by the grace of Scepta preference."

Tappiolus bowed, as did the others from within their *Cabriolins*. Two of these were Asians, while the third distinctly Mediterranean, swarthy and tan. It was true. Harris had been drawn into an uncontracted role, and cast in an eternal play — without top billing. And this smug asshole, who looked like a cheap version of Valentino, was his co-star, and a critic on vintage film, to boot. *Vintage film?* Harris never considered the efficacy of his own legacy, or lack of one.

"Sir," he said to Kuriakis, bowing slightly as a concession. "I know you mean well and I am a pawn in the scheme of things, but I assure you, I'm not the man for the part."

Kuriakis extended the ring again. Harris balked, but this time looked to Arquebus for help. Arquebus urged compliance.

"Either you kiss it," Tappiolus snapped, "or throw your other boot at him. You have no other choices."

"No one does," said the Mediterranean man, who cocked his head and waved a small baton — a strange decorative stick.

"Sceptas choose us," Tappiolus said. "Only they can release us. You are a replacement for a recently released consort, so your fate is sealed."

"Released?"

"Not in the way you think, Harris," Arquebus said.

Harris felt the beach heat through his right sock and considered throwing his left boot, and then making a level run for it. *But to where?* He looked to *Mortis House*, Charminus posing alluringly at the door. If she held his fate, could there be much harm in smooching her father's ring. *Little risk*, he thought.

He bowed slightly, and then touched his lips to the jade ring. Gales of laughter rained from Tappiolus. Harris already hated the man, despite the short acquaintance.

3

"Brother," Tappiolus carped, still laughing. "Welcome to the Pod."

The horn sounded as *the terrerbyrd* swooped, pursued by the hunters in their *Cabriolins*. Kuriakis raised his staff, pointing it skyward. He shot a golden bolt at the beast, grazing it and altering its course toward shore.

"Enough pother," Kuriakis declared. "I came to the Plageris to hunt. We shall continue this discussion later." He grinned at Harris. "Come aloft with us."

The Elector retreated to his steed, which the two runners barely reined in. Another runner helped Kuriakis into the saddle.

"It is a fine day to chase up dinner," the Elector shouted. "Joella will want a feast and I shall not disappoint her." He pointed the staff at Harris. "Go aloft with Arquebus. As for the rest of you lazy blighters, enough dawdle. Enough pother. Aloft with you! Aloft!"

Nightmare rose on its hind legs, its emerald hoof pads flashing, its crimson snort steaming.

"Hoy!" the Elector shouted, and soon the great Kuriakis was aloft again, charging toward *the terrerbyrd*.

The Pod followed, each to their *Cabriolins*, cloaks flapping in the wind — batons aimed at the flying quarry — tom-toms and kazoos playing in their wake.

Arquebus touched Harris' shoulder.

"That business with the boot has endeared you to him," he remarked. "But I fear you have an enemy in Tappiolus."

Harris watched the Pod as they rose over the tide.

"They're flying high."

"Have you objections to flight? I hear the men of your time routinely fly."

"Yes, but in . . . bigger birds."

"Come aloft then — with me. We shall take it easy. No sense stoking your fears."

"I'm not afraid."

Harris just had made a film that had him in harness a host of times. He'd been required to do his own stunts, flying above a set with his crotch tethered in a ball-crushing harness suit. Arquebus bowed, and then escorted him to *the Cabriolin*.

"How does this thing go?" Harris asked.

"I shall manage it. Now is not the time for learning. Hold tightly to the railing and enjoy the view."

Harris grinned. The vehicle, simple — rudimentary even, consisted of a round platform loosely enclosed by three circumferential tubes, making the contraption look like a flying trash barrel. A raised panel displayed an array of lights, the controls, no doubt.

"No seat belts?" Harris asked, but there were no seats, so the question seemed lame.

He leaned his back on the railing while Arquebus played with the controls and rubbed some device pinned to his cloak. The craft lifted smoothly, drifting parallel to the shoreline. Harris grinned, a stiff breeze striking his gob and dancing through his hair. He saw Charminus on the veranda. She wore a purple gown, a cowl hooding her. Still alluring, Harris wondered why he would ever want to leave her. However, the thought wasn't his own, but telepathically implanted as he passed before her smile, an antidote to his escape plan. His reverie broke when he noticed the other one — the Trone, standing behind her mistress, toting a tray of refreshments.

"Who's that with Charminus?"

"Her Trone," Arquebus replied.

"I meant, what's her name?"

"Trones are not called by name."

Disappointing. He tried to shake off the Scepta's allure, which told him he pleased her and she wanted him again and again — for eternity.

Harris sighed, and then gazed skyward.

4

Skyward. *The Cabriolin* banked over waves, rising when it neared the Pod. The hunters assaulted *the terrerbyrd* with a battery of fiery flashes, which shot from their batons. Arquebus had a baton also, attached to the front railing. Harris perused it. A puzzle. No visible mechanism — trigger, hammer, buttons or barrels. He touched it.

"What is this thing?"

"*A Stick.*"

"*A Stick?*"

"That is what it is called. What else could it be?"

"I thought you'd call it a fire torch or a big bad bang-bang or something."

"No. Just *a Stick*."

"How does it . . ."

"It does nothing. The power comes from the operator, not *the Stick*. It merely focuses."

Harris took *the Stick* from its holder, bringing it to his eye. It was decorated, but otherwise it was as Arquebus declared — *a Stick*, made from a sturdy wood. The only mark he discerned, beside the decorations, was etched on a plate near the stub end — a *V* crisscrossed by two wavy lines.

"What's this symbol?"

"That is I, dear friend," Arquebus said. "The *V* is the sigil for my Scepta — the Scepta Soffira. The two waves declares me as her second consort. The first consort is Agrimentikos." He pointed ahead. "That is he, showing off for the Elector with his fancy dips and swirls. He still will not score a hit."

The man — Agrimentikos, was the Mediterranean.

"And why won't he score a hit?"

"He is a bad shot." Arquebus chuckled. "He is better quoting lines from Sophocles and Aristophanes. He does a wonderful *Opoponax*. But shooting? And even if he could shoot straight, none dares upstage Kuriakis."

"Do I detect rivalry between you and your co-consort?"

Arquebus leered.

"I know my place as you shall learn yours."

Harris watched Kuriakis the Great as he soared as nimbly as Perseus on Pegasus, teasing *the terrerbyrd*, while the Pod corralled it until it tuckered. Although the beast still dodged the flashes, it ceased attacking. The consorts shone now, edging closer to the prey than other Pod members. The younger men eased off, drifting to the periphery. The runners, who flew on strange electronic footgear, unfurled a net over the tide to catch *the byrd* when it was felled.

"Why aren't we joining the fray?" Harris asked.

"Time enough on another day. Even the Thirdlings fall back now."

"Thirdlings?"

Before Arquebus replied, one young man brought his *Cabriolin* near. He saluted Arquebus, who returned the salute with a nod.

Harris nodded also to match the custom. The younger man came so close, his *Cabriolin* nearly touched Arquebus' railing.

"Wonderful hunt today, father," the lad said.

"I should say. *The Scullery Dorgan* will be busy cooking tonight."

"Nothing like *byrd* in red sauce."

"Nothing like it." Arquebus turned and addressed Harris. "Where are my manners? Harris Cartwright, may I introduce you to Elypticus, my seventh son."

"His favorite, I might add," the Thirdling remarked. "Glad to make your acquaintance, lord and most honored to receive the salute of a consort of distinction." Elypticus bowed deeply, and then flashed Harris a grin. "Impressive bootwork back there, lord. I have never seen anything like it in all my life."

"Short as that has been," Arquebus remarked, drawing giggles from his son.

Harris smiled, and nodded again.

"Glad to meet you also," he said, and then addressed Arquebus. "Your son?"

"Do you doubt it, sir?" Arquebus replied, and then brightened. "I have a jolly idea — a Bardian inspiration if I do say so myself." He addressed his son now. "Mr. Cartwright has expressed a desire to join in the fray. How about giving him a wee taste?"

Elypticus winked, mischievously, and then opened his *Cabriolin* gate.

"It would be my pleasure," he said. "Jump. Come aboard, lord."

Harris hesitated, the gulf between the two vehicles being unsteady, but then leaped the gap landing in Thirdling Elypticus' care.

"Hold tight," Arquebus said. "And son, remember he is co-consort to the dark one. If he comes to harm, you might find yourself in dire straits."

Elypticus nodded again, closed the gate and sped off, Harris lurching in the sudden acceleration.

5

Harris regarded Elypticus, Sir John's Thirdling son. Although the lad was tall — a hand taller than Harris, his face was that of a twelve-year old. *Unsettling.*

"First time up?" Elypticus asked.

"Yes," Harris said, looking down.

The netting now crisscrossed the sea. Beneath it, the waves churned.

"You should hold fast to the rail." Harris gripped. "Better fasten about my waist."

Harris did so. Immediately, the lad shook his head, his helmet feathers whipping the air. The *Cabriolin* accelerated, rising at least two-hundred feet in a few seconds. Harris gasped, but liked the thrill. They continued to rise until the Pod were specks and *the terrerbyrd* was mosquito-size. It was liberating.

Harris glanced to the suns and the moons beyond. He saw *Mortis House*, now a squat protrusion, emerging from the dunes, its rear lost to the scrub. The Plageris was an island, the Bottleblue Sea vast. He searched for landmarks — the Statue of Liberty or the Empire State Building would be nice, but beyond the island's girt was an unending expanse of turquoise — no horizon — no sign he was in the round world still. *Odd.*

Elypticus gave a shout — a wild *woohoo*, and brought *the Cabriolin* higher and drove it faster.

"Hold tight, lord."

"Pretty fast," Harris said. "Maybe, too fast."

"Not a bit of it. I am free and away from Farn and my brothers and the duty rolls and patrols. The sky is clear here — never green. Nothing tethers me to promise or prophecy."

Before Harris puzzled out which *promise* and what *prophecy*, *the Cabriolin* dipped, falling seaward in a joy ride's hectic speed. His heart raced. *Exhilarating.* This bested the fastest roller coaster he had ridden, and he had ridden a few ballbusters. But *the Cabriolin's* angle was steep. His grip slipped. The netting came up fast. *The terrerbyrd* wailed, and then fell, blasted by the Elector's staff. Before *the Cabriolin* reached the Pod, Elypticus swerved sharply, almost dumping Harris out.

"Whoa," he gasped. "That was some ride, but . . ."

"Again," Elypticus shouted like the child Harris suspected.

Harris heard shouts from the other Thirdlings — warning shouts. He noticed the consorts gathering in formation. Still,

Elypticus shot for the sky, the wind nearly blowing Harris aloft. Fun was fun, but this seemed reckless. Then, down again, this time over the open sea. As they leveled off, Harris witnessed a wonder — a long brown object swimming through the waves. He recognized it, and, although it still amazed, panic suddenly gripped him.

"Not so close," he shouted.

But the moment swallowed the lad.

"We can get closer, lord. Shall we?"

"No."

Then *the Cabriolin* plunged again, this time directly over *the misancorpus*, which wasn't up for visitors. It whipped about, its massive torso leaping from the water, its jaws on a direct course for luncheon.

"Pull up," Harris screamed. "Pull up."

John Briarcliff's son, seventh or otherwise, must have had a death wish, because he flew *the Cabriolin* through *the misancorpus'* open jaws, making it to the other side just as the megateeth clamped shut.

"Woohoo."

Harris squeezed Elypticus' waist.

"Enough," he shouted. "Get us out of here."

"Whatever you say, lord."

Elypticus was suddenly demure. He leveled the vehicle and sped shoreward, a host of consorts and Thirdlings surrounding him as he halted, hovering over *Mortis House*, before landing. Harris released his death grip, pushing the gate open and leaping to the sand. He was dizzy, in part from motion, but also from inspecting *the misancorpus'* tonsils. He staggered as the other *Cabriolins* landed. Elypticus went prostrate at the base of the ramp.

"Forgive him, my lady," Arquebus said, addressing Charminus, who stood angrily on the veranda. "He is a rash boy, only three now, but one more year will see him either in control or dead."

Arquebus surveyed his contrite son. The runners hauled the netting from the water, dragging *the terrerbyrd's* corpse over the shore's slick. Kuriakis, on Nightmare, hovered at a distance, unwinding his steed from the heat of the hunt. The Elector seemed to reflect on events — chanting to the sea in a language Harris couldn't comprehend.

Harris struggled to stay standing; too many G's having pressed him silly. Sir John steadied him, while the others turned their attentions to the harvest.

"That was some ride," Harris said, still breathless. He glanced back at Elypticus, and then addressed Arquebus. "I hope he's not in trouble. He meant well, and I egged him on."

"What shall be, shall be," Arquebus replied.

Arquebus bowed to Charminus, a tribute to sculptured ice. She had removed the purple gown and stood now in her black denim, reminding Harris of his dilemma. The ride momentarily diluted any notions of escape, replacing them with prayers for survival.

"My lady," he muttered, the jade ring flashing.

Suddenly, Harris felt intoxicated. He lost his balance and knelt beside the penitent Elypticus.

"I am sorry, lord," Elypticus whispered. "The pain is fleeting and shall pass, I assure you."

Harris *did* feel a pain welling across his shoulders. He almost welcomed the end. However, it *did* subside, giving way to exhaustion. He didn't recall exactly when he lost consciousness. However, he certainly remembered waking, because when his eyes opened again, he was in a different place — a place devoid of sea and sand.

Chapter Eight

Yustichisqua

1

Many things unsettled Harris in this new life, not the least, *Mortis House's* ability to shift and change like a dune. Sometimes it was confined, while at other times it sprawled endlessly, or seemingly so. Like *the Cabriolins*, it was a vehicle, but elastic over time and place — putty stretched to the outer lands with its heels set firmly in Farn. Such were the estates of the nine Electors, each to their realm — each to their city. So when Harris opened his eyes again, *Mortis House* still engulfed him, but as it appeared in Farn — an acropolis on a hill overlooking Montjoy City.

He did not see this at first. What he first saw was a golden eye — a projection, which hovered beneath an archway — one of several niches in the rotunda where he laid as a centerpiece as if in state. The eye blinked, and then flickered. He recognized the eye as Charminus Montjoy's or, as he should say, the Scepta Charminus, his mistress. *The Eye* was the first thing he saw. The second was a lad draped in a brown robe — buckskins, his hair double braided and held by a purple headband. He couldn't be more than fifteen or sixteen. With downcast eyes and a servile pose, he knelt in a humble heap when Harris awoke.

"Where am I?" Harris asked.

He was stiff, his back sore. He no longer wore his street duds, and his boots were missing, although he recalled wearing only one before he passed out, the other having been heaved at a monstrous flying reptile. He did recall the ride in . . . what did they call it, *a Cabriolin*, the driver a baby-faced teenager, hopped up on the experience and finding a ride through a sea serpent's jaw the height of exhilaration. Or had it been a dream?

Harris felt his shoulders. He wore a fine blue cloak cinched with a sapphire brooch. He tried to read the brooch's sigil, but it angled away from him. Otherwise, he was naked beneath this new garment, the silk upon his skin arousing him.

"Where am I?" he asked again, this time to *the Eye*.

It flickered, faded, and then disappeared. He directed his attention to the brown heap at the side of the platform. He sat up, and then kicked the form.

"I asked a question," he said. "You could at least tell me where the fuck I am."

The lad looked up, a slight grin washing his face. Harris couldn't tell whether the question amused or startled him.

"Farn," the lad stammered, and then looked away.

Harris edged to the floor — a bright-white marble floor, which would no doubt be cold if he were not wearing fine sandals made from a material he couldn't quite place. Not leather. Nor cloth. Metal, perhaps, but fluid like mercury and a bit unpleasant when pressed to the floor, like stepping in mud.

"Who are you?" he asked the lad.

No answer. Harris took a step, found the experience strange, and then grasped the platform. He hunkered down to the lad.

"You understand me or you couldn't have told me where I am."

The lad shook his head.

"You have a tongue or you couldn't have answered me at all. So who are you?"

"Your Trone."

"My Trone? A servant?" Harris stood, and then sat again at the platform's edge. "Do I need a servant? I don't need anyone fetching for me. It goes completely against the grain. I mean, if you were an intern or a dresser or a wardrobe expert, it would be different. But a servant . . . or what did you call it — *my Trone*. I don't think so."

"Please, master," the lad said, inching forward, clasping his hands prayer-like. He had a strange device near his knee — a lamp of some kind. He took care not to disturb it. "If you reject me, they will turn me out of the palace and I shall be in harm's way."

Harris sat agape. He had a servant — a slave, assigned to him and trembling at the loss of his meager prospects.

"Well, I wouldn't want to put you in harm's way."

"Thank you, master."

"Don't call me master. It makes me want to puke."

"Have I displeased you, master?"

The lad grasped Harris' ankle and squeezed. *Embarrassing.* Harris shook his foot loose.

"Let me think," he mused. "What's your name?"

The servant bowed low.

"No name, master."

Harris balled his fist at the word *master*. He would be no man's better. However, was this a man? The lad wore funny sandals and seemed to float instead of walking. He could be a robot or an android. Maybe he had a number — like Trone450-APrime2. If so, it would be a designation still.

"Certainly, you must have a name."

The lad trembled, touching the lamp as if it were his touchstone. Harris lost patience. He awoke in a strange, sterile room under the scrutiny of a fuzzy eyeball and now bantered with a creature so fawning it made him nervous to be in its presence.

"Come, come," Harris snapped. "Your name?"

"We are not allowed to speak, master," the Trone muttered. "Not even your name. You are not to know I am here even. Why would you know my name if I am not here?"

"Of course you're here. I'm not blind. And I'm not treating you like . . . that lamp or . . . a table, even if you're . . . fetching me stuff, or whatever you do."

"I serve you in all things. They should have told you."

"There's lots of shit I don't know. This is one. You can bet there's more. Like what was that big eyeball when I awoke?"

"I cannot speak of *the Eye*. She will know and I will be punished."

Just so. The kid's here to serve Harris' needs, but he couldn't answer the first question. He hunkered down again, looking his Trone squarely in the face. The lad found difficulty in deflecting the glance. Looking at the master must have also been a taboo. Harris sighed — a desperate gasp filled with resignation.

"So you're my Trone."

"Trone, master. Yes."

"And what's a Trone?"

The lad trembled, but cocked his head and stammered.

"A Trone, master. A Cetrone. The people of Cetronia are the Trones, although I live in *the Kalugu* and not beyond the Forling in the Spice Mountains."

For a nonentity blending into hamper and sink, this lad had given Harris a heap of information, most unintelligible, but it was a start. Harris reached out to touch him. The Trone flinched, and then looked askance, as if deciding to run should *the Eye* reappear.

"So your people *do* have a name — and not a label. You must have a name too."

"You must not ask it, master. It is not done."

"It is, if I say so. That is, if you're supposed to serve me in all things."

"You want to know the name my mother gave me?"

"That would be the one," although Harris knew the one he sported wasn't the one his mother gave him.

"It is not easy for *the Ayelli* to say things in my language."

"Ayelli?"

"You are *Ayelli*, master."

"Ah — you're teaching me left and right here." Harris frowned. "What's your name? Stop beating around the bush. If I can't pronounce it, I'll give you a nickname like Spanky or Alfalfa."

"Alfalfa?"

"Don't sweat it. Just tell me. My knees are hurting."

The lad grinned and, in that grin, connection. Harris felt it — trust emerging from servitude.

"I am called Yustichisqua."

"Yusti . . ."

"Yustichisqua."

"Cheese-skwa."

"Yustichisqua."

"Yustichisqua. Now that's not so bad to pronounce. I sound like a Cetrone now."

"Do not say that, master. You dishonor yourself."

"How so?"

"We are never more than servants to *the Ayelli*. I am fortunate to serve here. If you were Cetrone, I could not serve you."

Harris stood again, raising Yustichisqua. The lad remained humble, looking away to divert familiarity.

"Have I missed something?" Harris asked.

"You are not like the others. But in time you shall learn how to treat me as *an Ayelli* does and all will be well."

"You're right. I'm not like the others. I'll learn if I decide to stay. But I'm not playing Simon Legree for any one. That part's not in my repertoire." Harris thought he heard someone coming —

footfalls in the distance. "You know, I've forgotten how to pronounce your name already."

"You should not use it, master. You should not even refer to me as Trone. Just wave or glance. I shall know."

"Nonsense. Pronounce it again."

"Yustichisqua, if you insist, master."

"What does it mean?"

Yustichisqua smiled, and then went demure.

"It means Baby Bird in my language."

"Baby Bird." Harris chuckled, but then decided it was a perfect fit . . . or near perfect. "I shall call you Little Bird. How's that?"

"You should not do me honor, master. But . . ."

"But what?"

"I am glad that you are not dismissing me. To do so would end my life and I live to . . ."

"I know. To serve me in all things. That may be your role in this B movie, but we'll work on a better scenario. I'm an A-list actor, you know."

Little Bird bowed, just as the footsteps became louder and the men entered.

2

Arquebus strolled across the rotunda's marble floor accompanied by an elaborately dressed man, who plodded in a studious fashion — trundling. Later Harris would learn this newcomer was a Zecronisian, a member of Farn's merchant and trading class — who served as go-betweens for *the Ayelli* and the artisan class — the Gurts. Zecronisians were island peoples and seafarers, but in Montjoy city they had their own enclave where they practiced their religion and not without criticism or occasional persecution. They walked slightly bent to accommodate a curious third leg, which extended when they needed to sit. This particular Zecronisian was Mordacai, the personal physician to Elector Kuriakis. Harris didn't know this at the time, but was bewildered by an array of devices the physician plied within a few minutes of his arrival.

"Sir John," Harris said. Then the physician rubbed Harris' arm quickly with a square box. It flashed red and soon a painful throb went directly to his shoulder. "What the fuck?"

"A blood sample," Arquebus said. "It is better you do not address me as Sir John. That is from a past long forgotten."

"You could have warned me. What's he need blood for? And your past is far from forgotten, if I recall."

"I try to forget it, and this is Mordacai, the court physician. He needs to analyze your innards and can do it with just one sample."

"I don't see why?" Harris observed the doctor glancing into the box and making an array of facial expressions — quite unnerving. "What is he anyway?"

"The physician, I told you."

"No. He looks like an extra from the set of *The Ten Commandments*."

"He is Zecronisian, a valuable race to the Montjoys and the other Elector houses. Zecronisians fulfill many useful purposes, as you shall see. Are you hungry?"

"Yes, I am."

Arquebus snapped his fingers and Little Bird twisted into action. He spun about and raced away, his feet never touching the marble.

"Where'd he go?"

"His duty is to keep you fed, clothed, remove your waste, prepare your surroundings for comfort and assure you adhere to your schedule."

"My schedule?"

Mordacai croaked, and then laughed. He held the flashing box high.

"Many Thirdlings this one shall have. Yes. He is more fertile than the other one."

"The other one?" Harris asked.

"Good news."

Mordacai bowed, continued to chuckle and departed, muttering — *Many Thirdlings. Many Thirdlings.*

"I don't understand," Harris said. "You know I'm not sticking around here."

"Go, then."

Arquebus cocked his head, and then drew Harris to the platform's edge. He sat. Harris noticed the man had a manuscript tucked under his arm.

"This place?" Harris said, gazing at the ceiling.

"Yours."

"You think I'm trapped here?"

"I know you are. You can run through the halls of *Mortis House* until your advantages evaporate, but you shall never find a portal back to our world."

"You sound like a man who's tried."

"Sir John tried. However, Arquebus calls this place home now."

Harris sighed. His soul, still restless in its goal, refused to surrender. But it was a puzzlement. It would take time to unravel. He stood, grimacing at the feel of the floor.

"You shall grow accustomed to the gravity," Arquebus said.

Harris slid to the nearest niche.

"For starters, what was with the big eyeball?"

"*The Eye* watches us all."

"It doesn't watch now."

"Confidence comes with learning, my friend, and learn you shall. When your Trone returns with nourishment, you shall dress properly and join me in another place — one of revelation."

Harris touched the walls of the niche. He noticed an inscription along the wainscoting.

Belmundus.

He thought of *the other one* — the previous consort. This must have been his quarters also. *Whatever happened to him?*

"Will I be told everything in this place of revelation?" he mused, tracing his hand over the inscription. He noticed the word also etched in the floor tiles. "Will you tell me about this *other one*?"

"He is best forgotten."

"So you say, but I might insist."

"Insist as you will, but patience runs thin with time, as you shall see. Tolerance comes with rank. You must be presented before you earn the right to insist."

Harris saw Little Bird on the threshold, holding a tray, and hesitating until Arquebus waved him in. Harris rejoined him at the platform. Little Bird retrieved a table and juggled the tray to a position convenient to Harris' reach. Although done easily, Harris noted the rope lamp was balanced on Little Bird's belt.

Arquebus observed this proceeding with scant patience. Once Little Bird had settled the tray, Arquebus nodded him off and came to the platform, waving the manuscript.

"Here," Arquebus said, handing it to Harris.

"Is this my schedule? If so, it's hefty."

"No. Your schedule is more fluid. This is your script."

"Script?"

Harris opened it to the first page.

Othellohito – A Tale of Tokugawa Japan

"Shakespeare? Japan?"

"We are actors and are required to perform beyond the bedroom."

Harris brushed through the pages.

"This doesn't look complete."

"Ah, you are familiar with the work."

"I know the title and read it during on-set tutoring. Never played it. But this version seems cockeyed. Set in Japan?"

Arquebus grinned companionably.

"Know this. The three Sceptas have specific tastes and demand their entertainments tailored to those tastes. For Soffira, strong stagecraft is required. For Charminus, *hamming it up* is essential. And Miracola needs the Oriental touch — thus the scene has shifted from Venice and Cyprus to Tokugawa Edo."

"I see."

However, Harris didn't see at all.

"You shall play *Cassioshima* with a twist, because Cassio survives in this version to mediate for Desdemona. Consort Hasamun will do the honors as *Desdemonayama*. Posan will play *Emiliasan* and Tappiolus does a wonderful villain as *Iagomoto*. Agrimentikos shall deliver his best *Lodovicomori* and I shall . . ."

Arquebus hopped up and bowed Thespian fashion.

"You'll play Othello."

"Othellohito."

"Sounds moronic."

"If they like it, you shall retain favor."

"And if they don't?"

"They shall love it, and you shall know your lines by the end of the week."

"Japanese or English, lines are lines. If I'm here by then, I'll know them. In fact, I'll be ready in a jiffy."

"Glad to hear it, whatever that means. Eat, and then meet me in an hour's time at the *Cartisforium*." Harris shrugged. "Your Trone will know the way."

"Oh, you mean Little Bird."

Arquebus' eyes opened wide — in anger, the first show of anger Harris had seen from him. Little Bird crumbled into a heap.

"Take care, my friend. If there is one thing not tolerated in *Mortis House,* it is any form of familiarity with the Trones. Mine has learned to keep its distance."

Harris saw a shadow beyond the threshold.

"This is my only warning to you. Trones are as the air — evident only when you breathe. When they are not about to do your bidding, they are beyond our thought or care." Arquebus softened. "You are new to it and I understand your human frailty, especially since your time came to decry the benefits of such human amenities. But Trones are not humans. They are scarcely beings." Arquebus clapped. "To *the Cartisforium* in one hour's time."

Harris knew this homily was meant as much for the Trone as a lesson in consortship, but Arquebus never gazed down at the brown buckskin heap. He nodded, and then marched away to his own shadowy servant.

3

Harris, stunned — anger welling, wasn't consumed by it. He knew he couldn't stay here and was committed to find the exit. Perhaps these inscriptions about his predecessor, *Belmundus*, held a key. The former consort wasn't here now. There must be a release hole — a portal back. The Sceptas drifted between the worlds, after all. This wasn't magic. There must be a science to it.

He glanced beyond the script — *Othellohito*, to the tray and the table.

"Little Bird," he muttered.

Yustichisqua uncrumpled, bowed and lifted the cover from the tray. Harris looked at what passed for food in Farn. On the platter, a golden mound of crispy critters arose — cockroaches perhaps. He grimaced. Beside it sat a bowl of purple mush laden with reddish twigs. He would need to be near starvation before he would dip a spoon here.

"What do you call that?" he asked Yustichisqua.

No answer. After Arquebus' diatribe, Yustichisqua had reverted to silence.

"I said, what do you call that?"

"Do not be angry, master. It is *measlybug* and *pertupa* stew. It is tasty, so I am told."

"*You* eat it then. Where I come from that wouldn't be served to a starving Ethiopian."

Then his heart panged. He was as unfair as Arquebus. Harris sighed. But no amount of intestinal fortitude would get him to take a taste. Not even a sniff.

Yustichisqua trembled. Harris noticed a tear welling in the lad's eye. His heart broke. He couldn't play the tyrant. There had to be recourse. Harris grinned and reached out. Yustichisqua pulled away.

"No, master. *The Eye.*"

"Fuck *the Eye*," he said, looking for the diaphanous pupil. "If you want me to be happy, then you'll serve me in all things."

"I shall, master."

"Then stop calling me *master*."

"I dare not."

"We'll find another term sufficiently humiliating to us both to satisfy my sensibilities and your servile requirements."

Yustichisqua sniffed, but nodded.

"As for food, where's the Big Mac?"

"I do not understand, mas . . ."

"How do you say *friend* in your language?"

"I dare not."

"Well, if you'll not serve me in this, how can you serve me at all?"

Little Bird clasped his hands together. He wept now, in earnest.

"I shall tell you. I shall tell you. It is . . . *oginali*."

"*Oginali*. Yes. You shall call me that. Who could know it? It will be our secret, Little Bird? Who could know it?"

"Few *Ayelli* know my language . . . *oginali*."

"Good then. If you would be so kind as to clear away this plate of shit and bring me something solid like . . ."

"*Bull catonin* or perhaps *terrerbyrd* flesh in cream sauce."

"Sounds good to me."

Little Bird covered the platter and lifted the tray. He began to float toward the threshold.

"Wait," Harris said. "Where are you going?"

"To the *Scullery Dorgan*, master . . . I mean, *oginali*." He grinned.

"I'll come with you."

"It would not be wise."

"Why?"

"Because you do not know the way and you must lead."

"Then I *shall* lead, and you'll whisper behind me where to go."

Harris managed to reach the doorway, the floor still feeling strange beneath his shoes. He wondered how Yustichisqua managed to float on his magic sandals. No time for answers. He would have plenty of those when he met with Arquebus in *the Cartisforium* — the place of revelation. Now he was hungry — famished. So he crossed the threshold and heard a gentle whisper behind him.

"To the right, *oginali*. To the right."

Chapter Nine

The Scullery Dorgan

1

Harris walked in darkness and in light, through rooms great and small, turning left and right at the whispered commands behind him. It was a long way to go for *terrerbyrd* flesh in cream sauce. However, he supposed Little Bird, on his floating footgear, covered more ground quicker when unencumbered by a slowpoke consort. On this progress, Harris passed other Trones, who turned their faces away and bowed. This zone didn't seem like the family living quarters — more a passageway between the living quarters and the scullery.

"Are we almost there?" Harris muttered.

No answer, but then he saw an archway ahead, bricked like an oven. He felt heat and smelt cooking aromas — delectable. He yearned for a pile of whatever was baking, and a tall mug of beer. Hell, he'd settle for a Diet Coke.

"We are here, *oginali*," Little Bird said.

Harris turned, waiting for Yustichisqua to open the door. However, the archway had no door, being bricked solid. Harris slapped it with his hand.

"What the fuck?" he muttered in frustration. "How do I get in?"

Little Bird bowed.

"You cannot."

"Are we starting that business again?" Harris snapped. "Protocols be damned. There's food in there and I could eat one of those *misancorpus'* whole . . . with a side of French fries."

Little Bird laughed, for the first time. He caught himself, and then bowed again. Harris was pleased with laughter at least. *Progress.*

"You cannot enter, *oginali*, because there is no door. I do not need a door, you see."

He proceeded to put his hand through the wall. Harris recalled seeing Charminus' Trone perform a similar trick back when *Mortis House* had been a creaky old Victorian.

"How did you do that?"

"We just can. I shall be quick."

Yustichisqua drifted through the bricks, disappearing. Harris slapped the wall again, and shook his head, puzzled and amused. He wondered if this was a trick he'd be taught. He made a mental note to ask Arquebus when he came for his Q&A. He had many questions, this the least. Harris wanted a full accounting of his predecessor, *Belmundus*, and more information on the House of Montjoy and why they plucked actors from their happy careers and made them copulate like breeders on a stud farm. Didn't Farn have men? And weren't there strong and tall Trones in this world to service the likes of Charminus? Of course, his primary question — where's the exit — stage right, couldn't be asked, because he knew Arquebus wouldn't tell him — either proscribed from doing so or he truly didn't know.

Harris stood in a long corridor before *the Scullery Dorgan* — a busy hallway, with Trones darting up and down and in and out, through walls and speeding over the cobbled floors like the Jetson's robot. The House of Montjoy must have become so dependant on these beings they kept them in motion around the clock.

But I'll wipe my own ass, he thought, *thank you very much.* Although, he hadn't recalled seeing a toilet since arriving in this world. He also hadn't gone either. Odd. He chalked it up to the lack of food and drink. Had he eaten the original slop Yustichisqua served him, he might have discovered the outhouse quickly.

Harris paced impatiently. One thing at a time. Food first. Poop and wipe later. The call of nature was never a mystery, but where and how it called might prove a surprise as it often had to the unwary traveler. And that is what he was, after all. He was a tourist in Acapulco or Shanghai, feeling his way around strange customs, languages and cultural quirks, like memorizing lines to a Shakespearean play set in Japan or wondering how the natives could walk through solid walls. Little things like that. Small puzzlements . . .

Suddenly, he confronted another Trone — a female — one he had seen several times. Charminus' Trone. He bowed to her, but she floated backwards, pressed her hand to her chest, and shook her head. She didn't speak. He suspected she was shocked by being noticed, just as Yustichisqua had been.

"Lady," Harris said, because she was fair beyond measure — dark-eyed and raven-haired. Her skin was pure white and silken. Her lips were full, but the rest of her was hidden beneath her long buckskin robe. Her purple headband was exactly as Little Bird's except it had a crystal teardrop suspended from its center, as if placing her above other Trones.

Harris bowed to her. She arched up, turned to flee, but then twirled about again.

"No," she snapped, a chastisement, indeed.

She plowed into the wall, disappearing beyond brick and mortar like so many of her race, which Arquebus likened to the air. In this respect, he was correct. Like air, she sustained the life of her mistress — a tragic thought to Harris, who would have preferred the mistress to have stayed on her side of the line and never stolen his life away.

2

As Harris stared at where this enchanting Trone disappeared, Yustichisqua popped through. Harris jumped, startled. Little Bird held a tray, but Harris' desire to know the woman had replaced his need for food. Or so he thought until Little Bird lifted the lid, revealing a moist slab of *terrerbyrd* drizzled in golden sauce and with a red berry garnish — cranberries, he hoped.

"Does this please you, master," Little Bird said.

Harris raised an eyebrow at the word *master.*

"It's divine, but . . ."

"I know. I am sorry . . . *oginali*. It is hard for me to remember."

"It'll settle in with use. Now give that to me."

"But should you not retire to your quarters? This is *the Scullery Dorgan*, a place not fit for you."

"I'll be fine," Harris said, sitting on the floor, his back propped by the warm wall. "Give it here."

He took the tray on his lap and looked for utensils. Little Bird produced a knife and a fork, a two-pronged dainty more designed for lobster claws than poultry, but better than nothing. Harris sliced some *terrerbyrd* and popped it in his mouth. Delicious — the sauce aromatically infused — mint or rosemary. He couldn't tell. But it wasn't cat urine or beaver shit, so he was fine with it. The berries weren't *cran*. He didn't know from which bush these fell, but they were sweet like plums and juicy like pomegranates. He sought something to drink.

"There is *mellowbeer* in your quarters, *oginali*. I thought you were dining there. I am sorry. I shall get some for you now."

"No. These berries are moist enough. I'll wash it down when we return . . ."

He almost said *home*, but shook off the thought and chewed another morsel of *terrerbyrd*.

"This is wonderful, Little Bird. But you'd know, wouldn't you."

Silence. Then it dawned on him Trones didn't eat this well.

"Did they feed you in there?" he asked, pointing over his shoulder.

"I shall have some *sqwallen* later this evening."

"What the hell is *sqwallen?*"

"It is porridge made from *jomar* and *quillerfoil*. It is nourishing."

Harris dropped his fork, cocking his head at the servant. Then he speared a slice of *terrerbyrd* and turned the handle around.

"Here. Have a taste."

"No, *oginali*. I am not permitted. It would kill me."

"Will it? Do you know or is it a taboo?"

"Taboo?"

"A rule of prevention."

"It is not permitted for me to taste your food."

"Truly? Then how do I know if my enemies aren't trying to poison me?"

"Enemies? How do you come to have enemies?"

"I'm sure I have some, and if not, I'm sure I'll get me some. If you want me to eat securely, I insist you taste my food. If it's poisoned, you'll get it first and I'll bury you with honor."

Little Bird grinned. He was no fool, Harris knew. The lad grasped the fork handle and cautiously brought the meat to his mouth. His lips trembled as the sauce dribbled down his chin. A tear welled as he swallowed. Then he turned the fork about, handing it back.

"I believe, *oginali*, your food is not poisoned."

"Not today, but I'll need your vigilance often and in larger amounts in the future."

Little Bird bowed.

"Boots!"

3

"Boots," came a voice from a man who towered over them.

It was Tappiolus. Yustichisqua quickly rolled aside into a buckskin heap. Harris speared more *terrerbyrd* and ate.

"You found my boots?" he asked, his mouth mushed. "If so, I'd like them back. A friend of mine called them *shitekickers* and I'd sure like to have them around if I need to kick the *shite* out of someone with an ass in need of kicking."

Tappiolus laughed.

"*Boots* is the name our lord calls you, now that you have impressed him with your skill at hurling footwear at *terrerbyrds*. That chunk you just swallowed might have had your heel print on it."

Harris swallowed, and then moistened his lips.

"Could be? I've played the part of a heel. I'm not sure what roles you've landed in that faraway time you crammed upon the screen, but I'm versatile."

He stood, handing the plate to Little Bird.

"Now that you have let him taste your meal," Tappiolus chided, "you will never see a full plate again. You need instruction about that lot. But I am not the one to teach you."

"I'm fortunate in that."

Tappiolus grinned, *Snidely Whiplashing* his mustache. His Trone cowered behind him, sneaking a peek at Little Bird.

"You have not been indoctrinated, so there is time for you to break the law ignorantly. However, despite your grasp at nobility, these beings cannot be allowed to run amok. Too many cram into the city's eastern ward, derelict and useless. They'll become a state expense if we allow them to thrive."

Harris frowned. He knew this speech was not directed at him, but was an insult for Little Bird and any Trone within earshot.

"Is *my* servant any of your business?" Harris asked.

"Yes, they all are. I am the Provost of the Palace Yunockers."

Harris noted Little Bird's cringe.

"And what, pray tell, are the Yunockers?"

"They are the enforcers employed to keep order," Tappiolus replied.

"The police."

"You might say so — you might also call them mercenaries, because their services are bought under treaty terms, their allegiance controlled by this hand."

"Your hand?"

"You will learn, Boots, idleness in the palace is a terrible bore, especially when your time is *down*."

"Down?"

"It is *down* now, and still you do not know it. I, on the other hand, am *up* now. Our Scepta is versatile, she can only have one of us at a time."

"Thank God for that."

Tappiolus grinned, nodded curtly and began to leave. Before he did, however, he stood over Yustichisqua.

"*Sqwallen* keeps them docile and useful, Boots. Anything beyond that makes their blood too high and mighty. When that happens, the Yunockers are the only answer."

Harris stood up to this man, his co-consort and brother-in-law. This talk upset Yustichisqua. One more word and Harris would use the knife for more than *terrerbyrd*. Blood would be spilt in *the Scullery Dorgan*. However, before this could go further, the woman returned. She emerged from the wall carrying a tray. She startled both men. Trones turned away. She covered her face, showing neither Tappiolus nor Boots any notice as she drifted from *the Scullery Dorgan*.

"Who is she?" Harris asked absently.

"A Trone like any other," Tappiolus snapped. "She is held in higher regard, because she serves a Scepta. But she enjoys no exception to the rules."

Harris sneered at Tappiolus.

"I can't believe you."

"I am not sure what you mean, Boots."

"I can't believe you came from the same world as me."

"And why not, Boots? Didn't the generation before you plunge the world into mass murder and genocide? And didn't the generation after that one rip itself apart with religious terror? That this is a world of order is a blessing, and that you weren't sucked dry and left like a prune to rot in the suns like most Scepta encounters, is a miracle. But I think you shall be better than the other one, because you have cursed and are a far worse actor."

Tappiolus marched off like a chief of police, especially one who was *up*. Harris had a sack full of questions unanswered, but hoped these would be addressed by Arquebus in *the Cartisforium*.

Chapter Ten

The Cartisforium

1

Harris needed a breath of air or at least a nap after the satisfying meal. *Mortis House* was confining. He wished to find a window, stick his head out and see what there was to see. But Yustichisqua hastened him.

"*Oginali,*" he instructed, "you must be dressed to attend business at *the Cartisforium.*"

There was no putting Little Bird off. So Harris led again, listening to the whispered directions through courts and corridors until reaching his threshold. When he crossed it, he noticed that word again — *Belmundus.* When he reached the platform bed, he interrupted Little Bird's fussing with Harris' clothing change — a cerulean tunic, a matching kilt and a bejeweled headdress, all intended for business in *the Cartisforium.*

"Tell me, Little Bird, did you know the other one — my predecessor?"

Little Bird nodded, but remained mute, laying out the clothing.

"Did you serve him?"

"No, *oginali.* He was served by another. But . . ."

"Well . . . speak up."

"All Trones know about him and . . . his refusal to do his duty. It is not a good thing to refuse your lot in life."

"But you're a native. We consorts are not. How can it be our lot in life? We're abducted from our worlds and set up as the masters over people who deserve better."

Yustichisqua paused, as if to consider this.

"Abducted?"

"Stolen."

"Stolen? That cannot be, *oginali.* You are chosen when the Scepta harvests — chosen to manage Montjoy and all in it. You are *Ayelli* and must make young lords and ladies — the Thirdlings. It has always been so. How we would survive otherwise, I do not know? But you are not . . . stolen, *oginali.* No. Not stolen."

Little Bird's sudden patriotic burst, misplaced as it was, charmed Harris. He disagreed with the lad on every point, but wouldn't debate the issue now. His mother had taught him, *truth* was achieved through reasoning and an examination of the facts. Harris was short on facts at the moment. But he was confident he'd have more after his meeting with Arquebus.

Little Bird presented Harris with a strange garment, which looked like a golden jock strap. Harris was positive that it *was* a jock strap and his servant meant to accost him with it. However, Little Bird hesitated, waiting patiently.

"Is that for me?" Harris asked.

"Yes, *oginali*. But I cannot proceed until you remove your *Columbincus*."

"My what?"

"Your *Columbincus*." Little Bird pointed to the brooch. "I am forbidden to touch it."

Harris touched it, and then played with the clasp to unfasten it — a strange arrangement, the clip twisted about a silver post on a spring hinge. It took a mighty snap to undo, and then the cinch had a mind of its own. It opened mechanically, flashing blue light.

"Interesting bit of bling," he noted. "You called it a Columb-what-sit?"

"*Columbincus*," Little Bird said, bowing. "Place it gently on your bed. It will shut itself down. It is not fully initiated, but even so, a Trone must not touch it. How did you say it? It is a *taboo*."

Smart lad, Harris thought.

He set *the Columbincus* on the bed and it turned off. Yustichisqua removed the cloak, leaving his *oginali* naked. Little Bird didn't appear ashamed or deflect his sight. He wrapped the golden jock strap around Harris' waist, adjusting it around the crotch with the professionalism of a backstage dresser — a matter of procedure, nothing more. He attached the knee length kilt, which Harris regarded as a pleated skirt, like the kind Mom once wore — only materially light and divine. Yustichisqua slipped the tunic over Harris' head with ease as if it was tailor-made. These weren't his predecessor's castoffs, although he had inherited *Belmundus'* living quarters.

The apparel suited him. Harris had always been attracted to wardrobe in his film work. He often wished he could keep a costume or three after the production. However, the finery always reverted to stock. But these fine duds were his and he didn't mean to give them back, even when he figured out how to flee the coop.

The last act of dressing was the coronation crown — the headdress. When worn, it lent Harris the look of a young *maharaja*. All he needed was a golden idol and a peacock fan and he'd be the envy of a hundred drooling wannabees in the casting queue. He wanted to strut, if he could manage it in these blasted slippery slippers. He did a grand shuffle instead, moving to a mirror near the niche at the rotunda's far end. He preened.

"Yes," he said. "That's the ticket. If I get to strut in these duds, it might be worth sticking around . . . for a short while."

He was irresistibly drawn to his image. He was a star, indeed. But it made no sense now, captive, with no acting prospects except an Elizabethan-Kabuki fabrication — *Othellohito*. He checked out his chin scar, which had flared. He thought to call Little Bird for make-up, but vanity is the emptiest of shows. Then the mirror reflected more than Harris' radiance. *The Eye* appeared.

"Fuck," he said, stepping back. "What are *you* looking at?"

"It does not speak, *master*. It only observes."

Yustichisqua had reverted to addressing him as *master*. Despite this, Harris didn't chastise him before *the Eye*. Little Bird draped a luxurious cape over his *master's* shoulders. Harris held it in place to keep it from falling. Then he remembered his *Columbincus* and retreated to the bed.

The brooch wasn't easy to resnap. It began buzzing the minute he touched it. As he struggled, he noticed a sigil emblazoned on its face — an Eye with two bisecting wavy lines. He knew the two lines meant *second consort*, but seeing *the Eye* on his *Columbincus*, unsettled him.

He fastened his cape, and then strutted around the room like Svengali at a Magician's convention, gliding across the rotunda. It was like ice skating. No golden ocular projection would daunt him, even if he was her captive. He came close enough to *the Eye* as to poke it out, then bowed mockingly, his right hand brushing the tiles.

"Your Majesty," he said, in a courtly accent. "Does this meet with your approbation, because if it doesn't, then *fuck ye* and *fuck ye well*."

The Eye shut down. Harris laughed. He expected Little Bird to be out of his skin with fear, but, surprisingly, Yustichisqua grinned, as if enjoying the show.

"I guess they'll be talking about me in *the Scullery Dorgan* as the rebellious consort — the next one out the door. *Yippee*. That's the goal. Out the door."

Little Bird stood, and then spun about.

"It is time for your business at *the Cartisforium, oginali*."

"Is it? Will they still let me in after I've told the Eye where to go?"

"It does not matter, *oginali*. You must go now or you will be late."

Harris bobbled his head, feeling the weight of the headdress.

"Mustn't be late, you know. Mustn't fuck with *the Eye's* schedule."

Little Bird tugged him to the threshold. Then, off Harris went, walking the corridors again, only this time dressed like a pasha in a henhouse.

2

Harris' new duds buoyed him. As he paraded through *Mortis House*, he surged with pride — unreconciled importance, while Trones and other functionaries turned their heads away in respect. He passed a gathering of Thirdlings, who clasped their hands together and bowed deeply. This pleased him, and he couldn't tell why. As a rogue carrot in this salad bowl, he sought to return to his roots. Yet, here he was, Little Bird in tow, whispering *to the right, oginali* and *to the left, oginali*, a grand show, acing any red carpet Harris had tread. The purpose eluded him, but something was baked into his kilt or headdress making him feel damned superior. He hammed it up as he had when he had showed up on set when he was ten and had assumed acting was all . . . well, acting. All surface expression — nothing deep or emoting. Nothing capturing character, truth, justice or the soul's radiance. Here he was again — little Harris Cartwright — the cute and cuddly variety, forgiven all trespasses as if they weren't true transgressions.

"Here, *oginali*."

Harris halted. The corridor was abandoned, except a distant heap two yards away — a heap Harris recognized as a Trone parked beyond his keeper's sight. Little Bird fluttered now like a real bird. He brushed Harris' cape, taking care not to touch *the Columbincus*. He straightened the headdress, and then brushed dandruff from the tunic. He did everything short of adjusting the golden jock strap.

"Any advice, Little Bird?"

"Advice from me, *oginali*? I would not dare."

Harris stood before a door — an ornate affair carved intricately with mythic themes, mostly unrecognizable beasts — a beaver with inordinately long teeth and a giraffe with a crocodilian head. He waited for Little Bird to open the door, but the portal opened automatically.

"Are you coming?" Harris asked.

"It is . . . a taboo."

"I see. How do I look?"

"I cannot say. There is nothing to adjust or correct. You are presentable."

"A reflection on you, Little Bird."

Harris waited for a response like *Thank you, oginali*, but Little Bird had already parked himself in the obiquitous heap. Harris stepped over the threshold.

"Do not say *fuck* in this place, *oginali*," Yustichisqua blurted.

Ah, Harris thought. *Advice, after all.*

The room, octagonal and darkly rich — wooden with more carved panels, focused on three stained-glass windows, reflecting light through rosy segments — portraits of women, one of whom he recognized as his Scepta. Who could mistake the dark hair, the golden eyes and the mass of deep purple bunting? The other two were decidedly different — a fair woman with golden hair and a white bridal gown, and a plump specimen with great jowls, triple chin and a crimson drape worn over a vast landscape of fat. Which was Soffira and which, Miracola?

At the room's center stood an octagonal table and on it, a jewel-encrusted book — a fat volume with a lock lording over a mosaic of emeralds, rubies, sapphires and diamonds. On the ceiling, the heavens were represented, seeming to move like a planetarium. Harris was not expert in astronomy and couldn't name one constellation, if the common set were represented. But they twinkled, nonetheless.

Harris walked around the table, his head craned toward the ceiling, but still attending to his top-heavy headdress. He heard the sound of cloth on cloth, and noticed a man standing back-turned in the shadows — a man who wore similar attire as Harris, only in emerald.

Harris stopped, attentive as the man spoke.

"What have you learned?"

"Sir John?"

Arquebus turned.

"You have had time to observe this world. What have you learned?"

Harris grinned, and then strolled toward the windows, pointing to the middle pane.

"I've learned this one has kidnapped me and has put me out to stud." He waved at the other two portraits. "These must be her sisters, Soffira and Miracola. I haven't a clue which is which."

"Soffira is fair, while Miracola is . . . ample."

"Ah. Then I've learned another thing." He paused. "I have also been taught to avoid calling you *Sir John*. Also, I dislike Pukola or Putedi stew, preferring the *terrerbyrd* in cream sauce." He spun about. "I love these outfits and mean to take one when I leave. When . . . I . . . leave."

Arquebus laughed, coming into the light. He seemed older now, draped in his consort attire. He sported an assortment of rings, chains and badges on his tunic. Harris, a tenderfoot, didn't have a merit badge to his credit.

"I've also learned to misbehave and to break rules," Harris said, grinning. "Although I guess I brought that knowledge with me . . . an asset to keep in the game."

"Rules are important," Arquebus said, sternly. "When you *pooh-pooh* them, others suffer and perhaps worse than you could imagine. To break them, you must first learn them. Rules can be and are enforced in Farn."

"Ah, the Yanidoodles or Yofunkies or whatever Tappiolus called them."

"Yunockers. You are learning well. But if you think your conduct before *the Eye* moved you to disfavor, learn this. You are an actor and have been drawn as an actor. She likes it when you ham it up, displaying flights of amusing fancy. It endears you to Scepta Charminus."

Harris sighed. He'd hoped they culled bad eggs early and he'd wake on the F Train to Coney Island. No such luck. He might have even locked himself in further with his childish display.

"I'll be as silent as a priest," Harris said.

"That might amuse her more. But know this. You have one prime role in this world."

"To fuck her." Harris gasped, not heeding Little Bird's advice. "Sorry."

"No matter," Arquebus replied. "You put it crudely, but a shag by any other name would be as correct."

"I share this duty with Tappiolus. He's told me as much."

"Sharing is good and keeps a person from exhaustion. Our Sceptas also renew their essence in other worlds — in the outlands, coming to men in dreams and at odd times, sucking their spirits dry. We are the lucky ones. We have proved worthy of life and have been given the opportunity to multiply."

"The Thirdlings?"

"Yes. But more on that after you finish your account of your observations."

Harris thought, and then touched his brooch.

"I know this is called *a Columbincus* and mine isn't fully up to speed."

"Ah. You did not learn that last part through observation. You have not learned to ignore your Trone. Learn this. If you continue that course, it will go harder on him than on you. That said, that *is* your *Columbincus* and, yes, it is not fully initialized — not up to speed."

Arquebus touched his own *Columbincus* — a brooch like Harris' only with a different sigil. It flashed green at his touch. Arquebus snapped it off easily — practice making perfect, evidently.

"Do you know where we are?" he asked.

"Farn."

"And, furthermore?"

"Mortis House."

"Yes, I am listening."

"*The Cartisforium.*"

"Exactly." Arquebus reached across the table toward the book. "You must know certain things, Harris Cartwright, to progress in this world. This is *the Book of Farn*. It contains the history, mystery and wisdom of the Nine Houses and their borderlands. It is a fine thing that we do not age, because it would take eternity to delve into the treasury of its knowledge. However, like a schoolboy with a primer, you shall learn much useful and enriching information within its pages."

"Is it in English?"

"It is in whatever language the reader knows. However, it does not preclude understanding."

"Like the Bible."

"Perhaps so, only the Bible is tucked in the margins of this work, if you can even find it. Even then, it is pure, lacking the faulty translations. It would be the truth direct."

"I see."

"Do you, my friend?"

Arquebus pushed his *Columbincus* into the Book of Farn's keyhole. The lock shuddered, and then unlatched. Slowly, the book fanned open, the brooch suspended above the pages. Steam arose from the binding as the volume filled the air with perfumed knowledge. Harris inhaled. No fear. It enraptured him. He watched as images emerged from the pages. He saw that the ceiling's astronomical gazetteer had been replaced by a different map — a fuzzy chandelier of geographical features.

He grinned, *the Cartisforium's* spice captivating him. Arquebus nodded like a professor about to deliver a geography lecture — an orientation to a new land.

"What you have learned thus far," he said, "can be gathered on a pinhead and thrown to the wind." He stretched his arms out and closed his eyes. "Behold *the Book of Farn*. Savor its lessons and listen to the guides. Remember and recall it all, because your life might depend upon it."

Harris touched his own *Columbincus*, which vibrated. He kept his hand over the sigil of *the Eye* and the two wavy lines in an attempt to amplify his newborn knowledge. The magic began and Harris Cartwright was plunged into this new world with renewed illusion. After all, illusion was the only life he knew.

Chapter Eleven

The Book of Farn

1

Harris' heart beat fast as the royal faces appeared successively — men and women crowned with sparkling caps and diadems. At first, fleeting forms, they registered no significance. Still, he reached out to touch them; a useless exercise, because these specters were merely impressions representing Farn's history.

"Behold Great Farn," Arquebus intoned. "Nine houses — Electors all, and graceful Memers and Sceptas and Seneschals. Regal houses — each to their lands and cities. Each controlling the bridles of government, the protectors of the Primordius Centrum."

Harris didn't absorb it. Instead, his attentions were glued on the map as it descended — a vast circle cuffed by mountains and seas — fertile lands between the cities and citadels, except for a desert which edged on the margins, abutting the mountains. The map turned and from each sector came the faces again, matching their appropriate place. Through the cloud, Harris saw Arquebus, his hands raised, pointing to the chart — the map that lent its name to *the Cartisforium*.

Harris saw a sprawling, shimmering red city, spires aloft and towers flaring, edged by a lava lake. Trees blazed, but despite the conflagration, their flowers blossomed unhindered. Above the embers arose a fantasy dome, rosy in the sunlight. Rockets jetted above the din and the aroma of roasts and stews and baking wafted up Harris' nose. Then, casting up from the fiery lake, were the projections of a man and woman, draped in a crimson cascade, which rippled from head to toe like boughs infested with fire ants.

"Cheelum, the Elector of Volcanium, keeper of the sacred fire," Arquebus said, his tone ample, swelling with heraldry.

The ruler of Volcanium clarified. His face dripped wax, satiny across his cheeks, highlighting silver eyes. Rubies and bloodstones festooned his gown. His crown, a spike shooting flame, pointed to the suns. He bowed toward Harris, who fumbled returning the gesture, unsure whether a projection would care for such courtesies. However, he didn't wish to vex a man on fire. Volcanium's Memer stood within Cheelum's flickering flame — a thin wick of a woman, dripping vermilion oil lacquered to her chin. Three flaming Seneschals preened nearby. They played cards and continued their gambling as the map continued to turn.

The fire world gave way to one of water. A tsunami rolled over the scene, crashing into a lighthouse, which shone across cottages and rough dwellings. The shore teemed with boats, the fishermen casting nets. From the distance, an azure crystalline bubble approached. Golden pylons shielded it from the surge. As the world turned, land arose forming a vast dune. A palace sat astride the sands, its walls wending down to a bustling oasis. Then, rain. Harris felt the spray kiss his chin and forehead.

"Yama, the Elector of Aquilium, watcher of the watery realm," Arquebus announced.

A willowy man's projection appeared, wearing a thin cord of seaweed and naught else. His crown, a conch shell; his skin, olive; his beard, white and split into two strands, glistening with sea-foam, each blown in a different direction. At his feet clung the crest of his palace, a hump capped by a nautilus shell. His Memer appeared. She, as naked as her husband, embraced modesty only with a well-placed scallop shell at a strategic anatomical point. Three Sceptas peeked from behind her. They giggled, and then revealed long flowing hair, which changed colors as they combed it with snapping razor clams.

The Elector of Aquilium lifted a dazzling turquoise chalice, toasting Harris. Harris nodded, and then Yama drank, foam escaping his mouth, his Memer catching it in her hands and spraying water over the Sceptas, as if baptizing them. Harris thought them a pleasant family, although Aquilium recalled a nudist colony. He could live with that, but probably not with the rain and the riptide.

Rotation again, the watery world dissolving into steam billows. Harris squinted, but he saw naught but clouds. The more he stared, the more he had the sensation of flying. He was aloft in the sky. A flock of swallows funneled nearby — a winged ballet. They wafted over an emerging scene — clouds spiked with gables and marshmallow roofs, like cakes at a county fair. The populace feathered about their business. The birds settled on a colossal statue, which over lorded the town. As Harris watched, the statue twitched, sending the flock into another funnel — a skyward *pas de deux*.

"Yunoli, the Elector of Aolium, champion of the air," Arquebus chanted.

The Elector transformed into a twister, his green cloak disrupting wherever he touched down. His cape, dotted with stars, was an elegant astral garment. The city below, thousands of flets, was now blown about like leaves in the wind — lily pads adrift on a lake. On each flet, an igloo-shaped dwelling set. These clustered onto the gingerbread cloudland roofs, while Yunoli shook his cloak. Harris caught an aroma of fresh mint, as if Aolium was hung with deodorizers. The Elector laughed, his Memer joining him in flight. Together they swept over pasturelands and roofs, blowing the flets hysterically. More than a few citizens slipped from their igloos, falling through the clouds to their death. The Sceptas arrived on the backs of swans. The Elector greeted them by balling into a pink nimbus cloud and blowing over their heads, setting them adrift. The Elector and his Memer laughed, a joke enjoyed before planting in the valley again, two statues waiting for another swallow flock to scare.

The map turned faster now. The sky darkened quickly. The ground thickened, the pastures giving way to a rugged landscape peppered by belching smokestacks and broiling furnaces. The city, no longer an idyllic place, had one ponderous purpose, its signatures brick and cobbled, gray and dingy. People hauled and toted and carried and dragged. The dwellings were row houses. Coal dust and oil slicks mucked the streets. Larger buildings came into view. One was eye-catching ugly — a cube lined with factory windows, standing fifty stories high, surrounded by ancillary buildings. Beyond, a range of hills slept and, beyond those, open pits. Cranes and 'dozers rolled about the landscape. Harris choked, covering his mouth in his tunic collar. From the pit emerged a rugged man in a sooty robe. But it wasn't a robe, but hide, charred by kilns and caked in coal dust. The man's lips, chapped and black, poked through crusted grime.

"Yeholu, the Elector of Terrastrium, master digger of Farn," Arquebus croaked.

This Elector was different from the others, as if he had drawn the Hephaestian role. Repulsive. Still, Harris couldn't see Yeholu beneath the muck — an earth denizen and director of an industrial realm. However, industry was essential, Harris supposed, and thus this lord of coal.

The Memer crawled low to the ground, sidling to Yeholu's feet. There were others, but Harris couldn't discerned them clearly. Were they Sceptas or Seneschals beneath the muck? The family promenaded, dog packs encircling them. Each family member cracked a whip often. How could this bunch slip into other worlds to draw their due? Their appearance would have clogged the front pages of *the Alien Invasion Daily*. Harris rejoiced when the map turned, because the Elector farted, and nothing was so vile in this world or any other.

The landscape leveled smoothly, and then arose, opening onto a valley, cuffed by a circumferential ridge — stadium time. Would the home team be taking the field? The amphitheater, dotted with brick and mortar monoliths, was geometrically pleasing and symmetrical. It suggested to Harris a set of toy blocks.

"Sestanum, the Elector of Protractus, dean of science," Arquebus said, sharply, and then coughed to get Harris' attention.

Harris shrugged, but then noticed the Elector, who was expertly camouflaged. Sestanum, a splinter man, shot up like bamboo from a tetrahedron, which spun at the center of the amphitheater. The geometric world burst with activity, silver disks transporting citizens over moving walkways and through connection tubes. What their business was Harris didn't know, but assumed it was scientific and inventive by the city's state. Sestanum revealed himself, more insect than human, his eyes bugged, his headpiece spiked and was adorned with slinkies. His cloak stiffly fanned like a vintage Cadillac. He operated a remote control, aiming at random objects which spun and flashed and buzzed and fussed. He aimed it a Harris, who ducked, averting mischief.

Sestanum's Memer, a short stocky woman, bounced on a pogo stick around her lord. Three Seneschals sprang over the tetrahedron, pointing remotes in their father's wake, shutting down the spinning and the flashing and the buzzing and the fuss. Harris was glad he hadn't been drawn into this bizarre realm, although he supposed Seneschals were incubi rather than succubae when visiting other worlds. *Where do they keep the werewolves and zombies*, he mused. *And what about the vampires?* As the map turned again, he might discover.

Mist covered the land — not airy stuff or watery spray, not choking coal dust, but a purple veil hiding everything. Harris saw no image, no building, no shape, nor natural formation. Just mist — violet and fuchsia mist. Then wisps flitted in and out. Soon they flickered, strengthening until a gray-cloaked haggard specter appeared, wielding a great staff. Faceless, it could have been the grim reaper but for the staff instead of a scythe.

"Dunaliski, the Elector of Magus, grand wizard of Farn," Arquebus whispered.

The wizard waved his staff through the mist. Harris tried to discern features, but even the gray cloak was . . . well, gray and at times formless as if Dunaliski and the mist came from the same unreferenced cloth. This Elector seemed Memerless. No Sceptas or Seneschals either. However, Harris heard murmurs — a woman's voice, and then birdcalls — crows, perhaps — maybe, ravens. This family sublimated form, hiding in an arcane world. This realm teemed with invisible citizenry.

Suddenly, Dunaliski vanished, mist whirling where he had stood. Harris was beset with a deep, abiding dread. He couldn't tell why. Vacancy stole his senses. He wanted to flee *the Cartisforium*. The map couldn't turn fast enough.

"Turn, already. Turn," he muttered.

It complied, a Cathedral emerging through the mist — a magnificent Gothic edifice, gargoyled and buttressed. However, its spire was a pagoda and a minaret protruded from the apse. A medieval city clung to its skirts, a town with eclectic architecture — western sloppy to Oriental fantasy, like the play Harris had been asked to learn.

"Lododi, the Elector of Pontifrax, Archbishop of Farn," Arquebus intoned.

Hymns resounded — a mass perhaps, but not in Latin. Perhaps Chinese. Harris couldn't tell. However, he did know a priest when he saw one. Lododi, invested and frocked in priestly garb, sported a miter cap reserved for a Cardinal, only in bright blue instead of scarlet. The Elector blessed the citizenry, which appeared in miniature, clustering in piazzas and about shrines, knees bent, hands crossing or clapping or performing shaker rituals. More startling, the Memer, as if an archbishop could have one, was clad like the town slut. A whore by any other name would do as well. She filled the holy coffers with more than prayers to the Virgin. One shiver from her ample chest could endow a bishopric.

Three Seneschals lurked by Lododi's vestments, stewards of the collection plate. Harris inhaled incense rising from the censer. He almost crossed himself, then recalled he was Presbyterian and didn't know one Chinese word. The choir burst into a loud *Gloria*, followed by a *Benedictus — Amen*. Then the map moved on, but Harris wished it hadn't, because the Ecclesiastical world faded fast and the world grew darker still.

Harris began to sweat — cold sweat, as if *something evil this way came*. The ground flattened, writhing with creepy crawlers — thousands of spidery legs, as if the graves of the nine worlds opened.

"Divert your eyes," Arquebus said.

However, before Harris could obey, he saw the next Elector — a misshapen beast — the epitome of Caliban with a monster's mug — one eye, a cleft nose and a horn growing from his forehead. He carried black armor, which he scarcely attempted to don. Something evil came.

2

"Grimakadarian, the Elector of Zin," Arquebus shuddered. "Keeper of Darkness."

Harris turned his face away, and then his back. He heard agonizing screams and torturous cries, at first distant, and then directly at hand, filling his heart and soul with dread. The shouts were painful, every chalkboard ever scratched by unworldly fingernails. Harris felt compelled to look, but, unlike Lot's wife or Orpheus on ascending from hell, he fought the urge, focusing his attention on the stained-glass windows. However, he smelled a vile stench. This was the inferno, which touched his own outland — a hop, skip and jump away from here, after all.

Harris trembled and cursed Arquebus, who stopped the map to impress upon him the luck of being drawn into Montjoy and not into the realm of Zin. It worked.

The cacophony lessened. The pandemonium faded. So did the stench. Slowly, Harris turned, hoping his pirouette wasn't premature. Arquebus clapped. Harris was pleasantly surprised. Before him spread a great metropolis, draping across three hills and cuffed by a desert on one side and a sea on the other. The place bustled and buzzed, overlooked by a stately house — a palace he recognized from his *Cabriolin* ride.

"Kuriakis, the Elector of Montjoy, rector Maximus and provost for the arts," Arquebus said, proudly.

Harris sighed. Why he felt pride, he couldn't tell, particularly since he set his prime objective to escape Montjoy's grip. However, after witnessing eight other options, Montjoy was the pick of the basket. The image of the great man himself, Kuriakis, sitting on his steed Nightmare was projected on this scene like a poster in a travel agency. Saddled on a milk-white unicorn, Joella the Fair, his Memer sat like nature's handmaiden. This was Harris' first sighting of the mother of Montjoy — as stunning and comely as Kuriakis was regal. Reclining on ottomans, the three Sceptas mimed their stained-glass poses.

Harris sighed. His tour of Farn was complete. Little did he know.

"So this is Great Farn in all its glory," he spouted to Arquebus.

"Know them all," Arquebus replied. "Hear their names and take them to heart and memory."

Arquebus placed his hands upon his heart, and then closed his eyes, reciting:

> *"Nine houses rule the world of Farn*
> *Balanced in perpetuum*
> *About Primordius Centrum —*
> *Volcanium holds the firebrands,*
> *Aquilium has the waters' keep,*
> *In Aolium's realm the air depends,*
> *While Terrastrium mines the earthen halls.*
> *Montjoy lifts the orb of art,*
> *Protractus totes and measures all.*
> *And Magus wields the wands of time*
> *While Pontifrax chants the holy rites*
> *To draw the portals twain aligned*
> *Into Zin and Zacker's care,*
> *Beyond the darkest brightest lair."*

"Nine houses," Harris muttered.

"Nine Elector houses," Arquebus echoed. "Cheelum, the fire lord of Volcanium, Yama, the water lord of Aquilium, Yunoli, the ruler of the sky in Aolium, and Yeholu, the earth liege at Terrastrium. Art is in our lord, Kuriakis' charge, while science lies with Sestanum of Protractus. The miraculous belongs to Dunaliski of Magus, while rites are Lododi of Pontifrax's domain. Zin and Zacker hold the keys to *the Primordius Centrum* — the portal binding all in light and darkness. Nine houses in Farn — each to its realm and purpose."

Harris glided beside the map as it continued to rotate.

"Fire, water, air and earth," he said.

"Just so."

"Art and science. Magic and religion."

"Exactly."

"Then the two keepers — light and darkness."

"You are a fast study, my friend," Arquebus replied. "You said true when you boasted on learning lines quickly."

Then Harris paused, regarding the world, which spread before him.

"Nine houses," he mused.

"Nine, precisely."

"But you have said ten names."

"Yes. You can disregard the last one — Zacker."

"Which is he?"

"Not displayed. Gone. Destroyed."

"And yet the verse isn't altered. Peculiar primer for a quick study."

"Grimakadarian of Zin holds the key to both light and darkness. It has been decreed."

"And this . . . this Primordial Rectum . . ."

"*Primordius Centrum*. It is the portal and the pillar to all that is — the transfer of energy for all worlds — inland and outland."

"And yet the tenth house has been destroyed? Did it fall into a black hole — *the Primordius . . . Centrum?*"

Arquebus raised his hands again. The map shimmered, transforming into something entirely different.

Chapter Twelve

Promise and Prophecy

1

A bright flash temporarily blinded Harris. He thought one of the suns went nova, but when the room settled, he could see the lands, which he had toured previously, were alive with activity. A diorama showed Farn at war — armies and hovercraft filling the terrain and sky — explosions over the towers and the flets and the smokestacks and the palaces. Whirligigs zoomed across a heaven dashed in flame and smoke.

Harris sat in a convenient chair, which he hadn't remembered being there before. He had been standing for a while and, considering the stress, sitting seemed like a good idea. However, once seated, the chair bucked, and then hovered over the table. Harris tried to wiggle free, but he didn't want to fall out, so he grasped the armrests and imbibed the chaos. Confusion. He couldn't separate the action, except the nine houses were embroiled in a conflict promising to destroy their world.

"War," Arquebus intoned, his voice lost in the rocketing rumble. "A great war in the time before Electors ruled supreme — before the Sceptas and Seneschals drew succor from the outlands. A conflict arising from power's gluttony — a desire for one to rule all. Arising from Zin."

Harris shut his eyes, not wishing to see Zin again, even the brief glimpse he had taken — a glimpse cloaking his mind in tar. However, as the chair spun about battlefields and besieged towns, he opened his eyes and saw Zin's darkness settling over the land.

"Grimakadarian pressed his dark key into the outlands," Arquebus said. "He intended to rule all worlds — to trump all houses, enslaving their children and gathering the inland peoples into the abyss. However, a challenge arose from the House of Zacker, who kept the key of light. Light shone across the realm, preventing Zin from easy victory. Light roused the houses to arms. But not every Elector supported light's cause.

"The spirit of *the Primordius Centrum* is the well-spring of all things, the source of balance and dominion. With this call to Light, the realm was neither balanced nor dominated. A civil war ensued.

Much was lost. Nothing gained. *The Primordius Centrum* broke precedence. It arose from slumber to restore order, but at a price. Peace was imposed, but never won.

"The lords of Farn became true Electors, each with an equal say to maintain the balance. But there were ten houses — no deciding vote for standoffs. Therefore, the House of Zacker was eliminated. The Nine Houses held power in tandem, Zacker paying for its intervention, for confounding dominion. The restoration of power frustrated Zin, but it held no dominion as it had wished. Fate rebuked the remaining houses — rebuked them with a promise and a prophecy. Binding was the declaration of *the Primordius Centrum*, becoming the law of the land — the law of imposed balance and stayed dominion."

The chair descended, replanting beside the table. It released Harris, who jumped to his feet. The diorama had faded — the war lesson retired. However, within the lingering mist arose an ashen figure, emerging from *the Book of Farn*. Only the figure's upper half was revealed — down to its waist, like a tree rooted within the tome. The figure was old, wizened and bearded, draped in a shimmering shawl — its eyes, weary — its countenance, sad. One hand pointed to the book — the other to the ceiling.

"Hear my words," it muttered, its voice frosty upon the land. "Hear my declaration, ye sons of Farn. I give thee this promise as a watchword for redemption. I wrap it in a prophecy, which shall steer thy courses until great *Solus* and *Dodecadatamus* converge and burn the moons of *Yeholo*."

So intoned *the Primordius Centrum* concerning the promise and the prophecy:

> *To each Elector three branches made*
> *Deigned as sons and daughters born,*
> *Renowned Sceptas and Seneschals*
> *But as towers apart shall grow,*
> *Never fruitful within their bounds,*
> *So to the outlands they must go,*
> *To gather succor into dough —*
> *The life force must they always hoe.*
> *But each may draw a double mate,*
> *And thus may sow and populate,*
> *A harvest to serve and ease their shade —*

A scattered horde as duty paid,
Smiling kin for the alliance trade,
But as mules these Thirdlings be,
Until there comes the mending free.
Then a fourth shall bloom in Farn
Uniting houses — the outlands darn
'til suns and moons reflect no more
And Zin and Zacker close the door.

2

Like the morning mist, the ancient spirit dissipated, a radiant blue glow sparkling over *the Book of Farn* in its wake. Harris thought this was a helluva way to teach history. It was like shooting at the class to give them the taste of flying bullets, and then have a frosty old talking head sum up with appropriate mystery. If every schoolroom had these visual aids, more students would get an A+.

The experience overwhelmed Harris. He raised his right hand adjusting his headdress, cock-eyed from the magic chair. Then he checked his *Columbincus* assuring the thing remained tightly clasped.

"Are you firmly in hand?" Arquebus asked.

"I guess so," Harris replied. "I mean, that was one helluva show — smoke and fire and the spooky proclamation — quite a lot to digest."

"Did you digest it?"

Harris thought. He couldn't recall the declaration for his life, except it placed limitations on the number of children the Electors could produce, and then blabbed on about those children — the Sceptas and Seneschals. The rest escaped him.

"I got the gist . . . ."

"You need more than the gist, my friend. It is the reason we are here."

Harris placed both hands on the table, looking squarely at his mentor.

"Enlighten me; and speak in simple terms — more along the lines of Shakespeare than Moses, if you please."

Arquebus grinned.

"Plain and simple. The Electors are immortal and need not produce progeny. However, they are fleshly and will make hay. In this, they are limited to a few times per year and make a great fuss about it — a festival."

"They have sex and we celebrate?"

"Precisely. However, they can have no issue beyond three children per house."

"The Sceptas . . ."

"And Seneschals. This second generation is neither immortal nor attracted to one another, either within or between their houses."

"Then how . . ."

"The outlands. They feed on life forces in the outlands. You have seen them as I have — in our nocturnal longings. When the Sceptas come, rarely does the sleeper awake. We, however, are the fortunate ones — we consorts. We have been drawn. Each Scepta and Seneschal can draw two consorts each. And thereby be fruitful and multiply."

"Children? Your children?"

"Our children — the Thirdlings. However, the rebuke is deep, and the promise deeper. While our spawn may marry between the houses and are useful in strategic alliances, they are mules — sterile."

"Then how does Farn . . . propagate?"

"The Thirdlings mature quickly. From birth to age three, they are adults, and at four they can be put out to farm between the houses. They can command legions of Yunockers or police the markets or be foreman in the manufactories. The Electors' blood is widespread across Great Farn."

Harris pondered this. Like Adam begetting his sons, how could this account for the rest of the population — the Trones for example. He raised his finger to ask, but Arquebus anticipated him.

"They are the inlanders," he replied. "They are Cetrone and Yunockers and Zecronisians and Gurts and other dwellers who have found their place under the Elector's rule. They are beyond the scope of prophecy — beyond the hope of promise."

"If the ruling house . . ."

"Our house."

"Whatever. If the . . . the houses are impotent except through our intervention and our offspring are sterile, what promise is that? Or is it punishment for the war — a bad joke with an ironic punch line?"

"That is not the promise," Arquebus said. "You were not attentive. Not all unions between Thirdlings will be barren. One will spark and blossom and the issue of that union will bring unity to the houses, restoring peace and tranquility to all worlds."

"Like a savior?"

"No. Like a *promise* — a covenant, if you wish to drift toward the biblical."

Harris preferred *the prosaic* to *the Mosaic*. It might resurrect Pontifrax and a round of *Hail Marys* in Chinese. It smelled of fish. The system seemed self-perpetuating, the Electors enforcing their cabals. However, Harris craved more knowledge on the inlanders. They appeared oppressed — an unsuspecting crop of souls preyed upon by a bunch of bucks and bitches in the middle of the night — dreams and hypnotism.

"The Trones," he began.

"I shall not speak of the Cetrone."

"Yes, the Cetrone."

Arquebus raised both arms and a flash shot above him. Harris postponed his inquiry in light of what came next. Behind Arquebus, flat to the wall, was a map — a real map — not a Disney World dark ride. As this map clarified, Harris observed a red flashing light at its center. Arquebus produced a long pointer — an old-fashioned teaching prop. He struck the red spot.

"We are here."

Harris moved quietly around the table, joining Arquebus and gazing at the chart — a Mall map without legends to the footgear or the names of the pizzerias in the food court.

"Is this Montjoy?"

"Montjoy City. Montjoy extends farther east across the desert to the mountains."

Arquebus shifted the pointer westward.

"You mean to the west."

"The east. The west is here."

He shifted the pointer eastward.

"Are we upside down and backward?"

"No. We are in Farn. Things differ here."

He moved the pointer up.

"Don't tell me . . . south."

"Correct."

"And we are standing in the center at the big red dot."

"Precisely."

"If we moved, would the dot move with us?"

"Precisely."

"Like GPS?"

"No. Like the red dot which tracks my *Columbincus*. Yours is not fully initiated and is not trackable yet."

Harris noticed other dots of different colors and brightness. He assumed these were *the Columbincus'* (or was it *the Columbinkae*) of other consorts and personages of importance. *Fascinating.*

"Then that's *Mortis House*," Harris mumbled.

Arquebus swept his pointer about the house and the environs.

"*Mortis House*, the Electoral Gardens and Pavilions and here . . . the Temple of Greary Gree. The precinct is called *Ayelli*."

"*Ayelli*," Harris repeated. He had heard the term before, from Yustichisqua's lips. "Quite the tourist town."

"Without the tourists." Arquebus' pointer went westward (old time East). "The Zecronisian settlement is here. We call it *Wudayleegu* by the Bottleblue Sea or *the Amaykwohi*."

"If you say so," Harris chuckled. "Am I expected to . . ."

"Expected." The pointer went northward (down). "The Market of the Gurts is called *Yuyutlu*, and the Garrison of the Yunockers — here to the South — *Yuganawu*."

"And the Trones?"

Arquebus frowned, but slapped the pointer to the east near the desert.

"*Kalugu*, only we refer to it never. It is just the eastern ward."

"*Kalugu*," Harris said, sharply. "That's an easy word. And the desert?"

"*Yinaga*, the Forling wasteland."

"Forling, it is," Harris said. "Is there to be a quiz?"

"A quiz?"

"An examination?"

"No examination. But you are expected to know core knowledge as a matter of survival. The book is always here for your reference — once your *Columbincus* is fully activated."

Harris touched the brooch. It flickered. It felt activated.

"When does that happen?"

"Tomorrow. You will be invested tomorrow. I and your other brothers-in-law consorts will greet you in the morning and escort you to meet the family."

"But I've already met the family."

"You have seen our lord, true; and have had a casual brush with Tappiolus. Those meetings do not count."

This mystified Harris. Was everything before the investiture a legal fiction?

"What if the family finds me unacceptable?"

"There is scant chance for that. Our lord already calls you 'Boots,' an endearment signaling your acceptance."

"But I had a predecessor, who was acceptable, but then managed to lose favor."

"You listen too much to Trone gossip."

"This is a history lesson, isn't it, Sir John . . . I mean, Arquebus? Shouldn't I know about my predecessor to prevent me from making the same mistakes?"

"I cannot answer that question."

"Will I find it in the book?"

Arquebus dropped the pointer and pushed his face into Harris'.

"That would be a mistake, friend."

"Should I ask Scepta Charminus about him?"

"I advise it not."

Harris suddenly felt this conversation's heat rising into his throat. He puckered his lips and clenched his fists.

"How do you expect me to learn all this crap and ignore the history most important to me? I see traces of him in every corner and crevice — spoken on the wind even. I need to know. I must know about Belmundus." Arquebus' eyebrows raised far above their natural limits. Then he laughed. "I'm not joking," Harris snapped. "I must know. Who was Belmundus?"

"You, my friend," Arquebus replied. "You are Belmundus."

"Me?"

"A name chosen by *the Primordius Centrum* and applied during your slumbers. You and none other are Lord Belmundus Montjoy, co-consort of Farn."

Arquebus bowed. Harris, trembling, turned and rushed across the threshold to his waiting Trone.

Chapter Thirteen

The Shoe on the Other Foot

1

"Belmundus," Harris muttered as he crossed the threshold, scarcely noticing Yustichisqua's humble heap.

"*Oginali*," Little Bird said

Harris looked down at this man, younger than he, but nearly as tall, squatting in submission like a slave from *Uncle Tom's Cabin*.

"Am I Belmundus?" he asked, half question, half declaration.

"Yes, *oginali*. Of course, you are. You are Lord Belmundus."

Harris closed his eyes, and then shook his head. He felt betrayed by this servant, who was tasked to guide him through the essentials. *Why didn't he tell him the mysterious word on the pillars and tiles was the heraldry of the new consort?*

"You are angry, *oginali* . . . master?"

At the word *master,* Harris flashed his eyes opened. He froze when Arquebus emerged, who nodded, and then swept past, his Trone padding behind him like a cur from the kennel.

"Yes," Harris snapped. "I'm angry, but only when you call me *master.*"

Harris stomped off in the opposite direction, correct or not. He heard Yustichisqua buzzing behind him.

I am Belmundus, Harris thought — a wretched thought, because someone had taken a liberty. His mother could name him, and she had — and an agent could derive a new name for him, consensually. But to have a frosty old spirit who dwelled in a hole pronounce a new name and expect it to stick — even to have it carved in the woodwork, was presumptuous.

"*Oginali*," Little Bird whispered. "This is not the way."

Harris halted, and then turned.

"I don't give a flying fuck where I wind up, Little Bird. I've just witnessed an abortion. I saw a bunch of pseudogods carve up the world and decide the fate of its inhabitants, as if everyone was just a pile of dog crap — and you're concerned I'm going the wrong way. I need some air."

"In that case, *oginali*, you are going the correct way."

Little Bird passed him, waving him forward around an array of square columns and across a courtyard crowned with an extravagant fountain, which spouted blue and pink water. Harris gave it scant attention and no praise. He truly needed a lung full of oxygen, or whatever passed for oxygen in this realm. He'd been cooped up too long in this cathouse.

Yustichisqua waved him on across the courtyard and under a gallery of archways, which formed a dark tunnel emerging into the night — onto a balcony. Harris was struck by crisp, clean air and a night sky draped with the three moons of *Yeholo* — ornaments on a vast ebony tree, Odin be praised. The moons were asymetrical, differing in size and brightness, the largest tinged blue, the midsized one, violet and the dwarf, pastel pink. Harris gasped, and then turned to Yustichisqua.

"What a sight," he said.

"Montjoy City. Not my city, but a wonder to behold at this height, *oginali*."

Harris clasped his *Columbincus*. The valley danced with light. He recalled the wall map, but the dark cloaked the detail needed to match these sights to the chart. He faced east, that is west if he weren't through the looking glass. The lights abruptly dimmed, falling away in the distance.

"The Forling Desert," he muttered.

"Yes," Little Bird said. "*Yinaga*, in my language." He pointed northward. "That way is *the Yuyutlu*, the great Gurt market, and there is *the Yuganawu*, the Yunocker stronghold."

"And the Cetrone?"

"Cetronia is not in Montjoy, but beyond *the Yinaga*, in *the Dodaloo* — the Spice Mountains."

"But Arquebus said . . ."

"True. He would say the Cetrone are denizens of the eastern ward, *the Kalugu*, but that is where we are kept when we are not serving."

"A ghetto," Harris muttered.

"Excuse me, *oginali*. I do not know this word."

"Nor should you."

Suddenly, Montjoy City's beauty faded in Harris' mind. He turned his attention to a slope dotted with lanterns, what he learned later were called *bronskers*. He assumed this was the gardens of *the Ayelli*. Yes, *the Ayelli* lorded over the land from this cathouse called *Mortis*. However, it overlooked a pool of toilers — Trones, Yunockers, Gurts and Zecronisians. Harris had met one Zecronisian — Mordacai. Perhaps some worker bees received better treatment than others. The Yunockers seemed an elite group — a military caste. However, the judge was still out on *the Yuyutlu* Gurts, whoever they might be. No doubt clung to *the Kalugu*. Harris knew it would be a pitiful place if it confined the Trones. Even from this height, light from *the Kalugu* shone like a bonfire — a raging conflagration contained by trenches and hoses — not the elegant *bronskers* which climbed *the Ayelli,* illuminating the nocturnal gardens.

"Has the air refreshed you, *oginali?*"

"Yes. Thank you, Little Bird. It has. The panorama is grand. I'd love to see it in daylight and up close and personal to assess it better."

"That may not be wise."

Harris turned to his servant — his Trone. He sounded like Arquebus — *do this, don't do that.* A strange world this, with many prohibitions and gratifications.

"Don't tell me. It's a taboo."

"No, *oginali*. Nothing is a taboo for you. You are Lord Belmundus, consort. Nothing is denied you."

"Then what prevents me?"

"Darkness perfumes Montjoy. Daylight reveals her faults. Here on the hill is best for you, *oginali*. Your life is blessed — glorious and happy."

Yustichisqua bowed. Harris laughed — an infectious laugh, because Little Bird grinned, and then chuckled.

"I've had enough air. Take me back to my chicken coop. My *glorious and happy* chicken coop."

"Chicken coop?"

"My suite — my residence."

"The Court of Lord Belmundus," Yustichisqua replied, and then turned and proceeded back through the tunnel.

"Blessed, my ass," Harris muttered and followed.

2

The Court of Lord Belmundus was as it was when Harris left it, only then he hadn't known it was the *court* of anything, and if he were to guess about Belmundus, it was another person — not him.

The suite seemed bigger now — a place for a high rolling big shot. That would be him. *Ho ho. Ha ha.* One thing bothered him — well, not one thing, but the next thing. Left to his own devices this place would become a colossal bore. Was there recreation — a gym for a workout? Where were the showers? The local multiplex? Couldn't he shuttle to the nearest rock club and do the hootchie kootchie with a bevy of lovely ladies . . . or men? Nothing was denied him, right? No taboos. He wasn't so gullible. These options weren't available. He didn't even know how to prepare for the dang-bang investiture ceremony. Maybe Yustichisqua had a deck of cards and they could play a few rounds of rummy. Then he passed a mirror — the same mirror where he had gawked at his new-fangled duds.

He paused, and then preened. He *did* look wonderful in this get-up.

"Lord Belmundus," he muttered.

That's a laugh. Why not Lord Butterfield or Mickey Higgenbottom, both characters he had played? *Belmundus. Ha!* He noticed the inscription again on pillars and posts — even one on the mirror.

"I guess Higgenbottom wouldn't fit the paving stones," he mused.

He thought of the Hollywood walk of stars. He hadn't done his yet — no hand and foot pirnts in the Chinese Theater courtyard either. However, he could imagine a star emblazoned with the word *Belmundus*. It might look better than *Cartwright* or *Kopfstutter*.

"Better than Lord Butterfield."

"Did you need something, *oginali?*"

"Yes. I need to take a piss."

Little Bird grinned, bowed and drifted off on his hovercraft footgear. He returned with a porcelain pot — something of Ming proportions, and quite ornate. It would be like peeing in *the Louvre*.

"I can manage myself," Harris said, as Little Bird lifted the kilt and poked at the golden jock strap.

"Take care not to soak your *asano*."

"*Asano?*"

"Your skirt."

"I've got good aim. You should worry if I might miss the pot altogether and hit your magic shoes."

Little Bird laughed again. Harris noticed the lad was laughing more, a sign of comfort, and a step up from the invisible man. Perhaps *the oginali's* lessons took hold. After Harris finished this awkward task, and considered what would happen when the inevitable bowel movement erupted, he trained his eyes on Little Bird's footgear. Amazing contraptions. All Cetrone wore them. Harris was surprised their legs didn't atrophy from disuse. Perhaps they had. When Yustichisqua returned from emptying the pot, Harris hunkered to inspect the footgear.

"Do you always wear these?"

"We must."

Another rule. Well, that goes without saying.

"What are they called?"

"*Digali sodi alasulo.*"

"What? That's a mouthful. *Digaliguli sewyourzuloo?*"

Little Bird laughed.

"*Digali sodi alasulo.* But the people of *the Ayelli* call them *zulus.*"

"*Zulus.* I can live with that." Harris touched them. Yustichisqua flinched. "How do they work?"

"I cannot tell. They just do so."

Harris gave him the fish-eye, but he supposed Yustichisqua wasn't a physicist.

"Let me try them on."

Little Bird looked horrified.

"It is a big, big taboo, *oginali.*"

"It would be fun. I could show you some skateboarding tricks, and you could laugh your ass off."

Little Bird shook his head.

"I do not know."

"What's there to know? I'm Lord Belmundus, the almighty ruler of this court. You're supposed to do what I ask. I pissed in the pot and ate the *terrerbyrd* and even looked to you for adjusting my jock strap. Can you deny a simple request — a try at your roller derby sandals?"

"*Zulus.*"

"Yes, *zulus.*"

Little Bird looked about, and then quietly removed his sandals. He bowed and handed them to Harris, who examined them. They were flat like Japanese clogs with leather straps to hold them in place. Underneath was a metallic grillwork, now silent and asleep. Harris slipped them on, tying each, grinning at Little Bird's nervous frown. Once clamped securely, Harris jumped to his feet.

"How do you turn them on?"

Yustichisqua touched a switch and Harris' feet tingled — burned even. He looked down and saw a green glow seeping from below like pond scum. He was thrown three feet in the air.

"This can't be right."

Little Bird was upright, pulling him down, but laughing a little.

"Funny, you think. Well, watch this."

Harris took a step, and the damned things took off, as if trying to escape. He waved his arms, attempting to keep balanced, but it didn't work. He dangled upside down, because *the zulus* found the ceiling. The kilt inverted, covering Harris' face. His *Columbincus* dangled precariously. Suddenly, *the Eye* appeared.

"Master," Little Bird shouted, pulling Harris down.

The *zulus* returned to the floor, but not before bucking like a ship in a storm. Harris went crashing to the tiles, his ass flat, but his feet lifted like a virgin on her wedding night. Yustichisqua leaped at the sandals, untying them and quickly returning them to his feet. He bowed before the Eye. Harris sat dumbly glaring at the golden orb.

"Get the fuck out of here," he snapped, waving his hand. "I'm the Lord in my Court, and I demand privacy."

It disappeared. Yustichisqua trembled, shivering into a heap, his entire body racked. Harris grasped him about the shoulders.

"Little Bird. Little Bird. It's okay."

"I am doomed, *oginali*." Yustichisqua wept. "You were good to me, and I shall always remember you, even when I am confined in *the Porias*."

"Nonsense."

Then came a knock at the door.

3

Before Harris could respond, the door opened and two tall figures, also on *zulus*, entered. They were dressed like extras in a remake of *Spartacus* — crimson capes, silver and leather armor and a feathered helmet. They carried *Sticks*. These were policemen. The Yunockers. Had to be.

The two officers floated across the court and hovered over Yustichisqua. One sported a black sash, which Harris assumed meant he was the ranking cop. The other did not, but had a turkey feather shoved in his epaulet. Little Bird trembled even more, if it were possible.

"What's the meaning of this intrusion?" Harris snapped.

"Pardon us, Lord Belmundus," said the ranking Yunocker, "but an infraction has been reported and must be remedied."

"An infraction?"

"*Zulu* removal is a capital offense," the turkey man said, and not ungraciously.

"*Zulu* removal?" Harris looked at Little Bird. "There they are — on his feet. You are mistaken."

"It was reported and there has been time enough for the infraction to be rectified."

"But once removed," yapped the second, "there is no rectification."

The Yunockers raised their *Sticks*.

"How dare you come into my quarters armed?" Harris snapped, trying out his best Lord Butterfield voice.

"We apologize for the fuss," the ranking Yunocker said, "but we have orders. If any insult has been construed, you may address it to the Scepta. But . . ."

The *Sticks* were raised. Little Bird cowered, prepared, no doubt, for pain or even death, Harris' anger grew. He raised his hand, but then thought hand-raising probably wouldn't deter them. So he slapped his *Columbincus*. The damned thing glowed and shot an unexpected bolt toward the ceiling. The Yunockers lowered their *Sticks* and glanced at each other. Doubt had been raised. Harris stepped between them and Yustichisqua.

"Who do you think you are?" Harris shouted. "Because, I know who I am. I am consort Belmundus Montjoy. If you dare interfere with me and mine, you shall feel the brunt of my anger. You would never survive it, even with a thousand *Sticks* and two thousand stones."

Harris balled his fists. The Yunockers backed away.

"You are not fully invested, my lord," said the black-sashed warrior. "Until then, we are not obliged to follow your every command."

Harris shook his fist, and then spit.

"I'm to be invested tomorrow. Go ahead and vex me tonight. Go ahead and stand on your petty book of orders. You might get the better of me now, but tomorrow afternoon, I'll be hunting black sashes and turkey feathers. Go ahead, gentlemen of the constabulary. Fuck with me, Lord Belmundus, if you dare. Go ahead and take your best shot. Leave me in the dust and explain to Lord Kuriakis in the morning that his new consort didn't appear for his investiture because you decided to play soldiers."

Terror blossomed across the collective constabulary faces. They bowed curtly, and then drifted backward, out and over the threshold, never daring to turn backs on this pissed-off lord of *the Ayelli* — this Lord Belmundus Montjoy, a man to be reckoned with.

4

Once the Yunockers departed and the door shut, Harris hunkered to Yustichisqua.

"Little Bird, Little Bird," he said. "You're safe now."

"No, I am not, *oginali*. They shall get me when I leave you."

"Then you won't leave. Don't let them make you cry."

Harris took his servant in his arms and patted his back.

"They do not make me cry, *oginali*. It is you. You make me cry." Little Bird glanced into Harris' eyes. "Never has anyone stood for me — ever. No one has placed themselves in the way of harm for weary Yustichisqua." He wept in earnest now. "No one has ever . . . ever been *oginali* to me."

"There, there. Weep then. That's worthy of tears, my friend. And you won't leave tonight. You won't drift down to the Ghetto and be given your shitty bowl of *sqwallen*."

Little Bird pushed away, suddenly concerned.

"If I cannot go to *the Scullery Dorgan*, you shall not eat."

"Then my belly will rumble tonight."

"But . . ."

"It'll rumble . . . and there's always that beer you brought. We'll get drunk together. That should settle us fine."

"Settle us fine?" Little Bird sniffed. "Where shall I sleep?"

"In a heap, in the corner." Harris laughed. "Well, you're used to it. True? And you don't think I'm giving up my comfy bed, do you?" He laughed again. "You can sleep beside me, if you can."

"I cannot. I will sleep at the foot of your bed."

"Like a dog?"

"Like a guardian."

Harris sighed. It was settled then. No food. Scant sleep. Perhaps some beer and, if that fucking *Eye* stayed shut, no more interruption from *the Gestapo*.

"Come. Undress me."

Harris drifted to the mirror. Little Bird fluttered behind him.

"Stand tall when you're alone with me," Harris said. "You do me no honor bent like a pretzel."

"A pretzel, *oginali?*"

"A strange twisted food from my land — a salty and crunchy snack. We'll probably want some before the night's out."

Harris felt hands on his shoulders, tugging at his cape. They hesitated. Then Harris remembered.

"Ah. *Columbincus.*"

He fumbled with the thing, but now it was more a companion, having come alive on cue. He wondered how it would be when *fully initiated.* Once removed, Yustichisqua slipped away the cape, and then attended to the tunic and *the asano.* This left Harris standing in the golden jockstrap before the mirror. Yustichisqua went to undo it, but Harris held to it fast. Little Bird retreated.

Harris glanced at the shimmering reflection.

"Who am I?" he mused.

Here he was — Harris Cartwright, formerly of stage and screen, naked to the world except for a golden swath. But who was he, really? He had never been truly Harris Cartwright. That was the wraith who filled many skins — many costumes and personas. Was he just another *run-of-the-mill Joe* — Humphrey Kopfstutter, the product of a Californian divorce? Now he was a champion. A protector of another spirit — a vibrant one, who knew nothing but sorrow and care.

"Who am I?" he mused as he peered into the glass. "I'm Lord Belmundus; and . . . I'm a star."

And at that moment he became one and would be so for the remainder of time.

Chapter Fourteen

The Food of the Gods

1

"*Oginali,*" came a whisper.

Harris hardly stirred. Exhausted and hungry, he wanted to sleep late. Yustichisqua's alarm clock voice roused Harris to look for the snooze button. He rolled over and almost fell from the platform. Then he sniffed. A sweet aroma captured him, and he turned, this time with eyes opened and saliva flowing.

"Is that a muffin?"

"A muffin, *oginali?* No, it is a *stewganasti.*"

Harris sat up.

"It doesn't look *nasty* to me. Give me some."

"Take it all, *oginali.*"

Little Bird pointed to a marble pedestal where set a tray filled with *stewganasti* of all sorts, and hot steaming brew — coffee perhaps. *And was that bacon and sausage?* Harris pulled some *nasty* muffin to his mouth and munched. Heavenly — as far from *nasty* as he was from slumber.

"You were brave to make *a Scullery Dorgan* run, Little Bird."

"Not so, *oginali.* The food was here when I awoke."

Harris suspected Arquebus might have sent a doggie bag, probably hearing about the previous evening's scuffle. Harris hopped over to the tray. He didn't recognize a thing.

"Is that coffee?"

"*Kawee?* Yes, *oginali.* And delicious *hawiya yukayosu, hawiya asdoyuwi* and *suweechi.*"

Little Bird poured *the kawee,* and then dumped gray stuff in it, which Harris took to be milk, probably from an unpronounceable member of the bovine family. This was soon confirmed, but it could use sugar.

"Sugar?" Little Bird shrugged.

"Sweeter."

"Ah. *caliseegee.*"

"Yes, that."

Little Bird opened a small crock of orange gravel and quickly plopped a handful into Harris' cup of *kawee*. Harris sipped again, and then grinned.

"I'll need to learn what things are called here."

"Whatever you call them, they become."

Harris lifted the cup.

"Then this is a Montjoy Latte with Orange Sweet Shit."

Little Bird smiled, hiding his face like a girl and tittered. Harris gladdened at Little Bird's improved mood.

Harris concentrated on the various *hawiya*, which he learned later was the term given to anything derived from *the adesigua*, which the Montjovians called *the pogo-pogo* — but pig by any other name was still bacon and sausage. These meats were salty and spicy, and complemented with *terrerbyrd* omelet — the aforementioned *suweechi* dish. If he ever got back to California he'd have a ball ordering in IHOP — two double sunnyside up *suweechis* with a sidecar of extra crispy *hawiya yukayosu* and a cup of *kawee*, hold *the orange sweet shit*, if you please.

Little Bird ate from a different bowl, stuff which looked like oatmeal, but dry and unappetizing.

"Is that *sqwallen*?" Harris asked.

"Yes, *oginali*."

Harris reached over, swiping the bowl. He gathered delectibles from the tray onto a plate.

"You eat what I eat."

"Then will you eat *sqwallen*?"

"Not if I can help it. How dare they bring me the tasty *nasty* muffins and make you eat crap."

"But *she* brought it."

"Who? Scepta Charminus?"

"No. The one who serves her."

Harris put his plate aside and sipped his *kawee*, struck by the thought of *the one who serves her*. He knew her — the Trone with the superiority complex. But she couldn't be bad, because she brought them food.

"Then it came from the Scepta," Harris said. "If her maid brought it, Charminus sent it."

"No, *oginali*. I believe . . . well, her servant acts according to her own wants and wishes. I say true."

Harris grinned.

"How do you know? Who is this Cetrone? What's her name?"

Little Bird frowned. He set his plate aside and turned back to his *sqwallen*. Harris thought to swipe the bowl again, but perhaps there was something in this feed the Cetrone required — craved. However, Harris craved to know the Trone maid's name. He couldn't tell why.

Little Bird finished quickly, and then went about setting out clothes — more elegant than yesterday, if it were possible.

"They will be here soon to escort you to the ceremony, *oginali*. I must prepare you."

"Where's the shower room?"

"You wish to bathe?"

"Well, I'm not putting on rich duds over a smelly body."

Yustichisqua brought his nose into Harris' armpit and sniffed. "But you do not smell."

"Like hell, I don't. I'm more like *Lord Bigdungass* than *Lord Belmundus*. So where's the shower?"

"Very well," Yustichisqua said. "Remove your *Columbincus* and I will prepare you."

Harris unsnapped his brooch, an act easier to master, and stripped before Little Bird could do it. Hot steam and gushing water would be a blessing. However, once naked, save for the golden jockstrap, Yustichisqua raised Lord Belmundus' arms. A light beam struck Harris — a blinding white flash. His skin tugged and tickled and tinged. Blue light followed, spiraling over his shoulder, wrapping him in tentacles. It lifted him, turning him like a cement mixer until a red light scanned him from below, pelting him with a material akin to gravel. It hurt.

"Get me out of this," Harris complained

"But *oginali*, you must wait for the green light."

It came — a rush of green, a funnel which pinched him, tossed him and drip-dried him. When it concluded, Harris was dumped to the tiles. He was clean, befuddled, and not amused, still looking forward to a real bath, which he guessed would evade him until he rented a cabana at the edge of the Bottleblue Sea, or as they called it, *the Amaykwohi*.

2

Arquebus arrived first with three Thirdlings. Harris recognized one to be the cowboy *Cabriolin* driver, Elypticus. Harris wondered if the other two were sons of Arquebus also. All three bowed, while Arquebus waved his hand spaciously. Two Trones carted in a large basket of fruit on a low cart, which the natives called a *dollywaggle*.

"Peaches," Harris said, grinning at the prospects.

"No, Lord Belmundus," Arquebus said. "They look like peaches, but they are *hiloseegi* fruit. Some are bitter, while others, sweet. You never know until you select one."

"I thank you."

"They are not from me. They are a gift from Agrimentikos, who shall be here shortly with the others. I had cargo Trones assigned to me, so I granted the boon and had them *dollywaggle* his gift here." He reached beneath his *Columbincus* and withdrew a green leather pouch. "This is my gift to you."

Harris opened his hand accepting it.

"Should I look?" he asked.

"You should. It is not much."

Harris unhitched the pouch and dumped a palm's worth of coins into his hand.

"Money."

"That it is. There are sixty *yedalas*. Not a king's ransom, but it will help you if you should choose to gamble or visit Xyftys, the Gurt tailor." Harris bowed. "My advice to you is a more valued gift."

"Oh," Harris said, reading the subtext. "So the word's got about?"

"That you have called out Buhippus in the line of his duty, yes."

"Buhippus? Is that the black sashed one or the turkey feather dude?"

"Black sash, and the captain of the Palace Yunockers. I am afraid that you have angered Tappiolus."

"He has my permission to boycott my big *whoop-dee-do* ceremony."

"He cannot. He will be here with the others and as civil as a python in the undergrowth. Today you are the golden consort. No one will dare reprimand you or . . . your property."

Arquebus stared at Yustichisqua, who averted his eyes.

"Little Bird," Harris snapped, as commanding as a drill sergeant. "Keep your eyes up. Stand to your full height. I won't have you as a groveling shadow."

"Yes, mast . . . yes, *oginali*."

Little Bird stood tall, nervously, but abandoned the groveling. Arquebus shook his head.

"Sir John," Harris said. "Can I call you Sir John in private?"

"We are not in private, Lord Belmundus. My sons are here and your Trone is within earshot. If *Sir John* is in the vicinity, he might hear you. But then again, he might not."

"I'll take my chances. Need I remind you I'm the golden consort today? I'm even sporting my best bling."

"Need I remind you, you have no concept of today's events."

That was true. Unlike the elaborate course Harris had undertaken in *the Cartisforium* on Farn history and geography, no one had sat him down to explain the Investiture Rite. Maybe it would be worse than the sandblasting shower.

"I assume I'll meet the family, or so you said."

"Yes. You say true. However, it shall occur in the Scarlet Chamber."

With this, the three Thirdlings bowed and the two Trones shuffled on their *zulus*.

"What's so special about the Scarlet Chamber?"

"It is comparable to Buckingham Palace," Arquebus said. "Only no established protocols to follow. You will be left to your own devices."

"Surely there must be protocols," Harris said. "This place is like a Chinese checker game. There's a regulation for every tick of the clock."

By omitting the scorecard, a consort, golden or otherwise, would have every opportunity to be his own undoing. Was that it? Harris guessed it was the point or the test.

"There are protocols. You need to discover them, Lord Belmundus. You need . . ."

The doors opened and four gentlemen entered — gentlemen whom Lord Belmundus had met before — the hunting Pod, now dressed to the nines. They wore similar silken tunics, capes and kilts (*asano*), only in different colors and accessories — gold, silver, ruby, and jade. When they walked, they sparkled like *Tiffany's* window. Behind each trawled a Trone — eyes downcast and contrite. They toted boxes — the gifts, Harris assumed, and he was correct in this assumption.

First to come forward was the senior consort, Agrimentikos —
he of the Mediterranean look. Draped in a jade-crusted cape, his
conical cap dazzled. Agrimentikos raised his arms in welcome.
Belmundus bowed.

"I thank you, lord," Harris said, pointing to the peaches, which
were not peaches.

"I grow them myself," Agrimentikos announced. "Once your
digestion becomes accustomed to them, you will be regular for an
eternity. What a gift! What a gift!"

He laughed and turned about, his brother consorts bowing to
him. He had been here the longest, drawn from a traveling
company of Thespians who had given a performance of *Oedipus
Rex* to an unappreciative crowd of Macedonians, as Agrimentikos
would tell you. During the performance, he noticed a divinity in
the amphitheater — a golden-haired Helen of Troy, who dazzled
him. So overwhelmed by her, the Chorus overtook his apostrophe
and he stood gaping before the few awake members of the
audience. She came to him again and again, this vision of beauty,
until he followed her to the Temple of Mithridates Major and
awoke exhausted, but delighted in *Mortis House.* He had served
and serviced Scepta Soffira ever since.

Agrimentikos clasped his co-consort Arquebus about the
shoulders.

"He appears to be a rare acquisition, brother. Look at his
profile and beauty — his youth. And he shall play *Cassioshima.*
You have given him the piece, have you not?"

"Yes, brother. He has had it since yesterday."

"Good. Good."

Agrimentikos strutted about like a man imagining even the
pillars as audience. Harris thought the man a *trip-and-a-half* and a
bloated old fart — but not so old, perhaps thirty-one or two, which
by ancient Athenian standards fell far short of Medicare.

Tappiolus stepped forward, grinning like . . . well, *a python in
the undergrowth.*

Here it comes, Harris thought. A lecture on calling out
Boohippy or Bulrushes or whatever the fuck his name is.

However, Tappiolus was pleasant and pointed to his Trone,
who raised a long box to the golden consort.

"For me?" Harris asked. "You shouldn't have. It's not even my
'hday."

"Why would I not present you with a gift on your day of days, Boots?"

Day of days. Good one. Hiss. Hiss. Hiss.

"Considering we already have had some differences of opinion . . ."

"Not true, brother. However, this gift will square things up between us."

Harris pawed the box, and then lifted the lid. Inside was a . . . *a Stick* — a beautifully crafted weapon of Farn with a silver band about the base and a gold one near the muzzle. Harris wondered if this was one of a matched set and, once taken, he and brother Tappiolus would go back to back, step ten paces, turn and fire.

"It is lovely, brother," Harris said. He snapped *the Stick* from its housing. It was light and balanced. "I'll be careful not to aim it at anything."

"It does not matter, yet. You cannot use it until tomorrow. Then I shall have the privilege of showing you its proper use. I and my captain of the guard, Buhippus. I believe you have met Buhippus."

"Can't recall the fellow," Harris said. "But I look forward to it."

He bowed, just as the last two consorts stepped toward him. They strode in tandem like a binary program. They were Oriental and the co-consorts to Miracola, who Harris recalled from the stained-glass windows as being . . . ample.

The first consort bowed — Hasamun, handsome and feminine — no more than twenty-five in appearance, but since he had been drawn from the Mikado's court theater near Kyoto while on an entertainment run north to the Shogunate at Edo castle, he was a sight older than he appeared. Hasamun had seen Miracola as a lustrous moon in the mists over a nighttime glade. He worshiped her immediately. He had been summoned by the Tokugawa warlord that evening to perform the ghost of *Kumasaka* in the *Noh* play of the same name. But he failed to show, greatly angering Tokugawa Ieyesu, because it was a three-man play, and one-third of the company had gone missing. Fortunately, a giant carp arose from the castle's koi pond and swallowed Hasamun — swallowed him to *Mortis House.*

Hasamun extended a flat box to Belmundus — a similar box in shape and size as Tappiolus'. Before Harris could accept it, the second consort came forward, with a twin box. Posan, older than Hasamun and Chinese, was a performer-playwright. He had been renowned for his drinking capacity and entertaining prostitutes into the wee hours of the morning at local wine pavilions. However, when the Mongols put an end to his Sung lords, Posan had been summoned to perform for the great Khan, who enjoyed a bit of untoward culture with exotic turns. Posan was rarely up to the task, preferring rice wine than the chopping block. He first saw Miracola's face on every pastry he ate and in every wine bucket he lifted. Soon this woman obsessed him and he brushed a play about her — even performed as Miracola before the Princess Wei-ch'i-k'ai-lung-fan. The play flopped and he fled the henchman. Fortunately, he hid in a fortuitous well and, when hoisted out, he was in Farn.

Posan bowed deeply and pushed his gift in front of Hasamun's. Hasamun grinned and pushed his out farther. There was a contest for precedence. Harris wasn't sure what to do. If he went for one over the other, would it be an insult? He held back. Then, the two consorts stood tall.

"Together," they said in unison and popped the lids.

"More *Sticks*?" Harris asked.

"No, brother," Hasamun replied.

He shook the gift loose, unfurling it.

"A painting?" Harris said.

"For the left side of your court." It was a watercolor peacock. "In a style my brother taught me to brush."

Hasamun bowed to Posan. Posan unfurled his gift — another painting, this one a wood blocked — a seaside scene in *Ukiyo-e* style.

"For the right side of your court, Lord Belmundus," Posan said. "My brother has taught me the art."

Then the two consorts bowed to each other. Harris felt he was in the presence of twins, but they were still distinguishable. Still, there was concordance, which pleased Harris. He accepted the paintings, handing them to Yustichisqua. Arquebus came close to Harris' ear.

"It is customary for the incoming consort to offer a small token of his appreciation," he whispered. "I only mention it, because it is ᠈ected."

Harris cocked his head. He wasn't prepared for this. He thought of the stale beer, beyond warm piss now, if any remained from last night. It was a source of comfort then. Now it was an empty bottle, the genie having escaped. He glanced at Little Bird, who pondered. Then Harris had a thought — a sly thought, which could compromise him. It would set precedents.

"Little Bird," he said. "Bring me your bowl."

"*Oginali?*"

"Do it."

"At once."

Yustichisqua rummaged below the pedestal for his bowl and brought it. He trembled. Harris sniffed the stuff. Vile, but he was resolved to do this. He dipped the spoon into the wallpapery paste, taking a massive dollop of the brown, gluttonous staple.

"You must not do this," Arquebus whispered.

Harris grinned. He witnessed the horror registered on all the faces, only encouraging him to complete the act.

"*Sqwallen,*" he declared. "Wonderful stuff."

He wrapped his mouth around the spoon and almost gagged. It was bitter and greasy, though it looked dry and sweet. There was a gamy aftertaste. However, he forced himself to swallow, and then pressed a satisfied grin across his lips. He pushed the bowl forward to his brother consorts. A sudden burst of laughter — gales of hilarity.

"Our new brother has a sense of humor," Agrimentikos shouted. "I like it. I like it well."

Harris shifted the bowl back to Little Bird, who looked worried. The two Trones weren't enjoying this either, looking to one another, uncomfortable at the gesture. Arquebus came around and placed his arm about Harris' shoulders.

"We have had our fun," Agrimentikos said. "But now it is time to proceed to the Scarlet Chamber."

Decorum descended on the company. They turned to the door and processed.

Chapter Fifteen

The Scarlet Chamber

1

It was the Red Carpet again, or so Harris thought. The corridor leading to the Scarlet Chamber was lined with Yunockers, attired in dress uniforms, or so Harris assumed. He hadn't seen so much brass and silver since he played a young cadet in *The Honor of the Point.* He admired the way the guards kept their poses, still and unbending while balanced on *zulus.* In niches, Romanesque statues stood interspersed with modern pieces — nudes *sans* fig leaves. Such *frou-frou* was proper in the court of the Provost of Art. Were these by famous sculptors? Was there room for fame in a land where the first generation still kicked the tires?

Agrimentikos led the way as senior consort, followed by Hasamun and Posan, who Harris came to regard collectively as Eng and Chang. Tappiolus and Arquebus marched side by side flanked by the three Thirdlings. Then came Belmundus like a bride held in reserve — the best for last, although *last* was a train of Trones led by Yustichisqua. Harris noticed Little Bird kept his head erect as ordered, but glared at the Yunockers, cautiously.

It pleased Harris, his servant staying the course, but he also realized he had forced the lad into a precarious zone. This world was new for Harris. Had he the right to graft his will here? However, did Montjoy have the right to force him into a life of privilege at free will's expense? He might need to tread lighter to find his way clear and not destroy his Trone in the bargain.

But wouldn't Little Bird be better off dead than subjugated to this enslavement?

As Harris tread this Red Carpet, he hugged confusion. The order of the universe should not be his concern. Life should begin and end with himself, because he could only know one path — his own. But that would make him a lone tree in a desert. There had to be something beyond the bark. The sap flowed somewhere. A puzzlement. *Mortis House* was shamefully comfortable to him. Yet, his soul rebelled against it and others might be liable for his rebellious actions.

This place replayed a Hollywood scene — a bubble designed for him and Tony and McCann and the rest of the cast to dwell — a realm of art and joy and self-expression, separated from fans, who clamored in the dark and shouted for autographs — who sucked on the teat of celebrity, assuring that hope to run along this wooly rug beneath a shower of flashes and interviews. A shared life, this, but was it? A puppet's life, this, but was it? Was he Mrs. Kopfstutter's little boy or Harris Cartwright of the twenty foot screen in high definition and sometimes 3D? Or was he . . . Lord Belmundus, the gigolo for a creature who sucked the life force from thousands, replicating from the sperm of a chosen few, who were promised by a tree stump from an eternal hole in the ground? Farn was like the world entire — a dilemma, unresolved and insoluble.

Here he was — again, processing with his fellow actors on a runway cordoned by glitzy security guards and cheered by fans trained to adulate him — dress him, shower him and even catch his pee in an ornate Ming vase. How different was this place from the other place? Why would he want to escape? Because it entered the same multiplex, the same Q&A session and was conducted on the same fucking Red Carpet, which he despised. So what could he do? He smiled like the actor he was, wrapped in his new cape. Beneath his *Columbincus* beat a star's heart, hot and rebellious, ready to nova and change the world about him.

From the Scarlet Chamber came merry music, exotic, but vaguely. A blend of *Rule Britannia* and the *Tennessee Waltz*. Floral fragrance blasted Harris, choking him. Orchids and roses and jasmine — separately delectable, but together gloomy. Perhaps this was his funeral? Would it be a Viking pyre like mighty Siegfried's in the Twilight of the Gods or a chippy-chippy chop chop chop, and then stuffed into a baggy?

The corridor opened into the hall. Arquebus drifted to his side, tugging him left, while Tappiolus and the Thirdlings drifted to his right. In the chamber clustered young men and women to the sidelines, their attire eclectic and stylized — hair primary-colored and sculpted, spiked or mushroomed, no two the same. Some Thirdlings wore glittered trousers, while others preened in starched dresses deltaring over boots or slippers, according to preference. Harris couldn't tell the girls from the boys. He was sure some male Thirdlings were decked in ball gowns and some females, judging by bust lines, were tuxedofied. He thought he had slipped into the East Village for the Halloween parade.

On the chamber's right, a curtain of capes and caftans draped the Zecronisian guests — turbaned or skull capped, and not a woman among them. Between them loitered strange creatures with olive skin — lizard-like with squat faces terminating in snouts. These were Gurts, Harris learned later, an inlander species, which most *Ayelli* avoided. The Gurts were artisans and craftsmen, who manufactured everything needed and admired in Montjoy. The Zecronisians were the go-betweens — a convenient arrangement.

At the chamber's left mustered the Palace guard — Yunockers. Their captain, Buhippus, with his prominent black sash, stood at their head. He nodded at Belmundus, but Harris suspected the gesture was as false as Tappiolus' congeniality. Behind the Yunockers heaped a brown wall of Trones, their eyes peeping to catch a glimpse of what they were forbidden to see. Still, they served and fetched and sanitized, so they formed a necessary fog in the nether reaches. Perhaps they were issued an extra ration of *sqwallen. Yuck*!

"Fine music," Arquebus said to Belmundus.

"Yes," Harris agreed, although he wouldn't describe it as such, because it reminded him of a score spun from old *Ben Hur* clips — when the slave girls titillate the Roman Governor.

Thinking of Roman Governors, Harris spotted his future father-in-law, although he guessed Kuriakis already claimed him as a son. The Elector sat on a throne, slightly elevated above his mate, the Memer Joella, whose eyes flirted with a tall man attired in Saran wrap. This man also wore a helmet topped by three antennae — a triple pig's ass crown — an escapee from the set of *Flash Gordon.*

"Who's that man?" Harris asked Arquebus.

"Ambassador Traggert of Protractus. There has been a conference among four of the realms. Protractus has been a sticking point."

"A sticking point?"

"No need for you to be concerned. No consort should. The realm's politics only concern us when our children are at stake, which *does* come around frequently. But since you have not set upon that course yet, there is even less need for you to consider Farn's complex inter-Elector relationships."

"I agree," Harris said as they neared a proscenium, which banded the dais. "I can't even remember the name of what I ate for breakfast. Complex enough."

"Things will come in time," Arquebus said.

Time, Harris thought. A sudden chill overcame him as he remembered he would be reported missing by all those near and dear. They would drag Central Park Lake for his body or put out an all-point bulletin coast-to-coast about a kidnapping. No ransom note, however.

"My poor mother," he muttered.

"Are you ill?" Arquebus asked.

Harris *was* ill. *It must be the Sqwallen*, he thought, because he was dizzy and he wanted his mother. Her face was before him. The orchestra strummed and the Thirdlings did a quirky dance as gracefully coordinated as foaling a horse. But this was a phantom in a rainstorm to Harris, because the Scarlet Chamber shifted. He held Arquebus' shoulder to keep from falling.

"*Oginali*," came a whisper. "Do not fall. Do not displease them. You must stay erect."

Harris felt steadier, but was overcast by loss and dread. Then, through a dash in the music, he saw *her* again — not his mother, but his kidnapper. Charminus processed into the chamber with two others, her sister Sceptas, no doubt. Harris was caught by the jade ring — that mesmerizing gem which had captured him before and often. He became stronger when passion bubbled from his spleen, overcoming his former weakness. With Little Bird at hand, Harris stood tall beside his brother consorts.

2

The court fell silent as the musicians raised their instruments and played a processional for the three Sceptas. Although his mistress entranced him, Harris listened to Arquebus' palaver intently.

"It might interest you, as you have an attraction to Trones, we *do* recognize their musical abilities."

Harris noted the orchestra consisted entirely of Cetrone, spruced up in their best beggar buckskins and headbands. He recognized the instruments, which approximated ones from the outlands. Later, Little Bird would tell him the big drum in the ivory casing was called a *yuyona* and the fart horns were called *yaholi*.

The strings were *atliyidee* and came in several sizes. The piano, the guitar and the organ were classified as *dikano geesti* — the big bellied guitar being *the boboli dikano geesti*, the narrow piano-harpsichord, *yutumi dikano geesti*, and the organ-fluty thing, *yutana dikano geesti.* Despite the odd names, Harris embraced the beautiful sound — a majestic tune — a march to a muffled drum beat and a sweet melody, arching over it while the Sceptas assumed their places on the dais. There followed a passel of floating Trones — children, uniform in stature and arrayed in two rows before Kuriakis. They bowed, and then filled the chamber with their glorious voices.

Thankful all are we for thee,
Elector Provost of the Arts,
All living things of Montjoy be
To keep thee in our beating hearts.
For our daily sqwallen give,
At thy wondrous grace we live,
Service to the Sceptas' smile,
We forever reconcile
As the children of the soil,
For Elector and our Memer toil,
All hail Joella, mother fair.
All hail our father, Provost rare,
All hail great Kuriakis,
All hail, all hail, all hail!

The tune was lovely beyond description, touching Harris' heart, distracting him from Charminus and her ring. But the words stirred more, inflaming him with the preponderance of Trone service. *They were taught from the earliest age to know their place.* It explained Yustichisqua's diffidence.

"So you see, Lord Belmundus," Arquebus whispered, "Trones have a place beyond the dustbins and lavatories. Our Memer holds a soft spot for them and, although we are bound to ignore them, she never permits mistreatment unless the rules are violated. Such charity abounds from Memer Joella."

"It's called *patronizing*," Harris muttered. "Recognize it for what it is."

Arquebus shook his head, but grinned — the knowing grin of a man acknowledging *naïveté*. A man expecting the bloom to fall from the rose. Perhaps today.

The children finished an encore of their hymn, and then bowed. Kuriakis stood and applauded, prompting acclaim from the court, even from the Sceptas, although begrudgingly, Harris observed.

"What fine singing," Kuriakis boomed, and then swept his hand toward his Memer, who nodded graciously.

Three Trones emerged from behind her throne, carrying baskets of *hiloseegi* fruit, distributing them to the children, who bowed in thanks to Joella. Agrimentikos shot a knowing smile to Belmundus. It said, *I grow them myself.* How useful. An ancient Greek grocer, convenient to pick the peaches to reward the help. Harris returned the grin. He liked the senior consort — jovial and convivial. Agrimentikos didn't spout regulations like Arquebus and Tappiolus. Nor was he a marionette like Posan and Hasamun,

The orchestra struck a livelier tune. The children's choir floated to the brown curtain of Trones. Four Thirdlings approached the throne, bowed, faced each other, and then did the herkiest jerkiest dance Harris had ever witnessed. It was like an unsprung clock exploding, coils flying apart. The couples clapped, out of time, and performed a few sloppy somersaults. When the music stopped, they continued like mimes at charades. Then they halted abruptly, bowed and withdrew. The crowd went wild, which mystified Harris. Still, the performance had significance for Kuriakis, because he stood again, this time wiping away tears, and then turning to Ambassador Traggert.

"Is there anything in Protractus to match its beauty?"

Traggert muttered a few unintelligible bleeps and blips, evidently the communication in the world of high science.

"I thought not," Kuriakis said.

He laughed, satisfied with the entertainment, and then raised his hand for silence. He glanced toward Harris. The moment was upon Lord Belmundus, no mistaking it. Harris awaited a solemn command to come forward from his fellow consorts. However, Kuriakis drew a deep breath, and then bellowed across the chamber.

"Boots!"

He laughed, dumbfounding Harris. He had received fair warning that the Elector had bestowed this nickname upon him.

Harris liked it. But he reckoned it would be a private nickname —
one allowed in intimate moments with the Elector. But no. Here it
was, and here it was bellowed again.

"Boots! Come forward and meet my daughters."

Harris took two steps, and then hesitated, waiting for
Yustichisqua to follow, but this was not protocol. To hell with that.

"Little Bird," he whispered.

Yustichisqua didn't move, but then he came, floating behind
like a shadow. Little Bird was already in trouble with the
Yunockers. What were the odds of them killing him twice? Now
anchored by Little Bird, Lord Belmundus emerged, striding toward
the throne. When he reached the proscenium, he recalled he was
never taught the rituals. But, what the hell, he had broken the rules
already having his Trone in tow, so no holds were barred. Harris
clasped his hands together, drawing them over his *Columbincus*,
and then bowed respectfully.

"Father," he said. "You have summoned me and I appear."

He recalled the line from some script or other — unproduced
no doubt. But he had a head full of lines and his voice could mimic
a host of expressions.

"Yes, Boots. Well done. Well done." Kuriakis stepped forward,
reaching for Harris' hand. "You are a fine specimen. I saw it when
you warded off *the terrer*byrd. I told Agrimentikos you will be a
fine addition to the court, didn't I, Agrimentikos?"

"Yes, my lord," the Greek said from the sideline.

"Thank you, father," Harris responded.

"Yes, yes." Kuriakis waved his hands toward his daughters.
"You know Charminus, without saying. You are her pick, after all.
But let me introduce you to my other daughters."

Harris looked to the two, who resembled their stained glass
images only in the flesh. Soffira was the lovelier of the two — of
the three, actually. She had blonde tresses, pure white skin —
whiter than Charminus', and rosy lips, more toward pink than
toward claret. Her eyes were blue like Harris'. She extended her
hand and Harris approached, grasping it.

"My pleasure, sister."

"Sister?" Soffira said, giggling, and then looked to Charminus.
"He is unlike the other one in this. You have my blessings with this
charmer."

Charminus frowned at first, probably sibling rivalry, but then parted her crimson lips in a sinister grin.

"Do not mistake his smooth tongue for the real thing, dear Soffira," she said. "Although glad he has manners, he is inclined . . . to buck. But we know how to tame."

"Good, good," Kuriakis exclaimed. "I like a bucker . . . but." He winked at Harris. "Not a rascally troublemaker, I hope. You know what I mean?"

Harris did. This was illusion after all. He'd be *Boots the wunderkind* as long as he was spirited within boundaries. Too much *buck* and he'd be sent to where his mysterious predecessor evaporated. Harris bowed to Kuriakis, and then to Soffira.

"And this is my eldest daughter," Kuriakis proclaimed. "Miracola, the Scepta of the great loom — the mistress of weaving."

Harris saw before him the *ample* Scepta, who in the outlands would be regarded as a candidate for the fat farm. She had auburn hair, three chins, cheeks as wide as Maine, breasts as blue ribbon as anything seen at the Iowa State Fair, and a backside, which required a reinforced throne, no doubt. He imagined the pain her Trones must suffer at unimaginable and unmentionable duties. Then he thought of Hasamun and Posan — thin young men. They must disappear in bed. Well, Hasamun saw her as a moon and Posan as a giant fish. But there was no accounting for tastes. She probably had a docile and wondrous personality.

"Sister," Harris said, tentatively.

"You may call me Scepta Miracola," she said, puffing the words out like a fortuneteller in a mechanical chance booth. "I do not even allow my sisters to call me *sister*."

Soffira laughed — an annoying laugh, while Charminus pouted, her lips pruning. Harris bowed again.

"Scepta Miracola," he said.

She raised an eyebrow, inspecting him in one glance.

"You are a fat one," she said. "Your co-consort is thinner." She glanced toward Tappiolus. "But Charminus always liked them with some heft and no bodily definition."

I work out, Harris thought. But he wasn't here to debate. So he bowed with acceptance, wondering how Weight Watchers would regard Miracola's assessment.

"Excellent," Kuriakis said.

He grasped Harris about the shoulders, ushering him to the Memer. This would be a difficult introduction. If Harris addressed the Memer as *mother*, he might drift into *sqwallen* induced morbidity. He gazed nervously at her. She was radiant — a combination of the Virgin Mary and the Queen of England — young Elizabeth, not old gouty Anne. Perhaps this wouldn't be difficult after all. He bowed low, his hand extended in an old fashioned, *thankee sai* gesture. He couldn't be courtlier.

"Mother," he said.

Joella stood, raising both hands. The court rumbled. Harris thought he was done in, crossing the protocol line, waiting for the Memer to scream, *off with his head.* But no. She opened her arms wide, and returned the bow graciously.

3

"Montjoy has thrived as the preserver of all things beautiful," Joella began. "In our fair land blows the Lilies of Murrow and the Roses of Scaladar, scenting the palaces of Farn and beyond. We harvest the Silk from *the Threadnickery* and weave the sheer Cloth of Trelaw. All the Electors reckon us as the center of grace and luxury, the sponsor of the Gurts manufactories in *the Yuyutlu* and the great market of *Wudayleegu* for the Zecronisians, from over the *Amaykwohi* Sea. Our militia is the most elegant and our *Kalugu* produces the most talented musicians and the most obedient Trones in Farn. To this the most beautiful children from the Forling to the sea grace our gardens. We are the quartermasters of all which is precious to the eye and tender to the nose; and display it for the ages on *the Ayelli*. This I say to you, dear outlander, whom *the Primordial Centrum* has christened Belmundus the Fair — Belmundus the Just — Belmundus the Bountiful. To you I say welcome. Add to our glory as many have done before you and many who follow shall over the cavalcade of time. Let my daughter's choice not shame the House of Montjoy. May you enjoy and ennoble the family name."

She extended her hand toward him. In it she held a ring — a jade ring, much like Charminus' only with his own sigil — the eye with two squiggles.

"Take this as a token of your mother's love and your father's earnest faith that you shall be fruitful and add to our population."

Harris stepped toward her, hesitating. He wasn't sure he could approach her, but how else could he take the ring, unless she tossed it. He plucked the ring from her grasp, and then, on impulse, kissed her hand.

"Thank you, mother."

"This is a day of gifting. Whatever your pleasure and want, ask it of me and it shall be granted."

He bowed again, but decided to save his request. You never know when you'll need a *get out of jail free card.*

Kuriakis clapped, and then waved the other consorts forward.

"It is time, my sons." He turned to Harris. "Boots, kneel before me."

Harris went to one knee, and then to both, bowing his head. The consorts gathered around him, placing hands upon him.

"Boots," Kuriakis intoned, and then chuckled. "I guess for this we need formality." He opened his hands wide — large hands with the shepherd's crook sigil tattooed on the palms. Harris recalled Charminus saying, *my father dabbles in magic.* Harris didn't doubt it. "Belmundus the Fair, the Just and the Bountiful, I pronounce you the second consort to my daughter, Charminus the Shimmering, Scepta to the House of Montjoy on this eighth day of *Ringus Mordantus* in the forty-two thousandth rotation about *Solus Dodecadatemus*, declared here *in Mortis House* before the court of *the Ayelli.*"

He touched Harris' *Columbincus*, which glowed sapphire blue. Harris felt a surge of power — warmth — a fire even from head to groin as if preparing him for Marathon sex with the Goth girl, Charminus the Shimmering. The ring, which he held in his palm, also shone. He quickly secured it on his right hand, but then thought better of this, and shifted it to his left ring finger. His brother consorts pulsed their lightning charms. When they released him, he turned to see his mistress — his kidnapper and now his keeper — standing before him. Was she his wife? He couldn't tell. This was like no coupling on the books. He was now officially one of the two batteries, which charged this lady's dildo. But Harris could have done worse. Besides, he was pinned by her mesmerizing ring. He could claim insanity and maintain the sanctity of his soul.

She raised him, gesturing into her arms. But when he drew close, she spun about, holding his hand only, raising it in hers — a signal for the crowd to go wild — applause and shouts of *Adadooski*, which Harris later learned meant *be fruitful — get crackin' and make those babies — those Thirdlings who fill this chamber to the rafters and nothing beyond.* Well, that's what it meant by implication.

One more step in the rite came now. A priest named Fagus Marius, a deacon in the Church of the Pontifraxian Orbitum, came forward, sent by the Elector of Pontifrax to bless the union, or as Harris regarded it, the abduction. The man was robed in black with a snowy shawl, and wore several crosses and ankhs and sephiras and pentacles. Harris wondered how the man could stay upright with this amount of metal and still swing his fiery censer. Fagus Marius swung it left, and then right. Harris thought one more swing and the thing would take off into the crowd.

"Hear the words of *the Primordius Centrum*," Fagus chanted, and then made his declaration:

> *"To each Elector three branches made*
> *Deigned as sons and daughters born,*
> *Renowned Sceptas and Seneschals*
> *But as towers apart shall grow,*
> *Never fruitful within their bonds,*
> *So to the outlands they must go,*
> *To gather succor into dough —*
> *The life force must they always hoe.*
> *But each may draw a double mate,*
> *And thus may sow and populate,*
> *A harvest to serve and ease their shade —*
> *A scattered horde as duty paid,*
> *Smiling kin for the alliance trade,*
> *But as mules these Thirdlings be,*
> *Until there comes the mending free.*
> *Then a fourth shall bloom in Farn*
> *Uniting houses — the outlands darn*
> *'til suns and moons reflect no more*
> *And Zin and Zacker close the door.*

The deacon made a strange sign of the cross — a Z-trace, and then clicked his tongue three times.

"May this union be the one to fulfill the promise — the promise of *the Spasatorum,* in the name of *Elohim al Fazir Galafindrus. Arkmo.*"

The entire chamber mumbled the word *Arkmo.* Then Charminus spun Belmundus around again to great applause and *Adadooski.*

4

"You are *up,*" Tappiolus said, grinning. "I need a rest."

Harris imagined a dozen wrecked hotel rooms. He hoped this time he'd remember the fun and not solely the exhaustion. Charminus gave Tappiolus a sly wink. Her Trone appeared behind her, catching Harris' attention. The woman was fetching in ways, which Charminus could never be. However, the dark haired beauty was appropriately servile before her mistress, and Charminus twitched until she regained Harris' attentions. Short lived, because Kuriakis clapped and paraded around the proscenium regally.

"Boots," he shouted. "Here, here, Boots. My gift to you."

Harris turned to see a draped object nearby the Yunockers ranks. At Kuriakis' command, Buhippus removed the drape, revealing the gift.

"Nice," Harris said like a teenager getting the keys to daddy's car.

It was *a Cabriolin.* His very own *Cabriolin.* Harris left Charminus and strolled to the machine. How did it operate? Could he master it? Could he soar over the Bottleblue Sea?

"Thank you . . . father."

"It will be here when you finish your rounds," Kuriakis announced, indicating the awaiting Scepta. "And I suppose you will need a replacement Trone."

Harris twisted about looking toward Yustichisqua, who immediately went to his knees, *zulus* spread outward.

"Replacement?" Harris asked. "But this Trone pleases me."

"That might well be, but he is a drifter from duty and this will not do. Especially since you are new to our ways."

Harris looked toward Buhippus, who grinned with satisfaction. Then he observed Charminus and her golden eyes. It was only one of those peepers that muddled the course.

"But father," Harris supplicated. "This Trone pleases me fine."

"We strive for perfection in the highest circles, Boots. This one is not an asset for Lord Belmundus. There are many others more disciplined."

Harris glanced at Little Bird, suddenly aware this was not the Cetrone's fault. It was his *oginali's* fault. Harris' insistence had brought Yustichisqua to this brink. He would probably be thrown to the dogs in *the Kalugu*; or worse — waste away with nothing but *sqwallen* in a Yunocker prison called *the Porias*. Harris swallowed hard — a bolt of air helping him brace for his next action. He bowed to Kuriakis, but shifted toward Joella, who still sat graciously on her throne.

"Mother," he said. "You promised me a gift."

"I did," she said.

"This Trone pleases me well."

She smiled at him, and then nodded toward Kuriakis, who grunted and threw his arms toward the ceiling. *Surrender.*

"My dear Lord Belmundus," she replied. "Would you waste your advantage on a worthless request? Surely you may keep this Trone, but there must be something better you have considered."

Harris touched first his *Columbincus,* and then his jade ring.

"Yes," he said. "I wish for this Trone to shed his *zulus* and walk as other creatures do upon the ground which holds us all."

A murmur rumbled through the hall, growing into a discussion. Harris looked to Arquebus, who shook his head. He saw Buhippus touch his *Stick*, perhaps preparing to suppress an insurrection of Trones. However, Joella gently raised her hand, and then stood. The hall melted to silence.

"Boots," Kuriakis snapped. "And would you have this creature walk beside you?"

"No, father. Behind me, as befitting his station."

Charminus came forward and grasped Belmundus by the arm.

"You forget yourself," she said, in a sharp tone, but still maintaining her public pose.

"Perhaps, I do," he confessed.

"You may keep this Trone," Kuriakis said. "As a gift from the Memer. As for shucking his *zulus*, he may do so in private in the confines of your court. But beyond that, he must adhere to the regulations."

Harris nodded, and then turned to his Trone.

"Yustichisqua," he said. "Rise and serve me."

Little Bird stood, tears draining into the edges of his lips. "Forever, *oginali*."

The music recommenced, and Belmundus bowed in turn to his brother consorts and to Soffira and Miracola. Charminus sent her Trone ahead to prepare the way, and then strode out of the Scarlet Chamber. Harris turned once again to Joella and Kuriakis. He nodded to Ambassador Traggert and to Deacon Fagus Marius. Finally, he raised his hands to the court. They shouted *Adadooski! Adadooski!*

"I am ready," Belmundus said to his Trone, although he was far from ready. "One day at a time," he muttered.

As he followed Charminus' wake, he heard the gentle buzz of Little Bird's *zulus*. Then the lad whispered something to him. Harris smiled, because Yustichisqua had bestowed a gift for the occasion.

"*Oginali*," he whispered. "Her name is Littafulchee and she is my cousin."

Adadooski!

Arkmo!

Part II

Exploring the Part

Chapter One

Following the Fold

1

Belmundus was *up* and stayed *up* for two weeks. *All hail youth in its exuberant blood flow!* Or so went *the Ayelli* proverb crafted by womenfolk, no doubt. Unlike the previous experiences, Harris recalled fragmentary moments. It wasn't all pleasure, because, although stamina blessed him, and his selection probably predicated on it, drilling for oil in the same field proved routine after two days, verging on tedium after a week. At two weeks, filled with *Corzanthe* and delectable tasty pastries and fruit, which Yustichisqua brought or Littafulchee toted, Harris had a hangover few had ever encountered and fewer would envy. While intoxicating on one hand, it begged for relief on the other. When he resisted the Scepta, she would put on her Goth girl routine, recapturing the passion, which had snagged him from the outlands — an art refined by an eternity of succubus need. However, whatever her feelings for the act, she had scant feelings for him. Harris was an object — a magic wand fulfilling the promise and perhaps the prophecy. Satiating the Scepta's spirit — the food which kept her alive, dwelled beyond him — beyond *Mortis House* and Montjoy — in the several worlds of the outlands, in the dreams of the unsuspecting, who would slumber hot and bothered, never to awake, depleted of testosterone. Loved ones would find these victims in the morning and declare a death by a heart attack or an aneurysm from a precondition. *Shame! Father of two. Successful businessman! Early death and much mourned.* Harris wondered whether Montjoy invested in the insurance policies these acts inspired. In any event, he might be exhausted, but he was alive and kicking.

At breaks, when they dined together, Harris would test the waters with general questions. As long as he stuck to generalities, the Scepta might answer. She told him the two suns of this world were named *Solus* and *Dodecadatamus*, and there were two suns in all the outlands. However, *Dodecadatamus* in some worlds orbited wide, making its approach beyond human reckoning. Every Thirdling knew as much. Once, he asked about *the zulus*.

"Why do you force Trones to wear those *zippy* shoes?"

"To serve us faster," she replied. "It is their shame, and they must recall it."

"What must they recall and why?" he asked.

"Their shame, of course. Because, they must. It is ordained."

"Who ordained it?"

She grinned, pointing to the ceiling, and then to the floor, but didn't venture an answer beyond that. Then, after a sip of *Corzanthe*, she calmly said, "Your Trone will murder you in your sleep."

"Not true."

"You regard yourself as liberator, but they cannot be liberated by those who rule. They can only be free when they regard us as weak and assailable. That is why we have Yunockers."

"But they wear *zulus* too."

"Yes, and for the same reason."

"I'd fear *the zippy* cops slitting my throat before I would my Trone."

"In your case, my dear Lord Belmundus, you might be correct."

He winced, although it had been his suggestion.

"Am I marked?" he asked.

"You have incurred Captain Buhippus' anger. He is an obedient servant, but given to command. Tappiolus barely controls him, though I have admonished him to demean Buhippus — to regard him with less importance. More like a trained *Tippagore* or *Hunting dragget*. Tappiolus would never condone easing *the zulu* rule."

"Does it really matter?" Harris asked, as if the conversation had veered to the political.

"Actually, to me, no," she snapped. "I am above such discussions. If a Trone — even my most obedient and trustworthy Trone, were to transgress the law, punishment would be swift and severe. *The Kalugu* brims with replacement candidates, compliant entities happier to serve in *Ayelli* than to starve in *Kalugu*."

She yawned. Harris fell silent. Then he changed to a subject closer to his interests.

"When am I to see the city?" he asked. "I've been shown maps and I see it from my perch, but it would please me to visit the wards and markets."

"It would please me not," she said. He pouted. "Perhaps someday," she added. "There are pleasures enough to keep you here. And Brunting Day approaches."

Brunting Day was a sacred festival set aside by Kuriakis and Joella for their coupling. They processed from their palaces to *the Scaladar* gardens to reap the adulation of Montjoy. Elector and Memer would entered the Temple of Greary Gree and dedicate their bodies to the divinity of Farn. The play Harris was to perform — the tidbit dubbed *Othellohito,* was scheduled at the garden amphitheater on Brunting Day.

Harris didn't press the subject further. Bored or enthusiastic, he still considered escape. But when his passion flagged, Charminus would enchant him with her ring. He became a zapped bug. He did learn about her ring. The sigil on its face, resembling a shepherd's crook, actually evoked the sacred plant, which grew around the Temple of Greary Gree. It was a finicky specimen, blooming once every ten years. It was called the Lily of Murrow, its flower used to brew a liquor so powerful when poured into a silver goblet, the vessel turned to gold. It was almost worth the price of admission to see it, but the event was a few years off. Why did these precious plants take so long to flower, when the Sceptas had a short six-week gestation period, and the Thirdlings went from infanthood to dancing *the herky jerky* in three years?

Harris also discovered when his own ring touched Charminus', it caused her eyes to roll in orgiastic rapture. She almost lost consciousness. So whenever he needed a break, he'd clamp his ring to hers — jade to jade. Was this the secret for *Ayelli* insemination, because during his first inning of being *up*, he failed to impregnate her? Maybe the rings had to be clanked at precisely the correct moment — some sacred plant weaving its perfume about the canopy of the great bed. However, except *the Book of Farn*, there were no ready books on Montjoy lovemaking. Harris wasn't anxious to visit *the Cartisforium* for fear the chapters on sex would display a map akin to the *Kama Sutra.* There was one curious ring-related action. Whenever Charminus called him to his session, the jade shone brightly. Harris was glad it didn't come with a siren or he'd be a walking broadcast for his horny mistress.

Harris asked Charminus a specific question, one too specific for her reply — a question, which Arquebus had warned him to avoid. He sensed Charminus was lulled to joy after their last round of passion. The opportunity was too good to let pass. He looked deeply into her golden eyes — those eyes, which could project into a huge spyglass, roaming the halls of *Mortis House*.

"Great Scepta," he said solemnly, as if asking permission to use the toilet. "May I ask a question, which burns in my soul?"

She nodded. He couldn't tell whether it was ascent or her usual shrug.

"Thank you," he said, sitting up. "What happened to my predecessor?"

Charminus closed her eyes, and then scrambled from the vast bed, summoning her Trone to bring a fresh shift, as if the question had soiled her. Harris summoned Yustichisqua for a fresh jockstrap — tit for tat. He never asked her that question again. Besides, his *up* time was almost *up*. The clock rang him out when Tappiolus bowed his way in, his own Trone in tow. Charminus left them alone — the changing of the guard.

"Is this the way it'll always be?" Harris asked, hoping under these arrangements co-consort paths would cross once every two weeks only.

"Sometimes, Boots," Tappiolus replied. "But she roves to the out worlds also. When it happens, you must pursue knitting *ganuggle* robes or growing *protastitorium* spuds or whatever young screen stars are accustomed to do when not thrashing in the bedroom."

"I generally read Cicero," Harris said, smugly — although he couldn't remember the last Greek or Roman he read. "And I fancy exotic languages. Perhaps I'll study Cetrone."

Tappiolus sneered — a canine scowl.

"You are testing me, Lord Belmundus. But remember, when it comes to Trones, I am not the only deterrent."

"Buhippus?" Harris asked. "Yes, I forgot *El Capitan* and his pogo stick."

"If I were you, sir," Tappiolus admonished. "I would devote your free time to your *Columbincus* and becoming proficient at controlling your *Cabriolin*."

"And there's Brunting Day."

"Yes." Tappiolus bowed smartly, like a *gendarme* in a French Foreign Legion film, only with Italian subtitles. "You are relieved to take your ease, Lord Belmundus."

What? No Boots? Harris would like to call Tappiolus, Shithead, but he didn't think it would fly unless Kuriakis initiated it. Instead, he returned the bow — smartly *á la the back lot.*

"Yes, Lord Tappiolus, I'll relieve myself."

Harris left his fellow consort fuming, but his gibes would improve with time.

2

Arquebus instructed Harris on the refinements of *the Columbincus*. It afforded many advantages, including a shield if a Trone should try to murder him in his sleep. It also powered his *Stick* and *Cabriolin*.

Firing *the Stick* was an art, Harris soon discovered. You just didn't point and shoot. Tappiolus had offered to teach him, but since the co-consort was now *up* and unavailable, Hasamun and Posan took his place. A difficult course of study this, because neither consort spoke often — mostly grunting, demonstrating *Stick* techniques through tug and push. Hasamun taught Harris how to hold *the Stick*. Grip it wide-side toward the body and narrow-side out. Otherwise the shooter could do himself injury. Next, the thumb was pressed along the decorative band, which ringed *the Stick's* midsection. The index finger must be rigid, the remaining fingers bowed against the weapon's underside for support. Harris dropped the damn thing before he managed the proper grip.

"If you hold it not correctly," Hasamun explained, "it will knock you backwards upon your rump."

"Or fly away over your hip," Posan added. "And then . . ."

He pointed to the sky, laughing. He laughed harder when Harris' *Stick* did exactly that. They scrambled up a tree to retrieve it.

"Maybe I should just use it as a club," he suggested.

Finally, he managed to power up *the Stick*, regardless where it flew. He accomplished this by holding his left hand over the sigil of his *Columbincus* and focusing his mind on *the Stick's* tip. This fired the dang thing up. Now it was a matter of aim.

"Practice on the birds," Hasamun said, pointing to a gaggle of scarlet tweeters, which perched on a branch.

"What did they do to me?" Harris asked.

"Just aim and see," Posan replied.

Harris shrugged, touched his *Columbincus*, lifted *the Stick,* held properly with thumb pressed, index finger stiff, and the rest, bowed. He *wished upon a star* the thing missed the sweet little birdies, which had done him no harm. However, when he lifted his arm, the birds squawked, displayed hideous teeth and dived at him.

"Holy crap," he cried.

The little devils were aiming for his head. Harris stepped back, tripping over a footstool. He heard Yustichisqua behind him, yelling — *fire, oginali. Fire!* Harris waved the weapon like a flag, spraying the incoming *kamikaze* birds with enough blue fire to stop them cold. They fell like scarlet raindrops at his feet.

Hasamun and Posan bowed, and then applauded. Harris waited for an *arkmo* and an *Adadooski*, but his brother consorts just helped him to his feet, while Little Bird fussed about the state of Lord Belmundus' *asano* and cape. Harris laughed.

"Not so cute, these birdies," he said, kicking one aside.

Yustichisqua gathered them in his *korinkle* — a knapsack as ubiquitous as his *waddly wazzoo.*

"Good eating, *oginali*. They are *porgeedasqui.*"

Tastes like chicken, Harris thought. But he had taken his first shot. He could become a big game hunter if Charminus allowed him to spread his wings and find the quarry. Chances seemed nil to no way. As for spreading his wings, that was left to Arquebus and the flying machine.

3

Cabriolins, Harris learned, were also *Columbincus* powered. Whatever powered the *Columbincus* remained a mystery, although he asked.

"There is a place where minerals are mined," Arquebus explained. "There the enriching stones lurk, coveted by the Electors as . . . as the source."

That didn't explain much. Were these minerals like *kryptonite* or *Dragonstone* — or were they the fabled paragons of power, which Hollywood scripts harvested whenever they needed a focal point for the ubiquitous *force* or the mystical essence, *ch'i*? Harris accepted the answer pat, as if Arquebus said *Cabriolins* were powered by *gas from the pump.* He decided to call the all-powerful mineral, *the stuff.* He needed to manipulate *the stuff,* because it was found in *Ayelli* inventions, most beyond his ken.

The *Cabriolin's* panel was simple — flat and smooth with five indented zones — ports. Harris had observed these when he first encountered Arquebus, and the roller-coaster ride with Elypticus.

"This turns the power on," Arquebus explained, touching the center zone.

"Like a car's ignition?"

"If that yields meaning to you, yes."

Arquebus lived in pre-automotive times, so Harris shut up and listened. Arquebus touched each of the zones in turn.

"Your navigation — much like a ship's wheel. Left — right — upward and downward."

"Simple enough."

Elypticus arrived in his vehicle, and bowed.

"Is Lord Belmundus ready to race?"

Harris grinned, and then positioned himself before the panel. He touched the center zone, but nothing occurred. Arquebus chuckled. Then Harris looked to Elypticus, who touched his chest, where a smaller version of a *Columbincus* was pinned. Harris nodded, and touched his left hand to his brooch, and then applied his hand to the power port. *The Cabriolin* shook, the central zone glowing ruby. Harris shifted his hand to the upper zone and . . .

"Wow," he said, looking to Arquebus, who held on for his life.

"Keep it steady," his teacher advised. "And no racing today. Just ride easy — right — left, and then down a little."

Harris felt the vehicle responding not only to his hand, but to his thoughts — gentle glide, easy bank, forward over *the Ayelli* and upward to the sky. Elypticus kept pace with him, winking and grinning — clearly itching for a race.

"Keep your eyes on the panel," Arquebus chided, because *Ayelli*'s beauty had captivated Harris' attentions.

His eyes drank the sights — the valley sloping toward the city, verdant, dotted with pavilions and fountains and shrines. The amphitheatre, where he would put forth his best *Cassioshima*, if he managed to learn his lines, spread beneath his *Cabriolin*. A rotunda dominated the hill — the Temple of Greary Gree.

Suddenly, Arquebus placed a hand on Harris' shoulder.

"Hover here. Go no further."

Harris didn't know how to stop the contraption, and shrugged. Arquebus came beside him.

"Just take your hand away and not too . . . "

But Harris jerked his hand up, and *the Cabriolin* began spinning like a top.

"Now what?" Harris cried, alarmed.

"Hands back on," Arquebus shouted. "Tickle the left and right ports together."

Harris did this until the gyration gradually stopped. Dizzy, he might donate his lunch to the landscape below.

"Gently remove your hand."

Done. Stopped and hovering. Elypticus laughed, but upon catching his father's eye, the lad puckered, nodded and turned his head away. From both north and south (or was it south and north) *a Cabriolin* convoy approached, two double lines of ten, driving at a lower altitude than Harris, but clearly drawing a boundary between *Ayelli* and Montjoy City.

"Who are they?"

"Yunockers," Arquebus explained. "The guardians of the gate."

"I don't see a gate."

"You will if you cross the line," Arquebus replied.

"So we're not allowed in the city? None of us?"

"Yes, on occasion — supervised. Tappiolus is, of course, as he is the Provost of the Yunocker and must inspect *the Yuganawu*. Agrimentikos goes frequently, but he has been here so long he is . . ."

Harris cocked his head. Arquebus was about to say *he is trusted to do so.* Harris was convinced.

"He's what?"

"Nothing. The longer you are here, the more freedoms you accrue."

Harris looked at Arquebus suspiciously. Sir John was suppressing something. It was plain from the man's expression — one of longing, and yet disgust. This, despite the actor's art.

"Sir John," Harris snapped. "Do you want to know what I think?"

"No one cares what we think, Lord Belmundus and do not call me, Sir John."

"Does it pain you?"

"That name is best left in the past."

Harris watched the guardian forces crisscross before them. It *was* a gate and it was locked.

"What if I put my hand in gear and edge us closer?" Harris asked, a trace of mischief in his voice.

"They would take you into custody."

"Custody? *An Ayelli* Lord in custody?"

"They would do it with civility and considerable apology, but they would do it all the same. They would escort you to your Scepta to await chastisement."

"And what if I resisted their escort?"

Arquebus grimaced.

"You are as troublesome as . . ."

"As whom? The other one?"

"No one."

"Do you know what I think?"

Arquebus didn't answer. However, this didn't stop Harris from mulling over answers in his mind. *I think we're kept from the city because there's a secret there. I bet there's a way out and I also bet my predecessor — old Mr. Troublesome, found his way and was . . . well, was gently chastised for the discovery. Probably thrown to the terrerbyrds.*

"Do you know what I think?" Harris repeated, and then caught Elypticus' eye. "I think I'm up for a race."

Arquebus shook his head.

"You are not ready. Besides, it would be no contest."

"You think I'd lose?"

"On the contrary. Elypticus would let you win at all costs."

Harris grinned. He waved at the Thirdling, who cocked his head suspiciously, like a parrot wondering where the cracker was hidden. Then he grasped the intent. Harris slammed his hand on the center panel, and then banked away from the gate. He dived fast and furiously, swooping over the amphitheater and the Temple of Greary Gree. Elypticus gave a war whoop (a childish one), but zoomed to the challenge.

"Try to make me win," Harris shouted. "That's what you think."

Harris accelerated over the gardens and raced so low he could almost pick some Roses of *Scaladar*. It was the best ride he had ever taken — exhilarating and even more gratifying, because he had a chiding, grumbling Arquebus gripping on the rail.

"Some driving lesson," Harris shouted.

Elypticus kept up, but pointed at the sky. Harris winced, trying to see what the Thirdling meant. Storm clouds were rolling in. Harris could hear the rumble of distant thunder.

"I must insist," Arquebus said. "I insist we end this foolishness, Lord Belmundus. Riding *a Cabriolin* in a tempest is not wise."

"Why not? The Yunockers do it."

It was true. It was already raining at the invisible gate. However, a militia is trained to maneuver to evade lightning strikes and perhaps even ratchet between the drops. So Harris banked hard and raced *the Cabriolin* back toward *Mortis House.*

Neck and neck with Elypticus, the Thirdling would fall back when they approached the terrace.

He will allow me to win at all costs.

Harris had another thing in mind. Within fifty yards of the portico, Harris lifted his hand abruptly from the controls. This halted *the Cabriolin* and put it into a violent tub spin, taking Elypticus by surprise as he passed his opponent, landing abruptly on the terrace. Harris replaced his hand on the left and right ports, feathering *the Cabriolin* into a steady hover. Arquebus was a wreck. However, tradition was even more so, because Lord Belmundus navigated his craft to the terrace having lost the race. There Elypticus sprawled prostrate on the marble tiles.

"What?" Harris asked, as Yustichisqua helped him disembark. "You are the victor, Elypticus. Congratulations."

"Forgive me, Lord Belmundus," the Thirdling wept. "I shall be mocked by all who see me from now and forever."

"What?"

Arquebus was furious. He kicked his son, and then turned to Harris, bowing deeply.

"Please forgive my son, Lord Belmundus. He shall be punished before the day is out for his presumption."

He rolled the Thirdling about the ground.

"Please," Harris protested. "He's done nothing wrong."

This didn't deter Arquebus, who lifted Elypticus by the scruff of his cape and dragged him away.

"*Oginali,*" Yustichisqua said, in an even tone. "The Thirdling has insulted you by winning the contest. It is disrespectful."

"But I let him win."

"That does not count. He must let you win."

"At all costs," Harris muttered.

The rain began to fall.

Chapter Two

Learning Lines

1

The rain began to fall and it seemed never to cease — no promise in the endless water's fall. Yustichisqua said it was the rainy season, when clouds blew in from the sea, buffeting the desert's dry heat. Sometimes it rained in the desert and, when it did, *the wadis* would fill with quickened sand, facilitating the Pod to hunt *Tippagores* and *Tyggers,* the beasts the Cetrone called *tludachi.*

Little Bird was gladdened on the weather and its persistence. It made the gardens of *the Ayelli* bloom, not to mention the growing lands beyond the hill, where many Cetrone bent their backs to the work. But it was hard work raising *jomar* and *quillerfoil,* the principle grain for *bupka* bread and s*qwallen,* although s*qwallen* had additives in its recipe — cement and *marijuana* came to Harris' mind, because the stuff was heavy on the tongue. He also had to account for the *high* he experienced after ingesting the stuff. Were the Cetrone permanently high? Yustichisqua appeared alert, although he was eating less and less *sqwallen.*

Lethargy embraced Harris in this so-called rainy season. Although he was kept from practicing with his *Stick* and from taking a spin about the gardens in his *Cabriolin,* it was the dustup with Elypticus that depressed him. Arquebus' treatment of the Thirdling infuriated Harris. He wanted to give him a piece of his mind, but then recalled these were family matters between a father and his son. Perhaps Arquebus feared that *the Eye* had captured the *Cabriolin* race. Did Soffira have a roving Eye also or a *Big Toe*? Harris wasn't sure, but he witnessed Arquebus' transformation from an admonishing mentor to a tyrannical father in a split second.

Harris considered seeking Elypticus and have a heart to heart with him — explaining to the lad that in the outlands pedestrians ran over children and didn't give it a second thought — that teenagers lived in an iPod haze, never considering the world about them. Winning a race was a good thing — something to crow about, not to shiver in the gutter. However, after Harris asked Little

Bird for directions to Elypticus' quarters, Yustichisqua balked.

"If you seek the Thirdling," Little Bird said, "you will further shame him. It overthrows his punishment."

"But he shouldn't be punished," Harris complained. He shrugged — a concession to Little Bird's advice. "I'll send him a gift then."

"He must send *you* a gift, *oginali*."

Sure enough, a gift eventually would arrive with one of Arquebus' Trones.

The whole affair was irksome, leaving Harris depressed. He retreated to the portico, listening to the rain. The drops chilled, cascading in a sheet from the overhang, past the balustrade and into the ravine below *Mortis House*.

Harris sighed, and turned to a review of his assignment, the play *Othellohito*. He had puttered about this for hours, scarcely concentrating on his lines. The rain sound was a narcotic — the sights even more. He couldn't see the distant city and the forbidden gate, but he discerned a haze kissing the valley below — the sky river collecting into a verdant glade about the cobbled gardens. The botanicals spread like a pinwheel from the Temple of Greary Gree. Occasionally, a *Cabriolin* raced by — sometimes singly; sometimes in tandem — Yunockers making their rounds of *the Ayelli*.

Lord Tappiolus was *up* these past two weeks and Harris wondered how he fared. Despite the boredom, Harris preferred being the master of his own time. He studied lines and wondered about the places beyond the boundary — the invisible gate. He would love to bridge it and explore the city, because it was there and — and for other reasons. He suspected his predecessor had discovered a portal or a mirror or a slit trench to escape this captivity. If it weren't so, Montjoy City wouldn't be off-limits. But even if his speculation was dead wrong, exploring the town would be a better occupation than reading this hack reworking of Shakespeare.

Harris broke mid-reverie, letting his eye rove. It settled on Little Bird, who mended his *waddly wazzoo*, a rope lamp, which all Cetrone used to navigate the dark corridors. The device mystified Harris — primitive wicks in a land with bright sconces and unsourced recessed lighting. But Little Bird mended the lamp as if it were sacred, more a symbol than a navigational device. At this moment, Yustichisqua looked up, cocked his head toward the sliding door of the inner court, and then got to his feet. Instinctively, he gathered his *zulus*, which, by Elector decree, he could shed in the privacy of the consort's chamber. He hesitated, and then looked to Harris as if to don them would be an insult.

"You best put them on," Harris said. "You never know who's at the door. It might be big fucking Buhippus himself."

Little Bird grinned, as he had whenever his master regaled him with friendly obscenities. Yustichisqua knew all the bad words. He was raised in *the Kalugu,* after all, *Mortis House's* refinement keeping such language at bay. But refreshingly not with Lord Belmundus. Gossip in *the Scullery Dorgan* had already noted the new consort's renegade attitude. But in time, all suspected Lord Belmundus would settle into the tyrannical ruthlessness enjoyed by all *Ayelli* nobility. The palace slaves didn't seem to resent the protocols, which set a stable atmosphere of expectation. From one generation to the next, they had survived the weight of a generation, which never departed. But this Lord Belmundus — he was a conversation piece where words were whispered behind *the terrapinsgi* soup cauldron.

So Little Bird grinned, and then slipped on his *zulus*.

Bing bong.

The door vibrated innocuously, and slid aside revealing a short Trone, who looked past Yustichisqua to see the master. Upon spotting him, he bowed curtly, crossing the threshold; but just. He carried a large basket covered by a green tea towel. Little Bird lifted the towel, peeking into the basket. He grinned, looking back at Lord Belmundus. Harris shrugged. Little Bird took the basket with two hands.

"Accepted," he snapped.

"Is it?" the Trone asked.

Little Bird looked again to Harris, who slipped from his balustrade perch and approached. Yustichisqua quickly returned his attention to the Trone, nodding and pushing him across the threshold.

Bing bong.

The door slid closed.

"What was that all about?"

Yustichisqua shucked his *zulus*, meeting the master halfway.

"It is the gift, *oginali*."

"Gift?" He glanced at the closed door. "You tossed a fellow Trone out? We should be more hospitable, Little Bird."

"You cannot appear too generous with this gift, *oginali*. It is a healing gift."

"Healing gift?"

"From the Thirdling."

"Elypticus?"

"Your acceptance will heal his shame. If you appear too anxious to return the favor, it would only shame him again. He would need to send you another gift."

"I'll never get used to these doings," Harris said, lifting the tea towel. "What is it? It looks like dead snakes. Maybe I was hasty accepting it."

"No, no, *oginali*. This is *mongerhide* — a delicacy — and very dear. It costs many *yedalas* — more than I have ever seen."

"Do we wear them or eat them?"

"You eat them, *oginali*. I cannot, but you must enjoy it."

Harris snapped the basket from his servant, waving him to follow. He returned to the portico and the rain and the script. He set the basket on a table and slipped off the tea towel. He held one of these strange *mongerhide* sticks to his eye.

"Slim Jims," he muttered, "although they're twisted like bugs in a Chinese market."

He grinned and bit into the end. Crunchy, but when saliva ran, it softened to a spicy morsel — between *pepperoni* and *anduoille*. Tasty juice trickled down his gullet.

"Slim Jims," he concluded. "Eat one."

Little Bird hesitated, glancing back at the wall, looking for *the Eye,* no doubt. Then he snatched one and quickly devoured it before anyone could see him. Harris laughed.

"Good," Little Bird murmured.

Yustichisqua grinned, the ruddy juice trickling down his mouth's crevices. He swallowed, and then snatched another.

"Better than *sqwallen*, eh, Little Bird?"

"Better, *oginali*."

"Fucking-A," Harris said, hugging him. "I don't care how many *yedalas* these Slim Jim taste-alikes cost. It's worth it if it makes you smile."

Harris munched as much *mongerhide* as he could, short of belly busting.

"Perhaps I should press more Thirdlings to shame."

Yustichisqua giggled, snickering down the crunchy delicacy.

"I do not advise it, *oginali,*" he said.

"Ah. You're my adviser now."

Little Bird immediately changed his demeanor to formal subservience, a posture Harris disliked. He was joshing, after all. Again in this culture, all was literal. He stood, raising Little Bird.

"Hear me," he said, wagging his finger. "I'm a prick sometimes, and even when I don't know it."

"No, *oginali.*"

"You have no idea what I'm talking about, do you?"

"No, *oginali.*"

"I'm still learning. I don't intend to cause anxiety or to bring punishments. But until I get my land legs, your advice is precious. Do you understand me now?"

"Yes, *oginali.*" Yustichisqua returned to his haunches. "But after you get these land leggings, shall Little Bird become as he was? I mean no offense and have delighted in feeling the ground under my toes and being able to speak in your presence and to eat wonderful foods — and see things no Trone is permitted to see."

Harris hunkered down, placing his hands on Little Bird's shoulders.

"You shall be as you are, however you are, when you are who you are. There's no going back, and even after I've figured this place out and find . . . and find my way home, you are changed forever . . . forever."

Little Bird nodded.

"It is a fearful thing."

"It is. Your fear will raise you. When you lack fear you become a slave."

"But I do not fear you."

"Fear me, Yustichisqua. I'll never harm you intentionally. But if you throw your lot in with me, you might just fall off a cliff."

Little Bird smiled. He nodded, and then touched Harris' forehead, a zone forbidden to touch.

"I will never fear you, even when you throw me off the cliff. I delight in the moments you have given, like the light of my *waddly wazzoo,* which burns strong now."

Harris stood and waited for Yustichisqua to join him at his side. Then he snatched a *mongerhide* stick, offering it to the lad.

Little Bird grinned, snatched one from the basket and offered it to Lord Belmundus. Thus the knots of trust are tied.

2

Incessant rain — a melody throughout the night; chilled fingers during the day. Lightning struck beyond the valley, never coming to *the Ayelli*, as if a force field shielded it from damage. No such shields protected Montjoy City. Harris saw fires glowing in the distant *Kalugu* and *the Yuyutlu*. Swarms of Yunockers raced on large *Cabriolins*, which Harris assumed were Farn's version of fire trucks. He also noticed the priorities — blazes in *the Yuyutlu* took preference, while *the Kalugu* was left to burn. Cruel Farn logic.

Harris grew listless. He couldn't sit around and munch *yedalas* worth of *mongerhide* all day or sip *yarrow tarrow* tea. He persisted in going over his lines of the worst script he had ever encountered. If this were truly Shakespeare, he would make an honorable effort worthy of his craft. But the script reflected the twisted tastes of the three Sceptas, making for crappy drama. *Othellohito* no longer had pretence to tragedy, since Desdemona (or *Desdemonayama*) magically comes back to life at the end and hooks up with *Cassioshima* in a hammy manner. Still, Brunting Day approached. The rain had forestalled it, but it would come. He would be ready.

He raised the script and read to himself, occasionally glancing up from the page.

> *"I found it in my mikaruni:*
> *And he himself confess'd but even now*
> *That there he dropp'd it for a special purpose*
> *Which wrought to his desire."*

Harris assumed that a *mikaruni* was a bedchamber, if the handkerchief in question was indeed the handkerchief in question. He closed the script, his finger keeping the place.

"I found it in my . . . *macaroni*," he laughed, drawing Little Bird's attention. "That's not right." Yustichisqua shrugged. "It's bad enough I'm contending with *Cetronian* and *Ayellian* and *What-the-fuck-onian*, I've gotta know Japanese too?"

Little Bird approached. He tapped the script, which Harris opened. His servant cocked his head and read the lines to himself.

"It is not Cetrone speech, *oginali*."

"How would you know?" Little Bird smiled. "You can read, you sly devil. I would think if there's an edict on what you can't eat and what you must wear on your tootsies, there'd be one helluva taboo about you reading."

"There is. We are allowed to learn how to read, but it is forbidden to teach us."

"That's nifty-shifty logic," Harris said, turning the script back 'round. He raised an eyebrow. "I've an idea which'll help me learn this shit."

"Help I will do."

Harris thrust the script into Little Bird's hands, pointing to a place on the page.

"Feed me lines."

"Feed you? But we just ate."

"Read the line, and that'll prompt me for *my* line."

Yustichisqua appeared eager, now that he understood the process. He raised the script close to his face.

"Can you see it?"

"Yes. We are partial to far seeing. Near seeing is a challenge."

Harris put that on his mental to-do list.

"Read."

Yustichisqua spoke:

"O the pernicious . . . catwhiff!"

Harris peeked.

"Caitiff. It's an old English word for a coward or a miserable bastard."

"Oh."

"Start again."

"O the pernicious caitiff!
How came you, Cassioshima, by that handkerchief
That was my wife's?"

Harris looked off into the rain and mumbled.

"I found it in my macaroni:
And he himself confess'd but even now
That there he dropp'd it for a special purpose

Which wrought to his desire."

Pause. Long pause.

"Next line."
"Yes, *oginali*." Yustichisqua trembled. "O fool! Fool! fool!"
He nodded. "Please forgive me, *oginali*."
Harris laughed but continued unabated and in full voice.

> *"There is besides in Roderikosan's letter,*
> *How he upbraids Iagomoto, that he made him*
> *Brave me upon the watch; whereon it came*
> *That I was cast: and even but now he spake,*
> *After long seeming dead, Iagomoto hurt him,*
> *Iagomoto set him on.*"

Little Bird's eyes widened, impressed by his master's deep voice. Recitation, not acting — not yet, but the germ brought forth another being and must have surprised Yustichisqua. *How many men lived inside Lord Belmundus?*
"Come, Little Bird. I believe the next line belongs to *Lodovicomori*."
Yustichisqua returned to the script.
"Yes, *oginali*. That is the name for the next say."
He read, slowly, and with temerity:

> *"You must forsake this . . . mikaruni, and go with*
> *   us:*
> *Your power and your command is taken off,*
> *And Cassioshima rules in Honshu. For this slave,*
> *If there be any cunning cruelty . . .*"

"Enough," Harris said. "You've done well."
"Thank you, *oginali*. I do not know what it means."
"Most people don't. Besides, we're just running lines. There's more to acting than that."
"I do not doubt it."
Harris took the script, rolled it, and then slapped it in his open palm.
"Who taught you how to read?"

Silence.

He was sorry he asked. The teacher had broken the law not the student. If *the Eye* should pop in now, it might think Harris held class.

"*She* did," Little Bird said, after hesitation.

"She?"

"Littafulchee."

"Your cousin."

Harris had a mental flash of the elusive Trone who served Charminus silently, but efficiently — a Trone whom other Trones gave wide berth. An attractive Trone — mysteriously alluring. Harris knew he might have stepped over the line with Yustichisqua, but when it came to Charminus', liberties were heresies and dismissal would probably result.

"But if it's a taboo to teach . . ."

Little Bird was circumspect.

"She teaches us when we are in *the Kalugu*. It is dangerous, but if she did not undertake it, our people would lose their heritage."

"Is heritage important to a people who grovel and live at death's edge?"

"We do not fear death, *oginali*. We fear pain — the lingering in dying, which the Yunockers can give effectively. *That* we fear. We, like you, do not live forever. You will live long and will cling to your youth. But your poor Yustichisqua grows old and dies — food for *the porcorporian*."

Harris sat with a thud. He hadn't considered life and death's dynamics in a community where the masters live forever or nearly so, and the population churns like sand in the wind.

"How sad," he said.

"No, *oginali*. We are bound to service. Our lives are hard, but they have been hard always, or so I have been told. To serve in silence is honorable. But we have a voice and it is alive. That is why Littafulchee has taught me to read the letters and to say the words."

"Cetrone."

"The ancestral speech prevails."

Suddenly, Harris had a revelation.

"So, Cetrone is the basic speech of Farn."

"It sits with others at the core."

This was true. The wards of Montjoy City all had Cetrone names — as did the instruments in the orchestra and the flora and the fauna. Even within the tasty name of *mongerhide* lingered a Cetrone root word, but it wasn't a mouthful Harris was prepared to swallow.

"Then," Harris mused, "the Cetrone have been around for a long time."

Little Bird smiled broadly.

"We are the people, *oginali*. *The Ayelli* came from another place. They took our land — the growing fields beyond the hills, and made many changes to the way we live. But as long as they are *the Ayelli*, we are content to serve them."

Harris soon learned *Ayelli* meant . . . *Invader.*

Chapter Three

The Weeping Road

1

Yustichisqua gazed into the rain, and then extended his hand to catch the drops. He grinned, and brought the sky drink to his lips, sipping it from his palm. He gained Harris' full attention.

"This is our land, *oginali*," Little Bird began. "From the hill to the valley to these drops of rain. Ours, but no longer."

"Did *the Ayelli* steal it?"

"Not *the Ayelli*," Yustichisqua replied, sadness in his voice. "They came later. We are the people, but not the only people in Farn. There are many rulers. The spirits of the realm decide for all when they decide at all."

The promise and prophecy, Harris thought.

"Can it be true?" he asked.

"True and final, although some believe there will come a time when we shall dwell in peace and breathe the free air again. We know now, land can be owned and taken. It was not a thing we knew to be true, but we know it drives others. It drove the Yunockers, who watched the Gurts and Zecronisians buy and sell land. Such things are hard to know, but are true, because they happen."

"Land is a possession, Little Bird. It's as true where I come from as it is here. If you don't have a deed, you're screwed."

Little Bird chuckled.

"Pieces of parchment and twigs notched with boundary marks. The Cetrone know that well . . . now. We even thought it to be in our best interest to adopt such ways. When the Yunockers first came into the valley, we called them *brothers*. They spoke a language close to ours. The Great Spirit settled them to our south, in the pastures of *Aweeyodayna*, where they lived in straw huts and ate braised *dayna* meat. They grew no *jomar* or *quillerfoil*. They harbored no *waddly wazzoos* to guide their spirits. When they hungered, the Cetrone took pity. We taught them to plant the seed and till the land. We let them settle on our borders so they could share in our bounty. But we knew not the measure of their greed — a people driven by possession and the ownership of land."

"The Cetrone were Good Samaritans," Harris said.

"If you call it so, *oginali*, then it is so."

Yustichisqua strode to a spot near his *waddly wazzoo*. Sadly, he looked to the lamp as if it were the only thing in his life deemed true. He sighed.

"They came to us for help. They thanked us and gave us gifts, which they said was payment for land. We took these, but regarded them as traditional gifts — unexpected but embraced as any nation would embrace another, especially much like our kin as were these Yunockers. They came into the valley like the tides upon *Plageris*. They built tall houses, which shadowed our simple *yehu*. They invited the Gurts to craft metal and *zulus*, to carve gemstones and shape pottery. They hosted a market with the Zecronisians who excelled at take and bring, making for commerce to other lands. The Zecronisians sold wares — wares made on the soil of the Cetrone ancestors."

"Sounds like an infestation to me," Harris said. "Farn's not unlike my world, where people impose on people at every turn, taking what's not theirs and pushing the natives aside."

"Then you understand, *oginali*. There is no surprise in it. You must see Montjoy as a place much like your own. You shall thrive here."

"No, Little Bird. Farn's like my world in some respects, but is foreign as shit in most everything else. I'll never be comfortable in a land where creatures are enslaved."

"But it is our fault we are so," Yustichisqua said, sitting beside his lamp. "When all the land was taken and the Cetrone had been paid these *gifts* — when they had bought buckets of *sqwallen* and retreated to *the Kalugu*, there was little more we could do. Then came *the Ayelli*. Their lands were beyond the mountains, but the great master took a shine to our valley. He bought the hill, and then claimed it in the name of the Great Spirit."

"There's always some god or other to make things right," Harris said. He hunkered down beside Little Bird. "But how is this the Cetrone's fault?"

"That is something lost in time, *oginali*. The Yunockers did not accept the Elector's rule. Oh, no. They arose to evict him from his hill. They attacked the palace and threatened to destroy his treasure houses. But the Elector's power is great. He needs no armies. With a wave of his great *Stick*, he paralyzed the Yunocker forces. After

the Yunockers were defeated, *the Ayelli* demanded *yedalas* —
many *yedalas*. And great stores of *jomar* and *quillerfoil*. The
Yunocker Grand Council sued for peace — a thing on the Elector's
mind also."

"But how did that affect the Cetrone?"

"We are a divided people, *oginali*. We have always been given
to factions. The villagers who owned land and had slaves wanted
to sign an obligation to the Grand Council for rewards. Others, the
people of *the Kalugu*, secretly sent a delegation to the Elector,
agreeing to serve the House of Montjoy in exchange for *the
Kalugu*. This shook the Yunocker hold over the eastern ward.
However, before the Cetrone could act with one voice, a treaty
between *the Ayelli* and the Yunockers was made. The Yunockers
could live in peace if they supplied the Elector with a police force.
The Elector also demanded the Cetrone serve his family upon the
hill. It has been so ever since."

"Sad."

"Sadder," Little Bird said, lifting his *waddly wazzoo*, allowing
it to dangle from its chain. "The Cetrone refused to comply,
rebelling against both Yunockers and *Ayelli*. There was much
bloodshed. We are a peaceful folk with few weapons, and had no
access to *Aniniya nayu* — the Power Stones, which the Yunockers
had in abundance from the trade with the Zecronisians."

"So, you were defeated."

"And downtrodden," Little Bird said, a tear glistening in his
eye. "It is a thing of the past — so long ago I only know it through
the Yodanado — the Whisperers. Then the Yunockers captured us,
putting us in cages — in long rows to hang upon the desert wall.
Many examples were made. Many Cetrone dried in the demon
suns. Others were imprisoned and tortured. But the lord Elector is
not a cruel man. He intervened. He commanded the Yunockers to
set free the Cetrone. And so it was decided we would be moved."

"Resettled?"

"Yes. Some remained in *the Kalugu*, because the House of
Montjoy needed servants. All others were to be set aside and
driven east to *the Dodaloo* — the Spice Mountains, many *yiyutli*
across the Forling desert."

"The Cetrone were marched across the desert?"

"Yes. No *zulus* to shield us from *the kowlinka* — the red sand.
The Yunockers prodded us onward. Many Cetrone fell from

exhaustion and torment. Great was the weeping. By our tears the trail was moistened. Those who survived the journey settled in *the Dodaloo* and are there still. It is called Cetronia. In days past, a ferry crossed the Forling to keep contact there, but such crossings are few now."

"But if Cetronia is across the desert, why are your people still in Montjoy — in *the Kalugu*?"

"We are not immortal, *oginali*. We live and die and breed and grow and multiply like all things except royal Farnians, who keep the spirit fires and are rewarded with long life and health everlasting. We are . . . stuck. We serve to manage it. It is our fault, after all. We were good hosts to the Yunockers and unable to come together to serve our interests over the invaders'. Our contracts hold us with few advantages. The Yunockers enforce our lives — which we give often. The past seems a bitter place, choosing being more painful than compliance."

Yustichisqua brought his *waddly wazzoo* closer, kindling it with a friction stone near the wick. It burst into flame, the light dim different from other light in Farn.

"And that, *oginali* is why places here are called by Cetrone names and not in *the Ayelli* language."

He closed his eyes and began to sway gently, singing a haunting song:

> *"Dsulasi dona owaynasa,*
> *Ulushoo ita ha yeeyasa,*
> *Awaydeesga akali*
> *Ustigunana digaswosdi."*

"How sad, Yustichisqua," Harris said. "What does it mean?" Little Bird opened his eyes.

> *"My feet go far from home,*
> *I fall because I roam,*
> *I tote my people's load,*
> *Along the weeping road."*

"The weeping road," Harris echoed, and knew he too was *Ayelli.*

2

Little Bird dowsed his lamp.

"I must get you something to eat, *oginali*. Perhaps, *chumwhat* porridge and the cheese of the *diluwopeen bear*."

"Sounds delectable," Harris said absently. "But I can wait. I want to hear more about the Cetrone."

"What more is there to tell? We are as we are and will remain so. There is peace when order is kept. Everyone knows their place. Steady grows the heart."

"Bullshit," Harris snapped. "Do you mean to tell me that none among you stir against these cruel overlords or your enemy?"

"It is true the Yunockers are our enemy. But in defeat there is no shame when the honor of the victors is revered."

"Bullshit, again and again, I say, bullshit."

"You may say it, *oginali*, and I may hear it, but here it stays like the rain upon the railing or the wick of my *waddly wazzoo*."

Harris didn't buy it. Cetrone history sat heavy on his conscience, as if he had caused the encroachment or ordered the resettlement. A fair-minded man, he had always been generous to his co-stars, never rivaling anyone for marquee space or top billing, despite the box office cut tied to it. His agent, a wily fox who must have had a *waddly wazzoo* of his own, because Harris had more than his share of top billing, handled those details. Still, this wasn't theater. This was a strange world — not his world. Yet, sitting in the storm and listening to Yustichisqua's tale, Harris' anger inflamed and with it — guilt. There must be a way to leverage his advantages as Lord Belmundus the Fair and the Just and the Big Muckyfuck to right these wrongs. Yet how? Centuries old wrongs, these . . . millennia perhaps — an eternity of darkness imprinted upon a people who had lost their will to fight. Grumble they might do behind *the chumwhat* porridge pots in *the Scullery Dorgan*, but nary a word against their overlords was spoken in public. Then, something occurred to him.

"Hey, wait a minute, Little Bird."

"You are hungry now, yes, *oginali*. I shall get you *the diluwopeen* cheese straight away."

"No. I just thought of something. You can walk through walls."

"Yes, I can."

"Then how the fuck can the Yunockers confine you in *the Kalugu?* You can just use that advantage to frustrate the crap out of their plans."

Yustichisqua grinned.

"I see what you are thinking, *oginali*. But the wall walking is the property of *kaybar nayu*, and not of all rocks and stones. It is not entirely within us, but in *the kaybar*. Just *kaybar*."

"*Kaybar?* I don't understand."

"I do not either. How it works is beyond me. But it is so, nonetheless. The Cetrone cannot feel *kaybar nayu*. We cannot even lift it. We can use building hoists to craft houses and walls made from it, as others can do. *The Ayelli* use it as a convenience so we may pass through it and serve them better, much like wearing *the zulus*. But wall walking has to do with our body's composition. It is like the Gurts' long tongue, which they can use to scratch their ears and catch lice crawling on their backs. The Zecronisians have a third leg growing like a tail from their backsides, which they extend and have a seat. And the Yunockers have a powerful sense of smell. They can sniff out a Cetrone at many *yiyutli* distance. However, none can pass through *the kaybar* as we can. But we cannot pass through other stone. So the walls around *the Kalugu* are made of *phitron nayu* and other materials like wood from the iron trees of the hillside or *glassifon* crafted in Gurt kilns and *ryyves*. They make strong *glassifon* there and we cannot penetrate it. Only *the kaybar*."

Suddenly, Yustichisqua jumped about as if dislodging a cricket from his loincloth.

"What is it?" Harris asked.

"Nothing," Little Bird replied. "I just wanted to show you that the tiles here are made of *phitron*. If they were made of *kaybar*, I would not be able to walk on them. In fact, in *the Kalugu*, the Yunockers have constructed traps for us — *kaybar* floors disguised to look like *phitron*. But when we step across them, we fall through into whatever they have waiting for us at the bottom. It forces us to wear our *zulus*."

"Crafty sons-of-bitches, aren't they?"

"If that is like *usona geetli,* I agree. But they are the victors."

"Bullshit, I say again." Then Harris winced. "But . . . but when you went through the wall, you didn't go naked. You had your duds on and your *zulus*. You can't tell me that you sprinkled them with fairy dust to make the trip."

Yustichisqua laughed.

"No, no. Whatever I wear will come too. We can extend this trait to whatever touches our body. Some things will get stuck. Remember, I also carried a tray of food back to you."

"Yes. That made it through."

"There was a plate of *fregallen* leaves which did not. The plate was empty, except for the sauce. I had forgotten *fregallen* leaves will not go through. They sometimes will not even pass through the body."

"And you were going to feed me those and wait until . . . but, wait. Does this mean, if I hold your hand when you pass through *the kaybar*, I can go through too?"

"I do not know, *oginali*. And I do not wish to try, because it could harm you."

"Oh, why not? Let's experiment."

Little Bird appeared terrified, and went to his knees suddenly. *The Eye* appeared in all its twitchy glory. Harris raised both hands.

"Now what, my dear mistress and ruler of my heart?"

He bowed to it, but of course, it was an eye and not a mouth, so it didn't say anything. It just stared at Yustichisqua as if it knew much had been said and the next act was beyond tolerance's pale.

Harris turned to his servant.

"Gather your lamp, Little Bird and let's take a walk in the rain."

"But master."

"No. We'll get ourselves soaked to the gills and perhaps catch something foul." He turned to *the Eye*. "And when my time comes *up*, perhaps I'll spend it sniffing and coughing and in need of Mordacai the Zecronisian. But if the great Scepta and my esteemed co-consort have a need to pry into my boring existence, I would prefer to slide in the slicks of mud in the temple garden. Perhaps the spirit of Greary Gree will be sympathetic to a persecuted actor who ducks both fans and audiences and . . ."

The Eye faded, and then disappeared. Harris giggled.

"I must remember that it hates diarrhea of the mouth. I rather it escapes me than I it, eh Little Bird?"

"I am glad we do not need to walk in the rain."

"Afraid to get wet?"

"No. I would need to keep you dry and that is a big effort. You are slightly taller than me and I must stretch to hold the wide *shlombrera* over your head. And I would need to repair your clothing and unmat your hair."

"I could have gone naked and worn a hat," Harris replied, laughing.

"You are a puzzle to me sometimes, *oginali*. Just like Hierarchus."

Harris suddenly rushed Little Bird, hunkering down in fury.

"Hierarchus? Did you say Hierarchus? Who is this Hierarchus?" Yustichisqua trembled and did not answer. "He was my predecessor, wasn't he?" No answer still. "Wasn't he?"

"Yes, *oginali*."

Harris pushed Little Bird over and began to maul him. Yustichisqua rolled into a ball. Harris was genuinely angry. Little Bird had claimed no knowledge of the predecessor. Now he mentioned his name.

"Please, master. Do not hurt your Little Bird."

Harris heard this, and stopped. But his anger wasn't assuaged. He jumped to his feet and swept out onto the portico, slamming both hands on the balustrade.

"*Oginali, oginali*," came the plea. "I did not know him. I swear to you. I did not lie when I said I did not know him."

"But you did know about him, Yustichisqua. Do all Trones manipulate their masters like you do?"

"How can they, *oginali*? Trones are not permitted to speak to their masters. They cannot. I cannot. But . . . but, I do."

And at great risk. Yes, Harris considered this. His rage subsided. He was rarely angry — in fact, he couldn't remember the last time he flew off the handle. Not even on *Plageris* by the Bottleblue Sea had he been as angry. Frustrated. Anxious. Snappy and caustic, even — but rage? No. It was the violation of trust that sparked him, and now he realized he may have jumped the gun. He eased off. He turned to Yustichisqua, who was on his knees like a slave before the foreman, begging to be spared the lash. This would not do. Harris went to him and lifted him up.

"Calm yourself, Little Bird. I'm sorry. I didn't mean to be so cruel."

Yustichisqua wept, and then Harris took him into his arms, like a lost child who sought parental caress.

"I was so afraid, *oginali*."

Afraid. Here was a being not afraid to live in the ghetto or shake off his zulus and risk expulsion, and yet he was afraid of the one person he should never fear. Perhaps it was the loss of . . . of what? Friendship? Protection? Love? Harris mentally promised he would never subject Little Bird to this again. Never.

"I wanted to tell you, *oginali* . . . to tell you his name and that he was troublesome to *the Ayelli* and turned away from Montjoy City. But you appeared to know as much. His Trone was also my cousin, and he was sent to a secret place in *the Kalugu* and never seen again."

"Then, if he was your cousin, then he was . . ."

"Yes. Littafulchee knows more than I do, but she is forbidden to say. She has never told me what Hierarchus was about, except he was different and rebellious. He did not amuse the Scepta Charminus. He was in trouble with Lord Tappiolus and . . . "

"Buhippus."

"Worse than that. Buhippus' brother, Tarhippus."

Belmundus sighed. He would ask no more. Thoughts of *kaybar* experimentation were set aside also. He wouldn't subject Little Bird to more. However, he would have liked to ask some questions to the lovely cousin. But how?

Harris walked Yustichisqua to the portico's edge. The rain was subsiding. Perhaps a slosh in the gardens was possible after all, but why bother if it couldn't piss off Charminus or Tappiolus. Instead, Harris cupped his hands and captured some rainwater dripping from the overhang. He brought it to his lips, tasting it. He then offered it to Little Bird, who came to this small pond and drank.

Chapter Four

Rehearsing Othellohito

1

The cascades ceased and the suns shone magnificently, drying hillside and valley. Harris could have anticipated easy days exploring the gardens, but it was his turn to be *up*. He planned to run the gauntlet nearest his quarters, Yustichisqua selecting the best trails and paths. However, Lord Tappiolus told Harris that the Scepta may have *kindled* — the term for the miraculously short gestation period these ladies underwent before popping out a Thirdling. Since there might be a question of paternity, Charminus decided to abstain from Lord Belmundus' charms until the matter was settled.

"I am positive it is mine, Boots," Tappiolus announced. "You have not ripened enough to know Charminus' cycles. I have fathered twelve Thirdlings in the last twenty-five years." Evidently, *kindling* wasn't an everyday occurrence. "You will improve with practice. Still, we must rule out beginner's luck."

Harris was content. He wasn't ready for fatherhood yet, especially the kind that sprouted from diapers to *Cabriolin* races in less than three years. That Tappiolus had insulted his colleague's manhood didn't bother Harris. Man, woman or lamppost — they were all the same to him when not under the influence of an evil fairy with a mysterious jade ring. Now he could explore *the Ayelli* at his ease.

After these tidings, another announcement came, cramping Harris' plans. The Elector was leaving on a diplomatic mission to Protractus, and then on to Volcanium. This meant Kuriakis' schedule would shift to accommodate his various pleasures, which included a review of new art acquisitions, a hunting expedition and, of course, Brunting Day.

With the festivities accelerated, rehearsals for *Othellohito* came to the fore. Arquebus told Harris to be performance ready for a rehearsal at the Amphitheater — this, at a moment's notice.

"They have given me your playing costume, *oginali*," Little Bird said. "But it is only to be worn for the performance and shall be set aside until Brunting Day."

"How do they know it fits?"

"They know it."

Harris remembered the first day, when Mordacai the Zecronisian ran his *tricorder-thingy* over him and pricked his finger for a blood sample. They knew his every measure from that reading, enough to send off to Madame Tussaud's for a waxwork double. So, Harris grabbed his script, gave it a once-over, and then departed for the rehearsal.

The gardens shimmered, especially after the rain. The buttery paving stones glistened under the suns. Fragrance assaulted Harris — gardenia, jasmine, rose and a sharp cinnamon aroma, although he would be hard pressed to identify the source bloom — a large floppy blossom, like a hibiscus or a moonflower. Roses he did see, these queens of the garden a universal truth.

Every twenty paces along the pathways stood sculptures — alabaster at base, but dabbed with brilliant colors. Nothing subtle. Nothing muted. No lambent shade. Purple and crimson predominated thin togas on tall nude women and even taller naked men, nary a fig leaf in sight.

The garden radiated from a central point and the paths crisscrossed forming small triangular patches sporting marigold bursts and dahlia parasols, triumphantly looming over waves of violets and periwinkles. Among these triangles stood benches, and on these benches sat Thirdlings — some playing card games; others plucking harp-like instruments; still others puffing flutes. Some danced a jerky bolero.

Harris was amused at Thirdling fashions — stiff apparel, asymmetric. Their hair was dyed to match lips and eyes. While they awaited diplomatic alliances with the Thirdlings from other realms, these brothers and sisters had time on their hands, although, Harris recalled Elypticus saying something about police work. Perhaps these Thirdlings were the youngest set — only two years old, and still on the path to useful work.

Central to these botanical pinwheels stood a gentle Rotunda — the Temple of Greary Gree. Harris hadn't asked after the spirit who dwelled within, if in residence. He was on information overload and hearing theology from Arquebus would mean he actually cared — and he didn't give a shit about religion in the outlands, so to take up its cause on *the Ayelli* hill would be self-defeating. Greary Gree may have been a sacred shrine or not, but periodically

Kuriakis and Joella came here for *Brunting*, which Harris considered a misspelled word. Sex between immortals by any other name . . . well, he didn't need an image.

The temple was a sight to see, the dome in the fashion of the Jefferson Memorial, only scarlet topped by a golden statue — probably of Greary Gree. The columns flared at their base and were decorated with mythical beasts. Upon closer inspection, Harris doubted this was mythology, because *a misancorpus* graced one column and a *terrerbyrd*, another. He didn't want to encounter either again — nor the bevy of other ominous beasts.

In the shadow of Greary Gree, a reflecting pool pitched circular and, beyond it, the Amphitheatre — a classical sugar bowl with perfect acoustics, he hoped — the kind demonstrated on *History Channel* specials, where a whisper could be heard in distant Volcanium.

"Some setup they have here, Little Bird," he mused, standing poolside, glancing down into the Amphitheatre.

"I do not understand, *oginali.*"

"*Ayelli* is a virtual Versailles." He turned to Yustichisqua, who shrugged. "That's a pleasure palace in the outlands built by a fancy dude who thought he was the Sun King." He looked to the two shining orbs above. "Here he'd do double duty. Versailles was an expression of wealth and power, built on the backs of the poor and the downtrodden."

"I see," Little Bird said. "A setup."

This was not the time or place for a discussion with someone who knew his own people's social history and approved the *status quo*. Besides, *the Eye* could pop from the reflecting pool and blink — Yunockers to follow.

Harris gazed down the long aisle, which sloped to the stage. There his fellow consorts were already rehearsing. A row of *Cabriolins* were parked along the proscenium. Still, Harris was happy to be on foot today, breathing the floral scents. Arquebus, spotting him, waved him on. Then Tappiolus marched up the aisle.

"Stay here, Little Bird," Harris said, noticing the other Trones gathered in an array of buckskin heaps in the upper rows.

Yustichisqua nodded, and then drifted to his place. Harris met Tappiolus halfway.

"Greetings, brother," Harris said, his hand and moxie extended. "I haven't missed the festivities, have I?"

"You have been long about it, Boots," Tappiolus snapped. "Our bit comes first. You have caused us a delay."

"My part's small compared to the lions of Cyprus, or should I say Edo."

"There was discipline when I plied my craft."

"But I'm a diva, don't you know."

"I do not doubt it," Tappiolus said, trudging back to the stage.

"Don't go away mad," Harris said, muttering beneath his breath the usual rejoinder — just *go away.*

2

The other consorts were congenial, as always. Hasamun preened in his feminine role as *Desdemonayama*, while Posan feigned coyness as the enraged wife, *Emiliasan*. However, Arquebus shone, having the best lines as the star — *Othellohito*. He also had a hand on the rewrite, juxtaposing the Bard's juiciest bits appropriately to catch the audience's vulnerability. And who would be this audience? Harris asked Agrimentikos. He spouted a long list of Thirdlings and related family lines generated by Farn political marriages. While some Thirdlings lived at their in-laws' courts — in Aolium, Volcanium and Protractus (the most fertile grounds for these mule alliances), others lived in Montjoy City. Also in the audience would be a cross-section of prominent Yunocker citizenry, a few distinguished and talented Gurts and the cream of the Zecronisian aristocracy. A demanding crowd invited by *the Brunting* couple and their fair daughters.

Harris did his bit — the little handkerchief scene with Tappiolus playing *Iagomoto*. Tappiolus was a hack, delivering his lines perfunctorily, which didn't inspire Harris to do much better. He was more inspired when running lines with Yustichisqua. The play would get off to a cold start, sending Kuriakis off to sleep, no doubt. Perhaps when the scenery was in place and costumes donned, things would pep up.

When Arquebus began his opening soliloquy, Harris was reassured. The man had an undeniable stage presence, unfettered from takes and retakes. One shot and a different one each performance was the hallmark. Harris imagined how Sir John Briarcliff must have dazzled an audience back in Whitechurch.

Hasamun slept on a bamboo mat, while Sir John approached as the doleful prince. He clapped, looking directly at Harris when delivering his lines:

> *"It is the cause, it is the cause, my soul —*
> *Let me not name it to you, you chaste stars —*
> *It is the cause. Yet I'll not shed her blood;*
> *Nor scar that whiter skin of hers than snow,*
> *And smooth as monumental alabaster.*
> *Yet she must die, else she'll betray more men."*

He then raised his hand over the sleeping *Desdemonayama*, and then closed his eyes as if to pray. But he did not pray. He bellowed:

> *"Put out the wazzoo, and then put out the wazzoo:*
> *If I quench thee, thou flaming minister,*
> *I can again thy former waddly wazzoo restore,*
> *Should I repent me: but once put out thy wazzoo,*
> *Thou cunning'st pattern of excelling nature,*
> *I know not where is that Volcanium heat*
> *That can thy kindle relume. When I have pluck'd the*
> *   Scaladar,*
> *I cannot give it vital growth again.*
> *It must needs wither: I'll smell it on the tree."*

Arquebus wept. Harris went to applaud, but halted, knowing this was unprofessional. Certainly some acclaim must be accorded to this master Thespian. Harris gazed toward the Trones, who slept, except . . . except Yustichisqua, whose wide eyes were fastened upon the stage, his mouth agape. Harris was pleased. He was less pleased by Agrimentikos, who interrupted the flow by reminding everyone this was a rehearsal and nothing but perfection was expected. Therefore, since Arquebus had been standing too close to the sleeping Hasamun, he was requested to repeat the soliloquy no less than three times, each with a different pose and a little less vehemence on *the waddly wazzoos.* Hasamun followed with a rejoinder — waking and questioning the lord. It was a queer interaction of styles, because, although the words were Elizabethan, the acting was Victorian slammed forcefully into *Noh* tradition — Hasamun exaggerating his words into sonorous lines — *Alaaaas my loooord!* and *be meeercifuuul.* Then he bobbed his head, contorting his arms. Harris didn't think it worked, but recalled, at the piece's conclusion, he would have a scene with Hasamun — a scene practiced with Yustichisqua, who just rattled the words off like a reading from a dictionary. Now they'd be singsong soupy with twitchy-kawitchy body language as a compensation for resonance. How would that fly with the Zecronisian aristocracy?

Harris didn't fret, because Agrimentikos interrupted so often with reruns, the chances of getting to the second entrance was slim to none. Then, as Harris gazed back again at Yustichisqua, his attention caught a new scene — a buckskin robe floating along the back row and out into the garden. Littafulchee.

Harris stood.

"You are not up yet," Agrimentikos said, not unkindly.

"I need a stretch," Harris explained. He pointed up and away. "I'll be taking my ease in the garden."

"Don't go far . . . and not forever."

"Just whistle and I'll be back in a flash."

Agrimentikos shrugged, as if he'd whistle, and then clapped to bring Posan on as *Emiliasan.* Harris chuckled, and then crept up the stairs, drifting toward the garden trellises. He saw Yustichisqua stir. Harris shook his head, patting the air. Little Bird took the meaning, returning to his seat.

Harris reached the top row, and then sighed. One thing was true. A whisper from the stage could be heard loud and clear up here — *the History Channel* vindicated.

3

Harris entered the arbor — a lambent spot, where cascades of a flowering vine spun golden, blooms reminiscent of wild snapdragons. Clumps of purple berries and pink leaves were interspersed. Rose bushes climbed trellises, a crimson riot mingled with tan buds and ivory blooms. These were the Roses of *Scaladar* Harris had heard in speeches and verbally embedded in the Bard's rewrite. On the path, back turned, floated Littafulchee, a conical basket swinging from her shoulder to capture floral cuttings. Charminus' boudoir was flooded with these floral tributes extraordinary. Littafulchee was the fair harvester.

Harris approached quietly taking care not to disturb any pebble under foot. He wouldn't startle this Cetrone maid. He feared she'd turn and flee. Turn she did, but flee she did not. She cocked her head, her crystal ornament dancing on her forehead. She nodded in greeting, and yet it could have been a departing gesture. Harris raised his right hand, placing it on his *Columbincus*. He bowed.

"No," she snapped. "No such honor must be paid, master."

"Please don't regard me as your master," he said, drawing closer.

Littafulchee glided backward a short distance, sighing. She returned to her work, a small shearing device emerging from her robe sleeve, liberating blossoms from their thorny home and gently arranging them in the basket.

"Please, do me the courtesy of listening," Harris said.

She hesitated as she cut, and then clipped the largest bloom from the trellis, leaving a two-foot stem. She slipped it into her cornucopia, never letting the blossom escape her gaze.

"You must know I'm unhappy here," Harris whispered.

She looked up and parted her lips as if to speak, but then closed them.

"I have much to learn," Harris continued, "and contentment is not in the stars. But I believe that the man who proceeded me as consort — the one named Hierarchus, found his freedom and, even if it means death, I would embrace it rather than be kept as the Scepta's plaything."

"You must not," she whispered, scarcely moving her lips. "You take liberties, master. I know. I see. It is dangerous."

"I don't mean to compromise you, Littafulchee, but I must know what you know about Hierarchus."

At his pronouncement of her name, she dropped the shears and spun about. Harris thought she would flee, but she came nearer.

"You must not say my name, master." He nodded brusquely. "I know how you know it and why you have come to me to ask about Lord Hierarchus. Yustichisqua should not be so free with words."

"As free as you are now?"

Anger rippled across her face. Harris was glad for it. Heat was better than ice. He grinned, but she retreated a few feet before retrieving her shears. He thought she might use them to drive him off. He came close, gripping her shoulders gently.

"Lord Belmundus," she snapped. "I am not your Trone. I serve the Scepta Charminus."

"But the Cetrone regard you with honor."

"They do not," she protested.

"They do. I see it in their actions when you approach. Now, I don't doubt they're within their rights to defer to your tenure, but denying that they do is misplaced and, frankly, it doesn't become you."

Littafulchee trembled. Her eyes met his, batting furiously as if dust had contaminated them. However, Harris didn't press further. He had said his say and she was not willing to tell him more. But she had spoken, and that was something. Since she was Charminus' Trone, he would see her again. He would seek clandestine opportunities to press her for further information about Hierarchus. She hadn't denied her knowledge, only objecting to Yustichisqua's loose lips.

Harris stepped back, clamped his hand again to his *Columbincus,* and bowed.

"I promise you," he said. "I'll not honor you in public or before *the Eye*. But I see you now. Don't forget it, because I'm in your hands, lady."

"*Oginali*," came a guttural whisper from behind him. "They are waiting for you to do the play acting."

"I'm coming, Little Bird."

Littafulchee glared at her cousin. Perhaps she'd chastise him. But, she just grunted and turned away, attending the Roses of *Scaladar*.

Harris faced Yustichisqua, who appeared frightened by this Trone — not the fear of punishment, but from a breach of trust. Little Bird had kicked off his *zulus* and walked with bare feet on the cobblestones. *Gutsy*. Evidently no one had noticed, otherwise Buhippus and the Yunocker guard would have invaded in a flash.

"Little Bird," Harris said. "You should wear your *zulus* here."

"I know, *oginali*. I kicked them off and forgot to slip them on."

"Let's not push it."

"At once, *oginali*."

Then came a voice from behind them — a sweet voice lost within the Roses of *Scaladar*. It said:

"If you leave us, Lord Belmundus, it would not please me."

Harris turned about fearful *the Eye* had shown up and Charminus was butting in on the conversation, but *the Eye* had no mouth. Littafulchee had spoken these words — words spoken to the blossoms. Harris was happy to hear them and thought to reply, but caught these words on the wind instead, filing them away for another day.

Chapter Five

Mustering the Pod

1

Harris never had the opportunity to rehearse his last scene with Hasamun, because, as he began his first line, Buhippus appeared with a Yunocker brigade. The Trones scattered to their master's *Cabriolins*. Yustichisqua huddled behind the first row, peering at Harris for protection. Harris hopped off the stage, preparing to confront the palace captain, but Tappiolus blocked his way.

"Boots," he snapped. "What business of yours is this?" Tappiolus turned to the chief, hands raised and head cocked. "We rehearse for the Brunting Day, good Buhippus. There is no reason to interrupt us."

Buhippus nodded, and then disembarked from his *Cabriolin*. He turned to Agrimentikos.

"Lord Agrimentikos, father of all consorts, pardon the intrusion, but we come as Great Kuriakis' vanguard."

"Truly?" Agrimentikos asked. He then walked past Buhippus, his eyes keen on the reflecting pool. "Where is our lord and father?"

Then, as if arising from the waters, *Nightmare* loomed on the amphitheatre's rim, his master in saddle. Three Trones and seven Thirdlings came forward, waving Montjoy banners — a black flag with a white Rose of *Scaladar* embroidered full square and center. The flags fluttered in the great gust caused by *Nightmare's* glide over the stairs, powerful hooves finding purchase beside Buhippus. The captain went to one knee. The consorts bowed deeply. The Trones were prostrate.

The Elector, in a merry mood, or so Harris thought given the broad smile brimming from beneath the martial visor, dismounted. Kuriakis removed his helmet, passing it to his chief Trone. The Elector went briskly to Agrimentikos, grasping the senior consort by the shoulder, bobbing in greeting.

"My lord and father," Agrimentikos said, "demote me if you must, but these proceedings are sacred. You may not spy upon us until *Brunting Day*."

Kuriakis laughed, and then hopped to the stage.

"Spy?" he laughed. "I have not seen a thing nor heard a line. So you are safe, Agrimentikos. The spirit of Greary Gree will not crush you between her pouting lips." He raised his arms. "However, it would please me if Joella not be told I came upon you in such a manner and at such a time." Agrimentikos struck his *Columbincus* humbly, and bowed. "Good. But I could not contain myself and am anxious to say to you all — my sons that I am in the hunting way — the mood striking me like Aolium thunder. How say you? Are you with me?"

The consorts animated, rushing the stage. Harris was swept up in the moment. A hunt would suit him. Tappiolus contravened.

"I believe Lord Belmundus may still be too gentle with his *Stick*," Tappiolus remarked. "Unless he can find his other boot to hit the mark."

The consorts laughed, not unkindly.

"At least I hit something, dear brother-in-law," Harris replied to Tappiolus, never frowning, but not bowing. Then he said to Kuriakis: "Father, will we be hunting *terrerbyrd* again?"

"No, Boots. There is no time to funnel us to Plageris. No. We to the Forling shall head."

The consorts cheered.

"The desert?" Harris asked.

"Yes, Boots," Kuriakis said. "There are creatures in the Forling more cunning and much tastier than the briskets that fly in Plageris' air." He laughed. "We shall be hunting *Tippagore*." He beamed. "And perhaps a *noya tludachi* or three."

"I think mayhap that Lord Belmundus should start with *grumperian* rat," Tappiolus said. "Although they are quick and might defeat his range."

Harris grinned, coming directly before Tappiolus, his nose near enough to smell the man's breakfast.

"I think I'm able to strike *your* ass at whatever range you manage and however fast you scurry."

Peals of laughter now — except from Trones and Yunockers, and decidedly not Tappiolus. The loudest bellow came from Kuriakis, so raucous that *Nightmare* joined with a dragonet whinny.

"Boots," Kuriakis said. "I know you met the Pod at Plageris and rode in *a Cabriolin* then. You have experienced the hunt's spirit. But as fledgling, you must follow protocol. Agrimentikos will guide you on the preparations for a muster and your Trone, who I know hears me, must assure your readiness . . . although I bet he is a fledgling too. But no matter." The Elector suddenly seemed in thought. "But no matter," he muttered again, and waved his hand. "At dawn, brave sirs and sons. By nightfall tomorrow we shall have a *Tippagore* feast."

Kuriakis jumped from the stage, grabbed his helmet from his Trone and leaped on Nightmare's back. He tugged the reins, the beast turning — flying toward the heavens. The Trones and Thirdlings receded like a carpet furled. Buhippus led his troops, departing in strict formation. Harris gazed to Agrimentikos, who grinned, and then to Tappiolus, who scowled. But it was Yustichisqua who emerged to tug him away and back up the garden path.

2

There were two orders of business before the dawn. Yustichisqua needed to assemble the hunting wardrobe and Harris wanted more information on the creatures of the Forling, particularly *the Tippagore*. Little Bird couldn't provide much information on the beast, because he had never seen one, let alone hunted one. He had never tasted its flesh or even heard stories told by *the Yodanado* in the *Kalugu* about the Forling, except that there was once a ferry to Cetronia, the homeland in the Spice Mountains. Harris had no choice but to shuttle over to the *Cartisforium* and use his *Columbincus* as a key for the first time.

The place was as he remembered it — as stuffy as a library and as quiet as a church. But why should it be otherwise? The wall map was gone, but the stained glass windows remained, as did the octagonal table, which held the bejeweled tome — *the Book of Farn*. Harris went alone, allowing Yustichisqua to assemble the hunting *accoutrement*. He wondered whether he could find *the Cartisforium* again, but his sense of direction didn't fail. Once inside the place, he shuffled about the table's edge until he stood where Arquebus had lectured. Was there a chant or recitation of *the Promise and Prophecy* needed to evoke information from the sacred book? He hoped not, because he hadn't committed the verses to memory, barely gripping its significance. So he shrugged, snapped off his *Columbincus* and stretched his hand over the book. One firm pat wedged his snazzy sapphire blue sigil into the cover.

"I hope there's an index, or at least a Table of Contents."

Harris had recently acquired an eReader, one of those new-fangled Kindle devices, which he found easy to navigate. But how does one wade through a book without an index. Perhaps he should just ask it a question like the Delphic Oracle. He cleared his throat.

"What is a *Tippagore?*" he declared, as if asking directions for the bus to LAX.

The book cover opened with a jar, the pages fanning like a cascading card trick. Harris jumped, hoping nothing would leap out and bite him. However, once this initial action slowed, a cloud emerged — a puffy, shapeless white cloud, which didn't remain shapeless for long. It soon changed colors — pink and gray, legs emerging, and then a head and a tail. It looked like a cow formed from cheese. Then the object floated toward him, coming to rest on the table. That's when it grew.

The beast turned solid — a long creature, tall at the withers, with eight massive pachyderm legs and a bull's head. Like a bull, it had short horns, but also a set of antlers like a water buffalo, and, like a boar, sported three menacing tusks. That was the front end. The back end was like shaggy carpet left on a line to dry. For a desert denizen, it came complete with enough territory to supply ten yurts and perhaps, like a camel, held vast reservoirs beneath its tapestry.

Massive. *The Tippagore*, at least thirty feet long and nine feet high, appeared more like a caterpillar in aerial perspective. Compaction would maintain a cool climate beneath its rug, Harris supposed. Now he knew why Kuriakis sought to hunt this beast. It probably moved like a tortoise and mooed like a cow. Unless the Pod came within range of its head, they could make short work of this dinner piece, assaulting those colossal tent poles — its legs.

Suddenly, *the Tippagore* stirred. It snorted, and then raised itself up on its haunches, scaling a height challenging to anyone flying overhead. Harris stepped away thinking the Book would demonstrate *the Tippagore's* full arsenal. However, more clouds appeared from within the pages. Several other animals emerged — ones not summoned, nor would they be unless Harris ordered a nightmare. A pack of wolf-like creatures, with as many heads as Cerberus, barked, although they sported forked tongues more serpentine than vulpine. A large specie of scorpion fell from the clouds, massive mandibles clicking like a Havana whore on the dance floor. Then there were rabbit thingies, with long fangs and three ears; and fire-spitting cats, which, from their size and camouflage, Harris assumed were *Dune Tyggers*. Quite an array and none happy outside the book's pages.

He had seen enough, but didn't know how to wrap things up. So he just reached over and snapped his fingers. That did the trick. The menagerie quickly puffed back into clouds, sucked into the book quicker than a NASCAR pile-up. The book slammed shut, the *Columbincus* flung from the keyhole and into Harris' hand, his library card expired, evidently. So much for the Farn version of the Kindle.

3

When Harris returned to his quarters, Yustichisqua was laying out the hunt clothing, even inspecting a change of duds for himself.

"You're shucking your buckskins?" Harris asked.

"I asked the other Trones. They said it does a consort great honor for Trones to match his colors when hunting." He bowed, and then held up a blue cape — a handsome garment, which Harris thought would be *taboo* as Trone apparel. Apparently, not. "It is my first hunt and . . . I am anxious, *oginali.*"

"It's mine too, so if we go down, we go down together." He laughed, but then considered — Yustichisqua hadn't seen the beastie assortment. What would he say when he encountered the Horny Rugrunner, especially when it reared to the heavens to nibble a *Cabriolin*. "Come, sit with me."

Yustichisqua folded the cape neatly, and then approached. Harris secretly grinned. The changes in this lad were readily apparent. He walked taller and . . . walked — *zululess*. He had treated his new garments beyond the respect it would accord honor to his lord — with a pride to ownership. Indeed, the earmarks of running afoul of the Yunockers was evident, pleasing Harris.

Once seated, Little Bird gazed attentively at his lord, waiting instructions. Harris struck an advisory tone.

"Little Bird," he said. "When we ride tomorrow . . ."

"We, *oginali?* Surely I cannot be in *the Cabriolin*. I must scoot behind you."

"How would you know where you must scoot if you haven't been on a hunt? I'm an ignorant ass when it comes to hunting protocols, so anything goes — and anything I say goes. Right?"

"Yes, *oginali*. But your actions will not provoke Lord Tappiolus. I will be blamed, because a Trone is supposed to know the rules and adhere to them. If the Yunockers question me, I cannot say Lord Belmundus has ordered it so. They will accuse me of failing to point out any breech."

"Bullshit," Harris said. "I will answer for your lapses, whether I encouraged them or not. If Lord Tappiolus makes issue, which he will not, I'll remind him I've been invested as a consort and rule my household as I see fit."

"Then . . . I am your household?"

"You are. Does it make you sad?"

Little Bird looked away shyly.

"No, *oginali*. I am used well — very well indeed, if I am your household."

"So, you'll ride in my *Cabriolin* and for a specific reason."

"For ballast?"

"No — although, I hadn't thought of that. But you've never seen *a Tippagore*."

Yustichisqua blanched — clearly uneasy.

"You saw it, *oginali* — in the *Cartisforium*? Was it hideous?"

Harris stood, stretching his arms wide. He puckered his face, and then made horns — then antlers, and finally tusks. Yustichisqua's eyes popped.

"And it's massive, with eight monstrous legs and skin as shaggy as a sheep dog. It could take out a whole Yunocker squadron, if it tried. But somehow I don't think it's naturally aggressive."

"But it is fierce, if you say it is so big and ugly."

"Yes, but I wouldn't be surprised if it ate cactus or sage brush or whatever the fuck grows in the Forling. Otherwise it would be a sight smaller and on shorter legs — and be like a lizard. I saw more dangerous things in *the Cartisforium*."

He pointed to his teeth, and then made three rabbit ears. He concluded the charade with his best impersonation of a scorpion with a large snapping claw.

"*Gasuntsgi*," Yustichisqua stammered, imitating the rabbit-thing, "and *Porcorporian* — the sand creepers. I have seen those. They come to the edge of *the Kalugu* and try to penetrate the walls."

"So, you see, I want you in my *Cabriolin*, because I can't afford to lose you to a swiping paw or well-aimed claw."

Little Bird looked worried, and then sat again. Harris joined him.

"Don't sweat it, kiddo," he said. "The best way to brush troubles aside is to distract your mind. Why don't you show me my hunting duds."

Yustichisqua darted over to the clothing array on the sleeping platform. He held up a scanty leather jockstrap etched on the crotch with Lord Belmundus' sigil.

"That's a statement," Harris laughed.

"I guess when *the Tippagore* tries to attack you, *oginali*, he may go for your *gugubasti* — genitals."

"I believe the fiercest *Tippagores* are females — pissed-off mothers. But we'll do our best to save my balls, because they don't belong to me any more, do they?"

Yustichisqua blushed, but raised Lord Belmundus' breastplate — a heavy piece of armor made of what he learned later was *conontoroy*, plated with two mosaic rows of *lapis lazuli* and turquoise. Harris snatched it.

"This'll tire me out," he said. "Is there a cape to match?"

He saw the cape clearly, so the question was moot. Still, Little Bird lovingly presented the blue bolt for inspection. It was identical to his except dotted with sapphires and filigreed with golden thread.

"A thing of beauty," Little Bird said. "I have never touched so fine a garment."

"It'll be a mess in the desert," Harris said, draping it over one shoulder and his right arm. "The sweat rings I'll make. But I guess I can afford it — or at least, Charminus can."

He gazed at the bed to the remaining gear — an assortment of ropes and clubs and *Sticks* and a sword. He went for that, raising it to his eye. When he did, *the Eye* appeared in its niche. He turned, thinking to poke it out. Instead, he regarded the weapon fondly. A matching dagger rested beside it.

"What a thing this is, Little Bird? An old-fashioned swashbuckler."

"It is for show, *oginali*," he said. "You use your *Stick* for the hunting. The sword is a sign of your rank."

"Maybe so, but with one of these on my jockstrap, I might stand a better chance in a pinch."

He glanced at the golden *Eye*, and decided to greet his mistress. He strolled over, the sword held high. He bowed.

"Blessed evening, dear mistress," he said, softly. "I hear you are with child, as they say — kindled. Maybe its mine, although I suspect my gracious brother, who shares my pleasures, has hit the jackpot again." He bowed deeply this time. It was strange holding a one-way conversation with part of a Cyclops. However, getting no feedback was fine with him. He raised the sword. "I thank you for this as I go out with our father to hunt the mighty *Tippagore*. I've used fine weapons on many sets. I trained with the best fencing master in the business — *Messer. Jardierne de Valois*."

Harris grinned, and then struck the first fencing pose. "*En Garde*." Then, in a flash, *advance,* followed with a loud *appel*, sweeping backwards in a *glissade*, followed by two *lunges* and a *parry* of an invisible attacker. He *redoublement*, and then *quillioned* before raising the weapon in a *grand salute. The Eye* winked, faded, and then disappeared.

"Aha, Madam," Harris said, bowing to nothing, and then turning to Yustichisqua, and bowing again.

Little Bird applauded.

"You know how," he said.

"Well, this isn't the sword for such things. Fencing swords are called *rapiers*, but this broad thing could do damage, where *a rapier* would be a pin to *a Tippagore*." He laughed. "I've given the old gal entertainment enough for the evening, eh? I mean, she's suffering without either consort for a while."

Harris returned to the bed, found the scabbard, and then tried to figure out how it attached to his leather jockstrap. As he monkeyed with the problem, Little Bird sorted the remaining gear into a wooden box to be mounted inside *the Cabriolin*. Then he held out the other weapon for his master's inspection.

"What do we have here?"

A knife. A six-inch dagger of the Marine variety, with a long mean blade, which could slice off wads of *terrerbyrd* in a pinch. Its hilt, unadorned except for a small sapphire at the grasp, emblazoned an etching of Lord Belmundus' sigil. This fine blade was sheathed in leather. Harris weighed it in his hand.

"Some heft here," he said. "A combat knife. I wielded one like it on the set of *Okinawa — Island of Death.*" He watched Yustichisqua's eyes, which never left the weapon. Suddenly, Harris was struck by an idea. "Here."

Little Bird took the dagger and proceeded to place it in the wooden box.

"No, Little Bird. Not there. I'm giving this to you. A gift."

"Me, *oginali?* I cannot. It is a Lord's weapon."

"And what if you need to defend yourself in the Forling? What if you need to protect me?"

Little Bird frowned, but then grinned. He inspected the dagger, and then touched it to his headband, bowing to his lord.

"I have never had such a gift, *oginali.*"

"Neither have I, Yustichisqua. Neither have I."

Once sorted, Harris tried for sleep, but it wouldn't come, the hunt's prospects keeping him up. He was afraid, but welcomed the chance to go beyond the confines of the invisible gate. He sat at bed's edge and peered at the moonlight. Only one moon was full, the others slivers, but soon all three faded as *Solus,* and then *Dodecadatemus* edged over into the sky. Dawn arrived. He would be riding with the Pod. Soon Yustichisqua would be a busy engine, wrapping him in fine new hunting clothes.

Harris arose and went onto the portico. His *Cabriolin* was idled on its pedestal. He had taken his sword with him. He raised it to the rising suns.

"*En Garde,*" he challenged, loud enough to stir Little Bird, beginning the ever-present engine.

Chapter Six

Hunting the Tippagore

1

At this world's edge, the suns rose. Dawn flooded the sky with crimson beauty. Harris stood in his *Cabriolin* with Yustichisqua perched behind him. They cut fine figures — a regal mass of blue silk, Lord and squire, ready for the hunt. As Harris gazed over *the Ayelli*, he saw stars twinkling on the borderlands of night, but soon realized these were lights from dozens of *Cabriolins* and *zulus* in the distance — his brother consorts and their Thirdling children with Trones in tow, all hovering over the valley. The Pod had assembled. A brace of *Cabriolins* approached Harris' in his high perch. The first arrival was Arquebus.

"Are you secured?" Arquebus asked. "It will be a fine day for the hunt, but a foray into the Forling is fraught with danger. Heed Agrimentikos and his instructions."

"I'm ready for it, Sir John," Harris said, uncaring about his form of address.

This man would always be Sir John Briarcliff to him, despite title and protocol. Harris nodded a welcome to Elypticus, who drifted beside his father in a separate *Cabriolin*. Harris thought to thank the Thirdling for the *mongerhide*, but recalled Little Birds' words concerning honor among Thirdlings. Elypticus bowed deeply, just as Agrimentikos arrived.

"Ah, Lord Belmundus," Agrimentikos shouted, warmly. "I see you flout the rules already, your Trone riding astern."

"I resist rules which defy logic, honorable brother," Harris replied, touching his *Columbincus* in salute. "This Trone's mine — for my exclusive use. Am I correct?"

"Absolutely," Agrimentikos replied.

"Wasn't his conduct scrutinized in the Scarlet Chamber?"

"Undoubtedly."

"Did it survive my mistress' approbation?"

"Tenuously."

"And didn't the fair Joella grant me my heart's wish?"

"Most graciously."

"Confirmed and upheld by Kuriakis himself?"

"Case won, Lord Belmundus. I have no objections."

"Then, neither I nor my Trone have broken the rules."

"That might be disputed by Captain Buhippus," Arquebus inserted. "Lord Tappiolus would have a word on the subject also."

"Let him sue me."

"That is not his style, my friend," Arquebus replied, moving aside when Agrimentikos landed on the portico.

"Look yonder, Lord Belmundus," Agrimentikos said. "You have left the outlands — worlds of grief and misery. You embrace a place with purpose, one filled with beauty. You must admit its charm."

Harris did admit its charm — its mystery and its puzzlement. However, arrayed before him was an army of hunters — predators no different from the outland he had left. Besides, Farn wouldn't be his first choice of substitute realms. But he needed a respite from *Mortis House*, if just for a little while. The prospects of a real hunt — not a cinematic setup with booms and cranes and green screens and fall nets and harnesses, was exhilarating. He grinned at Agrimentikos.

"I'll admit there's much in Farn that's reassuring. But I've seen only the inside of this fucking palace and this small circuit of gardens. I long to see the world beyond the invisible gate. I'll explore it with my *Stick* in hand, my brothers racing at my side and my Cetrone at my back."

"Well, that is a novel view, Lord Belmundus," Agrimentikos said. He cocked his head, gazing into Yustichisqua's eyes. "I have watched these people for more years than you can know and, unlike the Yunockers or my brothers, I see value in their knowledge of the land, of music and their empathy for others. If you can control the wildness inside this lad — a wildness not evident at first glance, then I will be the last to object to your household's management." He brought his face into Little Bird's. "You are wild, are you not? Admit it. Beneath your *sqwallen-*addled façade, lurks a Dune Tygger ready to pounce. I can see it."

Little Bird trembled, not answering.

"That's it, Lord Agrimentikos," Harris said. "I have my *Stick* in hand, a sword on my belt and a knife wielding *Dune Tygger* at my back. Can anyone doubt my potency?"

Agrimentikos grinned, and touched Yustichisqua's headband.

"Still, I would keep that dagger out of Lord Tappiolus' sight. He enforces the rules. He is a game of *grusoker*. We can control him at most times, but his arm can stretch beyond us, kidnapping authority from Scepta Charminus and anointing those who serve him."

Agrimentikos straightened over his *Cabriolin's* helm. His Thirdlings — six of them, hovering at a distance, maneuvered into a V formation around Arquebus' entourage. Agrimentikos raised his *Stick*.

"Here begins the adventure of my brother, Lord Belmundus the Just," he announced in his booming Macedonian voice. "He comes to the Pod with an iron heart and a Dune Tygger at his back."

Three Trones floated from the shadows, raising twisted horns, and then blew, echoing across *the Ayelli*. Other, more distant horns were blown, bellowing the air with foregone victory. Then from the palace emerged *Nightmare*, his master on his back. The Pod drifted slowly until Kuriakis assumed its head, raising his staff, blue lightning flashing skyward. The journey to the Forling had begun. The hunt was on.

2

Rushing through the invisible gate over a fathomless ravine, the Pod swept past the Yunocker legions, who hovered as the Elector rode *Nightmare* onward. Harris gazed about like a child set loose in an amusement park. He viewed the gateway with awe, because, although invisible, there was a hint of it — an atmospheric change when his *Cabriolin* crossed. The Yunockers stood reverently in their vehicles, fists clapped to their hearts in a salute — humbled by the House of Montjoy. This now Harris included as Lord Belmundus. He returned the salute, touching his right hand over his left, crossing his *Columbincus*. The Yunockers stirred at this.

"They think you mean to fire at them, *oginali*," Yustichisqua whispered.

Harris immediately restored his right hand to its navigating position and nodded his thanks to Little Bird. Agrimentikos smiled, probably aware *the Dune Tygger at Lord Belmundus' back* had provided proper guidance. Arquebus didn't seem as content. Tappiolus regarded Yustichisqua suspiciously. However, under the circumstance and Agrimentikos' tutelage, Tappiolus could not voice his objections, nor press his legal credentials.

When the Pod reached the city, Harris sighed with both wonder and puzzlement. Although he could see only rooftops and the street grid, he had a good view of an urban landscape. To the left, a wash of Oriental minarets and pagodas punctuated a long valley, which led to the coast. He couldn't see *the Amaykwola*, but the morning haze promised that a sea was out there somewhere.

"Little Bird," he whispered.

"That is *the Wudayleegu*, the Zecronisian ward, *oginali*."

"Ah."

Harris looked to the right. A riot of color — awnings and pastel huts, and smoke of various hues hung like a canopy — vast and waking with activity.

"Is that the market?" he asked Yustichisqua.

"Yes, *oginali*, *the Yuyutlu*, where the Gurts make the goods and craft the stones. There the Zecronisians negotiate the selling and the trading."

The Pod crossed the city center, where the marketplace spilled into a sprawl of square buildings. *Symmetry*. Some buildings were tall across the Pod's path, but the majority were low and squat. One was walled — a fortress arising like a dark tidal wave. Yustichisqua grunted as they passed it.

"What's that place?"

"*The Yuganawu, oginali*. The place of the governing."

"But I thought the government was in *the Ayelli*."

"No. *The Ayelli* is the place of the ruler, but the Yunockers govern from *the Yuganawu*, and below us are their homes. The Cetrone serve the Yunockers also and are very much in this place — the central ward of the city. We are subjected to the governing."

Harris scanned the place from the heights. Cold and geometric — much like photos he recalled of Hitler's dream for Nuremburg. Other fortresses arose to the east (or to the west by Farn reckoning).

"And those?" Harris asked.

"*The Porias* and *the Katorias* — the old and new prisons, *oginali*." Yustichisqua slid around the *Cabriolin*'s railing so his face could be seen. "The old one is for the peoples of Montjoy, made of *kaybar* and secure. The new one is for the Cetrone, built with *Phitron* and impenetrable."

Phitron — the black stone. That explained what Harris saw next, on the right and lost to a night black wall — a secure zone, much like the Phitron prison, only larger and patrolled by Yunockers, like wasps about a hive.

"*The Kalugu?*" he asked.

"Yes," Yustichisqua replied. "My home. The place where we are drawn from when in service until *the reaptide* takes us away."

"I can't see over the walls, Little Bird."

"You may never see it, *oginali.* May the spirits of my *waddly wazzoo* keep you from seeing it. It would burden your heart — and yours is a good heart, *oginali.*"

Harris turned his head toward Agrimentikos, who had fixed his stare upon Little Bird. The old consort knew the Trone would tell the tale of *the Kalugu* sympathetically. But it didn't matter. It couldn't be helped. Not with a thousand *Cabriolins* or a dozen *Nightmares*. The place was off-limits to *the* Ayelli by a treaty crafted in good faith.

This world was as it was — places set and, like a water clock or the two suns and three moons, churned on a never ending course despite well-meaning thoughts from an actor drawn from the outer world — despite the hem and haw of a young servant, even if he was a *Dune Tygger at his back*. Agrimentikos knew. But it was Arquebus who had worrisome eyes. It was Tappiolus who had captured the plot, simmering it as the Pod reached the Montjoy's city walls.

3

The walls were high and gated — a real gate this time, branched with barbed wire and heavily guarded. The gate was opened out of respect for the Elector, but it could have remained shut — Kuriakis easily guiding *Nightmare* over the razor-sharp spirals, which could never pretend to hold back immortality.

Once across the wall, the vast red desert astonished Harris. He careened to see the other side. He could not. A heat wave baked his face like strolling inside a pizza oven. Below, scrub — a dark defile with scant vegetation edged by drifting crimson sand.

"It's so red," he muttered.

"*Kowlinka,*" Little Bird said. "It is called *kowlinka* and is used to make pots in *the Yuyutlu.*"

"Good to know."

When the Pod cleared the margins, a line of dunes arose suddenly. These writhed with activity — a hot wind, the red drifts rippling like the tide, but also something beneath them.

"They are there," Yustichisqua said, fear in his voice. "*The Porcorporian.*"

Harris stared down to see which denizen from *the Cartisforium* Little Bird described. Soon there was no doubt. From the drifting sand, an occasional claw emerged, and then a scaly back and an ugly scorpion-like thing called *the Porcorporian* — gross and ferocious. It chased things called *Gasuntsgi*, vampire bunny rabbits, which would, no doubt, suck anything dry given the chance. Small. Their outlines could be seen hopping about the drifting terrain, claws clapping at their tails. Then, as fast as they appeared, they were gone, down rabbit holes beneath the sand.

Horns blasted. Harris' brother consorts hooted and hollered — war whoops. Something was a-foot, but not *a Tippagore*, but something feline — worthy of war whooping.

Dune Tyggers prowled in a five pack — lavender and furry, a bit larger than outland tigers, but similar in most respects otherwise — stripes (deep purple) and lethal teeth — the scimitars of old Smilidon of the La Brea — the Saber Toothed tiger.

"Hoy, Lord Belmundus," Agrimentikos shouted. "Follow me and we shall bag one as an exercise in straight shooting."

Harris nodded. He felt Yustichisqua cinch about his waist. Then he dipped his *Cabriolin* over the lead *Tygger*.

"*Noya Tludachi*," Agrimentikos shouted.

"Excuse me?"

"*Noya Tludachi, oginali*," Little Bird muttered. "It is the name for *the Dune Tygger.*"

"Ah," Harris said, drawing up his *Stick*, holding it lance-like. "They're beautiful creatures. It's a shame to zap one."

"Good eating," Yustichisqua said.

It was always about the belly. However, in the case of Kuriakis' hunting parties, the hunt was *priority one*. Harris watched his brethren and their assault team assail *the tludachi*, a spark cloud rising above the dunes. He glanced at Agrimentikos, and then at Arquebus, *Sticks* close at hand. Agrimentikos nodded, giving Harris the honor of the first shot — a difficult honor to redeem. This wasn't a movie set with green screen and CGI animation. The creature was flesh and didn't wake this morning knowing a bunch of wild-ass guys would stream across its home with lightning rods and sear its fur. Still, Harris was Lord Belmundus now. Mercy on the hunt would be misconstrued as *pussy galore.* So he clenched his *Stick* as Eng and Chang had taught, and then steadied his *Cabriolin,* recalling the exact spot on his *Columbincus* supporting accurate shooting.

"One, two, three," he muttered, and then fired.

"Yes," Agrimentikos shouted.

Elypticus hooted. Arquebus grinned. Harris had landed his first strike, directly through the beast's right eye. As *the Cabriolin* hovered over the downed *Tygger*, Harris felt the marksman's pride, but also a hunter's pain. *The Noya Tludachi* was a beautiful creature, its fur reminding Harris of many *Red Carpet* coats. The beast was in pain, still thrashing about. It swiped its paw up to its assailants, but three more bolts brought it down finally. Agrimentikos came to Harris' side. He beamed like a proud parent.

"Good work, Lord Belmundus."

"Boots," came a cry from above. It was Kuriakis, standing high in *Nightmare's* stirrups. He waved his wand in triumph. "That shot shall be etched on the pillars of Greary Gree, it will."

Harris could hear the shouts of the other consorts and Thirdlings.

Boots! Boots! Boots!

He was certain Lord Tappiolus' voice was not in this threnody.

4

The horns blared again. The cymbals crashed. The drums beat. All attention was drawn away from *the Dune Tyggers*, because *the Tippagore* had been found. Kuriakis raised his staff like a lance and the Pod went aloft. Harris had difficulty keeping abreast with Agrimentikos, *the Cabriolin* showing signs of a power loss. Perhaps it was running out of gas. But how could that be? Harris looked to Little Bird.

"Perhaps the heat, *oginali.* Perhaps much *kowlinka* in the intake."

"Perhaps."

However, they were aloft and on the make. Agrimentikos didn't care whether his charge was trailing. The Elector, always given the honor of felling the quarry, there was no need to rush. Harris spotted the beast — a marvel.

"It's much smaller than the one in the library," he muttered.

"I am glad for that, *oginali*."

"But smaller might mean fiercer."

The Tippagore, about twenty feet long and as rug-like as an Afghan hound, trundled, bristling — puffs of red sand spewing from its nostrils. It's horns, sharp — it's tusks, at the ready. But the Pod, an airborne force, defied tusks. Harris soon discovered their use. When Hasamun and Posan's squad circled the lumbering beast, it turned and reared — its elephantine legs poised to kick, its ram-like head twitching wildly. The tusks caught the legs of two Trones and, when they fell, the beast stomped them into a bloodstain.

"Did you see that, *oginali*?" Little Bird squealed.

"We'll stay clear unless we're needed," Harris replied. "I think I've made my mark on that *tludachi* thing."

The Pod rushed the beast, which galloped along the dunes, more sure-footed than could be anticipated. However, the Pod corralled it on the flat scrub, where it continued to rear, threatening with its natural armor. Still, it showed signs of tiring. Harris hovered lower and at a distance, especially when Kuriakis went in for the kill. He couldn't witness that. He drifted further away, but close enough not to be called a coward. No one watched him, or so he thought.

As he drifted further, the stench of *the Tippagore* heightened. The beast emitted a skunk odor with notes of petroleum products. Harris expected that the further away he drifted, the fewer stenches he'd experience. Maybe the beast, downed and dying, intensified its odor. Then Little Bird tugged on Harris' cape.

"*Oginali*."

Harris turned. Directly behind him was another Tippagore, larger than the first.

"Holy crap," he stammered, slamming his hand on *the Cabriolin* altitude button. "That's the motherfucker I saw in *the Cartisforium*."

It was — a thirty footer and uttering heart-rending wails at the events just over the dune. Harris pounded his hand on the controls. No response. Then, when *the* Cabriolin jerked into action, it went sideways, directly into the beast's jaws.

"Turn, turn, *oginali*."

"I'm trying."

He took a deep breath, trying the *up* button again. No go. Then the side navigations. An evil thought crossed his mind. His *Cabriolin* might be a lemon and to be returned to the show room. Perhaps someone tampered with it. Suddenly, the controls kicked in — not the up, but side to side. This kicked him back from the tusks, providing him a tour of the beast's massive length — its long tented carpeting. Harris saw activity there other than legs.

"What the fuck?"

"I see baby *Tippagores*," Little Bird said, almost gleefully.

"Nothing like a pissed off Mamagore. We'd better get out of here . . . fast."

However, before they could paddle away in this half-assed contraption, the Pod arrived, whooping and howling at their luck — finding a second and larger quarry for *the Scullery Dorgan*. Hell, this one would feed *the Ayelli* for a month.

The mother *Tippagore* whined. Harris thought it was a cry for her mate, who was being carved by the cargo Trones even as she called. She couldn't trundle away, because she had at least a dozen suckling baby *Tippagores* attached to a mammary assembly line. She was doomed, and perhaps baby *Tippagore* was a delicacy in *the Ayelli*, like veal cutlet.

Harris landed his dickey *Cabriolin* just as Tappiolus arrived.

"I must admit, Boots," Tappiolus remarked, "this is a find which will give you an advantage in Charminus' bed."

"It's the female," Harris said, and not as a point of information. "She's suckling her young. Let her be."

"Now there is a novel idea which will give us a good laugh."

Harris disembarked, marching toward his fellow consort, *Stick* in hand.

"I said, let her be."

The Tippagore watched this exchange, whimpering like a wounded puppy.

"Ah. Lord Belmundus is soft for the beast. How tender."

The rest of the Pod landed with Thirdlings and Trones assembled behind Tappiolus. Still, Harris rushed forward at a run. He raised his *Stick*.

"Stop this at once," Agrimentikos shouted. "What will this prove, Lord Belmundus? We have come to hunt and hunt we must."

"And hunt we shall," came the booming voice of the Elector on *Nightmare*. "Lower your *Stick*, Boots."

Harris halted. He trembled, lowering his *Stick*, and then facing Kuriakis.

"Father," he said. "This *Tippagore* protects her young, which suckle beneath her. Pass her by, I beg you."

"But Boots. This is a wonderful specimen — docile. An easy kill."

Harris dropped his *Stick* and went to one knee.

"Where I'm from, father, we take pity on the helpless. You have good quarry already. Spare this one."

"But why?"

"If you kill her, future hunts will be jeopardized. Her young will not grow to maturity. *Tippagores* may become rarer than they are now. Endangered even."

He scored a point, and he knew it. However, the silence was interrupted by a collective gasp. He saw everyone distracted. He turned to see a raised claw and an approaching jaw. *A porcorporian* had popped from its lair for a midday feast — co-consort would do nicely.

Harris shuffled backward, reaching for his *Stick*. However, someone had kicked it away. No question whom. He also had a flash no one — not consort, not Thirdling, not Elector had raised a *Stick* in his defense. Perhaps, they were surprised. The thing approached fast.

So this is how I die, he thought.

A painful death, one wrought by broken bones and spurting blood. How he wished for his stunt double. Then the *porcorporian* chattered, shuddering. Its claw slipped sideways in the lurch, but the beast collapsed a few feet from Harris' all-too-famous boots. Green ooze poured from the creature's skull. Someone had thrown something at the critter. Then, from atop the dead thing, stood a lad — dagger in hand.

"*Oginali.*"

5

"Arrest that Trone," Tappiolus shouted.

Harris stood, turned and gasped.

"What are you talking about?"

"That Trone has a weapon," Tappiolus cried, waving his hand for his Thirdlings to surround Little Bird.

Yustichisqua stood bemused on *the porcorporian's* crown. The only sound beyond the wind came from *the Tippagore*, which grunted its approval. Harris kneeled to Kuriakis, who scratched his head. Such bravery could not be rewarded with an arrest.

"If we allow Trones to be armed, Boots," Kuriakis said, fatherly, "they would murder us in our sleep."

"Open your eyes, father," Harris replied. "This Trone saved the life of his lord, while everyone else stood around with their fingers up their asses. How is that for murdering me in my sleep?"

Kuriakis rubbed his beard, looking to the other consorts, who hung noncommittal expressions.

"That might be so," Tappiolus said, "but it is a matter of convenience. To have such a weapon, and then to use it, is unprecedented."

"It is," Harris shouted.

"And where did he get the thing?" Tappiolus carped.

"I gave it to him," Harris replied. "My gift."

Murmuring now and light discussion. Thirdling hands cuffed comments. Even *the Tippagore* commented with a grunt. Harris saw he would not get a fair hearing. He'd have more success saving Mama *Tippagore*. The time for pleading was over. Harris stood tall, facing the Pod, raising his right hand high, and pressing his left one on his *Columbincus*.

"I am Lord Belmundus the Just," he shouted. "You named me so. I come to you with valor and honor." He pointed to Little Bird. "I ride with my *Stick* glowing strong and with *a Dune Tygger* at my back. Behold Lord Belmundus' *Noya tludachi*."

Harris bowed to his Trone. Everyone gasped. Tappiolus waved his hand again to set the arrest in motion, but Yustichisqua raised the dagger, placing it against his heart. Suddenly, every Trone on that scrubby field grunted and knelt. Tappiolus halted.

"Be still, Lord Tappiolus," Kuriakis commanded. "We have a singular demonstration of allegiance, which cannot be dismissed as criminality. No. No. It cannot." Kuriakis looked to Harris, shaking his head, as if he still couldn't fathom the breach of protocol. Still, who ruled here? Who had the key to order? "Boots, you are a quandary. Leave it to my daughter to draw an anomaly from the outer lands. She brought us Tappiolus, who has been given great responsibility, and then we had Lord . . . well, never mind. Not all choices are wise. As for you, I believe you are a hunter at heart. You have vision. So . . . so, I decree this. You may run your household as you will if it does not inspire others to thwart the law. Monitoring will be strict." He pointed to Yustichisqua. "I will send you a bejeweled case for that gift — a royal gift to be sure. Never doubt it. In its case, you may admire it when you say your spirit prayers to your *waddly wazzoo.*"

Yustichisqua lowered the dagger, and then knelt on the cartilage mess. Kuriakis grinned, and then faced *the Tippagore.*

"As for you, madam cow, raise your babies well, for some day they will grace *Ayelli* feasts and fill many Montjoy bellies. Today my son has been your champion. Go in peace."

Kuriakis reared on *Nightmare* and charged off toward the heavens. Tappiolus stormed to his *Cabriolin*, leading the Pod toward the city. Harris stood beside *the porcorporian* carcass. He gazed at *the Tippagore*, which nodded, whining no more.

Agrimentikos was at the ready. Because Harris' *Cabriolin* would be abandoned, Elypticus would ferry Lord Belmundus and his *Dune Tygger* back to *the Ayelli.*

Yustichisqua jumped off *the porcorporian*, coming to Harris' side. He knelt, grasping his master's *asana*, abjectly weeping into it. Harris swept the garment out of Little Bird's hands, raising him.

"You shall never kneel to me again, Yustichisqua. Never; for as long as I breathe."

Shallow promise that, because, with Tappiolus on watch, that breathless day could be tomorrow.

Chapter Seven

Admiration, Fear and Wonder

1

Harris had much to ponder and understand. He had become a source of admiration, fear and wonder wherever he went in *the Ayelli*. Except Tappiolus, Harris' fellow consorts and their Thirdlings showed admiration for him, as did the Sceptas. After returning from the hunt, his quarters were cluttered with gifts — an assortment of green liquids, that Yustichisqua said were the rare wines of Aquilium. These were from Soffira, whose second son was married to the third daughter of Scepta Asa of Aquilium. Miracola gave Harris a new chair, which was shaped like a tree stump, cushioned with cottony stuffing, far more comfortable for sitting than the bed's edge. She also sent greetings in a poem, which verged on the lewd. Other tributes came from Thirdlings and brother consorts — some gifts delectable to the taste, others keepsakes for a growing souvenir shelf in a mathum museum.

Despite this admiration, Tappiolus sent a Yunocker squadron twice daily to Lord Belmundus' quarters apparently to protect him from his *armed and dangerous* Trone and any bloodlust exercise which could ensue. When Harris protested to Charminus, she feigned indifference — apathy even, noting that Tappiolus had his brother consort's welfare at heart.

Since the hunt, Harris pondered Tappiolus' motives. That his co-consort was secure in Charminus' lust was beyond doubt. She had seven Thirdlings by him and, as it proved, the eighth — the current kindling, was his also, according to Mordacai the Zecronisian. Harris also discovered *the Eye*, indeed Charminus' eye, was a projection of her real eye and controlled by Tappiolus, independent of the Scepta. Harris no longer bowed to it or addressed it as *my lady*, because it was a device implanted by his brother-in-law — a device, which could appear in several places simultaneously throughout *the Ayelli* and probably across Montjoy city. Harris protested its use to Charminus.

"*The Eye* demeans your reputation," Harris argued. "You're an object of beauty and grace — a ruler upon this hill, my lady. But *the Eye* has made you an object of fear and, dare I say it . . . hatred."

Charminus only grinned, tossing her hair back. She cared not for such things. If the Trones loved or feared her, it made no difference to her. *If it kept order*, she noted, *Tappiolus can use my belly button*. It was useless for Harris to protest. Still, Charminus wasn't the spy — the Big Sister. Having *Big Brother-in-law* was less intimidating. *At least I could kick him in the balls.* Charminus couldn't care less whether Trones donned *zulus* or danced the herky-jerky before the Temple of Greary Gree.

Harris stayed as clear of Tappiolus as much as possible. He advised Yustichisqua to do the same. He was certain his *Cabriolin* had been tampered with on the hunt — confirmed by Tappiolus' satisfied look when it had failed, and then his response to Little Bird's actions to save his lord's life. Tappiolus' motives eluded Harris, but the intent was clear. Perhaps it was jealousy, Kuriakis' favor.

Admiration, fear and wonder.

Yes, *wonder*, because whenever Harris went abroad — a casual jaunt along the corridors or a sweep through the gardens for fresh air, Trones would stop, nod and clutch their hands to their chests. They didn't do this for any other consort or Thirdling. Harris questioned Yustichisqua.

"You bowed to me, *oginali*," Little Bird replied. "No lord has ever bowed to a Trone. And you refuse to let me bow to you. No Trone has ever been released from the obligation. The Cetrone mark your way in wonder, *oginali*. You give them hope. So they bow to you on my behalf."

Harris was uncomfortable with this honor. In a repressive land, such respect could prove dangerous. It could spawn jealousies and resentments. It had, and he knew it — Lord Tappiolus a case in point. As for *hope*, there was *hope* before he had been drawn here. There is always hope, even in the darkest corners of the deepest holes. Weren't the swag lamps all Cetrone kept, a sign of that hope? Still, public honor from the slaves of Farn made him as uneasy as Tappiolus' undue scrutiny. The more the Trones bowed, the greater that scrutiny became. Tension mounted.

The Sceptas' favor and Kuriakis bending the rules in Belmundus' favor further fanned resentments. He should have taken it in stride — preening and floating about regally, an easement against the lingering hope for escape. However, some days he wanted to hide in his quarters, meditating on the paintings Eng and Chang had gifted, and waiting for the inevitable intrusion of Buhippus and turkey-feather man, who would bow, greet him civilly, and then inspect the place for weapons, perhaps. Buhippus would always sniff the beautiful display case, which housed Yustichisqua's dagger. Kuriakis, good on his word, sent the box over. Little Bird sealed his weapon in it, displaying it prominently on a shelf beside Harris' own tributary gifts. It was to that dagger the Yunockers drifted every day — twice a day, checking the latch and the position of the blade, assuring that Belmundus' *Noya Tludachi* hadn't been using it to slice fruit or *Ayelli* throats. It was like theater, Harris thought. And why not? *Mortis House* was one big picture show — admission high, popcorn buttered and complete with appropriately rated previews.

Admiration, fear and wonder.

Then came Brunting Day.

2

Yustichisqua had delivered Harris' costume for *Othellohito* to the changing area at the amphitheatre before returning to prepare for the Brunting Day rituals. He donned a new cloak — a silver one, which shimmered in starlight. Harris had decided both consort and Trone would be a matched set and, although Lord Belmundus' colors were sapphire, Harris whipped up a silver alternative for Brunting Day. He had ordered a new cloak from the resident Gurt tailor, Xyftys, whose handiwork was admired — too much so to allow him to hide in *the Yuyutlu* behind a veil of Zecronisian banter and barter. Lord Belmundus' new garment was silver trimmed with blue pearls and azure diamonds right down to its hem and, although Yustichisqua's garment lacked the gem work, there could be no doubt whom he served when wrapped in his silvery drape.

Still, Yustichisqua was reticent with these liberties. However, with Kuriakis' decree ringing in his ears, he was willing to lean more toward his good fortune, apparently. As he dressed Harris, he peered into the mirror, obviously pleased. Then, breaking this brief reverie, he squared his master's shoulders and inspected the full effect of Lord Belmundus.

Admiration, fear and wonder.

"Your script, *oginali*," Little Bird said. "Do not forget it."

"No need for it," Harris replied. "I know it pat. The role's straight-forward."

"But you missed many words the last time we . . . as you say, *ran the lines*."

"Not missed, Yustichisqua. *Ad lib'd.* With Lord Hasamun's sparse characterization as *Desdemonayama*, I can ramble a bit — make improvements as the mood strikes me."

Yustichisqua straightened the drape of Harris' cloak, coming dangerously close to the *Columbincus.* Harris turned, and then swept aside, leaving Little Bird alone in the mirror.

"Look at you, my friend," he said. "What an improvement over that shadow who crept behind me, refusing to tell me his name."

"It seems long ago, *oginali*."

"Things change in a flash if you go with the flow. This evening you'll ride to the Temple of Greary Gree in my *Cabriolin* and . . . you won't wear your *zulus*."

"I will take them all the same," Little Bird replied. "You never know."

"True. I'm guided by your wisdom."

But Harris knew wisdom didn't guide these actions. Raw responses to the environment did.

Admiration, fear and wonder.

Together, Lord and squire overtook the portico and mounted a new *Cabriolin*, a gift from Joella Montjoy, who had the new one engraved with her favors directly above Charminus' sigil and Belmundus' own double squiggle. It was another source of pride which fed jealousy's bedevilment, but if there was one possession Harris appreciated from *Mortis House,* it was his *Cabriolin.* He wished they came in niftier colors — like teal. But they were always plain black with silver sigils as if they came directly from Henry Ford's assembly line. What could you do with a flying platform anyway?

The curtain of evening fell as Harris navigated his cart the short distance from his portico to the Temple of Greary Gree, where a solemn ritual would be performed before the reflecting pool. As he gazed over *the Ayelli*, dusk wrapped its fingers about a serpentine trail of light, which wended up the hill from the city. Thousands of lamps came — an impressive sight.

"They come," Yustichisqua said. "The Cetrone from the city climb the summit to honor the Elector. They have lit their *waddly wazzoos* to offer their sparks, because the Proctor blesses them on this Brunting Day."

"But the Elector and his Memer can Brunt all they want, Little Bird. The spooky jingle which speaks about promises and prophecy says they've reached their kiddy limit."

"But it is sacred to all who live in Montjoy, *oginali*, and this blesses the *jomar* and *quillerfoil* crop."

"Yes," Harris muttered. "All hail to the Almighty *sqwallen* bowl." He heard Little Bird grunt. "You don't miss it, do you? The *sqwallen*, I mean. Vile stuff."

"My head is much clearer without it, *oginali*. But it does settle anxiety."

"I bet it does. I used to smoke, but I kicked the habit quickly."

No response to this. They were approaching the reflecting pool, where throngs of citizens stood layered and jockeying for position for the best view, no doubt. Most were Thirdlings, but Harris spotted several posh Zecronisians and a few well-heeled Gurts. The Yunockers were here in force, forming a perimeter, Buhippus at the fore.

On a throne in the temple's portico sat Kuriakis, Joella to his right. To his left sat the three Sceptas, Charminus great with child — any day now. Arrayed on the right (Harris' point of destination) were his brother consorts and their Trones.

"Well, I'll be," Harris said delighted as he touched down.

Agrimentikos had reattired his Trones in new cloaks, as did Hasamun and Posan. The servants were on *zulus* and didn't ride in the *Cabriolins*, but Harris may have inadvertently touched off a trend, which tenuously made inroads at the highest levels.

Admiration, fear and wonder.

Arquebus' Trones were still in buck skins, and Tappiolus, red-faced and clearly put off by these changes, had his Trones heaped beside his *Cabriolin*, faces hidden and bodies turned away — an abject gesture to their lord's intention to enforce entrenchment. However, only Yustichisqua arrived in a consort's *Cabriolin*. And Little Bird's attire outshone most Thirdlings. When he stepped from the vehicle behind his lord, he stepped *zululess*. He bowed when Harris did, but otherwise stood as straight as the temple's columns.

"Boots," Kuriakis said as a greeting, but said no more.

"Father," Harris replied, bowing first to Kuriakis, and then to Joella, mouthing the word *mother*. She raised her hand and nodded graciously. Harris went to one knee before Charminus. "Mistress mine," he said, much like an actor would, "you blossom like the cherry tree on the brink of spring. Someday you shall kindle my offshoots and, on that day, I shall be the happiest man alive."

Charminus grinned, and touched her belly. Harris touched his *Columbincus.*

"High praise," she said. "And I believe it is purloined from some work you have encountered, no doubt."

"No doubt," Harris said. "Would I honor you otherwise?"

Charminus grinned again, pleased by his admission. Tappiolus stepped forward.

"Lord Belmundus," he muttered. "This ritual is not about you . . . this time. Your grandiloquent public display before our Scepta upstages our father."

Upstage. There was a word Harris knew well. He withdrew to the sidelines to watch the Brunting Day ritual unfold.

3

The perimeter dispersed to allow the Cetrone pilgrims entry — an endless train of humble buckskins and headbands, each holding their lamps beneath their chins — a ghostly procession. At best, Cetrone faces were downcast. Now lit in the ambient glow of their *waddly wazzoos*, high-toned features revealed careworn chiseled faces. Harris glanced toward his Scepta — toward the tall Cetrone who stood behind her. Littafulchee didn't hide her face — her eyes drawn away from the reflecting pool, as if contemplating another ritual altogether. Her face wasn't care worn, bearing a different history. Harris wished he could read her thoughts and pick her brain — to learn the secrets. He sensed many secrets — not the least the fate of his predecessor, Hierarchus.

As the Cetrone reached the pool, floating on *zulus*, they fanned into a semi-circle, edging the audience aside. Reaching midpoint, they halted, facing the throne, the procession's leaders bowing, and then cupping their lamp wicks deterring the evening breeze.

Kuriakis stood, raised his arms as if to embrace the procession. He took three steps down the stairs to the pool's edge.

"What gift have you brought the Memer and I?" he asked, ceremoniously.

The two lead Cetrone swung their lamps, and then touched them to the pool. A blue drizzle of light kissed the surface, and soon a pastel glow engulfed the waters. Kuriakis waved his staff over the pool.

"Let the waters rise," he said. "Let the sky blossom with an Elector's blessing, May this be proof of our good intentions — a sign for the fields to thrive for yet another season."

Blue and pink jets fountained high over the assembly. This water ballet captivated Harris. The fanned spray transformed into fiery sparks and soon the sky filled with fireworks greeted with appreciative gasps. Harris recalled evenings on Santa Monica Pier sitting beside his mother and watching the Luminous Chrysanthemums and the Rose Bombs engage the night sky over an invisible sea. Suddenly, he was homesick. He looked away, but his eye caught Yustichisqua's, who must have read his master's sadness. Harris shook his head, returning his attention to the entertainment. Great cries of *Adadooski* and *Arkmo* rang forth as Kuriakis waved his arms, conducting these dancing waters and the floral fireworks display.

As the show progressed, the Cetrone lit small votives from their *waddly wazzoos*, bowing as they did. They floated each along the edge of the pool forming a flotilla of prayer and devotion. With each act, a Cetrone muttered thanks, and then departed, proceeding down the hill.

Littafulchee moved beyond Charminus' chair. Harris watched her as she bowed to Joella, and then drifted to the pool, joining in the votive ceremony. She kissed a candle, touching it to her crystal before tapping it on her *waddly wazzoo*, which gave her vessel a gentle spin when it entered the water. She turned, facing Kuriakis. The other consorts and Scepta Trones came forward, Yustichisqua included. A mixed bag now, some in impressive cloaks and others as drab as a woodland thicket, they held their lamps firmly, drifting to the pool to perform the votive rite. They all floated, except one — a renegade, who walked there on his mother-given feet, thanks to his lord's instigation. Perhaps Little Bird should have slipped his *zulus* on for this act, thus avoiding the radical risk.

Admiration, fear and wonder.

However, *radical* colored the evening. When Yustichisqua reached the pool, he did something unexpected — something, which hushed all *Adadooskis* and choked every *Arkmo*.

After lighting his candle and launching his boat, Little Bird turned to Kuriakis and bowed deeply, but then turned to his cousin, Littafulchee and knelt, kissing the hem of her cloak. Such majesty dumbfounded the assembly. Harris looked to Tappiolus, who twitched and to Buhippus, who had his hand on his *Stick*, but always he had his hand on his *Stick*. What surprised Harris most was Littafulchee's unflinching response. She gently raised Little Bird and tapped his hand as if to admonish him for an unseemly gesture. However, as the Trones returned to their consorts and Sceptas, Joella stood, pointing to Little Bird.

"I have heard much about you," she said to Yustichisqua. "They whisper your name in the corridors outside my quarters. Of course, I pay them no heed as your name is of no consequence, but still it is spoken. Perhaps Lord Belmundus should listen to the whispers."

Was this an admonishment? Harris wondered. It was gently spoken — almost an invitation to continue the precedent, however, more likely designed to place comments at a distance. Harris could not let it pass.

"Mother," he said. "You gave me this Trone as a gift. He saved my life in the Forling, so your gift accounts for my presence this evening. If not for his bravery, my mistress would be seeking another in the outlands. For such bravery from one so low and base, I've bestowed upon this Trone some creature privileges of limited consequence, all of which I hope are within my dominion to grant. If not, dear mother, I'll withdraw them and seek the advice of my mistress on how such bravery from those who dwell in the shadows can be recognized by those who are saved."

He came forward and bowed — a crapshoot, but the Memer had a soft spot in her heart for him, one which matched Kuriakis' paternal ember.

"Boots," Kuriakis remarked at a distance. "The liberty this Trone has taken is to honor a female in our presence. A few bits of shiny cloth and the lack of *zulus* do not offend us. But such a display . . ."

"Ah," Harris said. He turned to Little Bird, and then to Littafulchee. He wagged a finger at both. "This may seem an impropriety. I see. I see." He came close to Joella, lowered his voice and beckoned for her ear. "Mother, these Trones are kin. Nothing more. They have saluted as a cousin salutes a cousin."

Joella grinned, but otherwise remained fixed on Yustichisqua. Kuriakis had caught only the last bit, but enough to dispel his concerns. He raised his hands again and continued conducting the ritual, the water jets flaring high and fireworks letting loose. The world animated again.

Admiration, fear and wonder.

Harris roughly gathered Little Bird to the *Cabriolin*, a show to be sure, but enough to assuage anger — all but one. Littafulchee appeared distraught as she floated back to Charminus like a *Duenna* loosed on a virgin. She pouted, and then turned her face away from Harris. Charminus appeared unconcerned, chatting with Soffira, probably about the last cascading lilac display, which had trickled from the heavens and into the pool.

When the final candle was floated and the last Trone drifted away from *the Ayelli*, Kuriakis calmed the blessing display amidst new rounds of *Adadooski* and *Arkmo*. He clapped, gathering their pleasure with arms spread wide. Like old King Cole, he laughed. He didn't call for his pipe and his bowl (or his fiddlers three), but escorted his Memer to her seat and called for the next phase of the entertainment.

"Agrimentikos," he shouted. "While we have our refreshments, prepare to pleasure us with the play. My daughters have spoken of nothing else for the last two weeks. We are eager for it. Do the honors, if you please."

Agrimentikos bowed, and then waved to the consorts to proceed to the amphitheatre. Harris welcomed the break.

"*Oginali*," Little Bird said. "We must hurry. You are in the first scene and you have yet to dress."

Harris gazed at the lad. His brush with what might have amounted to high treason didn't seem to faze him. Yes, Yustichisqua had come a long way. *Or was it the lack of sqwallen?* Harris thought. Still, Little Bird hopped into the *Cabriolin*, nodding to his master to make haste — a novel turnabout.

As Harris mounted his cart, he glanced back at his Scepta, who still bantered with her sisters while reaching for a purple pastry. He noticed Littafulchee's stone glance, detracting from her beauty.

Yet, she was worthy of the public honor Little Bird paid her. But why was such honor paid?

Harris shrugged, slapping his hand on his *Columbincus*, prepared to jet down the bank into the arena.

"Hurry, *oginali*. The costume is complex and you must wear it properly. It will take time to place you in it."

Harris touched the dashboard, and the *Cabriolin* left the Temple of Greary Gree.

Admiration, fear and wonder.

Chapter Eight

The Play's the Thing

1

The stage was set — a floral beauty, silk draped and topped by a crimson *Torii*, giving the audience a peek at Mount Fuji through the portal. As the guests hustled to their seats, the consort cast crammed the backstage dressing rooms to don their costumes — costumes matching *the Edo* set.

"It will be hot," Yustichisqua remarked as he hoisted turquoise shoulder flairs across Harris' back. "Let me secure them so they do not fall."

"Tight," Harris said, wiggling to test them. "It'll be a balancing act, but . . . "

He glanced into a floor-length mirror. He had never worn such a costume — not even for *The Magic Planet*, which had some dandy duds for its star. Silk cascaded down his chest concealing his *Columbincus*. A broad *obi* cinched his *asano*, while the shoulder flairs were *portieres sans* curtain rod. On his head, a tall chimney hat arose complete with stiff side paddles, recalling the handlebars on an old *hand-me-down* Schwinn. The make-up was *Kabuki* and applied quickly — clown white, charcoal eyeliner, sanguine lip balm and chicken tracks near the tear ducts to give an impression of epicanthic eyes.

"Do they wear such things in the outer world, *oginali*?" Little Bird asked.

"They do," Harris replied. "And with *getas* on my feet, I'll be lucky not to fall off the stage and into the Elector's lap." He laughed. "My face needs work."

"No time, *oginali*. I hear the guests going silent."

"How can you hear them going silent, Little Bird? Think what you said and . . ."

"Boots."

Tappiolus had materialized as *Iagomoto* — a dreadful sight. He wore a pointed cap, a leonine black wig, and was draped in purple silk cinched by a death-white sash. His face Harlequin's, half happy — half sad, a genuine sign to the audience his character was a tortured spirit not to be trusted beyond his crow taloned shoulder flairs.

"Are we up?"

"No doubt."

Harris gave him a turn on the *getas,* and then darted past the dressing area. He tripped onto the stage, greeted by applause and a few *Adadooskis*. He spotted the Elector and his Memer, centerpieces in the front row, the Sceptas sitting to their right and dignitaries at their left. He saw the Protractusian ambassador and the Bishop of Titipu, or whatever Fagus Marius was called officially in Pontifrax. Harris couldn't see beyond them, but he assumed Thirdlings and other prominent citizens, not to mention a heap of Yunockers filled the place to the bleachers.

He bowed slightly to acknowledge the applause, and then produced the handkerchief in question — *the raison d'etre* for this opening scene. Once waved, Tappiolus began his lines.

The scene could have been flawless had Tappiolus stuck to the rehearsed *shtick*. But no. *Iagomoto* upstaged Harris, who was forced to deliver his lines at an unnatural angle. When he shuffled on his *getas,* Tappiolus gazed down and grinned. The gesture provoked audience twitter, which regarded it as a sight gag. It stepped on Harris' lines. Things didn't improve. Tappiolus made grandiloquent work of his short speech, elongating it until it drew attention away from his partner in dialog. Then, when Harris responded, Tappiolus turned his back, exiting stage-right, leaving *Cassioshima* to fumble with his short speech, and then trip to an inelegant exit, his shoulder flairs bouncing like a wounded angel. He was livid.

Harris balled his fists and sought his co-consort, but Little Bird caught him on the fly.

"*Oginali,*" he said. "What has happened? That is not the way it goes."

"I know," Harris muttered, fuming. "Where's that fucker? I'll rip him a new *obi* hole."

"He is preparing for his next entrance, *oginali.*"

"I think I'll help him onto the stage."

However, when Harris tripped over the backstage props to let his anger fly, Agrimentikos blocked the way, a finger to his lips.

"They can hear you," he whispered, pointing to the stage.

Arquebus was on tap as *Othellohito.* Harris sucked his gut in and hung on the stage legs, trying his best to push his anger down to his spleen. He watched Arquebus, black-faced as any proper *Othellohito* should be, in a *samurai* robe with long sword and hair tapped in a bun. Arquebus spun lines like a gossamer web over the audience. It was *that* speech again — the one which had mesmerized Harris at rehearsal.

He can't go wrong with that, Harris thought, and forgot he had just laid an egg in public, thanks to Tappiolus.

Suddenly, Posan stood beside him. Posan, as *Emiliasan,* was draped in a green-silk robe, but less ornate than the rest of the cast because *Emiliasan* was a servant. He looked to Harris, his starch-white face rouged at the cheeks and outlined at the chin — the illusion of middle age.

Arquebus finished his deed — *Othellohito* smothering the sleeping *Desdemonayama* after a bantering about the sun and the moon and the stars. Hasamun spoke his lines with an annoying clip in a high-pitched lady's voice. He underscored each line with hand gestures and facial knots, managing to translate his emotional state across the gulf betwixt him and audience. In the end, the pillow came down — a proper smothering.

Posan glanced at Harris, winked, and then took a deep breath before delivering his off-stage lines.

"My lord, my lord! what, ho! my lord, my lord!"

Arquebus turned and looked toward the wings, directly at Harris. He turned back to the couch and that heap of Japanese frills — Hasamun.

"What noise is this? Not dead? not yet quite dead?
I that am cruel am yet merciful;
I would not have thee linger in thy pain: So, so."

Posan clapped.

"What, ho! my lord, my lord!"

"Who's there?"

Pause, Posan counting to three with his fingers raised.

"O, good my lord, I would speak a word with you!"

The action commenced.

2

Harris started counting. Part of the action was true to Shakespeare, but much had been altered to accommodate the Sceptas' tastes and follow the Memer's insistence for a happy ending. Drama and thunder was acceptable — edge of your seat *stürm und strang*, but, in the end, all must be well. It would not serve to have the Elector and his lady disappear into the Greary Gree depressed. First, *Emiliasan* would discover the body, and then *Iagomoto's* villainy would be revealed. Arquebus would have another moment — the shining moment, just as he plunged a dagger into his heart. But then *Cassioshima* would spring out and save the day in the silliest turn of events Harris had ever encountered. His script had serviceable lines full of jollity — like Jupiter on high or Mercury at the gates of Olympus. His performance would be appreciated for what it was and no more. He would have a small opportunity to point out *Iagomoto's* villainy before turning the stage over to Agrimentikos as *Lodovicomori*, who'd close the piece with a stately speech about honor and love and the weather and whatever moved him. Curtain (well, there was no curtain), applause (or *Adadooskis*) and perhaps a plate of those delicious prune buns, which everyone enjoyed. So Harris counted — first aloud, and then with his internal clock.

"Villany, villany, villany!"

Emiliasan screamed — a bloodcurdling wail, raising the spirit in Greary Gree, if in residence.

> *"Villany, villany, villany!*
> *I think upon't, I think: I smell't: O villany.*
> *I thought so then: — I'll kill myself for grief:*
> *O villany, villany!"*

Tappiolus, the target of these lines, responded angrily:

"What, are you mad? I charge you, get you home."

Emiliasan spun, her robes twirling — a nice effect, if not out-of-place. She fell in a heap before *Othellohito* and *Lodovicomori*.

> *"Good gentlemen, let me have leave to speak:*
> *'Tis proper I obey him, but not now.*
> *Perchance, Iagomoto, I will ne'er go home."*

Suddenly, Arquebus raised his hands and threw himself upon the couch.

> *"O! O! O!"*

Posan crawled along the floor just short of *Othellohito's* robes. With one pleading hand, shaking like a willow tree, Posan had his moment in the moon.

> *"Nay, lay thee down and roar;*
> *For thou hast kill'd the sweetest innocent*
> *That e'er did lift up eye."*

But Arquebus confronted her, flying from the couch and shaking his fists at Posan.

> *"O, she was foul!"*

He turned to *Lodovicomori*:

> *"I scarce did know you, uncle: there lies your niece,*
> *Whose breath, indeed, these hands have newly*
> *   stopp'd:*
> *I know this act shows horrible and grim."*

Harris watched the action, still counting. He needed his rhythm now. He wound his soul like a clock when all hell broke loose on stage as *Othellohito* explained the case — his wife's adulterous actions with foul *Cassioshima*, who still lived — drat him! And how the handkerchief was the evidence. Ask *Iagomoto. He'll tell yer!*

Posan popped up like a crocus in May.

> *"O thou dull Moor! that handkerchief thou speak'st*
> > *of*
> *I found by fortune and did give my husband;*
> *For often, with a solemn earnestness,*
> *More than indeed belong'd to such a trifle,*
> *He begg'd of me to steal it."*

Tappiolus lurched forth in character as Tappiolus, not to say *Iagomoto.*

> *"Villanous whore!"*

Emiliasan protested vehemently.

> *"She give it Cassioshima! no, alas! I found it,*
> *And I did give 't my husband."*

> *"Filth, thou liest!"*

> *"By heaven, I do not, I do not, gentlemen.*
> *O murderous coxcomb! what should such a fool*
> *Do with so good a woman?"*

Arquebus trembled, gripping the air like a tiger, rushing *Iagomoto.*

> *"Are there no stones in heaven*
> *But what serve for the thunder? — Precious*
> > *villain!"*

"*Oginali*, the time is near."

"Yes," Harris stammered, and hoped Little Bird would keep quiet now.

Just as Arquebus reached Posan, Tappiolus stabbed his wife in the back, shouting to the audience (who hissed) and dashing to the exit almost plowing into Harris.

"Out of the way, Boots," he grumbled.

Harris ignored him and continued to count. His moment approached.

3

Arquebus began screaming like a banshee, and turned to Agrimentikos (as *Lodovicomori*) and brandished a dagger — a blade not unlike the one Harris had gifted to Little Bird. He pressed the blade to his chest, pinched in agony.

Count, count, count.

> *"Behold, I have a weapon;*
> *A better never did itself sustain*
> *Upon a soldier's thigh: I have seen the day,*
> *That, with this little arm and this good sword,*
> *I have made my way through more impediments*
> *Than twenty times your stop: but, O vain boast!"*

Arquebus swept about the stage, the blade alternating between his breast and the man who would alter his course.

Count, count, count.

> *"Who can control his fate? 'tis not so now.*
> *Be not afraid, though you do see me weapon'd;*
> *Here is my journey's end, here is my butt,*
> *And very sea-mark of my utmost sail.*
> *Do you go back dismay'd? 'tis a lost fear;*
> *Man but a rush against Othellohito's breast,*
> *And he retires. Where should Othellohito go?"*

He glanced sadly to *Desdemonayama*, and choked back his tears.

> *"Now, how dost thou look now? O ill-starr'd*
> *   wench!*
> *Pale as thy smock! when we shall meet at compt,*
> *This look of thine will hurl my soul from heaven,*
> *And fiends will snatch at it. Cold, cold, my girl!*
> *Even like thy chastity. O cursed slave!"*

He raised his hand high, the hilt clasped in his fists, ready to drive the weapon home.

Count, count, count.

> *"Whip me, ye devils,*
> *From the possession of this heavenly sight!*
> *Blow me about in winds! roast me in sulfur!*
> *Wash me in steep-down gulfs of liquid fire!*
> *O Desdemonayama! Desdemonayama! dead!*
> *Oh! Oh! Oh!"*

This was the moment. Yustichisqua gave his master a push. Harris leaped across the stage, his *getas* impeding progress. But he was infused with the intensity of Arquebus' craft. Harris rushed Arquebus, preventing the inevitable thrust.

> *"Hold thy hand from thy tender breast,*
> *As your mistress yet breathes the evening air."*

Arquebus turned, and Hasamun heaved his chest, the silks rustling. The audience gasped collectively. Harris glided about the couch and raised his hands to frame his lily-white face.

> *"See the gentle mist of life arising from her lips;*
> *The swell of her bosom ever gaining to combat the*
> *gates*
> *Of the hell you would compel her to dwel inl."*

Arquebus turned, about to deliver his next line. But Harris moved, the moment captured by the action.

> *"Sweet friend and captain mine,*
> *Who has taught me the spirit that moves a mortal*
> *soul to war,*
> *And devises the boundaries sweeping a man to*
> *peace,*
> *I implore thee by the love I bear thee to lower thy*
> *beauteous hand*
> *And grieve no more for past offenses."*

Arquebus lowered his hand and began his lines. But Harris grasped his arm — passionately.

> *"If ever a sweet prince did rise upon the air of strife*
> *to guide me,*
> *You, dear friend, have led me to all my*
> *understanding,*
> *Like a father lost in the haze of time's o'erbearing*
> *discipline.*
> *Ah! Ah! Wondrous Othellohito, doubt never your*
> *dear son, for as a son I am,*
> *And like he born from the world of war and peace*
> *Shall settle this stern skirmish between thy*
> *conscience and his mistress."*

He turned to Hasamun, who had delicately raised himself to find a place to insert his lines, no doubt. Not finding it, he sat in wonder. Harris bowed, and then pulled Arquebus' hand toward Hasamun's.

> *"Like the moons in the wake of dawn, may you be*
> *reconciled,*
> *For never was there a quarrel between you.*
> *Good lady forgive my lord for his anxiety and acts,*
> *For you have suffered, but he had suffered all the*
> *more for the love of you.*
> *Pity be thy name, dear soul and take his hand in*
> *gentle c'ress,*
> *Take it and find renewed love within the dawn."*

From where these words were born, Harris couldn't tell. They exploded from him as he joined severed love, and then kissed their hands. Arquebus seemed at a complete loss, but no anger crossed his face. Instead, he clasped Hasamun about the shoulders and covered him with kisses. Harris spread his arms like an eagle, and looked toward the heaped body of *Emiliasan*.

> *"Good Lodovicomori, see that a medico attends to*
> *this faithful woman's wounds,*

For I can see they are not fatal unless the blood has
seeped to the soil in full measure."

Agrimentikos looked to Posan, who stirred. Then Tappiolus strode in from the wings. It looked as if he were about to engage in a bit of extempore himself. But Harris pointed at him.

"Away with him and place him at the bar."

The audience burst into rapturous applause.
Adadooski. Adadooski. Adadooski.
Slowly, Harris bowed, keeping in character as the peacemaker instead of that *deus ex machina,* which had been scribbled for him. He had managed to end the play, although he suspected that Agrimentikos, whose final speech came next, would deliver it, because it was proper. However, Agrimentikos came forward and bowed deeply to Harris, and then raised his hands to signify the piece had been concluded.

4

"Boots," Kuriakis shouted, his voice ringing from one end of the amphitheatre to the other. "Who would have thought such talent dwelled in one so young and within an actor from the flickersphere?" He applauded, amidst the continual cheering and *Adadooski*s. "Such a performance — such presence cannot go unrewarded."

Harris bowed to the Elector, but had enough sense to reach for his brother consorts for a group bow.

"I'm sorry," he whispered to Arquebus.

"Do not be," Arquebus replied. "It was sheer genius. I have not seen such a performance in an age. It came from your lips like Athena born of Zeus."

"Except the last line," Harris admitted. "That was from *The Pirates of Penzance.*"

"The Pirates of what?"

Harris realized Gilbert and Sullivan had their run after Sir John's slip into Farn.

"Never mind. Someday I'll whistle some of it for you."

While the cast preened, Harris observed Kuriakis, who conferred first with Charminus, and then with a wealthy

Zecronisian, whom he later learned was Nikodemos, the chief of the *Zocor* sect — big wigs of the *Wudayleegu*. When the accolades diminished, Kuriakis raised his hand for silence.

"Boots," he shouted again. "Come to me, son."

Harris looked to Agrimentikos, who grinned and to Tappiolus, who didn't. He jumped down awkwardly in his *getas*, and decided he'd be flat on his face if he continued to wear them — so he kicked them off. He knelt before the Elector, who raised him.

"Where is your *Columbincus?*" he asked.

"Under this mound of silk."

"Show it here," Kuriakis snapped, smiling broadly, glancing at Joella, and then to Charminus.

Harris tried his best to push aside the silks, but finally let the shoulder flairs fall, and the *obi* unhitch. Silk is impossible to obliterate. Slipping off his top jacket, he revealed his *Columbincus.* Kuriakis raised his staff, and then brought it down on Harris' head — hard, if he didn't know better. Kuriakis touched the *Columbincus.* It glowed its sapphire shine, but an amber stone appeared above the central gem. It flickered once, and shot a beam over the audience's head. They reacted with *Adadooskis.*

"Lord Belmundus," Kuriakis said. "Since you have expressed an interest to see Montjoy, I charge you with an important responsibility. From this moment, you are appointed the Provost of the *Yuyutlu.* The enforcement of market regulations and fair practices are under your stern eye. May you do me proud . . . Boots."

Harris gasped, and then lowered his head.

"Father," he said, "I'm speechless."

Kuriakis laughed.

"Now, now, none of that. For a man who has just enraptured all *Ayelli* with a speech as long as the Forling is wide, I would not call you speechless."

Everyone present could agree with that. Harris stood and noticed that everyone was bowing to him, even Tappiolus, who probably cringed in the gesture. Only two did not bow — Littafulchee, who appeared afraid of the act, and Yustichisqua, who had sworn an oath never to bow to Lord Belmundus again. The first puzzled Harris, but the second pleased him beyond measure — almost beyond being appointed as the Provost of the *Yuyutlu.*

Chapter Nine

Danuwa and Taleenay

1

In Brunting Day's afterglow, activity swept Harris. Kuriakis had bestowed an honor on him. But Harris soon realized it wasn't an empty show — a title without responsibilities. Evidently, there had not been a Provost — *a Didaniyisgi* appointed in Montjoy since Tappiolus' captaincy of the Yunockers. Duties and obligations were attached to the title. Of course, he was obliged to both the Elector and Scepta Charminus. She had suggested this reward, most likely responding to Harris' insistence on visiting Montjoy. Now he would go, not as a tourist, but as some mucky-muck *Ayelli* with his own entourage. His first act was to thank Charminus.

The Scepta remained unconcerned, regarding the thanks as excessive and, shortly thereafter, went into labor. The gestation period may have been brief in Farn, still birthing was painful. Harris didn't stick around to see or hear it, although Charminus' wails could be heard throughout *Mortis House.* Instead, Harris commiserated with Tappiolus, who appeared unconcerned.

"She will not die in the act," he explained. "When it is born, send around a gift and nothing more will be said on the matter."

More to the point, Tappiolus had an interest in Harris' choice of marshals. A *Didaniyisgi* was required to choose three marshals — *the Danuwa*, to aid him in his tasks — an entourage, if you will. These he would select from the Thirdlings. Harris' own choice would have been from Soffira and Miracola's established Thirdling pool, but the rules were firm. *The Danuwa* must represent each Scepta — thus, one Thirdling from each household. So, Harris chose Parnasus, Posan's sixth son from Miracola's brood and Elypticus from Soffira's, in part to make amends to the lad for his treatment after the *Cabriolin* race. Still, Harris needed to select one of Tappiolus' offspring — reluctantly. Tappiolus would certainly seed the selection with a spy. Who needed *the Eye* when a whole body would do fine if not better? To balance things, Harris decided upon Mihela, Tappiolus' fourth daughter. She had many of Charminus' traits, but Harris could live with those.

"Mihela is destined for Aolium," Tappiolus explained. "Daughters are easy pieces in the political game, Boots. No, no, no. I insist you choose from among my sons. In fact, I have one who could benefit from the light touch of this experience and the easy tasks."

And if this son needed to break out, Harris thought, *why hadn't Tappiolus employed him as Danuwa in his own captaincy?*

"Yes, Boots, I insist you cast a favorable eye on Melonius."

Harris found it curious that Melonius happened to be standing about ready to appear at a finger's click. He was handsome enough and going on four years old — a bit short by Thirdling standards, perhaps five foot eight, but he grinned like a porcupine and had an inquisitive eye.

Yes, the Eye.

"Why, here he is, Boots."

Melonius approached, bowing.

"Lord Belmundus," he said, his voice squeaking and his manner ingratiating.

No wonder no female Thirdling from the other realms held an interest in this one. Still, Harris had to pick someone from Charminus' brood. He wished he had cavorted with them, to judge them better.

"Your father tells me you have an adventuresome spirit," Harris said, in his best interviewing voice.

"I might," Melonius replied. "One needs to take adventures to know if the spirit favors them."

Queer thought.

"Would you like to tag along with me to *the Yuyutlu* and see if adventure suits you?"

"Who else have you chosen?"

"Parnasus and Elypticus," Harris replied.

"They still need to be confirmed," Tappiolus chuffed.

"As would your son," Harris countered. "Now that Brunting has finished and our lady has drawn her mother's attention to the new baby, I believe our lord is free to evaluate my choices."

"And who shall act as your *Taleenay*?" Melonius asked.

The *Taleenay* acted as the Provost's right-hand — his second, and was usually appointed from the three *Danuwa,* but not always. Harris saw the game. Tappiolus was maneuvering his son into *the Taleenay's* position. But Harris already had resolved the issue.

"Yustichisqua is my *Taleenay*."

Tappiolus flinched, his lower jaw jittering. He turned away.

"Who is this Yustichisqua?" Melonius asked. "From which Scepta's brood is he?"

"Enough," Tappiolus snapped. "Yustichisqua is Lord Belmundus' Trone."

"His Trone?"

"My *Noya Tludachi*," Harris replied. "If you join with me, Melonius, you must see things in a new light."

Melonius glanced at his father, his expression clearly asking *must I, father?* Of course, he must. This Thirdling was useless as a pawn in the foreseeable future. His only use, besides singing witty songs to damsel Thirdlings or playing *grusoker* with his pals, was to be his father's eyes and ears against this *new light*.

"I believe," Tappiolus said to Melonius. "I believe my brother is an experimenter, commendable on some level. Our lord, Kuriakis might support experimentation within reason. So, Melonius, if Lord Belmundus decides on you, you must be thankful for the opportunity and accept your company as designed."

No joy stood in the eyes of either father or son. Still, Melonius no more commanded his fate than any Thirdling. So he grinned dimly and bowed to Harris — a half-assed bow without conviction. When Parnasus had accepted the appointment, he performed a hand ceremony Posan had taught him — a tradition of Shantung province. Elypticus had accepted the appointment sprawled on his chest, weeping thanks to Lord Belmundus. Harris would need to be happy with Melonius' nod, because no other ready choice was available in Charminus' brood.

"Then, it's decided," Harris said. "Come to me tomorrow and we shall deck you out in a uniform." He turned to Tappiolus. "Don't fret, brother. Yustichisqua will not murder your son in his sleep. Even though I'm permitting him to retrieve his dagger from the holy display case."

"Is that wise?"

"Wisdom has nothing to do with it, brother."

"Will our lord approve?"

"We shall see." Harris winked. "We shall see."

2

As the season ripened and Harris prepared to leave for his post, Kuriakis stirred. When Kuriakis stirred, all creatures knew it.

"The sky is green today," Yustichisqua noted. "The Elector stirs."

Harris confirmed the unusual hue which wrapped the sky. He had expected it. Both Arquebus and Agrimentikos had warned him about anxieties brewing in other realms. Neither consort gave a precise explanation. However, political conflict had been looming for a few centuries and would not easily dissipate.

"It is a matter of *the aniniya*," Agrimentikos noted.

Aniniya was that precious power source — the mineral Harris called *the stuff*. Mined in Terrastrium, it did not belong to that realm exclusively. The Terrastriums thrived on *Aniniya*, but seldom transformed it beyond its raw state, only shaping it for the bare requirements, crafting it into lamps and weapons and excavation tools. Otherwise they exported *the stuff*. Collective laws regulated *aniniya's* application in Farn, or so Agrimentikos told Harris. However, Farn law went beyond everyone except Electors and their councils. Evidently, changes in *aniniya* production drew concern from Protractus and Aolium, Montjoy's chief allies.

"The lord of Zin has been active lately," Arquebus explained.

Harris remembered Zin from his orientation at *the Cartisforium*. Zin's projection was so horrific, he had kept his eyes shut. The stench still lingered in recall. But neither Arquebus nor Agrimentikos offered specifics about Zin's current activities, because consorts possessed no such detailed knowledge.

"We are not the arbitrators of realms," Arquebus stated. "The less we understand the better."

Harris was made of sterner stuff. He was curious — inquisitive, especially when others withheld information intentionally. Still, he had too much on his mind to undertake a study of Farn politics and metallurgical regulations. That was the Electors' job. His was to mitigate disputes between local merchants and artisans, inlander cultures beyond his ken at the moment. He would depend upon Little Bird to give him a leg up.

Little Bird seemed to know much for one so young. Harris only hoped by appointing Yustichisqua as his second — the *Taleenay*, he hadn't doomed him to punishment. Tappiolus might be a bastard, but had enough commonality to suggest that Kuriakis sometimes acted upon whim. Certainly, allowing a Trone free will was whimsical. Definitely, Harris' appointment as *Didaniyisgi* had been novel too.

"Such a sky," Yustichisqua repeated. "When it hangs like this, the Elector is anxious."

"Like a mood ring?" Harris asked. "Where I come from there's a stone that changes color with mood swings. Body temperature broadcasts change."

"Ah," Little Bird said. "The sky is like that sometimes. It tells us when rain is coming or dust storms — even snow. But when it is green, it tells us the Elector stirs about his palace. We should take care, *oginali.*"

We should, Harris thought. *A good time to get out of Dodge.*

Then the three *Danuwa* arrived, accompanied by Buhippus and seven Yunockers.

"Lord Belmundus," Buhippus said, nodding graciously. "Prepare to leave, if you will."

"Is it wise under the circumstances?" Harris asked, pointing to the sky.

"It is," came a voice from behind the squadron. Agrimentikos. "Your choices have been confirmed. We should leave immediately."

"Brother," Harris said. "I'm anxious to get going, but why the hurry; and why do I need this *posse?*"

He swept his hand past Buhippus and the squadron.

"Ah. *Posse*, you say," Agrimentikos replied. "I know this term from Tappiolus. It is a deputation of men charged temporarily with legal authority, is it not?"

"Yes."

"I assure you, there is nothing temporary about it," Agrimentikos said. "These Yunockers have been assigned to your safety. Captain Buhippus will attend us to assure the case."

"To assure the case," Buhippus echoed.

The three *Danuwa* came forward.

"We have come, Lord Belmundus," Elypticus announced, much passion in his voice.

"I am ready to serve," Parnasus echoed.

This lad was tall and willowy, a replica of his father, Posan. He had none of his mother's fleshy acreage. Harris had taken a shine to him, choosing him over several other Thirdlings in Miracola's brood. Harris noticed Melonius remained silent — no bow or nod or expression, except a hint of arrogance. Melonius' nose twitched as if he smelled a bad odor.

Harris turned to Yustichisqua.

"Little Bird," he said. "Take my marshals to their new uniforms."

Yustichisqua touched his belt — a new belt, where his dagger hung. His hand tapped the hilt, his adaptation of a salute. As *Taleenay*, he also wore a new uniform — a crimson tunic, a leather kilt, a short silver cape and a small gold box cap with a sapphire top button and tied beneath his chin so he wouldn't lose it in the wind. Simple and sleek, but impressive compared with many outfits worn by Thirdlings in the *Ayelli*.

Little Bird led the *Danuwa* into a dressing room. They followed tenuously, as if to do so would recognize this Trone as their better. The fact that Lord Belmundus had named him *Taleenay* swept all questions aside. For a moment, Harris thought Melonius wouldn't follow, but Agrimentikos came forward, placing his arm around the recalcitrant Thirdling's shoulder.

"Ah, a new uniform, Melonius," he said. "Let me see what my brother consort has concocted for you three."

Agrimentikos winked at Harris, and then ushered Melonius away, leaving Lord Belmundus alone with his unwanted guard and their proud captain.

3

After a nervous silence, Harris dared to stare down Buhippus, who had taken a sentry's stance on his *zulus*.

"The sky is different today, captain," Harris said. "I know the significance."

"Do you now, my lord?" Buhippus said, bristling. "With luck, the Elector will mount his steed and proceed to Protractus to conclude his business. Until then, Montjoy shall be a gloomy place. The Sceptas will be out of sorts. The Thirdlings will not play games. *The Scullery Dorgan* will go on half rations. Even the garden will withhold its fragrance. The sooner we descend into the valley, the better."

"An ill omen, you think?"

Buhippus drifted to Harris' side.

"I would not concern yourself with Lord Kuriakis' disposition. When the sky is . . . that color, he sometimes changes his mind about things. Lord Agrimentikos feared our lord might recall his generosity in this quarter of the household, even though he had issued his confirmation of your selections. Lord Agrimentikos feared the Elector might pay you a visit. He still might do so."

"He has never done it before, but he would be welcomed, I assure you."

Buhippus laughed. Harris didn't care for the mirth, especially at his expense.

"Trust me, my lord; you would not want to chance it."

"I know he sometimes acts upon a whim," Harris said. "But he certainly hasn't acted in secret."

"He can be private or public as he sees fit. It doesn't matter." Buhippus came close to Harris' eye. "Kuriakis *is* Montjoy. If he farts, we all smell it. If he dances with the Memer, we all rejoice. But when the sky turns . . ." He pointed.

Time to get out of Dodge.

"I thank you for the warning," Harris said, reluctantly.

"We are not enemies, Lord Belmundus." Buhippus let his feet touch the ground. "The fact that I am regulated by Lord Tappiolus has on no occasion shaded my judgment of you or your actions."

"Are you my judge?"

"I am a Yunocker. We are the heirs to the valley."

"That means your people conquered it like a bunch of Aztecs dancing over the people of the corn."

Buhippus cocked his head, clearly missing the allusion.

"We were the masters of the land, true," he said. "The Cetrones once held that distinction, but they are saddled by the promise and prophecy. We are not. *The Ayelli* are saddled by it also. The Yunockers are still the masters of our race. Greater powers have transformed us into tributaries, but not slaves, Lord Belmundus. Not slaves."

Harris was glad to hear these words, because they informed, although he had no idea what *the promise and prophecy* had to do with the relationship of the conquered, the masters and the House of Montjoy.

"I have much to learn," Harris admitted.

"You have, and in that gap you have cast aside sacred order. I must tell you that I am tolerant — more tolerant than most Yunockers."

Harris was puzzled. He had regarded Buhippus as an unmitigated bigot.

"You refer to my treatment of Yustichisqua."

"Trones are not treated by *the Ayelli*. They serve. They are an extension of want and fulfillment. They fetch, carry and, in Montjoy they are the shadows of this world. How you have convinced the Elector to permit a slave to be addressed, shuck the *zulus*, wear finery, carry a weapon and be titled, is beyond me. However, I am tolerant and respectful. I recognize as truth anything called as such by the great Kuriakis. And to that end, I can admire you, Lord Belmundus, for taking a sacred vessel and dashing it on the tiles without cutting your feet on the shards."

Buhippus bowed.

"I have much to learn, captain, but I also have much to teach."

"I am tolerant, but I am a poor student when the lessons defy natural order. One kernel in an ear of *quillerfoil* can rot the entire crop. However, a harvest can be destroyed before reaped and pounded into use."

Harris grinned.

"Is that a warning, Buhippus?"

"Advice, my lord. Many have no capacity for tolerance. Some are standing behind me now. If I were not here, they might have drawn their *Sticks* and removed your new *Taleenay*'s cap, and perhaps might have inadvertently taken off his head. In the valley, you will find many who hold these sentiments to their hearts, and some who would harvest the *quillerfoil* with flame and not apologize later."

Harris sighed. At least the man was being honest. Perhaps Buhippus would prove essential to this enterprise. Harris pictured wagons filled with vigilantes in white hoods riding through the valley, snatching every *uppity* Cetrone within reach and lynching them on the nearest *phitron* wall. He had more questions for this chief Yunocker, but before he could engage his next sentence, Agrimentikos returned with a dazzling display of *Danuwa*.

4

"Brilliant," Harris said, applauding his three marshals as they reentered the hall.

Uniform, except in color — Elypticus in ivory, Parnasus in goldenrod and Melonius in mauve. Each *Danuwa* wore a metallic tunic with pleated kilt. Each sported a braided belt with an array of badges and weapons — a dagger, a *Stick* and a short sword. Three capes rustled in the breeze, and, upon their noggins, helmets topped with tanager plumes like fiery cock crests. They bowed (Melonius a bit off the mark), stunning to behold — an extension of their lord's ermine cape and golden-laurel lid.

"Xyftys does splendid work," Agrimentikos remarked.

"He does, indeed," Harris said. "I must send a gift around to express my satisfaction."

"Please, Lord Belmundus," Agrimentikos coached. "You mean to spoil all the races. If you were to overpay Xyftys, the price of mending our socks will increase by three *yedalas* a pair. Leave well enough alone. He is overpriced as it is. Besides, you must learn about the economy now that you are in charge of the marketplace."

Harris agreed with this sentiment. He had much to learn. However, he was proud of this sight — his three *Danuwa* and his *Taleenay*, arrayed before a squadron of turkey-feathered Yunockers and one cocky captain of the guard. They would make an impressive entrance into *the Wudayleegu*. The Zecronisian reception committee couldn't fail to regard their new Provost with respect. Still, they hadn't had a Provost within the memory of a single lifetime, so the novelty might be just that. Despite his elation, Harris recognized vanity when he saw it and spotted his own particularly well. He was a star, after all. He shook it off, looked toward the sky and grimaced.

"If only the Elector didn't stir," he muttered.

"It will fade when he departs for the council," Agrimentikos said. "It is best we depart while it is pale green. When it turns olive, we would best be grounded." He looked toward Buhippus. "Good captain, what strategy do you propose?"

"Our *Cabriolins* are standing at the ready," he replied. "I shall lead with half my squadron. *The Didaniyisgi* will follow with his *Taleenay*. The three *Danuwa* can V-form behind him. Then you, my lord can stay as drogue. We shall bypass Montjoy and the *Yuyutlu*."

"Bypass the city?" Harris asked.

"Yes, my lord. It is best to go through the *Yugda Yustiganu*."

"The Yugda . . ."

"*Yugda Yustiganu, oginali*," Little Bird said. "The Ravine Road going to the sea and the *Wudayleegu*."

"Wise," Agrimentikos remarked.

"But isn't that like sneaking in the back door?" Harris asked.

"While the Elector stirs," Buhippus explained, "any large *Cabriolin* convoy approaching Montjoy or *the Yuyutlu* would cause undue anxiety."

"Besides, Lord Belmundus," Agrimentikos said, "it would be improper for you to be introduced into the marketplace before meeting with the Zocor council. Nikodemos can be a prickly character when he wants to press his authority."

Harris nodded his assent, and then raised his arms toward his *Danuwa*.

"I have one more gift for each," he said. "Yustichisqua."

Little Bird scurried to a display case in the *mathom* collection, snatching three small velvet boxes. He carried these to Harris, who took them up.

"Here! Catch!" He tossed them unceremoniously to each of the marshals, who, unprepared, fumbled to catch them. "Well, open them. Open them."

As *the Danuwa* flipped the box lids up, their faces blossomed collectively. Even Melonius' dour puss changed for the better.

"Rings," Elypticus announced, popping his out and holding it to his eye.

"Not just rings," Harris said. "They are seals of your authority to be used when I am away attending the Scepta and you are toiling on my behalf."

Parnasus slipped his ring on, and then knelt.

"Now, none of that," Harris said. He glanced to Buhippus. "I'm not a king or a blue-blood and I don't cotton kindly to all this bowing and scraping. I'm just a kid from California who just happened to have my fly opened on a moonlit night near the Bowery."

"Not so," Agrimentikos chided. "You were selected and drawn for your strength of character and for your ability to portray the noblest of your race. Never think or say otherwise. Whether you wish those about you to bow and scrape is another matter and depends on . . ." He pointed to the sky. "It depends on the color of the sky and how our world is tuned to the lord of these realms. Never forget it, Lord Belmundus."

Harris shrugged, but looked again at the sky. No matter how he would ultimately handle the obeisance of others, it was time *to get out of Dodge* or at least drift down from *the Ayelli* through the *Yugda Yustiganu* and arrive at the edge of the sea.

Chapter Ten

In the Wudayleegu

1

A mist hung across the invisible gate. A Yunocker convoy met Lord Belmundus' entourage, halting Buhippus short of the boundary between *the Ayelli* and Montjoy proper. While Buhippus explained their mission to the guards, Harris glanced at the gulf below, which separated hill from valley. The terrain puzzled him.

"Little Bird," he said. "What lies at that pit's bottom?"

"I do not know, *oginali*. There are many tales and rumors."

Harris twisted, glancing at his Dune Tygger, who seemed to know everything else.

"You can tell me. I can keep a secret."

"There is nothing to tell," Yustichisqua replied, shrugging. "I cross the pit on *zulus*. My *waddly wazzoo* does not stay lit when I pass. Some say it is a passage between the realms of light and darkness. As children, we are told *the Zinbear* dwells below — a monster with twelve heads that devours light, extinguishing it forever. But it is a tale to scare children. We shall never know, because no one, not even the Elector ventures there."

Harris regarded the rift, realizing it grew shallower at one end and, at that end, it formed a promontory, cutting the hills into a canyon.

"And there?"

"That is *the Yugda Yustiganu, oginali*."

"Our way?"

"Yes. That is why *the Zinbear* stories must be false. If true, it could climb out and devour all the light in Montjoy."

"Which it hasn't."

"No. There is light to spare, for we keep it sacred for all. A thankless task, but our duty."

Harris saw that. Why did a people, who preserved light in a land powered by *the stuff* be regarded abysmally?

"We are summoned, *oginali*."

Harris saw Buhippus signal him to come, so he maneuvered *the Cabriolin* to the fore, Agrimentikos joining him. Two lords were better than one. However, what caused the delay, Harris couldn't guess. Wisely, he announced himself.

"What seems to be the hold up, Captain Buhippus?"

"It is unseemly to keep consorts in queue," Agrimentikos complained.

Buhippus raised his hand, indicating his regal charges.

"Here is proof enough," Buhippus said to the sentries. "Proof that *the Ayelli* travel during *Yichiyusti*."

"Green sky days," Little Bird whispered to Harris as his ever-present translator.

"Indeed," Harris piped. "I'm the new *Didaniyisgi* of *the Yuyutlu* and I go to *the Wudayleegu* through *the Yugda Yustiganu*. How dare you question the Elector's mandate?"

The sentry twitched, and then bowed. Buhippus grinned, and Agrimentikos nodded as if to say *that was a mouthful, but you nailed it.* Harris was an actor, after all, and lines are lines. However, he wouldn't chance repeating that *mouthful* any time soon.

"Pardon us, Lord Belmundus," the sentry said. "It has not been the custom for *the Ayelli* to travel during *Yichiyusti*." He pointed skyward. "However, I now see that you do."

"And I shall." Harris turned his *Cabriolin* about, returning to his place in the formation. "Lead on, Captain Buhippus," he shouted.

The sentries parted and the entourage crossed *the Zinbear's* lair, steeply banking right, following the promontory to *the Yugda*'s entrance.

"How did I do?" Belmundus whispered to Yustichisqua.

"I must teach you the correct pronunciation on some words, *oginali*, but I think you were clear enough."

"Well, we're jugging through *the Yugda*, aren't we?" He laughed, and glanced through the approaching mist, which clung to the canyon's walls.

The *Yugda Yustiganu* was alpine, although the two mountains forming the ravine weren't precipitously high. However, the gorge was deep. The haze lent it a charged atmosphere — one wrapped in mystery. Harris kept an eye on the verdant slopes, where shadows drifted. He thought of *the Zinbear*, Mama Monster leading baby monsters along the cleft to lash at *the Cabriolins*. Then he spotted flocks of lavender sheep — or at least they looked like sheep, larger than the kind that jumped dream fences, but fleecy, nonetheless.

"*Awidena*," Yustichisqua said. "Good to wear, to eat and to drink."

"A regular department store on legs," Harris remarked. "And those?"

"*Tludachi*," Little Bird said.

"Tyggers?" Harris mused. "They look more like lions than the beast I killed in the Forling."

"These are *Odala Tludachi* — Mountain Tyggers."

They appeared as fierce as their majestic Serengeti cousins, stalking their prey until the chase began, although sheep were no contest for lions or tyggers or *Zinbears* — life in all its food-chain elegance in universal, even in this realm's membrane.

Ahead, the mist dispelled, the green sky palled, shrouding the land gap. Buhippus banked left, and then right, and then left again following *the Yugda's* sharp contour. As they maneuvered, they descended to a lower altitude. The vegetation — wild *jomar* and voluntary *quillerfoil,* brushed beneath *the Cabriolin* jets as they skirted *the Yugda's* ledge. Then the land fell away, a rift opening over symmetric fields — acreage of manicured farmland. Harris was hooded farmers tilling, while others tended the small gardens. He couldn't tell whether these were Cetrone or Yunockers. Perhaps, both. But the sights were fleeting, because the rift widened, dropping off into majestic palisades. Beyond was . . . the sea.

"*The Amaykwohi*," Yustichisqua gasped. "I have never seen it, *oginali.* My mother once told me of it. She was born near here before the invasion."

"Before the invasion?"

"Yes, *oginali.*"

Harris supposed there was more than one invasion — Yunocker, *Ayelli*, Montjoy and perhaps a team of hot coal-dancing Hottentots for all he knew, so he didn't dissect the history behind this statement. But Yustichisqua's amazement took him — a boy's enlightenment, as if he had seen his first bare breast in a brothel's quiet shadow. But this wasn't a bare breast. This was the sea — vast and powerful, stretching to the beyond — no horizon, because there were no horizons in Farn — only sky, and today that sky was as green as the *Yugda Yustiganu.*

"It's beautiful," Harris said, as *the Cabriolins* dipped over a town.

"You have seen it before, *oginali?*"

"Not this sea, although all seas might be one sea connecting distant shores."

This gave him the idea the sea could be a portal of sorts. He remembered in the Plageris the sea could have bordered Coney Island, or so he had hoped. He peered down at the town.

"Is that *the Wudayleegu?*"

"The Zecronisian quarter. Yes."

Agrimentikos' *Cabriolin* inched beside Harris'.

"Look and see, brother," Agrimentikos harked — a merry hark, in opposition to the sky's gloom. *"The Wudayleegu."*

A forest of minarets and pagodas towered over a sprawl of tent-like structures — yurts and pavilions, which could have been tents. If these were stone, it was the most elastic stone Harris had ever encountered. A palace stood at the town's center, a bulbous dome dominating the roof's twist — an inverted replica of the Guggenheim, to Harris' mind. Then his breath hitched. Despite the fantastic architecture, the port captivated more.

A swath of docks hugged the sea girt — bays wide and narrow and fully deployed to the shipping business. Despite the gloomy advent of *Yichiyusti*, the port buzzed with activity. If less active now because of the green sky, it must be hectic under blue skies. However, what took Harris' breath away were the ships, an eclectic assortment of sailing ships — some single-masted in *trireme* style, others three-masted caravels. Tug boats were also docked. They could have come from New York Harbor. *Daubs* from the Indian Ocean and junks from the South China Sea plied the waves. So many sails flapped with a symphony of so many styles confirming *the Amaykwohi* as the connective tissue between the realms and the outlands.

These ships must come from somewhere . . . and they must be going back. Harris' heart pounded. Where there are ports, there are ships and where there are ships, there are sailors and sailors . . . tell tales. Yes, sailors tell tales of places and, perhaps in those tales was a grain that tasted like Brooklyn or, better yet, Santa Monica, somewhere on the other side of these waters, her amusement pier spreading a welcome mat at the far side of the world. It had to be so.

Harris closed his eyes and descended into the world of the Zecronisians.

2

Buhippus brought the convoy down in a grassy park before the palace. He raised his hand to keep everyone in their *Cabriolins*.

"Why are we waiting?" Harris mused.

"I know not, *oginali*."

"The Zecronisians are given to ritual," Agrimentikos stated. "Although they are tributary to *the Ayelli* and bow to the House of Montjoy, they must still welcome us formally. We are a delegation."

A horn sounded and a beast resembling a small elephant, only fully carpeted with two trunks and horns instead of tusks, approached, a richly attired Zecronisian riding in a *howdah* on the beast's back. Two squadrons of half-naked soldiers marched on each side of the beast, holding halberds at one o'clock. Floating on each flank were Yunockers, *zulus* firmly in place — *Sticks* drawn. The Zecronisians' third leg flapped behind them like a tail and, when the procession stopped, the legs extended, allowing them to sit — fleshy tripods. The Zecronisians Harris had encountered on *the Ayelli* were fully robed and decorously attired, never displaying their third appendage.

Buhippus dismounted from his *Cabriolin,* and then approached Harris.

"Lord Belmundus," he said, bowing. "The Zocor delegate is here to welcome you to *the Wudayleegu*. However, he is merely an usher in Nikodemos' household. You are expected to express indignation to this slight. It is a breach in protocol. He will tell you, after many apologies, it is not a slight, but in keeping with the green sky. Otherwise, Nikodemos would have come in person. However, your response to the insult is expected and will be tolerated as it is customary."

Harris twitched. He wasn't in the least insulted. Sending an elephant, a squad of three-legged men and an array of Yunockers seemed a fine reception to him. However, Agrimentikos' words echoed in his mind.

The Zecronisians are given to ritual.

"Well," Harris muttered to the captain, "I'm an actor, am I not? I can do *insulted* and *slighted*. Watch and learn."

"I need not learn things I can do without pretense, my lord."

Buhippus grinned, and bowed again. Harris pointed to the ground, and Yustichisqua disembarked, nodding to the Provost. Harris hopped down, turning to his *Danuwa* three, who came to his side. Glancing at each in turn, he gave Agrimentikos a sly look — the fish-eye and a wink.

"Follow my lead, my brave and worthy marshals."

Harris strutted to the entourage, who kept to their third legs. The Yunockers fidgeted, sniffing and disconsolate. But Buhippus raised his *Stick*, returning them to order. Harris knew these warriors had sniffed Yustichisqua. The sight of a richly adorned Trone out of *zulus* upset their apple cart. Buhippus was deterrent enough.

The delegate stood in his *howdah*, the beast — which Harris later learned was called a *gufa* (he would call it a *Goofy Goofer*), rested with the ease of a meadowed cow. The delegate waved open hands in welcome. He was an old man, a fact Harris half regretted.

"*Didaniyisgi Belmundus,*" the old man croaked. "Welcome to *the Wudayleegu*, where you shall find our spirits atuned to aid your mission to the *Yuyutlu*. Long have the Zecronisians looked to the Elector's support to preserve the balance of the marketplace."

Harris turned his back on the old man. The attendants grunted — an expected reaction.

"I'm appalled," Harris shouted. "I'm a deputy from *the Ayelli*, appointed by the Great Kuriakis. I've traveled far and long. And what do I find? Am I greeted by Nikodemos? Has the Zocor turned out to celebrate my arrival? Is there a general celebration — a feast, dancing girls, the port closed in my honor? Where is the band? Just a single farting horn and an array of naked minions. I've a mind to return to *the Ayelli* and ask the Zocor council to come and fetch me, after they apologize to the Elector and . . . to Memer Joella."

All this time, he winked at his entourage. He turned again to the old man. Harris stood like Samson challenging the Philistines. The minions retracted their third legs, helping *the gufa* to its feet.

"Lord Belmundus," the old man whimpered. "Lord Belmundus. Lord Belmundus."

Get on with it, Harris thought.

"I'm here. I'm listening."

"Forgive our appalling display, but you must realize it is *Yichiyusti*. What greater insult could we level upon Great Kuriakis than to celebrate your arrival when he stirs? I promise you a grander welcome when the sky turns. We welcome friend and stranger alike, but when it comes to the new *Didaniyisgi,* we shall declare a holiday . . . but not during *Yichiyusti."*

Harris nodded.

"I understand," he said, coolly. "I expect accommodations for me and my fellows, which exceed your own."

"Indeed, it shall be so." The delegate pointed to a ridge of buildings at the park's far end — buildings made from that tent-like material, pliant as silk, but resilient like alabaster. "Until the heavens smile again, you shall know no want."

Suddenly, one of the Yunockers drifted to the *howdah* and whispered something to the old one.

"Ah," the delegate said. "Yes. How foolish of me. You are all welcomed here, but we shall offer a separate and comfortable room for your Trone."

He bowed, but before he could raise his head, Harris threw off the actor, jumping into a rage.

"I have no Trone," he shouted. "How dare you, sir? How dare you separate the *Didaniyisgi* from his *Taleenay?"*

Harris reached *the gufa*, whose big ivory eyes gazed sheepishly at him. But the minions were alarmed. So were the Yunockers. This sudden genuine burst of ire wasn't in the script. Harris raised his *Stick,* and then drew his sword.

"Let every one hear me," he shouted. "I shall not repeat it. All members of my household, regardless of race, culture or position are worthy of me, and I am worthy of Kuriakis. Insult my *Taleenay* and you will find yourself at my sword's edge. Say it twice and I promise summary justice."

Buhippus intervened, as did Agrimentikos. They didn't chastise Harris or cast him in a bad light, but since two of *the Danuwa* appeared fierce enough to go to the mat for their Provost, it was clear the delegate had made a colossal error.

"Apologize at once to the *Didaniyisgi*," Buhippus snapped.

He also glanced to the Yunockers — those with the delegate and those with the Provost.

"At once, Lord Belmundus," the old one wailed. "I did not realize that you . . . that you."

"Leave it at that," Buhippus said. "Now, I am sure Lord Belmundus the Just, whose magnanimity goes beyond all doubt, will accept your apology for all the transgressions laid at his feet on this field of honor."

Harris blew out a long bull's snort, but one of relief. He glanced at Yustichisqua, who appeared near tears. This was enough to stir Harris again, but he turned about like a spoiled child. Perhaps he *was* a spoiled child. Then his glance caught the Yunockers, and then Melonius. If it wasn't for Kuriakis' support, Little Bird would be a goner. Harris stood firm.

"Accepted," he shouted, and then with less intensity, he nodded. "Accepted. Lead us to these most excellent quarters that shall leave me and mine without want."

The old one sat, relief blossoming across his face. The *gufa* was poked into motion and the delegation trundled toward the tent-like accommodations. Harris' entourage remounted their *Cabriolins*. The crisis was over.

"I guess I went overboard," Harris muttered as he passed Buhippus and Agrimentikos.

"An actor's prerogative," Agrimentikos noted.

"Never apologize, my lord," Buhippus said. "It is a sign of weakness if you are to be who you are."

Harris stopped, glancing deeply into Buhippus' eyes. Yes, there was value having this policeman along for the ride.

"Good of you to say it, captain."

"It makes me neither friend nor enemy, my lord. But it is easier to keep you alive if you exude an authoritative spark. If you were to let them take *the Taleenay* away to separate quarters, you would have been appointing a new *Taleenay* in the morning."

Harris shuddered. When would this world give him the peace of mind he craved? He supposed it was much like all places.

He hopped into the *Cabriolin*, grasping Yustichisqua's arm.

"A close call, my friend," he said.

Little Bird touched his dagger in the new salute.

"I have used this before, *oginali*. If needed, I would use it again."

Harris was glad to hear it.

The entourage moved slowly behind the trundling Goofy Goofer toward the most excellent quarters in *the Wudayleegu.*.

Chapter Eleven

Garan the Gucheeda

1

Lord Belmundus was taken to the Pavilion of Light or *Lyspykyn* in Gurt, the language of building in the *Wudayleegu*. Harris thought it aptly named because the rippling pseudocanvas of stone proved thin and porous, *the Yichiyusti* green sky seeping through, adding a mossy glow to the billowy light that rippled across floor tiles. The main room had been prepared to entertain the entourage — platforms piled like ziggurats, covered with victuals of untold variety. Harris didn't recognized the banquet food, nor did Yustichisqua. Still, the aromas were delectable. Many stomachs rumbled, but also many eyes stared at a dozen scantily clad maidens, who coaxed their guests to feast. A curiously dressed steward presided. He had olive skin and a protruding jaw. A Gurt. He greeted Lords Belmundus and Agrimentikos.

"I am Fytzyfu," he said. "I am here to attend to your every need. May I suggest you retire to your rooms before the feast and shake the travel from your cloaks."

He bowed again.

"Good notion, that," Harris said to all, although he saw the Yunockers drooling for the women and *the Danuwa* salivating for the food. It should have been the other way around. Still, he signaled to Agrimentikos, who cocked his head. "Shall we?"

"You rest, Lord Belmundus," Agrimentikos replied. "I see a particular beauty who shall shake the travel from my cloak better than a bounce on soft satin."

He winked, drifting past Fytzyfu to a voluptuous green-haired Zecronisian, who sported three globular breasts (like a pawn shop's marquee). She beckoned him with her third leg.

"Very well," Harris said, and then looked to Fytzyfu for directions.

The rooms were partitioned from the central court by that wondrous material — a fascination to Harris. He touched the walls as he entered his assigned quarters, glancing at Yustichisqua for an explanation.

"I do not know, *oginali*." Little Bird brought his hand to it, trying to penetrate it. "It is not *kaybar*. That I would know."

"Yes. Whatever it is, it beats plastic."

"Plastic?"

"A material used for all kinds of shit in my world — pliable and elastic, but not biodegradable."

"Biodegradable?"

"Never mind. I guess your quarters are through there." Then he thought. "You might want to find yourself one of those lassies and have yourself an evening of it."

"Lassies?"

"The women, Little Bird. Don't you do women in *the Kalugu?*"

"Of course, we do. That is why *the Kalugu* is over populated. Our menfolk have difficulty keeping control over their *gugubasgi* — penises."

"Well, if that's the case . . ."

"But these . . . lassies are not Cetrone."

"That doesn't seem to bother anyone else."

"It would bother them because I am Cetrone. They would not share their bed with me."

"Not even for many *yedalas*."

"Not for one of the moons, would they. Cetrone mate only with Cetrone."

Harris tried the bed — soft as *awidena* fleece. He rubbed his hands along its length.

"I'll sleep tonight."

"Then, *oginali*, you will not be riding a Zecronisian lassie also?"

"Don't be a smart-ass, Yustichisqua. After fucking Charminus for two weeks straight, this is a holiday. I don't understand how Agrimentikos can jump into the saddle so fast."

"He has been with Scepta Soffira for centuries, *oginali*. I guess he craves some *caliseegee* in his *kawee*."

Centuries, Harris thought. A chill overcame him.

"Your analysis isn't comforting."

"Perhaps after a few centuries, you will seek variety too."

Harris had to laugh. He sat on the bed. He was ferociously hungry, but wasn't sure whether the aromas were attached to things he could eat or things which could eat him.

"I'm hungry."

"I shall fetch you a plate, *oginali*."

But before Harris could stop Yustichisqua to tell him he'd get his own food, *the Taleenay* darted off. He was replaced by Captain Buhippus, who entered, bowed, and then waited on the sidelines like an *Odala Tludachi* surveying the flock. He made Harris nervous.

"Is there something you need, captain?" Harris asked.

"Yes, my lord. But I have learned to suppress my sexual appetite while on duty. It dulls the acuity and opens the way to undetected conspiracy."

"You see assassins in the shadows."

"Most assassins dwell in the shadows, my lord. But not all."

"Then they aren't assassins, captain," Harris said, the banter better than the silence. "They're ruthless killers."

"I agree."

"Perhaps you can do me a service."

"It is my primary function on this excursion."

"Could you ask my *Danuwa* to attend me?"

Buhippus nodded, turned on his *zulus* and disappeared beyond the pliant walls. He was replaced by Fytzyfu, who entered like P.T. Barnum. He looked a bit like the famous humbug — dressed in a red ringmaster's robe, a turban on his head, and a monocle pasted into his eye socket. Harris waited for the spiel: *ladies and gentlemen, in this ring we have Lord Belmundus, the Didaniyisgi of the Yuyutlu, who will demonstrate a remarkable feat of celibacy.*

"Can I help you . . . Fizzitu, is it?"

"Fytzyfu, Lord Belmundus. I am checking if all things are to your liking." He bowed again, his turban bouncing like Jell-O. "You have not eaten yet and have not touched the lovely breasts provided for your easement."

"My *Taleenay* is preparing a plate for me, and you must know, I'm the consort to the Scepta Charminus."

Of course, with Agrimentikos playing the part of a Macedonian bull, the explanation didn't hold water.

"Remarkable," Fytzyfu replied. "Perhaps some music?"

Harris heard music playing in the distant rooms. He imagined his Yunocker guards having tossed off their *zulus* and now did *the Yuganawu* jig with the three-breasted cuties.

"Thank you, I'm fine." Then he thought. "You could answer a question for me, however."

"Anything."

"The walls of this pavilion — they're like butterfly wings, yet as solid as *phitron*. How's it possible?"

"Ah. It is a specialty of Gurt manufactory. It is called *mopyn*. It is made not from stone, but from Gurt excrement mixed with *zugginak* milk."

Harris wiped his hands again on the bed fleece.

Excrement.

"Zugginak?"

Fytzyfu shrugged, but Yustichisqua returned at that moment.

"Little Bird," Harris said. "What's a *zugginak*?"

Yustichisqua appeared upset and almost dropped the two plates and the jug. Once steadied, he set one plate down and brought the other plate (and the jug) to Harris.

"*Zugginaks* are ferocious dogs the Yunockers train to sniff out Trones."

"Oh."

"Why ask?"

"It seems their milk, when mixed with Gurt shit, hardens into . . ." He raised his hands to the ceiling . . . "into this wonderfully elastic material."

"*Mopyn*," Fytzyfu confirmed. "Can I answer anything else for Lord Belmundus?"

"No, thank you."

The steward bowed his way out. Harris checked if the Gurt had left a stinky calling card on the threshold. He hadn't.

2

In Fytzyfu's wake, Buhippus returned, *the Danuwa* in tow.

"Ah, my marshals," Harris said, bouncing to his feet and greeting them with open arms. "Are you settled into rooms yet?"

Elypticus attempted to answer, but his mouth was full, the crumbs of a flaky pastry spluttering. Parnasus was no better. Only Melonius could speak without spraying the air.

"We have been eating, my lord," Melonius said, plaintively. "We still sample the many delicacies."

"Sorry," Harris said. "I didn't mean to spoil your feasting, but I wanted to be sure you're making the best of it off the hill. Have you selected something beyond meat and potatoes, lads?"

Elypticus glanced at Parnasus, who appeared sheepish. Melonius shrugged.

"I believe Lord Agrimentikos means to take them all," Melonius said. "I have better things to do with my *yedalas.*"

"*Yedalas?*" Harris asked. "These ladies are there for the taking, aren't they?"

"They are," Buhippus stated. "For you and Agrimentikos they are diplomatically programmed to fulfill your every need and not look beyond it. But for the rest, we must reckon our pleasures with a gratuity befitting our rank and station."

"Really?" He observed his three *Danuwa*. When Melonius had stated his need to conserve his *yedalas*, the others appeared glum — eating their way through the feast for consolation. "Do I sense a lack of *yedalas* here?"

Parnasus cocked his head. Elypticus scuffed the ground.

"My lord," Buhippus interceded. "My men are paid and paid well. Warriors always thrive in service to Kuriakis. But Thirdlings are a managed commodity and paid nothing for the privilege."

"Yustichisqua," Harris said. "My purse."

Little Bird put down his leg of *whatever*, wiped his hand on his *naperonus* and plunged his hand to his belt for the purse. He relinquished it to Harris, who stopped him.

"No, no. As my *Taleenay*, you make the disbursements." He looked to *the Danuwa*. "Will five *yedalas* each be enough?" Melonius shook his head like a bucking bull. "No. How about six, then?"

"I need no charity," Melonius snapped.

Parnasus and Elypticus appeared desperate, as if they would grab their colleague by the legs and dump him.

"Come, come," Harris said, approaching Melonius. "Your hand, sir." Melonius scowled. "Yustichisqua, bring it here."

"Not from *his* hands," Melonius said. "Charity is shameful enough, but to be a beggar to such a thing, I will not do it."

"You will, sir," Harris howled. "It's a gift. I'll decide on a regular stipend after I consult with Agrimentikos. And if you won't accept it as a gift, regard it as an advance in pay."

"Put it on my account," Melonius snapped. "I do not mean to lower myself to these Zecronisian she-wolves, and certainly not with *yedalas* handled by your *Taleenay*."

He bowed curtly and departed, leaving Harris more bemused than angry. On some level, he understood prejudice's root — a learned bedevilment not easily dispelled by a simple *say-so* or a few acts of generosity. He turned to the remaining *Danuwa*.

"Gentleman, are you disinclined to romp in a field of triple-breasted beauties?"

"No, my lord," Parnasus said, without thinking.

"I would take it as a kindness," Elypticus echoed.

Harris sensed two instant erections. Were these lads weak and Melonius strong?

Bull-headed, most likely. *I need to talk with that lad,* Harris thought.

"You're not above taking the disbursement from *the Taleenay's* hand?"

"He is *the Taleenay,* my lord," Parnasus replied.

"I regard him as an equal," Elypticus remarked.

These rejoinders were too readily plied, but in light of *boner wood,* what else could he expect?

"Very well, lads," he said.

Harris nodded at Little Bird, who counted out six *yedalas* each, placing them into outstretched hands. He counted out six more.

"*Oginali?*"

"Start an account for *Danuwa* Melonius. Enter it as a credit."

Little Bird returned *the yedalas* to the purse, and then retrieved a small writing book from his *korinkle*. With a charcoal stick, he made the entry. Harris noticed Buhippus shaking his head, most likely realizing this Trone could write — probably could read too.

Harris returned to his plate. He was voraciously hungry. He nodded to *the Danuwa's* thank you bows and noticed Buhippus retreated also.

"Captain Buhippus," Harris called. "A word with you, please."

Buhippus floated over, passing Yustichisqua, cocking his head to observe the notations in the book.

"He has a fair hand," the captain remarked. "You have done a fine job with his learning."

"Good try, captain," Harris said. "I haven't broken that law. The lad came to me fully baked and you're not to pursue the history of his learning."

"I shall regard it as a mystery. I presume you wish to ask me about Melonius."

"I understand Melonius," Harris replied. "Tappiolus is his father and I assume he's been raised in the lap of the Yunocker guards. Melonius isn't a mystery to me. Remember, he wasn't my first choice. But he'll need a good heart to heart with me. Either that or a spanking."

Buhippus chuckled.

"He might spank back."

"Would he raise a hand to his lord?"

"If provoked, Melonius would raise a hand to Kuriakis himself." Buhippus turned serious. "Some mysteries are best not revealed, so I will not pursue their revelation."

"*Touché*. But I have a request. I wish to explore the port."

"I suggest you stay in *the Lyspykyn* until summoned by the Zocor council. It is still *Yichiyusti*."

"I thank you for your advice, but . . ." Harris poked through a mound of what looked like purple potatoes. "What the fuck is this?"

Little Bird was on the spot. He poked his finger in the pile, and then tasted it.

"You will like it, *oginali. Pukas midaskoos* — the root of the *midas* herb. Very tasty."

Harris forked some, sniffed, and then licked his utensil clean.

"Very good." He noticed Buhippus' amazement . . . again. "Yustichisqua's my food taster, captain. You never know when someone shits in the spaghetti. Now, as for your advice, I think I'll finish this plate of bones and drippings, lick all *the midas* root I can get . . . it tastes a bit like carrots, only minty . . . then, I'll proceed to explore the docks."

Buhippus' lip twitched. He clapped his *zulu* heels together, and bowed curtly.

"Whatever my lord desires," he snapped. "Only . . . I insist on accompanying you."

"Absolutely. Yustichisqua will come also. And if you would be so kind to tell Melonius I'll need one of my marshals. Since he chooses not to copulate with the Zecronisian sirens, he's *the Danuwa* of the day."

"He will not like that, my lord."

"Too bad — tough titties, and all that rot. I'll be ready within the hour."

He continued to eat, feeling more despotic than ever in his life.

"Very well, my lord," Buhippus croaked, and then turned on his *zulus*, departing.

Harris washed his meal down with the bubbling green liquor which Yustichisqua had ported with the plate.

"Little Bird, I'll have another plate of Pukis . . ."

"*Pukas midaskoos, oginali.*"

"That's it, although I can't believe anyone would call food, *puke*. But it's really very good. Maybe we'll get the recipe and bring it back up the hill."

Yes, never so despotic in his life.

3

Despite the bilious sky of *Yichiyusti*, the port glistened under the shipping's tall timbers, beckoning to *wanderlust* travelers to sail to freedom. The wharves were bleached with gulls — birds which, despite their name (*delfins*), looked like familiar scavengers from home. They had black beaks, red eyes and a pink stripe running lengthwise across their wings, but they had only one head and two legs, which Harris took as an imprint to normality.

The port bustled — carts piled high with boxes and rickshaws pulled to and from vessels. His and Melonius' *Cabriolins* were the only hover crafts in sight. Hearty conversation boomed, the salty kind, with *cuss* words, and Harris hoped he'd meet an ancient tar who'd tell him of lands afar and countries nearby, mayhap.

"It makes me dizzy," Yustichisqua said. "So many Zecronisians. So many Gurts."

"I think it'll be like this in *the Yuyutlu*."

"I have never traveled to *the Yuyutlu* either, *oginali*. But if commerce is like this, I suppose you are correct."

"I'm right at home here, Little Bird."

"Is this like your realm in the outlands?"

"No. Not a bit. It's like a movie set — tall ships and Shanghai vessels — the Indian trade and the New York docks of a hundred years ago or more. But . . . this is not a replica. There's nothing like it in the stacks of Prop shack number four, I assure you."

Little Bird was silent. Harris glanced at Melonius, who wore a permanent mask of disgust. For a Thirdling with xenophobic leanings, this trip was the ticket to hell. His attitude, however, didn't register to the passers-by, who were engrossed in their business. Buhippus remained vigilant, hovering in the margins.

Occasionally, another Yunocker would stop and confer with him. Harris supposed the Yunockers were *the law and order* for the entire port. Whatever Buhippus said to these policeman, they left Lord Belmundus unmolested and, more importantly, they kept away from Yustichisqua.

Harris pushed away from the dour Melonius and settled between two impressive vessels — a caravel with a high decorated fo'c'stle and a three-masted junk with crimson sails, two semifurled. Perhaps it would sail soon. Between these vessels, Harris viewed the sea — endless and unbounded by the green sky, which, despite the law of vanishing points, provided no horizon.

"The sea is large, *oginali*. I think it is dangerous for those who do not know its ways."

"I've always loved the sea, but rarely ventured out. A little surfing, but I stink at it."

He sighed, and then stared across the ripples, his sight skipping like a stone over the surface. *The Amaykwohi* was calm, but he bet it could kick up in a storm. He imagined it teeming with life — everything from jellyfish to *misancorpus*. Where was the opposite shore — the place the Zecronisians called home?

"I know your thinking, but you are wrong-minded, my lord," came a gravelly voice.

It startled Harris and repelled Yustichisqua. A man stood beside them — a Zecronisian merchant, perhaps, draped in gold and crimson silk and wearing a broad sombrero, which reminded Harris of a lid from a *Marco Polo* rerun. The man exuded Venice in all its republican glory.

"How would you know what I'm thinking?" Harris asked. "And even if you could read my thoughts, how can you say they're wrong-minded?"

"I know men, my lord. I also know eyes and longing and the vision of those who seek to go to sea." He bowed, and then pointed to the bay. "Such men seek lands afar — exotic places to escape the mundane. But I also have eyes, which see you, my lord. You are already far afield. You think to escape to your home . . . across this sea."

"You're a clever devil, aren't you?"

"Clever? Yes. A devil, definitely." He bowed again, removing his hat, this time like one of the musketeers. "I am Garan — Garan *the Gucheeda.*"

Yustichisqua gasped.

"That means *outlaw*, *oginali*."

"True," Garan said, pride in his voice. "*Gucheeda* fits me fine, as does *Fumarca* and *Harandu* and *Jamabispa*, all terms for an unprincipled wielder of opportunity and advantage. However, I am also *the Deegosgi* for both the port and *the Yuyutlu*."

"*Deegosgi?*" Harris asked, more from Little Bird than from this bold stranger.

"It means Arbitrator," Yustichisqua replied. "Although I do not understand how *a Gucheeda* can also be *a Deegosgi*."

"Can a Trone be *a Taleenay*, for so you must be?" Garan nodded, grinning with a sinister tinge. "And because I am *Deegosgi* of *the Yuyutlu*, I have anticipated the *Didiniyisgi's* arrival and assume you are Lord Belmundus." He bowed again, a gesture getting on Harris' nerves. "You *are* Lord Belmundus, are you not?"

"Last time I looked in a mirror, I was," Harris snapped. "I'm still confused." He pointed to the sea. "How do you know that my . . . my home is not on these sea lanes?"

"Because, my lord, *the Amaykwohi* does not touch the outlands. In fact, it is not a sea. It is a vast lake."

Harris twitched, and then looked to the waters, blinking away his hopes. He spit.

"There. I've added to its volume."

Garan laughed. Buhippus drifted over.

"Is there a problem, my lord?"

"No, captain. This man is the Arbitrator for the marketplace and has sought me out — an introduction, because we'll be working toward the same aim." He glanced at Garan. "Have I stated the facts correctly, Mr. Garan?"

"As Arbitrator, my lord, I hope our views will align, but when they diverge, it will not be for a want of trying."

"Which means Yustichisqua will need to watch my purse carefully and I'll need to count the silverware after Mr. Garan's visits."

Garan laughed. Buhippus didn't. He sniffed, giving the Arbitrator a leer. Harris raised his hand.

"We'll be fine, captain. Truly."

Garan pulled back, giving Buhippus an inquisitive glance. However, the captain nodded and floated back to his sentry position.

"Yunockers make me nervous," Garan said. "They are always trying to question me — inspecting my papers and poking into my goods."

"Looking for contraband, perhaps," Yustichisqua said, boldly.

"Little Bird," Harris snapped. "There's no need to be on the defensive."

"No need," Garan said. "You are old enough to know that some seek better callings. It certainly looks like you have made a good start."

Little Bird grunted, but did not reply. This talk puzzled Harris, but no more than the usual chatter which grazed his head when among Farnfolk.

"So, Mr. Garan . . . you're an official and an outlaw — a nice pairing, because where I come from most officials are outlaws, only we elect them to their positions. Then, when they pick our pockets and pinch our asses, we complain and vote them in again."

He laughed.

"You will find my rewards are within the acceptable range of Zecronisian standards, my lord," Garan remarked. "This ship — *the Ponsetossit*," he said, pointing to the caravel, "is mine. I never question whence the cargo comes, and always know its destination. I pay my port taxes to enter and *the griffies* to unload and to cart. I tip the port master and sprinkle *yedalas* across the hands of the Yunockers, although they still prod and poke if the amount is not to their expectations. I am a respectable investor in the sea trade."

"Then why are you called *the Gucheeda*?" Harris asked.

"I will tell you, *oginali*," Yustichisqua replied. "It is not the transport which is illegal. It is the cargo."

"Little Bird," Harris reprimanded. "I don't know what's got into you." Then he glanced at Garan. One glance and he saw Yustichisqua was correct. But Harris didn't care if Garan was smuggling *Hula* girls or *Dead Sea Scrolls* — this wasn't his jurisdiction. If he had to enforce contraband's flow into *the Yuyutlu*, then it might become his concern, but he didn't know it . . . yet. He returned his attention to Little Bird. "As my *Taleenay*, you represent me."

Yustichisqua pouted, and then nodded to Garan.

"I shall mind my tongue, Garan *the Deegosgi*."

"Do not concern yourself about it, sir," Garan said. "It is not seemly for you to give homage to me. I respect my elders."

Harris twitched, and then looked at Yustichisqua, his eyebrows knitting.

"How much longer must I stay here, my lord?" came an intrusive voice.

Melonius had wafted over in his *Cabriolin*, fidgeting impatiently.

"When I'm ready to leave, sir," Harris snapped. "That's how long."

Melonius blew an angry sigh, and then, upon seeing Garan, slammed his hand on his *Cabriolin* panel and scooted to Buhippus.

"When we return to *the Lyspykyn*," Harris shouted after him, "you're to see me." Several heads turned, but Melonius had soured Harris' mood. "I've got to set him right," he muttered. Then he looked for Garan, but the man had departed. "Where'd he go?"

"He is fast, *oginali,* and smooth."

"The denizens of this world are unpredictable, or so I'm learning," he said, staring at Yustichisqua. "He said, he respects his elders. What did that mean?"

Little Bird lowered his eyes. Harris had come to think of Yustichisqua as a fifteen or sixteen-year old lad. However, there had been comments, like Little Bird's reference to his mother being born before the invasion, and now Garan's doff to his age.

"Just how old are you, Yustichisqua?"

"It is hard to say, *oginali.* The years differ in length, depending on our transit around *Solus*. Some years are longer — when *Dodecadatamus* rules."

"Tell me."

"Between fifty-two and fifty-seven, *oginali*." Harris cocked his head in amazement. "I am the same age as when I met you. It cannot be helped."

"No, it can't."

"We live long lives, the Cetrone. We do not live forever, and certainly we die in the many. I am very young in my clan. You are my first master. Have I offended you? I would die if I did so."

Harris softened.

"No. I'm just surprised and feel . . . feel a bit foolish. Now you're *my* elder and I should look to *you* for guidance."

"You always have, *oginali*."

Harris laughed. The laugh grew into a roar, blossoming across the docks, drawing the attention of *griffies* and drovers alike.

"Your people grow at a snail's pace, while the Thirdlings sprout in three years. Next you'll tell me the Gurts are grown on trees and fall like fruit."

"No, *oginali*. Gurts grow from seed sown in the ground."

Harris balked, but Yustichisqua laughed now.

"I think that's the first joke you've ever told me, Little Bird."

"Joke? It is a jest to make you easier in mind, now that you have learned your home cannot be reached on Garan's great ship."

Harris stretched, sucking in the sea air. He looked to the green sky, and then to his *Taleenay*.

"Come on, old man. Let's get back to *the Lyspykyn*. I have a *Danuwa* to chastise."

"Old man?" Yustichisqua asked. "I will always be your Little Bird, *oginali*. Even when I am two-hundred and you are too ancient to stand erect."

Harris was glad, because he had one touchstone in this topsy-turvy world, even though this touchstone was upside down and backward.

Adadooski! Arkmo!

Chapter Twelve

A Game of Grusoker

1

Harris didn't know what to tell Melonius. No doubt, the lad needed a stern lecture on a topic which would turn him around — a parental talk. But Harris wasn't a parent. Neither was he the executive type, logically laying out a situation with goals and rewards — boardroom stuff. He had played the warrior and pirate parts, but he would show up on set with his memorized lines, prepared for a real leader — the director, who inspired his innate talents with snippets and numerous takes, later to be spliced into a tale for his adoring fans to savor in the dark. Harris aspired to be a director, but in the future. That Melonius was bred a bigot, Harris knew. However, this *Danuwa* was also a renegade — a rebel against authority. Melonius disliked his assignment and bucked at every turn. He mirrored Harris' captive spirit — locked in a world he didn't choose.

How could Harris convince Melonius to turn over a new leaf, when he was unwilling to do so himself? Yet, in this legal fiction as *the Didaniyisgi*, a foreign culture sucked him into being a representative and defender. Be off the leash wasn't a gift. Harris was at a loss on how to handle Melonius. Still, it had to be done.

His first inclination was to summon Melonius to the Provosts' quarters and dress him down officially — a Lord to his minion. But this approach would stiffen the *Danuwa's* neck, or so Harris thought. So he considered a group meeting with all three *Danuwas* — safety in numbers. However, the stern message might infect Elypticus and Parnasus, toughening hidden issues between the Provost and his marshals. It would single out Melonius before his peers. Harris considered Buhippus' words about Melonius' unpredictable temperament. The lad had to be cooled or an eruption could take down Harris and Yustichisqua. Stab now and apologize later. No. Concessions were in order, leveling the playing ground. He would meet Melonius on his own turf. So Harris asked Yustichisqua to stay behind and told Captain Buhippus to guard from a distance. *The Didaniyisgi* was visiting Melonius' quarters.

Beyond the central hall, still set with a feast, lay a honeycomb of small rooms with *mopyn* walls. Harris peeked into one room after another hoping to discover Melonius' quarters. After the fourth intrusion, he almost gave up, having interrupted much *devil-may-care*. Then, he stumbled into Parnasus' room, the young *Danuwa* sprawled in the aftermath of six *yedalas'* worth of Zecronisian sexual congress. The object of that shimmy, sat up, her triple bust line jiggling in alarm.

"Excuse me," Harris blurted. "I've got the wrong room."

Parnasus stirred, sitting bolt upright, and then falling butt naked off the bed onto the buttery tiles. He scrambled to his feet, grabbing a fleece to cover his flaccid noodle and drooping globes.

"My lord," he stammered.

Harris found it hard not to laugh, less from a sense of the ridiculous, and more from empathy, having been caught in similar positions, but never with a bodacious purple-haired Amazon. Although, there was this guy named Bruce.

"No, no, Parnasus," Harris said, backing out of the room. "Carry on. Carry on." He went to leave, stopped, and then turned to his *flagrante delecti Danuwa*. "Where's Melonius' room? This place's laid out like a fun house."

He chuckled, because most residents were having fun.

"My lord," Parnasus responded, "Melonius is across the corridor and one door to the right."

"I looked there," Harris said.

He had — a dim room with its occupant absent.

"He might be in the gaming room, three rooms further."

"Ah," Harris said, nodding, and then winking, a gesture causing Parnasus to blush. "I'll give it a try. Carry on. Carry on."

He chuckled as he left, feeling much like a patronizing ensign on the Love Boat. He followed the twisted corridor to the gaming room, and then hesitated. He didn't want to confront Melonius in the company of others — especially in the middle of a hot poker game, or whatever they played in Farn.

I'll wave him off and we'll retire to his quarters. That's it.

Harris entered the room. Melonius was there — alone and engrossed in a document. He didn't notice Harris arrive. If games were played here, they had moved on to the brothel kind. The air was redolent of smoke, the kind he had encountered wherever Yunockers took their ease. He assumed there had been gambling, the aftermath as evidence. Suddenly, Melonius looked up, twitching, but neither rising nor bowing. Not even a nod.

"You here?" he said, as if he had sought this refuge from *the Didaniyisgi*. He furled the document, and began to leave. "You are too late to play *grusoker*. They would have cleaned you out."

"No, wait. I didn't come here to gamble. As for *grusoker*, put it on your to-do list to teach me how to play. Are you good at it?"

"I can afford my own whores, if I am so inclined."

"But you're not."

"Not these. I told you . . ." He nodded and began to leave.

"I'm looking for you."

Melonius halted.

"I told you we must talk," Harris continued.

"You did not tell me," Melonius said, turning sharply. "You scolded me in public and threatened to put me right."

Harris sighed. He pointed to a chair — the one Melonius recently had vacated. The *Danuwa* hesitated, then marched to it and sat again, crossing his arms impatiently.

"Listen," Harris said, softening. "I'm sorry I blew my top on the docks."

"It is not your place to apologize to me."

"You might be correct," Harris said, pulling up a chair. "But you must know this. What you expect me to be, I'm not. If you'd uncross your arms, I'd take it as a sign of respect."

"And if I do not respect you, what course will you take?"

"Not the one you want. I know you hope I'll send you back up the hill. And perhaps it would be best for me and you and for every motherfucking creature that crosses your path, but it's not going to happen, because I chose you to be my *Danuwa*."

"You did not choose me. My father chose."

"His wishes weighed heavily in the choice, but by your mother's magic jade ring, there's a reason you're it. There's a reason for everything, and even if you picked every *Scaladar* around Great Greary Gree's asshole, you're sticking around for that reason."

Melonius' eyes drifted, thought kicking in, no doubt. It might not have been critical thought — more a puzzlement of Harris' unusual confrontational style. Still, Melonius took a bracing breath and uncrossed his arms. Harris smiled.

2

"I'm not who you think I am, Melonius," Harris began. "An outsider from a different world — yes. But I'm not a good fit when it comes to commanding others. I like my freedom — cherish it. Until I slipped one evening into temptation's harmful path, I was my own man. But the Scepta went a-hunting and I was as slow as *a Tippagore*."

"When a Scepta has chosen," Melonius said, "none can resist."

"I believe a stronger man could have."

"Stronger men die in their sleep on that score. Like my father, you are here for a single purpose and *this* is not it."

"You're right," Harris said, cocking his head. "You're as right as right can be. But, as you can see, I'm not on the hill now. I've been given a long leash."

"And I, a short one."

Melonius turned his head away, glancing at a nearby gaming table, the site of his evening's victory at *grusoker*.

"You see," Harris remarked. "We have something in common and should make the best of it."

"You are here, because my mother has put you at a distance."

"Has she?" Harris wondered. Kuriakis was the moving spirit, but Charminus had planted the thought — got the ball rolling. Perhaps this little nipper was correct. But did it matter? "If so, Melonius, we still have something in common, because your father pushed you into my way. You mustn't be the joy of his heart."

Melonius frowned.

"It does not surprise me," he snapped. "He has resisted my desires to enter the marriage pool and become a useful extension of the clan like my brothers and sisters. Instead, he saddles me with . . ."

"With me." Harris chuckled. "I know, I'm a living hell. I take you for adventurous rides in *the Yugda*, furnish you with spiffy new apparel, put you in the way of pretty heifers to ride until dawn, show you the port and, above all, take time to talk to you now, because I know your insides are churning."

"You do not know me."

"I may never know you, Melonius, and frankly, I'm not sure it's worth my time. However, you are my *Danuwa*, and you must function. I must trust you."

"I can be trusted."

"I want to believe that. I want to think if I asked you to represent me in *the Yuyutlu* I wouldn't return to find a trail of tortured Cetrone, pissed off Gurts and a rebellion of Zecronisian merchants."

"I am not so stupid."

"No, but you seem to hate them all. And . . . I understand it."

Melonius gave him an incredulous look.

"You are the oath breaker . . . my lord." He bowed, as if to ameliorate the accusation. "You have raised your Trone to a dangerous position. You treat the Gurts with civility and regard the Zecronisians as equals. We are *the Ayelli*, my lord. You may be from a different world, but you are *Ayelli* now."

"*Ayelli* means *invader*, doesn't it? So my *Taleenay* tells me."

"He has told you correctly. We are the *invaders* and the *conquerors.*"

"And you are how old, Melonius? You remember the invasion, do you?"

"We are told."

"Schooled in it at *the Cartisforium*. Very real and gripping too, I bet. I missed that segment, and I'm glad I did. My world's different, but not so removed from *the Ayelli* way of thinking."

"I am not convinced," Melonius chuffed. "You bring foreign ways to us and are trying to make us think as you do. It is working on Parnasus and Elypticus. Even Kuriakis is charmed by it — and that disturbs me."

"Nothing like a political consciousness." Harris reached over and touched Melonius' knee, peering into his eyes. "My world is riddled with hate and is tormented by intolerance. My people enslaved a whole race and pushed other races aside. My world bled for a decade — a span of years where millions were rounded up and placed in . . . in *Kalugus*, and executed for being who they were. Millions fell to bombs and bullets and hellfire. And when I was drawn away, religious intolerance, so vile it condemned us by the tenants proclaimed as our saving grace, plagued civilization. No, Melonius. Hate and intolerance enslaves those who practice it. It destroys their targets. Both are lost forever in a cloud so thick, darkness wins over light."

Melonius pushed Harris' hand away. However, he didn't dispute these remarks. They might not have penetrated his bull head. The words could have been hornets, buzzing about his temples, threatening to sting, but never doing so.

"We have laws, my lord."

"No law trumps hope, Melonius. No darkness is so powerful that light is forever extinguished. Think about it. I'm not asking you to raise a flag and join me in a crusade. This isn't a holy mission. I've been appointed Kuriakis' representative to safeguard *Ayelli* interests in the marketplace, a position which hasn't been filled within anyone's memory. Sounds like a make-work post to me." He grinned, detecting a slight change in Melonius' expression. "But what the fuck, we should show them all that a *Yuyutlu* without a *Didaniyisgi* is like a whore with only one tit. Help me with this, and then you can scurry off to Volcanium or Aolium and marry the daughter of the Seneschal of Bippity-boo, and I . . ." He winked. "I shall find a hole to slip back into the hostile, violent, volatile world I lost — a world with a sliver of hope. Help me trust you, Melonius. That's all I ask."

The *Danuwa* nodded, curtly.

3

"You have found him," came a voice.

Parnasus, now fully dressed, stood on the threshold, Elypticus peeping over his shoulder. Harris turned.

"Yes, lads," he chortled. "Seek and ye shall find. Your partner in crime was about to show me how to play . . . glunocker?"

"*Grusoker*," Melonius said, shrugging.

"My favorite game," Elypticus piped, crossing the threshold. "You need at least three players."

"You are not a good player," Melonius said.

"Good enough," Elypticus replied, scooting to the gaming table. "Come, Parnasus, help me set up."

Parnasus bowed to Harris, and then proceeded to the table. Harris looked to Melonius, who still hadn't cottoned to the idea, no doubt.

"I like games, Melonius," Harris said, "and I'll bet this one is better than the one we've been playing."

Melonius wandered to the table, sitting in the round. Harris joined him.

"Yustichisqua handles my purse, so I'm playing on credit. Does anyone object?"

"How can we?" Elypticus said. "We are playing with your *yedalas.*"

Parnasus laughed and clasped his coins in his hand.

"Then the question goes to Melonius," Harris said, "whose luck has given him a fistful of Yunocker *yedalas.*"

"The best way to learn is to listen and watch," Melonius said. "I will explain, but you will not understand until you see a few rounds."

"Shoot," Harris said.

Elypticus pressed a button and the board elevated slightly from the table. It was an attractive playing surface — round and richly carved. There were blue slots for *the yedalas*, the bets no doubt, and a track with holes circumnavigating a bright-green slab. In the holes, or at least in what Harris assumed was the starting position, were ivory pegs — a cribbage arrangement. Then Melonius pressed another button and seven dice materialized centerboard. Harris grinned at the pretty things — three pyramids, three tetrahedrons and an octahedron — pearl white with blue and red markings, which Harris had come to recognize as Farn numbers.

"First we shake these," Elypticus said, passing the dice to Parnasus, who gave them a good rattle, barely able to contain them in his hands. "And let them fall onto *the gorettle.*"

Parnasus dropped the stones in the center of the board — in an area which lit with a flash of green, and then with a warm, cozy blue. Elypticus scanned the dice with his index finger, calculating.

"Two *yedalas*," Melonius said.

"Is it two?" Parnasus replied, cocking his head, looking for himself.

"Trust me." He glanced at Harris. "We calculate the bet based on the arrangement of the stones, and then divide their position by the numbers appearing on the face-ups. The side stones, turned inward, are discounted — we subtract that amount, and then look to the mother rock." He pointed to the octahedron. "If it has an even number, we deduct one. If odd, we add one, and if it is blank, it is a wash."

"I think it is only one," Parnasus said,

"Two," Melonius quibbled.

"It *is* two, Parnasus," Elypticus said. "See, this one with the five, faces this one with the three."

Parnasus squinted, and then took two *yedalas* and slipped them into the slots. He moved a peg forward. Harris was befuddled. Never strong at math, he would stink at the Farn variety. He hoped he'd fare better in the marketplace. Elypticus took his turn at tossing.

"Oh, *bogger*," he said. "Three. That is much."

He frowned, but placed his wager in a separate slot and moved a peg forward two spaces. Melonius grinned, took up the stones in two hands, gave them a stylized rattle as if he could control luck's vagary. Down they went.

"Free ride," he exclaimed.

"I think they are rigged somehow," Elypticus said.

"You know they are not," Melonius exclaimed, and then clasped his fingers together in greed. He turned to Harris.

"Now that the bidding is set, the play begins." He pressed a button and a stack of tiles levitated above the board. Swiftly, they were dealt to each player, who caught them and quickly hid them behind the low boundary of the table's edge. Harris peeked at Melonius' set. There were tiles in four colors — red, yellow, green and blue, and only on the face. The backs were golden. Each had a Farn number, but Harris could see script sigils on some.

"Watch," Melonius said. "We shall play this first rubber slowly."

Another stack appeared centerboard — in *the gorettle*. Melonius turned over a tile.

"This is a blue four," he said. He pointed at Parnasus to his right, counter-clockwise. "Now Parnasus will attempt to match either color or number. Do so, Parnasus."

Parnasus placed a tile.

"A green four," Parnasus said.

Elypticus placed a tile atop this one.

"A green seven," he said.

"The play comes to me," Melonius explained. "You can see, I can play one of several tiles. If I want the play to continue to Parnasus, I will play another number. But if I wish the play to return to Elypticus, I will place a sigil." He pointed to one. "There are four sigils to each color — a sun, a moon, a star and a comet. This turns the play."

He played a comet.

"Blue comet," Elypticus said, playing a blue number. "Blue seven."

"Green seven," Parnasus declared, playing his tile.

"Yellow seven," Melonius said, and suddenly their hands went to the stack, slapping it hard.

"*Grusoker*," Elypticus and Parnasus both shouted.

"I got it," Elypticus snapped.

"I think I did," Parnasus complained.

"It does not matter," Melonius said. "I announced the three in a row to demonstrate."

"Oh," Elypticus said. "Take it, brother,"

"No, brother," Parnasus replied.

Melonius snapped his hand over it.

"*Grusoker*, then." He grinned and gathered the entire stack. "Do not pout. You know the rules."

Harris laughed.

"But who gets *the yedalas?*"

"They accumulate, my lord," Melonius said. "Whoever gets the full stack gets the ransom."

"It seems easy," Harris said.

Melonius grinned, and then nodded to his fellow players. Parnasus' hand went to the stack, revealing the next tile. Elypticus played a number, Melonius a sigil, reversing play, quickly, and so it went. Harris could hardly see their hands flying as the play went about and about, punctuated by slapping hands and cries of *grusoker.* There were several debates over false starts with the slaps, but the game was vigorous — stopping briefly for a toss of the dice, new bets and peg advancement. He wanted to ask about the pegs, but could barely keep track of the flying tiles, the slaps and the shouts. Finally, the last slap came crashing down in *the gorettle*, and Melonius declared himself the victor. Harris roared and clapped.

Elypticus and Parnasus appeared crestfallen, but shook their brother *Danuwa's* hand.

"It looks like I'll need to pay you lads more often to keep you in *grusoker* money," Harris announced. "But I might not need to pay Melonius anything if this is an example of his gambling skills."

Melonius nodded to Harris. It wasn't kinship, but ground had been established. However, Harris might need to win some *yedalas* before Melonius would consider the playing ground level, but at least there was a playing ground now.

"Ah, *grusoker!*" came a hearty hail over the threshold.

"Lord Agrimentikos," Harris said. "Are you a player?"

"I might have invented the game back when we called it Egyptian Ratscrew, but I have not played at it in years."

Buhippus was at his side and, behind them, Yustichisqua.

"My lords," Buhippus said. "There is no time for such play."

"Why, what's happened?" Harris asked.

"The sky, *oginali*," Yustichisqua said. "It has turned."

"Yes," Agrimentikos declared. "*Yichiyusti* is finished. Kuriakis no longer stirs."

"We will be summoned to the Zocor council," Buhippus said.

Harris turned to his *Danuwa*. The dank, smoke-laden air of the gaming pit seemed perfumed now.

"My loyal *Danuwa*," Harris said. "I will continue to learn this fascinating game on another day. Perhaps, I'll get good at it and whip your *asanos*. But now we must fulfill our duty. Let's sparkle for the council, now that our lord no longer stirs. Let *the Ayelli* make its mark."

"That is the spirit," Agrimentikos said.

Harris glanced at Melonius, who appeared less recalcitrant, although he wasn't dancing the herky-jerky. Harris looked to his trusty *Taleenay*.

"Little Bird," he called. "Time to shine. Time to sparkle."

Yustichisqua nodded and slapped his dagger's hilt. Harris slapped his *Columbincus*. There was nothing like a game of *grusoker*, played with the highest stakes.

Chapter Thirteen

Time to Shine — Time to Sparkle

1

At *Yichiyusti*'s end, the sky shone turquoise. *Solus* and *Dodecadatamus* were two butter pats melting in the heavens. Outside *the Lyspykyn*, the revels began — banners and dancers and musicians, generating a festival where there had been gloom. Harris rode in his *Cabriolin*, Yustichisqua holding tightly to the railing. *The Danuwa* rode in formation beside throngs of Gurts and Zecronisians, who sang and juggled and skipped and hopped on two or three legs, each to nature's accordance. Elypticus, pie-eyed, beamed at the sights — the scantily clad women, who twisted and shook like puddings on a rack. Parnasus puckered, as if to blow a kiss to an odalisque, who reclined in a sedan, carried by four hulks on their tripod legs. Melonius kept his eyes front, but Harris saw them occasionally leering at one reveler or another.

Buhippus was in the fore, his vanguard Yunockers clearing a way through the crowd.

Banners whipped across canopies as *the Didiniyisgi's* cortege entered the principal boulevard of *the Wudayleegu* — a broad thoroughfare lined with sandstone buildings with palladium doorways; off-kiltered, because these buildings mushroomed into a fantasy array — minarets, pagodas, *stupas*, ziggurats, beehives, bulbous domes and other *pietra dura*. Green and yellow pigeons swarmed above the roofs, reflecting like bees in a riot of gold, jade, *lapis lazuli* and peridot tiles.

"Astounding," Harris said. "It's like the set for *Gandhi* or perhaps *The Last Emperor*."

"*Oginali*," Little Bird noted. "It is like *a fungimus* forest."

"I know what you mean," Harris replied, although he hadn't a clue.

"*The Wudayleegu* is the pride of Montjoy," Agrimentikos said, his *Cabriolin* sidling to Harris'. "The interiors are what you would expect. Lord Kuriakis visits twice a year to gape at the architecture and to acquire a few oddments for the Museum."

"The Zecronisians are quite the builders," Harris remarked.

"The Gurts are the builders, Lord Belmundus," Agrimentikos replied. "They are remarkably ugly creatures with the lowest of habits, but from them emerge . . ." He waved his hand beneath the shadows cast by palaces and pavilions. "All this and more." He tugged at his cloak. "More."

As they penetrated the boulevard, the crowd thickened. Soon, the Provost's cortege resembled a parade, becoming the center of attention. Sidelines formed. Banners waved. Welcome shouts assailed Harris, assaulting all his senses. Should he raise his hand like the Queen and give a little twist? Instead, he held his head high and arched his shoulders. Yustichisqua imitated this, as did the three *Danuwa*. This stance was met with acclaim, swelling with many *Adadooskis* and *Arkmos*, although other words resonated, shouts of *bobyfysmagu* and *jipjipjiptipu* or something like them. Harris hoped they were the equivalent to *Ayelli* praise words. Otherwise, he would need a *Cabriolin* hooded with protection — the Farn version of the Pope-mobile.

At the end of the boulevard loomed *the Zocorpykyn — the Wudayleegu's* Custom House — the chief building of the city. Harris recalled it when they had dropped out of the *Yugda*. It impressed him then and impressed him now. A full skirt of *mopyn* swept from a two-hundred foot pinnacle in a graceful spiral to a broad veranda. A series of arches braced a rotund glass façade.

"How does it remain standing?" Harris mused.

He glanced to his *Danuwa*. All three craned their necks to survey *the Zocorpykyn*. Then, along side their entourage appeared a floating platform — a stiff magic carpet, if Harris let his imagination wander. On it sat (in their tripod fashion) trumpeters and a single drummer. They raised their instruments in unison and blasted away. The sonorous fanfare was an intricate composition, probably reserved for special occasions. On the opposite side, another carried more drums and an organ-like instrument, a Zecronisian master filling in melodies and descants, weaving like Liberace on his best night.

"Welcome to *the Zocorpykyn*, Lord Belmundus and company," came a voice that cut through from another float, which swerved before the cortege. It was Mr. Fytzyfu with a corps of *the Lyspykyn* dancers. "It is an honor the Elector favors *the Wudayleegu* with his *Didaniyisgi*."

Harris touched his *Columbincus* and, at that, the trumpeters blew a salute. Buhippus gazed back, a grin blossoming across his face.

"*Oginali,*" Yustichisqua muttered. "They are happy to see us."

"Time to sparkle, old man. Time to shine."

As they approached the façade, wide glass doors shimmered, and then opened. The surrounding terraces were overhung with citizenry, cheering and applauding. Harris saluted as the procession entered *the Zocorpykyn.*

Inside, a foyer widened into an auditorium — wide enough to accommodate the floating band. A chorus sang in the hall's recesses. It sounded to Harris like a hymn, but with oriental overtones — somewhere between *the Hatikvah* and *Chopsticks.* He looked to Agrimentikos, whose congenial smile gave way to astonishment. Elypticus looked as if he would lay an egg, while Parnasus trembled, with delight perhaps, but it might have been awe. Melonius shook his head affirming the proper respect accorded to *Ayelli.*

Time to shine. Time to sparkle.

The audience hall brimmed with the Zecronisian aristocracy, all upstanding and cheering. If Harris had been a gladiator seeking a *thumbs-up or down,* he couldn't have expected a more rousing response. The auditorium lacked seats, the population having their own retractable anatomical stools.

Harris gazed across a sea of silk, satin, gems, turbans, twists, mortarboards, shawls, gagoos and bling. He also noticed pockets of similarly attired Gurts, their low foreheads and olive skin setting them apart from *the Wudayleegu* crowd.

The bands drifted to the auditorium's front, settling into niches as if they were iPods slipped into portable speakers. On the dais, three rows of dignitaries sat — the Zocor Council, wearing white shawls streaked blue and fringed green. Some wore round fur hats, while most had small boxes strapped to their noggins. They bowed repeatedly to each other as they spoke. First row members seemed more prominant, their robes brightly colored — arrayed in rainbow order, violet to red. The three centerpiece men wore green. Harris recognized Nikodemos and assumed this was the council. He later learned the three were the *Byllymycky,* chosen by a Zecronisian-Gurts caucus. Evidently, Gurt power went beyond their craft, sharing spiritual kinship with the Zecronisians. Still, the Zocor

Council sat as *the Wudayleegu's* spiritual spearhead and *the Byllymycky*, the council's supreme authority.

The trumpets blared again. The chorus changed its tune to a simple sing-song hymn, which Harris swore was *Jesus loves me, this I know.* He almost joined in, but exercised restraint. Buhippus led his Yunockers, both the vanguard and the drogues as a bumper, buffering the crowd. Agrimentikos parked his *Cabriolin*, facing the dais, and then disembarked, his Trone heaped beside the vehicle. Harris signaled *the Danuwa* to land, and, then maneuvered his *Cabriolin* behind Agrimentikos'.

The crowd cheered again when Harris stepped out, led by Yustichisqua. Harris noticed Agrimentikos bowing deeply to the council. *Protocol.* But one glance from Buhippus and Harris knew a *Didaniyisgi* didn't bow so readily. However, his entourage should.

"Bow, Little Bird," he whispered.

Yustichisqua made deep obeisance before *the Byllymycky*. *The Danuwa* followed suit. The crowd cheered.

Then, Nikodemos stood, raising both hands. The auditorium fell silent, except one errant flute, which had missed a beat and lingered awkwardly in the solemnity.

2

"Lord Agrimentikos," Nikodemos said. "What gift has Kuriakis the Great sent to his subjects in *the Wudayleegu?*"

"A rare gift, indeed, Grand Councilor Nikodemos," Agrimentikos replied, his voice booming to fill *the Zocorpykyn*. "*A Didaniyisgi* for *the Yuyutlu*, to abnegate injustice and regulate the trade." Agrimentikos bowed. "My great lord is pleased with his subjects, both Zecronisian and Gurt, who have come together in harmony for the good of all Montjoy — an age of prosperity, like nowhere else in Farn. To that he wishes to make perfect what is already a paragon to all observers."

The two other chief councilors stood. They bowed graciously to Agrimentikos. Then one spoke — the one to Nikodemos' left — the one called Altacantris.

"Long have we wished for a better presence in *the Yuyutlu* to replace the Yunocker regulators. *The Yuganawu* already has much to enforce within its precincts and within *the Kalugu*."

"General Tarhippus cannot be in all places," Mumpfredis (the other councilor) added. "Although he manages."

"That he does," Agrimentikos said, gazing at Buhippus, who appeared grave.

"We understand having *a Didaniyisgi* is like having Kuriakis' heart and soul in our midst," Nikodemos said.

"Our greatest joy," Altacantris echoed.

"Without a doubt," Mumpfredis underscored.

"There is much to see and much to know," Altacantris said.

"*The Ayelli* are omniscient," Mumpfredis added, smarmily.

"There is much to ingest, but Kuriakis' proxy must have a hearty appetite, even if he is so young," Altacantris continued.

"So young," Mumpfredis noted.

Harris understood these statements. The council didn't want Kuriakis' interference, but what could they do? They had operated for millennia without a provost, and whatever law enforcement necessary was provided by the Yunocker regulators under some honcho named Tarhippus. They doubted this gift from *the Ayelli* could learn in so short a time, despite the doctrine that everything from the hill was sacrosanct and all-knowing. In fact, this gift was young — too young to inspire much confidence, but also too young to make much difference, and thus not a threat. So the Zocor Council had assembled, threw this welcoming shindig, complete with floating trumpets, choral interlude, every third leg in *the Wudayleegu* and a packed house shouting their *bobyfysmagus* and *jipjipjiptipus*. Everyone loved a party, didn't they? But Harris was not another pretty face. He was here to turn his *make-work* assignment into a way to learn how to escape his servitude. This was a time to sparkle — a time to shine. Before Agrimentikos continued his babble or Altacantris and Mumpfredis delivered more left-handed insults, Harris stomped to the dais, slapping his *Columbincus.* He signaled his *Danuwa* and *Taleenay* to join him.

"Thank you for your kind words and confidence," Harris said, as if acting before a full house — the actual case. "I mean to do my father's will, learn what there is to learn, and discard things unworthy of my time and effort."

The three councilors looked to each other, and then sat on their extendable bottoms. Worry crossed Nikodemos' face.

"Lord Belmundus," he said, respectfully, but with the authority of owning this turf. "You are welcomed to our fair port and will be supported in every way to fulfill your father's wishes. However, the Zocor Council must follow certain forms."

"They must be ancient forms," Harris said, "considering there hasn't been *a Didaniyisgi* within anyone's memory."

"They *are* ancient, but must still be followed. Your father would not have us do otherwise."

"Absolutely," Harris said, and then touched his *Columbincus* again. "I would never set aside rituals and honored practices despite their fragility." He bowed for the first time. "I'm not so bold to dispatch established ways without first learning them. Only a fool sets aside misunderstood practices."

"Yes," Nikodemos said. "We are of the same mind." He clapped and Garan the *Gucheeda* appeared near the bandstand — accompanied by a Gurt, who sported several insignias on his cloak, perhaps denoting loftiness. Between them floated a book — a very large book. "This is Garan *the Deegosgi* — the Arbitrator of *the Yuyutlu*." Garan bowed, and winked. "And Cyprytop, Archon Supreme. Garan is the master of *the Book of Adjustments* and Cyprytop oversees the Gurt *ryyves*. Garan will support you in understanding the many regulations of the marketplace. Cyprytop will guide you to the chief centers of manufactory and trade."

Harris nodded to both Arbitrator and Archon Supreme. They returned his bow.

"The book is quite thick," Harris stated. "A little light reading to keep me busy."

"Are you up to the challenge, Lord Belmundus?" Nikodemos boomed.

Harris regarded the book, the Gurt and, finally, Garan, whom he knew was more *Gucheeda* than *Deegosgi*. He read Garan's face as surely as he read Yustichisqua's. *Odd.* Still, it spoke volumes saying: *time to sparkle — time to shine.* Harris turned, facing Nikodemos and his cronies.

"It is not proper to pose such questions to me, *an Ayelli* and consort to a Scepta, sir."

Nikodemos grinned. *Not so young, after all.* He shook his head, and then stood.

"Forgiveness, my lord."

The crowd rumbled, as if they expected a tag team match between the old councilor and cronies, and *the Didaniyisgi* and his Thirdling estate. But Harris moved quickly toward Garan and

Cyprytop. He placed his hand on the book, but, seeing a notch on the cover — a keyhole like *the Book of Farn's*, Harris snapped his *Columbincus* from his cloak and tossed it in the air. The blue sigil glowed, coming to rest in the notch. Suddenly, the book opened, a tornado of numbers and charts and products funneling to *the Zocorpykyn's* ceiling. The audience burst into applause.

Adadooski. Bobyfysmagu. Arkmos. Jipjipjiptipu.

Harris had deduced the ancient ritual. No objections came from any member of the Zocor Council. The only cautionary note came from another quarter.

3

Harris and his entourage retired to an anteroom behind the auditorium, where the crowd's assault on the senses was replaced by a buffet of Zecronisian delicacies. Harris left the food choices to Yustichisqua and never questioned a thing on the platter. Fytzyfu introduced him to the more eminent council members. Harris made small talk with each, trying to imagine himself to be like Caesar at a senatorial reception, although recalling how *that* went in the end.

The *Byllymycky* expressed amazement at Lord Belmundus' ability to open *the Book of Adjustments* in the proper manner, unleashing the elements of trade balance for all to see. Nikodemos explained that Cyprytop and Garan would conduct him to *the Yuyutlu* that afternoon, where the provost could assess the market and the manufactories.

"You shall take up residence in *the Myrkpykyn*," Nikodemos said. "It is not elegant, but serviceable. You are welcome to refurnish it to your tastes, but *the Myrkpykyn* is a functioning establishment for the conduct of business and not designed for *Ayelli* pleasures. I have been to the hilltop and have seen *Ayelli* standards. *The Myrkpykyn* is not up to those standards."

Harris couldn't fathom the fuss. *The Myrkpykyn* was as it was. His time would be divided between *the Yuyutlu* and Charminus' bed. A rundown hut at the edge of the marketplace would be paradise compared to trampolining on the Scepta under her jade ring's spell. Garan dovecoted him — a relief, because there was too much pretense among the Zocor Council.

"My lord," Garan began, nibbling on what had been a lizard's tail. "I never underestimated your talent."

"You've never seen me in action."

"Ah. You refer to stage acting. True?"

"To an actor, *action* has a particular meaning."

Garan swallowed, and then grinned, a runnel of blood dripping from his lip's corner.

"Perhaps I saw an actor when you confronted *the Byllymycky*," he whispered. "I assumed you would bow and scrape to them. But I was wrong. You *acted* as a consort."

"I *am* a consort."

"One of a different shade, I suspect." He nodded toward Yustichisqua, who gobbled a pile of *pukas midaskoos*. "I anticipate a more liberal take on *the Book of Adjustments* than the standard interpretation and application."

"Don't reveal whats' normal, so I can repaint with a fresh can."

Garan laughed, then demured when Buhippus approached.

"I recommend you take advantage of the slumber chambers before we leave, my lord," Garan said. "The itinerary is hectic and you may not see a bed again until tomorrow."

"I'll consider it," Harris said, but Garan and his lizard tail faded into the cloud of guests.

"My lord," Buhippus said. "I have received the travel plan for you to review."

"Captain," Harris said, incredulously. "Because I haven't a clue where I am or where I'm going, except to inspect factories and sweat shops, and to land in sub-standard housing, I'll leave the arrangements to you. If you need help, enlist Melonius."

"What happened to the imperious consort I beheld today?" Buhippus remarked. "Inconsistency will reveal the sham."

"Sham? That I depend on you there's no doubt. If I command informally, don't construe it as weakness."

"Unfortunately, my lord, there is an issue which requires you to wear steel more consistently."

"Issue?" Harris set his plate down and moved away from prying ears. "The council seems harmless enough. Powerful, but when confronted by Kuriakis' mandate, harmless."

"A mandate you have," Buhippus said, "but, until now, the enforcement of rules in *the Yuyutlu* has been under another's jurisdiction, who some might interpret as overlapping your mandate."

"General Tarhippus."

"Just so. And I have learned from Nikodemos that Tarhippus has been informed of your assignment and purpose through the postern system — and nothing has been sent to him directly from the Zocor Council."

"But his orders would come from Kuriakis," Harris remarked.

"Yes. But the general is slow to read dispatches. His jurisdiction is wide and busy. He is a hands-on commander."

Harris scratched his chin. He had heard Tarhippus' name invoked and always in whispers, as if said too loudly, the general would appear — an avoidable event.

"Perhaps a visit to the general's headquarters should be my first point of business."

"It should. But he resides in *the Yuganawu.* The Zocor Council should have invited him here to greet you. It would have been a pissing contest, but at least the first round would have been on Zecronisian turf."

Harris burbled his lips.

"You know him well, captain."

"He is my brother, my lord."

"Ah, then I have the advantage."

"None that I know." Buhippus bowed. "I will speak on your behalf. I am bound to do so."

"You are also bound to protect me."

"Yes . . . with the meager forces meant as your escort. But it is not an army." Harris sighed. "I only warn you, my lord, so you wear balls of steel and have your *Stick* always at the ready."

"For that I thank you. I've porcelain balls, being Charminus' bedfellow, but I might fare better with my sword. *Sticks* are too much like magic wands for me. Besides, it's still hit or miss."

He noticed Yustichisqua silently loitering on the margins, probably loathed to interrupt a conversation with Buhippus.

"I think your *Taleenay* has words for you, my lord," Buhippus said, turning away.

"Yes, Little Bird."

"*Oginali,* Garan advises us to rest before we depart."

"I agree."

"I have found the rooms."

Agrimentikos was here now.

"Brother," he said, "you made an impression on these decadent folk. They cannot cease praising your tornado display."

"I don't think that'll impress General Tarhippus."

Agrimentikos frowned.

"That gentleman is most effective at his tasks. I hope he finds the boundaries between your role and his; otherwise I fear upstaging will result."

Harris thought of Tappiolus during the performance of *Othellohito*. It never ceased, this life upon the wicked stage.

He didn't feel like sleeping, but he assumed that Yustichisqua would have a fit if he didn't try.

"Bedrooms, you say, Little Bird."

"Yes, *oginali*," the *Taleenay* replied.

Harris looked about, spotting Parnasus. He waved him over.

"Yes, my lord."

"Gather your two colleagues and follow us for some well deserved rest."

"Rest, my lord?"

"Don't question it. If we're to remain sparkling and shiny, we need to sleep away the tarnish."

Parnasus grinned, bowed, and then scurried away, hopping to see over the heads of the guests. Harris grasped Agrimentikos' hand.

"Will you be coming with us, brother?"

"Here my part ends, Lord Belmundus. I shall tarry with the Zecronisian ladies for a day or two, then drift up the hill to Soffira's bed sheets. It is my time to be *up*, and Arquebus deserves a well-earned rest." He patted Harris' hand. "Make your brothers proud, Lord Belmundus. Find the limits of your task and keep well within them. Expectations are like clouds at best and are like reflections at worst. Stay strong. Impress, but . . ." He inclined toward Harris' ear and whispered. "Do not become too popular."

This star shouldn't sparkle too brightly or shine beyond the task. A funny world, this.

Chapter Fourteen

Trouble at Ryyve Aniniya

1

"All the fabrics of Montjoy are made here by *the Ryyve Gudi*," Cyprytop explained, his hand sweeping across what seemed miles of looms and spindles.

Harris and his entourage, called in *the Yuyutlu, the Seegoniga* — the blue ones, owing to *the Didaniyisgi's* blue cloak and sigil, had traveled to the marketplace through a toll tunnel, operated by the Zecronisian *Department of Hyryods* (Tariffs). Once in the bazaar's thick, negotiating *Cabriolins* in narrow lanes and alleys, under awnings and over low stalls, Garan and Cyprytop guided *the Seegoniga* into the factory zone, the district of *the Ryyves* or guilds. Their first stop was *the Ryyve Pykyn*, where the master builders of Montjoy enjoyed particular prosperity — masons carving *kaybar* and *phitron* and *banibara* into building blocks for every edifice in the city and the port.

"Is this where they make *mopyn*?" Harris asked Cyprytop.

Cyprytop, a Gurt, who exuded an aristocratic air, held his nose and coughed.

"My lord does not wish to visit there today," he said. "That is not a stone mason's *Ryyve,* but a place were cows are milked and sewers flow. You shall visit it when the time is proper. Even Tarhippus stays clear of *the Ryyve Mopyn* if he can."

Harris recalled *mopyn*, the Gurt plastic molding material, made from pressed milk and Gurt shit without a quarry in sight.

"I understand," Harris said, looking to Garan, who grinned. Garan always grinned, a latch to secrets, Harris supposed. "Who among my *Danuwa* will take responsibility for the *Ryyve Mopyn*?" he asked, using the proper syntax for the Gurt word for *guild* (*ryyve*) and the manufactured product.

"Sounds like a job for Melonius," Elypticus said, laughter upon his lip.

"Sounds like a job for *the Taleenay*," Melonius replied, but then appeared abashed by his boldness.

"*Danuwa* Melonius," Yustichisqua said, "any Cetrone lucky enough to rule *the mopyn* pits would reap wealth beyond a Thirdling's imagination."

Harris grinned, happy Little Bird could hold his own when insulted.

Now they were at *the Ryyve Gudi,* where Harris' blue cloak had originated, spun from the furry *awidena,* sheep he had seen grazing in *the Yugda.*

"Tell me, Cyprytop," Harris asked, "how do they spin the cloth so fine for Xyftys finishing touches?"

Harris rubbed his cloak, which didn't feel wooly, the expected texture of sheep. Garan answered.

"The secret is in the water, my lord."

"Such is our secret," Cyprytop said, giving Garan the fish-eye. "We do not reveal it readily, but since you are *the Didaniyisgi,* I suppose you must see. Come."

The *Seegoniga* followed their Gurt conductor and, after words with the foreman, who seemed cross that these strangers trespassed beyond the first stages of *the Ryyve,* Cyprytop waved them forward.

"What you see must not be reported casually to acquaintances and friends, my lord," Cyprytop stated, his long tongue snapping a fly, which buzzed near his head. "If our methods were known, the monopoly would be impossible to preserve. *The Hyryods* would be exorbitant. We would lose our advantage."

"I understand, sir," Harris said.

Harris walked carefully, because the ground was slimy, the looms spewing oil from their heddles. The fabric stretched to the ceiling and soon *the Seegoniga* walked beneath a canopy of every shade and color cloth imaginable. Reaching the roof's gap, it fluttered in the breeze, drying, before tugged onto rolling machines — a spool for each color, each standing upright fifty feet tall. As far as Harris could see were columns of silky thimbles.

Harris reached the end of the weaving floor. Here the ground fell away, a river rushing through the building — a rusty rapids flecked with gossamer knots. Several rickety sluices channeled this brew into pipes, funneling it back to the weaving floor. Trones filtered the water with long paddles, catching strange creepy crawlers in nets.

"It smells like bananas in here," Harris said.

"More like *fuveratski*," Parnasus said. "I am not fond of *fuveratski*."

Whatever caused the sweet sickly smell, it swam in the water.

"The work is dangerous," Garan said. "*The googani* is akin to *the porcorporian* from the Forling. But they secrete a powerful elastic. When it washes *the awidena* fleece, the resulting yarn turns soft and pliant."

Suddenly, *a googani* emerged, its tarantula legs sweeping to the sluice, catching a Trone, who struggled for a moment, and then disappeared into the creature's mandibles. The other Trones cowered, putting their paddles down. The victim's legs kicked, and a terrible crunch could be heard. Harris drew his sword, but Garan parried it. Elypticus and Parnasus had their hands on their *Sticks*. Yustichisqua wrapped his fingers around his dagger's hilt.

"No, my lord," Garan stammered. "You must not interfere with the process."

"Process?" Harris shouted. "I'm watching a big fucking bug feed on Cetrone laborers so its oily bristles can pollute the waters for a better sheen on my fucking cloak. That's barbarous."

"Only one Trone a day is sacrificed, my lord," Cyprytop explained. "They are expendable and worth less than the cloth."

Harris balled his fists, but Melonius grasped his shoulder.

"It might seem appalling, my lord," he whispered, "especially since *the Taleenay* is here to witness it. But it is the practice you are sworn to uphold."

Harris clenched his teeth, but listened to Melonius' reason — a justification for murder — much like saying *we sacrifice only one virgin a day to the Cyclops, but look at the perks* — thousands of upright bolts of silk made from sheep fleece — gold spun from straw. The bananary *fuveratski* stench from *the googani* got to him now.

"We need our Trones," Cyprytop explained. "They comb the water for *googani* eggs to hatch and keep production high. We could not afford to lose more than one Trone a day."

Harris closed his eyes and counted to ten. No chance of overturning this process, although he might later convince the Gurts to feed *the googani* a *gufa* or a can of tuna fish.

"No wonder you keep this a secret," he muttered, resignation in his voice. "I've seen enough. What's next?"

2

Next up, *the Ryyve Sulasgi* — the ceramics factory. It was on the far side of *the Yuyutlu* bounded by *the Yuganawu* — the Yunocker quarters, its skyline dominated by the high fortress and the old and new prisons. To reach *the Ryyve Sulasgi, the Seegoniga* had to pass through the open marketplace — a *free-for-all* zone, where any Gurt who could hammer or chisel or bake or lick a postage stamp could setup shop to deal with their Zecronisian go betweens — agents called *the Augustii.* The open market was called *the Doonedin* by the Yunockers and *the Byybykyyip* by the Gurts.

"Most disputes occur in *the Byybykyyip,* my lord," Cyprytop explained as the *Cabriolins* zoomed through the traffic maze and dust. "Many *Gucheeda* here."

Garan laughed.

"I suppose it's a pickpocket's heaven," Harris remarked.

"Each seller here is without a *Ryyve,* my lord, because the resident has not qualified to work in the *Vyrjyts.*"

"*Vyrjyts?* " Harris asked.

"A work zone," Cyprytop said.

"My lord," Garan explained, "it is basic, but you must understand. Every Gurt is born attached to a craft. It is determined by family heritage. Weavers become weavers. Potters become potters. Bakers become . . ."

"I get the idea. It sounds like feudalism to me."

"Feudalism?" Cyprytop asked.

"A system where everyone is born to a state and cannot escape it."

"We are not Trones," Cyprytop complained. "Gurts are skilled, taught by parents from an early age. But there are too many skills and not enough *Vyrjyts,* so all Gurts must qualify."

"A test?"

"Exactly so, my lord," Cyprytop continued. "The standards are high. Even if a baker Gurt can make fine *bupka* in the pail and bubble manner, with gritty *prysyst* and sweet *mollicops,* it does not mean she will earn her *Vyrjyt.* Her *bupka* must be carefully judged against the semiannual candidates for the bequest and if it exceeds standards, she is rewarded a *Vyrjyt* in the *Ryyve Bomertoss,* where the finest *bupka* is baked. That leaves many *bupka* bakers without a *Vyrjyt*. So they setup their fires and bring their pails to bubble into *the Byybykyyip*. Yunocker households are fond of *bupka*. Their women come to the *Byybykyyip* daily and seek *the Augustii* to negotiate for cheap *bupka*."

"Sounds like a free for all."

"It is, my lord," Garan said. "My job, when I am in port, is to settle cases between unscrupulous *Doonedin* Gurts, who sell shoddy *pimpsqua* or defective *perpadranum* using a less than honest *Augustii* in the palaver."

"And my occupation," Cyprytop added, "is to assure that *the Hyryods* are administered fairly and Garan does not win every case."

Harris glimpsed at the many squabbles under the awnings and in the stalls. Perhaps these were heated negotiations between Zecronisian agents, called *Augustii* and the non-*Vyrjyt* Gurts. However, he also noticed Yunocker regulators at every turn and the first civilian Yunockers he had encountered — comely women in stylish skirts and fashionable *zulus*, some with children in tow. Older men wearing sharp tunics, perusing goods on racks and shelves, shadowed by *Augustii* ready to strike a bargain with a resident Gurt.

"Why the middlemen, Garan?" Harris asked. "Why can't the Yunockers shop and pay a tagged price directly to the deserving shopowner?"

"My lord, *the Augustii* own the shops, and the Yunockers will not deal with the Gurts."

"That jacks up the price of doing business, I imagine."

"They are men of pedigree," Garan said. "The saying goes: One Yunocker's morning spit is worth more than all the Trones in *the Kalugu*."

"I don't see any Trones."

"Not in the *Doonedin*, my lord. In *the Ryyves* for the dirty jobs and in the shadows for the night soil. Except to serve in rich households and on *the Ayelli,* Trones do not exist." He glanced at Yustichisqua. "There are exceptions, no doubt — exceptions which might prove interesting in this environment."

No doubts there.

They had reached *the Ryyve Sulasgi*, where everything clay was formed. Harris wondered if he would see old-fashioned pottery forms or more bloodletting — pigments made of macerated body parts. Still, *the Seegoniga's Cabriolins* parked in a small courtyard, where they were greeted by the chief agents (*the Ryyvytys*) of *the Sulasgi* manufactory. They bowed.

"Is all prepared?" Cyprytop asked.

"Yes, Archon Supreme," they said in unison, voices matched precisely as if automated. Even their tongue snaps were synchronized.

"All is well," Cyprytop remarked, and then turned to Garan. "You have not visited *the Sulasgi* kilns for many years, great *Deegosgi.*

"Has it changed?"

"Perfection cannot be made more perfect."

Garan faced Harris.

"Cyprytop does not exaggerate, my lord. If you have never seen ceramics manufactured or glass blown, you shall be impressed."

"I've been to *Pottery Barn*," Harris replied, and he had, and he had seen glass blown in Wheeling, West Virginia, when his mother took him to a spa at the beginning of his Thespian career. "Clay, wheels, fire and brimstone."

Garan grinned, and then bowed.

"As you will, my lord."

The courtyard door opened — two Fort Laramie-style impalements, revealing their secrets inside. Harris gasped. He heard the other members of his crew mutter. The inner sanctum was vast — the opposite side beyond sight. In perfect array sat at least a thousand Gurts at potters' wheels, hugging and caressing and otherwise sculpting the clay into every imaginable shape. The wheels hummed, as did the potters — a whistling song which kept their long tongues lashing, creating rims and flutes and spouts and funnels. Slowly, Cyprytop conducted *the Seegoniga* down the central aisle. The potters bowed gently as they passed, each indicating their current production with a whip of the tongue.

Behind each potter, heaps of broken shards were hilled, and behind these, completed vessels sat — bowls, vases, jugs, trays, and crenulated water *vargos,* used as canteens. Other Gurts carried the unfired forms on stretchers to the yard's far wall. Like beehives, the kilns lined the walls — countless ovens, fire in their bellies and smoke in their stacks. Like chefs at a pizzeria, the kiln Gurts peeled the clay forms into the bake zones. Other Gurts cut underglaze designs in the crockery before shuffling the finished forms into tempered ovens.

"Here we finish the daily ware," Cyprytop said, indicating a large vat of milky substance, which stank like a thousand elephant farts.

"How can they stand it?" Harris said.

He noticed the aroma seize Elypticus and Parnasus, who choked. Melonius took the stench in stride, but did make a face, covering his mouth. Yustichisqua didn't flinch. Nor did Garan.

"It is *Tygger* piss," Garan said. "The Gurts use it for emulsification. The more delicate work — over glaze painting and bejeweling is accomplished at the far end of the yard."

"I'll take your word for it," Harris said, his eyes tearing. "I think I've seen and smelt enough. I'm impressed, Cyprytop. I've never seen so vast an operation."

"It is the heart of my people," Cyprytop replied.

The two *Ryyvytys* bowed in unison and muttered something about their delight in pleasing *the Sakwoladi.*

"What did they call me?" Harris asked.

"Not you, my lord," Garan said. "Your entire crew."

"*The Seegoniga?*"

"Yes, only they said it in Gurt — *Sakwoladi*, which means bluebirds, considering you travel in the air; although the word *seegoniga* refers to the blue holly bush."

Harris smiled, but the stench was too much to keep him here longer. He backed away into the pottery zone, where the air was less tart and the singing trumped him sweetly.

3

"Funny," Harris remarked to Yustichisqua, "I've often called you my *Noya Tludachi*, yet I never considered what that meant if you pissed in my cart."

Little Bird laughed.

"It is a common smell in *the Kalugu*, where *Tyggers* are kept in pits to assure we wear *zulus*."

That explained Little Bird's reaction or no reaction to the smell. But *the Kalugu* must be an unbearable place to dwell in with air so foul.

The Seegoniga (or now perhaps, *the Sakwoladi*) sped away from *the Ryyve Sulasgi*. Harris hoped today's tour was over. The afternoon grew late and he would have liked to settle into his digs before nightfall. He anticipated *the Myrkpykyn* to be a scabby place to bunk and hoped it didn't reek of *Tygger* piss. However, his hopes were dashed, although as *the Didaniyisgi* he could command the tour end. But what loomed ahead fascinated him — a tall cinder block building with high parapets and protective spikes, flashing Tesla-style voltage along the perimeter. It could have been a prison, because it was surrounded by an armed Yunocker force. Fort Knox came to mind.

"What's this place?" he asked Garan.

"*The Ryyve Aniniya,*" Garan replied. "Here is where . . ."

"They make *the stuff,*" Harris said. "That's the shit of the gods. No wonder the place looks like a lockup."

"They do not make it here, my lord," Garan explained. "They fashion it here. *Aniniya* is mined in Terrastrium and, by treaty and contract, it is distributed among the nine realms. Each place exports their quota here, where Gurt artisans apply their skills."

"High tension here," Cyprytop stated.

Harris glanced up at the electrified fortification and didn't doubt it. However, he soon learned this comment was not scientific, but sociological. *Aniniya* was the most valuable commodity in Farn and each realm was jealous of its quantity and its application. The haggling between *Augustii* and *Ryyvytys* in *the Ryyve Aniniya* sometimes reached fever pitch, as it did today.

The *Seegoniga* did not abandon their *Cabriolins* here as in other *Ryyves.* This *Ryyve's* inner sanctum was partitioned into several factories. Cyprytop relinquished his tour guide position to Buhippus, who negotiated each zone militaristically, palavering with the various Yunocker guards regulating each production line. From a silent distance, Harris witnessed the manufacturing of *Sticks* — an armory of every size weapon, including some he had not encountered before — even one which looked like a tank, or rather an *Aniniya* Armadillo. There were also flying contraptions — strafe bombers perhaps, being assembled beside *Cabriolins* of assorted sizes and shapes. But in *the zulu* factory, *the Seegoniga* faced trouble.

The factory, a roundhouse, was honeycombed with streets punctuated with stalls and awnings, much like *the Byybykyyip,.* Each *zulu* maker could negotiate his own price and each *Augustii* could level the best *Hyryods* from the resident *Ryyvytys.* The haggling noise was tremendous, but centered on one heated discussion. *The Ryyvyty* lashed his tongue at the *Augustii*, who thrust his third leg under the Gurt's belly, pulling him to the ground. *The Seegoniga* landed, Buhippus raising his hand to keep them in their *Cabriolins.*

A troop of Yunockers came on the scene, but the fight continued, more Gurts and *Augustii* joining into the fray.

"What do we do?" Harris asked Garan.

"If this were any other *Ryyve*, we would be separating the combatants and mediating the cause."

"But . . ."

"Stay put and hope."

"Hope what?"

"Hope that . . ."

Hope went through the roof, because suddenly a fierce cry came from the far end of the street. Gurts fled and *Augustii* cleared a path. A snapping sound was followed by painful wailing. Yunocker guards pushed the crowd back.

"What the fuck?" Harris stammered.

He caught Buhippus' eye. It said, *stay put . . . my lord.* Cyprytop shook his head, while Garan hid behind *the Cabriolin.* Before them, charging forth like Lucifer rising, was a Yunocker like no other. His face was broad and mean, with thick, angry lips and eyes set far apart — too far spaced to be friendly. His helmet was fiery — literally. It was on fire. His *Cabriolin* was ablaze also and, instead of a *Stick*, he wielded a ferocious whip — what Yustichisqua had called *a gwasdi.* Before him roared three dog-like creatures, *zugginaks*, and they were hungry and snarling and snapping at the crowd. They leaped forward and soon attacked Harris' *Cabriolin.* Yustichisqua cowered.

"Help me, *oginali.*"

Harris drew his sword and swung, missing *the zugginak* closest to the left thruster. Elypticus fired his *Stick,* but missed. Parnasus drew, but before he aimed, Buhippus was on the spot with a whistle. *The zugginaks* cowered.

"If you kill Tarhippus' *zugginaks,* my lord," Buhippus said, tensely, "it will be more trouble than it is worth."

"Tarhippus?" Harris asked, and then looked toward the monster charging, now out of his fiery *Cabriolin* and lashing his whip at anything in his course.

"A Trone in *the Ryyve Aniniya*," Tarhippus roared. "I shall hang every man who let that Trone pass through these gates."

The whip lashed out, striking Harris' *Cabriolin* just a hairbreadth from Yustichisqua, who now crouched on the ground, shivering.

"What has brought you here?" Buhippus shouted, a stupid question to be sure, but one catching Tarhippus' attention.

"Buhippus?" the General growled. "I do not understand. Why would *you* permit this infraction? Infraction!"

"Must I hang too, brother? You are here to regulate a dispute, not to chastise the new *Didaniyisgi's Taleenay*."

Tarhippus' eyes opened wider than Harris thought possible. He gazed at the Provost and peered over the edge of the Cabriolin.

"I do not see *a Taleenay*. I see a bog sucking Trone in this *Ryyve* of *Ryyves*."

"He is my *Taleenay*," Harris snapped, nerves bubbling to the surface. "And these are my *Danuwa*, and those are your fucking dogs, and if you don't want to lose one under my sword, you'd best get back into your fucking *Cabriolin* and ride out from whence you came."

Tarhippus' face went redder — his flaming helmet, volcanic. He raised his *gwasdi,* but Buhippus slapped his *Stick* on his brother's arm.

"This is our lord Kuriakis' Provost, brother. To harm him will bring *the Ayelli* down upon your head and the heads of all Yunockers."

"You were sent your orders," Harris said, tenuously.

Tarhippus trembled, and then looked to Buhippus.

"*The Didaniyisgi*, you say?"

"Yes."

The general laughed, a terrifying howl, which brought whomever wasn't on their knees already, down. "Why did you not say so?"

"I did," Harris barked. "My orders are as clear as yours."

"Are they?"

"I rule *the Yuyutlu*."

"Rule?" Tarhippus laughed. Buhippus gave Harris a cautionary glance. "I believe you meant to say, *mediate* or *piss over the heads of the Augustii*. Your orders do not trump the rules, and to bring a Trone into *the Ryyve Aniniya*, especially one decked out as a lord and traveling without *zulus* in *a Cabriolin,* is more than rule breaking. It is an infraction. Infraction! It is an invalidation of your warrant, sir."

"It is not," Harris shouted. "I am the son of Kuriakis. I am the consort to Scepta Charminus. Even if I chose to enter here with an army of Cetrone, you'd have to take your *gwasdi* and shove it up your ass."

The crowd gasped. Tarhippus raised an eyebrow, bringing his face close to Harris'. It was a horrible visage to behold, with a brimstone stench, which nearly trumped *the Tygger* piss. Then Tarhippus whipped about and pointed to two Yunockers.

"Arrest those *Ryyvytys* and *the Augustii.* Bring them to *the Katorias* to await my pleasure, and . . ." He shook his fist at Yustichisqua, "arrest this . . . thing in costume, and toss him in *the Porias* to await my pleasure."

Harris swung the sword, but missed. Yustichisqua drew his dagger.

"Armed," Tarhippus shouted. "This Trone is armed. Infraction! Infraction!"

Buhippus intervened, grasping his brother's shoulders and tossing him aside. Tarhippus pushed back, but Buhippus threatened with his *Stick.* Yunockers on both sides bellied up for a fight.

"Brother," Buhippus said, "I am as opposed as you are to the arming of a Trone, but when a Trone is elevated by Kuriakis' consent to *Taleenay,* neither you nor I can question it."

"Kuriakis approved this abomination?"

"Yes, and we are the enforcers of the law and the law is Montjoy — and Kuriakis is the Elector in Montjoy. He is the law. He can never be . . . an infraction. Do not forget yourself, brother. Do not give way to your fiery soul. If you do, we shall all be lost."

Tarhippus trembled, and then snorted. He turned to Harris and pointed, but Harris pointed to the Yunockers.

"Release those men to my charge," Harris commanded. "They shall be brought to the *Myrkpykyn* for my decision on any penalties incurred for this disturbance." The *two Ryyvytys* and *the Augustii* rushed into the custody of *the Seegoniga* Yunockers. "As for laying a hand on my *Taleenay,* General Tarhippus. Any violation of my deputies will be regarded as grounds for your immediate dismissal. You can shine fleece in *the Ryyve Sulasgi* for the balance of your days. You can swim with *the googani*, which you closely resemble."

Tarhippus spit, but didn't dispute any further. He turned his back to Harris and gathered his *zugginaks* about his heels.

"One more thing, General Tarhippus," Harris said. Tarhippus turned again. "I realize you believe you are enforcing the rules today, so I will not press you further for any breach in protocol. However, I insist you greet me in an appropriate fashion."

Tarhippus grinned.

"I did not kill your Trone today. Take it as my welcome to the *Yuyutlu* . . . my . . . lord."

Tarhippus mounted his *Cabriolin* and sped off through the alley, the Yunockers shaken by their commander's inability to bring down fire on the new provost's head. Harris helped Yustichisqua to his feet and saw Garan peep from beneath a stall. Cyprytop attended to the custody of the prisoners. Harris faced his *Danuwa*, who bowed to him, even Melonius, who touched his Thirdling *Columbincus*.

"Captain Buhippus," Harris said, not looking to the man. "I hope I haven't compromised you with your brother."

"We are blood, my lord, but we were compromised in the cradle."

"I'm not looking for praise or anything, but did I totally fuck this up or what?"

"No, my lord. In fact, there is hope your porcelain balls might still turn to steel."

Harris grinned. Right now those balls were tired and made of puff pastry.

Chapter Fifteen

The Judgment of Harris

1

The *Myrkpykyn* was everything Harris had expected — a low two-story building with a judicial façade, a peppering of offices and a courtroom — musty and underutilized. Above the courtroom, at the back, as an afterthought, was a loft with two small bedrooms, more for convenience than comfort, although *the Myrkpykyn* staff had readied them for *the Didaniyisgi's* use — one room for him and one for his *Seegoniga*. A kingsized bed was chucked in the room reserved for the Provost and four platforms were erected for *the Seegoniga's* easement. Harris inspected the rooms soon after his arrival, giving them a cursory glance. He told Cyprytop that the space was adequate to the purpose and in line with Nikodemus' description. Harris wanted to occupy his room at once, but business prevailed. So, he descended to the courtroom to hear the case and deliver his judgment against the two *Ryyvytys* and *the Augustii* from *the Ryyve Aniniya*. He hadn't a notion on how to proceed and would rely upon Garan's experience and Cyprytop's knowledge. Somehow he'd muddle through.

Two *bronskers* (*the aniniya* fueled lamps ubiquitous to Montjoy) lit the courtroom harshly, not having the soft glow of *waddly wazzoos*. Still, they chased the shadows as night fell. Four Gurt attendants polished the empty gallery — a reviewing stand, six rows high and steeply inclined, like bleachers in a gymnasium. Two others helped Cyprytop install *The Book of Adjustment* in a prominent position beside *a bronsker*, a position Harris assumed it had enjoyed for centuries.

Harris entered from the second story directly to his place on the high bench overlooking the court. Guided by Garan, *the Danuwa* found places lower down beneath Harris' bench. Garan ushered Yustichisqua lower still, to a solitary chair at ground level and central to the proceedings. The prisoner's dock, a cage opposite the gallery, was empty, the defendants absent, probably held in cells beneath *the Myrkpykyn*. Harris sat on the hard seat — not comfortable and not conducive for sleeping. Nonetheless, he closed his eyes, resting them.

The day had been long — too many *Ryyves* — too many factories. Harris was dreadfully tired. He wished to postpone these proceedings until the morning, but Cyprytop needed to return to his family and Garan to his ship. Harris didn't want to detain the prisoners unduly, although they were prisoners and he was exhausted. So he rested his eyes and wished everyone would hurry.

Harris listened to Elypticus and Parnasus whispering like children in church. He couldn't make out the words and wondered why they whispered in an empty courtroom. Perhaps the austere room induced silence. As he listened to his *Danuwa* susurrate, he daydreamed, and not pleasantly. He saw *the googani*, its tentacles batting a dozen Trones from the sluice bank, blood coursing the flume while the monster dined. He smelled the emulsion vat in *the Ryyve Sulasgi*. Pew. The traffic in *the Byybykyyip* besieged him. He shuddered. He heard the snap of *the gwasdi* and the barking *zugginaks*. Tarhippus' face came upon him in a flash, its chilling mask a terror to recall. Harris awoke abruptly, muttering a single word, which emblazoned his heart.

"Infractions."

"My lord," Garan said, close to his ear. "Yes, infractions."

"Infractions," Harris said again, this time with conviction. He tried to mask the fact he was asleep by beginning a discussion on jurisprudence. He was awake, but not sure where he was, until he saw *the Danuwa* staring at him, and then Little Bird's terrified expression.

"Sorry," Harris said. "I dozed off. Sorry." He looked to Garan. "This has been an overlong day. If I could postpone this until tomorrow I would, but . . ."

He glanced at the empty courtroom, now no longer empty. When the gallery filled, he couldn't tell. Who these people were, went beyond him, but a mixed audience of Gurts, Zecronisians and Yunockers sat attentively musing on the somnambulistic behavior of their new *Didaniyisgi*.

Harris scanned the room, his gaze settling on the prisoners. *When did they arrive?* The *Ryyvytys* might have been twins — either a family resemblance or a Gurt trait. Harris recalled the *duo* who had greeted him in *the Ryyve Sulasgi* — synchronized automatons. But these prisoners' eyes were sad and careworn, perhaps worrying about their fate.

Perhaps from weariness like their Didaniyisgi.

The *Augustii* seemed less distressed, wrapped in an elegant gold cloak, now smeared with mud from the scuffle.

Harris turned to Garan, who bowed.

"You are expected to say a few words, my lord," Garan said in a low voice.

Nice.

He had said more than a few words to Tarhippus, and where did that get him? This was his first case. He worked without a net. That wasn't precisely true. He had *the Danuwa* in the next row down, his faithful Dune Tygger front and center, Garan as *Deegosgi* or *Gucheeda* or whatever other title he sported this evening, Cyprytop as the Archon Supreme and . . . and Buhippus. Harris careened.

"Where's Captain Buhippus?" he asked.

"Below stairs, my lord, preparing to enforce your will," Garan replied.

"Ah," Harris said. "Preparing the thumbscrews, no doubt."

"Excuse me?"

"Never mind. A few words, you say."

He cleared his throat, and then stood. The gallery crowd stirred, bowing their heads as if they anticipated holy communion. He raised his hand, signaling for heads to rise. He wanted to see their eyes, although his own were lidded.

"Good people of *the Yuyutlu*," he began, and since he heard no grunting, he said it again. "Good people of *the Yuyutlu*, I realize these proceedings have been convened in my father's name since time immemorial under a proxy of Archons and *Deegosgis*. Now *the Ayelli* will manage it directly. I am your *Didaniyisgi* and these are my *Danuwa*."

The three Thirdlings nodded in recognition. Yustichisqua knew better to do so. Harris decided not to push his *Taleenay* on this crowd — a doff to political necessity. It was bad enough he didn't know what he was doing, it would be worse if he lit a fuse he couldn't dowse. Then, he pointed to *the Book of Adjustments*.

"The law is the true embodiment of everything that's excellent. It has no kind of fault or flaw and I intend to embody the law." He had encountered this phrase somewhere in his stagecraft, but the exact source escaped him at the moment. Gilbert & Sullivan's *Iolanthe* came briefly to mind, but no matter. Any good line in a pinch. "I mean to press the heads of first offenders softly; those who commit lesser . . . infractions." The word stopped in his throat. "Yes, infractions, dealt with harshly in other jurisdictions." The crowd murmured. The Tarhippus reference hit its mark. "But I am *your Didaniyisgi* and no other. I use a velvet glove. And know this. The hand that gloves me conceals none other than the loving hand of your Elector . . . Kuriakis the Great."

He raised both arms high, looking to the ceiling cracks. The gallery crowd met this gesture with approbation — applauding and letting loose with shouts of *adadooski, arkmo, bobyfysmagu* and *jipjipjiptipu.* They even banged their feet on the gallery wood — two or three, according to the species.

Harris glanced at Cyprytop, who grinned, his tongue lashing his approval. Garan appeared humble, a charm that didn't become him. Harris thought — *Uriah Heep.* But he depended on *the Deegosgi* for guidance; for the next step, in fact. So he watched carefully until it came — a wink. Harris sat. Enough said.

Four Gurt staffers entered the courtroom carrying four scrolls. They trundled ceremoniously to *the Taleenay*, and then stopped. Yustichisqua stared at them, puzzled; and then, taking the hint, he extended his hands, receiving the scrolls one at a time. He nodded, and then looked to Cyprytop, whose tongue pointed to Harris. Little Bird stood, carefully toting these scrolls to the aisle's end, and then carrying them up to Harris. *The Didaniyisgi* took them with as much pomp as he could imagine, and he could imagine much pomp. Garan seemed pleased.

"Thank you, *Taleenay*," Harris intoned.

This caused a stir in the gallery, the acknowledgment that *the Trone in the room* was the second-in-command.

"With humility, *oginali*," Yustichisqua replied, garnering a frown from Garan. "I mean, my lord."

The frown converted into an approving grin.

Harris cut the scroll's strings and unfurled one. He perused the first — chicken-scratch — an unintelligible scrawl of Zecronisian characters. He grinned, and then unfurled the others in succession — reading (or not, because he couldn't), nodding and performing this pantomime until Cyprytop stood.

A gong sounded. Cyprytop strutted to a position before the prisoner dock. He placed his hands behind his back like Clarence Darrow at the Scope's Monkey Trial. He snapped his tongue and addressed the cage.

"Gypysyp of *Ryyve Aniniya*," he chanted. "You have been brought to *the Myrkpykyn* because you disturbed the peace of your *Ryyve* by contesting *the Hyryod* of Ricktus Morphinus, *Augustii spinctus* of said *Ryyve*. How say you?"

"I did so, Archon Supreme," Gypysyp squeaked, and then bowed.

Gong.

Cyprytop turned about, faced the gallery and grinned. He cracked his knuckles and continued addressing the cage.

"Rypchypy of *Ryyve Aniniya*," he intoned. "You also have been brought to *the Myrkpykyn* because you also disturbed the peace of your *Ryyve* by contesting *the Hyryod* of the same Ricktus Morphinus, *Augustii spinctus* of aforesaid *Ryyve*. How say you?"

"I did so, Archon Supreme," Rypchypy grunted, "and would do so again if so provoked."

The gallery buzzed. Cyprytop snapped his tongue clear around his head, but didn't react further. Harris assumed these boring proceedings were the standard fare in *the Myrkpykyn*. However, as the noise increased, he looked about the desk for a gavel or something to curb the audience in case of an insurrection. No gavel.

Some courtroom this, where the judge didn't have a hammer to keep order. Harris thought. *Judge Judy would be appalled.*

Harris stood suddenly — not a radical move, but it did the trick. The room came to order. Cyprytop bowed in gratitude, but how order was restored without a presiding judge, Harris couldn't guess? He leaned forward and whispered to his *Danuwa*.

"Watch and learn."

Gong.

Cyprytop continued.

"Ricktus Morphinus, *Augustii spinctus* of zone *zulus* of *the Ryyve Aniniya*, you have been brought to *the Myrkpykyn* because you contributed to a riot by assaulting these *Ryyvytys* before many witnesses. How say you?"

Ricktus Morphinus raised his palms, and then looked to the ceiling as if calling the faithful to prayer.

"I have not been brought to *the Myrkpykyn* for the reason you say."

Cyprytop looked concerned. The gallery became restless again. Harris prepared to stand — his gavel *in absentia*.

"No, Archon Supreme," *the Augustii* murmured. "This was not my destined place. Tarhippus the Regulator ordered me to *the Katorias* to be interrogated by *the Fantin* and punished under *the Book of Pain.* But I was spared. I was spared. No such cruelty for me. I am here in *the Myrkpykyn* by the grace of *the Didaniyisgi.*" Ricktus Morphinus faced Harris, and then knelt, his head disappearing behind the holding dock wall. "So say I," he muttered. "So say I to the man who has saved my life, thank you, my lord."

"So say I," Gypysyp shouted. "Thank you, my lord."

"And I," Rypchypy echoed. "So say I."

Then together, they raised their eyes to Harris.

"So say we."

The *Ryyvytys* disappeared behind the dock wall, their weeping clearly heard. The gallery exploded.

Adadooski.

Arkmo.

Bobyfysmagu.

Jipjipjiptipu.

Harris slowly stood as the applause wafted over him like honey, buoying him with a sense he had changed the course of *Yuyutlu* administration when he intervened and saved these men from Tarhippus' clutches. It was like dropping a house in Munchkinland. He glanced toward Garan, who shrugged, and then toward Cyprytop, who grinned.

Harris scooped up the scrolls, flapping them like flags. He held them to his chest, and then descended from his lofty spot, signaling *the Danuwa* and *Taleenay* to join him. Buhippus showed up with three Yunockers, no doubt stirred by the commotion. Had *the Didaniyisgi* run amok and incited insurrection? But when Harris reached the courtroom floor, the gallery crowd hushed.

"Elypticus," he said in a low voice. "I need light."

Elypticus looked to Parnasus, and then they separated, each retrieving *a bronsker*, returning to Harris and lifting the lamps high.

"Yustichisqua, I need more light."

"Yes, *oginali.*"

Little Bird knelt and unfastened his *waddly wazzoo* from his belt, the rope lamp at once glowing. Slowly, Yustichisqua kindled it, and then held it high, illuminating Harris' angelic visage.

"Melonius," Harris said.

"Yes, my lord."

"More light, if you please."

Melonius touched his *Columbincus*, and a light jet umbrellated around *the Seegoniga,* enclosing them in a shimmering membrane. The gallery audience hummed with wonder. Garan and Cyprytop approached on the perimeter.

"A new day has dawned for *the Yuyutlu,*" Harris proclaimed. "Light shall replace darkness and justice shall prevail. Leniency shall be the example and the stern claw of *the Book of Adjustment* shall be reserved for egregious infractions only . . . infractions of commerce. Social law is not the law of *the Yuyutlu* or *the Yuganawu,* but the jurisdiction of Kuriakis and *the Ayelli,* who purge such judgments in a superior light."

He paused to see if the gallery cheered. They didn't.

They should know what they are getting in me, he thought. *My imprint is more important than the ability to enforce it, but they'll think twice before they arbitrarily condemn a Trone on my watch.*

He inclined his ear to the bubble's edge.

"Archon Supreme."

"Yes, my lord."

"What is the harshest punishment I may mete out on these prisoners?"

Cyprytop frowned, his grave eyes perusing the dock.

"You may fine *the Ryyvytys* as much as one-thousand *yedalas.* You may suspend *the Augustii* from duties for three months."

He bowed, awaiting Harris' decision.

"*Deegosgi,* " Harris said.

"Yes, my lord," Garan responded.

"What do you recommend under the circumstances, considering this is my first pronouncement and I have declared *a new dawn?*"

"You could set them free."

"Impossible."

"You might apply them to a social cause of worth and excellence."

Harris cocked his head.

"How so?"

"These *Ryyvytys* traffic in *zulus,* my lord, footwear mandated to all residents of *the Kalugu.* Many Cetrone are restricted because they lack *zulus*, which they must wear. If the artisans who supply these *Ryyvytys* were to donate a few pair of *zulus* to the *Kalugu*, it would be significant — a social cause of worth and excellence. *The Augustii spinctus* is permitted entry into *the Kalugu*, and could thereby deliver the goods."

Garan bowed deeply, while Harris considered these words. He clapped. Melonius released his hand from his *Columbincus*, and the bubble burst. Harris stepped toward Buhippus, waving the fragmented scrolls.

"Captain Buhippus," he said.

"My lord."

"Hear my sentence and prepare to make it so."

Harris tried to keep a straight face. Everyone was so serious, but the words he uttered sounded like an old Cecil B. DeMille epic — lines from *The Ten Commandments*, when Debra Padget didn't break a sweat in the heat of Egypt and muttered her dramatic *Moses, Moses, Moses* to that hack, Charlton Heston. So, like Edward G. Robinson extolling *the Calf of Gold*, Harris moistened his lips and waited for the prisoners to stand, the Yunockers pulling them up.

"*Ryyvyty* Gypysyp and *Ryyvyty* Rypchypy, you shall prepare two pairs of *zulus* daily in perpetuity as a donation for the betterment of Farn, and Ricktus Morphinus, you shall act as agent and deliver these donations to *the Kalugu* for distribution to those fellow creatures who have done your bidding since the outland peoples invaded this fair valley and placed the Cetrone into servitude. This is my judgment and final word."

"But my lord," Ricktus said. "The expense will be great."

"Cheaper than *the Katorias*."

Ricktus shuddered, and then bowed.

"Thank you, my lord. I am beholding to you, my lord."

"Then tell your fellow *Augustii* about the new dawn in *the Yuyutlu*." He looked to the two *Ryyvyty*, who grinned and also bowed. "Tell all." He looked to Buhippus, who remained steely, his expression noncommittal. "Return them to *Ryyve Aniniya* . . . gently and courteously. They shall keep the peace now, I trust."

Harris regarded the now-stunned gallery. The crowd was either amazed at his clemency or bemused by his foolishness. Perhaps they expressed collective incredulity, but the moment was too ripe for Harris to let pass. He threw the scrolls to the floor, and then stomped them flat.

"Case closed," he shouted, and then marched to his *Seegoniga*. It was a long day and the wee upstairs cubby beckoned him.

2

The bedroom was small and Harris now shared it with Yustichisqua, who had relinquished his place in the adjoining room to the Thirdlings.

"You deserve to stay with them," Harris said.

"Yes, *oginali,* but there are better ways to ease their thinking. It is better I sleep at your feet again."

"Nonsense," Harris replied. "There's room in this bed for two."

Little Bird nodded and prepared for sleep. Harris gazed out the window — a skylight in the roof's bevel. The night was fair, the moons hanging among the stars like Christmas ornaments.

"Sometimes I believe Farn isn't so bad," Harris mused.

"It is beautiful at times, *oginali,* even to the sons of slaves."

"I'm sorry about that ruckus in *Ryyve Aniniya*."

Little Bird sat beside him on the bed, his *waddly wazzoo* prepared for evening prayers. It kindled low.

"I was frightened," Yustichisqua said, "but the General never would have taken me. You know this to be true."

Harris pictured Yustichisqua lashing out at Tarhippus, the dagger lodged in that hideous face — right between those wide spaced eyes. But Yustichisqua never could have succeeded. When Tappiolus had threatened Yustichisqua in the Forling, Little Bird had poised the dagger at his own heart. That's what his *Taleenay* meant to do in the *Ryyve Aniniya*. He would have taken his own life rather than be hauled to *the Porias*, where he would receive no trial — just a sentence — the only one sentence in *the Porias*.

"Sometimes I regret I ever gifted you that knife, Little Bird."

"If you hadn't, *oginali*, you would have been *porcorporian* food."

Harris chuckled.

"You are true and faithful."

"We are *oginali* — friends. The Cetrone do not take this lightly."

Harris sighed. He had many acting jobs in Farn — opportunities to fulfill roles and not even being paid *scale*, although the perks of being Lord Belmundus could be considered the perk of perks — even the unlimited sex with an enchantress. Some would call it lucky. But perhaps his greatest reward was a realization. *There was more to life than acting.* Today he had been a VIP-deluxe — escorted through *the Ryyves*, surviving the wrath of the most feared personage in Montjoy and rising like cream in the role as Judge — *the Didaniyisgi of the Yuyutlu*. But sitting here beside this lad of fifty or fifty-seven, the acting fell by the wayside. Harris recalled his life in that other place — the one that was fading.

He looked through the skylight again, regarding the moons of Farn. He recalled his last gig on *The Magic Planet* — his fun on the set, with the director and with . . . with Tony. He missed the drone of cockney commentary from that Dorsetshire sissy. He missed normal dinners — steak and French Fries instead of *suweechee* and *mongerhide.* He longed for untrammeled love and sex, instead of jade-ring driven lust. He saw his sister's face and heard the dulcet sounds of her shepherding voice. And Mom . . . the guide of all guides. An errant tear rolled down his cheek, salty to the taste.

"*Oginali,*" Yustichisqua whispered. "The outlands are far away."

"Far away, Little Bird," Harris sniffed. "Thoughts of them unman me."

"My homeland is far away too. Beyond the Forling in the Spice Mountains."

"Do you miss it?"

"I have never seen it."

Harris turned, drying his tears.

"How sad."

"Someday the ferry will fly again and Cosawta will find a way to steer the course. It is my only hope."

"Until then?"

"Until then, I am your *Taleenay* and *oginali*, and I am content. But I know you look beyond me."

Harris turned away, peering out the window again. He saw the charcoal outline of *the Kalugu* in the distance. To have made it this far was good, but not good enough. There were other places to know.

"You seek the secrets of my people, *oginali,*" Yustichisqua said. "You want to go to *the Kalugu* and know what there is to know."

Yes, that was the ticket. Hierarchus knew the way and may have found it.

Harris squinted, sharpening his view of the distant *phitron* walls. Moonlight caught a corner of one tower — an ugly claw proclaiming cruelty. He closed his eyes, barring the night orbs' strange sight over the landscape. Instead, he saw a single Moon, full and bright, reflected in a shimmering ocean. He could hear the waves crashing on the jetties and the heels of pedestrians strolling on the pier. He caught the aroma of cotton candy and corn dogs. Yes, he needed to know the secrets of *the Kalugu* so he could recapture the brilliance of his own Moon — the one shining on his Mom in Santa Monica.

Part III

Takes and Retakes

Chapter One

The Gulliwailit Bridge

1

"There it is," Harris said, raising his hand, halting *the Danuwa*. The *Cabriolins* clustered behind him. Yustichisqua took his usual place in Lord Belmundus' vehicle. He sighed, shaking his head, probably recalling the sadness dwelling behind the walls. At *the Seegoniga's* backs, Montjoy City buzzed prosperously — Yunocker folk soaring from place to place, unconcerned for those who lived beyond the bridge over *the gulliwailit* — the black stream separating *the Yuganawu* from *the Kalugu*.

"What's our chances?" Harris asked Little Bird. "Do you think we can crack this safe open today and glimpse the inner workings?"

"I know the inner workings, *oginali*. No day is a good day to cross this bridge."

Harris leaned forward, shading his eyes. *The phitron* walls, ebony and pitted with sharp metallic netting called *yuyenihi* — an impenetrable razor demon, were formidable and heavily controlled by the gate guardians. These guards checked every Trone's *gollywi* — a brand on the upper forearm near the elbow, which proclaimed clan affiliation — *alisoqua* (bear), *chisqua* (bird), *geetli* (dog), *tlugu* (tree), or *seegoniga* (blue holly). Yustichisqua had the bird clan mark burned into his flesh. Harris had seen it and wondered what cruelty led the Yunockers to brand the Cetrone like cattle. He later learned these marks were self-imposed and worn proudly. That the Yunockers used *gollywi* to sort by clans and that they served as indelible passports into *the Kalugu* was a matter of convenience. That Harris' entourage had been given a clan name by the Gurts and Zecronisians — *seegoniga*, was significant.

Harris had explored Montjoy during his first three months as *the Didaniyisgi*. The Yunockers were a privileged race, although several classes emphasized social stratification. The city burghers, *the praeters*, lived in mansions around the central plazas and owned estates in the foothills. *The majorin* class went to business — record-keeping, *yedalas* trading, and *aniniya* speculation. They lived in neat neighborhoods surrounding downtown central. *The minorin* — shopkeepers, clerks and petty regulators, fended as best they could in rental plots and small holdings in the suburbs, although they commuted to their employment on speedy *zulus*. Finally, *the regulati* were Yunocker policeman, militia, enforcers, prison guards and peacekeepers. They lived in several strategic barracks around Montjoy. There were so many *regulati*, the city seemed to be a police state. However, although *the Ayelli* controlled the Yunocker, *the regulatis* specialized in policing the Trone population, which was considerable.

The Cetrone left a significant mark upon the landscape. The oldest structures in town were Georgian-style dwellings, constructed of *banibara* and *phitron*, with *kaybar* doors, which would have barred anyone but Cetrones from entering. However, Yunockers, mostly *majorins*, now occupied these houses, retaining *the kaybar* doors for servant Trones to conveniently enter to perform their duties. *Praeter* estates sprawled behind high gates and parapets. Gurt designed and constructed, these mansions competed for attention among the status sensitive *praeters*. Harris made a special note of one unusual feature of buildings in Montjoy. Beside each was constructed a low *phitron* kettle-shaped building, black and miserable — as ubiquitous as chimneys in Victorian London. These were *the kaleezo* and housed the Trones when they weren't about their duties or in *the Kalugu*. Huddled out of sight, their *waddly wazzoos* lit for scant but true light, Cetrone servants sang their hymns at night to the spirits who had made them, but who had abandoned them to cruel masters. Cetrone were only free to return to *the Kalugu* when their contracts had expired, and pnly then to renew them, if luck prevailed.

"I served *the praeters* of the House of Guranitos," Yustichisqua told Harris on one of their spins about *the Yuganawu*. "I scrubbed pots and waited tables. They were not cruel to me and occasionally allowed me to drift up to *the Ayelli* in the procession to Greary Gree. But when my contract expired, I returned to *the chisqua* clan in *the Kalugu*. It made me sad. At least in *the kaleezo* of Master Guranitos, I could sing my songs and kindle my light. But in *the Kalugu, the regulati* pestered me incessantly. There I was fed *sqwallen,* until my cousin Littafulchee saved me, recommending me for service at *Mortis House*. That is when I met you, *oginali.*"

The Trone's plight in *the Yuganawu* distressed Harris. However, he recognized Yunocker society's structure and its apartheid creed. The Yunockers ignored their servants unless a pot was cracked or a jewel had gone missing. Then General Tarhippus' crew would sweep the refuse away to *the Porias*, the prison for Trones — *phitron* built, secure and mostly vacant, because few Trones lasted more than a day, *the Porias'* crematorium kept busy.

Harris spent his days in *the Myrkpykyn* adjudicating *Yuyutlu* disputes, many now because word had spread. The new *Didaniyisgi* was fair and had declared a new dawn. But unlike his first judgments, the courtroom was rarely packed and ceremony had fallen by the wayside. Cyprytop occasionally turned up to defend a prominent *Augustii*, but mostly he sent his opinions in writing — writing which Harris still couldn't decipher. But Garan could. *The Deegosgi* was present at all proceedings and beyond them. He'd show up at all hours to chatter about happenings in this *Ryyve* or that *Ryyve*. Harris found Garan fascinating, especially when he spoke of travels to *the Makronican Islands* in the *Amaykwohi Sea*. This was the home of *the Finistrians*, a tribe of pearl fishers, who harvested pearls as big as ostrich eggs, which said much about the oysters.

Harris still had his other duties — his reason for being. Lord Belmundus trekked back to Charminus' bed when he was *up*, Little Bird in tow. Yustichisqua reverted to Trone on those weeks, serving Lord Belmundus from *the Scullery Dorgan* beside his cousin Littafulchee, who waited always upon the Scepta. Harris rarely remembered these stints with Charminus, the ring's power a powerful narcotic, which made the time fleet and the sex go unnoticed, at least to him. He wondered where his sex drive went. At nineteen, his sexual vigor was spent. Even an enticing three-breasted Zecronisian siren or a cute muscle boy from Montjoy couldn't hold his interest.

In his absence from *the Myrkpykyn*, his *Danuwa* held court, heard cases and passed judgments. They made the daily rounds in *the Yuyutlu* and into *the Yuganawu*. Garan oversaw the cases and Buhippus, when he wasn't back in *Mortis House*, which also drew him away as Captain of the Palace Guard, oversaw *the Danuwa*. These overseers reported to Harris favorably. Elypticus and Parnasus were enthusiastic in their attention to details, while Melonius kept the judgments fair, but not reckless. Melonius had evolved into a level-headed asset, although he still wasn't much fun when confronting non-*Ayellians*.

One thing disturbed Harris. Elypticus reported that, in Harris' absence, *the Eye* appeared more often. Because Harris would be in bed with the owner of that *Eye*, Charminus was not the spy. She had no interest in any discussion of *the Didaniyisgi* duties and couldn't care less whether *the Ryyves* were on fire or the *Yuyutlu* froze. Like most *Ayelli*, on their remote hill, including Kuriakis and Joella, so long as the goods were delivered and the homage paid, Montjoy could dance the herky-jerky. Harris concluded Tappiolus was the originator of these *Eye* events and wondered what interest his co-consort had for events in *the Yuyutlu*. Tappiolus, despite his position as Provost of the Yunocker forces, never went to Montjoy. He never intervened in *regulati* affairs and never attempted to govern Tarhippus. No one governed Tarhippus except Kuriakis, perhaps. Harris concluded Tappiolus' interest was Tarhippus' interest. *The Eye* spied for the General — no need for contact with *the Didaniyisgi.* Case closed.

2

"What's our chances?" Harris asked Little Bird. "Shall we cross it today?"

Harris had come to this brink before and had asked this question often. His hesitation was steeled by Yustichisqua's replies and *the Danuwa's* reluctance. This wasn't Lord Belmundus' jurisdiction, after all. He should let it be. But Harris thirsted not for what he knew — the distress of the Trones, but for something he guessed. Behind *the Kalugu's* walls a secret was deliberately withheld from the world. Harris would know this secret.

"What's our chances, Little Bird?"

"Cross it, *oginali.*"

Harris glanced at his *Taleenay*, as if this challenge was a mockery. He then looked at *the Danuwa*. Elypticus fidgeted, but Elypticus always fidgeted. Parnasus shrugged. Melonius, however, nodded and spoke:

"Everyone needs to die someday, my lord. Today is as good as any other."

"We shall not die," Harris said, and edged his *Cabriolin* forward.

As the four *Seegoniga* crossed the *gulliwailit* bridge, the creek's acrid smell invaded their nostrils. Not Yustichisqua's. He peered over *the Cabriolin's* side. There, peering up at him were

Trones who trundled either to their servitude or to their ghetto existence. They floated by on their *zulus* trying not to disturb a lord from *the Ayelli* in his passage. However, the sight of one of their own borne in style caused many blinks and fearsome glances.

"It is difficult, *oginali,*" Little Bird said. "I once crossed this bridge as they do, and now I return in a guise they cannot comprehend."

"You mustn't let it disturb you, old man," Harris said. "The world's filled with change and I bring a new dawn."

Harris almost believed this, although words were pointless. Words may have changed the course of history in his realm, but here they flared like entertainments on a hot summer's night. He glanced at the sky, which had turned from its merry blue to a foreboding gray.

So long as it isn't green, he thought, remembering *yichiyusti,* when Kuriakis stirred.

"Ahead, my lord," Melonius said.

Harris saw them — five Yunockers meeting him before the bridge's end. They came on *zulus* with three *zugginaks.* Yustichisqua trembled.

"They will kill me, *oginali.*"

"Over my dead body," Harris said.

That might not have been reassuring. Harris halted when the lead Yunocker drifted forward. The guard sniffed.

"Why is that Trone in your *Cabriolin*, sir?" he snapped, pointing directly at Yustichisqua.

"He is my *Taleenay*. I am . . ."

"We know who you are, Lord Belmundus. We have watched you from afar on many days when you make rounds in Montjoy." The guard nodded, but still pointed. "That does not mean you can treat your Trone with special privileges in *the Yuganawu*."

"This isn't your concern, sir," Harris said. "As *the Didaniyisgi,* my warrants are from Kuriakis. I choose my staff as you can see."

He indicated *the Danuwa,* who placed hands on their *Columbincus'* in unison.

The guard brought his *Stick* to the ready as if *the Seegoniga* had brooked a challenge and meant to do battle on the bridge. The other guards moved forward, *the zugginaks* pulling on their restraints, growling over gobs of snot dripping from their jowls. Yustichisqua's hand went to his dagger.

"We mean to pass, sir," Harris said, his voice steady and in command.

"*Ayelli* are not permitted in *the Kalugu.*"

"I don't see why not, unless you mean to hide the pitiable conditions of the Cetrone from the eyes of your overlords."

This brought the guard closer, waving *the Stick.*

"Your Trone may enter, if he dares," the guard snapped. "He must first shed that rich robe and put on *zulus* as the law demands. Then he may join his brethren to trek across *the gulliwailit* and present his *gollywi* to enter." He looked to Little Bird, defiantly. "Show us your *gollywi* . . . Trone."

Harris moved his *Cabriolin* closer, so much so, the guards nearly set *the zugginaks* loose.

"You shall address him as Yustichisqua, *Taleenay of the Yuyutlu,*" Harris shouted. "He is far above you in rank and position, master of this piss bridge."

Harris heard Melonius whisper *mistake, my lord,* and perhaps he *had* gone too far. The guard slammed his *Stick* on *the Cabriolin's* rail. Yustichisqua drew his dagger, which provoked the guard to grimace, bubbling with surprise and anger. Harris drew his sword. Sword against *Stick* — an interesting match. Hard to guess the outcome, but Harris' experience on the set of *The Magic Planet* won that battle, but not today. He brought the sword down on *the Stick,* splitting the guard's weapon in two, *the Aniniya* core slipping to the ground and rolling to the bridge's edge. Then the precious core fell into *the gulliwailit.* The guard screamed and the other four came forward. Melonius drew his *Stick.* Elypticus cleared the Trones aside. Parnasus charged to Harris' side. *The zugginaks* were loosed.

Unfortunately, *zugginaks* were dumb creatures driven by scent and not by their masters. They only knew a Trone's scent and not necessarily the whiff of a dagger-wielding, fancy dressed Trone in a *Cabriolin.* They attacked the Trones nearest their jaws, sending a mob of servants fleeing back to *the Yuganawu* or sideways over the bridge and into *the gulliwailit.*

Harris was shocked. This was not his intention. Yustichisqua whimpered as *zugginaks* bit and chomped at *zulus,* legs and torsos.

Harris raised his sword.

"Stop this madness," he shouted. "I, Lord Belmundus, command you to stop."

Suddenly, through the guards came another Yunocker, a whistle in his ugly maw. He blew it and *the zugginaks* returned to his side as calm as chipmunks. It was General Tarhippus, this time without his fiery *Cabriolin, gwasdi* and power *zulus*. He strode like the king of the bridge, which he was — a Troll in all but grace.

"Lord Belmundus," he said firmly, but without the peppery spice of their first encounter. "What brings you to *the Kalugu* today?"

"General Tarhippus," Harris stammered, off his guard. "I didn't expect to see you . . ."

"Most people do not expect to see me," he said wryly, and then smiled — a sardonic grin which sent chills to anyone seeing it, including his guards. A dangerous grin. "But I must remind you, despite your exalted position in the eyes of Gurts and Zecronisians and, I might add, the Elector on High, you are not permitted to tour *the Kalugu*."

"Why not?"

"*Ayelli* are excluded here. It is a matter of treaty. "

"I see no purpose in such a treaty."

"You would not, I daresay, because you are . . . a newcomer to our fair and honorable city. You have brought unsettling changes, especially in your views toward the conquered." He indicated the suffering and mutilated Cetrone struggling to cross the bridge. "It will serve no purpose in the end. Still we must allow . . . newcomers their moment in the sun." He laughed. "However, I respect you, Lord Belmundus. I might even invite you to my palace for dinner and to explore the best prison cell in *the Katorias*, but *the Kalugu* is off-limits to you." He looked to Yustichisqua. "And despite my captain's suggestion that your Trone . . . excuse me, your *Taleenay* may enter if appropriately altered, I say no. We have enough stirring in *the Kalugu*. I will not offer unseemly examples. Even your *Danuwa* cannot enter, because they are *Ayelli,* though one is the son of our Provost. No, no, no, no."

"Lord Tappiolus would be forbidden entry?"

"Absolutely, although he would never dare so much." Tarhippus nodded, condescendingly. "Even the one who did dare enter did not find his way out of the labyrinth."

Hierarchus, Harris thought. He wanted to toss his sword at Tarhippus' head, and then make a mad dash onward through the gates. The general taunted him. Then from behind *the Danuwa* came another voice.

"My lord," Buhippus said. "It is best you retreat from here. You have won a victory on this bridge, for no one has ever stood his ground as you have today."

Harris heard these words. They entered his heart like balm. He didn't achieve his goal, but everyone in Montjoy City would know there had been a showdown on *the gulliwailit* bridge between the powers in this land, of which he was now one. He sheathed his sword. His pride arose, despite the sadness of the massacred Trones. Perhaps they were better off dead, but not maimed and wounded — mixed justification. There would be time later to analyze his actions and be remorseful.

"General Tarhippus," he said, in a loud voice. "I shall honor the treaty, but know this. If you are inclined to invite me to your table, I'll find a conflict in my schedule."

"Ah, a shame," Tarhippus roared. "My table is a fine one. But I still extend my invitation to put you in the best cell in *the Katorias* when the time comes, as it surely shall."

Harris raised his hand. He backed his *Cabriolin* over the bridge, *the Danuwa* following suit. They never turned their backs on Tarhippus. It would be unwise to do so. When upon the other side, Buhippus shook his head and nodded.

"What were you thinking, my lord?" he growled, still appropriately humble.

"You know what I'm thinking, captain, otherwise you wouldn't be here now."

"My brother will make good on his promise."

"I don't doubt it, but before I take up residence in his jail, I mean to bring a new dawn inside those walls."

"I fear the Trones will not appreciate your effort," Buhippus said.

"You are wrong," Yustichisqua snapped. "Thousands of *waddly wazzoos* are ready to be kindled."

Harris glared at Little Bird. *What revolutionary sentiment was this?* Harris expected anger to flare from Buhippus, but it didn't come. The captain just sighed, and then moved across the bridge to his brother, no doubt to tie up loose ends in what would be called in ages hence, *the Incident at the Gulliwailit Bridge*, the day Boots of Montjoy commenced the revolution — new dawn that it would become.

Chapter Two

Wisgi and Charpgris

1

Night and rain crept over *the Myrkpykyn's* roof, the former like a shroud — the latter like a leaky faucet. Harris sat at the bed's edge, Yustichisqua nearby. Water dripped through crevices, puddling on the floor. A steady cascade ran along the bevel's seams, the drips caught in a cylindrical pot, which Little Bird had found in the basement. The day's heat had escaped, seeming never to return. Even *the waddly wazzoo* brought no solace into the gloom of *the Didaniyisgi's* quarters.

Harris pouted, the gloom aiding his thoughts — thoughts of failure about *the Gulliwailit Bridge*. He cursed his lack of control and Tarhippus' mastery. He regretted the loss of Trone life at *zugginak* expense. He sighed for the jumpers in the murky creek. Above all, he cursed the ambivalence of *the regulati*. What was one Trone or another? *The Kalugu* had an ample supply for every household in Montjoy — a surplus, permitting warehoused labor beyond measure.

"It's my fault," he muttered.

Yustichisqua gazed at him.

"Do not blame yourself, *oginali*. Trones die daily. If these had not been attacked or taken the more painless course, they would have died tomorrow or the next day."

"Or lived to be old men and women."

"To what purpose, *oginali*?" Yustichisqua asked.

Harris sighed. If the Cetrone lacked hope, Little Bird was correct. Nothing mattered to aid them. Yet, Yustichisqua had been bettered — more comfortable and raised in status, despite the prevailing prejudice. Harris sighed again, the rain's chill pounding the skylight, raising his skin into goose-flesh.

"When will this rain stop?" he mused, gazing through the water-streaked panes.

"It always stops," Yustichisqua noted. "I should seek another pot. This one is nealy full."

"I'll go," Harris said, leaping off the bed. "I need the stretch."

Little Bird nodded, having learned not to argue with Lord Belmundus. He checked the water level, and then tended his *wazzly wazzoo*. Harris shuddered. Despondency was foreign to him, but he feared it as a prelude to depression, a state which never had found him.

On the landing, he heard *the Danuwa* discussing the day's events. They didn't argue. Elypticus and Parnasus expressed marvel at *the Didaniyisgi's* stand against Tarhippus. Melonius was silent, but then told Parnasus to mop the floor.

I must ask Cyprytop about the roof's condition, Harris thought. *There must be a maintenance Ryyve.*

Harris entered the courtroom from top level, hesitating to survey the darkness engulfing it. Except lightning flashes, the place was shadowy — almost Gothic. He wondered how Buhippus and the guards fared in the basement. Drier, perhaps, away from the roof. But perhaps the ground seeped through the cells, provoking a need for galoshes or whatever the Gurt's called them. He soon would know, in his quest for a replacement pot, wouldn't he?

As he began his descent into this room, which seemed taken straight from a mystery book — *Rebecca* or *Wuthering Heights*, he discerned a huddled figure near the doorway. It crouched beside an oversized sack set on a rolling cart, which the residents of *the Byybykyyip* called *a dollywangle*.

"Who's there?" he asked. "Is that you, captain?"

The figure moved forward, wrapped like a street beggar, wads of gauze dripping across the floor like a mummy arisen from a swamp. Harris wished he had lit the big *bronsker*, which sat beside *the Book of Adjustment*. But since court wasn't in session, he made do with the small *aniniya*-powered hand lamp called a *birripsun*. However, he hadn't taken one with him on this errand. *Fool.* As the figure approached, Harris backed up to the bench.

"No cases are being heard this evening," he snapped. "Come back in the morning . . . if it isn't raining."

Then the man shucked his wet garments, revealing a familiar face.

"Garan?"

Garan lit his *birrupsun*, shining it beneath his chin. *Eerie.*

"Sorry I startled you, my lord."

Harris wasn't amused. He approached *the Deegosgi*, and then passed him by.

"Am I not welcomed?"

"I need to see a man about a pot," Harris blurted. "The fucking roof leaks and I didn't bring a swim suit."

"Wait," Garan said. "I bring gifts." He pointed to the sack. "Gifts that include an epoxy, which seals most anything, including seeping roofs."

Harris halted.

"You're not just saying that to put me in a better mood, because I'm not sure I want my mood changed."

Garan bowed.

"My lord, I know your mood. It is understandable."

"You know my mood?"

"Yes."

"You may *think* you know it." Harris pointed to the windows. Thunder clapped. Lightning flashed. "The weather's the weather and it'll pass, or so my *Taleenay* assures me. But my mood embraces me like a python, tightening as time goes on."

"Python, my lord? I believe I know this word. It is a snake. Yes?"

"Yes."

"Much like *the bolliganga*, only found in your world in a place called *Afrikat*. True?"

"Near enough."

Harris returned to Garan.

"Yes. I hear much and say much. I have heard about your victory at *the Gulliwailit Bridge*."

"Victory?"

"Yes. You stood your ground against the tyrant and challenged *the Treaty of Parazell*."

Harris hadn't a clue. He remembered Buhippus touting a victory and the guard invoking some treaty during the contest, but *Parazell? What the hell?*

"*Parazell?*"

"A pact between the Yunocker council and Kuriakis giving *the Yuganawu* control over Trone traffic, distribution and maintenance."

"Like slavery."

"Not precisely, my lord. Slavery entails commodity trading, which harvests profits and includes ownership. This is not so. The Cetrone are a conquered people." He shrugged. "The Yunockers are also a conquered people. The promise of a limitless and free labor source was an opportunity too dear for Kuriakis to resist. The pact gives *the Ayelli* the cream of Trone services in a steady flow. In exchange, *Mortis House* is prohibited from interfering with the trade or the affairs of *the Kalugu.* The Treaty states: *Ayelli* are not permitted to set foot in *the Kalugu.*"

"But that's not true," Harris said. Garan sucked in his breath. "I know that Lord Hierarchus entered *the Kalugu.*"

"I know you know. You aspire to follow his footsteps." He drew Harris aside, near the lowest bench. "But Lord Hierarchus' course is not your course."

"Why?" Harris pressed. "Because I failed to gain entrance today?"

"No," Garan said, coming near Harris' ear. "No, my lord. You *shall* enter. I am sure of it. But you will not suffer his fate. You shall not be caught, because I, Garan *the Gucheeda, the Deegosgi, the Fumarca, the Harandu* and *the Jamabispa,* will help you succeed."

Thunder clapped.
Lightning flashed.

2

Yustichisqua appeared at the top of the court, waving his *waddly wazzoo. The Danuwa* also appeared, each holding *a birrupsun.*

"*Oginali,* the pot is nearly full."

Harris looked to Garan, and then to *the Seegoniga.*

"Garan has something to plug the leaks," Harris said.

Garan went to the sack, shuffling inside it until he found a pyramid-shaped container.

"*Jupsim,*" he announced.

Yustichisqua hurried down the stairs, *the Danuwa* following.

"Just the thing," Little Bird said, retrieving it, and then hastening back up to remedy the roof.

"Return when finished, *Taleenay,*" Garan called. "I have more gifts." He looked to *the Danuwa.* "Yes, many gifts." He returned to the sack, retrieving a basket. "*Mongerhide.*"

Elypticus brightened, and accepted the basket enthusiastically.

"I have longed for the taste of it, *Deegosgi,*" he said. "Thank you."

"I like that stuff too," Harris said.

"And . . . *bolingara* wine." Garan held up two flasks of green liquid. Parnasus retrieved these. "And . . . if you can lend me a hand . . ."

He struggled with a large box. It was a wonder he could have toted it here on his small *dollywaggle*. Melonius helped him hoist it out, and then grinned.

"You may have saved the day, *Deegosgi,*" Melonius said. He turned to the others. "A *grusoker* board."

"Complete with every asset," Garan said, breathlessly. "In this weather and with court business slow, I thought you might find it a profitable investment for lost hours."

"*That* we shall," Melonius said.

The other *Danuwa* grasped *the grusoker* board's sides and, together, they retreated with the game, the snack and the booze, chattering like schoolboys released from their studies.

"You're a good man, Garan," Harris said.

"That should keep them distracted."

"Distracted?"

"Yes, my lord. It's best they keep to their room and slam *the gorettle*, forgetting the hours, and even the days."

Harris cocked his head. Garan's grin turned impish. *Mongerhide, bolingara* and *grusoker* would be a diversion, but from what? There was more to this game than dice and tiles. Yustichisqua appeared topside, *the jupsim* bucket in one hand, and his *waddly wazzoo* in the other. Garan waved to him.

"*Taleenay*, come see what more I have."

Yustichisqua set the bucket aside and trotted down the staircase.

"What other gifts did you bring, sir?" Harris asked. "Somehow I think you mean to fill my lost hours too."

"Would that it was as simple as *grusoker,*" Garan said, bowing and returning to the sack.

"*Grusoker* isn't simple," Harris replied.

Yustichisqua raised his light. Garan drew out a bottle — more wine, perhaps.

"Is it *brantsgi*?" Little Bird asked.

"Better than *brantsgi*," Garan replied. "*Wisgi.*"

Yustichisqua sighed, and in that susurration, Harris knew this liquor exceeded every beverage in the realm. Garan popped out two glasses and set them on the bleacher railing.

"Do you mean to get us shit-faced, Garan?" Harris said as he watched the golden *wisgi* glow in the dim light — amber and familiar.

"If you mean by that, *drunk*," Garan replied, "this elixir will do that. It will also warm your soul to any task. That is my purpose. The task is daunting and this *wisgi* is rare — from my private stock."

"Private stock, eh?" Harris said.

"*Oginali*, it is the stuff of legend. I have never tasted it, but I have heard there is magic in the blend and it will give a coward courage."

"Are we cowards, Garan?" Harris asked.

"Nothing like it," Garan replied, finishing the pouring. "But a little *wisgi* on a foul night in the darkness of extinguished justice goes a long way to restore resolve and fortitude."

The three glasses beckoned, catching the lightning flashes and tossing them back to the night. Harris grasped his glass firmly. He raised it to his nose, and sniffed.

Familiar.

"I know this drink," he said.

"I would not be surprised," Garan replied.

Yustichisqua lifted his glass, and then downed it in one go — neither toast nor preparation. He choked, grasping his throat. But after the first reaction, he grinned and licked the rim. Harris drank. Garan swallowed also.

"Yes," Harris remarked. "It's good to know you can get something like this in Montjoy."

Garan polished off his portion, and then lifted the bottle to pour three more. When the bottle came into the light, Harris twitched. He saw the label — black with white lettering: It read:

Jim Beam — Black

He grabbed the neck, bringing the flask to his eye.

"Where did you get this?" he stammered. "You said it's from your private stock, but unless you keep your booze cellar in

Kentucky, I suspect you reached far afield for this. Where did you get it, sir?"

Garan grabbed the bottle and continued to pour. When he finished filling the last glass, he secured the cap and set *the wisgi* bottle on the railing.

"I have been to *the Dodingdaten,* my lord. There are many wares there which few in Montjoy have seen."

Yustichisqua stopped drinking midgulp. Harris winced.

"Where the hell's *the Dodingdaten?*" he asked.

"Beyond Cetronia, *oginali,*" Little Bird stammered. "And you have been there, *Deegosgi?*"

"Yes," Garan said. "Drink up."

3

The happy sounds of *grusoker* echoed from the upper rooms almost trumping the thunder and lightning. Harris huddled with Garan and Little Bird about the bottle, the warmth from *Kentucky* or *the Dodingdaten* sliding him toward new comfort levels.

"*The Dodingdaten* is a strange place, my lord," Garan said. "The inhabitants are not as we are."

"We?" Harris asked.

"They are like you, but have not been drawn by the Sceptas. But they *are* from the outlands."

Harris poured more *wisgi* and heaved it down his gullet. The liquid's bite was less now and his astonishment mellowed.

"And just where did these *the Didingydatenonians* come from? How'd they get here?"

"It is a mystery, my lord. They slipped through the portals, which connect the worlds, but those portals are lost to knowledge. *The Dodingdatens* cluster in an enclave near Cetronia. They avoid Montjoy, although they are *Fumarcans* — land pirates."

"Like you, Garan."

Garan nodded, affirming one of his titles.

"Piracy takes many forms, my lord. I am the same on both land and sea. Others call me by these names. I accept them as honors or curses. It matters not."

"But you've been there, you say — to these *Fumarcans?*"

"Yes. In years past. Before I ferried across the Forling, I explored the Spice Mountains and came upon the enclave. Few have survived an encounter with them. Cetrone, who keep the

fires, avoid *the Dodingdaten*, although when *Fumarcans* need
supplies, they make forays into the Cetrone camps and villages. I
have since traveled there by sea and there is some intercourse
between the peoples of *the Dodaloo*, which might prove beneficial
for everyone . . . under controlled conditions. But *the Fumarcans*
are driven by self need and can be ferocious when provoked — and
they are easily provoked, my lord."

"But you survived?"

"I am clever when it comes to surviving, my lord. I plan
carefully and ahead. As a trader, I had interesting goods at my
disposal. I bartered well for items attractive to me — things
catching my fancy."

"Like a shit load of *wisgi?*"

"*Wisgi*," Yustichisqua slurred, raising his glass for more.

"I believe you've reached your limit, Little Bird, but . . ."

Harris poured him a half-glass. Yustichisqua grinned, downed
it and began to doze.

"Yes, my lord, *wisgi* is rare and I managed to barter five and
twenty bottles."

"That would keep us happy for a while."

"Happiness is not my aim." He leaned forward. "I have brought
other gifts tonight."

"Truly? What could be better than this?"

"Truly," Garan said.

Garan went to the sack, dragging it to the railing, *the
dollywaggle* rattling when pulled. He whipped out two black
cloaks — ugly things with thick cowls.

"I don't need blankets, Garan."

"Blankets? These are not blankets, my lord. They are the
official cloaks of *the Augustii spinctus*." He brought the garments
closer, rubbing the surface on his cheek. "They may look poor, but
they will cover you well and mark you as *a Ryyve* official."

"For what purpose?"

"Surely you can think of the purpose." He sniffed at the cowl.
"Waterproof, they are, the *jupsim* sewn into the weave."

Yustichisqua stirred. He peered at the cloaks.

"Have you slain *the Augustii* who wore these?" Little Bird
asked. "They would not give these up freely."

Harris touched the cloak. *Disguises.* He recalled Garan's
pledge to get him into *the Kalugu.*

"Will it work?" he stammered, sobering fast. "Won't the guards question a Zecronisian entering the keep?"

"Two *Augustii spinctus*, with warrants to transport *zulus* into *the mordanka* — the quartermaster general — warrants signed by *the Didaniyisgi* himself as a settlement for a dispute within *the Ryyve Aniniya* — no. No questions."

Garan popped out the warrant. Harris grabbed it and tried to read it.

"That's my signature and seal alright, but like most crap I sign, I can't read it."

"You trusted me then," Garan said, tapping the seal.

"I'll trust you now."

"But *Deegosgi*," Yustichisqua asked. "Am I to go?"

"Of course. But I will not be entering. You know *the Kalugu* and will know where to take Lord Belmundus."

"Yes, but I will spoil everything. *The zugginaks* will sniff me out and kill me, and then *the regulati* will arrest my lord."

Garan grinned, and then reached into his cloak, producing a flask. He popped the cork and brought it under *Yustichisqua's* nose. Little Bird grinned, but didn't react otherwise. Harris sniffed it.

"Oh, my God, what the fuck's that? It stinks like an outhouse in the forest."

"*Charpgris, oginali. Tludachi* piss."

"You have smelt it before, my lord," Garan said. "At *the Ryyve Sulasgi. The Taleenay* will wear some — hands, cheeks and behind the ears, and *zugginaks* and *regulati* will not detect him as a Trone."

Harris sniffed it again, and then corked the flask. He tapped Little Bird's noggin.

"Well, I'm not kissing you, old man, but if it works, it works."

"I am happy to have it," Yustichisqua said, "but when we enter the grounds, it still will be dangerous for me. I must wear *zulus* to cross the pit bridges. No *Augustii* wears *zulus*."

"Ah," Garan replied, grinning.

He went to the sack again and dragged out two pairs of boots.

"*Shitekickers*," Harris said, grabbing for one. "Now these I'll wear."

"*Borabas*," Garan proclaimed.

"For me?" Yustichisqua said, touching the soft black boot, his hand trembling. "I have never known things so beautiful."

Harris smiled as he watched Little Bird sniff the heel and inspect the sole.

"These boots, my lord, are reinforced with *phitron* soles, crafted to be light and durable. These should keep your *Taleenay* from falling through the *kaybar* bridges and into the pits."

Yustichisqua stood, shaky from drink, and then bowed to Garan.

"I know you are grateful, *Taleenay*," Garan warned, "but remember, I do not send you home, but as a guide to Lord Belmundus."

"I shall always be his guide, and his . . . *oginali*."

He hiccupped.

Harris pulled on one boot, and then the other, Yustichisqua helping with the last push. Harris stood and strutted about, perhaps looking for a mirror in a shoe store.

"How did you know my size, Garan?"

"The wonder of *borabas* are they fit all feet equally."

"One size fits all," Harris muttered. "Sweet."

Yustichisqua donned his *borabas* and clopped about, grinning at the music they made.

"So, we're set to go," Harris announced.

Grusoker!

The laughter aloft gave Harris pause.

"Yes, my lord, *your Danawu* are distracted now. *The bolingara* and *mongerhide* will put them to sleep for many hours. I will stay here and tell them the Scepta called you away in the night."

"They won't believe it."

"But if they are loyal and faithful, they will not question it. However, I fear you must tell Captain Buhippus the truth and trust the strength of his warrants."

"But he's Tarhippus' brother."

"Still, the captain must know, otherwise he will question your whereabouts and pursue you. Since you leave your *Cabriolin* behind, it must be stored from sight. I am not equipped to move it." He touched his *Columbincus-free* breast. "I lack the appropriate power."

Harris glanced toward the entrance — to the basement staircase. He turned to Yustichisqua.

"One more drink, Little Bird — what my Uncle Andy called *Dutch courage*."

Yustichisqua poured the last of *the wisgi* into the glasses, and the three conspirators downed the stiffener.

"One more thing," Garan said, patting his backside. "You will need to wear a pad at the rear."

"Excuse me? "

"Zecronisians have three legs, my lord and waddle like *gukpeckyns* or hadn't you noticed?" He winked. "The prosthetic is uncomfortable, but provides the appropriate credibility."

"If we must."

"You must. Be thankful you are not a Zecronisian woman or you would need to wear a third breast."

He laughed, and then bowed. Harris grasped Garan's hand, and then his arm, shaking it warmly.

"I owe you one."

"Yes, you do. My payment will be on account, if I live to collect it. For now you must test loyalty's waters."

He pointed to the basement's entrance.

Thunder clapped.

Lightning flashed.

Grusoker.

Chapter Three

In Enemy Country

1

Thunder clapped.
Lightning flashed.

The *Byybykyyip* swallowed two travelers as they dodged in the shadows — two *Augustii spinctae* abroad in an ungainly fashion at an ungodly hour, dragging *a dollywaggle of zulus* noisily over the cobblestones and gutters. Harris struggled with the prosthetic third leg, which pitched him forward like an old crone. The leg wasn't extended, but pinched his waist unnaturally. It competed with his sword and *Stick*, which flopped uneasily beneath the cloak. He noticed Yustichisqua's angle, more severe because his *waddly wazzoo* dangled from his neck, secured from view by a harness Garan had whipped up from remnants of gauze. Together, they hauled *the dollywaggle*, which became heavier as they progressed, potholes and mud patches contributing to the challenge.

What was this challenge compared to Harris' conference with Captain Buhippus? Buhippus had guessed *the Didaniyisgi's* purpose before he revealed it, but still, the consequences were in doubt. However, when told plainly, no detail hidden, Buhippus gave a disapproving grunt and shrugged.

You are my lord, he said. *I serve my warrant and not my family. But I must caution you. You are violating a treaty, which, if known, will undo your position both here and on the hill.*

Harris understood this and appreciated Buhippus' candor, and said as much. However, his chief concern was whether Buhippus would report the violation to his brother. *The Didaniyisgi* placed the captain in a precarious position. But if both clung to the fiction that Lord Belmundus never paid him a visit and Garan's explanation was believable, the chief of the Palace Yunockers only would be judged a fool — far better than a traitor.

You realize the Sceptas are abroad in the outlands and your reason for absence is negated.

Harris knew this, but few others did — surely not his *Danuwa* or Garan. But Tappiolus would be on the hoof, spying as he did when Charminus was out sapping men's life force. Harris would chance the excuse, although he would tell Garan, who might frame it better. Harris thanked Buhippus, who said that no thanks was required, because the interview had never taken place.

Harris embraced a tenuous trust in the captain. Now, having cleared *the Byybykyyip* without hearing *gwasdi* snaps and *zugginak* howls, his faith in Buhippus improved. His faith in the weather did not. The rain pelted them. He was dry, thankfully, because the *jupsim*-woven cloak repelled all liquids. It hardened the material into a shell, Harris reckoning he had become a turtle and the cloak — his carapace.

Jupsim repelled liquid, but not smells. Yustichisqua had dowsed himself with *charpgris*, that Tygger piss perfume, which marinated him into a cesspool. He had applied it to cheeks, ears, chest, armpits and groin, making him repulsive to any creature not accustomed to the stink. Harris choked during the haul through *the Byybykyyip*.

"I am sorry, *oginali,*" Yustichisqua said as they shuffled along. "I do not smell a thing, but I know you are offended."

"So long as it throws the bad guys off your scent, old man, I'll suffer." Harris choked again. "You'd think the rain would wash it away."

"It lingers," Yustichisqua said.

"Tell me about it."

Suddenly, the road improved. Harris halted, considering the change.

"We have come to *the Yuganawu*," Little Bird said. "We call it *the Yugodohi — Enemy Country*. You have never noted the road change, because you are always in *the Cabriolin*. But I know it from old. The going will be better for *dollywaggle* pulling, but more dangerous. More Yunockers."

"I don't see anyone out in this weather."

Harris continued hauling the wagon like an old bag woman from *the stetl*. The third leg pinched his balls and he moaned. He heard Little Bird laugh. He wanted to hit his friend over the head with the leg, but realized Little Bird must be suffering from the same testicular pain with the added attraction of a kettled *waddly wazzoo* trying to free itself under his carapace.

"You stink," Harris said, in response, and then chuckled at the obvious.

"Like a Tygger pissing, *oginali*. You have always called me your *Noya Tludachi*. Now you know why."

They hauled *the dollywaggle* up an incline into the business district, a grand plaza devoid of pedestrians at this hour, although *bronksers* were lit in the windows and faces peered into the storm. The buildings were an eclectic mix, sleek Art Deco straight from Albert Speer's sketch book, and sandstone Georgian, remnants of a distant time when the Cetrone ruled Montjoy, their homeland and settlement. The *Nuremburg-rally-style* buildings were closed now, transactions finished by this time, but *the majorin*-occupied Cetrone houses stirred in the tempest. As the disguised *Augustii spinctae* passed *the kaybar* front doors, a few opened, *majorin* citizens noting who crept through the plaza at this hour and in this inclemency. A few heads popped out from *the kaleezos*, the servants also curious.

"*Oginali*," Yustichisqua said, fearfully. "The Yunockers will see me as Garan has disguised me, but the Cetrone will know that I am one of them."

"Let us hope they don't tell their . . . their masters."

"They do not speak to their masters," Little Bird said, "But we are a naturally gossiping people. By morning our passage will be known in every *kaleezo* in the city."

"You exaggerate."

"Do I? I worry, because when Cetrone gossip, their masters notice. Curiosity might spur questioning, and then . . ."

"And then the game is up. Let's boogie then."

Yustichisqua didn't ask, but picked up the pace despite the ball-pinching pain. Soon, they cleared the square and slipped through an alleyway. However, coming toward them were several *birrupsun* beacons.

2

Three *regulati* approached swiftly on *zulus*, their *birrupsuns* shining through the rain streaks.

"We should run, *oginali*," Yustichisqua whispered.

"Hold your ground. We've nothing to fear. We're two *Augustii spinctae* taking a *dollywaggle* of *zulus* to *the Kalugu* under the warrant signed by a big fucky-wucker from the *Yuyutlu*." He laughed. "Just stay calm and don't speak. I know you're older than me in dog-years, but we're Zecronisians now and I outrank you. I have the bigger third leg."

Little Bird giggled nervously, but Harris wasn't convinced. They needed to stay vigilant.

The *regulati* patrol slowed, hovering across the path.

"So late, gentlemen," the chief one said. "And in such weather."

"Yes," Harris said, gruffly as befitting his hunched over, painful position. "Business is business and orders are orders. My business does not recognize time or weather."

The other two *regulati* came around the back and poked *the dollywaggle.*

"*Zulus,*" Harris said, anticipating the question. "*Zulus* for *the Kalugu mordanka.*"

"I suppose you have that in writing," the patrol leader commanded. "Your *gufawpup.*"

Harris had no idea what *a gufawpup* was, but Little Bird came to their aid.

"Better than a *gufawpup*, sir," Yustichisqua replied. "We have a warrant from *the Didaniyisgi of the Yuyutlu*, enjoined to a case settlement from *the Myrkpykyn.*"

"Truly?"

Harris reached into his cloak, grasping the document. He opened it quickly, displaying the seal.

"Do you recognize the seal?" he asked.

He flashed it, then, fearing the rain, he slipped it back into his cloak. While in there, his hand grasped the hilt of his sword — just in case.

"I do," the leader said. "Although, I see no reason for an increase in *zulu* supply to *the Kalugu.* If a Trone cannot be shod, it should fall into *the Deetsuneeli* and become *Tludachi* food."

"Orders are orders," Harris said, bowing slightly. "And . . ."

"I know. The weather is the weather. We do our duty in the storm as we do it in the suns-shine. Pass on."

The patrol regrouped and continued to the plaza, disappearing in the turn.

"I am liked to die, *oginali*," Little Bird said.

"You did well," Harris replied, giving *the dollywaggle* a tug. "What the fuck's *a gufawpup.* Some kind of laughing dog?"

"No. A permit for a shipment of goods."

"A freight bill. Good thinking on your part."

"They wanted papers and we have papers."

"We also have third legs shoved up our asses, but we're not there yet."

They shuffled on to another plaza — a smaller one lined with shops. A stopped up drain had caused street flooding, a river running through it. Harris gaped at the obstacle, and then sat on *the dollywaggle*, pondering the next step.

3

"We have *zulus*," Yustichisqua suggested. "We could fly over it."

"With this get-up? And we need *the dollywaggle* to tote our shit."

"Do we, *oginali*? *The zulus* are in sacks. We could carry them just as easily as we can struggle with *the dollywaggle*."

"I see. We fly over the puddle with the sacks and return to our *Zecronisian* selves on the other side. But what if we're seen."

"This is a shopping zone. No one buying or selling at this hour. And no houses around."

"Good point. *Zulus*? I hate wearing those things. Will they fit over our *borabas*?"

"*Borabas* adjust to accommodate all sizes — inner and outer."

"One size fits all." He stood. "Let's give it a shot. It's either that or doing the backstroke wearing cloaks."

"The *jupsim* would let us float."

"I'm joking, old man. But a dip in the bathtub would wash it away." Suddenly, he paused, grinning. "You know, those *regulati* didn't detect you. The piss really works."

"Yes, *oginali*. I was happy when they didn't guess that I am not *an Augustii*."

"That's reassuring. It makes your *Night in the Sewer* fragrance almost bearable." He gazed at *the dollywaggle*. "I'm not going to miss dragging the little red wagon, although I suppose we'll need to buy a new one for Garan."

Yustichisqua rustled through the sacks, finding two pairs of *zulus*. He helped Harris don one pair over *the borabas,* and then slipped a pair on himself, activating them with a side switch. He almost slipped into the lake.

"It has been some time, *oginali.*"

Harris switched his on and hovered an inch above the ground.
"It's been longer for me."

He remembered the only time he tried to maneuver on *zulus*.
He had only been in Farn for a few days and nearly caused
Yustichisqua's arrest. He was upended and landed on his ass then.
Now he not only had to remain upstanding, he had to tote a sack of
zulus while being weighed down by a sword, a *Stick* and a third-
leg, not to mention a heavily cowled cloak . . . in the teeming rain.

"This ain't gonna work."

"Yes, *oginali*, it will. I shall guide you. We will go slowly."

Harris felt the brace of Yustichisqua's hand under his elbow.
They rose together over the flood, the sacks swaying in the wind.
Thunder clapped. Lightning flashed. But the two *Augustii*
impostors floated over the water. Harris could feel himself
tumbling, like a tot first learning to ride a bicycle. But each time he
wavered, Yustichisqua compensated by lifting Harris' elbow.

It was a short trip, but hectic, the wind trying to blow them off
course. But they made it to the other side and drifted along another
lane until reaching dry ground, where the drains worked. Harris
landed, but as he touched down, *the Eye* appeared.

"Crap," he muttered.

Tappiolus was on the prowl. With Charminus abroad, the co-
consort could invade privacies without restraint. That *the Eye*
appeared at an unlikely spot, a god-awful hour and in ominous
weather, convinced Harris that Buhippus might be unreliable, if
Lord Tappiolus knew about this excursion and sought to interrupt
it.

"Kick the switch, *oginali*," Yustichisqua whispered.

Harris tripped his feet under the cloak, trying to kick the button
to deactivate *the zulus*. After a few misses, he connected. The
cursed footwear ceased vibrating. Little Bird succeeded also.

"Ignore the spy," Harris said. "We are *Augustii spinctae.* Act
the part."

Harris adjusted the sack on his back, leaning forward. He
limped like *Quasimodo*, because he felt like *Quasimodo*. Bring on
those bells. Steadily, he passed *the Eye*, not giving it another
thought. He had the urge to flip his finger and bellow a *fuck you,
brother-in-law*, but he kept to his role and trundled into the next
alleyway, not looking back. He heard the familiar *whoosh*, which
occurred when *the Eye* faded.

"I believe *the equa anatoli* has gone, *oginali*."

"If you mean *the Eye*, yep. We beat it this time."

They reached the end of this alley. Harris felt beat. The sack was heavy. His back ached. He kicked *the zulus* off, and replaced them in his sack. Water dripped from the end of his nose and, although he was dry beneath, the steady downpour drove him loony. Perhaps he should have waited for a starry night to undertake this mission. But a starry night would have been fraught with many *regulati* and citizens.

"There," Yustichisqua said.

Harris glanced into the rain swept clearing, which loomed before him. He recognized the spot — a place he'd been many times on his tour of *the Yuganawu*. Here he had pondered *the Kalugu* from a distance at the edge of *the Gulliwailit*. Perhaps a hundred yards away was *the Bridge — the Bridge over Troubled Waters*.

4

Crossing the bridge, Harris put enemy country, what Yustichisqua called *the Yugodohi*, behind him. He had crossed this bridge yesterday, but, on reconsideration, it was a rash try to knock at *the Kalugu's* gates. Now he tried to carry out the same feat with subterfuge. The longer he hobbled like an old man, the more like an old man he felt. He'd need a massage when he returned to *the Myrkpykyn — if* he returned to *the Myrkpykyn*.

All was black and bleak on *the Gulliwailit Bridge* — the road, the creek, the pylons — the backdrop of *phitron* walls. Coming toward Harris and Yustichisqua, three Trones floated, their buckskins soaked. They came close, but upon seeing Yustichisqua, bowed and continued their journey to *the Yugodohi*, no doubt an early shift of night soil collectors.

"They smell worse than you," Harris muttered.

"I did detect it also, *oginali*, but you would stink too if you dived into the muck and carried *the fuggipantis*."

Harris didn't want to know. The moment of truth had come. He had passed the scene of yesterday's *brouhaha* — where Tarhippus had confronted him. No signs remained of Trone blood, the rain a natural scrub brush. Still, Harris experienced a chill.

As they approached *the Kalugu's* gate, the guard, luck of the draw — the same one encountered yesterday, didn't meet them halfway. Harris hoped there was no reason for a challenge. He reached for his papers, certain they'd be scrutinized. Two *zugginaks* stirred, coming to the guard's heels, then cocked their heads and retreated to a dry spot under the portcullis.

"Rather late for a delivery," the guard said.

"I do not control the weather, sir," Harris replied, preparing to whip out the warrant.

"No *dollywaggle* this time?"

"Light load . . ."

"And two of you porting, I see, instead of the usual one."

Ricktus Morphinus probably made this run alone. Harris wished he had known that tidbit, but the guard had all the answers. How convenient.

"Exactly so," Harris said, bowing, although he didn't have far to go with the gesture.

As Yustichisqua came under the portcullis, the guard sniffed as if detecting *the blood of an Englishmun*. But the reaction passed, only serving Harris' jitters.

"You *Augustii* will do anything for *yedalas*."

"Not anything, sir. I would not put my hand in your *zugginak's* mouth for every *yedala* in *the Yuyutlu*."

"Now, I would have bet you would," the guard said.

Two other guards were slouching near the wall. They waved to *the Augustii* as if the errand was regular, if not late. Harris didn't react, not knowing Ricktus Morphinus' usual response. However, the sentry guard suddenly raised *a burripsun*, shining it in Yustichisqua's face. Little Bird deflected the light.

"It is as I thought," the guard snapped, laughing. "Zecronisians are near blind."

"Yes," Harris concurred, pulling Yustichisqua forward. "Our eyes are sensitive. That is why we are hooded and cloaked. Please deflect your *birrupsun*, sir.*"*

"Since when do I take my orders from you?"

"Never," Harris said, bowing to assure that his own face was lower than the light. "But in the spirit of cooperation, let us pass in darkness to *the mordanka*."

Yustichisqua had proceeded through the gate, while Harris made deep gestures to the guard as if begging for crumbs from a baker. The sentry guard enjoyed the servility of a man who was, by law, not a servant. Harris could see satisfaction welling in the sentry's eyes and wished he could draw his sword and cut those eyeballs out. How light-sensitive would *they* be? But the other two guards joined him in a congratulatory mood. It was late, stormy and these minions were bored, no doubt. Tormenting two Zecronisian agents would be good entertainment to chase the hours until morning.

"Ah, go to *the mordanka*," the sentry said. "I get my share every time you pass through, so what do I care?"

His share? How did this operation work? Harris had to remember Garan as *a Gucheeda* as well as *a Deegosgi*. Shady dealings profited the unscrupulous. Perhaps this was the grease which let this plan work.

"Thank you," Harris blurted, thinking something else.

Harris turned and followed Yustichisqua, who progressed into the courtyard. He caught up to Little Bird at the edge of a gallery — a narrow street, where Yustichisqua had hesitated.

"We did it, old man," Harris said. "*The Treaty of Parazell* has been broken. I'd love to tell them to wipe their asses with it, but . . . you know. They'd . . . well, you know."

"They would kill us, and still may, *oginali*."

A thunderous roar sounded, the storm, no doubt. But there *was* doubt. The rain lashed at the path before them — a latticework stone causeway, which spanned whatever roared beneath it.

"*The Deetsuneeli*," Yustichisqua mumbled, fear in the word. "*The Place Where Death Crosses*."

"We're prepared for this, old man."

"I hope these *borabas* work."

"I'm sure they will."

"For you, there is no question. You can walk on *phitron* and *kaybar* . . ."

"I can walk on *fuggipantis* too." Little Bird giggled, nervously. "You didn't think I knew what that meant, did you?"

"It will not matter if *the Tludachi* eats me."

On cue, the Tygger roared, his *charpgris* stink striking Harris between the nostrils.

"Well, in the words of Melonius: Everyone needs to die someday. Tonight's as good as any other."

"If I should slip through," Yustichisqua said, "let me slip."

"Like hell, I will."

"Really, *oginali*. If I fall and you are touching me, you shall fall too."

"So that's how it works," Harris said, grinning. "I thought so. But I'm wearing *borabas*. Won't that leave me hanging upside down if my boots get caught?"

"But *Tludachi* can jump and . . ." Yustichisqua gazed into Harris' eyes, a grin spreading across his face. "I see what you mean."

He lifted his foot and stepped onto *the Place Where Death Crosses*.

The tludachi roared.

Chapter Four

The Place Where Death Crosses

1

Yustichisqua lifted his foot and stepped onto *the Place Where Death Crosses.*

The tludachi roared.

The foot came down lightly at first, Little Bird expecting to seep through *the Deetsuneeli* and collapse into awaiting jaws. But *the borabas* held, *the phitron* a saving grace between the Cetrone and his fate.

"I am walking, *oginali,*" he whispered, tears rolling down his cheeks.

"It's a good thing, walking," Harris said, moving him along.

The *tludachi* leaped to the latticework, clawing through the slats. Harris' comfort in *the borabas'* efficacy to keep Yustichisqua from falling was earnest, but if *the Tygger* clawed its way through, the boots would be useless.

"Let's move it along, old man," he said. "This racket will bring the guards."

"But we are *Augustii.*"

"I don't care if we're Christ walking on water. The faster I clear this plank, the better I'll feel."

A second *tludachi* joined its mate. The ground shook now, the growls unnerving Harris, who nearly dropped the sack and ran. He tugged Yustichisqua forward, a difficult task while bent by a third leg pinch.

The *Place Where Death Crosses* seemed endless, extending to a far wall. Harris hoped it wasn't a dead-end. More *tludachi* joined the ruckus, the floor vibrating with their wrath. Their stench far exceeded Yustichisqua's *charpgris* splashes. The planking buckled and rose under the beasts' power.

"They will break through, *oginali,*"

"How can they? It's *kaybar*. I thought *kaybar* kept everything at bay except Cetrone."

"But the seams are separating."

So they were, and between them, a paw slapped topside. Harris leaped over it. Little Bird hesitated, turning to retreat.

"Jump it," Harris barked. "Jump it now."

Little Bird hopped over the swiping paw. The beast's anger flared more, now that its quarry evaded him. Harris jogged, tough in this get-up. Yustichisqua plodded behind him. The end was in sight, but another seam opened, wider than the first. *A tludachi* head popped up, its saber teeth bristling in the rain.

"Shit," Harris said, stopping short, barring Yustichisqua's progress. "Perhaps Melonius' statement'll come true."

The paw swiped at them, but poor purchase and the beast's weight dragged it back into the pit.

"Now," Harris shouted. "Jump now."

He pitched forward, pulling Little Bird, *the zulu* sacks rattling. Leaping the gap could prove fatal, because the cargo weighed them down. They leaped, hitting the other side like two tumbleweeds, rolling to the plank's end.

"Help, *oginali*."

Little Bird's leg straddled *the kaybar*. It plunged through, *borabas* and all. Harris grabbed him, risking a trip himself, but he was well grounded. He took Little Bird into his arms and fell backward, ripping Yustichisqua's leg out of the pit. They both panted in the rain as *the tludachi* tried unsuccessfully to break out. The ruckus was menacing, but the beasts fell into angry fighting, which promised to thin their population by one.

"Are you alright?" Harris asked.

"I shat on my extra leg, perhaps."

Harris laughed, but knew they had to get going.

"Well, with the stinks around here, I won't notice it."

He helped Yustichisqua up.

"I'm glad that's over," he said.

"But we will need to cross it again when we leave, *oginali*."

"Always a source of cheer, you are. Which way now?"

The wall was not a dead-end, but forced them to choose — a dilemma in the true sense of the word.

"*The mordanka* is that way," Little Bird said, pointing left.

"We're not going to *the mordanka*."

"Then we shall go the other way."

Yustichisqua turned right, leading Harris into the heart of *the Kalugu*.

2

The way narrowed — dark — the street crooked — the houses, hovels. The rain didn't improve their appearance. The lightning highlighted the disrepair. Harris sighed at the sight.

How can anyone live here?

Yustichisqua shuffled. Along walls and in niches, Cetrone sat, inert as if dead. Harris thought they might be dead, but the occasional twitch and pipe glow told him this the living suffering. The tangle of streets cut through vacant lots where Cetrone slept. Women suckled babies unsheltered from the elements. Children sat, wide-eyed and big bellied, too weak to beg for whatever these *Augustii* travelers carried in the *korinkles*.

"Little Bird," Harris whispered, as if in a morgue. "What is this place?"

"*The Banetuckle, oginali — the Place of Desperation.*"

"Little Bird," Harris whispered again. "Why are they outside in this weather?"

"It does not matter, *oginali*. Most places are infested with *morggus* and *bettlebuds*. Not good for eating. The rain soothes the bites."

"They look so forlorn — dreamy."

"It is *the sqwallen. The regulati* administer a dose twice a day to keep order here, now that these Cetrone have left *the yehu* — the clan districts."

"Barbaric."

Harris noticed the waifs went barefoot.

"I thought wearing *zulus* was the law."

"These Cetrone have sold their *zulus* to pay for *sqwallen.*"

"Pay for it?"

"Yes." Yustichisqua gazed into Harris' eyes. "These people have lost *gollywi* support and shelter. They come here to die. Without *zulus,* they cannot leave *the Kalugu.* Without *zulus,* they violate the regulations. They will be taken to *the Porias* or suffer in *the reaptide.*"

Harris stared at the dismal lot — helpless souls, crawling if not sleeping. People without hope, waiting for . . . for what? *The Porias? The reaptide,* whatever that could be?

"The Yunockers can't be such bastards," he muttered.

"They are the enemy. They are the conquerors. It is expensive to transport all *the Banetuckle* to *the Porias* and set their bones on fire. *The zugginaks* will pass this way and feed on the living. The already dead will feed *the tludachi*."

Harris clenched his fists. He stared at faces as they passed. An old man drooled into his beard, his headband buckled by the rain. His woman might have been dead, her eyes closed, her old breasts sagging beneath her buckskins, but she hiccupped, showing the rag-tag vestiges of life, such as it was.

A young man squatted, his fingers in a bowl of gruel — *sqwallen*, his eyes flashing at his neighbors, fearing they might ask him to share it. Most were too weak to stir, but upon seeing *the Augustii spinctae*, the man clutched the bowl to his shallow chest and spit as a warning.

A child sat in a puddle, naked and drenched. He splashed his feet, looking for his toes. His belly bulged, but he appeared bright enough. Harris thought to take him in his arms and give him shelter. But could he sweep all the children under *the Augustii's* cloak? Could he save them from the death, which already crept here?

A young woman chatted to the night, a furtive conversation with the thunder. When Harris passed, she stopped, staring at him accusingly, as if she hated all foreigners, especially interlopers from *the Byybykyyip*. She gnashed her teeth, and then stuck out her tongue. Harris turned to Little Bird.

"Take me away from this."

"We are almost there, *oginali*."

Harris hurried into the next alley — another horror scene, where several men fought for the attentions of a girl, who didn't seem to care who won her. She flirted, raising her buckskins, showing her lopsided breasts. Her belly was scarred, raising her audience's temperament. She ran in a circle, two geezers trying to catch her, stepping over human debris — the already dead or dying.

Harris pushed Little Bird forward. He prayed the next turn would take him away from these sights. It did not.

Shadows mulled aimlessly, hundreds searching for nothing — empty beings treading in the driving rain, moaning vacant words. Harris couldn't comprehend them. *Zombie*. Only these forms were still living. He halted, but Little Bird proceeded.

How can he walk among them?

Harris' breath hitched. He trembled and began to weep. Still, he pushed his way forward, lost souls easily swept aside with a brush from his cloak. The street seemed endless. The gutters spilt refuse. The pavement crept with depravity. A picture of Hell, only it wasn't a picture.

"When?" he whispered to Yustichisqua.

"We are near, *oginali*."

They turned a corner and, as if a boundary had been crossed, the street was quiet and empty, except a few Cetrone, who roved on *zulus* between houses. The dwellings didn't improve, but the district kept their horrors indoors.

Harris hastened to Yustichisqua's side.

"Where are we now?" he stammered.

"The district of *the chisqua* clan. My clan. Near *the chisqua yehu* — the bird clan house."

"Then let's get there, before . . . before . . ."

Harris shook, his head swimming. The tears gushed now. He sobbed, and drifted to the street's edge, sitting in a heap, the cloak clustered about his cowl, the sack sinking to the ground.

"*Oginali*," Yustichisqua said, coming to him, holding his hand. "I am sorry this makes you sad, but it is in this sadness you know the truth."

"I'd rather have the lie, old man."

Harris rocked, gasping for air. The world was gone — all worlds were gone, both inner and outer. The actor had fled. The heart bled. If he never saw another soul, he could not forget *the Banetuckle of the Kalugu*. He squeezed the rain and looked to the lightning. He roared like *a tludachi*.

"Bring me back the lie, Yustichisqua," he shouted. "I should've never come here. I should've left the treaty intact."

Little Bird took him into his arms.

"No, *oginali*. Your eyes are the ones that see, while all others are blind. You are the new dawn. You were *my* new dawn, and so shall it be for all who come to know you."

Harris wrapped his arms about this friend of friends, rocking him until he recalled they sat in a torrent with an unfulfilled mission.

Harris tried to block these horrors from his mind, but how could he? Had the secret of *the Kalugu* been revealed to be a graveyard unlike any other? He quivered to think on it. He had little time to ponder, because Yustichisqua marched steadily onward through several lanes and streets lined by a labyrinth of shattered hovels. Few Cetrone were abroad in this neighborhood. The sack seemed heavier as if *the zulus* had become lodestones, each able to redeem a life.

Yustichisqua halted, turning toward an ancient hovel — a black house with a wide front. Through display windows, Harris saw dim light, most likely *waddly wazzoos.*

"This is the place, *oginali.* This is *the chisqua yehu* — the bird clan house."

"It doesn't look promising," Harris remarked. "Has it always been so gloomy?"

"It is the best way to hide secrets — to blend into the surroundings." He raised his hand to the rain, catching the drops and bringing the moisture to his lips. "My clan's heart is kept within, although we must take care. *The regulati* come at *reaptide.*"

Harris didn't ask. *Reaptide* sounded ominous and he had his fill of *ominous* for the night. Yustichisqua peered through the window. Then he opened the door — made of *phitron* to prevent easy passage. He held it for Harris, who crossed the threshold. Harris' first instinct was to let his cowl slip, but when he reached for it, Yustichisqua grunted.

"Not yet, *oginali.*"

Harris moved forward into a wide hall arrayed with mats and low beds — a hospital, perhaps. Most were occupied by sleeping Cetrone. Beside some were *waddly wazzoos*, dimly burning. Most wore *zulus*, powered down, clamped from heel to toe. Beside all were bowls of vicious gruel — *sqwallen.*

"Is this a dormitory?" he whispered.

"It is a den," Little Bird replied.

A sqwallen den.

These slumberers were lost in a numb world. Some snored, while others stirred lightly. A few mumbled, and then one sat up. Harris paused. This one stared blankly at the intruders, then reached for his bowl, spooned some gray slime to his lips, swallowed, and, after a few grumbles, returned to his dream state.

"I don't understand," Harris said.

"The clan administers daily doses, in comfort and at a discount."

Harris shook his head.

"Unbelievable."

"Not so loud," Yustichisqua warned.

"Why? They're all asleep."

"Not all. They hear us and know. And the spooner will be at hand."

"The spooner?"

At that, one *waddly wazzoo* shone brightly from the far end of the hall.

"Who stirs there?" came a gruff voice.

"Do not answer, *oginali*."

Harris obeyed, walking toward the light. An old Cetrone stood in the aisle.

"I said, who stirs there?" He waved his *waddly wazzoo*. "Who . . . Oh, it is you *Augustii* Ricktus. How odd that you have come so late and in such weather. And so close to *reaptide*. And you have brought an assistant." The Cetrone came closer, holding *the waddly wazzoo* higher. He had a crooked nose and wispy hair constrained by a dirty purple headband. His buckskins had seen better days. "And you have two sacks. How did you manage to get them past *the mordanka*? Or have you struck a new bargain?" He shook the light. "Have you . . ." His breath hitched. "You are not Ricktus Morphinus. Where is *the Augustii spinctus*? Is there a new arrangement?"

Harris let the cowl slip. It was time.

"You are not even Zecronisian," the man snapped.

Little Bird also uncovered.

"Hold your tongue, Talqwah," he muttered.

"Yustichisqua? You here?" Talqwah drifted back on his *zulus*. "And disguised. What foolery is this?"

Harris let the sack fall and rushed the spooner of *the chisqua yehu*. The cloak slipped farther, revealing *the Columbincus*. Talqwah gasped, and then tried to bow.

"You are *Ayelli*," he stammered. "You cannot be here."

"I'm *the Didaniyisgi of the Yuyutlu*."

"Lord Belmundus," Talqwah yelped, pushing back. "We will be undone."

"Enough, Talqwah," Yustichisqua said.

"You know you cannot be here, Yustichisqua," the spooner said. "You do not wear *zulus* and your eyes are clear of *sqwallen.*"

"I am not the only one free of the spell," Little Bird said.

Talqwah raised his *waddly wazzoo*, swinging it about as if to signal, but Little Bird drew his dagger and thrust it into the lamp's base. Talqwah, horrified, dropped it and crouched on the floor.

"Profanity," he stammered.

"I am sorry, uncle, but you left me no choice."

"Uncle?" Harris asked.

"This is the clan house, *oginali*. We are all blood kin."

"You are not," Talqwah spit, getting to his *zulus* and moving toward the dormitory.

"If you raise the alarm," Yustichisqua said, "*the regulati* will come before *reaptide* and we shall all be put in *the Porias.*"

Talqwah grunted, but returned. He retrieved his damaged *waddly wazzoo*, mumbling as he inspected the knife hole.

"I cannot believe you would do this, Yustichisqua. I cannot."

"I am sorry. *The Yodanado* can bless it again and all will be fine."

Harris hunkered down to Talqwah.

"I mean no disrespect and bring you no harm."

"You bring us our death, Lord Belmundus. You seek passage to the outlands, like the other one had. But it is not here."

"Lord Hierarchus *was* here? The Treaty has been broken before?"

"We do not speak of him."

"Tell him," Yustichisqua said. "I would do it, but I do not know."

Talqwah diverted his eyes from Harris.

"He brought us much pain," he murmured.

Harris grasped the spooner's shoulders.

"I've seen pain, sir — much pain — here — tonight. Don't blame others for your inability to stand up to these demons. Don't blame me or any other." He shook Talqwah, who scowled. "Did Lord Hierarchus break the treaty?"

"Yes," Talqwah growled. "But *the regulati* did not announce it to all Montjoy. Lord Tarhippus commanded us to silence. No more was said about it."

"Until now."

"Why have you come?" Talqwah asked, pushing back on his *zulus*. "Have you come to barter *the zulus* and make your profit? If so, give me your cargo and I shall dispose of it as I will. But leave — you and the renegade."

"We have come to see *the Yodanado*," Yustichisqua said.

"You want to enter *the siti?*" Talqwah asked. "Impossible. They will not see you. They do not bless renegades. They do not sanction the tainted."

"I shall see for myself." Yustichisqua displayed his *waddly wazzoo*, holding it high in his left hand. In his right hand, the dagger threatened again. "I remember the way to *the siti*. Step aside, uncle."

"You would not dare," Talqwah grumbled. "It is too close to *reaptide*."

"We do dare," Harris replied, not having a clue where *the siti* was or who *the Yodanado* were. But Yustichisqua had a plan and it was better than arguing with an old man in a room filled with drugged Cetrone on the brink of *reaptide*, whatever that was. "And you shall lead us."

"But my lamp is . . ."

"My light will show the way," Yustichisqua said. "We will not leave you here to bargain with *the regulati* for your skin at our expense. We shall dispose of our cargo in our own way and in our own time." Little Bird brandished the knife. "You may complain of me to the council and have me stripped and beaten, but for now, do as I say, uncle, or I will have one less relative to call me renegade."

Harris, shocked by Little Bird's gumption, took up the sack and pushed the spooner forward. Talqwah reluctantly floated toward the back wall. A beaded curtain hid the way. He pushed through it, and quickly went beyond Little Bird and Harris.

"He will escape us, *oginali*," Yustichisqua said. "He has always been wily. That is why he is *the yehu* spooner. I will run ahead and keep him from slipping away."

Harris nodded and pushed through the beadwork. The room on the other side was pitch-dark. He saw the faint twinkle of Talqwah's damaged *waddly wazzoo* and Yustichisqua's brighter light pursuing. He also heard the padding of *borabas*. But he lost his bearings in the dark. There could be surprises which *zulus* would skirt, but clodhoppers could not — a box, a chair, a footstool — vermin, perhaps. He tried to keep pace, the third leg a deterrent, because it came loose and promised to trip him. Then both beacons disappeared. He panicked. He felt his way forward, one hand extended, until it hit another beaded curtain. He pushed through into light — into a larger hall.

Yustichisqua had halted, corralling his uncle. He waited for Harris to catch up. The old spooner complained, offering several reasons not to go farther. Harris reached them, slamming the sack to the ground.

"I can't take this get-up anymore," he said, wiggling out of the cloak. "And this leg is so far up my ass, I might marry it."

"*Oginali*," Yustichisqua protested. "We need to remain *Augustii spinctae* to escape."

"Do we?"

Little Bird considered, grinned, and then shucked his cloak also. Emerging before the spooner of *the chisqua yehu* were two noble specimens perfectly primed for the executioner if *reaptide* should sweep through.

"That's better," Harris said, adjusting his sword, *Stick* and his *Columbincus*.

He shouldered the sack again and nodded to proceed. Little Bird held high his *waddly wazzoo*, revealing a barrel vaulted hall, hung with triangular tiles in rainbow colors. When the light struck them, they chimed as if caught in a breeze. Talqwah sighed. Humming drifted from a distant place. Not so distant, Harris realized. Perhaps from the next hall.

"What lies beyond that panel?" he asked Yustichisqua.

"*The siti*," Little Bird said, bowing his head. "The temple of *the Yodanado* — the Whisperers."

Talqwah trembled, shaking his head.

"You are our undoing, Lord Belmundus," he said. "They will not sacrifice the clan for your curiosity. Not even for two sacks of *zulus*."

"Then we shall all die together," Harris said. "I have it on good authority that any day is as good as any other."

Talqwah slid the wall panel aside, revealing *the siti*.

Chapter Five

Whisperers and Ferrymen

1

Harris crossed the threshold into *the siti.* Although dim on the periphery, it appeared to be a rotunda with a glass dome — the material reminding him of the Gurt plastic, *mopyn,* because it scalloped overhead, catching the storm, the rain washing in rivers. In *the siti's* center were seven conical-shapes — tepees or volcanoes, each six feet tall, topped by a sleeping head. Harris realized these were Cetrone — impressive Cetrone, their buckskins stiffly forming each cone, a banded head inanimate at the summit. Old heads and feminine.

"*The Yodanado, oginali,*" Yustichisqua said. "The Whisperers, sacred to *the chisqua yehu.*"

"And not to be disturbed," Talqwah snapped. "Do so at your risk."

Yustichisqua ignored him, approaching the array, humbly, but with his *waddly wazzoo* raised. Talqwah muttered, and then turned to leave.

"Stay," Harris said. "If they decide to punish us, you'll share in the pain."

"You are our bane, Lord Belmundus."

"I've lived so long to be so honored."

As the light struck *the Yodanado,* Harris regarded the crones — cheeks cracked and worn — lips as thick as Goodyears and hair, ashen. Each wore a different crystal at their headband's peak. They could be sisters — weird sisters perhaps, recalling the Scottish Play, but these were seven in number — not three.

Suddenly, one opened her eyes in a flash. Her pupils were yellowing.

"Who calls Euforsee? Who disturbs my run with the wolves?"

The others opened their eyes, but did not speak. Yustichisqua bowed, trembling.

"It is I," he stammered.

"Yustichisqua, son of Killowa and Talapinkwalp, who left these halls to serve *the Ayelli.* Much I have heard about you. Much that disturbs." She grinned. "Much that pleases."

"I have come to ask . . ."

"You need not tell me. We know why you come. You have brought the interloper."

Harris stepped forward and bowed, assuming he had earned a new title — a dubious one, but one befitting his current treaty-breaking status.

"I'm here, great one," he said.

"I am neither great nor one," she said. "I am Euforsee, the voice of my sisters, who choose to speak through me."

The heads nodded in unison. Harris thought they spoke. He heard the humming again, but didn't comprehend it. Talqwah slipped between Harris and *the Yodanado*.

"Forgive me, Euforsee," he grunted. "They forced me to show them the way. They broke my lamp." He lifted it. "Bless it so it might be restored."

"Ah, spooner Talqwah. Such wounds to the lamp are hard to repair."

"Hard?"

"It has been punctured by *a brashun blade*."

"*Brashun?*" Talqwah gasped, and looked to Yustichisqua. "What have you done?"

Yustichisqua drew his dagger, staring at it.

"*Brashun?*" he stammered. "I had no idea."

"It is not *your* blade," Euforsee said. "It was a gift from another, who wears a sword of the same metal."

Harris grasped the hilt of his sword, but dared not draw it, afraid to offend the crone.

"I don't understand," he said.

"Lord Belmundus," she replied. "*Ayelli* are not permitted here."

"I know, but something compelled me to come."

Suddenly, the entire *Yodanado* cackled, a disturbing humor, stirring fear in Harris' soul. Was he a source of amusement? He didn't recall telling a joke.

"I compelled you," Euforsee said, suddenly stern and commanding. Her crystal shone bright white. "I, Euforsee of *the chisqua Yodanado* compelled you to come here, as I compelled the other one to cross *the Deetsuneeli*. He stood where you stand now and looked into my eyes. I saw the abyss that was his soul and knew he was not the one I sought."

Harris came closer, the light drawing him.

"What do you see in my eyes, Euforsee of *the chisqua Yodanado*?"

"Magic," she said. "I see the universe unleashed. I see Zacker rise and Zin fall. I see the one I seek."

She closed her eyes and went silent. Harris trembled. He had no idea what these words meant. However, Yustichisqua had crumbled into a heap, shivering. Harris hunkered down to him.

"Little Bird, are you ill?"

"Never ill, *oginali*. She speaks to me. She sings to my soul."

"Sings?"

"She tells me to assure your safety in all things. She charges me to be your *Taleenay* and your *Noya Tludachi*."

"You're that already," Harris said.

"Yes, by my choice. But now I am compelled to do it until I close my eyes. Until my *waddly wazzoo* fades into the darkness of Zin."

"Lord Belmundus," Euforsee chanted above the humming and the storm. Her eyes were open again. Harris stood. "You seek a way to return to your world."

"Is there a portal here?"

"No portals here except those built by the enemy, and they lead to *reaptide*."

"There must be a way back."

"There are many ways to return and you shall find them in time, but know this. If you seek a way home, you have already found it."

Harris' hand went to the hilt of his sword — *the brashun bladed* gift from the Elector. The move was visceral. He could easily swing at these talking volcanoes and lopped their heads off into a sticky pile. But he stayed his hand. Disappointment caused the move. Disappointment caused him to stay it. Sadness engulfed him.

"It is a happy time for us," Euforsee said.

"Happy," Talqwah snapped. "My lamp has gone out."

"Fuck you, Talqwah," Harris said, sick of the old man's temperament. "Your lamp's out because you were a pain in the ass. My lamp's out because I was too dumb to zip up my fly. I would have done better to overdose on some wacky shit and be a sensational headline on Twitter."

Talqwah wept. Harris felt bad. He shouldn't have taken it out on the spooner. He tapped his shoulder, trying to console him. Then he touched the dead *waddly wazzoo* and a spark grew from his fingertips. The light spawned an ember and the lamp sizzled — a faint kindling.

"My lord," Talqwah said, bowing, and then kissing Harris' hand. "You are the bright light. You have the spark."

Harris sighed. He didn't understand this, but felt a surge of unfathomable happiness.

Euforsee spoke, her voice filling *the siti*, overtaking the thunder and lightning:

> *To each Elector three branches made*
> *Deigned as sons and daughters born,*
> *Renowned Sceptas and Seneschals*
> *But as towers apart shall grow,*
> *Never fruitful within their bonds,*
> *So to the outlands they must go,*
> *To gather succor into dough —*
> *The life force must they always hoe.*
> *But each may draw a double mate,*
> *And thus may sow and populate,*
> *A harvest to serve and ease their shade —*
> *A scattered horde as duty paid,*
> *Smiling kin for the alliance trade,*
> *But as mules these Thirdlings be,*
> *Until there comes the mending free.*
> *Then a fourth shall bloom in Farn*
> *Uniting houses — the outlands darn*
> *'til suns and moons reflect no more*
> *And Zin and Zacker close the door.*

Harris stood.

"Promise and Prophecy," he stammered.

Then he heard a song from a remote corner of the room, the voice sweet and feminine — the tune enough to break his heart.

> *In the mountain's meadow shade,*
> *Sighed a sad, but lonely maid,*
> *Gazing at the cloudless sky,*

Dreaming worlds to multiply,
Lighting lands with glowing love
From the lamp of truth above.
Faraway mountain, faraway glade,
Sighs this most unhappy maid.

Beyond the Forling sings a heart
From her true love far apart,
Waiting in the nave of love
For the hawk to claim his dove.
And join her in the fire's heat,
And with his tears wash weary feet.
Faraway mountain, faraway glade,
Sighs this most unhappy maid.

I serve a mistress stern and still
Who rules upon the conqueror's hill,
I bring her all. I am her slave,
A spirit trapped within a cave,
But know I now that it is he,
Who comes aloft to set me free.
Faraway mountain, faraway glade,
Sighs this most, most hopeful maid.

Harris grasped Yustichisqua to his side and stared toward *the siti's* periphery. Emerging from the shadows came the singer — Littafulchee.

2

"My lady," Yustichisqua said, bowing.

Harris nodded and started to her side, but Littafulchee held her hand up in a stopping gesture.

"This is a raw intrusion, Lord Belmundus, but one I must accept."

"Intrusion?" Harris said, although how could it be anything else, unbidden as it was?

Littafulchee glared at Little Bird.

"Yustichisqua, you are emboldened by your new status. But recall that few acknowledge it. Your openness to embrace the ways of *the Ayelli* have not gone unnoticed here."

"I am not *Ayelli,* cousin," he protested. "I am still a servant of the light."

"Perhaps the best we have," Euforsee chanted, chiding the proud Littafulchee, who nodded as a concession.

"Silver cloak and *brashun blades* become you," Littafulchee said to Yustichisqua, and then looked toward Harris. "You seemed puzzled, my lord."

"A mystery flies with my every breath."

"It is to be expected, my lord."

"And you are here, Littafulchee."

"My lady on the hill — your mistress, has gone hunting in the outlands. When she does, I come here. Is that why you are here now?"

"I am here to seek answers."

"You would be better to seek questions, Lord Belmundus. The answers are easy, while the questions are difficult."

Harris grinned at this lovely maiden, whose voice enchanted and whose eyes were magnets. If she meant to tease him with conundrums, she succeeded. If she intended to engage in tricky conversation, she had hit the mark. He bowed.

"You have every advantage here, Littafulchee the Divine," he said, irony in his voice. "I come in this storm at great risk to witness great sorrow, and you choose to banter with me before these mystic oracles as if you are one of them."

Suddenly, all seven *Yodanado* raised their arms, each holding *a waddly wazzoo.* The effect startled Harris.

"Littafulchee of the Zacker," Euforsee intoned. "The time to question has fled. The hour to enlist is at hand."

Littafulchee bowed, and then turned to Harris. She extended her hand. He hesitated, but took it.

"Come with me, Lord Belmundus. Bring your cargo and your *Taleenay,* and you shall see what we are about." She looked to Talqwah. "Spooner, return to *the yehu.* Lock the doors and prepared to secure the sleepers for *reaptide.* Not one under your care must succumb."

Talqwah seized his *waddly wazzoo* lovingly, and then bowed to Littafulchee. He backed away into the shadows, returning to his post. Littafulchee raised her lamp and drifted on her *zulus,* leading Harris and Little Bird away from *the siti* into the shadows — through the place where she had sung. There, an archway pierced blackly into the room — a sinister corridor lit only by the *waddly wazzoos*.

"Where are you taking me?" Harris asked.

"To the questions," she replied. "You must listen and learn. You must accept the harshness of what we are about."

"Must I?"

"*The Yodanado* say you shall. Whether you come to it by degrees or embrace it all at once, I cannot tell." She led them through the darkness. "Yustichisqua will aid you, but he must also find his way to it, because these are the deepest secrets we hold and few know them. Only those who live or die for these secrets know them."

These words pierced Harris' mind like *a brashun blade,* enigmas from a philosopher's tome — an argument from Aristotle — an equation from Euclid. Logic underpinned the lot, but logic was like kettle steam, evaporating before it scalded with understanding.

They emerged into an open courtyard, blanketed by the rain. Harris missed his *jupsim* cloak, now that his hair began to mat. Littafulchee pulled him and Little Bird under a portico and waited. Across the ground spread a colorful tarpaulin — rainbow-colored, drenched and puddled. Harris saw it was attached to a huge cargo box — no, a basket, reminiscent of a gondola — the kind carried beneath balloons, only it was oddly shaped — birdlike. A figure emerged from behind it — a diminutive Cetrone, protected from the downpour by a silk sheet. It didn't do much good, because the man was dripping, water running down the bridge of his nose to the bow of his lip. He approached Littafulchee on dim *zulus,* bowing, but not having the good sense to come in out of the rain.

"My lady," he said, his voice high-pitched like a sparrow chirping. "My lady! My lady!"

"Where is he, Tomatly?" she asked.

"He has taken too much *sqwallen,* I fear, and sleeps inside the ferry." He pointed to the basket, which was covered with the same silk material which poorly sheltered Tomatly.

"This is not good, Tomatly," Littafulchee said, sternly. "You should not have let him take so much, if any."

"But the Seneschal is strong and can crush poor Tomatly with his big hands. I can guide him with advice and he can nod to me in agreement, but he does what he wants in the end. He said, a little bit more, Tomatly, and I said, no more, my lord. And he said, more please. And I said . . ."

"Enough, Tomatly. You do your duty poorly, but who else could do it?" She landed on the ground and poked about under her buckskins for a flask. "Here," she said. "Do your duty now."

Tomatly took the flask and drifted back to the basket, poking around inside.

"Cousin," Little Bird said, "what brew is this?"

"*Pilocarpinus*," she muttered.

"Rare, *oginali*, and the only antidote for *sqwallen* overdoses."

"Why so rare?" Harris asked.

"Because General Tarhippus has confiscated every bottle from every *mordanka* in Montjoy," Littafulchee replied.

"Not every *mordanka*," Harris said.

"*The mordanka* in *the Kalugu* will do anything for profit, as you shall see," she said. "They pilfer goods and sell them for profit. They engage in many illegal transactions, including the one that allowed that flask and . . . the one which allows your illicit trade in *zulus*."

Harris let his cargo sack slide.

"These *zulus* are for the needy, and are not part of an illicit trade," he snapped. "I saw so many people waiting to die in that place called . . . I can't remember. I don't want to remember, but I don't ever want to forget."

"*The Banetuckle,*" Yustichisqua said. "*The Didaniyisgi* is correct, cousin. We bring these *zulus* here so those who need to survive *the reaptide* can do so."

Littafulchee sighed, and then shook her head.

"I said you must accept the harshness of what we are about. Those who need *zulus* have given them away freely, knowing *the mordanka regulati* will trade them for more valuable goods — knowing *the regulati* trade is with *the chisqua yehu* and our ferryman."

Yustichisqua's eyes opened wide.

"Cosawta is engaged in the contraband trade?" Yustichisqua cried. "It is dishonorable, cousin. It is killing our own people."

"Those that die, die willingly," she whispered. "A sacrifice."

"Hold on here," Harris said. "I'm not following you. Are you telling me there's a black market in *zulus* and I've been unwittingly feeding it?"

"If you mean by *black market*, an illicit trade, yes. But before you are judgmental and irrational, as I know you can be, hear me."

"I'm listening and it better be good . . . my lady."

Harris' anger was real, but it was also steeped in disappointment. Littafulchee was intelligent, fair and attractive. She epitomized a purity in his mind — a paragon of femininity. Such idealizations are not easily assailed. He would hear her out, but nothing could justify the suffering he had witnessed in *the Banetuckle*.

Littafulchee reached into the sack and pulled out a single *zulu*. She turned it over and released the tread which held the mechanism together. With a quick twist, the power element — the battery, slipped into her hand. She held it up.

"*Aniniya*," she announced.

"That is so," Yustichisqua confirmed. "But only enough to lift and carry us." He turned to Harris, touching the housing. "It reacts to *the conontoroy*."

"What are you talking about?" Harris asked.

"*The aniniya*," Yustichisqua explained, "reacts to this other mineral — *conontoroy*. It is not a powerful interaction, but enough to fit the purpose. But I do not understand what end would be achieved by removing the power source from *zulus* when the people need them intact."

"You lack vision, Yustichisqua," Littafulchee said. "It is still *aniniya*."

"But not enough to make . . . weapons. And not enough even to power *a Cabriolin*." He turned to Harris. "*Cabriolins* depend on the reaction of *aniniya* with another mineral — *yustunalla*. A more powerful reaction, but I do not see an illicit trade in *Cabriolins*."

Littafulchee waved *the aniniya* about Yustichisqua's head, drawing him to silence.

"Listen and learn, Lord Belmundus. *Aniniya* is not the most valuable mineral in Farn. There are three minerals which interact with *aniniya* — *conontoroy*, *yustunalla* and . . ." She pointed to Harris' chest. He twitched.

"*Columbincus*?" he stammered.

"Yes. *Columbincus*. Not mined in Terrastrium and long since depleted in the bowels of Zin. Each realm cherishes its supply for its ability to interact with *aniniya*. "

Harris touched his brooch. Suddenly, he sensed he wore something akin to the Hope Diamond.

"All *Ayelli* have some form of this," he said.

"Yes, and there's a tincture of it in every *Stick* made and stored in *the Ryyve Aniniya*. But it is rare, and the Yunockers want it more than anything else, because they have enough *aniniya,* but lack a supply of *Columbincus.*"

"Then it is dangerous for *the Didaniyisgi* to wear his brooch," Yustichisqua said. "Or even the gems worn by *the Danuwa.*"

"No Yunocker would dare deprive *an Ayelli* official of his credentials*.* "

"Kuriakis must have an unlimited supply of the stuff," Harris mused. "I mean, he wears it from head to toe, and the Sceptas and my Memer wear it too. All Thirdlings sport one, and the consorts also. But I've never seen a stockpile."

"It is in plain sight," she said. "What place is revered above all others in *the Ayelli?*"

"The Temple of Greary Gree?" Harris said.

"Exactly so. A warehouse awaiting for enough *aniniya* to create an arsenal beyond imagination."

"That still doesn't explain *the zulu* trade," Harris snapped.

"Yes, it does," Littafulchee replied. "Beyond Greary Gree, the closest source of *Columbincus* is beyond the Forling . . . in Cetronia."

"We have a *Columbincus* mine in Cetronia?" Yustichisqua asked.

"No. Better. We have dealings with the *Fumarcans* of *the Dodingdaten.* "

Harris remembered Garan's tale of his dealings with these pirates, who had inspired a barter trade system. Then he remembered who convinced him to send *the zulus* into *the Kalugu* with Ricktus Morphinus.

"Garan," he stammered.

"He is *a Gucheeda,*" Yustichisqua grumbled.

"He is a friend to our cause," Littafulchee said.

"Cause?" Harris said.

"Yes," she replied. "You shall see. *The regulati* of *the Kalugu mordanka* take a few *zulus* to barter for goods, but allow the rest to come here, where they are transported by the ferryman." She pointed to the basket, and then to the open, rain-flooded ceiling gap in the roof — a way out of the place. "He takes *the zulus* to Cetronia to trade for *Columbincus*. He returns with small amounts, but enough to be worth the risk for these greedy *regulati*. They then trade *the Columbincus* to General Tarhippus. He does not care where it comes from, although be sure of it, he knows. He uses it to power his *aniniya* weaponry, his *gwasdi* and such."

"But you're arming your enemy?"

"Our enemy is brave, but stupid," she said, with too much passion in her voice for Harris' tastes. "They are arming us. *The zulus* provide us with a stockpile of *aniniya* and we have enough *Columbincus* to make a difference when the time comes."

"The time?" Harris said, his mind cloud parting. "You're planning an uprising."

Thunder cracked.

Lightning flashed.

"*Adadooski*," Yustichisqua shouted.

"Hush," Littafulchee said. "The uprising has not come and may not for some time. But those who sacrifice their lives now will be redeemed when the light comes again."

Yustichisqua knelt before her, grasping her hem. She didn't deter him. Harris wasn't sure what to think. He had just had a lesson in Farn metallurgy and also one on greed, the universal type. On one hand, his spirit was buoyed that these people weren't lambs brought to slaughter, and yet they brought their own to the altar as payment for future payback. He wasn't sure who the enemy was — the Yunockers, no doubt, but did this include *the Ayelli*, who also kept their feet on Cetrone backs? Or was there another, unseen enemy, lurking in the deepest, darkest corners of Farn?

3

Staggering toward them was a tall man — the resuscitated Ferryman, who wore no buckskins nor *zulus*. His step seemed unsure, *a sqwallen* hangover perhaps or could it be the antidote — rare *Pilocarpinus,* probably derived from the *jub-jub* bird's pancreas. Yustichisqua, who had resumed his stance, now bowed again. Harris just nodded as the man approached, steadied by Tomatly.

"Brother," Littafulchee said, "you disappoint me when you follow the old ways."

"You know better than to scold me in front of strangers," he said.

Instead of buckskins, the man wore a loin cloth and a tight leather tunic — something in the Samson class. He had bulging muscles, unlike any Cetrone Harris had ever encountered. His crystal wasn't suspended from a headband, but implanted in his forehead like a Hindu Tika.

"These are not strangers, brother," Littafulchee said. "Look closer."

The man squinted through the sheets of rain. He frowned, and then brightened.

"Is that cousin Yustichisqua?" he asked.

"Yes, Cosawta," Little Bird replied. "I have returned."

"Good for you. I have heard of your exploits. Acknowledged as a hero by the Elector and toting a dagger made of *brashun*."

"A gift from *the Didaniyisgi*," Little Bird said, meekly. "And I did not know it had *a brashun blade* until moments ago."

"In any case," Cosawta replied, "we can use another pair of balls here. There is too much deprecation and *waddly wazzoo* waving in the *yehu* . . ."

"And *sqwallen* pigs, also," Littafulchee added.

"You are too pure, sister. You need a consort. Another tale." He laughed, and then stared at Harris. "But . . . can this be . . . has the treaty been broken again?"

"It has," Harris said.

"Lord Belmundus?"

"It is I."

Cosawta reached out and hugged Harris, taking him by surprise. The man's grip was formidable. An ill-planned but well-intentioned squeeze could have driven the life from any man. Harris choked.

"Ah, this is a good day for this *yehu*. Good day. The fucking treaty is busted again, and this time by the man of the hour."

Harris was astonished. He had never heard a Cetrone curse before. In fact, no one in Farn seemed to use profanity. He instantly liked this man — this Cosawta, the Ferryman. But what did he ferry? Harris had no time to ask, because a sudden alarm sounded — a klaxon, howling across the rooftops. Tomatly cowered as did Yustichisqua. Littafulchee sighed and Cosawta shook his fists.

"*Reaptide,*" he shouted.

"Lord Belmundus," Littafulchee said. "Follow us to *the sustiya* — a place of safety."

The klaxon unnerved Harris, but more so the barks — *the zugginaks*, and the screams of those caught in their jaws. He glanced at the terror flooding Yustichisqua's face. No question hesitating now. To *the sustiya* they would go, and hide and wait for the passing of *reaptide.*

Chapter Six

Reaptide

1

What Harris could not see, he certainly could imagine. The klaxon couldn't drown the agony beyond *the yehu* walls. *The regulati* shouted commands above wailing women and pleading men. This didn't appear to be willing sacrifices for a promised uprising. Barbarity raised its head beneath *the zugginak's* barking and *the tludachi's* roar. Harris wondered what he would see when he wended his way through *the Banetuckle* to *the Deetsaneeli* and *the Gulliwailit Bridge.* Straddling *the Kalugu* walls seemed the better option to escape, now that he had shucked his *Augustii* disguise.

Littafulchee held his hand as she floated ahead, her *waddly wazzoo* lighting the course like fairy dust through *the yehu's* gloomy corridors and rain-drenched courtyards. With each courtyard, the sounds of *reaptide* intensified horribly. Harris heard breaking glass and the sizzle of *Sticks* firing. *Resisters? How could the sqwallen-addled Cetrone resist such wanton slaughter? Or was mercy afoot in the Kalugu?*

Yustichisqua wept, not from cowardice, but from a deep remembrance. He had lived here. Death's raging swarm was as natural to him as caring for his rope lamp. Perhaps *reaptide* laid heavier on his mind now that he was *sqwallen-free* and exposed to freedom's light.

Harris touched Little Bird's shoulder.

"I shall be fine, *oginali*. I recall my brother, lost at *reaptide*." *How sad.*

"Come quickly," Littafulchee insisted. "We near *the sustiya.*"

"It is just ahead," Cosawta boomed, pushing Tomatly, the diminutive Cetrone propelled on his *zulus*, his *waddly wazzoo* waving in the breeze.

The last courtyard ended in a narrow alley. Drenched walls cascaded in a waterfall overflowing the gutters. *Thunder cracked. Lightning flashed.* A strange building appeared ahead — gumdrop-shaped with no visible door. But when Harris reached it, he found the entrance down a short flight and over a causeway. The outside deceived, because inside it was large, rotund and receded deep into a cistern spun to a spiraling causeway, funneling into an abyss.

Littafulchee and Tomatly's *zulus* wisked down the causeway. Harris and Yustichisqua's heavy *phitron* footsteps clanked beneath their *borabas*.

"You could wake *the Zinbear* with those boots," Cosawta quipped, laughing, his own tread heavy, but silent. "Garan's resourcefulness reflects in your gear, Lord Belmundus. Your squire pounds away like *a Dodingdaten Fumarca*."

"I am no such thing," Little Bird protested. "I am *the Taleenay*."

"And so *the Book of Light* shall record for future generations of Cetrone," Cosawta said.

Harris found this banter uneasy, the klaxon still raging above the storm — the massacre relentlessly beyond his sight.

"How can you bear it?" he asked Littafulchee. "*The reaptide?*"

"How can you say I do?" she replied. "To dwell in *the Kalugu* is not to dwell at all, Lord Belmundus. You may think me callous to their plight, but it is my plight also. No Cetrone has gone untouched by *the regulati* and their expedient means. If we had been the conquerors, our hearts would have been sensitive to the vanquished. There would be no *reaptide* and never *the yuluyi* — *the weeping road*."

Harris recalled Yustichisqua's sad song about the trail of tears, which forced the Cetrone from their homes in Montjoy across the Forling to the Spice Mountains. He heard Little Bird's furtive weeping now, even as *the Taleenay* stomped down the gangway into the *the sustiya's* bowels.

"I don't know what to think," Harris said. "There's been travail in my world too, although it never touched me directly. In my country, there's diversity — many suffer, while many others thrive. But we do it by our own management. We're dealt the cards and play them to our best abilities. I must admit, we often forget we're privileged among the races. In my world, there's more yearning than aspiration — more blind eyes turned from the realities that undo us."

Littafulchee paused, hovering. She studied Harris like a schoolmarm inspecting a fresh candidate.

"Do not turn a blind eye to *the reaptide*," she said. "Listen to the klaxon, but also hear your *Taleenay's* sobbing."

Harris didn't know how to respond. Was he chastised? Did this stern Cetrone lady scorned all other worlds? How could she and still remain beyond self-indictment? As Littafulchee continued down the gangway, Harris glanced at Yustichisqua, who sniffled, but otherwise stood tall.

"I am fine, *oginali*," he said. "I was just recalling another *reaptide* — the one that took my mother."

"I'm sorry," Harris whispered.

"Do not be so," Little Bird sighed. "She was not in *the Banetuckle*, and was *sqwallen*-free. She rushed into the street because I was abroad and she would have me safe. But I had already found my way into *the yehu*, only she did not know it. The doors were locked to her and she could not come in for safety." He choked, his eyes batting away tears. "As I watched through the window, *the zugginaks* took her. She died on their first bite, so suffered little. I suffered more."

Harris touched Yustichisqua's shoulder to ease the pain, a modest gesture, which went far to soothe him. Harris thought of his own mother — a lady who would run into the jaws of Pit Bulls and Dobermans to keep him safe. It was a difficult image to encompass, so he shook his head and hastened on his course.

2

In *the sustiya's* deepest haunt, the klaxon was finally muffled, the barking hushed. The storm, still heard, reflected lightning through the gumdrop roof down the shaft to the floor. These flashes revealed a treasure warehouse covered in the gossamer cloth, which most Cetrone used to weave their underwear.

Cosawta halted, raising his arms over the vast trove.

"The destination for the trade," he announced. "Your efforts are heaped beneath these rugs, Lord Belmundus." He reached for one, pulling it aside grandly. "*Aniniya.*" He pulled another. "*Aniniya.*" And another. "Everywhere, *Aniniya.*"

Yustichisqua danced about the skirts. He beamed, his tears having abated.

"We could take on Tarhippus himself with so much *aniniya*," he declared with uncustomary brashness.

"But it must be fitted into *Sticks* first," Tomatly twittered. He pointed to other piles — crafted wooden rods and metal rings. "It is not easy to fit them."

Harris stared at the stockpile, moving closer for a better look, but when he came to the skirt, his brooch shone its brightest blue. He grasped it, and then noticed his sword flickered as if joining in an elemental convocation.

"What the fuck?" he said, turning to Littafulchee apologetically. She wasn't fazed.

"Fuck, you say," Cosawta said, roaring. "I agree." He dared to touch Harris' *Columbincus*. "This is the stuff of gods and Electors."

"I am no god," Harris said quickly. "I'm just a stranger tossed into Farn by the sex kitten from hell."

Cosawta winked.

"Do not be so harsh upon your Scepta," he said. "She is compelled by law to exhibit her abilities in your unsuspecting world. Many others would regard you as a lucky *sonofabitch* to spend many weeks playing between Charminus' legs."

"Brother," Littafulchee snapped. "You forget yourself. Recall that when Lord Belmundus and Lord Tappiolus perform their consort duties, I am present — serving and waiting. I must pretend it does not happen."

"Well, sister, you cannot be titillated by the sight, but Yustichisqua has a prime seat for it." He laughed, and then patted Little Bird's back. "Eh, Yustichisqua?"

"I scarcely notice," Little Bird replied.

"Is there something wrong with you?" Cosawta asked.

"Nothing," Little Bird said, pawing *the aniniya*. "It is my *oginali's* occupation. He must do it as he is a consort. I am there to keep him clean and revive him after the act."

"Revive him?"

Harris pushed Cosawta's hand off the brooch.

"Please," he said. "I never remember my . . . my encounters with Charminus. She flashes her ring and, the next thing I know, Little Bird is beside me, waking me and feeding me my favorite shit from *the Scullery Dorgan*. It's like . . . how can I say it?"

"It is like consuming *sqwallen*," Littafulchee said.

That was it — nail hit on the head. The ring and *Corzanthe* combination kept him attentive to Charminus. He was no more than a dildo, and his batteries were low, because all his urges were spent. However, he was uncomfortable talking about this in current company — company who was present when he went between

Charminus' legs. It was tasteless to discuss such things during the current carnage devastating *the Banetuckle*.

"Enough," he said. "Why has my *Columbincus* come alive? Why does my sword flicker?"

"And my dagger?" Yustichisqua added.

Littafulchee dared touch the brooch also, but unlike Cosawta's corsair slap, her touch caressed, the light dancing between her fingers.

"*The Columbincus* awakes because your heart does, Lord Belmundus. The power is not in the stone, but inside you. That is why we can chance *the regulati* trade for small amounts of *Columbincus* without much fear. Their spirit is hollow and, except powering a few weapons, they cannot extend their souls to find the true measure."

"And I can?" Harris asked.

"You have," she said, her hand wandering to his chest. "You have the spark within you. It is the spark which makes you *Ayelli*. Charminus drew you from many, because she harvests only men who have the spark."

"But . . ."

Littafulchee lowered her eyes, and removed her hand. She clasped them about her *waddly wazzoo,* which brightened.

"You have power, Lord Belmundus," she said. "How much power is to be revealed, but you must trust your instincts. *The Yodanado* are correct. I would not think it, but I trust them. You have power."

Cosawta roared.

"You light our world," he shouted. "You can light up this whole fucking pile of *aniniya.*"

"Only," Littafulchee whispered, "you must learn how to do it."

3

Harris turned aside, this woman's words alluring — his passions stirred.

"And yet you can let your people fall into *zugginak* jaws," he said.

"It is not I who do it, Lord Belmundus," she explained softly. *"The reaptide* has been with us since the defeat times — since *the regulati* rebuilt *the Kalugu,* turning it into the place of confinement. I do not do these things. Until there is change, I must accept it as the way."

Harris walked across *the aniniya*, his *Columbincus* flickering. His sword answered it, so Harris drew it. It was a beautiful thing. He had failed to notice it before. He had many prop blades in his career — some weighted fine for use, while others showpieces studded with a gallery of sham gems. This sword was simple — sleek and scantily decorated. But its blade shimmered, alternating between blue and silver. Its glow strengthened. The question wasn't why it glowed, but how he caused it to glow.

"Is this a *brashun blade*?" he asked Cosawta. "Does that mean I'll win when I tangle with General Tarhippus?"

"Do not press your luck," Cosawta replied. "Unless you have the discipline, a flashing weapon will only serve to light the way to your destruction. But, when mastered, you could vanquish a squad of Yunockers with a single thrust."

Harris balanced the weapon, and grinned.

"Who can teach me?" he mumbled.

"Now there is a question. You cannot throw shit against the wind and expect it to come back as sweet *mollicop*."

"What the fuck does that mean?"

"It means," Cosawta said, grasping Harris' wrist, forcing the sword back into its scabbard. "It means, only an Elector can teach you the full mastery of this sword."

"I don't think Kuriakis is likely to do that."

"I do not know, but I believe you are correct."

"Then what's the point?"

Cosawta laughed. He strode over *the aniniya*, reaching the top of the pile. There he stood, fists balled and handled to his waist.

"Have some vision, Lord Belmundus." He swept his hand across the stockpile. "If you stood at the front of a thousand Cetrone with your sword ablaze, they would not ask you to perform miracles. They would follow you and assume a man who had such power did not need to flaunt it." He grinned. "Look at me. Am I a sight for anyone to behold? *The regulati* address me with respect and not for any secret weapon, but for my appearance, my arrogance and my muscles. I fly a ferry. They need *Columbincus.* I can navigate across the Forling to Cetronia and *the Dodingdaten.*"

Suddenly, he glanced into the darkness, his eyes wide — his lips quivering.

"There is a place beyond this hell, Lord Belmundus, where the air is touched with the scent of cinnamon. The waters flow clear and the rills shine with gemstones. It is the place of the mountain meadow's shade." He sighed. "And I, Cosawta of the Zacker, take wing in my ferry and carry the contraband across the dunes to the homeland." He turned. "Of course, it is not really the homeland. This is our home, now beshatted with Yunockers and every fucking foreigner who drifts in for profit. Do not think the shit of a million *tludachi* is less sweet than one fucking Yunocker who turns his head in disdain and calls to the hellhounds to eat our flesh — to scourge our hearts." He raised his arms, his fists clenched to the lightning. "We are the defeated and yet they did not defeat us. We are destined to rise again and slay the darkness and, if these Yunockers and the spawn of Electors come between us and our destiny, so be it. They shall know a worse *reaptide.* And you shall bring it to them, Lord Belmundus."

Harris backed away. Cosawta's ethereal recall of traveling over the desert in a balloon to a fairytale kingdom now had transformed into a vision of *Armageddon.* It unsettled Harris. Yustichisqua and Tomatly looked at the ferryman with admiration. Littafulchee stood supportive, but tense, as if engaged in some pledge of allegiance. However, she broke the moment.

"Lord Belmundus," she said. "Your sword is an alloy of Farn's most powerful metals."

Harris unsheathed the sword and regarded it again. It still flickered. Little Bird stared at his dagger also. It seemed to be having a conversation with its bigger brother.

"It is *aniniya*," Harris replied, as if Littafulchee's statement was a quiz.

"Yes," she said. "*Aniniya* and . . ."

"*Columbincus*," he said.

"Exactly so," Cosawta echoed, hopping from his summit. "You should name the fucking thing."

"Name it?" Harris asked. "You mean like *Excalibur* or *Sting?*"

"Name it what you will, because it will be your companion."

Harris grinned, brandishing it in his hand. If this was a prop, he'd be thanking a craftsman from the art department, but the person owed thanks for this beauty probably didn't need the thanks. *The Elector's Gift*, he thought, but that was presumption. Then it came to him in a flash.

"*Tony*," he said. "I'll call it *Tony*."

"*Tony, oginali?*" Little Bird asked. "What does this word mean?"

"It's a name — short for Anthony."

"*Tony?*" Cosawta said.

"You would've liked him," Harris replied. "Full of F-words, like you."

"With daring, I would hope."

"Buck naked forceful brass balls — that's Tony to a T."

"*Tony*, it shall be," Littafulchee said.

Harris turned to Yustichisqua.

"Name your dagger, old man."

"Name it?"

"Of course. If you're going to stand behind me and watch my back, I'd like to know I'm protected by a noble blade with a snappy name."

Little Bird grinned, pondering.

"*Gasohisgi*," he said. "It means — I got your back."

Harris laughed.

"*Gaso* . . . whatever. You most certainly do."

4

The klaxon sounded again — distant, but distinct.

"It is over," Littafulchee said.

"It is over. It is over," Tomatly squeaked, dancing about on his *zulus*.

"Thank God," Harris replied.

"You must leave here now," Litafulchee said, pulling him forward.

"I don't think so," Harris protested. "I'm not stepping over the remains in *the Banetuckle*. We've chucked our disguises. We'd be in Tarhippus' grip the second we emerged."

"You misunderstand me," Littafulchee explained. "You will leave by a secret way — an ancient method *the regulati* do not know."

"How can they not know?"

"I told you," she replied. "They are courageous, but stupid."

Cosawta grasped Harris' elbow, walking him toward the gangway. He pointed to a spot one third up *the sustiya*.

"*The sustiya* has stood before the time of *yuyuli*. It served our leaders in council. They made provisions for the quick getaway." He winked. "In those days, they fled a different enemy, but one enemy is much like another."

"So there's a secret way out of *the Kalugu*."

And in, he thought.

"Few know it," Littafulchee said. She looked to Yustichisqua. "Few should know."

He bowed.

"There is a *kaybar* wall to the outside through that passageway," Cosawta said. "There you shall go and pass through."

"How does that help me?" Harris protested. "I can't walk through *kaybar* like some people I know."

"Do not be thick. Surely you can manage it."

Harris thought. *How?* Then he recalled Yustichisqua's request not to catch him if he fell into the pit. He looked to Little Bird.

"Yes," Yustichisqua said. "I can pull you through, *oginali*."

"Can you? I mean, all of me will come? I won't leave my spleen stuck in some wall, will I?"

"Hardly," Cosawta said. He touched the *Columbincus*. "The only question is whether your sigil and sword will follow you. Some things are naturally resistant to the transference. But do not worry. If you leave one of these beauties behind, I shall find a fucking use for it, you can bet."

"I bet," Harris said. "So, let's go, before I decide to take rooms in the palace and weigh other options."

"No other options," Littafulchee said. "I must return to *the yehu* when the time beckons me."

She bowed. Harris realized she was departing and not leading him to the escape hatch.

"Come with me," he stammered. "At least to *the kaybar* wall."

"I cannot," she said. "There is much to do after *reaptide*. I will need to supervise it. My brother will take you there."

Harris sighed. He wanted to be in her company. He wanted a quiet picnic on the stacks of *aniniya* bars — another song from her sweet lips. She would tell him the story of her life and he'd brag about his filmography and drop the names of his A-list co-stars. It would be wonderful. But no. She had to supervise the mopping up of fields of blood and torn limbs and severed heads, and he — he had to hold Yustichisqua's hand and travel through a stone wall. *Pity*.

Harris gazed into Littafulchee's eyes. They spoke to him. Then, he leaned forward, daring to kiss her, but she was there first. His passions drove him mad, but he knew pressing further would ruin his chances, if he had chances.

"I'm sorry," he whispered, smacking his lips.

"Do not be," she said, quietly. "Remember, I do not capture you with a charmed ring. My gifts are given. When given, they are a treasure rarer even than your *Columbincus*."

Harris' sword flickered. He glanced to Yustichisqua who smiled — approval even, not that Harris needed his approval. Perhaps he did. So he bowed to Littafulchee as she drifted past him and onto the gangway.

"You are a lucky *sonofabitch*, Lord Belmundus," Cosawta said. "My sister is an uncommon Cetrone and has never kissed anyone other than our mother, as far as I know. I am surprised you are still standing."

He roared, and then led his tour up the gangway to the mysterious corridor, ferryman that he was.

Chapter Seven

From the Jaws of Death

1

The wall differed from its surroundings, although in the dark could have been missed. However, by *waddly wazzoo* light, the difference could be discerned by anyone directed to it.

"We call it *the Yudolayda Asdodi — the Secret D*oor."

"*The Secret Door —* that's what I'll call it," Harris said. "Since it's a secret, it'd be foolish to learn another mouthful of Cetrone."

"As you will, Lord Belmundus." Cosawta touched the door, his hand seeping through. "On the opposite side it is marked with a *Z* — in crimson, like the blood of our fallen."

"Ah, like the mark of *Zorro.*"

"Whatever the fuck you need to recall it, you have my permission. Just remember, once outside you must move fast. The door opens near *the Porias,* and *the regulati* frequent the passageways."

Harris nodded, sucked in his breath and prepared for the experience. He wasn't keen on being transported through solid matter. He didn't rush it, because his body wasn't designed to do it. This wasn't a Hollywood device — a transporter backed up with Spockian logic, the infallible kind found in the Science Fiction world.

Yustichisqua reached out and grasped Harris' hand.

"Are you prepared, *oginali?*"

"No, but do it before I change my mind."

Harris felt a tug, and then a frosty tearing at his flesh, like sandblasting through ice. No pain, but discomfiture — like pulling a tooth with Novocaine. After a moment of suspension, the world stopped — his mind entertaining weird thoughts of being encased in a stone shroud and interred in a crypt. Not pleasant. He wouldn't recommend this to the general public. Although less painful than waiting in a security line at an airport, it was more stressful. Then, he emerged into the light — his rocky tomb shucked, his shoulders jiggling like baby bird wings.

"Fuck," he muttered. "That's one helluva downer, old man."

"You have survived and come through it," Yustichisqua said. "And the rain has stopped."

Harris turned, checking his legs and arms, and then regarded the sky, the clouds parting on a clear morning.

"I hope all my internal organs made it through."

"If not, you will know soon enough."

"You're not a joker, Little Bird, so this ain't a good time to become one."

"Sorry, *oginali*."

Harris looked at Yustichisqua's belt. The dagger — the one he named *gasohisgi* — was missing.

"It's gone," Harris gasped. "Your dagger."

He looked for his sword — *Tony*, but it made it through.

"No, *oginali*, I moved *gasohisgi* to my back belt loop." He slipped it out, displaying the *brashun blade.* "I feared such *blades* might be the exception to transference."

"Obviously not," Harris said, sighing with relief. He turned, observing the wall. It had the *Z* — that crimson mark of *Zorro* emblazoned across it, like graffiti, marking gang territory.

"*Z* marks the spot," he mused.

"We must go, *oginali,*"

Yustichisqua pointed to the building across the way — a ziggurat of *phitron*, as black as *the Kalugu* and as inspirational as *Golgotha.*

"*The Porias,*" Little Bird said. "The shame of shames. I would be away from it."

"I agree. Which way?"

Yustichisqua didn't stop to decide, but took off on a course away from the *old* prison. Harris followed as fast as *phitron*-soled boots could take him. They darted down alleys and across byways until they stood before the *new* prison — *the Katorias.*

"Is this any better?" Harris asked. "Do you know where we are?"

Little Bird was silent, but soon darted into another alley, one alive with morning activity — Trones sweeping gutters and taking out waste. The sight of one of their kind running without *zulus* and masquerading as *an Ayelli* drew many stares.

Soon *minorins* were out and about their business, doors opening with Yunockers drifting over the pavement on their way to business. Harris heard the niceties of the day, which to a Yunocker was *well met neighbor. May your feet speed you well to good gain and profit.* Two racing *Ayelli* would pique their interest, especially when sensitive Yunocker noses detected a Cetrone in their midst and not one who toiled or labored. Yustichisqua would be obvious, because *the charpgris* stink potion had worn off and he had failed to reanoint himself. He also toted a *waddly wazzoo.*

"Stop at the next intersection, old man," Harris shouted. "There are too many *minorins* to go unnoticed."

"I agree, *oginali*. I am your liability. Perhaps I should seek *a kaleezo* to shelter me."

"There's no guarantee they'd let you in, and if they did, you'd probably be detected quicker than not. No. Just hold up here and let me think."

"If we get to *the Yuyutlu*, we can get lost among the crowd."

"Yes, but I'm disoriented. Which way is it to the boundary?"

Yustichisqua shrugged, and then pointed to *the Columbincus*. "It glows," he said.

Harris grasped it, the sapphire light seeping through his fingers. "Now that's a dead giveaway."

"But you are *the Didaniyisgi* and can be here."

"Yes, in my *Cabriolin* and escorted. Not on foot with . . . with you."

"I shall find *a kaleezo*."

"No, old man." Harris touched Little Bird's shoulder. "You're never a liability. If we're meant to be caught today, we'll be caught together. We can slash our way out of it with . . . *Tony* and . . . your dagger."

"*Gasohisgi*."

"*Gasolino*," Harris laughed. "It'd make a great Saturday matinee — a buttered popcorn delight."

Yustichisqua grinned, but then grimaced.

"Be prepared to slash, *oginali*."

Harris gazed down the street.

"Shit."

A *regulati* brigade approach, aiming at them. The morning greeters more likely reported the oddity of two trespassers off *zulus* and wearing cloaks, rushing between the early street sweepers.

"Do we run, *oginali*?"

"Too late."

The leader was in *a Cabriolin*, with two other *Cabriolins* in drogue. The chief Yunocker sped to the intersection, his craft hovering. He turned to Harris, waving *a Stick* — non-threatening — like a symphony conductor.

"Lord Belmundus," he said, sternly. "You had best be on your way."

"Captain Buhippus?"

And behind him were Elypticus and Melonius.

"We were searching for you, my lord," Elypticus said.

"When you touched your *Columbincus*," Melonius added. "Ours homed in on the signal."

Buhippus took off, his Yunocker escort behind him. Elypticus opened *the Cabriolin* gate.

"Come aboard, sir," he said. "I promise not to take you into the jaws of *a misancorpus*."

"You can do what you please, Elypticus, so long as you take me the fuck out of here."

He rushed to *the Cabriolin*, hopping to the platform. He then gazed back at Yustichisqua, who hesitated. Melonius quietly opened his gate.

"*Taleenay*," he said.

Yustichisqua bowed and ran to *the Cabriolin*. Melonius kept silent, closed the gate and proceeded.

"Now," Harris said. "There's hope in this universe after all."

2

Harris continued his weekly visits to *the Kalugu* through *the Yudolayda Asdodi*, his *Augustii spinctus* disguise renewed, two sacks of *zulus* delivered to *the sustiya* with each visit. Yustichisqua always attended, welcomed by Cosawta as *Gasohisgi awudoli* — *He who has the back of hope*. It probably gave Little Bird a big head, but Harris didn't mind. He enjoyed watching his former Trone's confidence inflated to heroic proportions. Little Bird was accepted more as *the Taleenay* and, in the *Myrkpykyn*, neither Gurts nor Zecronisians questioned business transactions with a Cetrone. Even Buhippus seemed more at ease — a matter of compliance more than acceptance, but it was one less goal for Harris to achieve. Yustichisqua could achieve it on his own.

Garan outfitted them — cloaks, extra legs, *zulus* and the lovely *eau de charpgris*, which Little Bird rarely applied now that they entered through the wall marked *Z* (for *Zorro*). Ricktus Morphinus continued entering by the main gate, so Cosawta's *sustiya* stockpile grew incrementally, the greed of *the regulati mordanka* assuaged without interruption. When Harris exited through the secret door, he would slap his *Columbincus* and two *Danuwa* would arrive to taxi him and Yustichisqua back to *the Myrkpykyn*. This activity became routine. What interrupted this clandestine barter was predictable. When Charminus returned, Harris would be *up*. He wended his way back to *the Ayelli* and became co-consort again, Little Bird in tow to act as potboy.

Charminus hadn't changed. She was as fascinating as always, ring on finger, *Corzanthe* to lip, full breasted and legs spread. However, Harris found a difference. This came about after a disturbing conversation with Lord Tappiolus, who chastised Harris for relying too heavily on *the Danuwa* for *Myrkpykyn* business.

"Is this a complaint from your son?" Harris asked.

"No. I have not seen my son since he has taken up his post with you."

"Then, is it your roving eye telling you these young men have become responsible members of the legislative community in *the Yuyutlu*?"

"There are those who watch."

Harris thought perhaps Captain Buhippus had detected and reported on *the Didaniyisgi's* activities, but if that had occurred, this conversation with Tappiolus wouldn't be a mild chastisement about shirking responsibility, but a treasonable accusation or an indictment laid at Kuriakis' feet. However, Harris trusted Buhippus, oddly enough. The Yunocker Palace chief had many opportunities to turn Lord Belmundus in and hadn't. As for Melonius, although still too serious for the average four-year old Thirdling, he was angrier at his father than his father's co-consort. Melonius had been denied a shot at the endowments of the diplomatic marriage pool generally extended to Thirdlings as honors.

"I've given my *Danuwa* a strong sense of leadership," Harris explained, annoyed to do so, "which will serve *the Ayelli* in the future."

"This is not Boston or Chicago, Lord Belmundus," Tappiolus quipped. "They do not need lessons in civics as civics does not apply in this world. Our lord has much on his mind concerning the other realms — shadows which stir and cannot be disciplined by noble-minded rule-abiders among the Thirdlings. If you give them notions of hope, their sense of importance will be their downfall when they confront the real world — a courtship with a fire maid from Volcanium or a splash with a daughter of Aquilium."

"Well, I'm not teaching them to firefight or to swim the backstroke," Harris said. "But their duties will help them stand when others are forced to sit. It's my belief you wished to sideline Melonius and being my *Danuwa* was a good way to punish him. As it turns out, he's invaluable to me. I rely on his accounting sense and even his social conscience has been stirred."

Tappiolus raised an eyebrow.

"As his father, I must draw the line there."

"As his father, you already have drawn the line, and that line nearly had him in a noose. Fortunately, his eyes are fully opened and his mind forming judgments. Now, I can't say I agree with his conclusions, because his original assumptions were contaminated, but at least he's slipping away from the carefully taught prejudices. He's developing his own wicked brand. I can't ask more from a free-thinking man."

Tappiolus boiled over, but Harris left him choking on his own paternal shortcomings. He had managed to transfer paternity to a surrogate and it backfired.

"As for your fucking *Eye*," Harris said, a parting shot delivered over his shoulder, "take care I don't find the plug and ask Charminus to pull it."

Of course, Charminus would never deny Tappiolus his use of *The Eye*, because she didn't care about such things. She knew little of the world beyond her bedstead and the dream world of the outlands. That she cared for her consorts was true. Harris knew it and took care not to stir jealousy. If Tappiolus discovered the secret door and the weekly trips into *the Kalugu*, it would be Kuriakis who'd have Harris' hide, not Charminus. But if she knew his heart smoldered for her Trone, she would liquidate him in the bowels of Greary Gree. The problem surfaced when Littafulchee attended her mistress while Harris was *up*.

Charminus' ring captivated him, as always, but when Littafulchee brought her trays from *the Scullery Dorgan*, Harris found himself resisting Charminus' power and — Charminus noticed this. Fortunately, she didn't realize it was her Trone causing the drift.

"Lord Belmundus," she said, resentment in her voice. "Are you ill?"

"No, my lady," he replied, settling his head on her breasts. "I'm always happy when I'm here with you."

"I hope your duties in the marketplace have not caused you to fuss about them when you are here."

"No, my lady. *The Myrkpykyn* runs smoothly, even when I am here. My *Danuwa* attends to business well."

"There, then," she said, stroking his hair. "Your mind should be clear of all distractions."

However, it was not. He imagined the hand to be Littafulchee's and, with the Trone's aroma in the room as she served, it was hard to be *up* for the Scepta. He wondered how Littafulchee felt seeing him entangled in Charminus' arms, her breasts, her legs — and then to watch him as he explored her geography better than a Spanish conquistador. It unnerved him. But if Charminus suspected, the jig would be up. So he mustered his complaint about Tappiolus as a distraction.

"Charminus," he said, passionately. "I haven't been honest."

"Why, Lord Belmundus, what is your ailment?"

"None, but . . . I am saddled with Lord Tappiolus and his constant prying into my affairs."

"He is the Provost."

"Yes. I respect that. However, he uses your *Eye* to spy on my every move."

"We have discussed this before, Harris," she said.

When she used his real name, it was from annoyance and a sign for him to desist.

"I know, dearest. And I would not bring it up again if it were not that he has taken it upon himself to chastise me for doing a good job with his own son . . . your son, Melonius."

"Melonius is not my favorite."

"He could be . . . now, Charminus . . . dearest. He has many qualities you prize. I know, because I've distilled them in him, and they are qualities you admire in me."

Charminus gazed at him, sharply, but with renewed patience.

"And this worries you to distraction?" she asked. "It keeps you off your form that a son of mine is raised to betterment and you are chastised for it?"

"It is *The Eye* and Tappiolus' wanton use of it putting me off my form."

She grinned, and then hugged him

"I shall speak to Lord Tappiolus, and perhaps I should see Melonius — perhaps reappraise him for . . . marriage. My father has returned from serious negotiations in Protractus." She suddenly demurred. "A shadow grows again. He has concerns."

"A shadow?"

"You need not worry," she said. "Put aside care. Let it not distract you from your best form. I shall ask Lord Tappiolus to be less obtrusive with you. I cannot deny him *The Eye.* As Provost he needs it, but he can apply it more rationally in your case."

Harris assessed that Tappiolus would likely increase his spying, but the request threw Charminus off the scent. Now if only Littafulchee's scent were somewhere other than *Mortis House*, Harris could get on with his occupation.

3

In *the sustiya*, Harris sat on the piles of *aniniya* awaiting Littafulchee to come. Yustichisqua helped Tomatly stack the bars, and then arrange wooden sticks in neat rows. Cosawta sat at a distance, brooding. He had fallen off the wagon again — his *sqwallen* habit taking him out of commission for a week. However, a liberal dose of *pilocarpinus* had him back on the road to recovery. He grumbled and spat. Harris dared not disturb him. The man was powerful, even in this state, and could have landed a lethal blow before apologizing at the inquest.

Harris found *the sustiya* an odd place — a silo more than a sacred Cetrone citadel. He also thought it odd it went undetected by *the regulati.* Surely, if they partnered with Cosawta as the ferryman for their barter-trade across the Forling, they would suspect the surplus would be stored somewhere. It's ironic how, when greed is paramount, convenient blindness aids the beneficiaries.

Littafulchee appeared on the gangway, toting a basket. As she drifted down on her *zulus*, Harris had a guilt pang. That basket was for him — victuals of his favorite *mongerhide* and special treats for Yustichisqua. The food had been surreptitiously lifted from *the Scullery Dorgan* and brought here perilously. Still, as Littafulchee drifted toward him, Harris couldn't shake the idea of her service to Charminus — carrying the tray and rattling *the Corzanthe* bottle and goblets. He didn't want this service now. Yet, as she approached, he was taken by her grace — her deportment ritualistically applied. She was like no other being he had ever encountered. Still, she was Cetrone, but he had encountered other Cetrone women. Littafulchee towered above them. All Cetrone treated her with respect and she deigned it acceptable, like an affectionate mother. She was above the common lot. Harris would know why.

Cosawta grunted, turning at the prospects of the picnic. He certainly was welcomed to it. In fact, it was more his than Harris'. But the ferryman hesitated, perhaps seeing the sweet melting of temperament between *the Didaniyisgi* and the Cetrone maid, his sister.

"Sweet lady," Harris said, rising.

She curtsied.

"Lord Belmundus. We are well met."

"Always, when devoid of the Scepta."

"Always," she said, raising the basket.

He took it, setting it on the stockpile. Yustichisqua inched forward, peeking in.

"It is for all," Littafulchee announced.

"Only offer it to Cosawta first, old man."

This removed the basket (with company) from Littafulchee. Harris took her hand and led her aside. He stared into her eyes, only to be diverted by her crystal ornament.

"Fear not," she said. "It is a simple gem from Cetronia — a *lyricadim* — worn for show and not for power."

"Although I suspect its power lies in its prestige," Harris said.

"You may think it, Lord Belmundus."

"I would know it, my lady," he said. He pulled her gently into his arms. She didn't resist. "I would know who you are, Littafulchee of the Zacker."

"You have named me."

"I have wondered. I realize the *Z* on the Secret Door does not stand for *Zorro*."

"*Zorro?*"

"A poor joke, my lady. But it could stand for *Zin*." She frowned, and pulled away. "I didn't mean to offend, only Lord Tappiolus has spoken of a shadow growing across Farn and, as a consort, I know my lessons in *Promise and Prophecy*."

"Zin is a hard word for any in Farn to hear," she said. "You should know it and not speak its name. As for Zacker — Zacker is no more." She turned. "You see before you the blood line of a fallen house, but only drops remain, not enough to raise Farn's hope."

"Only Cetronia's?"

"Perhaps," she said. "But you are that hope now."

Cosawta stood beside them, having listened to this *tête-à-tête* unnoticed. His eyes were swollen and tearful, as if in the pronouncement of the lost realm of Zacker, his heart would burst.

"We must not speak of it, sister," he said, turning away.

"It saddens him," she said to Harris. "I pray you, Lord Belmundus, do not drive him to *the sqwallen* with such talk." She bowed. "Gather your thoughts among *the mongerhide* and be settled in this. We look to free the Cetrone from bondage, but Zacker is long gone. Let it be so."

Cosawta whimpered like a child, falling into Littafulchee's arms. This hadn't been Harris' plan. He wanted to know if he stood in the presence of the descendants of the fallen house, but he would have been content to listen to legends — history with a sad, but conclusive ending. Instead, he received a brutal confirmation of this blood line and watched, while brother and sister caressed. Caressing is what he intended, but not among the siblings.

Littafulchee and Cosawta drifted away to a place of consolation. Yustichisqua sat beside Harris now, munching a strip of *mongerhide*.

"What do *you* know about Zacker, old man?" Harris asked.

"I am too young to know much, *oginali*."

"Only being fifty-two or so."

"Yes. What is there to know? How important would it be?"

"Aren't you curious about your heritage?"

Yustichisqua knelt, lifting his *waddly wazzoo*.

"I know about *the yuyuli*."

"The Weeping Road — yes. Fascinating, but there's more to it, and you know it."

"Do I?"

"Aren't you curious?"

"Cetrone gossip much and tell many tales, *oginali*, but mostly about other Cetrone and to no advantage as most have no advantages."

"But you do."

Yustichisqua stood.

"When I want to know things, I ponder my *waddly wazzoo*. In its light, I sometimes see things."

"See things?"

"It is the light of truth, *oginali*. That is why all Cetrone carry one and protect it dearly. It is like a book to us, keeping all knowledge."

"All knowledge," Harris mused. He grabbed a *mongerhide* strip from the basket. Tomatly came close, so he pushed the food nearer, letting the diminutive Cetrone help himself. "A book, you say."

"Yes," Yustichisqua said. "But there are no books on Cetrone history. But why should there be? Our history is simple. We were happy in Montjoy until the Yunockers came. We helped them and called them our brothers. They took our help and then took our land and then our freedom. They were the enemy before *the Ayelli* arrived on the hill. Then all people decided to hate us and send most away beyond the Forling never again to be a bother. Just the slaves are here."

"Still, beyond the Forling there are free Cetrone."

"That is why we work here," Tomatly piped up. "Someday they will come and help us overthrow the heavy yoke, they will."

"They?" Harris mused. "I believe you're right, Tomatly."

"Yes, yes," he twittered. "I am right because the Seneschal believes this to be so."

Seneschal?

Harris stood. Yustichisqua gathered the basket.

"Leave it for our friend here," Harris said.

"Are we leaving, *oginali?*"

"Yes. It's time to consult *my* book of knowledge."

Yustichisqua grinned.

"We are not scheduled to be in *Mortis House.*"

"We are not scheduled to be in *the Kalugu* either, but does that stop *the Didaniyisgi* and his *Taleenay?*"

"But I cannot enter *the Cartisforium, oginali.*"

"Why not, old man? No door is barred to you as long as I've a say-so."

"Do you have a say-so in that?"

"Who knows?" he said. "And who cares? Come."

Little Bird grinned and handed the basket to Tomatly, who hovered on his *zulus* like a moth over daisies.

"I am going to where no Cetrone has ever been," he said to Tomatly. "*The Cartisforium.*"

Tomatly grunted and slipped into the shadows to eat to his heart's delight the delicacies of *the Scullery Dorgan*, surreptitiously lifted and precariously brought by his mistress, Littafulchee of Zacker. He cared not for this *Cartisforium*, wherever or whatever that might be.

Chapter Eight

The Shades of Zacker

1

The door of *the Cartisforium* was made of *kaybar*, a puzzlement to Harris, because the place barred Trones. However, Yustichisqua offered to pull him through, an experience Harris declined. Although having plunged into *the sustiya* a dozen or more times through *the kaybar* wall, Harris found the journey through solid objects as unnatural as it was uncomfortable.

"Let me hold the door for you," Harris told Yustichisqua, who giggled, entering the octagonal inner sanctum.

Giggles soon dissipated, Little Bird struck dumb by the austere place. The three Sceptas' shimmering light shone through the stained-glass effigies. Awestruck, he bowed, and then knelt.

"They won't bite," Harris said. "And this ain't church," although the spirits of time stirred.

"If I am arrested here, *oginali*," Little Bird explained, "I will end my days in *the Porias.*"

"From what I've been told, that's a short in and out."

"I do not wish to burn."

Harris gazed at his *Taleenay*. Perhaps this was the most daring of trespasses.

"If you wish to leave and bow like an inflated rug in the hallway, you're welcomed to do so. I'll think no less of you."

Yustichisqua gazed back toward the door, and then sighed.

"But I would think less of me, *oginali.*"

"Then let the show begin."

Harris guided Little Bird to the octagonal altar's far side. *The Book of Farn* was anchored like a galleon on a mahogany sea. The relic flickered when Harris approached it.

"It knows me," he said. "I wonder if it guesses what I'll be asking?"

"You might be the first one to ask it."

"I probably am. Nobody seems to give a shit about Zacker."

At the word *Zacker*, the book's cover opened, the pages rustling, and then it snapped shut, the lock as secure as a nun's vow. Harris cocked his head, grasping his *Columbincus*, which already commenced glowing. *Tony* flickered, as did Yustichisqua's dagger — *gasohisgi.*

"You have action on your belt, old man."

Little Bird snapped his hand over the hilt, and then gazed at *the Book of Farn.* Harris unclasped *the Columbincus* from his cloak and pounded it into the keyhole.

"Tell me about the House of Zacker," he said — simply, not elaborating.

He assumed he could fine-tune the inquiry as revelations peeled from the onion.

The *Columbincus* turned in the latch and the cover opened again, this time slowly, the book cleaving to a point midtome. Like his inquiry concerning *Tippagores*, a cloud arose from the vellum, forming and reforming. Harris couldn't discern the emerging shape — perhaps a map. But the cloud turned rust-colored, and then divided into seven cloudlets — biscuit dough readied for the oven. Each hovered over the altar, forming funnels, wide side down, and then settling in a circle. The light faded. These funnels sprouted arms and heads — ancient female heads.

"*The Yodanado,*" Yustichisqua gasped.

"A projection, Little Bird," Harris said, but watched intently as *waddly wazzoos* kindled and humming began. The central crone opened her eyes.

"Lord Belmundus has come," Euforsee said, her voice hollow, but clear. "We knew he would, because he is destined to do so."

She held up her *waddly wazzoo.* Yustichisqua cowered.

"Who is there in the shadows?" she asked. "Is that *Yustichisqua, son of Kittowa?"*

Little Bird grunted.

"We have come," Harris said. "I would know . . ."

"You shall, but first you must listen and learn — watch and understand. You must hold these secrets in your heart, too tender they to tell the world, because hearts are cold to it. Other hearts are tenderer still and would be crushed by the reminder." She stared at Yustichisqua. "Kittowa's son, be prepared to weep, but be prepared to give your life for the fate this inquiry reveals."

She waited for his reply. He grunted, but did not turn his eyes away.

"Good, then. Good . . . all is well as we unwrap the past and let the light come forth."

With the word *light*, the room went dark — abysmally dark, encouraging Harris to join Yustichisqua in grunting. The humming continued, and one dim *waddly wazzoo* drifted to the altar's center. It brightened gradually until it revealed a circle of thrones, and a tree stump mid table. Harris recognized the figure emerging from the stump — *the Primordius Centrum*. Harris prepared to hear the incantation of *the Promise and Prophecy* again. It seemed appropriate. The last time *the Yodanado* had assembled, Euforsee had chanted it. The first time he heard it was from the grim specter that grew at odds within this tree. Instead, *the Primordius Centrum* raised an accusatory hand and pointed at the figures planted on the ten thrones — the Electors of Farn.

2

Harris recognized the rulers of the realm — Cheelum of Volcanium, Yama of Aquilium, Yunoli of Aolium, Yeholu of Terrastrium, Sestanum of Protractus, Dunaliski of Magus, Lododi of Pontifrax, Kuriakis of Montjoy and two others — both new to him. One he guessed was the Lord of Zin and, as he guessed, he heard Euforsee whisper *Grimakadarian, Lord of Darkness*. Harris shuddered, looking to Yustichisqua, who nodded, having received the same whisper. As unsettling as this voice was, Harris was glad for the annotation. He dared not look at Grimakadarian, for fear of being turned to stone or silly putty. In his first visit here, watching the cavalcade of the nine realms, Zin had unnerved him. Arquebus had commanded Harris to shut his eyes when Zin appeared. But now, as his attention drifted to the dark Elector's black throne, the images of hell were suppressed. Grimakadarian was clad in ebony armor like a pot belly stove.

Harris regarded the other unknown figure, who sat on a lucid crystal throne.

Enitachopco, the Lord of Light, came the whisper.

"Zacker," Harris muttered.

The Elector of Zacker, if such was his title, was tall and pale with a snowy beard. His robes, buckskin, tapered at the foot into a broad skirt. He wore a purple band around his forehead and a golden crystal embedded between his eyes and a patch over one of those eyes.

Harris shuddered as he recalled other such countenances, but was held in check when *the Primordius Ce*ntrum raised his hand, pointing to Enitachopco, crimson light bands shooting through spidery fingers.

"Balance has returned to Farn," the creaky voice from the stump proclaimed. "Zin must fade to darkness and Zacker must be banished from our sight. Montjoy shall acquire the Hill of Greary Gree to house the tribute treasures of Farn. The people of Zacker shall descend into the valley and scratch the soil for the realm's benefit. There they shall be kept from the heights by Grimakadarian's dark beast."

The Zinbear, came the whisper.

Enitachopco arose, tall and sturdy under the crimson beams. He bowed. The Electors arose and also bowed. Harris expected *the Promise and Prophecy* to be chanted now, but he must have missed that show and was watching the finale — the destruction of Zacker as a realm. Grimakadarian laughed, and turned from his throne. The ground shook as he plodded his way back into darkness.

The mirage of the Electors faded into purple haze. *The Primordius Centrum* dimmed and slipped back into his stump. Only the glowing *waddly wazzoo* remained, now at Enitachopco's feet. He bent to raised it on its rope, and then kissed it.

Darkness again — briefly. The scene shifted to a regally decorated room, crowned with two thrones and a host of courtiers, each decked in rich tan buckskin robes. Each engaged in weeping — lamentations overcoming *the Cartisforium's* hum.

"The Scarlet Chamber, *oginali*."

"Yes, but that's not Kuriakis and Joella on the thrones."

On the thrones in the Scarlet Chamber on the Hill of Greary Gree sat Enitachopco, the fallen Elector of Zacker and his darkly beautiful Memer — strangely familiar.

Hedonacaria, came the whispered voice of Euforsee. *Our lady, rest her soul.*

Harris was suddenly sad. The humming encompassed the lamentations. Behind the Elector's throne sat his three children, two Sceptas and a Seneschal. Harris grasped Yustichisqua's arm.

"I see her, *oginali*," Little Bird said.

"And another one, sitting beside her."

"And he is there too. How can it be? This is ages past — many thousands of turns around *Solus* and *Dodecadatemus*."

"I can't guess."

It was undeniable. Littafulchee and her brother sat behind the thrones, and between them, another Scepta — a younger version of Littafulchee. The humming encompassed all. The lamentations tore at Harris' heart, and yet at the sight of Littafulchee, his heart raced — raced with passion — raced with wonder.

Enitachopco stood, raising *the waddly wazzoo*, which swung on its rope as if taking attendance.

"My children," he said, his voice sad, but steady. "The light shall never fail us. But Farn must rest from battle. Both sides are ordered to retreat. We, my sad children, must leave our sublime hill and descend into the valley called *cetronus morbidus* and reap to keep the promise alive. *The Prophecy* shall be our final say, but until then, the world will use us as it will."

He turned, *the waddly wazzoo* sparking traces of light. The Scarlet Chamber faded, transforming into a marble temple — a rotunda. At its center, on an altar, lay the Memer Hedonacaria, her eyes closed — her hands clasping Lilies of Murrow. The rotunda's walls were transparent like an architect's rendering, clearly an effect from *the Book of Farn*. Harris finally was viewing the interior of the Temple of Greary Gree.

The children of Hedonacaria wept, clasping their mother's hem, while their father raised *the waddly wazzoo* high. Littafulchee clamped her sister within her embrace, while Cosawta consoled them, but to little avail, his face bathed in tears. The sparks from the lamp wreathed their heads — a benediction blessing from their father, who stroked his Memer's hair.

"Farewell, sweet Hedonacaria, dear mother and wife," Enitachopco wept. "You have been sacrificed for the realms and shall watch us from this hill until the time arrives, when the Deliverer opens the chambers of Zin and floods the dark halls with light. That is *the Promise.* That is *the Prophecy.* It is from the loins of Zacker that the Spasatorium shall rise, and from no other."

He turned to the mournful.

"Children of Zacker," he invoked. "Descend from here and be as you are — pure and merciful. Keep the truth at hand always."

The two Sceptas raised their lamps, receiving their father's light. The Seneschal took *the waddly* wazzoo from Enitachopco. The children arose and floated to the mournful, kindling all the lamps — all the first *waddly wazzoos* — light taken from *the Primordius Centrum.* The light was passed, each courtier's lamp igniting the next, until the Temple was ablaze. When all lamps were lit, the Zacker, like a million fireflies, arose on their *zulus* and drifted down the hill.

Understanding dawned on Harris.

"That's why they return on Brunting Day," he said. "The Temple's sacred."

Yustichisqua wept.

"I thought it was to see Lord Kuriakis' fireworks. I am a fool, *oginali.*"

"No," came Euforsee's voice, clear and trumping the vision. She emerged at the altar's center. "No, son of Kittowa. You are no fool. You finally have come to the knowledge of who you are."

"I am Cetrone."

"You are a child of Zacker, pure and merciful, who has taken the full measure of the task — a part in *the Promise and Prophecy.* In that you must be less pure and a deal less merciful. You must be *the Noya Tludachi* for the Deliverer of our light."

Suddenly, each of *the Yodanado* raised their arms and *waddly wazzoos* like lanterns at a train crossing. Harris, startled, stepped back. *The Book of Farn* snapped shut. The latch twisted, spitting *the Columbincus* out, forcefully. It flew across the altar, hitting Harris on the forehead. He caught it, closing his fist. *The Yodanado* were gone, and *the book* rattled ominously as if to say *one question per customer and you've had more than your share today.*

3

"I'm not sure what I just saw," Harris said, affixing the brooch to his cloak.

"I know what I saw," Little Bird exclaimed.

"Yes, I know you know." Harris grasped his shoulder. "I wonder whether it's true."

"It is difficult for me," Yustichisqua said. "I have been Cetrone all my life and now I am something else altogether."

"You're the same as you've always been," Harris replied, knowing that statement was the biggest falsehood of the hour. "I mean, you're different because you've changed yourself."

"With your help. But to learn these things makes more questions — questions I did not have before."

"I bet."

"And did you see him — Cosawta — a Seneschal?"

"We've heard Tomatly call him that, but I thought it was honorary."

"It is honorary, *oginali*. An ancient honor. He must be older than . . ."

"Mud . . . and so must she." Harris twitched. "Jesus Christ. So . . . must . . . she. And if she's a Scepta, I've stepped in shit again. Am I a sucker for all the succubae in creation?"

"She is not like Charminus," Little Bird protested.

"Who knows? But you're right about one thing. There's a shit load of new questions. And who was the other Scepta?"

Both fell silent until a sound at the far end of *the Cartisforium* shook them out of their reverie. Someone had entered.

"Tappiolus," Harris whispered, pulling Yustichisqua into an alcove. "Shit."

"I will burn today, for sure, *oginali*, and just when I have learned I am a child of Zacker."

"Pure and merciful."

Yustichisqua grinned, and then drew *gasohisgi*. Harris stopped him.

"What are you doing?"

"Being less pure and a deal less merciful."

"And more stupid. That'd have us both burnt today. Put it away."

Yustichisqua complied. Harris peeked around a column and watched Tappiolus circumnavigate the altar, drifting to the stained-glass windows. Harris looked for the nearest exit, but it was the door directly within Tappiolus' view.

His attention drifted to a place under the altar. Was there a space beneath the table — enough for two interlopers on their way to prison — one for *the Katorias,* the other for *the Porias.* Then he pushed farther into the alcove, examining the walls. Solid.

"I guess our library card is about to expire, old man."

"No, *oginali*." Yustichisqua pushed his arm through the wall. "*Kaybar*. Give me your hand."

Harris shook his head, but complied. Little Bird pulled him through, Harris hated this mode of transport. But at least he knew now why the walls were porous for the Cetrone, or rather the Children of Zacker, who constructed them, no doubt, when Enitachopco and Hedonacaria ruled the world of light from the Hill of Great Greary Gree.

Chapter Nine

Defiance

1

Harris wasted no time addressing these open questions. He was armed now with a history or, at least, a flicker-show revealing much, but begging more. Yustichisqua was anxious also. It helped to have Little Bird at hand to discuss the various points observed in *the Cartisforium*. But it served only to focus on several points, points which Harris hoped Littafulchee and Cosawta could resolve. Somehow he thought the Scepta and Seneschal of the Zacker would not be forthcoming, given their response during their last encounter in *the sustiya*. Therefore, Harris hastened to return to *the Myrkpykyn* to be outfitted for the routine crossing through the secret portal into *the Kalugu*. Garan was curious. The haste was apparent and Lord Belmundus and his *Taleenay* appeared preoccupied. Still, Garan only regarded them with unaccustomed silence and complied with cloaks, third legs and two sacks of *zulus*.

In broad daylight, *the Didaniyisgi* and his *Taleenay* went as fast as their *borabas* could take them from the boundary where Elypticus and Parnasus released them from *Cabriolins*. It would be presumptive to allow anyone to know where *the Yudolayda Asdodi* was located. So, once released from their ride, the two shuffled down the alleyways through *the Yuganawu* past *the Katorias* to the cornerstone of *the Porias*.

"Quickly," Harris said, his *zulu* sack slung low. "The way's clear."

He glanced across the wide avenue, which separated *the Porias* from *the Kalugu*, and dashed to the niche where *the kaybar* door with its crimson *Z* stood. Here he waited for Yustichisqua to adjust his sack and ready his hand for the transference. When prepared, Harris grasped Little Bird's wrist tightly and took a deep breath, bracing for the plunge through solid matter.

"*Torpeda*," Yustichisqua stammered, the closest thing he had ever come to a curse word.

They hadn't budged.

"What's wrong?"

"My hand will not go through."

"What?"

Suddenly, from the adjacent wall, *The Eye* appeared. Harris twisted about, bringing his cowl up, covering his face. Yustichisqua tried to penetrate *the kaybar* again, but failed. *The Eye* was steady and drew closer, closer than Harris ever had seen it. He bowed quickly to it.

"We are about our business," he said, disguising his voice to sound like Ricktus Morphinus', knowing Tappiolus would recognize Lord Belmundus' voice. However, there was little disguising Yustichisqua's flustered plea.

"*Oginali.*"

"Hush," Harris croaked. "We are being observed doing our business." He bowed again and shook the sack. "Doing . . . our . . . business."

The *Eye* faded, but danger did not. From positions about the wall, *regulati* revealed themselves, having been concealed. As they stood, a Cabriolin raced to the alley's end, blocking any escape route. From the platform came the voice of the guard whom Harris hated most — the one who had confronted him at *the Gulliwailit Bridge*. The guard waved *a Stick* about, directing his escort to be wary against all contingencies.

"Gentlemen," he said to *the Augustii spinctus*, floating to them on his zulus. "I am the Officer of the Day, Warder Villamorticus, and have received a communication there has been a security breach in Sector 451."

"Sector 451?" Harris asked, still disguising his voice. "I am sorry to hear it, Warder Villamorticus. If we see anything, we shall report it at once."

Villamorticus laughed, coming closer.

"You do not understand."

He approached the secret door. Harris noticed *the Z* no longer blazed crimson, but was now motley-brown as if glazed over with some substance that deflected Yustichisqua's natural abilities. *Had the regulati discovered the Yudolayda Asdodi? Was the jig up?* His first response was to quietly tap his *Columbincus* and hope for the best. He then produced his papers.

"It is not for me to understand, Warder," Harris said, pouring on the actor. "I have a warrant to deliver *zulus* to *the mordanka*. I do so often, as you well know."

"Ah," Villamorticus said, seizing the papers. "You usually come through the front door." He perused the warrant, but Harris knew the Warder wasn't reading. He shook the paper and turned to the ambush crew. "It is odd to see them this far from *the Gulliwailit Bridge*, although . . ." He grinned, and then laughed, pointing at Harris. "I could have sworn I saw you cross the bridge but an hour ago."

The *regulati* grunted in agreement.

"Impossible," Harris said. "I am here."

"Yes, you are, Ricktus Morphinus." Villamorticus came closer. "You are here and . . . there, because I let you pass into *the Kalugu* and, oddly, you were alone." He sniffed. "Your assistant was absent." He sniffed again.

Shit, Harris thought. *No charpgris. He's not wearing charpgris.*

"No assistant whatsoever," Villamorticus said, and then went to Yustichisqua. He sniffed again. "I smell a Trone."

He waved his *Stick*, and two *regulati* rushed Little Bird, pulling off his cowl. Harris lowered his owm cowl, and then tossed his sack and robe aside. The jig was up, all for the lack of Tygger piss. He drew *Tony*, but before he could raise it high enough to do damage, Villamorticus disarmed him.

"*Oginali*," Little Bird shouted, drawing *gasohisgi*.

Villamorticus aimed his *Stick*, preparing to shoot, but Harris rushed him, knocking the Warder off his *zulus*. Yustichisqua stabbed first at the air, and then at his assailants. He drew blood — the leg of a Yunocker, who screamed like a fire alarm in the night. Villamorticus regained his feet, and then his balance. A dozen *regulati* tackled Harris and, as Yustichisqua leaped over them to the rescue, he was caught about the waist, battered by Villamorticus' *Stick*.

"Where did you get that dagger?" he shouted at Yustichisqua.

"From your mother's ass," Little Bird shouted, and then spit, spraying the Warder's cheek.

"You shall pay for that," Villamorticus stammered. He straddled Harris. "As for you, Lord Belmundus, I have been waiting for your return."

"I've broken your fucking treaty," Harris shouted. "And if you so much as harm a hair on my *Taleenay's* head, Lord Kuriakis will have you executed for interfering with his pleasure."

Villamorticus laughed, infecting the others, who had a good chuckle at Harris' expense. A wide wagon *Cabriolin* arrived now, what the Yunockers called a *pokiepen* — *an aniniya*-powered paddy wagon, only open to the air, for ignominy value. Villamorticus ordered his prisoners thrown into *the pokiepen*, their hands tied with *gondercoils.* They were mustered away from Sector 451.

"Are you hurt, *oginali*?"

Yustichisqua had landed on Harris' legs. They were in a tangle. *The pokiepen* moved swiftly.

"I'm just fine and dandy," Harris grumbled. "I think this is the day Melonius predicted."

"I am sorry," Yustichisqua said, sniffling. "I should have put on the piss."

"You should have."

"But it offends you."

"It offends me more now, but what can I say?"

Little Bird wept. He clutched his *waddly wazzoo*, which he had managed to retain.

"I have lost *gasohisgi.*"

"*Tony's* in the shitter too, but . . ." He touched his *Columbincus* again. "I don't know why they didn't take this."

"They would not dare," Yustichisqua whispered. "Perhaps you can kill us before they can."

"What are you nuts? If I get to use it, it won't be on us, but . . ."

"Keep silent," Villamorticus shouted. "There will be time enough to talk when General Tarhippus arrives. Until then, I do not want any talking."

Harris sighed. He gazed at Yustichisqua, who looked both terrified and like a holy terror. Harris winked at him. They untangled their legs and pushed up to peek above *the pokiepen's* rim. They were crossing *the Gulliwailit.*

2

The *pokiepen* halted and the prisoners were jostled to their feet. Harris squinted in the sunlight as the entourage had stopped just short of *the Kalugu's* main entrance — the portcullis. He could see *the Deetsuneeli* — *the Place Where Death Crosses* just beyond, *the tludachi* growling beneath *the kaybar* plank.

"Out," Villamorticus commanded, and Harris and Yustichisqua were tossed to the bridge.

A small crowd of Trones gathered to watch the proceeding, mystified, no doubt, that an *Ayelli* would be treated so roughly, and that he'd be accompanied by one of their own.

"Well," Harris said, defiantly, "I've already broken your fucking treaty, so I won't stand on ceremony when the triumph is mine."

Gasps from the crowd gave evidence of the news, which had been rumored, but now confirmed.

"You have broken nothing, Lord Belmundus," Villamorticus said, gleefully. "I have only witnessed a Zecronisian trader pass through these gates — *an Augustii spinctus*, who had a warrant to do so. *Ayelli* can never trespass here, but . . ." He glanced at Yustichisqua. "But it is fitting this low mutt has returned home for chastisement. He shall enter and enter now, only . . ." Villamorticus touched Little Bird's feet and *the borabas* disintegrated, leaving Yustichisqua in bare feet. "*The tludachi* are hungry, and it is feeding time."

He pushed Yustichisqua forward. Harris tried to bolt, but was held fast by *the regulati* and *the gondercoils*. He did manage to move under the portcullis's overhang.

"*Oginali,*" Yustichisqua cried. "Must I die like this?"

"No," Harris cried. "You can't go like this. This is shit, you know." He kicked his captors, but they grabbed his legs. "Old man, hold tight."

"*Oginali,* think of me. Do not forget your Little Bird."

Harris trembled, weeping like an infant — unmanly and horribly out of character. He swung his body about, but his restraint was total. He watched as Villamorticus pushed Yustichisqua forward to *the Deetsuneeli*, the planks buckling as *the tludachi* sensed flesh and blood. Yustichisqua gazed back at Harris, tears in his eyes, then he smiled — and in that smile Harris knew the undying loyalty and faith of one person for another. The son of Kittowa had accepted his fate and was grateful for the days when he was privileged to be in service to *the Didaniyisgi of the Yuyutlu.*

Villamorticus pushed and Yustichisqua snarled, and then raised his foot for the plunge into a horrific deat. Harris prayed it would be quick. He knew it wouldn't be painless. The foot hovered, and then . . .

. . . it never struck the plank. Two hands came from above, snatching Yustichisqua around the waist, suspending him over the plank.

"My lady," Harris sighed, and wept now for prayers answered.

Littafulchee hovered on her *zulus*, her arms now snapped across Little Bird's torso. Beside her, Cosawta outstretched his hands. The air bent and light wavered as the power of the Seneschal of Zacker swept through the portcullis and snatched *Tony* and *gasohisgi* from Villamorticus' *Cabriolin*. The Warder attempted to catch the sword, but caught the dagger in his chest instead. The *brashun blade* quickly ripped through the flesh to the neck, and then severed the main artery, a fountain of blood covering *the regulati*, who tried to save their leader.

Then Harris felt a tug and *the gondercoils* fell.

"My lord," came a voice.

"Elypticus?"

"We are all here." Elypticus clutched Harris in his arms and dumped him into his *Cabriolin*. "We must flee."

Harris glanced through the portcullis. Yustichisqua was safe and Cosawta wielded both *brashun blades*.

"No, Elypticus," Harris said. "We must storm this place."

"Impossible, my lord."

Cosawta raised *Tony* and shot a beam to *the Deetsuneeli*, the planks bursting into a thousand *kaybar* splinters. *The tludachi* escaped — three Tyggers, mad with hunger, plunging their claws into *the regulati* and sending the Trone crowd fleeing back over the bridge — screams, howls and panic. Harris still urged Elypticus to enter, but Littafulchee, hovering, stared at him — her head ornament flashing gold — a bolt as rampant as *the tludachi*. It struck Harris' *Columbincus*. He held his chest.

Flee my love. Flee.

Elypticus needed no further prompting. He turned *the Cabriolin* around, *regulatis* trying to stop him, probably seeking a way out before *the tludachi* reached them. Harris saw Melonius on the right flank and Parnasus on the left. They had been firing their *Sticks* at *regulati* on the parapet, covering Elypticus in the rescue. As *the Cabriolin* raced over the bridge, all three *Danuwa* gathered to protect their lord. Melonius shouted to Elypticus.

"*The Taleenay?*"

"Saved by his own kind," Elypticus replied.

"My poor Little Bird," Harris wept, but grasped Elypticus' shoulders and hugged him tightly. "My dear, faithful *Danuwa*."

Buhippus met them on the other side.

3

"Thank you," Harris said to Captain Buhippus as he joined the race.

"Do not thank me, Lord Belmundus. You are not safe. Every *regulati* in *the Yuganawu* has been alerted to your capture at *the Kalugu* and has been mustered to escort you to your prison cell. Now that all hell has broken loose, the orders will be changed. My brother has been known to shoot to kill and to investigate after the fact."

The *Seegoniga* were on their last ride together. They sped through the narrow lanes and alleys of Montjoy, uncaring who was blown over by their jets. Many *minorins* cursed as they passed. Many *majorins* shook fists. *Praeters* snapped their windows shut, most likely expecting a revolution, preparing to sweep their *kaleezos* clean of vermin.

"Where do we go?" Harris shouted across to Buhippus.

"We must split up."

"Split up?" Parnasus asked. "There is safety in numbers."

"That makes sense," Melonius agreed.

"I will not argue with you, young sirs," Buhippus growled. "If you wish to make a stand against a Yunocker army, you are welcomed to do so. I will depart your company now and seek the seclusion that a cabin grants."

"No," Harris said.

"But, my lord," Elypticus protested. "We are likened to family."

"And like family," Harris replied, "we must assure something of us remains." He looked to Buhippus. "We are at your mercy, captain."

"Not so. There will be no mercy here, especially if we are caught. By separating, our target is widened and harder to hit." He pointed to the next intersection. "Parnasus, you turn left there." They approached. Parnasus shook his head, but when they crossed the street, he veered away, and immediately disappeared down another lane to avoid an approaching *regulati* squad.

"Greary Gree watch over him," Harris said, and thought of the sacred Zacker who was interred in the temple.

"Melonius," Buhippus shouted. "You are next. East for you, and then north to *the Yuyutlu*. They will seek him at *the Myrkpykyn*, but they must find you."

Melonius shrugged, and when the intersection approached, he nodded to Harris.

"It has been my honor, my lord."

Harris choked back a tear, and then nodded. Melonius was gone, and Harris hoped not forever.

"I shall lead you to the boundary," Buhippus said. "Elypticus, ride true. We will make for the invisible gate and retreat up the hill."

"They will not let us pass," Elypticus stated.

"We may not ask them," Buhippus said.

Elypticus bucked, and then accelerated. Buhippus turned up the wide avenue, which led to *the Ayelli*. Harris braced himself for a rugged crossing. There was no question of security at this gate. It would have been alerted to events from the start and the patrols would not be fooled by fancy talk or trickery.

"We are about to die, my lord," Elypticus said. "But remember, I have flown through the jaws of *the misancorpus* and survived. Perhaps we shall try the same game with *the Zinbear*."

Harris shuddered at the thought of *the abyss* that separated *the Great Hill of Greary Gree* from *the cetronus morbicus*. It was the world of Zin — Grimakadarian's dark beast.

"May Hedonacaria be with us," he murmured.

"Who?" Elypticus asked.

"Someday, lad. Someday."

"I hope we see the end of this day, my lord."

"So do I."

Buhippus slowed as they reached *the abyss* and the invisible gate. Two patrols of Yunockers approached from both flanks, like a vise to catch any fly who tried to penetrate the swatter. Suddenly, the two patrols surrounded Behippus and crew.

"Your business," shouted the squad leader.

"To *the Ayelli*," Buhippus replied. "I know you. You are Fyndicapus of the Seventh Legion."

"Yes, sir. And I know you."

"Then let me pass."

"I wish I could oblige, but . . ."

"But if he did," came a booming voice, "I would have his balls bronzed and displayed in my library as a reminder of the price of disobeying orders."

Fyndicapus nodded.

Buhippus sighed, but bucked up.

"Brother," he said.

Tarhippus approached, his fiery *Cabriolin* as ominous as certain death. He whipped his *gwasdi* toward Elypticus, the lash coming near the Thirdling's hand.

"Yes, brother, and I see you have captured the fugitive, or . . . I hope I do not misconstrue your efforts here. You were bringing this cargo home to me?"

"No, brother," Buhippus said. "My orders are for Lord Belmundus' safety. That is my prime directive. He could cut your head off and I still would need to protect him."

"Commendable, but misplaced in this instance. But you were always a follower of orders and never an interpreter. Now, we all respect *the Ayelli* for what they are, but this renegade from their tribe has broken treaties and cultural laws. How Kuriakis maintains that this one should live and still maintain the peace of Montjoy is beyond me? However, he is my prisoner now, brother, so . . . whisk aside."

Buhippus did not. But filial piety was also a hallmark of Yunocker courage and Harris did not expect Buhippus to raise *a Stick* to his brother. Buhippus did not clear the way, but he did not resist beyond that. Tarhippus lashed his *gwasdi* at his brother, the tip piercing Buhippus' ear. The captain winced and stopped the blood flow with his palm.

"That is punishment enough for you, brother," Tarhippus said. "When you decide to defy me again, look in the glass and recall your pierced ear. You may want to dangle a bauble from it as a constant reminder."

Tarhippus reached Elypticus' *Cabriolin*. He glared at the Thirdling, and then at Harris. He made a mock bow.

"*Didaniyisgi*," Tarhippus said, laughing. "You are out in strange company after allegedly breaking *the Treaty of Parazell*."

"I broke your fucking treaty," Harris said.

"I know no such thing. We must investigate the claim. But until then, you and this misguided Thirdling shall be my guests in the best that my worst can afford at *the Katorias*."

"My father shall know of this, sir," Elypticus protested.

Tarhippus came close, his brutal face pushed into Elypticus'.

"I am sure he knows. If you were not *Ayelli*, I would lift your young ass out of your vehicle and let you fall . . . down, down, down . . . into *the Zinbear's* jaws." He snorted. "I might still do it. I mean, what is an upstart Thirdling who tried to attack me with his *Stick* to a General of *the Yuganawu*? What would Lord Arquebus say to me?" Tarhippus leaned back and howled. "He would require two baskets of *mongerhide* and a dozen Zecronisian wenches, an event that would be overcompensation for satisfying *the Zinbear's* appetite."

"Please," Harris said. "Take us to *the Katorias*, if that's your plan. Don't browbeat us with you comic-opera humor."

Tarhippus snarled, and looked back at his brother.

"You are a poor judge of heroes, brother. This one is a tosser."

"My Lord Belmundus," Buhippus said. "Forgive me for failing in my duty to protect you. I shall report to your Scepta and supplicate at the feet of the Memer to intercede."

"Thank you, captain. I regret my plight has cost you your ear and soured relationships within your family."

"I *do* regret the loss of my ear."

Tarhippus trembled with rage. He started after Buhippus.

"Off with you, sad offspring of a noble line. That you did not die at birth will always be my regret."

Buhippus nodded, and then departed up the hill. Tarhippus ranted, flailing his *gwasdis* in all directions, occasionally striking members of the patrols. Then, he stopped and pointed at Harris.

"You are mine and when I have finished with you, you will wish your were raped by every consort in Farn. You shall find no pleasure in it." He looked to Fyndicapus. "Take them to *the Katorias*."

Harris squeezed Elypticus' waist.

"I am sorry for this, sweet Elypticus."

"So am I, my lord."

Fyndicapus bumped *the Cabriolin*, now surrounded by the patrol. They left Tarhippus still ranting under the invisible gate, cursing his brother and all creatures who audaciously embrace defiance.

Chapter Ten

The Katorias

1

It was built with malice — the ultimate dark place for Yunockers who broke the rules and Zecronisians who disregarded their warrants and Gurts who proved vexatious. Never had the place contained Cetrone, because the walls were built sturdy — of *kaybar*. A special place girded by *phitron* was reserved for Cetrone — *the Porias*, both detention area and crematorium. Compared to *the Porias*, *the Katorias* was an easier place. The prison was never meant to hold a lawbreaker beyond interrogation and punishment. It was a means to an end, not the end itself. And only once before in the history of *the Katorias* had *an Ayelli* been incarcerated in its bowels. Now there were two — another proud rule-breaking consort and a misguided Thirdling. It was the talk of Montjoy — rumors abounding. But a political crisis set on the outcome. Discussion went apace and strategy was discussed. Still, in the dark hold, uncaring and above it all, sat Lord Belmundus and his faithful *Danuwa*, Elypticus the Good, seventh son of Lord Arquebus.

Harris shivered in the dark dampness of his cell, Elypticus cowering beside him. Light streamed down from a distant port several stories above them, but was too faint to do much good at ground level. Beyond their iron bars, other prisoners moaned, mostly from hunger, but Harris suspected a few had been through the interrogation process, because Yunocker guards, *the Fantin,* had swooped in, banging on grates and dragging detainees in *gondercoils* over the crosswalk. It would be only a matter of time when the guards would rattle Harris' cage for a similar exercise.

He was saddened by Elypticus' state. The lad had been spoiled by good food and fresh air. This atmosphere was stale, reeking of urine from the slop bucket provided for the purpose. Food consisted of stale *bupka* soaked in sour *bolingara*, so putrid Harris could barely get it past his nose, much less his lips. Still they had retained their cloaks, which provided warmth, and *the Fantin* hadn't taken their *Columbincus'*, although the brooches dimmed, as if ineffectual when dejected and spurned. Harris recalled the notion that *Columbincus* power resided in the heart of the wearer. If so, his should be dead, because his heart was broken, leveled by ignominy. Mostly, he missed Yustichisqua — and not the constant servant in waiting. It was true. Despite Harris' distaste for being served, he had become accustomed to Little Bird's constant attention to the details of wardrobe and toilet. Perhaps this was an adjunct to acting. But it went beyond that. Yustichisqua's devotion was like air to Harris and, now removed, he found it difficult to breathe without him.

Elypticus gasped.

"Are you ill?" Harris asked.

"I am desperately ill, my lord."

"I wish I had a basket of *mongerhide* and a flagon of *brantsgi* for you, but I'm afraid it won't get any better than shit in a pail."

Elypticus sighed.

"My illness comes from shame, not hunger."

Harris straightened the Thirdling's shoulders.

"You've nothing to be ashamed of, my friend. You saved my life."

"It was my duty to do so," Elypticus replied, attempting to genuflect.

"Enough of that, sir," Harris chided. "Look around you. We're both in the same fucking soup. Your attention to protocol gets us nowhere, so stow it. When you realize we've a real problem instead of accepting this dump, you'll feel a helluva lot better. Don't look at this place and call it fate."

"Fate, it is," Elypticus said. "We are destined to it."

Harris shook his head.

"Bullshit. That's Trone thinking. I would expect a *sqwallen*-head to spout crap like that, but not *an Ayelli.*"

Elypticus grinned, but then covered his face.

"I am a Trone, my lord."

"No, you're not."

"We are all Trones."

Harris pushed away from *the kaybar*, kneeling beside his cellmate.

"How do you figure that? Have you seen me giving in to them yet?"

"We all have surrendered, my lord." Elypticus sighed again, this time tinged with anger, an emotion Harris had never seen him display. "The Trones bow to all, but the Yunockers also bend their necks to the lords on the hill. The Thirdlings are fated to it also. We are raised like *awidena,* to be sacrificed when the time comes — like a game of *grusoker.* We are mated to goblins and hags — Thirdlings who breathe fire and have no faces, playing the game to see who will lay seed in barren fields. We try and try and never succeed, all for the sake of the one chance promised. Thousands of spawn, fated to try our luck, not for life, but for a miracle never to be, because . . . I do not believe it can happen. I believe we have been punished for the Electors' folly and their warfare. So long as Thirdlings are sent between the realms to frolic between the legs, the Electors hope for the Spasatorum."

"You don't believe in it, do you?"

"Do you, my lord?" Elypticus clasped the wall and pulled himself up. The dim light from the distant port struck his tender cheeks, catching a glistening of tears. "We are all Trones. And the consorts are at the top of the tree, forced to make us, so the game can go onward and onward, never ending." He turned to Harris. "I am ashamed because I have failed you, but I am glad that *this* Trone will find release from his Thirdling fate. I will not find the shores of a distant beast, who will ride me until I am sore and sorry, until I fade beside *the Pulveris Stream*, where my body will melt in the rippling tide and be lost to all memory."

Harris stood, grasping Elypticus' arm, and then pulling him into an embrace.

"With those words, you are truer to me than you know. You haven't failed me, Elypticus. You've come to this realization on your own and, in my world, we call that wisdom — a rare gift and not one to melt in *the Pulveris Stream*."

"Do you say true, my lord?"

"I say true, Elypticus."

Harris hugged him tightly, and then drew him back to *the kaybar*. He picked up the pail, lifting it to his nose.

"I can't tell whether this is food or waste," he muttered.

He threw the pail against the metal bars, the racket stirring the other inmates, like feeding time at the zoo. *A Fantin* swooped down, hitting the grate with his *Stick*.

"Prisoner Belmundus," the guard snapped. "If you disrupt the gallery again, you shall lose a finger."

Harris shot *the Fantin* a finger, and then both fingers. He wasn't sure whether this was a valid Farn expression of disrespect, but he was in no mood to moon the guard. Elypticus was on his feet again.

"Bring us something to eat that I can eat," he demanded.

"You can eat my *Stick*, young whelp," *the Fantin* shouted. "I shall shove it in your mouth and fire away. You might find *the aniniya* aftertaste a bit harsh for your refined taste, but you should have thought about that before you assaulted *a regulati*."

"I did not assault *a regulati*," Elypticus protested.

The guard pounded his *Stick* on the bars. The shouts from the other inmates increased and several *Fantin* joined the first, yelling expletives to quell the restless — promises of digit loss, cessation of feeding and other useless threats, which hopeless men disregard. Then, *the Fantin* warden arrived. Harris hoped Tarhippus would pay him a visit too. He had reserved the mooning for the General and perhaps a loud and sour *bupka* fart. But the warden, a pompous jackass who rarely spoke and only sneered, broke his customary silence with a single word.

"Visitor," he said, his supercilious voice cutting through the clatter.

Harris pulled up to the bars to see who accompanied the warden and shuddered upon recognition. Lord Tappiolus had come to gloat.

2

"Boots!"

"Fuck you, Tappiolus and *the Cabriolin* you rode in on."

"*Cliché* to the end, Lord Belmundus, or should I say, Prisoner Belmundus."

"Stick to *Boots*, if you're smart."

Tappiolus pushed aside *the Fantin*, allowing the warden to repeat his announcement, but with a more pronounced sense of importance.

"Visitor," he snapped.

"I'm not at home," Harris replied, and then receded into the darkness, standing with Elypticus.

"I have come to assess your condition," Tappiolus said.

"Is Charminus upset that my dick didn't show up on time?"

"You are not *up* this week. But even so, she is disturbed by the circumstances and is distracted."

"Distracted?"

Tappiolus waved the warden aside and came close to the bars.

"You have broken our father's heart, Boots."

"Why should he care?" Harris asked. "He's only interested in hunting and Brunting and making nice with the other Electors."

"For the gain of Montjoy and for Farn." Tappiolus rattled the grate. "You have brought much harm to the household. I cannot forgive you."

Harris charged the bars, shaking them vigorously, setting Tappiolus back and the warden forward.

"If harm has been brought to the household, you've brought it with your pompous attitude and your fucking spying. I should have blasted *The Eye* when I had the chance. Now you've cooked my goose and my *Danuwa* and . . ."

". . . your *Taleenay*?" Tappiolus snarled. "With that Trone you cooked your own bird. But he will be found and brought to *the Porias*, where he belongs."

"You haven't found him?" Harris gasped. He grinned. "Good. You can use two *Eyes* and you'll never find him, you two-bit apple-pinching porn star."

Tappiolus rushed the grate again, clasping his fingers around Harris', the two consorts, nose to chin now through the bars. Elypticus emerged from the shadows, but took a half-measure, shaking his fists and glaring at the warden.

"You are your own destruction, Boots."

"I'm still here." Harris tensed his jaw and poked his tongue through the gap in his teeth. "I suppose I'll be tried on the hill and kept caged in Charminus' bedroom."

Tappiolus pushed back.

"A tribunal," he said. "Yes. I do not understand it, but the household still is saddened by your plight. You spin a magical sympathy over them — even Kuriakis, who wept when he heard you were taken."

"Despite the broken treaty?"

"The treaty has not been broken."

Harris pushed back now, cocking his head.

"What are you about, sir? Why are you here? Surely not to tell me the family sends their regards and will cheer my case at trial."

"No, Boots. Such may be the case, but I doubt you will ever come to trial."

"Ah," Harris said, turning to Elypticus. "They mean to poison us." He regarded the food pail. "Probably already have. We'll be swimming in your *Pulveris Stream* very soon, I bet."

"Nothing so subtle, Boots," Tappiolus snarled. Harris sighed, and returned to the bars. "You must be interrogated. General Tarhippus is a thorough interrogator. He will apply pain to much of your body until you admit your guilt."

"I'm guilty," Harris said. "I did it. I broke the fucking treaty. I don't need interrogation."

"There is a rumor to that effect, Boots, but no confirmation."

Harris turned back to the darkness, and then raised his hands high.

"It's no rumor, sir. I broke the fucking Treaty of Para-fucking-zell."

"Perhaps you have, and perhaps you will admit it. But *the regulati* are fastidious concerning protocols and interrogation as a point of procedure. There are many questions to be settled — much paperwork and affidavits before you gasp your last breath . . . under General Tarhippus' blades."

"Damn you, Tappiolus, there are hundreds of witnesses."

"Witnesses, Boots? There are no witnesses."

"How about the shithead brigade of *regulati* at the gate and on the bridge?"

"Dead, I am afraid."

"Dead?"

"Killed to the last Yunocker." He drew close now, grinning. "You would be surprised how efficient a hungry *tludachi* can be."

"*The tludachi?*"

"Yes. They escaped their pit and killed every witness to your infraction."

"Not true," Elypticus said. "There are four living witnesses."

"You mean yourself, young pup?"

Elypticus came forward, anger on his brow, righteousness on his lip.

"I drove *the Cabriolin* and saw it all. I will swear on Lord Belmundus' behalf, and so will the others."

"Your word wears thin, Seventh Son of Lord Arquebus. You have crushed your father's soul."

"No," Elypticus gasped, twitching as if kicked in the belly. "I would never dishonor my father."

"Never? You are in *the Katorias*, young pup. What honor do you rain down on your mother? I believe you will see Tarhippus' blades before Lord Belmundus chokes on his last crust of *bupka*."

"But I am not the only witness."

"Do not think about my son."

"Where's Melonius?" Harris asked.

"Why should you care? You sent him to *the Myrkpykyn* to be swept in the net set to capture you." Tappiolus shrugged. "That boy has always been a disappointment."

"He didn't follow your mold, you mean," Harris said. "You planted him to spy on me, and he showed his more honorable side."

"You refer to his unfilial side. But he will be rewarded. I have decided to farm him to the mating pool. He will be suitably matched to a mud maiden from Terrastrium — someone suitable to the political landscape and dismal to his lungs. He shall spend his days wondering whether he has skin beneath the muck and ash in his underground home."

"You bastard," Harris said.

"He is my son and . . . he has found filial respect. As for Captain Buhippus, he is not my concern. As a witness, he is poor and answerable to his brother."

Harris grunted and pounded the bars.

"You wouldn't discharge a man of honor?"

"I have no use for honorable men, Boots. I also have no need to know his fate, although I suspect he shall become *a zugginak* keeper under Tarhippus' *gwasdis*."

"And Parnasus?" Elypticus asked.

"We shall find him — be sure of it."

"So, there *is* one witness on the lam," Harris said.

"Only a matter of time," Tappiolus replied. "So, Lord Belmundus, I predicted you would be trouble from the first time I spied you at Pelargis."

He bowed mockingly, and then turned away.

"Come back here, you bastard," Harris shouted. "I demand to be taken to Kuriakis at once. There's no need to interrogate me. No need."

The warden nodded his respects, and then followed Lord Tappiolus. *The Fantin*s rattled their *Sticks* along the bars, catching Harris' hand. He jumped back, clenched his fists and brought them to his head. He stared at his *Columbincus*. It pulsed dimly. He supposed when it faded completely, he'd be dead — doing the backstroke in the fabled *Pulveris Stream* — he and Elypticus.

"My lord," Elypticus said, his voice trembling. "I am sorry."

"Don't be sorry," Harris muttered. "You've been faithful."

"I am sorry you are so angry," he said, grasping Harris' arms and dragging them down to his sides. "That was Lord Tappiolus' purpose. He came to make you angry and he has succeeded."

"Trones," Harris snapped. He shook his head. "You're right, Elypticus. We are Trones. They pull our strings and we dance the funky chicken."

"I have never danced like that, my lord."

Harris grinned, a laugh deflating his ire.

"No, you haven't. I've seen you do *the herky-jerky,* and you slam down a good hand of *grusoker.*"

"I wish we had the game board here now."

Harris put his arm around Elypticus' shoulder and pulled him down to the wall.

"We should sit and wait."

"For the blades to scrape our skins?"

"You're cheery, ain't you?" Harris patted *the Danuwa's* hand. "No. We should just sit here and tell each other the story of our lives. I mean, yours is short and might be a vamp to pleasure. But mine is *socko*, filled with thrills and chills, although pretty hum-drum until I met a certain Gothgirl on the red carpet of my last film."

Elypticus appeared bemused, but kept his eyes trained on Lord Belmundus.

"It'll while away the time," Harris suggested.

"I am listening, my lord."

"Well, try to keep up with me." Harris squeezed the lad's hand. "I was born Humphrey Kopfstutter in a place called California."

Elypticus chuckled.

"A funny name, my lord."

"Humphrey?"

"No. Calipornica."

Now, Harris laughed.

"Just how funny, you'll never know. My mother worried that I had way too much energy and decided to funnel it into modeling, which suited me fine, because I was only eight. Of course, that's only four years older than you are now. I was a real cutie and was spotted by an agent, who thought I'd be good as a street urchin in a Dickens remake and . . ."

Harris looked at his audience, who had drifted off to sleep. He patted Elypticus' hand.

"Good idea."

Harris shut his own eyes. He prayed, and he wasn't sure to whom — the God of his Father (who left him high and dry when he was a baby) or to Greary Gree, the beauty ensconced on Hedonacaria's bier. He sighed for poor Melonius, who would creep about Terrastrium like a toad. He worried about Captain Buhippus — an honorable man, despite allegiance and orders. He prayed Parnasus was holed up safely where no one could find him. Then he thought of his poor Little Bird and wept. But as he drifted to melancholy, a danger more potent than hunger, he was swept by the sight of brave Cosawta wielding the *brashun blades* and Littafulchee — she who had captured his heart. He hoped they would shelter Yustichisqua. Such thoughts wafted him to sleep, until his dreams became polluted by visions of Charminus' misplaced worry and Kuriakis' careworn disappointment. When *The Eye* invaded the dream, he stirred, just before Tarhippus came riding through the mindscape, his *Cabriolin* shooting fire; his *gwasdis* inciting a pack of a dozen *zugginaks*.

Harris awoke abruptly.

The cell was darker, if possible. Elypticus snored. However, Harris sensed another presence. Was his tormentor quietly watching them from the shadows?

"Who's there?" Harris whispered.

He saw an outline moving. He scurried to his feet as this form emerged into the scant light.

"Garan?" Harris exclaimed.

Garan *the Gucheeda* bowed, his hand extended.

"At your service, my lord."

Chapter Eleven

Curfew

1

Harris shook Elypticus awake, and then grasped Garan's arm.

"Did I sleep so deeply?" Harris asked. "I don't recall them tossing you in here with us?"

Garan placed his finger to his lips, and then scurried to the bars, looking along the crosswalk.

"Is that Garan?" Elypticus asked.

"It is I," Garan whispered. "Be steady and calm. Do not arouse attention."

Harris grabbed Garan's arm again.

"But how . . . and why? Did they throw you in here for aiding me with the Zecronisian get-up?"

"No, my lord. No one has *tossed* Garan *the Gucheeda* anywhere." He looked about again, and then drew Harris back into the shadows. "I have come to take you and the young *Danuwa* away from *the Katorias.*"

"Away? How did you get in here in the first place?"

Harris glanced to the crosswalk, looking for Garan's means of entry.

"You shall find nothing there, my lord."

Garan placed his finger to the side of his nose, and then moved to the wall. With one quick poke, he thrust his arm through *the Kaybar.* Elypticus twitched. Harris cocked his head.

"How does a Zecronisian do that trick?" he asked.

Garan pulled his arm back, and then threw off his cloak. Harris was impressed, because Garan wore a fine silver tunic and a full-length scarlet *asano.* Then Garan bent over and tugged at his backside, pulling off his prosthetic third leg.

"He is not a Zecronisian," Elypticus exclaimed.

"Not so loud, my friend," Garan cautioned. "I am, and forever shall be, a Cetrone."

"Cetrone," Harris gasped. "I don't believe this."

"Believe it, Lord Belmundus and be grateful that I am what I am."

That certainly explained how Garan managed to join them in the cell. Garan thrust his hand into a side pouch and withdrew two sausages.

"*Mongerhide*, anyone?"

Elypticus nearly tackled Garan, while Harris politely took it, slowly bringing it to his nose and sniffing. Then he savored a bite, lovingly.

Divine.

"Bless you, Garan," he said. "You wouldn't happen to have a flagon of *brantsgi* shoved up your ass too? Hell, I'd settle for *bolingara* . . . if it ain't too sour."

"The drink is in *the Cabriolins.*"

"*Cabriolins?*" Elypticus muttered between chews. "Where have you parked *Cabriolins?*"

"Safely and hidden, young sir," Garan replied. "We have little time for discussion. We must hasten to these vehicles and be off before the tormentors come to claim you."

"Now would be a good time," Harris said.

He chomped a piece of *mongerhide* and wolfed it. Without liquid, it was tough. Nonetheless, his taste buds celebrated in cut time.

"I do not understand, my lord," Elypticus said. "Will we cut through the bars and join you on the roof?"

"The walls, young sir," Garan explained. "The walls are our means of escape."

"I do not see how."

"Elypticus, trust him," Harris said. "It's an old Cetrone trick, only I've never seen it performed as a three-person daisy chain."

"It will work with ten," Garan said. "There is risk. Not in the numbers, but in the walls' thickness."

"I don't understand," Harris said.

Garan offered him another *mongerhide* stick, which Harris greedily took, and then divided it, giving half to Elypticus, who bowed.

"The walls you have traversed until now, my lord," Garan explained. "Those walls went directly through. These prison walls do not face the outside."

"You mean it'll be a long trip."

"Considerably."

Harris touched Elypticus' forearm.

"This wall business is not pleasant at the best of times, lad. I'm just warning you. It might prove miserable."

"It is better than remaining here, my lord."

"You say true."

"True," Garan confirmed. "But should we fail, you both may become a permanent part of Gurt architecture."

Harris sighed.

"We'll chance it. Will everything pass through?" He touched his *Columbincus*. "Because this thing's as dead as a fly on a toad."

"You need *the Columbincus*, my lord. How else can you drive *a Cabriolin?*"

"But how . . ."

"One step at a time," Garan said. "If you should melt into *the kaybar*, there will be one fewer step to consider."

He shrugged, and then extended his hand. Harris took it. Elypticus still appeared puzzled, but Harris grasped his *Danuwa's* hand.

"Prepare for a shock," Harris announced. "Swallow hard and gird your loins."

Elypticus dropped the remains of *the mongerhide,* and then clenched his thighs. He was as ready as ever he would be, no doubt.

"I say farewell to *the Katorias*," Elypticus whispered.

"Goodbye, Tarhippus," Harris shouted. "You motherfucker."

Garan grinned, and then jumped through *the kaybar* wall, taking his three-person daisy chain with him.

2

Harris grasped tightly to two different hands during the passage. If he had let go of either — disaster. The usual weight of traveling through solids sat on his chest like a herd of *Tippagores.* His eyes itched, and then pained. He could see nothing except the tan texture of the substance which tried to smother him. These were precisely the sensations he had experienced when Yustichisqua pulled him through *the Yudolayda Asdodi.* But this trip seemed endless. As the thick flood of walls pounded him, he tried to call to Elypticus, but Harris' mouth was stopped — his tongue petrified. He wasn't sure whether he was breathing. He could be dead, except he felt the changes in contour — twists and turns through the several buttresses, which held *the Katorias* secure on its foundations. Harris wanted to scream, but his throat had turned to sandpaper. His skin seemed to emulsify, first bubbling and then, like mortar, began to set and harden. The thought terrified him.

I'm turning to stone. I'll be a memorial plaque to a foolish attempt to escape Tarhippus' clutches.

He couldn't feel the hands. They were gone. Or were they? His fingers pained, like frost biting knuckles in the dead of January, and then, like popping corn on bare palms over an open fire, they stung with agony. Suddenly, the frozen hand melted and he could feel Garan's grip. He sensed a cessation of pressure. He recognized the end — a good end.

Release.

Harris emerged into sunslight, falling to the pavement, still anchored to Elypticus' grasp. *The Danuwa* flew out also, but staggered, vomiting his *mongerhide* feast. He crashed to the ground.

"Elypticus," Harris cried.

Garan attended *the Danuwa*, shaking the lad's limp arms.

"He is alive, my lord," Garan said. "But he has the bending sickness."

"The bends?" Harris said, alarmed, struggling to Elypticus' side, shaking him. "He needs depressurization."

"He needs liquid," Garan said, and then scurried to *the Cabriolins*, parked beside a utility shed.

Harris twisted about. He noticed they had landed in an abandoned alley, perhaps one used to haul waste — not a place for a respectable Yunocker, much less *a Fantin*. He put his ear to Elypticus' chest and listened for his heart. It still beat, but not strongly . He lifted *the Danawu's* head as Garan came with *an awidena* skin of *brantsgi*, raising it to Elypticus' lips and squeezing the green liquid into his mouth, gushing. Elypticus didn't swallow at first, but then he choked. *The brantsgi* sprayed, and the lad opened his eyes.

"My lord," he gasped.

"You'll be fine, Elypticus," Harris muttered.

He grabbed *the brantsgi* skin and gave him another swig, and then listened to for a heartbeat again. Stronger.

"I thought I'd lost you."

"I am ill," Elypticus grunted.

"Will you puke again?"

Elypticus shook his head, and tried to rise. He wasn't successful. Harris helped him, but was shaky from the transference through the *kaybar*.

"Garan."

Garan grabbed Elypticus' legs.

"Take his shoulders, my lord. Get him to *the Cabriolin*."

Harris struggled. Between them, they managed to lug *the Danuwa* to *the Cabriolin*. They slung him in. Harris breathlessly sat at its base.

"Now what?" He touched his *Columbincus*. "I'm out of gas. How do we power these suckers up?"

Garan bowed, and then darted into the second *Cabriolin*. He hopped back, holding a sight for sore eyes.

"*Tony*?" Harris gasped, reaching for *the brashun blade.*

"Take its hilt, my lord."

Harris touched it, and sparks flew through his fingers. He felt an energy surge. When he grasped the hilt and balanced the sword over his legs, his *Columbincus* came to life.

"*Adadooski*," he said. "But how did you get this?"

"Your *Taleenay* has been busy."

Harris shuffled to his feet.

"Yustichisqua? Where is he? Is he here?"

"No, my lord. But his presence will be felt."

"Is he safe?"

"Very much so. He is with the keepers of *the sustiya*. I paid them a visit. Your *brashun blade* was in Yustichisqua's care. He knew you would need it, so he asked me to use it wisely and well." Garan bowed. "I have."

Garan hopped into the other *Cabriolin*, and returned holding Elypticus' brooch.

"You can't touch that," Harris said.

Garan gave him the fish eye.

"I am surprised you say so, Lord Belmundus — you, a subscriber to change. You, the iconoclast."

"Iconoclast?"

"A word I learned in *the Dodingdaten*. Besides, we must be parted. The young *Danuwa* cannot operate his vehicle. So, if you please, my lord, take your *brashun blade* and touch it to this brooch."

Garan snapped *the Columbincus* on his silver tunic. Harris thought it an odd bauble for a wiry Cetrone, but someone needed to carry Elypticus to safety. The brooch shone.

"I'll follow you," Harris said.

"No, my lord. I said we must be parted. You must depart Montjoy."

Depart Montjoy. Where would I go? Coney Island? Not likely.

"What the fuck are you talking about, Garan? I've nowhere to go."

"Yes, my lord. You do."

"Not up the hill. I don't think *the Ayelli* will forgive me, however much sympathy I've garnered. Tappiolus'd have my hide back in *the Katorias.*"

"Not back to *Mortis House.*"

"*The Kalugu?*"

That was an idea — to *the sustiya* and to brother and sister and Little Bird.

"No, my lord. You must go east."

"East?" He stopped to think. "You mean west."

"I mean to the Forling and beyond."

"The Forling?"

"You must disappear. I shall take the young *Danuwa* to my ship. No one will seek him there. He shall sail to *the Finistrians.*"

Harris trembled. The thought of the Forling — that terrible desert, had as much promise as *the Katorias.*

"What will I do in the Forling?"

"Nothing. Cross it. Head for the Spice Mountains."

"Cetronia?"

Garan patted Harris' hand, and then bowed low.

"You must leave now, my lord. They have discovered your escape."

"How do you know that?"

A klaxon sounded.

"It shall be some time before they realize you are outside the walls. They will think you crept through a hidden pipe and still wander *the Katorias*. But soon they will realize their mistake."

"They're stupid," Harris replied, thinking of Littafulchee.

"They are, but not so stupid as you might think,"

Harris peeked in on Elypticus, who glanced up weakly.

"My lord," Elypticus said. "I have failed you."

Harris leaned down and kissed his *Danuwa's* forehead.

"We may never meet again, Elypticus, but listen to me. If ever I were to choose a son, you would be the one."

Elypticus smiled dimly. Harris fought back tears, and then quickly went to his *Cabriolin*. He tossed *Tony* in. He saw a sack fastened to the cab.

"Supplies," Garan said. "Packed by your *Taleenay's* hand."

"Yustichisqua? I guess he still has my back."

"He shall always do his part on your behalf, my lord." Garan bowed. "Power up and get to the Forling gate before it shuts for midday curfew."

"How can I thank you, Garan?"

"Live, my lord, and when I see you next, I shall demand a princely sum."

Harris saluted *the Gucheeda*, and then touched his hand to *the Columbincus*. *The Cabriolin* revved and lifted cleanly away from the shed. Harris sniffed the free air and fled.

3

The klaxon could be heard throughout Montjoy, alerting the citizenry to an escape. *The Praeters* poked with their spyglasses from perches on their estates. *Majorin* stopped business, emerging onto the street, looking in all directions. *Minorin* donned helmets and did their civic duty, policing alleyways and cubbies. *The regulati* were assembled, patrolling every street.

Harris found his way blocked at every turn, so he eased *the Cabriolin* into the shadows of *the Kaleezos*, hoping Trone curiosity would stir nothing more than gossip. Still, he hovered in the shadows, moving forward too slow to fulfill Garan's directive — getting to the Forling Gate before the curfew.

The Gurts from *the Ryyve Aniniya* mined the desert's edge — a fine red sand called *kowlinka*, a principal ingredient for a translucent material akin to glass. The work was dangerous, the heat debilitating and *porcorporians* occasionally emerged to snap up a meal. More dangerous were *the gasuntsgi*, vampire rabbits which poked their fangs from dens, like gophers, thriving on every blood-type from Gurt to Yunocker. These hazards caused the Gurts to work in three short shifts from mid-morning to midday surrounded by *regulati* guards, who patrolled the site (also in shifts), blasting the fauna with their *Sticks*. It was considered the worst duty for a Yunocker — almost punitive. When these shifts changed, the Forling Gate was opened, and then immediately shut. With the last shift came a curfew, the gate remaining closed for the evening. It was this curfew Harris had to beat. With klaxons blaring and every Yunocker in Montjoy on the alert, the task seemed doomed to failure.

Harris drifted stealthily past the wall of a prominent *Praeter* estate. Traffic was sparse here, the privilege of residency. A service lane ran adjacent to the wall. No *minorin, majorin* or *regulati* kept vigil along this path. Harris accelerated, jetting beside the wall. He could see the Montjoy defenses in the distance — a high parapet which secured the city from the desert critters. He could even feel the heat wave beyond it. By his calculations, the lane ended at a tangle of *kaleezos* which hugged the battlements. If he could reach these beehive dwellings undetected, he might approach the Forling gate at an unexpected angle. *Surprise.* He had been to the gate on his many tours and knew two guard towers flanked it.

"Great," he muttered. "It'll be like diving into a tea cup from a high board."

He considered returning to *the Yuyutlu* boundaries, leaving fortress *Yuganawu* at his back. Perhaps Garan could find another berth on his ship for a wayward consort. But a *Didaniyisgi* on the lam would draw attention to *the Wudayleegu* and Garan's grand caravel would be sunk in the harbor.

"No," he muttered. "He's done enough. I won't compromise him."

Harris girded his shoulders, slapped his *Columbincus* and prepared to make a turn at the *kaleezos*. Had it not been for the resident *Praeter*, who hung from his widow-walk with a powerful telescope, Harris would have gone undetected. But a new klaxon and a red flare marked his progress.

"Shit," he said, banking around *kaleezo* roofs.

The Trones peeped, their eyes wide — their mouths shut. Had they known who he was? Did they know he had been the one who broke the Treaty of Parazell? Harris didn't have time to sort friend from foe. He angled past eaves and clipped gutters, emerging onto the wide plaza before the gate. Two *regulati* patrols approached — one from behind and one from across the plaza. It wouldn't be long before they'd be shooting, unless they had orders to capture him alive. Why deprive General Tarhippus of his fun? Harris could think of several reasons.

He turned sharply. The gate was closing as a line of thunderstruck Gurts and their escorts returned from *the kowlinka* fields. Harris pumped his *Columbincus,* accelerating. He saw the guards in the two towers alert to his approach. They hastened to close the gate. They signaled one another, hitting the lock buttons with ever-increasing desperation.

The two patrols merged. Harris braced for a *Stick* blast. He wondered how it felt, but decided he preferred ignorance on that score. However, *the regulati* didn't fire. Harris was correct in his assumption, evidently. Tarhippus wanted to flay him alive — so much more entertaining than explaining to Lord Kuriakis why the prisoner had escaped and the inquisition went astray.

Suddenly, *a Stick* fired, but not from the rear. It blasted the left tower, confusing Harris. Why would the Gurt escorts fire at the guard in the left tower? Then another blast struck the right tower. The gate froze, both guards incapacitated. Harris didn't look a gift horse in the mouth. But as he approached the exit, another series of blasts pelted the towers. Then he saw a rogue *Cabriolin* — one he recognized.

"Parnasus," he muttered, and then shouted. "Parnasus."

"Hurry, my lord," Parnasus replied, shooting over Harris' head at the approaching patrols.

The patrols finally came alive, their *Sticks* blazing. Harris looked for his *Stick*, but the holder was empty. He only had *Tony* and he wasn't sure how to fire it. Cut, yes. Slice, definitely. However, although he saw Cosawta blast away with *the brashun blade*, this art still eluded Lord Belmundus.

Parnasus scaled the heights, his *Cabriolin* taking a few hits. But he rushed the tower.

"Hurry, my lord," he shouted.

Harris knew. Parnasus was attempting to man the gate controls.

The patrols closed in. If Harris didn't manage to get through the gate now, he'd be so much Spam in a can. He girded his ass cheeks and pumped his *Columbincus* again. *The Cabriolin* surged. He held on tightly. The space between the portals was spare, so Harris needed to focus. He leaned forward, blasts now flying over his shoulder as if, short of killing him, *the regulati* wanted to wing him — a painful deterrent, keeping him alive and kicking for their sadistic chief.

Gurts went prostrate before the approaching horde. *The regulati* escort still seemed confused, but two got their act together and pursued Parnasus. *The Danuwa* fired an amazingly accurate shot, knocking them from their *Cabriolin*, sending them plummeting. Their vehicle slammed into the gate, shattering.

It came to this. Harris slipped through the gate by the narrowest of margins. The patrol needed to cut their speed if they were to avoid a pileup. In single file, they could slip through the gate and pursue him. That was the anticipated scenario. Then the gate began to close. *The Danawu* had achieved his goal.

"Good work, Parnasus," Harris muttered, but then choked on these words.

As Harris heard *the regulati* scream when they crashed into the gate, he imagined Yunocker carnage — flies caught in a zapper, falling into a metallic heap, entertaining the Gurts. Still, he trembled at the thought of brave Parnasus. He would be shot down or captured — sacrificed like *an awidena* in a mutton stew. It would be a miserable end for a brave warrior.

Harris stared ahead, the dry desert heat blasting his brow. The red sand — *the kowlinka*, was kicked up in a whirlwind. He sensed many eyes — *porcorporian, gasuntsgi* and even the dangerous *noya tludachi*, watching him as a moveable feast served on a speedy platter. The prospects leveled — *the Katorias versus the Forling*. However, he preferred nourishing an ugly *porcorporian* than giving Tarhippus a single moment's satisfaction.

"Poor, brave Parnasus," he muttered, tears forming, but drying before they could run. "I must have done something good to deserve the likes of you."

He bowed his head — silence before him — silence behind him. He had escaped General Tarhippus' cruelty. Would he fare better in the Forling, an unforgiving land? Silence. A telling silence. Despite the hungry eyes, the silence told him true. He was alone and might have discovered the last round-up — a tomb for Lord Belmundus.

"All curtains come down," he mused, and sighed.

But the only audience listening wanted to eat him for dinner.

Part IV
Cut, and Check the Gate

Chapter One

Oh, Home on the Range

1

Dizzy from the heat, Lord Belmundus jetted in a direct line into the red dust of the Forling. He had much on his mind and shut out the movement of *the porcorporians* beneath him. They shifted through the sand like silverfish — lethal silverfish, with lobster claws and tarantula jaws. He kept *the Cabriolin* as high as possible and steady in the crosscurrents. However, he had no confirmation of his direction, because the magneto on the vehicle's compass was missing indicators. Besides, east was west and south was north in this bass-ackward world. Who knew whether there was an equivalent to time zones or interfarn date lines?

Medians and longitudinal navigation was the least of Harris' worries. General Tarhippus would send a brigade after him. Why they hadn't lifted high over the gates and chased him when they had the chance was a mystery. But they were stupid, after all. Then he wondered why he didn't do the same. It could have been the swirls of *yuyenihi* — the razor-sharp barbed-wire used effectively in *the Yuganawu*. Still, he wanted to put many miles between him and the gate before the suns set and the soft glow of the three moons played their nocturne for the Forling's critters.

As the wind played in his hair, a terrible thought struck him. He was alone. It was the first time he was pitched into solitude since *the Plageris*, and even that was short-lived, having the company of the blue-headed stupid-birds and the ballet of *the misancorpus* — until Arquebus showed up with his Bardian welcoming speeches. Nothing balletic struck him watching the dunes ripple with *the porcorporians*. No consort from the Old Vic was on the horizon with a rendition of Prospero. Hell, there was no horizon, but there never had been in Farn, so why should he expect one now? But the sudden thought of being a solitary sentient on an expanse of blowing red sand was frightening. Then, his *Columbincus* flashed and *the Cabriolin* choked — a chug-chug that didn't bode well. In fact, he recalled such a chug-chug on his last visit to the Forling. Then he attributed it to sabotage. What were the chances of driving another lemon? What were the chances

Lord Tappiolus found this one vehicle in a thousand to remove the spark plugs?

"Shit," Harris said, as *the Cabriolin* descended.

It didn't stop. Lower, it leveled off and flew better, but it slowed to a rate which wouldn't beat *the suns-set* or a *porcorporian's* claws. It wouldn't outrun *a gasuntsgi* at a rapid hop. He released his hand from his *Columbincus* and *the Cabriolin* shut down. At least, he knew why it quit now. He let it hover to the ground. He gazed in every direction expecting to see the desert rush at him — *noya tludachi* galloping with their saber teeth raised for the kill. He anticipated a lobster claw — hold the drawn butter, if you please.

His hand went to *Tony's* hilt. He might not know how to fire this thing like a light-saber, but he had had enough training on the set of *The Magic Planet* to slice more than bologna. Then his sight fell on *the korinkle* — the knapsack.

"Let's see what my Little Bird packed for me," he murmured, squatting in the cab.

The *korinkle* was laced tightly. Beside it were three *awidena* skins filled with what he hoped would be water, but what was probably *brantsgi* — better for the cold Forling nights. Inside the sack were assorted trays, sealed with wax. There was an ample supply of *mongerhide*. Although tasty, it was easier on the entry than on the stinging exit. Three loaves of *bupka*, the good kind with *prysyst* and *mollicops*. He held another container to his eye.

"*Jipjipjiptipu*," he said in a high-pitched tone. Tasty *fungimus* — Zecronisian mushrooms. "I'll be farting for an eternity."

Other containers were packed with *yukayosu*, *asdoyuwi*, *suweechi* and the delicious *stewganasti*. Whatever these things were, Harris would need them to stay alive. He then spotted two smaller tubs, one marked with a black symbol he recognized — *for sleeping*, and the other, a red sigil — *for waking*. He opened the first and sniffed.

"*Sqwallen*," he said. "Old man, what were you thinking?"

Then he paused. The evil *jomar-quillerfoil* porridge was a drug, after all. It had its uses. The other tub was the antidote, *pilocarpinus*, although Harris couldn't figure out how one administered the solution when under the influence of the problem. He tucked them away in *the korinkle*. Then his hand hit something wedged in the bottom — a cloth-wrapped object. He pulled it out, letting the outer shell fall aside.

"*Zulus*," He grinned. "These'll come in handy, I bet."

Then he regarded the cloth — a cloak, and no mere shoddy poncho, but a cloak coated with *jupsim*. He also found two *borripsuns*. He checked them out, flashing them about the cab. He stood. He could use these now, because night was spreading her pall across the Forling. The dunes became silhouettes against the emerging moons as first *Solus* disappeared, and then *Dodecadatamus*. Nothing else was revealed. Perhaps the fauna of the Forling retired for the night. Somehow he doubted that. He thought he saw the flashes of eyes bouncing back in *the borripsuns'* glow. He raised *Tony*, which illuminated the periphery. Dozens of critters scurried. They didn't look like anything he had seen in daylight or in his research at *the Cartisforium*. He shuddered.

"It's gonna be a long night," he said, and turned *Tony* off.

2

Long and cold. The temperature dropped at least thirty degrees in a matter of a half-hour. *The Didaniyisgi* wasn't dressed for the climate change. He shivered for at least an hour until he resorted to *the jupsim* cloak. He was immediately warmed. The miracle Gurt coating, which nature hardened against moisture, proved an excellent insulation. What other properties did it have? Was it *porcorporian* proof? Could it stop a saber tooth at a single bound? He was thankful for the restored warmth and hunkered down in *the Cabriolin*.

He slept in fits and starts, but just when sleep settled in, it was shattered by merciless cries — banshees stirring the souls of the dead. More probably, *the tludachi* found a *night-whatever* or a *nocturnal-what's-it,* something with three heads and grisly gills — greatly roaring in the dark, howling to the moons in its final death-cry. Harris also heard footsteps — thunderous, sand shaking movement. He was tempted to pop up and shine *a birrupsun* across the desert, but decided he'd rather not know. Perhaps it was large enough to keep him safe, unless its appetite exceeded its curiosity. In that case, he wouldn't much worry. He'd be digested all the same. Finally, wrapped in the cloak, thanking Yustichisqua for the forethought, he dozed into a deep dreamless sleep.

He stirred in the morning chill, *the jupsim* cloak now cooling him as insulation does. He wasn't sure where he was — the previous day's events swallowed in the recesses of his mental state. No dreams — just a vacuum of the body shutting down for repairs, the brain drifting to sleep like a damaged *Cabriolin*. He was numb, but did feel a sharp pain in his foot, which he thought odd, because he wore *borabas*. He glanced down the length of the cloak at his exposed foot. He saw his toes — the lower portion of his boot torn away. Clamped on his foot was a pugnacious creature, sucking on his instep.

"Fuck," Harris screamed, shaking his foot.

The damn thing — *a gasuntsgi*, didn't pause, but chomped down in a different place. Harris yelped, kicking with his other foot, a fully-*borabas'd* foot with heavy *phitron* soles. The grotesque rabbit screeched, first in pain, and then threateningly. But it let go.

Harris grabbed *Tony,* and with a single swipe, decapitated the beast, blood (probably his own) spraying the cab thickly. Harris kicked the creature out. But when he tried to stand on *the gasuntsgi*-bitten foot, he collapsed — the foot numb, as if injected with an anesthetic, which it probably was. He glanced around the edge of *the Cabriolin*. He was surrounded by *gasuntsgi*. They hopped toward the vehicle, their vampire fangs ready for a drink.

"Christ," he muttered. "There's not enough of me to satisfy them all. I'll be dead in twenty minutes."

He felt light-headed, but managed to hop on his one foot to the control panel. He touched his *Columbincus*, which responded like a charm. *The Cabriolin*, however, wasn't as responsive. It revved, choked, lifted a few inches from the sand, and then set back down. Harris tried again, this time managing to move forward, but not up. He could have been driving an old Volkswagen — one trailed by the Halloween bunnies. Still, there was enough oomph to distance himself from the vampire crew.

"I'm glad they don't fly like bats," he thought, and then banished the thought from his mind, thinking the ears might convert into wings. Thankfully not.

The foot pained him, and yet it was numb. He hoped these funny bunnies weren't toxic, although there was a good chance they were. Even so, if he didn't stop the bleeding, he'd be in *la-la land* soon. So he chanced landing over the next dune. He glanced about for his pursuers, but they had given up — he hoped.

Harris cropped to the side of *the Cabriolin*, examining the foot. Two sets of punctures were evident, and both oozed red and black. The red was his, but the black was *the gasuntsgi's* contribution. He dove into *the korinkle* and unwrapped a loaf of *bupka*. He bit down and chewed (he was hungry and couldn't help himself). He reached for *an awidena* skin and drank some *brantsgi*.

"*Wisgi,*" he said, smiling. "Bless that Garan."

But *wisgi* was a good thing now, and not to drink. He used the bread wrapper to wipe the wound, and then sopped up the rest with *the bupka*. He wasn't that hungry after all, and there were priorities. He then took *a mongerhide* stick, bit down and poured *the wisgi* over his foot.

"Man, that hurts," he gasped. "Motherfucker and the bunny you hopped in on."

He bit *the mongerhide* in twain, and then carefully replaced it in *the korinkle*. The foot throbbed.

"How am I supposed to get across this fucking desert like this?" he muttered. "I might as well hitch a ride on the first *porcorporian* I see and let it perform the amputation."

Then he had an idea. Well, not an idea, but an instinctive reaction. He raised *Tony* and struck his *Columbincus*. Then he touched *the brashun blade* to the punctures. They clotted and the blood stopped flowing.

"Thank God."

But the pain was unyielding, and the numbness unabated. Then another idea dawned on him. He shuffled through *the korinkle* for *the sqwallen*. He opened the top. He wasn't sure whether he should use it as a poultice or to swallow it. The stuff was vile and narcotic. He sniffed it and choked. Then he espied the sigil — *for sleeping*. Sleeping was the last thing he wanted to do, so he took a glop of *sqwallen* and spread it over his foot.

"Looks like pigeon shit," he muttered.

But he felt better instantly. He couldn't imagine what the stuff did to the innards, but he did. He had seen the poor souls of *the Banetuckle*. He hopped to his feet, and headed for the control panel. He pounded his *Columbincus* and touched the controls. *The Cabriolin* spluttered, rising slightly, flickered, and then gave up the ghost.

3

Harris was not in an analytical mood. Why *the Cabriolin* ceased to function was not in his ken. He wasn't a Gurt mechanic nor did he have a driver's manual. There was no glove compartment in the thing with a step-by-step, and no Farn equivalent to AAA. He didn't panic. He had anticipated this contingency when he first landed the contraption last night. But the prospects didn't delight him either. He sighed and stared numbly out at the Forling — dune after dune of unforgiving red sand. He shrugged. He would have got out and kicked the damn thing, but with his foot in this condition, it would be self-defeating. He went to *the korinkle* and dove into the bottom.

"It's *zulu* time."

Harris was glad Yustichisqua had the foresight to include a pair of these, but now that he tried to slip them on, he was confronted by a left foot which had swelled to a considerable size. *Zulus* weren't *one size fits all* like *the borabas*. He managed to strap on the heel, but the instep flapped loose. Once engaged, the thing would flip-flop at will and he'd be on his ass in a flash. He studied the problem, thinking that the best way to get the things on was to chop off his toes. He shook his head and grinned at the thought. It was improbable, but when push came to shove, he might need to shove. Then he looked to *the birrupsun* wrappers — cloth and just the right length to twist into ropes. So he tied one to his instep, giving it a tight yank. Even with *the sqwallen* and *the wisgi*, the pain shot up to his kneecap.

"If I live to tell Mom about this one, it won't be clean," he muttered.

He completed the task and switched on the *zulus*. He managed to hover upright, the Gerry rigging staying in place. He filled *the korinkle* with as much loot as he could, grabbed *Tony* and slung *the awidena* skins over his shoulders.

"Perhaps I'll make it to Cetronia by Christmas," he said, and zipped out of *the Cabriolin*

Zulu travel was slow, by comparison, but slow-go was better than no-go on any day. The heat raged now, so he adjusted the cloak to cover his head. *The jupsim* was insulation still — no air conditioning, but cooler by any standard. The dunes were high. Without *the zulus*, he would have taken all morning just to clear one. As it was, the weight of *the korinkle* and the skins kept him low to the ground. In fact, as he reached the crest, he wasn't sure he'd clear it. He stopped to survey the landscape from here.

He sighed. Dune after dune and nothing more. No mountains in the distance and he was far from Montjoy's walls — a good thing perhaps, but it completed his solitary confinement. His foot ached and the slight hum of *the zulus* made his soles itch. He was thirsty, but didn't want to guzzle the wine or the booze, fearing depletion and perhaps unwanted drunkenness. Water's what he needed, because he sweated profusely, even under *the jupsim* cloak.

Down this dune and up the next and down and up — countless times. Each dune was much like the next. One thing absent were the critters. Perhaps he had ventured into a zone even the fauna shunned. As he pondered this, the answer came to him — all at once. He reached the bottom of a dune — a valley with many blind spots — boulders and scrub. He thought it would be a good time to rest, when from beneath him, a claw rushed up — *a porcorporian*, which had patiently waited for room service. If Harris was lucky, he could have veered aside and avoided the mandible, but no such luck. Surprise was complete and his foot — the bum left one, was caught in the creature's claw. *Agony.*

Harris tumbled over, the *korinkle* flung to the dunes and *Tony* tossed aside. *The awidena* skins crashed to the ground, splitting open, the wonderful liquor feeding the red sand. Harris choked back tears. He wiggled his foot, but it was snagged. He reached for *Tony*, but it was beyond him.

Dragged. *The porcorporian* tugged Harris, but he turned over on his back and, with his *phitron* boot, slammed the beast in the nose — if it was a nose. It winced, loosening its grip. Harris was still stuck, but another twist of his foot and the makeshift ties on *the zulu* fell away, leaving *the porcorporian* with *an aniniya* sandal, and nothing more, Harris scrabbled through the sand, reaching *Tony*. But *the porcorporian* attacked.

Harris stood, barely balancing on one foot, wielding his sword with both hands. He struck the thing, drawing green blood. It was maimed, but still determined to feed. It made a clicking sound — enragement, no doubt. Harris prepared to engage the thing again, but soon had double trouble. *Two tludachi* roared from the dunes. They galloped down, the red sand puffing before them, their saber teeth bared for the attack. Harris prepared to greet them with *Tony*. He struck his *Columbincus* trying to coax *the brashun blade* to shoot fire or brimstone or just a projection to scare the damn things away. He would have settled for old *I Luv Lucy* reruns. Nothing. He raised the sword. At least he'd get the lead *tludachi* and perhaps that would deter its partner. But as the beast approached, a shadow cast over them. A pair of tusks ripped through the lead *Tygger*, and a trunk dispatched the other. Another shadow stomped, and *the porcorporian* was pulverized beneath a gigantic stump.

Harris stood transfixed, his mouth agape, *Tony* loose in his hand. He looked up at this newcomer, his breath hitching, trying to determine whether this was still a contest for dinner. The pain in his foot flew up his thigh to his groin and his belly. He was overcome and tottered. The beast cast a wide shadow over him as he collapsed in a full-fledged swoon.

The Tippagore had arrived.

Chapter Two

Shades of Yorick

1

Pain's reality stirred Harris from another dreamless sleep. He had vague recollections of night's passage and another sunrise. His head wasn't clear. He sat in the sand, brushing his cloak and clutching first *Tony,* and then his *Columbincus.*

"*The korinkle,*" he stammered, and then swept the ground. Then he remembered. "Lost. And my *wisgi.*"

He had a raging thirst, which matched his utter pain — the foot throbbing, so much so he could see it pulsating, blackening under a roadmap of veins. He shook his head, took a deep breath, and then looked about. In the distance he saw the bull *Tippagore*, an apartment house-size beast, filtering the sand for nourishment, much like a whale filters plankton. Then he heard a grunt, turned and saw the bigger member of the species — the female, as tall as the bull, but like a freight train. Her tusks and horns blazed in the sunlight. At first Harris panicked, remembering the power of these beasts and their crushing defeat of the other critters. However, when his eyes met the female's, he knew. This was the Mama *Tippagore* — the one he had saved from Kuriakis' staff. She must have found herself another mate, because her sheltering shell protected a new crop of *Tippababies*. Yes, this was the one, and she remembered.

"Damn," Harris said, managing to rise painfully. He bowed, and the beast nodded. "You remember me, my lady. You do. Well, speak of casting bread upon the waters."

This loaf had returned ninety fold, like a freight train. She returned the favor, saving his life. He bowed again.

"I thank you."

The *Tippagore* nodded again and moo'd — a deep moan, melodious and befitting a Valkyrie, but Harris couldn't recall a sweeter *thank you* in his life. Suddenly, the pain shot to his knee and he keeled over, using *Tony* to keep him from plowing into the dune. His thirst overcame him and he began to choke. Madame *Tippagore* swayed in alarm and called to her mate, who answered with a booming hark. Then the female moved toward Harris. He thought she might accidentally crush him with good intentions. He pushed back, falling on his rump. Mama beast raised her foot, flipping her shaggy shell up, revealing the latest crop of pups, all drinking copious amounts of *Tippamilk*. Harris staggered. He couldn't believe the intent. She had extended an invitation.

Slowly, he crept, hopping on one *zulu*, dragging his *gasuntsgi* foot behind him like a Somerset-Maugham throwback. As he approached, he gazed into the beast's eyes — beautifully blue and tender. He shuffled beneath the moving tent. The babies had hooked their adolescent tusks to Mama's hide, and sucked her teats like lords and ladies at a banquet table. He glanced back at Mama, and she waggled her head — a clear *be my guest*.

Harris slipped beneath the shag, and once there, the rug engulfed him. He tried to find purchase to steady himself, but he didn't have tusks. But he did have *Tony*.

"Forgive me," he muttered, and then slid *Tony* into a flap of flesh. *Mama* groaned, but didn't evict him. "Gracious lady. Gracious, gracious lady."

Once in position, Harris hooked his arm around *Tony*'s hilt. The flap tightened. The stench was akin to the monkey house at the zoo, but he had tolerated the indelicate odor of *charpgris*, so he could survive this. He heard the array of babies sucking and moaning with delight. The thought of being weaned at his age was not so terrible considering his thirst. He felt for the nipple, *Tony*'s glow guiding his hands.

"Big," he murmured, squeezing, a warm thick trickle coursing his cheeks.

Harris kissed it, and then engorged this wonder of nature, which saved his life. Mama grunted, trumpeting her approval.

2

Swaying. Gentle swaying rocked this new found baby — this waif cast upon the Forling sea. As the cow trundled the red sands, like a ship upon the waves, Harris found comfort. Even his foot seemed to throb less. The drink had been sweet and he had had his fill of it. His stomach growled less, although a rumble danced through his bowels, perhaps in thanks. He still heard his brothers and sisters caressing Mama's wonders. He was in heaven. Perhaps he had died and this was heaven — his reincarnation as a beast. For the first time in some while, he dreamed — pleasant remembrances of his sister at play and his mother sitting on the pier in Santa Monica, the sun blazing over her floppy hat. Then the wind blew and she held the rim. *Humphrey*, she called. *Don't go too far. I'll take you on the Ferris Wheel in a moment, dear. Just let me rest here. The sun is warm and feels good. Be good for Mama. Be good.*

"I am good, Mama," Harris murmured, his eyes half-shut in *Tony's* glare. "Mama."

He had a new Mama now, at least for the moment — a day and a night, as she trundled over dune and valley, filtering the sand bugs and digesting the source of the sweet milk, which gave him life. He caressed her, kissing her, ashamed he had pierced her with his blade. But he felt stronger now, although he didn't want to leave her shelter, but he had no choice, because the swaying ceased, and the flap opened. The suns' glare near blinded him, but he released his legs and tumbled to the sand, taking *Tony* with him. His foot ached, but the pain seemed less. It was still useless to propel him far. He limped severely, but managed to come face to face with *the Tippagore.*

Both beasts were there — the cow mooing, the bull snorting. Harris bowed awkwardly to both. He couldn't thank them enough, nor would thanks be appropriate, because these creatures had returned a favor. But Harris wasn't sure if he was part of a new family or whether this was where the train stopped. Then, the bull reared and spit, a chunk of flesh falling at Harris' feet. He jumped back, nearly falling. It was a leg bone and haunch, chewed at the edges, but with enough skin and fur to be identified.

"*Tludachi,*" Harris muttered, cautiously approaching it.

The haunch had enough meat on it for a small village, but there was also rot. The bull nodded, and then turned away, seeking its meal of choice — microscopic critters in the sand. Harris speculated. *porcorporians* probably ambushed *the tludachi* and feasted until Mr. Tippagore chased them off, harvesting a haunch for his human guest. Harris crouched beside it. He reached under the skin, a mass of sinew and muscle — not appetizing. But he knew if he didn't imitate an animal and chomp down, he'd be dead by tomorrow. So, he knelt, bringing his face to the shin. He gagged, a stench so foul to conjure outhouse images. He started with a lick, his tongue stretched and trembling, if a tongue could tremble. The taste was metallic, but he had got to first base, so he

dipped his face close, his nose poking through the sinews. *Putrid.*
It was like diving head first into a dumpster. Then he counted
mentally to ten and bit down, ripping a chunk of flesh and skin and
fur, a flag waggling from his teeth. He chewed and choked. He
swallowed a little, the gristle stopping in his throat. He shook his
head, his eyes tearing. His chest heaved and he spewed the slop to
the red sand. He coughed and spit, holding his stomach.

"Great," he gasped. "Now I've got a belly to match my fucking
foot."

He looked back at the haunch and choked again. But as he held
his chest, *the Columbincus* shone brightly and, as if answering it,
Tony lit like a candle. Harris grasped the hilt, amazed at this action.
Then he plunged *the brashun blade* into the haunch, where it
smoldered. A few minutes later, he had roast *tludachi* and settled
down to a meal.

3

Harris never returned to *the Tippagore's* hospitable teat. Water
would be a problem, but he managed to wring enough blood from
the haunch to satisfy his needs for the evening. When *the
Tippagores* moved on, however, he packed as much meat as he
could carry, using *the jupsim* cloak as a makeshift *korinkle*, and
followed them. They were easy to lumber behind, because . . . they
lumbered. He hoped the bull might scavenge another meal for him,
but he supposed he could spear something with *Tony*, now that he
could get it to throw a flame. It wasn't much of a flame, but it was
a start and could boil water for tea if he should happen to meet
Thomas Lipton. If pressed, he was not above flirting with Mama to
see if the flap would rise and the milk bar open again. More
important, the Forling fauna stayed clear of *the Tippagores*.

A passing exigency, Harris tried to plan his next move, but it
wasn't promising. The beasts were slow and didn't seem to belong
to a herd. There was no *Tippatown* on this map. They were also
moving in a circle. *Solus* and *Dodecadatamus* indicated the
mountains were in the opposite direction. The priority, however,
was the foot. It flared at least ten times a day, forcing Harris to
pretzel in agony. But he did attempt to activate the sole remaining
zulu. At first, it was an idiot's effort, like riding a pogo stick in the
mud. But after two days of trying, Harris could stay aloft on one
zulu like the clown on the unicycle. Unfortunately, the minute the

rabbit-bitten foot flared, the pain would knock him asunder and he'd need to rest after each episode.

For four days, Harris semihovered and crunched behind *the Tippagores.* Then the liquids ran out and the thirst returned. The meat was gone the next day. He began to fall behind, and then he could no longer keep his balance on *the zulu.* He thought to use *Tony* to cauterise the wound. Cutting his foot off was an option. If he could withstand the pain and not pass out, cauterization would be a blessing. Then the pain would pass and so would this wild thinking. As he fell farther behind, his new family didn't wait. They accepted the inevitable. So did he. That night he saw eyes flashing in the darkness and knew the margin grew wide and the critters were here.

"So, this is how it ends," he said to the dawn, with no *Tippagore* in sight.

He glanced to the dunes. His thirst pinched his throat. His stomach belched fire. His foot went beyond pain. Then he saw the eyes — the flashing nearby. *Tludachi* or *gasuntsgi*, he wasn't sure. He knew it wasn't *a porcorporian.* Those bastards would come at him from beneath the sand and go for the belly. Perhaps it was a new terror. He stared at the eyes, and then realized they pulsed. His *Columbincus* seemed to answer them. His curiosity piqued. So he tried to get to his *zulu* and meet this new horror head on.

Surprisingly, *the zulu* held him and he slowly cruised to a cleft in the dune, the red sand shifting over a clump wedged beneath it. He hopped to the ground and crawled toward it.

"Damn," he stammered. "I know this."

He touched his *Columbincus*, and then scrambled to the mound, clearing it with his hands. He gasped, sitting back. It was a skeleton — rib cage. *Tludachi? A meal, perhaps?*

"No," he said. "Human and . . ."

His fingers pried through the cavity. He brushed the sand from the spine. A skull rolled to his knees. He stopped it from rolling down the dune. He lifted it briefly, and then thrust his hand into the rib cage, grasping the pulsating gem which he had mistaken for an eye. It was . . . *a Columbincus.* He raised it to the light, examining it.

"*The Eye* and two wavy lines," he muttered, and then looked to the skull. "So here you are . . . Lord Hierarchus." He sighed. "Here you are and . . . and here am I."

4

Harris drew the skull to his chest, hugging it close. He began to weep, rocking as he sobbed. He stared at the skeleton and the flickering of *the Columbincus* clutched in his hand. The road had ended. The desert's expanse had claimed him as it had his predecessor. He wondered what Hierarchus looked like, now as he embraced his skull. Images of youth and slyness overcame him. The impurities of existence washed through his soul. Here was a man with the spark, but the spark didn't keep him from this finality.

Harris rocked, gasping. He licked the tears from his cheeks and shook his head.

"I don't want to die," he muttered, the full force of the Forling pressing his mind. "I don't."

Then he looked to the sky and shouted:

"I'm only nineteen, for fuck's sake. I don't want to die. I don't . . ."

His throat clogged and he dropped the skull. Tears prevented him from watching it roll.

"I don't . . . I don't want to . . . die."

Then anger replaced abandonment and, despite the pain, he stood, wiping his nose and his eyes. He faltered, unsteady on the dune. He glanced down. The rib cage still flickered. He swallowed hard, and then poked through the cavity, where another object lay near the surface. He grasped it and yanked. Glowing in his hand was *a brashun blade*, a twin to *Tony*.

"His sword," Harris stammered, still sniffing. "Much good it did him."

Still, he raised it to the sky as if to pierce the suns.

"I shall call you *Hierarchus*, doomed though I be."

His hand trembled. He glanced at the second *Columbincus* again and decided to snap it beside his own. The clasp was sticky, but he had acquired the knack, and clasped it beneath its twin. Then both *Columbincus'* flashed. He had never seen such a reaction from his. *Tony* also flashed, as did *Hierarchus*. Suddenly, Harris was spun about like a firecracker, falling to the sand. He retrieved the second sword, because he had dropped it, and when he scrambled for it, the brooch ceased to glow. However, he no longer wore two *Columbincus'*. Instead, he had an enormous sapphire-colored gem pulsating on a single brooch — a double stone. The prospects scared him, fearing he had somehow polluted his own lifeline. Then he remembered he hadn't much life left. He sat with a thump beside the remains of his predecessor and looked to the sky again. The dust had kicked up and visibility dwindled. A glimmer of hope crossed his mind and he longed for his surrogate family — *the Tippagores*. So he rolled to his knees, secured his scant truck and switched on *the zulu* to begin a painful descent. When he passed the skull, he felt like kicking it like a soccer ball, but he hadn't a free foot for it.

5

The sand kicked up furiously. Harris wrapped his cloak about his head, covering his mouth, Bedouin-fashion. He couldn't stay aloft on *the zulu*, so he walked or hopped or hobbled. The wind howled. He expected a claw to pop from beneath the sand and do him in, but perhaps *the porcorporians* preferred fair-weather hunting. If the critters didn't get him, his hunger or the infection would. Then he looked skyward to whatever sky could be seen.

"Shit," he muttered.

He saw the outline of *a terrerbyrd.*

"No wonder the critters are in hiding. And I don't even have a boot."

The thing flew low, and he wasn't sure it was *a terrerbyrd*, because, to his faulty knowledge, these reptiles were native to *the Plageris*. But perhaps this was a cousin — *a horrorbyrd* or *a sandy flicker-fucker*. It cast a significant shadow, but passed him. He tried to follow its course, but it disappeared beyond the next dune. His foot flared and he counted to ten, waiting for the agony to pass. When it did, he shuffled slowly up the dune, but visibility was appalling. He sighed and trundled on. Then he saw them — *the Tippagores,* or the outline of a big backside.

"Thank God," he muttered.

He moved forward, but the big butt disappeared. *A mirage?* It was bound to happen. He looked again. The globular ass of the beast drifted in and out of view. He was sure it was a mirage, because it had psychedelic coloring — a tapestry of stripes in the colors of the rainbow.

"Foot gone. Eyes failing. Brain fried."

He switched on *the zulu*. If *the Tippagore*s were ahead, he'd catch them faster this way. But when *the aniniya sandal* revved, it tipped him forward and he crashed to the sand, his face slamming to *the kowlinka*. He spit out the grit and began weeping again. The fates had conspired to keep him alive to play with his soul. *Torture*. He didn't wish for death, but he certainly didn't want to dance with it. He crept forward, looking for the backsides.

"Gone."

His breath hitched. He waited for his life to flash before him like the pundits assured it would. He glanced up. The mirage appeared again. Color and silver flaring. The colors were brighter and the silver drew near. He blinked, but sand encrusted his eyes. Then the foot flared again and he knew it would be for the last time. He clenched his fists, and clasped his eyes shut. His teeth gnashed to counter the agony. But now his mind was going. He saw things — colors, *Tippagore* butts and shimmering silver. Now he heard voices on the wind. He expected this. He expected the calls of his sister and his mother. Next he'd hear the angels and see God, if forgiven his sins. The voices came. The voice. *One voice.*

"*Oginali.*"

Harris opened his eyes. A vision came toward him — silver blowing in the wind. A cloak . . . and a runner.

"*Oginali.*"

"Little Bird?" he whispered. He pushed up from the sand. "Little Bird?"

Yustichisqua hastened to him. Harris mistrusted this vision. *Mirages. Mirages.* But no. *The Tippagore* butt clarified in the distance. Not the backend of a beast, but . . . a balloon — the ferry.

"*Oginali.*"

"Yustichisqua," Harris rasped.

Little Bird rushed him, catching him as Harris fell again. Yustichisqua held him tightly, rocking him, brushing his hair through his fingers, weeping without shame or hesitation.

"I have come for you, *oginali*. Your Little Bird has come."

Harris grasped his double *Columbincus* and kissed Yustichisqua's hand. All pain subsided and, if he had died and this was heaven, an angel indeed had come.

Chapter Three

The Gananadana

1

Harris opened crusted eyes. *Startled.* He sweat, and yet had chills. He was tucked beneath a double cloak and felt the ground beneath him sway. It wasn't ground, exactly — matting, perhaps, but he was too startled to analyze it, because the face hovering above him was familiar, but unexpected.

"Tomatly?" he muttered.

"You are awake, my lord," the diminutive Cetrone gushed, and then turned his head aside and shouted. "He is awake. He is awake."

This call brought two other faces over Harris.

"*Oginali,*" Yustichisqua said, grasping Harris' hands, rubbing them. "You are still warm. You have fever."

Harris latched onto Little Bird's hands and tried to pull up.

"Not so fast, Lord Belmundus," carped the other attendee, the broad and muscular Cosawta.

"Where am I?"

"Not dead," the Seneschal said. "A fucking mess, as they say in *the Dodingdaten*, but enough remaining to reintroduce you to life."

"You are still ill," Yustichisqua said.

"Where am I, old man?" Harris panted.

"On *the Gananadana, oginali.*"

"The what?"

"My ship," Cosawta replied. "An airship with modified gondola, *jupsim* strength canopies, a true rudder and flying under full *waddly wazzoo* power."

"The ferry? A balloon?"

"Give that man a *seegar*," Cosawta drawled. "Welcome to my *Gananadana.*"

Harris tried to prop himself up again, but fell back to the mat, Yustichisqua adjusted the cloaking. Tomatly brought a rag and dribbled water over Harris' lips.

"Thank you," he gasped. "I've had nothing to drink except . . . well, you wouldn't believe it."

He grasped Yustichisqua's shoulders, and succeeded to push up, finally. He looked about the gondola — the basket he had seen in *the Kalugu*, only it was spacious like the poop deck of a sailing vessel. In fact, Cosawta gripped a steering mechanism — a rudder. Five *waddly wazzoos* formed a ring beneath the canopy, their light regulating the balloon's mass — a huge blimp, striped with the colors of the rainbow. Harris recalled seeing it through the red dust of the desert, thinking it was a *Tippagore* butt.

"Impressive," he muttered.

"It is the finest *Gananadana* to sail these skies," Cosawta said.

"Why don't you just call it a fucking balloon?" Harris mused, weakly.

"I may be Seneschal, but you are Lord Belmundus of *the Columbincus*. Your wish is granted." Cosawta yanked on the rudder. "But I say, it's the biggest fucking balloon to cross *the Yinaga.*"

He laughed, and then was joined by his sister, who stood beside him, perhaps to chide him for the language.

"My lady," Harris said, trembling. He felt dizzy and slumped back to the mat. "My lady. You're here?"

Littafulchee knelt beside him, her buckskin robes brushing his face. She touched his forehead, and then kissed it.

"I'm blessed," Harris said.

"You are, Lord Belmundus. We have been searching for you for many days and thought you were lost to us." She touched *the Columbincus*. "But this signaled us, even through *the kowlinka* winds. We know this sigil's call."

He clasped his hand over hers.

"My lady," he whispered. "Stay with me."

"Where am I to go? It is a fearsome drop from this gondola to the dunes."

"Dunes? We are still in the Forling?"

"Yes, *oginali,*" Yustichisqua said, a voice reminding Harris the world was still with him, although he would have enjoyed the sole company of the lady. "You must rest, if you are to recover."

"Your wound has festered," Littafulchee said. "Your fever has been high. Let us hope it has broken."

"Time will tell," Tomatly squeaked. "Time will tell."

"Time," Harris mumbled.

He still had pain in the foot, but less so.

"Time will take you to *the asi-asa*, where the medicine women will know the best course," Littafulchee said. She kissed his forehead. "Until then, you must slumber . . . my love."

He smiled as she moved away, sitting at Cosawta's feet as he steered *the Gananadana — the big fucking balloon*. Harris closed his eyes. He heard the hiss of *the waddly wazzoos* and Tomatly's high-pitched chatter. He grasped at the cloak, but found a hand. Was it *her* hand? No. He knew this hand, and he clutched it tightly.

"Thank you, old man," Harris whispered, and then drifted back to slumber.

2

The fever broke and Harris was hungry. He scrabbled from slumber, seeking Tomatly's rag, but was greeted with a gobblet of *brantsgi*. Ah, heaven in a cup. Yustichisqua had cold *hawiya yukayosu*. Harris bolted it faster than he had bolted the roast *tludachi* he had braised with *Tony*. This *hawiya* was the most delicious *pogo-pogo* he had ever eaten, although only the second time he had eaten it. He drank more, and then Yustichisqua fed him *hiloseegi* fruit slices. These were better than kissing, although they made him pucker. With each morsel, he felt strength coursing through his body. Yet, he was racked with pain — the weariness of running a marathon with the added dimension of a bum demon foot.

He paused, looking about the gondola again. The sky was different — green.

"*Yichiyusti*," he muttered. "He stirs. Kuriakis stirs."

"He does that," Cosawta bellowed from the rudder. "Your escape has probably put him in a shitty mood."

"Not anger, surely?" Harris said. "I'm his Boots."

"Boots or flutes," Cosawta replied. "He always has been a moody cuss, and I have known him longer than you."

Longer. A few thousand years longer.

"Little Bird, help me up."

"It is too soon, *oginali*."

"You're a doctor now?"

"When no medicine woman is near, I must be who I must be."

"Help me up."

Yustichisqua reluctantly lent Harris his shoulder. *Dizzy and unsteady*. Little Bird became his crutch. The foot, still useless, could have been a numb stump for all the good it did. Harris grabbed the edge of the gondola, and then sighed.

"What a glorious sight."

"It is just the fucking Forling beneath the big fucking balloon," Cosawta said, laughing.

"*The ganigonads*," Harris said, chuckling feebly under the circumstances.

The red *kowlinka* dunes spread for miles in all directions. Even from this height, and they were high, no mountains loomed in the distance. The gondola sported two fake wings and a *terrerbyrd* prow. So he hadn't imagined seeing a *terrerbyrd* when so desperate in the desert.

"It's bird shaped," he said, stating the obvious.

"It keeps the nasties at bay," Cosawta replied. "Scares the shit out of them. Besides, I like it. It appeals to my bizarre sense of humor."

Harris leaned over the side, gingerly. The gondola, larger than he had remembered it in the rain-soaked courtyard in *the Kalugu*, was weighed down with an undercarriage of cargo. As he gazed across the Forling, he spotted two massive creatures lumbering along. He recognized them at once.

"There they are," he stammered, pointing.

"They are *Tippagores, oginali*."

"They are family, Little Bird." He turned toward the rudder, where Littafulchee now stood. He nodded to her. "When I was attacked by *the porcorporian* and *tludachi, the Tippagores* killed them and then . . . and then they offered me their hospitality for days. I would have died long before you found me if it hadn't been for Mr. and Mrs. T'gore." He smiled, but then twitched. "Where's *Tony?*"

Yustichisqua pointed to a bale abutting the gondola. Both swords were stuck upright in the bale. Harris sighed with relief.

"Interesting question that begs," Cosawta said. "How does one go into the desert with one *brashun blade* and emerge with two. I have never known these things to have babies."

"And your *Columbincus*," Littafulchee remarked. "It has enlarged — doubled."

Harris touched his brooch, and then bowed.

"Only one sword is mine," he said, "and I fear I might have spoiled my powerful gemstone."

"How so?" Cosawta grumbled. "Worlds might turn on your brooch's power, sir. Take care with such things."

Harris brightened.

"I've learned one trick." He waggled his fingers and *Tony* shone. In fact, both swords illuminated.

"Good first step," Cosawta said. "Both are responding to you. Excellent."

Littafulchee approached, her hands extended. Harris reached for her and almost fell, but Yustichisqua steadied him. Harris grasped her hands, and she pulled him to the base of the rudder. He sat beside her, Tomatly hunkering nearby.

"Go on," Cosawta said, tugging at the rudder. "We have questions."

"So have I."

"You first, Lord Belmundus. We are not a puzzlement, but you are."

"Are you ready to tell us the sadness of your journey," Littafulchee asked, "and how you came so far, surviving with so little?"

"And so much," Cosawta said.

"Brother," Littafulchee chided. "We will wait, if we must. There are still many leagues to travel and Lord Belmundus has just stirred from his nightmare."

At the word *stirred* and *nightmare*, Harris looked to *the Yichiyusti* sky and thought of Kuriakis on his giant steed, brooding about the gardens near Greary Gree. He didn't want to upset his father-in-law. He never had a beef with the man, who was always indulgent when it came to Boots of Montjoy. He sighed.

"I suppose now is as good as any to tell you." He looked to Yustichisqua, who retrieved *the hiloseegi* slices. "No, old man. Come sit and listen."

Harris patted the gondola's planks and looked to the sky again.

3

The memories of his journey were painful, so he kept it short and simple. He told them about his escape, which they had helped engineer through Garan. But he also admitted his worry for Elypticus and Parnasus. He cursed *the Cabriolin* and its failure.

"*Cabriolins* cannot withstand *the kowlinka*," Cosawta explained. "You must fly high above the dust. If you fly low or land, you risk gumming the works." He raised his hands to *the Gananadana*. "Why do you think we cross *the Yinaga* in the big fucking balloon?"

Harris was glad to know this, because the loss of not one, but two *Cabriolins* in the Forling puzzled him.

"There is a solution," Cosawta said. "The Culpeepers and their *Seecoys*."

"Brother," Littafulchee said. "This is not the time."

Harris would have liked to hear more about the solution, but Littafulchee was correct, so he continued, relating the night of terror when *the gasuntsgi* chewed his boot and bit his foot. Yustichisqua was delighted Harris had used the contents in *the korinkle* for first aid, particularly *the bupka* as a medical mop. He expressed pleasure upon hearing the account of balancing on one *zulu*.

"I remember when you could not stand on two, *oginali*."

But then came the crisis. Harris spoke of *the porcorporian* and *the tludachi* and *the Tippagores*. He spoke of Mama *Tippagore's* nurturing care, but omitted the weaning and glossed over the affair with *the tludachi* haunch, except to say it was an advance on his knowledge of *Tony* — the heating and the eating of it.

"No wonder we could not find you," Cosawta said. "We knew you were crossing the Forling. Garan told us as much. But *Tippagores* traverse in wide circles. We might have passed your trail many times and mistaken it for the beast's normal track."

"I realized I was drifting and, when I did, I decided to follow the suns' course. But the desert denizens let me be when in the big ones' harbor."

"Wise decision," Cosawta said.

"I have never known these beasts to be kind," Littafulchee said. "You must have impressed them."

Harris looked to Yustichisqua.

"The female was the one we saved from the Pod."

"A good thing, *oginali*."

"Unfortunately, the weaker I became, my ability to keep up faded and ended. Then I saw . . ." He touched his *Columbincus*.

Littafulchee sighed and came close to him.

"You saw your *Columbincus*?" she asked.

"*His Columbincus.*" He pointed to the swords. "I found the remains of Lord Hierarchus."

Cosawta let loose the rudder. Littafulchee turned her face away. Harris sensed fear. Cosawta withdrew one sword from the bale, and held it high.

"Lord Hierarchus' sword?" Cosawta mused.

"I have named it after him."

"We need no reminder of him," Littafulchee said. "He had not the spark, as you do."

Harris grasped Yustichisqua's shoulder, pushing up and toward the rudder.

"What am I missing here?" he protested. "I found bones in the red dunes. They could have been anyone's bones, but they wore the sigil of Scepta Charminus, and when I drew it onto my cloak, it fused with my brooch forming a double *Columbincus.*"

"It would do that, Lord Belmundus," Cosawta said, tentatively. "The gems were mined from the same vein. They *are* the same. They would congeal, but . . . but the question is whether it is a fateful sign or a happy juxtaposition."

"I say, it is a sign," Yustichisqua said, his opinion put off by Littafulchee.

"I say, we must seek others to say." She leaned into Harris, her eyes steady, spooking him. "Lord Hierarchus did not care for anyone except Lord Hierarchus. He was not favored among the consorts and he tricked his Trone to bring him into *the Kalugu.* The Treaty was broken with no benefit. His Trone was thrown in *the Porias* and condemned to burning. Hierarchus' infraction was ignored, for fear the broken treaty would cause a distasteful incident between *the Yuganawu* and *the Ayelli.* "

"Hierarchus was as mercenary as . . . well, as mercenary as me," Cosawta said, brashly. "But I was born to it and mean to end the tyranny of *the Kalugu.* Hierarchus was looking for an exit portal and thought he found it when he learned about *the Dodingdaten.*"

"Is there an exit in *the Dodingdaten?*" Harris asked.

"Why should there be?" Cosawta replied.

"Garan has told me *the Fumarca* have come from the outlands against their will. Most men forced to such change usually buck against it."

"Like you, Lord Belmundus?"

"I buck," he said, and then looked to Littafulchee. "I buck, but in my quest to find a portal home, I wouldn't trample friends."

"Ah," Cosawta said. "Hierarchus had no friends. He pissed off Tarhippus and was hunted by *the regulati*."

"That's not a difficult accomplishment," Harris replied.

"Except Lord Tappiolus aided Hierarchus to flee across the Forling, where . . . where he was never heard from again."

"Until now," Harris said, reaching for the sword. Cosawta reluctantly gave it up. Harris weighed it in his hand, but it wearied him. "What will I do with two *brashun blades*?"

"Three," Yustichisqua said, unsheathing *gasohisgi*.

Cosawta laughed. Littafulchee raised her hand for silence. She listened, and then turned her head toward the west.

"They come," she muttered. "You shall see what can be done with three *brashun blades* and perhaps the mystery of a double *Columbincus* will be revealed." She grasped Harris' shoulders. "I pray to the purest light that you have not been polluted by Lord Hierarchus' soul. I pray your spark is still intact."

Tomatly hopped to *the Gananadana's* rim and pointed.

"They come, my lord. They come."

Harris squinted. In the distance — from the west that would be east, an array of *Cabriolin* flashes hung fire above the dunes. They had come, indeed.

Chapter Four

The Pursuers

1

"They pursue you, *oginali*."

"How can that be?" Harris mused. "Cosawta, how can that be? You said *Cabriolins* were sensitive to *the kowlinka*."

"They are, Lord Belmundus. And I say true, or as you say, speak good poop." Cosawta joined him at the rim. "These *Cabriolins* fly high above the perils. I give them credit, because they travel far and must be driven by weary men. But weary men are easily defeated."

"Unless there are two to *a Cabriolin*."

"You say true again," Cosawta replied, nodding at the prospects.

Harris felt a sharp pain in his foot and staggered backwards into Yustichisqua's arms.

"We must hide you, *oginali*."

"They do not know you are here," Littafulchee said. "*The Gananadana* is on a trading run. They will try to board us, but they cannot be sure you are here."

"They will not board us," Cosawta said. "They have no precedent to interfere with my run. Not one fucking *regulati* shall set *a zulu* aboard this bird, sister."

"I won't hide," Harris said, regaining his footing. "I won't allow them to attack my friends. I won't go peaceably."

"Nor should you," Cosawta said, glaring at his sister, and then at Yustichisqua.

Little Bird drew *gasohisgi* and flourished it, ready to defend Lord Belmundus, but Harris eased Yustichisqua's hand.

"I trust you and *the brashun blade*, old man, but I might just need you to prop me up while I try using this thing." He clutched *Tony*. "I'm pretty new at it."

"You shall do just fine," Cosawta said. "May I have the use of the other one?"

"*Hierarchus?*" Harris nodded. "I can barely illuminate one sword, much less two. Be my guest, although I have a feeling you didn't need to ask permission."

"Just being polite," Cosawta said, raising *Hierarchus* to his eye, and grinning. "Yes. This is the ticket. We shall ram the shit out of those bastards." He then waved his arms toward the canopy. "*The Gananadana* is constructed well and can withstand the onslaught. *Jupsim* coats her hide and resists most any volley within reason. Of course, mass assault might poke a hole in her and . . . well, it just takes one hole and down we go. *Porcorporian* food." He laughed. "Tomatly."

"Yes, my lord."

"Take us down."

"Yes, my lord. Down. Down."

Tomatly buzzed about on his *zulus*, flitting to the *waddly wazzoos,* lowering their temperament. *The Gananadana* began to descend.

"We're landing?" Harris asked.

"Not if I can help it," Cosawta said.

"The lower we are," Littafulchee explained, "the lower they must come and . . ."

"The more fatal *the kowlinka*," Harris said, understanding her drift.

"Just so," Cosawta said. "Besides, it is easier to shoot them in the ass than in the head. They will try to prevent it, no doubt, but the only way they can is to fly lower than us. Tomatly is a master big fucking balloonist. Is that not correct, Tomatly?"

"*The Gananadana* is my friend," he squeaked.

Harris smiled, despite the pain. Amusement replaced fear. However, he could see Yustichisqua was far from amused. Little Bird fretted, still clutching *gasohisgi* in a defensive stance. Harris eased to the matting. No sense of pushing his luck.

"Now," he announced, "if I could only get off a few practice shots."

"Not up, my lord," Tomatly called, as he adjusted the power sources. "You must take care of the canopy. The outside is coated, but the inside is not."

"Our Achilles heel," Cosawta said. "But *the regulati* do not know of it."

"They are brave, but stupid," Harris muttered.

"Still, brother," Litttafulchee added. "Even the stupid are lucky sometimes."

"You say true, sister." He looked to the green sky. "You say very true."

2

The squadron approached — a dozen Yunockers at first glance. Harris couldn't tell for sure. They spread into a solid formation as they approached *the big fucking balloon*. They arrogantly meant to overwhelm it by a frontal assault and a quick flanking movement. The strategy was as broadcast as hash. They slowed, taking their positions.

"You should hide, *oginali*," Yustichisqua whispered. "There is a trap door to the cargo bay. If they should wound *the Gananadana* and we land, they will search for you. I will secure the hatch so no one finds it."

"Listen to me, old man," Harris said, annoyance in his voice. "Would you respect me if you let me hide?"

"I would. You are injured. You are ill. You must survive."

"You're hysterical, Yustichisqua. On this jaunt across the desert, I've almost died three times and I'm still here." He pointed to the sky. "Besides, it's *Yichiyusti*. It's gloomy enough when Kuriakis stirs. I don't need your negative vibes."

"I am sorry, *oginali.*"

"Be sorry, but be brave. You're brave. I've seen it at every turn. I owe my life to your bravery and devotion. But trust me in this. If this thing crashes to the dunes, my nine lives run out. I won't regret it. I'd regret more living if the rest of you died." He clenched through the pain, but then wiped a tear from Little Bird's eye. "Now, you're so much older than me, old man. I mean to be the immortal my spark promises, and you have a few thousand years more to go. I say true."

Little Bird sighed, and then grasped *gasohisgi*.

"Let them come, then," he said.

"You say true."

Harris watched the array spread. He counted again. He thought there were thirteen *Cabriolins* and, as he expected, there were two men in each, allowing one to sleep while the other drove across the dangerous expanse — day and night — night and day. What they ate and drank was a matter for speculation, but these must be General Tarhippus' elite *regulati* — very brave and, Harris hoped, very stupid.

"Here they come," Cosawta said, aiming *Hierarchus* at the lead vehicle.

Tomatly lowered *the Gananadana* more, within a yard of the Forling. This sudden shift caught the lead *Cabriolin* by surprise, and he broke off the attack. But the left flank vehicle continued, giving Cosawta a clear shot at its power box. He fired *Hierarchus*.

The bolt drove through *the Cabriolin's* chassis, spinning it out of control. Both occupants leaped out, plummeting to the dunes. The vehicle burst into flames.

"Good shot, my lord," Tomatly shouted.

"Brother," Littafulchee said, preparing her own weapon, the crystal which dangled from her headband. "There is no question now of our intent. Was that wise?"

"What does wisdom have to do with warfare, sister?"

"We are of a different nature."

"We are, but must rise to the occasion and meet the enemy on *our* terms."

Littafulchee sighed. She clearly had different notions, but would not change course now.

"We are the aggressors, Lord Belmundus," she said. "Now we must play the part."

"I'm used to playing parts, my lady," Harris said, raising *Tony*.

Harris focused on *the brashun blade*, but *Tony*, as pretty as it was, flickering and winking, didn't illuminate. He shook it and waved it, but nothing stirred. He glanced to Cosawta for help, because the squad had recovered from their surprise and were descending like dive bombers. Cosawta grinned, and nodded toward *the Columbincus*,

"Right," Harris said, and touched the brooch.

Still, nothing. He looked up. He could see the features of *the regulati* now. Too close for trial and error, and yet too far to use *Tony* as a baloney slicer. He saw Yustichisqua raise *gasohisgi*, the little blade flickering, and then ablaze.

"How did you do that?" Harris stammered, just as his foot shot the worse pain blitz yet. The agony went through his chest and up his elbow. Then, one massive strike on his *Columbincus* and *Tony* came alive with terrible wrath. "Bingo."

A bolt, bigger, but less controlled than *Hierarchus'*, slammed into the lead *Cabriolin*, knocking it off course, but not out of commission. However, the attack broke off again, the squad regrouping.

Harris felt like cheering — cartwheels, perhaps and a human pyramid. But before he could shout *adadooski*, his foot conspired again, this time knocking him off his feet. He crashed to the mat.

"*Oginali*," Yustichisqua shouted. "Are you hit?"

"No, old man. Not by *a Stick*, but by my fucking bunny bite.*"*

Yustichisqua quickly examined the foot.

"You must lie down," he said.

"I'm already down, old man."

Littafulchee was there, dragging Harris reluctantly under the cloaking.

"Do not resist me, Lord Belmundus," she said.

And he could not. If he were destined to die today in this battle under the green sky, at least he'd have a pleasant last view of this woman.

"Did you see the shot, my lady?" he murmured. "It stopped the attack."

"It was a wonderful effort," she said, examining the foot, and then hoisting the cloak over him.

"You say true?"

"I say true. But you must remain here and let us defend the ship. You have done your part."

"Great fucking shot, Lord Belmundus," Cosawta shouted. "Tomatly, raise her." The balloon shifted skyward. "Let them climb for us now," Cosawta said, "now that their engines are fucked by *the kowlinka*."

Harris tried to sit up, but Littafulchee slammed him down, and not with loving grace. She meant business. Yustichisqua nodded, and then scurried to his defensive position. Harris didn't try to rise again. He listened to Cosawta's colorful ranting as he described the squad's difficulties. Cosawta shot two more *Cabriolin*s down and, when *the porcorporians* emerged for their feast, he cheered them as if at a Roman circus. *The Gananadana* raised and lowered, and then raised again, until it act became strategy. Tomatly buzzed like a firefly, enjoying every moment of the ride. Harris was miserable.

Then the unexpected happened. One *Cabriolin* outflanked the balloon and bumped the gondola's side. It flew level with the ship, the driver peering down at Harris.

"He is here," he shouted back to the remaining squad.

Yustichisqua was on the spot, shooting *gasohisgi*, knocking one of *the regulati* into the gondola. At first stunned, the man recovered and drew his *Stick*, aiming it at Harris. Harris shuffled out from beneath the cloaking, grasping for *Tony*, but he was too off balanced to get off another one of his *great fucking shots*. He expected *the Stick* to blast him, but it didn't. It only held him at bay.

The driver, still in the *Cabriolin*, aimed his *Stick* at Cosawta. They weren't there to kill Lord Belmundus. They were there to capture him. Harris dropped *Tony* rather than risk Cosawta, but, as *the regulati* relaxed, Yustichisqua rushed him, plunging *the brashun blade* into his side.

"Shoot," the driver shouted, but *the regulati* had stumbled, holding his side and dropping his *Stick*.

Harris scrabbled for *Tony*, but before he could, the driver took a shot at Cosawta — missing, but enough to stir Tomatly into action. The driver aimed his *Stick* at the balloon master — up into the canopy. Littafulchee shouted, her crystal ablaze. The driver was stunned, and then knocked out of his vehicle by a blast from outside *the Gananadana*.

Harris scrambled to the edge, peering at the squadron. They hovered haplessly, surrounded by another squadron — at least twenty *Cabriolins*. He recognized the drivers.

"Brothers," he stammered, weeping.

He released his grip on the rim and fell back to the matting.

3

Harris awoke to two new faces — new, but old.

"Arquebus?" he muttered. "Agrimentikos?"

"Yes," Agrimentikos blustered. "We are here. All are here, except Lord Tappiolus, the instigator for the pursuit squadron. He has been chastised."

Agrimentikos swept his hand up toward the sky — blue again.

"Our lord no longer stirs," Arquebus declared. "You are safe and he is content."

Harris grasped Arquebus' shoulders, weeping.

"Why have you done this, brother? I abandoned *the Ayelli*."

"But *the Ayelli* have not abandoned you," Agrimentikos boomed. "Although the next time you decide to give chase to General Tarhippus, I, for one, would appreciate a vacation at *the*

Plageris. The Forling is good for a day's outing, but a week here lies heavy on the chest." He turned to Cosawta, who sat on the bale, nursing *Hierarchus*, polishing the blade. "And the next time you have us as company, Lord Cosawta, please have decent wine. This *brantsgi* is not worth the trip."

"We had a fine *wisgi* procured by Garan the *Gucheeda*, but I am afraid it went to fucking waste on Lord Belmundus. In fact, he fed it to the Forling."

While Cosawta laughed, Littafulchee stepped up to Agrimentikos.

"We have been spared by *the Ayelli*," she said. "This is true. But I do not mean to return to service."

"You should have never been in service," Arquebus said. "It is injudicious of me to say it, because I have followed the admonishments to the letter, but I see change coming."

"Change does not come of its own doing, Lord Arquebus," Littafulchee said. "Change in Farn is a forthright battle, displeasing to the Elector. Thus we cannot depend upon it."

"By rights," Arquebus said, "we should return Lord Belmundus to his Scepta."

"By what right?" Littafulchee said. "Who is to say he is not already with his Scepta?"

Agrimentikos knelt. Harris pushed up, Yustichisqua's ever-ready shoulder available. He stared at this woman, this gracious lady, who embodied beauty and wisdom and starch. What had she meant? It left no doubt, except, if true, his free will had flown south again. Still, he was not under interdiction — no mesmerizing jade ring. Not even the crystal compelled him. Littafulchee's soul beckoned saying *live, my love and be worthy*.

"I shall not be returning to Montjoy," Harris announced. "At least not as an indentured servant." Arquebus appeared disturbed by this, turning away. "I meant no insult, Sir John. Each man must find his way. Every role must fit the player. I am miscast as *an Ayelli*."

"But this one fits you better?" Arquebus asked.

"I don't know. I'll read the script and decide for myself. My agent's back in California."

Agrimentikos laughed, rising again.

"Your brothers Hasamun and Posan beckon us to leave," he said. "We still search for Parnasus."

"Parnasus," Harris gasped. "He's alive?"

"We do not know . . . Boots," Arquebus said, grinning. He kissed Harris' forehead. "You saved my Elypticus and I thank you for it. He *is* the favorite of my seven. If he died, I would have sought *the Pulveris Springs* and wept 'til the end of time. But you saved him and he is safe on a distant shore across *the Amaykwohi Sea.*"

Harris bowed. Arquebus arose, and then stared at Yustichisqua. "Forgive me," he said. "I was wrong to doubt your humanity." Yustichisqua bowed.

"Do not bow to me," Arquebus said. "*The Ayelli* must change someday. My eyes are fully open to our awful situation. I shall await Lord Belmundus' return." He stared at Harris. "Play your part well and the accolades will enshrine you in the places we prize most."

The two consorts stood at the brink of *the Gananadana. The Cabriolins* swept by and they boarded. Harris scrambled painfully to the gondola's edge. He caught his brothers' waves — all four, surrounded by Thirdlings, who escorted the remnants of *the regulati* squadron over *the kowlinka* just as *Solus* and *Dodecadatamus* tinged the sky red.

Chapter Five

Dodaloo

1

"*Dodaloo*," Tomatly shouted. He zoomed near Harris' head, and then somersaulted to the bale, performing a midair jig. "*Dodaloo*."

Harris raised his bulk on his elbow and grinned. Despite the pain, Tomatly's excitement was infectious.

"Doodle-dee-loo-doo to you too," Harris said, laughing.

"No, *oginali*," Yustichisqua said, equally excited. "He sees them."

"I see them. I see them."

Cosawta pulled hard on the rudder and roared. He sang in a booming baritone voice:

> *"Pull me hard and push me soft,*
> *Drift we 'neath the morning's dew,*
> *Come we from the clouds aloft*
> *Into the air of the Dodaloo."*

"*Dodaloo. Dodaloo.*" Tomatly cried.

Littafulchee emerged from her spot aft, her buckskins gently sweeping the deck. She poised her hands, her fingers springboards.

"*Dodaloo*," she murmured, and then touched her hand to her crystal.

Cosawta slammed one palm on the rudder, and the other to his shin. Harris thought the man would join the dance, but again, he sang.

> *"Fire me high and blaze me low,*
> *Rise the steam of kaseegee brew,*
> *I, my Gananadana row,*
> *To my heart in the Dodaloo."*

"*Dodaloo. Dodaloo.*"

"*Dodaloo*," Harris muttered, tentatively.

Yustichisqua helped him rise to the gondola's rim. He pointed. In the distance, a mountain range cut through the Forling.

"Mountains," Harris gasped.

"*The Dodaloo*," Yustichisqua explained. "The Spice Mountains."

"Home," Littafulchee hummed. "Just a little way now, Lord Belmundus, and you shall see where the Cetrone have been exiled. Still, we call it home, because my father has made it so."

"Your father?"

"You know of whom I speak."

Harris knew. He realized the Scepta and Seneschal had heard the tale of his research trip to *the Cartisforium*, thanks to Yustichisqua. No matter. The oil to lubricate the mysteries might flow freer without harboring secrets.

"I do, my lady, but . . ."

She placed her fingers to his lips and pointed toward *the Dodaloo*. The peaks were cloaked in blue-green mist, a haven from the Forling's shifting red dunes.

"There we shall see to your wound," she said.

"It feels better already," he replied.

Her perfume intoxicated him. Harris wanted to wrap his arms about her neck and cover her in kisses. But the mood was too merry — bright cheers of *Dodaloo*, and now a horn tooted — Tomatly producing a recorder, which the Cetrone called *a yahuli*. He piped a catchy tune as he continued his midair dance. To this melody Cosawta tapped on the rudder, and then on a *yuyona*, a tom-tom which hung from the canopy. Yustichisqua bobbed his head to the rhythm, and Harris' heart filled with joy, something which had evaded him for some time.

"Soon you shall see home, Yustichisqua," Littafulchee said.

"I have never seen it," he replied, and then turned to Harris. "*Oginali*, I have heard many tales of Cetronia."

"You've sung them to me, too," Harris said. "You serenaded me with the history of the Weeping Road, if you recall?"

"My voice is poor compared to most," Little Bird said. "But I look forward to hearing the sounds of *Echota* and of *Comastee*."

"Heigh-ho," Cosawta shouted over *the yahuli*, giving two hard thumps on *the yuyona*. "You shall have *selu gadu*, Yustichisqua."

Yustichisqua closed his eyes, his lips puckering, his tongue moistening them with expectation.

"*Selu gadu*," he murmured. "I have only tasted it once. My mother made it." He opened his eyes. "*Oginali*, the bread of Cetronia has no peer, but it is rare in *the Kalugu*."

"Illegal," Littafulchee said. "There was a time when we grew and harvested fields of *selu* and pounded the ears' yellow teeth into a fine powder to make *the gadu*. But the Yunockers turned *the selu* fields into *quillerfoil*, and instead of *the gadu*, we were forced to *the sqwallen*."

"*Selu gadu*," Tomatly shouted, and then played *the yahuli* like a train whistle.

"*Oginali*," Yustichisqua said, lost in a memory. "I remember the day. My mother came to me and showed me a small package of yellow grain and she smiled." He paused and sighed. "She always smiled, even in *reaptide*. But she said to me — *Usti, Usti*. This day I will find clear water and *awidena* fat and shall make *the selu gadu*."

"Are you talking about corn bread?" Harris asked.

"If you say so, *oginali*, it is so. But it was golden and fine, and hot and creamy with *awidena* fat. My tongue cries for it."

"You shall have it again," Cosawta shouted, banging *the yuyona* with rapid thumping.

"I shall have it," Yustichisqua said. "And you shall have some too, *oginali*."

Harris smiled. Even though his foot trobbed faster than *the yuyona*, he could see the anticipation in Little Bird's eyes blending with the memory of his mother's secret act. How many times had Harris had corn bread, corn muffins, corn cake and cornflakes and never given it another thought? But now he remembered his mother's pumpkin pie and felt the warm charge of her absence. He hoped *the selu gadu* was as fulfilling as his mother's pumpkin pie.

"I will love every morsel," he said to Yustichisqua.

"It is the taste of home," Littafulchee added, standing.

She moved toward Tomatly, and then rested on her heels. Looking to the sky, she raised her hand in pantomime.

> "*The wind calls and the golden ears listen,*" she
>   sang.
> "*The yellow teeth smile to the suns' two eyes,*
> *Then the heads will nod in prayer*
> *To Memer Hedonacaria's care*

Who blesses the selu on the vine
And kisses the waters to make pure wine
To wash the golden sands to loaves,
And raise the gadu in our stoves.
The hot and sweet our tongues to numb
In the breaking of the crumb,
Holy gadu, delighted foam,
The gift of light, of hearth and home."

2

Harris watched over the rim for as long as he could bear it. But weariness overcame him, although *the Dodaloo* neared. His eyes drooped and the pain returned. He worried about the wound. He would think the throbbing would subside under Littafulchee's care. However, the foot was bluish and the skin around the punctures still oozed, despite the a fresh bandage and a healthful application of *sqwallen*. Even *the pilocarpinus,* which Littafulchee insisted he drink, only made him wearier. So, with the mountains coming ever closer, he slumped to slumber, the horn and drum drifting to white noise. When he awoke, the aroma of pine engulfed him.

"The Forling is past," Littafulchee said. "We are in *the Dodaloo.*"

Harris sat up, too quickly, his affliction reminding him that the mat was his friend. Still, he wanted to see the change of scenery. Yustichisqua stood nearby, his face rapt with wonder. Harris could see the landscape across Little Bird's cheeks — the purity of waterfalls cascading down precipitous crevices into pure pools of light. He could see the conifers dancing in Yustichisqua's eyes and the excitement of hawks hunting over boughs and streams. Then Yustichisqua turned and smiled at Harris.

"Old man," Harris stammered, and then nodded.

Yustichisqua came to him, extending his arms.

"*Oginali,* you cannot miss this wonder, even if I hold you on my shoulders."

Harris pushed up painfully. Littafulchee hoisted, while Yustichisqua pulled. Then Cosawta gave them a boost, which did the trick. He didn't stay beside them, *the Gananadana* more dependant now on a keen rudder. Harris gripped the gondola's rim and gazed at the panorama. Mist hugged the valleys, the taller trees poking above the fog. The natural cloak kept much of this universe in mystery, but ahead was a craggy peak — shaped like a wizard's cap. Several other mountains hugged this ridge forming a chain, which melted into the smoky curtain.

"Mount Talasee," Littafulchee said. "It can be seen from all points of Cetronia, and throughout *the Dodingdaten*."

"It's magnificent."

"So thought my father, but it is also precipitous and hides its secrets from us."

Harris had questions now, but the sheer wonder before his eyes dashed them into the spleen.

The gondola creaked scaling the heights toward Mount Talasee. The air chilled and the fresh pine aromas blended with juniper and a hint of frost. Harris enjoyed the breeze's cool blanket because he was *off-and-on* feverish. Then *the Gananadana* descended into a valley. As it came across a verdant ravine, a rainbow sprang from the highlands to the rocky cleavage. His anticipation grew. Yustichisqua fidgeted, hopping around the gondola's rim, looking over the side, enjoying the rush of a river below. Then the aromas changed to sweet baking.

"Heaven touches me," Harris said, inhaling.

"We are not far now," Littafulchee said. "Echota is over the next crest."

The balloon glided through the ravine, the cargo bay mirrored in the rushing stream. The ravine gave way to an expanse, the land falling away into the valley. The waters crashed below in a thin ribbon to a pristine pool. And beyond that, Harris spotted the town — a cluster of tumblers, roofs reminding him of *the kaleezos*, only brilliantly decorated with symbols — line drawings, heralding to the sky a union of spirit and reason. Far to the west (or east, if Farn held true), another rambling of towers and tumblers stood.

"Comastee," Littafulchee said. "The colony town, and beyond this, the infringers — the *Fumarca* of *the Dodingdaten*."

Harris strained to see *the Dodingdaten*, a place paramount in his interests. However, it was too distant. Perhaps in the mist he spotted a rampart, but it might have been another ridge. He returned his attention to the approaching Echota, his heart settling his pain. He wanted to land this great behemoth — this big fucking balloon, and have a decent meal of *whatever* crawled out of the mountains, and wash it down with a cup of *whatever* blended with the pristine pool. And the *selu gadu*. Yes, the merry bread of the

Cetrone. Then he heard music on the air. Bright and rhythmic. It toyed with his lips and buzzed his ear.

"Birdsong?" he asked Littafulchee.

"Bird and bear and dog and tree and blue," she said. "The clans have gathered."

"They have spied *the Gananadana*," Cosawta said. "Yes, we shall have a splendid welcome — a big fucking fuss."

"As it should be, brother," Littafulchee said, smiling gently at the Echota roofs. "As it should be for our homecoming."

3

High over the trees they came — came to the song of a hundred *yuyona*. The home fires burned and the voices rose in welcome — sweet tones of praise pouring from heart into throats. Over *the kaleezo* roofs they flew — roofs red, roofs yellow and purple and tan and, the highest and most rotund, those blue for *the seegoniga* clan. Finally, they settled softly in the plaza, *the Gananadana* caught by a hundred hands, hitching and guiding it. Then the music swept Harris to a moment of ecstasy.

The Cetrone formed lines grouped by clan. First came *the alisoqua*, the bear clan in their rich yellow robes and feather bonnets. They spun and sang, some on *zulus*, others not. They waved their *waddly wazzoos* wildly about the base of *the Gananadana*. Then came *the chisqua*, the bird clan in red shirts and cream white skirts, strumming the great bellied guitars — *the Boboli dikano geesti*, singing enchantingly. Yustichisqua squeezed Harris' shoulder at the sight of his clansmen. Then *the yahuli* band tooted clarion blasts as *the geetli*, the dog clan swept in, trailing purple cloaks and hoops, which they spun around their waists like dervishes. The music switched to a stately march, accompanied by the golden voices of *the tlugu*, the tree clan, dressed in soft tan buckskins laced with silver bells, tingling on the wind. This heralded the royal clan, the blue holly — *seegoniga*, in shimmering turquoise gowns and garters of golden feathers. Egret headdress' blew in the breeze as *the seegoniga* swung their *waddly wazzoos*. The harmony of light brought all the clans to the dance, people branded by *the gollywi*, the proud sigils of birth and ritual. Such did the Cetrone greet their Scepta and Seneschal home.

Harris clutched *Tony* and his *Columbincus*. He wanted to join in the singing, the dancing and the rich assortment of instrumental expressions, but all he could do was take it in — take it to his heart. These were the downtrodden of Farn, enslaved in *the Kalugu*, ground to dust by the Yunockers and subservient to *the Ayelli*. These were the people in their exile, but people still — rich in culture and tradition. These were the people standing about *the Gananadana* to hail their royalty, and he, Lord Belmundus — the Enemy, stood in their midst. He felt embraced, but also a prisoner again — drawn by different passions into this feathery, watery, breezy world of music and baking aromas. Harris Cartwright had arrived in Echota.

Cosawta leaped to the bale and stretched his arms, embracing the air. The Cetrone ceased their singing and dancing, bowing curtly at the waist, one foot forward, their hands extended. Harris had never witnessed this brand of homage. He had seen the Cetrone bow — always bowing, but in subservience to overlords. What did that bow mean if this one was the true bow of respect?

"Brothers and sisters," Cosawta shouted. "We have come again on the wings of *the Gananadana*, our belly filled with *aniniya* for the cause. And I bring other treasures."

He pointed to Harris.

Harris thought Cosawta was indicating Littafulchee, but she stirred, taking Harris' elbow, guiding him upright, Yustichisqua on his other flank. Harris was at a loss. He was caught by a thousand eyes, who regarded him anxiously. He tried to bow, but Littafulchee tightened her grip and he stopped midgesture.

"This is Lord Belmundus," she said. "He is *Ayelli*."

The crowd gasped in unison. Eyes averted in puzzlement.

"He has the spark," Cosawta said. "And he is our friend."

A great *ahhhh* floated across the plaza.

"Who shall tell Enitachopco of our return?" Cosawta bellowed.

Three *chisqua* stepped forward, bowed their special bow and departed.

"We need Nayowee," Littafulchee announced. "Lord Belmundus has sacrificed much to come. While crossing *the Yinaga*, he was attacked by *gasuntsgi*. He harbors their fire."

Another gasp, and three *alisoqua* stepped forward, performed the bow and departed.

"Send a light to Comastee," Cosawta said. "Bring a flame to *the Dodingdaten*. Tell the peoples of Watoge and Nuckasee that the time has come. Announce to the Toqua and the Sittiquo that we prepare to fulfill our destiny. Let Keowee and Tricentee join the council. The day has come and soon the skies above Mount Talasee will fill with new birds to cross *the Yinaga* and return our children home."

The drumming recommenced — the dancing too. The plaza moved to a joyous choreography — moves developed in the dim dawn of time and learned from the cradle. The dance flared capes and skirts. Feathers flew to the high trees.

Harris was overwhelmed. He trembled, held upright only by Littafulchee and Yustichisqua's tight grip.

"You must not fall," Littafulchee whispered. "Your ease is coming, but until then, you must let your double *Columbincus* shine above their celebrations."

"I will try," Harris replied. It was becoming an effort now. Then, while he watched the enthusiasm of the clans and their celebration, he had a perilous thought. "Am I on the menu?"

Littafulchee chuckled.

"You have already been consumed, my love," she said. "That happened when you stepped into *Mortis House*. You have been a mighty feast since."

Tomatly buzzed about distributing *the Gananadana's waddly wazzoos* to their proper owners — the royal crew and Yustichisqua. The lamps flared at their owner's touch. Then, through the hurley-burley in the plaza, the three *alisoqua* returned, their feather bonnets shaking as they ran, a stretcher held between them. Behind, hobbling on a cane, came an old woman — *seegoniga* by her dress. Her hair was gray and long, partially sweeping the ground. She used her stick to clear the way, her hand waving away dancers.

"Is this my ride?" Harris asked.

"It is," Littafulchee said, as the stretcher was set before *the Gananadana*, the three bearers kneeling.

The old woman marched over the litter to the edge of the gondola. She bowed, almost imperceptibly, because she was so bent as to be bowed already.

"Lord Cosawta," she muttered, her voice like a shop saw. "I have been summoned."

"If you please, holy Nayowee," Cosawta replied, "we seek your hospitality."

He indicated Harris, who nodded. Nayowee turned sharply toward Harris, shaking her cane in his direction.

"Come forward, you of *the Ayelli*," she rasped.

Harris tried to walk, but the foot was paralyzed. Yustichisqua propped him up, while Tomatly led the way, his *waddly wazzoo* trailing a gentle gray smoke. Littafulchee moved Harris forward, slowly. Nayowee impatiently banged her cane on the stretcher.

"Here, here," she said. "Put him here."

Cosawta stepped forward now, his *waddly wazzoo* brightest of all. The crowd hummed, a soft hymn thrumming the air. Harris felt it as balm. He looked at the stretcher, which beckoned him to rest and slumber. He gazed into Nayowee's terrible eyes. They were crimson and sap green and her nose was as crooked as an eel. He had glimmers of being baked in an oven like Hansel and Gretel. As he approached the stretcher, the voices grew louder, the song forming a relentless melody — a short tune of five or six notes, repeated over and over in graceful beauty.

"Easy, my love," Littafulchee said, helping Harris to the stretcher.

"I am here, *oginali*," Yustichisqua whispered. "I will not leave you. I will not, and I say true."

Harris grasped Little Bird's hand. The world was in that hand. He felt drowsy as Nayowee stuck her face in his, her blunt breath as sappy as her eyes. She examined his mouth, and then his arms, and then touched his *Columbincus*.

"Yes, yes," she muttered. "This will help you fine. But for this, you would not be here in Nayowee's care."

"Do you say true?" Harris muttered.

Nayowee looked to Littafulchee.

"He speaks like one of us," she cackled.

"He is one of us," Littafulchee said. "Holy Nayowee, save this one . . . for me. Save this one."

"Ah," she said, continuing her examination. "I see the situation. *Gasuntsgi* or no *gasuntsgi*. This one has been bitten where he already mends and, under such auspices, miracles can be performed, my lady." She suddenly looked toward Cosawta. "We go to *the asi-asa*. But I am tired and it is far for me to walk after my coming. I am not usually summoned, you know."

Cosawta bowed — the special bow, and raised Nayowee in his arms, her cane braced on his back, her long tresses trailing in the dust.

"To *the asi-asa*," she growled.

The song continued as *the alisoqua* raised the stretcher and carried Harris behind Cosawta and his human cargo. Harris felt the world fading — the melody of six notes bathing him in light and slumber as the stretcher swayed.

"I am here, *oginali*," came the voice, now in a dream.

"Do you . . . say . . . true?"

"I say true. I say true."

Chapter Six

The Asi-asa

1

Harris awoke, surprised that he had. His dreams were filled with color and music and no more. Faces eluded him. Voices, if he could remember them, babbled in Cetrone. He seemed to rock in *the Gananadana* again, but the sights were vacuous — the aromas, smoky. When his eyes opened, he saw a smoky canopy above him — a conical tent, which barreled down to form a rotunda, lit at intervals by *waddly wazzoos*. His chest heaved, drawing in the sweet lingering smoke.

"Yustichisqua," he muttered, turning his head, looking for Little Bird.

"Yustichisqua," came a gravelly voice. "Be still, and make no fuss."

It was the old woman, who hovered beside him, her spidery fingers twisting a nest of kindling, the smoke weaving between her knuckles. She blew the smoke toward him.

"Inhale it," she said. "Take it in your chest and let it do its work."

Harris resisted at first, because the smoke was like drinking pure honey. But it was too heavy to be resisted. Soon, he breathed easily and felt its wondrous power.

"My foot?" he stammered, suddenly realizing he couldn't feel it. "My foot?"

"It is still there, you *gosaka gaheeni*," she cackled. "Although you should be concerned, I suppose. I thought to chop it off and make your toes into a necklace. Now, that would make Nayowee's day, to have a chain of *Ayelli* toes dangling from her gobbler's neck." She laughed again, and blew more smoke at him. "Be easy, Lord of the Spark. Nayowee is a good and loyal subject of Zacker. When a Scepta pleads for something precious to her, I oblige." She frowned. "But it took much of my effort to allow your foot to remain. Sad to say, it will never be as it was, to run and hop and play at your *Ayelli* games. No, no. But it will take your weight again, once your vitals are restored to balance. Inhale. Breathe

Nayowee's smoke and the ages shall kiss you with their healing, they will."

Harris found himself floating again — *the Gananadana* swaying above the Forling, then into *Dodaloo*, and then onto the plaza. He heard the clan chants greeting their leaders home. Pleasant visions now — not just colors and vaporous aromas, but sweetness and warmth. He drifted and slept, locked in another world entirely. Such was Nayowee's cure.

2

When Harris' eyes opened again, *the asi-asa* was dim, the smoke dissipating. He was groggy, but his breathing had improved. He had to pee — fiercely. Yustichisqua was there on cue, without being called.

"Are you better, *oginali*?" Little Bird asked, anxiously. "Your color is better."

"I need to pee, old man."

"Again?"

Again? Harris thought. But he supposed Little Bird had accommodated him while he slept.

"Help me up."

"No need."

Yustichisqua slid a porcelain pot under the blanketing, and Harris found heaven. As he sighed in relief, Yustichisqua fumbled with a parcel, anxious to show Harris its contents.

"I'm finished," Harris said. "What do you have there?"

Yustichisqua slipped the pot out, covering it with gauze. Then he wiped his hands and raised a golden loaf of bread above his head as if it were a prize.

"*Selu gadu*," he announced. "It is still warm."

Harris pushed up, his lips moistening as he drank in the aroma of sweet corn. Yustichisqua broke off a piece, and then broke that piece in two. He slathered the two halves with a buttery substance, and then bowed to it. He handed one half to Harris, but held his hand up.

"Do not eat yet, *oginali*."

Harris just wanted to pop it in his mouth and savor it, but Little Bird raised his *waddly wazzoo*, shining the lamp over the bread.

"*Selu awudoli sgi-aniyo lunikwo, arkmo*."

Harris blinked.

"Arkmo," Little Bird prodded.

"Amen," Harris said, and then without further delay, wolfed the bread. "Yes, yes. It's everything you said it would be."

"There is plenty, *oginali.* You can eat it slowly and there will still be more."

Harris grinned, golden crumbs pouring from his maw. They laughed.

"Up," Nayowee cried. "If you can devour *selu gadu* obscenely and find a moment of merriment, you cannot be loitering in my *asi-asa.*"

The old woman thrust her fist into the *selu gadu,* taking a huge chunk and gobbling it, her several teeth managing fine.

"You are to leave here, *oginali,*" Yustichisqua explained. "*A kaleezo* has been prepared for us."

Harris gazed to his foot. It looked like a piece of alabaster, but he wiggled his toes. The pain had subsided, but full feeling had not returned.

"Am I healed?"

"No," Nayowee rasped; "You shall never be fully healed. You should be dead, you should. But I am the best healer in Farn and when my lady asks me to keep you alive, I will oblige her."

Nayowee hovered over the foot, poking it with her stick.

"You exhausted my stock of *pulverkempin* and *ruptus* weed. Very rare and hard to find." She pointed to the ceiling. "Lord Cosawta will need to ascend Mount Talasee to replenish my supply."

Harris bowed.

"How can I repay you, my lady?"

"Do not call me a lady, fine stick of *an Ayelli.* I am a potter's daughter from the extinct *kibanaquo* clan. *The seegoniga* have adopted me, and they remind me of the fact every chance they get. Royal mucketymucks. Never a moment out of their sight." She waved her hand dismissively. "As for payment, I shall send you *a gufawpup,* payment upon receipt. Now, get up and let me see how you fare."

She poked him with her cane. Yustichisqua helped him to his feet. Harris was dizzy — to be expected after the ordeal. He couldn't tell whether his foot held him or not, because he couldn't feel it. He knew it was there, but it tingled slightly and was wooden. He tried to take a step and almost fell.

"Steady, *oginali*. I shall catch you."

"Let him fall, if he must," Nayowee said. "He shall be a mass of bruises before the week is out. You must fashion a cane for him."

"A cane?" Harris muttered. "I don't want to walk like . . ."

"Like an old woman?" Nayowee cackled. "I have managed for over a thousand years and have used this cane for half that time." She turned to Yustichisqua. "Fashion a cane to make him proud. One he can use to bash over your head when you fail to bring him his pot."

"I am his *Taleenay*, not his Trone," Little Bird snapped.

"Is that what they call it now? Fancy words. Well, who am I to stop the course of fancy words. Just make it so or I will show you how I make a *Taleenay* hee-haw like an *assinoki*."

Yustichisqua buttressed Harris, and then nudged him toward a bench.

"Sit and rest."

"He has been resting for too long," Nayowee said. "It is best he practices how to use his gammers."

"How long have I been resting?" Harris asked.

"Long enough."

"For thirty-seven moons' rises, *oginali*."

"Thirty-seven days?" Harris took a step, and tottered to the bench, landing on his ass, barely. "I've been out of it for over a month?"

"You have been tended well," Nayowee said. "And many have come and gone through this *asi-asa*, cooing and blowing smoke on your behalf. I have not had a moment's rest." Nayowee pushed her face into his. "When I first saw your foot, I was overjoyed. Long I had wanted a necklace of *Ayelli* toes. If *the seegoniga* did not regard you as a lost treasure, I would have saved your foot, but taken those toes." She swept her hands to his feet. "Maybe two . . . as payment."

"Leave my fucking toes alone."

"You say that now, but for many days and nights I had the opportunity." She clutched her chest. "It would have been a fine necklace hanging between these ancient breasts. They would call me fashionable again. But . . . but I shall be compensated in better ways. So keep your toes, and be gone with you."

Harris shook his head. He didn't know whether to take these words for truth or bandied bullshit. He was overwhelmed by questions.

"Where is your cousin, Yustichisqua?"

"Which?"

"Littafulchee."

"Ah. She is waiting in *the kaleezo*."

"Waiting for me?"

"I am not sure what she does. She is always a mystery to me. As for Cosawta, he waits outside."

"Visitors," Nayowee said. "Always visitors."

"He has come daily to see you, *oginali*. You are awake now and should see him."

"I cannot keep him out," Nayowee said. "You — *Taleenay*, tell them to come in and be brief. Take the piss pot out with you."

"Them?" Harris asked.

"He comes with others," Little Bird said.

Yustichisqua retrieved *the selu gadu*, placing it on the bench, and then gathered the pot, pushing past the old woman, who snarled at him.

"Yes, Lord Belmundus, your *Taleenay* will make you a fine cane, I am sure of it."

Harris pressed his left hand to his *Columbincus* and his other to *Tony*, which trailed beside his good leg. Nayowee hobbled to a large cauldron at the opposite end of *the asi-asa*. There she chanted prayers and threw scraps of meat into the roiling liquid. Harris glanced down at his toes and shook his head, thinking of the weenies his mother used to throw into the bean pot. He was glad to have his toes, useless or not — better on his foot than in a stew or around the crone's wrinkled neck.

3

Cosawta entered *the asi-asa*, ducking to avoid hitting his headdress on the door flap. Two shorter men walked beside him, removing their hats and waving them beneath their noses — a sweat house not much to their custom, Harris supposed. They were dressed the same, like barkers at a fair — dirty plaid trousers, sweaty white high collared-shirts, and skimmers, which they now briskly waved to clear the air of smoke.

"Not much of a *bed sit* here," one said. He sported a handlebar mustache, unkempt and dotted with undergrowth. "Bit of a Dunny, I'd say."

"No Dunny budgies, I was hoping. But one can't say it," replied the other, clean of mustache, but heavily pocked on one cheek.

Odd fellows.

Harris wondered what language they spoke. It had a British twang, but the words were foreign. Cosawta swept his hand in a gesture of welcome, but more as a presentation element.

"This is Lord Belmundus, lads," he said. "Best fucking find in Farn."

The two gents cocked their heads — each in a different direction, and then looked to each other, before returning their skimmers to their heads, and doffing them like gentlemen in waiting.

"I'll be Gobsmacked," Mr. Mustache said. "If it isn't London to a brick."

"As sure as me old Fella finds it a piece of piss," Mr. Smoothie said.

Both bowed, and came forward. Harris lurched back, because they stank of rum and body odor. Evidently, wherever Cosawta dug these fellows up, they didn't believe in a bath. Of course, Harris sat in a cloud of sweat house smoke, which trumped the visitor's potency. They had indicated as much, or so he thought.

"He's a power house," Mustache said.

"Two fold *Comlumbinkie*."

They turned to Cosawta, who grinned.

"I told you true, lads. A find of finds."

"Excuse me," Harris piped up. "Am I some fucking treasure chest dug up from the Forling, Cosawta? Am I going to be sold to the fucking highest bidder in some slave market? Are these the . . . the bleedin' auctioneers?"

Both men laughed.

"Bleedin'," Smoothie said. "Good try, mate."

"Mate?" Harris asked. "Are you from . . ."

"From *the Dodingdaten*," Cosawta answered.

Harris gasped, B O and all.

"*Fumarca?*"

"Now, now, let's not go callin' us by names," Mustache snapped.

"But Garan told me the residents of *the Dodingdaten* were . . ."

"Fookin' *Fumarca*?" Smoothie said. "Garan would say that, he would. He's a bleedin' Goocheedee, after all. What would he know?"

"We do have names," Mustache insisted.

"Do tell," Harris asked. "You could have fooled me."

"I'm Morris Culpeeper," Mustache replied.

"And I'm his fair dinkum brother, Laurence . . . Culpeeper."

"I'm Harris Cartwright." Harris extended his hand, but the brothers only bowed.

"No, you're not," Morris said. "You're Lord Belmundus, although from which arse-hole outland you dropped in from is a matter of discussion, ain't it?"

"I'm from California," Harris replied.

"A bleedin' Seppo," Laurence said.

"A Yank by any other name," Morris echoed.

"We're from Brisvegas," Laurence said.

"I don't know that place," Harris confessed. "But you sound a bit Australian to me."

"Australian? You bet your fookin' chunder we're Aussie."

"From Brisbane," Morris said. "We're not your Whacker or your Tassie."

"Nor no Corn Eater."

Harris grinned. He hadn't a clue what they said, but it was a delightful change from the sonorous Cetrone *sgis* and *sguos*.

"Well," he replied, "it's good to know I'm not alone."

"You're alone," Morris said, his voice darkening. "Did you expect us from the DoDingoDatenus to be spun Fairy Floss, you daft drongo?"

"You're as alone here as alone there," Laurence said. "You're stuck in the muck with a bevy of fuck. But once you get to know us, you'll come to see there's no good search like the one you've given up on."

"Given up?"

Morris came close, stink and all. He winked.

"There's no way out, if you know what I mean. At least, you were drawn to it — taken by the sexy kittens and given a little naughty."

"We flopped in," Laurence said. "A stroll in the outback — a pit in the bush."

"I look-see'd in there, and said, 'Larry, is that a bit o' flash down the gully.' And he said, 'I think you're right, Moe, or I'm not a Larrikin.'"

Harris chuckled at the thought of being addressed by Moe and Larry and wondered if it meant Cosawta was Curly.

"'Well,' says I, 'I'm up for a bit of bush bashing if there be a golden Swede at the bottom.' So we took the plunge, and when we came out on the other side, we were in a land of fire."

"Terrastrium," Cosawta said.

"Terrastrium?" Harris replied, remembering the hellhole in question.

"It took a pull to find our way out of there," Moe said. "Glad we did, too."

"Hotbed of Kero, that," Larry added. "But that yarn's a long one."

"We're not in this fookin' Asses-assis to talk about our adventures on the fiery storm," Moe said. "We're here to fossick — to see if what this Figjam Cetronian tells us is truth or just plain plonk."

Harris grinned, barely able to keep from a full belly laugh. Although these men — the Culpeeper brothers from Brisbane, shattered any hope *the Dodingdaten* held the secret to an escape. The fact they were speaking some variant of English, which was less intelligible than the most arcane expressions in Farn, tickled his ribs. He looked to Cosawta.

"Just what have you told these men, Cosawta?"

Cosawta cocked his head.

"I have told them you are Lord Belmundus, the co-consort of the Scepta Charminus of *the Ayelli*. And you have the spark."

"All consorts have the spark, whatever the fuck that means," Harris said.

The Culpeepers grinned, looking to each other excitedly.

"You say true, my lord," Cosawta said. "But you also have crossed the Forling, the first *Ayelli* to do so. You have brought a gentle view of the Cetrone and wear a double *Columbincus*. You have two *brashun blades*."

Harris touched his *Columbincus*, and then *Tony's* hilt.

"I have only one sword."

Cosawta nodded, and then produced *Hierarchus* from beneath his robe. He extended it to Harris, who thought to let the Seneschal keep it, but a fire within told him to take and keep it. Cosawta did not express regret when *Hierarchus* was laid across Lord Belmundus' lap. Harris suddenly felt authoritative, despite his lingering dizziness.

"Gentleman," he said, spaciously. "I'm glad for the attention. It's true I have much metallurgy of worth about my being, but is that any reason to come court me?"

"Court you?' Moe said. "You've got the wrong notion there, Harris Cartwright."

Perhaps it was an error to use his real (or, at least, his stage) name.

"We've come to tell you," Larry snapped, pointing to *Hierarchus*, and then to *Tony*. "You're the poop in our jib, but we're the ridgy-didge road train."

"Ridgy-didge?" Harris asked.

"The *genyuwine* fookin' article. The rip-snorters of the DoDingoDatenus."

"Rip-snorters?"

"Engineers," Cosawta said. "Inventors."

"Ah!" Harris recalled the names now from his journey in *the Gananadana. The Culpeeper's and their Seecoys*. "I seem to recall something you said now, only your sister made you put it off."

"Put it off, I have. And put it further off, we must. But I could not keep these fucker-jammers at bay any longer, or . . ."

"We'd become unproductive," Moe said. "Nothing like showing us the Scratchy before we take the bait."

"We're not Maori sheepshaggers, you know."

The brothers laughed.

"And this invention?" Harris asked.

"Inventions," Moe corrected. "We shite them by the gross and piss them like an archer's artifice."

"Our drawing board's bigger than this busker's donger."

"You must come and see," Moe said.

"I'd love too, but . . ."

"Under the stoker, ain't we?" Larry said. "And we much understand it. Wouldn't want you to drop dead on us."

"No," Cosawta said. "My sister would have your balls in a hitching."

"Wouldn't want that," Larry said.

"Miss Little Fulchy has a definite view on things, she does. Never risk goin' up against her wishes."

They both bowed to Cosawta.

"So what is this thing you want me to see?" Harris asked.

"You'll see it soon enough," Moe said.

"Whatever you does do, or doesn't do," Larry said, "it'll make a turn of events, don't you doubt it."

"*Seecoys*," Harris announced.

"He knows it," Moe said.

"Mind reader, he."

"No. I've heard about it. Some kind of new *Cabriolin*."

The brothers roared.

"*Cabrioshite*," Moe said. "*Seecoys* are nothing like them."

"Those Gurt motherbonkers had no notion of design."

"No notion."

Suddenly, a cane broke through the conversation, Nayowee pounding her way between them.

"You disturb my smoke with your piss stench and *zugginak* shit talk of flying *dollywaggles*. This is a house of healing." She snarled at Cosawta, who nodded obediently. "Where is that *Taleenay* to take you away from me, Lord Belmundus?"

"I am here," Yustichisqua said from the doorway.

"Come take this brood from my fires. I can do no more and need to hibernate as an old woman should."

4

The Culpeeper brothers turned and left quickly, their skimmers fanning briskly. Cosawta bowed to Lord Belmundus, and then to Nayowee.

"Just go," she rankled. "Just go."

Harris watched the Seneschal depart. It had been an interesting interview, but it exhausted him. He tried to rise off the bench, but Yustichisqua pinned him down.

"No, *oginali*. I have brought you assistance."

Little Bird opened *a korinkle*, taking out a pair of *zulus*.

"Can I wear those?" Harris asked, recalling his odd foot size.

"I have crafted these over the days, *oginali*. They will fit, and I will guide you so you do not lose balance."

"He needs to walk," Nayowee shouted. "How will he learn to walk if he does not walk?"

"I agree," Little Bird said. "But today he shall move in comfort."

"Oh, yes, *Taleenay*. Now you are the medicine woman with eons of knowledge of these things. When I say he must walk, he must walk."

Nayowee pushed *the zulus* aside, but Yustichisqua retrieved them and hit her stick away. He glanced angrily into her eyes.

"I am not afraid of you, old woman," he shouted. "This is my *oginali*. You have done your best, and I appreciate it. But I know what he needs and it is not another moment of pain and suffering. He shall wear *the zulus* today. Tomorrow . . . we . . . shall . . . see."

Nayowee raised her cane, surely to whack Little Bird unconscious, but Harris caught the stick, and eased it to the ground.

"Mother Nayowee," he said sweetly. "I wait for your *gufawpup*, but I must insist my *Taleenay* perform his warrant. Can you repair a man's honor when it is forgone? Is there a balm in your cauldron to heal that which is not broken?"

Nayowee shook her head, puckered her lips, as if to spit, and then turned back to her potions, grumbling with every step. Yustichisqua raised the alabaster foot and carefully attached *the zulu*. He had installed special padding to assure comfort. When it was secure, he looked into Harris' eyes. Gratitude shone there.

"The other foot, *oginali*."

Harris obliged him.

"That will be some *gufawpup* when it arrives, old man."

"It will only cost you a toe, *oginali* . . . and perhaps one of my fingers."

Chapter Seven

Enitachopco's Say

1

Daylight stung Harris' eyes, the suns-light piercing the high trees onto the plaza. At his appearance, children playing pole ball in *an asorba* grove, stopped to gawk at the awkward sight of *an Ayelli* guided by a Cetrone and balancing precariously on *zulus*. Harris, aware of these stares and others from sweepers in the square and smokers lounging before *kaleezos*, didn't know whether he was expected to nod and wave. Surely, some act was required, because when he passed a gang of *geetli* men, who dug for *byudra* roots, they stopped and bowed deeply, their right legs extended respectfully.

"What do I do, old man?" Harris whispered to Yustichisqua.

"You say: *O-see-yo.*"

Harris slowed, and carefully turned, unsteady on the *zulus*, his leg comfortable, but unfeeling. He took a deep breath, and then said the words.

"*O-see-yo.*"

The men raised their faces and grinned.

"*Toe-hee-ju,*" they replied variously. "*Toe-hee-ju.*"

Harris nodded, and then continued his course.

"How did I do?"

"Fine, *oginali.*"

"What did I say?"

"Just a greeting. *How do I find you?*"

"And their reply?"

"*Fine, sir, and how are you?*"

"I should have thanked them." He turned, the men bowing again. "Well, old man. What do I say?"

"*A-ni-lo-li-ga.*"

"That's a mouthful."

"Then just say, *O-see-an-i*, and smile."

Harris grinned.

"*O-see-an-i,*" he said. "*A-ni-lolabrigita.*"

The *byudra* diggers looked puzzled, then laughed.

"I believe they took your meaning, *oginali*. We shall work on such things, we will."

"Ah, now you're the teacher, eh?"

"I am the one holding you steady."

That was true.

Harris continued through the plaza, stopping to greet anyone who bowed, trying his *o-see-yo*, and managing to approximate his thanks. He reached *the kaleezo's* door. There he paused.

"Are you pulling me through?" he asked, regarding the heavy portal. "I've never been keen on wall travel, and now I might be too weak to pass through intact."

"No, *oginali*. There is no *kaybar* in Cetronia."

"No kaybar?"

"How can we handle it when we pass through it easily? We cannot lift it. It evades our touch."

True enough. Harris was glad to hear it. He inspected *the kaleezo*. Like most, it was a roundhouse with black walls. However, the roof was a checkerboard of red and white shingles — whimsical.

"And this is for us?" he asked.

"It will serve until change."

There was a notion — *change.*

Yustichisqua pushed the portal open, and tugged Harris into the roundhouse. It was cool and floral scented. He recognized Littafulchee's aroma — the Rose of *Scaladar*. The inner walls were decorated with sigils — white strokes in a language he couldn't decipher. It wasn't Zecronisian script, which also eluded him. Those sigils were painfully brittle. These were soft, curved and reminiscent of the Latin alphabet, but not quite. At intervals, *waddly wazzoo's* were hitched to lampposts. He counted six. Two unlit *bronskers* stood sentinel to a second chamber. Harris scanned the room until his focus found the center and fell on visitors.

Visitors already?

He counted four men huddled in buckskins and smoking pipes — sweet, aromatic smoke, but not like tobacco or hemp — lavender incense, perhaps. Then Littafulchee entered from the second room. The four men stirred, looking toward Harris for the first time.

Harris was at a loss. The *zulus* hampered him now, so he pulled on Yustichisqua, managing to step forward. Littafulchee curtsied.

Harris tried to make the respectful bow, but it was too awkward, so he grasped Little Bird as a crutch, completing his welcome like a drunken sailor. Among the four men, one was prominent. Harris recognized him — an ashen man, with fine white braids and wispy beard. The old man wore a patch over his right eye. Harris had never met this man, but he had witnessed his image in *the Cartisforium*. This was the Elector of Zacker.

Harris tried his drunken bow again.

"Great lord," he said.

"It is Enitachopco," Yustichisqua whispered.

"*O-see-yo*, Enitachopco," Harris said like a native.

Enitachopco removed the pipe and glanced at his three companions — all aged Cetrone. They laughed gently. Harris wondered if his welcome was regarded as foolish. Then Enitachopco took a long draw on the pipe, and lifted his left hand.

"You know my name, Lord Belmundus?" he asked, his voice resonating beyond his reedy frame. "Yet we have not met."

Littafulchee hunkered down beside her father, whispering in his ear.

"Ah," Enitachopco said. "You have seen our history in the room I had set aside to recall times past. Then I have no advantages in your company, sir. No advantages, which is much to my liking."

"My lord," Harris said. "I know only images. The rest is speculation."

"Be comforted, weary spirit from the hill," Enitachopco said. "Speculation is all we have in this lifetime."

"Time has wrapped us in haphazard," said the old man to Enitachopco's right — the ancient who wore a bright-green feathery shawl.

"It has neither boundary nor center," remarked the old man to the left, who had a twitch, his cheek dancing with each syllable.

The third man was silent.

"Approach me, Lord Belmundus," Enitachopco commanded.

Harris hobbled to the center, cautiously, yet drawn by the blend of lavender and roses. He caught Littafulchee's glance and felt easier. Little Bird guided him, assuring a steady approach.

"You asked me: *How do I find you?*" Enitachopco said. "To that I make reply." He drew again on the pipe, letting the smoke curl from his lips like steam from a volcano. "I am the saddest of men,"

Harris sighed. He sensed truth, but that didn't make the prospects brighter.

"I'm sorry to hear it, my lord."

"I am also the most joyous of our race." He grinned, and then snapped his hand, grasping Harris by the chin, drawing him in — face to face. "I am in the company of like souls. Sometimes sad. Sometimes glad. But never more than what we are and what we shall become. And here you are — the promise for the future. I see it in your eyes and know it by your trace. So you ask me: *How do I find you?* To this I reply: You find me better now for your coming. You find me content in the knowledge that I shall return this dreadful night to he who shadowed my heart. He who *still* shadows my heart." He released Harris, who tumbled backward, landing on the spot opposite. "That is how you find me, Lord Belmundus, now that I have found you."

"The passage of time and the journey of wind are subtle brothers," said the green feathered man.

"Light and dark are two cheeks upon a single face," added the twitchy fellow.

The other warrior kept his silence — his poignant silence.

2

Littafulchee moved to the wall, returning with her *waddly wazzoo*. She signaled Yustichisqua to retrieve the other lamps, setting them in the center beside their owner's right knee. This left *the kaleezo* in darkness, save the center, where the glow recalled a hundred campfires for Harris. He wondered when the marshmallows would be brought forth and the S'mores ritual commence. Instead, Enitachopco raised his *waddly wazzoo*, or rather, the light from within it — separated, levitating above Harris.

"Light and dark are two cheeks upon a single face," the Elector intoned, and then sighed again. "We are a broken people, Lord Belmundus and would be mended. But this mending is slow, like the dimming of stars and the growing of mountains. Yet mend we shall."

The lamp light drifted over the green caped warrior.

"Coweeshee," Enitachopco said. "My brother and clan head of *alisoqua*, the bear."

Coweeshee grunted. Harris nodded respectfully. The lamp light drifted over the man with the twitch.

"Elejoy," Enitachopco said. "My brother and clan head of *geetli*, the dog."

Elejoy raised his pipe and sneered. Harris nodded, and the lamp light moved on, illuminating the silent warrior.

"Tucharechee," Enitachopco said. "My brother and clan head of *tlugu*, the tree."

Tucharechee remained silent and did not stir. Harris followed suit and did not nod. The lamp light returned to the center, hovering above Enitachopco.

"I head the Cetrone and was Elector of Zacker," he said. "I keep my rule over *the seegoniga*, the blue of the evening star and the holly bush."

He raised his hands and the light drifted back into his *waddly wazzoo*. Harris, seated, bent at the waist and tried to touch his head to *the kaleezo's floor*. Then, he looked up, gazing at Littafulchee.

"But who leads *the chisqua*, the bird clan?"

All present sighed, a hollow gust, which stole any joy which may have lurked within the circle.

"Dead," Enitachopco intoned. The clan heads raised their arms — even Tucharechee. "May *the Primordius Centrum* hold him close to the eternal hearth."

Yustichisqua wept. Harris touched his arm, but Little Bird covered his face, tears cascading relentlessly.

"Old man," Harris said, reaching for his friend's shoulders. "I'm sorry if . . ."

"It is cleansing for him to weep," Littafulchee said.

Harris regarded this strange assembly, arms raised or faces covered. These rituals were beyond him. But he asked the question and this was the answer.

"I'm sorry to evoke the memory of the lost clan head," Harris muttered. "Forgive me."

Yustichisqua uncovered his eyes, wiping his tears.

"No need for your sorrow, *oginali*," he said. "He was called Kittowa, and he died in *the Kalugu*. I do not remember him, but I recall my mother's weeping."

Suddenly, the truth dawned on Harris.

"He was your father?"

"You say true, *oginali*," Little Bird said.

"My youngest brother," Enitachopco replied. "And it is good that his son has finally returned to us."

"A sad reminder in our midst," Coweeshee said.

"You bear his image like moons reflecting suns," Elejoy echoed.

Then the silent one — Tucharechee, stirred, pointing at Yustichisqua.

"You must perform *Chewohe* and be worthy of him."

Yustichisqua bowed low, his face buried in his hands again.

"Does he think he can return to us, to be our blood and not perform *Chewohe*?" Tucharechee snapped.

"*Chewohe* is a choice, brother, and our nephew must consider his position," Enitachopco replied. He extended his pipe to Little Bird. "Come, smoke and consider."

Yustichisqua stirred. He crawled toward the Elector and took the offering. He puffed three times, weeping with each inhalation. Then he turned to Littafulchee.

"Cousin," he said. "I weep not because I must perform *Chewohe*. I weep because my *oginali* must do the same if destiny befalls him, and I would be of the same clan as he."

"Ah," murmured the clan heads, shaking their hands, comprehension removing doubt.

Doubts, however, clung to Harris.

"What is *Chewohe*?" he asked. "And why is it my destiny to perform it?"

"It is not your destiny to do anything beyond being our guest," Enitachopco said. "But if the spark is to grow, you should consider becoming my daughter's consort. In that choice lays the ritual of *Chewohe*."

Harris looked to Littafulchee, who raised her hands towards him. He wanted to rush across the space and gather her into his arms. But just as he had the thought, his jade ring shone — an echo from Charminus, a faint call to her bed across the Forling's expanse. He covered the ring, but the light danced between his fingers.

"She still owns you," Littafulchee said.

"She has never owned me," Harris snapped. He looked to Enitachopco. "No woman has ever owned me. Scepta Charminus charmed me and evoked her spells when she called me to her hayloft. I never remember the experience."

"But I do," Littafulchee said. "I served her and, in that, I served you."

Harris felt guilty. As Trone, this woman — the one who now had captured his heart — his true heart, had seen him buck naked and servicing the buxom daughter of Kuriakis — day after day into night after night. In fact, Littafulchee had witnessed Tappiolus at it also. Harris glanced to Yustichisqua, who shrugged. Little Bird had also been a witness. Harris felt ashamed.

"I am a wanton spirit," he muttered.

"No," Enitachopco said. "Few can resist Kuriakis' daughters and the web they weave. How many Thirdlings have you spawned by her?"

"None," Harris replied.

"Regard that as a favorable omen," Coweeshee said.

"She sought your spark, but could not draw it," Elejoy echoed.

Tucharechee returned to silence.

3

Harris considered this. Tappiolus had fathered a passel of Thirdlings and, although he had been at it longer than Harris, the fertile Scepta should have caught fire with at least one of Harris' sperm buds. He never considered the reasons for this, because he was so inured by sex with Charminus. He was content to retreat and recover from his weariness — to return to *the Myrkpykyn* and his scheme at *the Kalugu*. Now the lack confronted him. Perhaps this shortfall was his fault.

She sought your spark, but could not draw it.

What did that mean? And what was *Chewohe*? Harris imagined a painful ceremony, involving circumcision or hanging from *the Tree of Woe*. But he was already circumcised and the Forling was his *Tree of Woe*.

"You ask me to decide on this *Chewohe* ceremony without knowing the details?" he asked Enitachopco. "Is there a book? Do you have a branch of the local *Cartisforium* on this side of the desert?"

Enitachopco touched Harris' arm with fingers so icy they chilled him to the bone.

"Fear not, Lord Belmundus. Whatever the ritual entails, it is not central to your decision to carry your spark home."

Harris pushed the hand away.

"How do you know I have this spark? Everyone tells me I do, but I've never seen it or even felt it. And don't tell me it's my interaction with *the brashun blades* or my *Columbincus*. I've seen others interact — even Thirdlings. Hell, Yustichisqua can light *gasohisgi* with little effort."

Enitachopco glanced at Yustichisqua, who drew his dagger. The clan heads grinned with approval.

"Who's to say he doesn't have the spark too?" Harris protested. He realized he bordered on rudeness, and settled back. "I'm just saying, I'm ignorant of this *witchy-woo* stuff. I may be from California, but I have a foot in Missouri."

Enitachopco pointed to *a waddly wazzoo*, which had been set between his and Littafulchee's. It burned dimmer than the others.

"The lamp's light comes from a single source," Enitachopco explained. "We keep that light."

Harris knew this from his research trip. He had seen Enitachopco take the light from *the Primordius Centrum*. He had witnessed him ignite the lamps of his children at Greary Gree.

"It is a sacred light," Harris murmured.

"It dwells in a thousand lamps kept alive by the children of Zacker," Enitachopco said. "When a lamp is extinguished, the covenant is broken and the soul rends. My children in *the Kalugu* smolder their light each night at *reaptide*. My brother and his wife, the parents to this dear child, lit their son's lamp, but their lamp no longer burns." Enitachopco sighed. "There has been only one lamp ever extinguished and relit beyond *the Primordius Centrum*." He touched *the waddly wazzoo*. "Behold Talqwah's lamp."

Harris twitched.

"Talqwah?"

He recalled now. When Yustichisqua stabbed Talqwah's lamp with *gasohisgi*, the light was extinguished. Talqwah pleaded with *the whisperers* to rekindle it. They said it was impossible. But when Harris touched it, it came to life again. Was this their proof?

"But how could I acquire such skills?" he asked. "I mean, I don't remember shooting fire from my hands at home — even as a party trick."

"Your kind dwells in the light of a volatile world," Coweeshee said.

"They build engines to work for them and rely not on their inherent powers," Elejoy explained.

Tucharechee leaned forward, pointing with his pipe.

"You must perform *Chewohe* and fulfill your destiny."

"Choice," Enitachopco said.

"Choice," Littafulchee echoed, extending her arms again.

Harris glanced at the jade ring, the gift from Memer Joella, given with a different hope in mind. He covered the stone again with his hand. Suddenly, he longed for *the asi-asa* and Nayowee's grousing. He would have enjoyed another round of the Culpeeper brothers and their arcane chortling about their *Seecoys*. He would have welcomed even a day of reviewing cases at *the Myrkpykyn*, with Garan interpreting the chicken scratch and the *Danuwa* ushering the petty petitioners into the courtroom for *the Didaniyisgi's* rulings. As compelled as he felt to oblige this new supplication for his sperm and spark, this was not the essence he came to admire when he had glanced into that long gone and faraway mirror. Lord Belmundus had a choice, but he now sat crippled before a one-eyed Elector, who insisted on his say. That say was not quite over.

Chapter Eight

Two Cheeks Upon a Single Face

1

"Choice," Enitachopco said. "Choice has been our savior and downfall since the first ember kindled in these humble bones. It is choice again which decides the contour of the tide, Lord Belmundus. Your choice."

Harris sighed. He was in Las Vegas at the Blackjack tables, but with slimmer odds, because the upturned cards were as dicey as the downturned ones. It was unfair to place this choice on his head. At least Charminus wanted only one thing in endless supply. The fate of all existence didn't rest on his roll in the hay with her. Yet, perhaps it did.

"It's unfair,' he muttered.

While the brothers grimaced, Enitachopco eased into his accustomed sigh.

"Unfair would be to deny you a choice, sir," he replied, cocking his head.

Littafulchee grinned. Her choice seemed settled. Harris needed more information on which to base his decision, but he had a hunch this was all he would get. Still, Enitachopco, sensing needs, raised the pipe, puffed it, and then turned it toward his guest. Harris took it tentatively.

What would the surgeon general think?

Harris grasped the bowl loosely and the long stem tightly. The smoke already crept up the length, tugging at his lips. He inhaled, a cool blast filling his lungs like honey on pancakes. He grinned. He didn't expect this. Like *sqwallen*, this stuff would make him high — an easy target for manipulation — putty in the Elector's hands. Still, it relaxed him and clarified things. He returned the pipe to its owner.

"My own *choice* has dogged me until this time," Enitachopco said. "Grimakadarian assured the outcome and I, the fool, followed him to this oblivion."

"Out of darkness comes the light," Coweeshee said.

"Into darkness goes the light," Elejoy added.

"His choice did us in," Tucharechee muttered, tapping his forehead. "Go with correct thinking." He pounded his chest. "Ignore the songs of passion."

"He must choose," Littafulchee remarked, "but he need not choose today."

"Still, he must know," Tucharechee said.

"Yes, I must," Harris snapped. "I don't believe in buying a *pogo-pogo* in a poke."

Enitachopco smiled, and agreed, his shoulders easing into his robes, his eye blinking.

"Two keepers were there," he said. "Two. One for the keys to the door of darkness and the other the keeper of the key to the door of light." He nodded to each brother in turn. "Grimakadarian, to darkness — I, to light. But not all things in darkness are dark. Not all things in light are light. My darkness slept within me, but Grimakadarian's light walked beside him."

"I don't understand," Harris said.

"My mother," Littafulchee replied.

"Hedonacaria?" Harris muttered.

The three brothers bowed their heads, while Yustichisqua nodded in prayer toward his *waddly wazzoo*.

"The darkness consumed Grimakadarian's mistress, the Memer Borshalit. But light shone bright upon their daughter, Hedonacaria. I was young — but twenty eons old. I saw her lustrous robes — her wondrous breasts, and I was struck by the light from the darkness. She was drawn to the dark of my light. I wished her for my own. So . . ."

"So, he used the key of light to open the door to darkness," Tucharechee growled.

"A sin beyond understanding," Elejoy added.

"All for the passion of the dark maiden who walked in light," Coweeshee explained.

"I had made my choice."

"A choice giving the dark one an excuse to emerge into Farn and demand his place among the Electors," Elejoy said.

"It caused a fracas, which has gone unhealed until this day," Coweeshee added.

"Which is why *choice* is an evil thing and blind dictation is best," Tucharechee concluded.

Harris mulled this over. Suddenly, the light of darkness (or the darkness of light) dawned on him.

"You started the war?" he asked Enitachopco.

"I caused an imbalance leading to eons of unrest and turmoil," the Elector explained, the sigh gusting again. "I claimed my Memer. We loved each other deeply. She had my babies — the children of Zacker, but . . ."

"After the warfare," Elejoy said.

"After the turmoil," Coweeshee added.

"After all was said and done and the land burnt and many places spoiled," Tucharachee moaned. "Then the ground trembled and belched forth its arbiter and its harsh conviction."

"The conditions for peace were exacting," Littafulchee said.

"*The Promise and Prophecy*," Harris murmured, trying to recall it, chapter and verse.

The brothers nodded. They had driven the point home. Lord Belmundus had connected the dots and understood the full weight of the twilight — the blend of darkness and light, which engulfed the House of Zacker even as it sank into the Cetronian depths.

"We are banished, as you know," Enitachopco said. "We were exiled from our beacon hill and downtrodden by the enemy Yunocker. The Elector of Montjoy has custodianship over us and, although Kuriakis is an easy tyrant, he embodies time's tedium. He preserves order, assuring neither darkness nor light predominates in Farn."

"Order he keeps," Harris said. "But *the Kalugu* is an abomination."

"There are those who would not agree with you," Littafulchee said. "Even some in Cetronia."

"I can't believe that."

"Believe it," Elejoy remarked. "Even in this council we are not of one mind."

Tucharechee grunted.

"Many suffered to come here," Coweeshee explained. "Those who refused the journey, split our union — our good face. They became Trones and their descendants were born into the servitude of *the Kalugu* and suffer the heavy laws of the enemy. In Cetronia some view the nonconformers as renegades, who drew *the reaptide* by their own fatal choice."

Harris trembled. How could anyone witness *the reaptide* and blame the victim. Victims have often been blamed for their fate. He knew this from outland experiences and a solid grounding in twentieth-century history. He played a child in a concentration camp, after all. It was still a rueful notion in many places — in unlikely places and held by people who should know better.

"Where are your hearts?" Harris asked. "How can you ignore the plight of those who suffer at *reaptide?"*

"All have kin there," Tucharechee said. "I would lead warriors across the Forling until the red dust burned the skin from my feet. I would pound *the Kalugu* walls to a nub and free our kin. But I am but one of five."

"Of four," Elejoy said.

Tucharechee grunted.

"Brother, be at ease," Coweeshee concluded. "We await Lord Belmundus' choice."

"Back to that," Harris said.

Silence, natural to this council, resumed its place. Enitachopco returned to his pipe, while his brothers muttered. Yustichisqua tended his *waddly wazzoo*. However, Littafulchee came forward, touching Harris' shoulder. He enjoyed the touch, but knew it was not meant as encouragement, but to steady him.

"I had a sister," Littafulchee said.

"I saw her image in *the Cartisforium*," Harris replied.

"This I know, but you have never asked about her."

"There are many things I haven't asked, my lady. Many things which go beyond my caring — given the priorities."

Litttafulchee glanced down. Harris thought he might have insulted her — an insensitive remark against a long-gone sister. Enitachopco tapped his pipe in his palm.

"Hetafulchee was from the darkness in my heart," Enitachopco said, sadly. He tugged away his eyepatch, pointing to the empty socket. Ghastly. "Light and dark are two cheeks upon a single face. My eldest daughter bore her grandfather's mark. So he claimed her."

Enitachopco sat back. Harris could swear tears rolled down from this missing eye. Littafulchee comforted her father, but the brothers turned their backs with a single uniform gesture.

"She is with him still," the Elector wept. "Grimakadarian took her — his own granddaughter, as his Memer. There she sits at his hideous side, stoking the cold shades of night beyond the dark portal. But . . ." He leaned forward, his finger pointing to his eye socket. "But each night she calls me through the darkness. She says *Papa. Papa. I am cold in this grave. Hear me and be warned. He desires to come forth again and devour everything beneath his foot. Papa. Papa. I would be the queen of death for Farn and the inlands and outlands and lands for as far as light is chased. Papa. Papa. Be warned.*"

Suddenly, Enitachopco smiled, covering his eye crater again. He fastened onto Littafulchee's shoulder and stood. He was a full seven feet, a silvery ghost in his ancient buckskins and his feathery crown.

"So the light shall rise again, because we have been given *the Promise and the Prophecy* as a settlement between Zin and Zacker," he intoned. "One daughter has called me from the darkness and . . ." He clasped Littafulchee to his breast. "And one daughter has called me from the light. Thus my two cheeks make one face again to confront the long night of Zin. And you, Lord Belmundus — you are the spark — the new kindling in a plan which has no pattern nor rhythm, much like light itself, shimmering. You are the water to lave the desert to full bloom."

His brothers stood — each a colossus. They neither comforted him nor rallied to his plan. They nodded to Harris in turn, each gesture packed with a stern commandment to make a *choice* soon.

Enitachopco grasped Harris' hands, and brought them up to his lips. He patted them before kissing each finger, and then led his council and their *waddly wazzoos* through the *kaleezo's* portal. Harris stood in near darkness with Yustichisqua still puttering with his lamp and Littafulchee standing remorseless in her father's wake.

2

"Well," Harris said nervously, "we should light those *bronskers* so I don't trip over my fucking bum foot and land on my ass."

"I shall do it, *oginali.*"

"Wait," Littafulchee said. "There is much to digest and it is best done in dim light. Too much is revealed in *the bronskers' false candle.*"

She stretched her arms like a bird, and then pitched her head back, looking to the dark ceiling. Her chest heaved as if preparing for a ritual. Harris stood stunned, staggering in waves of rose scent, like a bee seeking pollen.

"Yustichisqua," Littafulchee said.

Little Bird came to her side, and then released her robe, pulling it apart, revealing her shift. He carefully placed the buckskin aside, and then continued to undress her until she stood naked before Lord Belmundus. Harris gasped. Her beauty went beyond reckoning. Her silkened skin danced in *the waddly wazzoo's* dim light. Her breasts were full, a harvest for his taking, but he hesitated, struck dumb by awkwardness.

"Behold me," Littafulchee said.

"The light brushes you, my lady," Harris whispered. "It doesn't do you justice."

He looked to Yustichisqua to light *the bronskers*, but Little Bird remained beside *the waddly wazzoo*. Of the three remaining lamps, two were bright enough to reveal the Scepta's contours — enough to highlight *the gollywi* branded between her breasts — the blue holly mark of *the seegoniga*. But Harris would see more, his eyes wandering to her waist and thighs. But there the darkness prevailed.

"I would see you in a better light," he whispered. "Let Little Bird light *the bronskers.*"

"If you wish to see what your choice will bring, my love, you must shine your light upon me."

Harris took that as an invitation. He shimmied in his robe until only his *Columbincus* held it fast to his shoulders. He unclasped the brooch, letting the robe tumble.

"Old man," he stammered.

Yustichisqua did what he had done so many times, removing Lord Belmundus' belt and swords, releasing his blouse and *asano*, letting it slip, until the beauty of Harris' manhood arose in all its glory. Still, despite these revelations, Harris made scant progress to win this maiden, who still kept her arms apart, keen to allow his eyes to drink in whatever the light afforded. But the invitation halted in the shadows.

Harris sighed deeply. To take a single step would unman him, invalid now beyond his stunning appearance. He cocked his head, sulkily, tempting Littafulchee to take the next step, but she remained adamant. Suddenly, Harris clenched his fists, intending to beat his chest like an ancestral primate, but as he raised his arms, a tremor whipped his wrists, seeping up to his elbow, and then to his neck. He winced, opening his hands, an unrelenting pressure released like a new kind of orgasm, unknown to him, and yet like the real thing. From his fingers shot golden plasma, striking the ground and the third, dormant *waddly wazzoo*. The lamp — his lamp, shook, a glow kindling within, and then — without. It dazzled, so brightly the entire *kaleezo* illuminated — the wall inscriptions, the decorative ridgepole, the stellar fresco on the ceiling — all brilliantly bathed with the light of this single lamp.

Harris stepped backward, nearly falling. Yustichisqua went to a heap, covering his face, weeping. Harris hoped for joy. Littafulchee brought her arms together, and then turned slowly, allowing Harris to see her fully and without shame. He reached for her, but she avoided his touch.

"You are heaven," he muttered.

"No, Lord Belmundus," she said, reaching for her shift. "I am a promise for your consideration. I am no man's reward. I am the child of light and destined for your spark, if you will share it."

"*Chewohe*," he muttered.

"It is your choice," she said. Yustichisqua attended her again, wrapping her in the shift, covering her breasts lovingly — *the gollywi* disappearing behind this curtain. "You will be loved by the Cetrone despite your decision, and I shall never think the worst of you should you choose to hold tightly to your freedom."

She raised her arms, Little Bird replacing her buckskins, fastening her barrel buttons. As Harris' *waddly wazzoo* diminished, she hunkered near him, touching his naked chest. Her fingers were warm. Harris' heart raced. He clutched her hand.

"May I steal a kiss?" he asked.

Littafulchee grinned, and turned to Yustichisqua.

"Cousin." Little Bird nodded, and then turned his face away. This assured, Littafulchee nodded to Harris, whispering. "Lord Belmundus, you may taste my lips, if it pleases you."

Harris leaned forward, touching her chin. Her eyes drank him in. He was falling from a mountaintop. He drew her close, bringing his lips to hers, tasting them again as he had briefly in *the sustiya*. But this was not a picnic. This was a compact sealed — a down-payment on a decision he had almost made — his choice conceded. Would he think better of his freedom after she departed? He didn't care at this moment, but sipped her like nectar quaffed — he the bee upon the roses, stealing pollen for the hive. Then, it was over.

"It is good," she said.

Yustichisqua turned and came to Harris' shoulders, grasping them in restraint. Harris thought this a wise move, because without Little Bird's soft reminder, Lord Belmundus would have drifted from gentle lover to randy ram in a flash. This was not foreplay, but a liberty granted — the soft light of a lover's consignment. He nodded, and reached for his *asano.* Yustichisqua obliged him.

As near darkness returned, Littafulchee withdrew, her *waddly wazzoo* swaying in her departure. Not another word was exchanged. Harris was drained — exhausted as if he had been with Charminus for the usual fortnight.

"Shall I light *the bronskers* now, *oginali?*"

"No, old man. I think I'll sit here half-naked in the dark for a while. I have much to consider."

Yustichisqua gathered his lamp and went into the next room, leaving Harris sitting in the dimmest light of all, much like a star gone *nova.*

Chapter Nine

Kanuwudi

1

Harris was on the mend or, as the Cetrone say, *kanuwudi*. This recovery process was important, because every Echotan respected it once it was declared, and declared it was by Nayowee, and then Enitachopco. Handbills printed in strange Latinesque letters were posted through the town stating that Lord Belmundus had made a deep sacrifice to come to Cetronia and must be allowed this period of *kanuwudi* before his purpose would be revealed. The Echotans discussed this purpose openly and didn't admit knowing it. However, if the Elector was concerned for his guest's recovery, every amenity and consideration would be accorded.

Cosawta visited many times, monitoring Harris' progress, chattering about finishing *kanuwudi*, and then attend to the business of inspecting the Culpeeper brothers' various inventions. Harris felt up to it, except their workshop was not at Echota, but at Comastee, over the mountains and through the woods — a bumpy journey for a man experiencing locomotive difficulties. However, Cosawta, as impatient as he appeared, followed the edict of *kanuwudi*.

"My father advises me not to push you too fucking hard, Lord Belmundus."

"Time for that later," Harris remarked.

The *kaleezo* had been aired and freshly strewn with aromatics, most scents beyond Harris' linguistic abilities to pronounce or even remember. The only one he recalled was a potent fuchsia nosegay called *pupernisgi*, which choked him. He requested its removal and Yustichisqua complied. *The bronskers* were lit and a steady flow of native foods arrived on schedule, supervised by Yustichisqua, although ported by lads from the various clans — each clan taking a turn. Harris supposed, since the foods were various — never the same on any given day, these were clan favorites and perhaps identity traces. He never quibbled with a dish. He ate every morsel of flesh passed beneath his nose, be it gritty, pulpy or tender. Most dishes came with an assortment of vegetables, mostly mashed and earthen in color (and sometimes in taste). The purple stuff was the best. Nonetheless, he insisted on a daily ration of *selu gadu*, and fortunately all the clans ate this bread as their staple, although even these came in a variety of textures, shades and toppings. He felt the pounds going on. His actor's instincts kicked in. He had to get moving or he'd be like one of those Hawaiian royals, too fat to move on their own — carried by two dozen doyens. Much could be said for *kanuwudi*, but too much recovery might require a subsequent *kanuwudi* — recovery from the recovery.

Despite Cosawta's visits, the confined life grew tedious for Harris. Sleeping was good. Eating was fine, but watching the suns' dance on *the kaleezo's* walls and the halo from the moons didn't suit Lord Belmundus. He pondered much and wondered long. He considered *Chewohe* and wondered why no one pressed him to decide. Perhaps it was proscribed during *kanuwudi*. Thinking about it, however, was not banished, especially when he drifted to Littafulchee's indelible image standing in the bright light of his *waddly wazzoo*, her breasts radiant and beckoning.

She had not visited him since that night, nor did he expect it. Absence would raise the stakes. He had fallen down the rabbit hole once — as Moe Culpeeper would have declared. Harris must be circumspect. Love and passion were real, but were they transient or permanent? Who could tell what brand marked any given romantic opportunity? His relationship with Charminus was simple — a contract with only one signature and not his. He knew the stakes, even if Cetronia didn't unanimously subscribe to Enitachopco's plan. Destiny was destiny, but that didn't make it a contract — as illogical as ice cream on spaghetti. Harris held absolute rein on his destiny. Everyone courted kismet, but no one needed to subscribe to it.

Still, Littafulchee didn't come and he longed for her. Yustichisqua *did* come, because he lived in the back room. However, after he attended to Harris' needs, Little Bird did as little birds do. He flew to other activities beyond Lord Belmundus' knowing. Yustichisqua returned to supervise feeding and assure that Harris exercised. *The zulus* were handy to get about *the kaleezo*, and Harris had become an expert, learning the vicarious contours of balance. However, the injured foot needed a workout. So Little Bird appeared one day with a cane.

"I feel like an old man, *old man*," Harris said, taking the cane in hand. "This is light."

"Hollow," Yustichisqua said.

"I don't think it'll do."

"Yes, yes." Yustichisqua tugged at *Tony*. "I made it so *the brashun blade* would fit inside. It will be sturdy enough and the cane will now serve two purposes."

Harris grinned, unfastening *Tony*, slipping it into the hollow tube. The hilt locked into place.

"Good thinking."

"And you still have the other one for fast action, if need be."

Harris touched *Hierarchus*. He leaned on the cane and hobbled. The foot was stiff — pain no longer the issue, but his limp was prominent. If he ever returned to life upon the wicked stage, he'd be playing Long John Silver or Richard III. But youth is impervious to such bleak thoughts, and Harris considered the cane and the foot and the limp a passing inconvenience. He didn't think he'd be hobbling 'til the grave.

"Now I can give it a good workout," he declared.

"But you can use *the zulus* also, *oginali*."

"Maybe we could go out."

"When *kanuwudi* has passed."

Harris shook his head and walked faster, ignoring the comment. He headed for the door.

"*Oginali*, you cannot go until *kanuwudi* has passed."

"I don't give a flying fuck for *kana-fucking-wudi*." He turned on Yustichisqua. "I'm climbing the walls. And I'm getting fat." He pinched his waistline, which yielded nothing, but to Harris it did — an imaginary layer of potential flab — the blossoming of a new and unwanted him. "So you can follow me or lead me or stay here and pick lint out of your ass, old man. I'm taking a walk or a limp or maybe I'll go learn how to do the village dance."

He turned and propelled toward the door, quite efficiently using his new friend — *friend Tony*. He grinned and grabbed at his independence, but when he reached the threshold, it was blocked.

"Going somewhere?" came the rasping voice of Nayowee.

"Shit," Harris barked. "It's old Mother Hubbard."

Nayowee had a cane of her own. She poked at him until he turned and fled back to his bed, cursing with every step.

"I am glad to see you abandon your flying sandals — a lazy man's excuse for locomotion," she snarled. She hit *Friend Tony* with her cane. "Solid stick," she cackled. "I suspect there is more to it than wood." She turned to Little Bird. "Perhaps a bit of *brashun.*"

"Yes," Little Bird snapped, quite unimpressed by the old woman. "He is still *the Didaniyisgi* and *an Ayelli* lord. He must carry his symbol of office. You said — make a cane, and so I did."

"And you did," Nayowee said, mimicking Little Bird's last say. "And very well too, which I would think was beyond your ken and kittle. But even Nayowee can be wrong on rare occasions."

"I'm going out," Harris said, standing again.

"Yes, you are," Nayowee snapped, pushing him back down with her stick. She then turned, threatening Yustichisqua, who had moved to retaliate this disrespect. "If you value your *waddly wazzoo,*" she replied, "you best heed me. I can cure any harm I might bring to you, but I can also walk away and let you fade beside the lamp."

Yustichisqua paced, but then sat beside Harris. They appeared like two schoolchildren kept back for detention, the crone lecturing them on tardiness or misspelling.

"Yes, you are going out," Nayowee explained.

"Is *kanuwudi* passed?" Harris asked.

"You said so," she remarked. "As I approached I heard you shout that *kana-fucking-wudi* has passed. So it must be so, if that is what you intended."

"I did."

"Then it is so, but . . . " She pointed her cane at his nose. "Lord Belmundus, Echota is not a pleasure park for your condescension. Even our nobility are useful."

"I understand."

"Do you? I want you to exercise your injury well. I want you to fill your lungs with fresh air, but teach your body the ways of this people."

Harris looked to Yustichisqua, who chuckled.

"What's so funny, old man?"

"She means for you to work."

"Yes," Nayowee affirmed. "Dig something. Learn to speak. Do solid things. Make *gugu.*"

"*Gugu?*"

"You must be good at that. It is good exercise."

He looked to Little Bird, who blushed, but then slid his right index finger into the fist of his left hand going back and forth.

"Oh," Harris declared, grinning. "*Gugu.*"

Nayowee laughed. She shuffled away, kicking *the zulus* as she passed.

"I shall be watching you, Lord Belmundus. *Kanuwudi* has passed and I shall be watching you."

Harris twisted about looking after the crone as she trundled over the threshold. He then turned to Yustichisqua.

"Well, I hope she's not watching all the time. It would certainly take the punch out of *gugu.*"

Yustichisqua laughed, and then helped Harris up, assuring *Friend Tony*'s firm stance.

2

In the days which followed, Harris had the time of his life. At first he progressed about his *kaleezo's* immediate neighborhood, drawing stares. Children whispered about his limp and men pointed to *Friend Tony* with admiration. Soon, Harris ignored their curiosity. He was accustomed to this as an A-List actor, who drew more attention just crossing Santa Monica Boulevard, only now he didn't wear a disguise. In his position, he couldn't hide from his neighbors. They knew who he was and wanted to know more. But he fastened his attentions on them and their activities. This settled the question. Soon, they regarded him as just another outlander — much like the occasional drifter from *the Dodingdaten.*

Harris pushed beyond the boundaries to the fields edging Echota. Here *the selu* was grown and he observed *the tlugu* clan tending the tall stalks, which grew toward the suns. Yustichisqua guided Harris through the stout rows, where he greeted the workers, men and women, picking the long ears. The crop was similar to corn, except the ears twisted into three husks, each a different color — yellow, purple and ruby. The silks reflected this and each pod looked like a voodoo rattle. The men reached for the ears, twisting them from the stalk, tossing them into a basket, which children dragged on *dollywaggles*. The women shucked the husks, separating the spiral ears into three sacks — yellow, purple and ruby. They sang, as all Cetrone did, rhythmic tunes born deep in the soil and secure in the light. Harris reached for a husk and, to his delight, a young *tlugu* maiden showed him how to shuck it properly. He tried his hand at it and, joined by Yustichisqua, worked beside *the dollywaggle* with a feeling he had earned his evening portion of *selu gadu.*

In an adjacent field, *geetli* folk dug *byudra* root. Harris found this more back breaking, but he learned the art of *the buggeroo* — the sharp digging tool, which managed, when pressed properly, both to lift the turnip-like rhizome from the soil and cut it from its roots cleanly. Another army of *dollywaggles* received *the byudra.* Harris found this work more tiring, but enjoyed sitting around in a circle, chewing a raw one, which he found pleasant, if not tart. His first bite raised gales of laughter from *the geetli* men, who were chastised for it by the *geetli* women. Harris also liked their songs better than *the selu* harvesters' — a steady beat to match the digging and a chorus of whoops to ease *the dollywaggle's* push and pull.

"I like these in a pie," Yustichisqua said shaking *a byudra* tuber. "When we were fortunate to get *a byudra* in *the Kalugu,* we guarded it with care, because the Yunockers also like the taste and they would take it. Five *byudras,* with plenty of *caliseegee,* makes a fine pie."

Harris imagined his mother's hot apple pie, and even more, a New York version with a thick wedge of sharp cheddar melting across the latticework. He sorely would have liked some pie. His wish came true, because, within a day, he explored the glories of *the adanadasga* — the Echotan bakery, *alisoqua* run and operated. Here *the selu gadu* was made — the kernels wrought into fine flour, and then mixed with spring water and *awidena* fat. The women shaped and pounded the loaves, while the men stoked the ovens. Hot as Harris found *the adanadasga,* he was intrigued by the industry — the uniform size of each loaf and the perfect rise before being popped into the ovens. Then they were stacked in lines in tall *perpadranum* — baskets sufficiently open to cool the bread for consumption. Harris manned the line, taking on his mash of *selu* meal, pushing it, shaping it and finally making a mess of it, much to *alisoqua* delight. Little Bird found it amusing, but did not offer to make it better. Finally, gentle hands came from behind Harris, taking his arms and guiding him through the process. He grinned as the loaf took shape. Perfection.

"I made bread," he exclaimed as if it were the first loaf in creation.

He then turned to thank the woman, but she was departing quickly.

"Littafulchee," he gasped.

He started after her, but Little Bird stopped him.

"She has been watching you, *oginali*, but I do not think she means for you to touch her again until . . ."

"Yes, yes," he stammered. "You're right."

"You must finish your bread, because it is not *gadu* yet. Just a popkin pleading for the fire."

Harris grinned. He was encouraged by his help mates, and even more pleased by his lump of *selu* dough. He looked for a *gorsatsgi* — the Cetrone equivalent to a pizza paddle, and, with the master *alisoqua* baker's assistance, slid his creation into the hot and fiery furnace. He turned to await the outcome only to be presented with a gift. *Byudra pie.*

"See, *oginali*. They like you here."

Harris grinned, grasping the plate.

"Get two forks, old man and we'll make short work of this."

<h1 style="text-align:center">3</h1>

Perfect pie. Perfect *selu gadu,* although Harris suspected even if the bread imploded, *the alisoqua* would have declared it a high-scoring ten. Over the next three days, he watched for Littafulchee observing him and, although he knew she tracked his moves, she kept circumspectly hidden. Nayowee was not as circumspect. While Harris was learning how to cure *awi-eeni* skins into *asano* in the *chisqua* tannery, Nayowee popped out from behind the stinkpots and accosted him with her cane, poking his leg, coming dangerously, if not injuriously, near his balls.

"You are working well, I see, but you must not undo my good mending, Lord Belmundus."

"I know what I'm about," he complained, having almost cut *the awi-eeni* skin too deeply. "You commanded me to learn, and learn I have."

"Making a great show of it," she cackled. "I'd like to see you make *asano* all day and night for a week, and then tell me what you have learned."

"If you wish it."

Nayowee poked *the awi-eeni* skin with her fingers.

"I do not wish it, nor do I command you. Your fear of me commands you." She laughed, and then came close to him, whispering. "And you are showing off for the maiden, I know. I know. Best road to *gugu*." She laughed hysterically, putting *the chisqua* tanners off their stride. "But from what I see, if you made all our *asano*, we would need to go naked for the lack of quality."

Harris cocked his head.

"Your work is fine, *oginali*," Yustichisqua snapped.

"What would you know about it, mighty *Taleenay*?" Nayowee asked.

Yustichisqua pushed the cane aside and stared down the old lady.

"I have handled the finest garments on *the Ayelli* and know the quality of every manner of *asano*. You only know the warts on the end of your nose."

"Yustichisqua," Harris said, worried they might be turned into slithering *bollinganga*.

"I shall leave you, Lord Belmundus," Nayowee snapped, turning, pushing the tanners aside. "You are in good hands." She turned. "At least, this one will not steer you astray of the mark."

Harris bowed curtly to her, noticing a shadow near the entrance and guessed who it might be.

After tanning, Harris observed *the seegoniga* building *kaleezos* and repairing the same. Houses in Cetronia were called *yehu*, although Harris had come to call them *kaleezos* only to learn this was the term for *slave quarters*. The construction was the same, but the intent was different. Still his own *yehu* was dubbed *the Kaleezo*, in deference to his ignorance and also because he liked the demeaning imprint it leant his brand. Too long this *Ayelli* lived in palaces. He learned the many uses of *jupsim*, a substance he was already glad to know — a coating which had saved his ass in the Forling. He watched Tomatly buzz around the deflated *Gananadana*, brushing a new coat of the stuff along each rib and rim.

Finally, after three weeks, he visited *the Deedaloquasdi* — the Cetrone school, where children of all clans learned language, writing, courtesy and tradition. He found the place infectious and the children loved him. Rarely did *big people* visit and here there were two. Harris mimicked their recitations and listened carefully to the wisdom from their teacher, a young *seegoniga* named Wanona, a pretty thing, with a smile the children came to caress with trust.

Harris exercised with the school, a morning drill of jumping jacks and *zulu* rolls, mixed with handstands and, most beneficial for him, a hopping routine, which made him fall at first — the children loving it. They jumped on him and tickled him. Best, he loved to dance *the alsagi*, a slow, swaying number, with hand gestures, which told the story of *the waddly wazzoo*. He was happy to have his own lamp now and could find the rhythm of light. The accompanying chant was simple to learn:

> *From the center of the world*
> *Comes the lamp which lights the way*
> *To the edge of darkness swirled,*
> *Separating night from day,*
> *Rock away lantern in shadows through*
> *Pure heart of fire, waddly wazzoo.*
> *Waddly wazzoo.*
> *Waddly wazzoo.*

However, what Harris loved best at *the Deedaloquasdi* was Yustichisqua's attentions to Wanona. It was evident Little Bird was smitten by the school teacher's smile, much like the children, but beyond it. When Wanona ran her language drills, Yustichisqua would stare guilelessly at her, and, better still, she winked at him, sending *the Taleenay* into rapturous sighs. Harris gathered him about the shoulders, squeezing with approval.

"She is mine," Little Bird whispered.

"Have you spoken to her yet?" Harris asked.

"No need, *oginali*. She is mine.*"*

Harris detected a need to provide amorous instruction — the gentle art of courtship, which he assumed could be adapted to the Cetrone way. However, Yustichisqua explained.

"I am fortunate, *oginali*. Wanona will be my mate if I decide to make *Chewohe*."

Harris grinned, but soon considered the situation. Yustichisqua had been promised this maidenly prize by the powers that be, if he performed *Chewohe*. But Little Bird was predicating his decision on Harris'. How's that for additional pressure? Harris was fighting a losing battle.

"I think it's time for me to pay a visit," Harris said.

"To my cousin?"

"Yes."

"But she may not see you, *oginali.*"

"She may not, but surely Cosawta will."

Chapter Ten

Journey to Comastee

1

Harris had been considering Cosawta's invitation to see the Culpeeper brother's inventions. He meant to consult Nayowee, but after the incident in the tannery, he wanted to avoid the mistress of *the asi-asa*. This was wishful thinking, but fiction or not, he endorsed it. Harris anticipated a visit from Cosawta because he had frequented *the kaleezo* during *kanuwudi*, but the Seneschal stayed away.

"He might be traveling again," he suggested to Yustichisqua.

"How so, *oginali*? Tomatly repairs *the Gananadana*."

"True."

So Harris sought Cosawta in his haven — *the Asowisdi* — the House of Light, a grand *yehu* — Echota's tallest building, spiraling above the trees. Enitachopco shunned it, and Littafulchee prefered to make her quarters in *the seegoniga* clan house. But Cosawta, true to form, had erected this monument to his unbridled position. Considering the Seneschal rarely dwelled in Cetronia, Harris wondered why this high-maintenance dwelling was required. *Chutzpah*, he supposed. Soon, he'd learn the secret.

As he approached *the Asowisdi* with Yustichisqua, a sharp, but familiar odor bit his nose.

"I know that stink," Harris muttered.

"It is *charpgris, oginali.*"

"Tiger piss?" He halted, raising a hand, preventing Yustichisqua's progress. "You didn't break a bottle of that shit, did you?"

"I do not carry it. No need. No Yunockers. Perhaps it is worn by the Seneschal's *Dodingdaten* companions."

"*Fumarcas?*"

He considered the Culpeeper brothers and their lack of bathing. But nothing human could ever approximate *charpgris'* stench. There could be only one explanation.

They looked to one another, and then to *the Asowisdi's* threshold. Two *seegoniga* warriors stood guard. Upon recognizing Lord Belmundus, they opened the doors. Harris tugged

Yustichisqua forward, nodding to the guards as he passed them. He entered into a spacious antechamber, wary, because the stink intensified.

"What is this place, old man?" Harris asked.

"I have never entered *the Asowisdi, oginali.* I think Lord Cosawta lives apart for strange reasons."

"Perhaps I should've sent him word to visit me."

Suddenly, a roar — a distinct feline calling card, came from behind the next array of closed doors. Yustichisqua clutched Harris, or could it have been the other way 'round?

"Perhaps we'll come another day," Harris suggested.

"Perhaps."

As they turned to leave, the inner doors opened, revealing the Seneschal imperiously standing on the threshold. Under leash, he held two *tludachi*, which pulled him forward upon seeing the visitors. Harris decided this visit might have been a bad idea. *The tludachi* roared in turn, and then together. Harris bolted as fast as his foot and *Friend Tony* would permit. Little Bird beat him to the exit. The guards laughed.

"Lord Belmundus," Cosawta shouted. "Do not worry. These fuckers are my pets — as tamed as *awidena* in the meadow."

The cats snarled, but when Cosawta tugged on the leashes, they calmed, withdrawing to his heel, sitting beside him like two stuffed armrests. He roared, and not unlike his *tludachi* pets.

"They need exercise," Cosawta explained. "I have many furries and slinkies in this shit house. That is why it is so accommodating. Would I need such amplitude for me alone? I have been in *the Kalugu.* But these little fuckers need a place to roam." He clapped, and the two guards attended the beasts, each taking a leash. "Give them an ample walk. Take them to *the pogo-pogo* pen for a tidbit."

Harris approached, cautiously. Yustichisqua walked in his shadow.

"You don't have many visitors, I suppose," Harris said.

"Bitch and Bastard," Cosawta exclaimed.

"Excuse me?"

"Their names." Cosawta clamped his arms about the neck of the male, rumpling its mass of lavender fur. It purred at his touch. "Bastard here." He then stroked the female's head. "Bitch does not like hugging." Bitch yawned, while Bastard snorted, and then made a small roar — a muffled sound, which Harris found discouraging. "I've mated them, Lord Belmundus. I have little *tludachi's* throughout this shithouse."

"Pisshouse," Harris replied, sniffing.

"So you say." Cosawta replied. "I am quite accustomed to the perfume. It suits me." He laughed again, releasing his pets to the guards — not guards after all, Harris realized, but two of many zookeepers. When Bitch and Bastard were out of sight (not before glancing back and displaying their saber teeth), Harris came to Cosawta's side, bowing slightly. Yustichisqua managed to step in a load of *tludachi* shit.

"*Torpeda,*" he swore.

"Lots of that about," Cosawta said. "Be glad you are not wearing *zulus* today."

He laughed, and then guided Harris through the inner doors.

A vaulted chamber was hung with caged birds, arising perhaps forty feet. Keepers tended them. Harris didn't feel any safer, remembering the scarlet tanager-like birdies when he learned how to fire his *Stick*. Those nasties — called *porgeedasqui*, had attacked him. Birds in Farn had a vicious streak, so Harris kept his eyes on the cages, hoping they were locked.

At the chamber's center sat an overstuffed red cushion ringed with bowls of *sqwallen*. The Seneschal was sequestered here beyond a menagerie. However, he didn't appear to be under the drug's influence.

"Take care," Cosawta said, throwing himself on the cushion. "Do not kick over my supply of relaxation. *Sqwallen* is rare in these parts, this batch cured for me, in particular, by Tomatly."

"Does he also administer *the pilocarpinus*?" Yustichisqua asked.

"Ah. You are bold before your Seneschal."

Little Bird bowed, but didn't appear contrite.

"I have no tolerance for *sqwallen*," he replied.

"Understandable from one who knows its allure and its . . ."

"Its curse."

"Just do not kick the bowls or get *tludachi* shit on my cushions."

Little Bird stepped back.

"We've intruded on your solace, Cosawta," Harris said, preamble to stammering an apology and making an escape. His gaze still darted between ceiling and cages. "Perhaps we should meet in my *kaleezo* as we have in the past."

"No, no," Cosawta said. "You had to see my shithouse sooner or later." He tapped the cane. "I see you mend well. Still, you need this device."

Harris grinned, stepped back and grasped the hilt firmly. He drew *Tony* from its scabbard, *the brashun blade* shimmering. Cosawta stood. The birds went wild — cackles and caws, squawks and hoots. Harris raised the sword, expecting to make chicken salad.

"They think you are attacking me."

"Oh," Harris said. He sheathed the sword. Calm was restored. "Such devotion."

"Yes," Cosawta replied.

He glanced down. From beneath the cushions slithered three *bolligangas*, each as thick as an elephant's leg and as long as an Amazon map. Yustichisqua went for *gasohisgi*, but Cosawta raised his hand.

"Retreat slowly," he suggested. "These are not as trained up as Bitch and Bastard are."

Harris moved back now.

"We'll be going," he said.

"Slowly," Cosawta replied. "And back out."

"We still need to talk," Harris said as he padded backwards, supported by *Friend Tony*.

"I know why you have come, Lord Belmundus, and I shall be happy to escort you to Comastee to see what I have longed to show you."

Harris nodded, glanced back at the door, where Bitch and Bastard were returning from their *pogo-pogo* meal, blood still dripping from their canines. He hesitated and thought Little Bird would lose his constraint on *gasohisgi*.

"Steady, old man," Harris muttered as the beasts passed within a foot on each side. Harris grinned at them. He thought he saw a gleam in Bastard's eyes, which said *dessert*. "Steady, old man."

Cosawta sat again, reaching for his *sqwallen*. The *bolligangas* coiled around his legs, their tongues caressing his knees. One inched up his arm and shared *the sqwallen*. Cosawta kissed its head, and then raised the bowl to Harris.

"Tomorrow at dawn, Lord Belmundus. I shall meet you and your bold *Taleenay* before your *kaleezo*. Wear *zulus* and pack *a korinkle* of whatever tickles your fancy. I promise you, I shall be alert, and free of this shit by then." He slurped the mush, pushing the snake aside. "Tomorrow I shall take you to Comastee where your fucking eyes will open wide to the wonders we have wrought."

Reaching the antechamber's threshold and clearing *the tludachi*, Harris turned and hobbled as fast as he could through the doors, Yustichisqua muttering behind him.

"*Torpeda,*" he spluttered. "I stepped in it again."

But the air freshened as they put *the Asowisdi* behind them.

2

Cosawta showed up the following morning, sober and without his pets. Instead, Tomatly attended him, impatient to begin the journey. Harris met the Seneschal outside *the kaleezo*, Yustichisqua still frosty from the previous day. Cosawta didn't seem to care.

"You handle yourself well on *zulus*, Lord Belmundus," he noted. "But I am glad you still tote your *brashun blades.*"

Harris clutched *Friend Tony* and nodded toward *Hierarchus*, which dangled from his belt. *A korinkle* was slung over his shoulders. He had to adjust his stance, because he wasn't accustomed to carrying this load while hovering on *zulus*. Yustichisqua carried two *korinkles*, the overspill of necessity.

"How far is it to Comastee?" Harris asked.

"Far enough," Cosawta replied. "But the country is fair and the weather is fine."

He lifted off on his *zulus*, Tomatly waving for Harris to follow. The experience was novel. Until now, the highest Harris had flown on *zulus* was over a big puddle in *the Yuganawu* — a short flight. Generally, he drifted no more than a few feet from the ground. Now he followed the Seneschal and his attendant over Echota's colorful rooftops, dodging tree branches and clan totems. Below him, *the budrya* diggers were up and at it. A few waved, but Harris feared dropping *Friend Tony*, so he didn't return the greeting. Yustichisqua flew beside him.

"Do you know where we're going, old man?"

"Comastee."

"I know that. Do you know the way?"

"Never have I been there, *oginali*, but I know it is on the other side of Mount Talasee, through *the Usquanigo,* up *the Itsayusi Yuweya* and over *the Ama Udali* to *the Didadusi.*"

"You don't say," Harris said, shaking his head. "Why don't I just nod off. You wake me when we fly over the rainbow."

"If we are fortunate, we shall see one."

Harris didn't pursue the explanation. He recalled seeing a rainbow on their first approach to Cetronia from the Forling. His only fear now was that Yustichisqua would tell him the name of the phenomena — probably a long-ass word like *bibiddybopiddybo.* He learned later it was simpler (although long) — *yunogolada.* Fortunately, rainbows were rare.

The *Usquanigo* turned out to be a valley — the Valley of Mystery, although Harris didn't know what *mystery* it held. Through it ran *the Itsayusi Yuweya* — the Green River, and it *was* green in the shadow of Mount Talasee's formidable walls. Pine aroma intoxicated the riverbanks and Harris was drawn to memories of pleasant outings at Yosemite. In fact, Mount Talasee's precipitous ridge reminded him of *El Capitan.*

"It is beautiful, *oginali*," Yustichisqua said. "I had heard tales of this valley, but never could I imagine it to be so lovely."

"Lovely, it is! Lovely, it is!" shouted Tomatly at the fore. "But in the waters many dangers dwell."

"Let's not go there," Harris said.

Cosawta laughed.

"If time permitted, I would cast a line into the stream and add to my fucking *atsadi* tanks. Good *torgentli* swim and hunt within these waters."

"Something to feed your *bolligangas*?" Harris asked.

"Ha! One *torgentli* male could swallow a *bolliganga* whole. "

Harris glanced at the rushing green waters, expecting the emergence of a fish so large it could ingest a python-size *bolliganga* — a fin or a silvery bulge beneath the verdant rush. But the river seemed bucolic — an invitation to picnic on its banks.

Cosawta dipped, pointing to a lush copse of broad-leafed trees — elders, perhaps. Harris was shy a botany lesson, so elm or elder was much the same to him. He supposed if he had known the Cetrone word, he would forget it as fast as he heard it.

They landed, Tomatly trotting ahead to a shady spot. The wind rustled and birdsong burst within the tree boughs. The diminutive

Cetrone opened his *korinkle,* producing his *waddly wazzoo.* He chanted and danced, whipping the lamp around until the birds arose like locusts, abandoning the branches.

"*Porgeedasqui,*" Yustichisqua said.

"Not boon companions for lunching," Cosawta explained.

Harris wasn't hungry; nor was he tired. *Zulu* travel was easy, despite the accusations of Nayowee on laziness. The lunch conversation was light, mostly because they chomped on *mongerhide* and drank *brantsgi.* Still, Harris was wary to ask about the locale, fearing a barrage of new Cetrone vocabulary. He had already forgotten the stuff Little Bird spluttered to this point in the journey, replacing the geographical references with his own — Mystery Valley, Green River, beastie fish and nasty birds.

Cosawta belched, and then stood.

"Enough," he announced. "We have fucking far to go."

He sprang to the air, Tomatly beckoning the nasty birds back to their branches. Harris gathered his *korinkle* and followed. Yustichisqua lingered to piss, but soon flew again beside his *oginali* through Mystery Valley over the Green River.

Soon, they avoided the riverbanks.

"*Sittoquo! Sittoquo!*" Tomatly shouted, and then placed a finger over his lips for silence.

Harris looked to Yustichisqua for an explanation.

"*The Sittoquo* is the sacred tree, *oginali,*" he whispered.

"Sacred? How so?"

"They grow near the portal of Zin. Enitachopco planted a grove near the ceremonial grounds where *Chewohe* is performed."

Harris immediately looked toward the grove — *the Sittoquo.* They were a twisted crop — gnarled boughs and metallic leaves — ominous, like the portals of Zin. Beyond them, a circumferential clearing was littered with stakes and water troughs — *the Chewohe* ceremonial grounds, he presumed.

"Tell me more," he said.

"You will know when you decide," Cosawta said, his gruff whisper cutting the breeze. "It is not proper to speak in places where *the Sittoquo* can hear you."

"Hear you?"

"You will know when you seek the knowledge, Lord Belmundus."

Harris swallowed hard, and then stared down at the trees — an ugly crop, like arboreal versions of Nayowee, waiting for his words to spin into gossip, passing it along the bough tips and the sharp edges of the leaves. Harris guessed he had found the valley's mystery. He kept his speculation to himself, because the flying party left the ceremonial grounds and approached a wide part of the river.

"*The Ama Udali*," Cosawta said.

A pool — no, a lake spread before them, reflecting both sky and mountain, but commanded more attention than either. Along its banks massed mounds of white crystals — blanched sand or quarried quartz. Harris couldn't tell which.

"What's that crust, old man?"

"*Ama.*"

"Salt?" Harris knew that word and should have been able to parse it with *Udali*, the word for lake. "A salt lake." *Where were the Mormons — their tabernacle and their mystical underwear?* "Amazing."

3

Harris glanced down at the waters, his image reflecting back. The distance was sufficient to ripple the picture, but the lake pristine enough to clarify it. Yustichisqua's imaged raced beside his, while Cosawta and Tomatly's led the way. *Exhilarating.*

Schools of fish darted below the lake's surface, a large predator's shadow pursuing them. Was this the dreaded *torgentli*? Harris couldn't tell. However, he hoped it didn't fly or leap. Whatever owned the shadow, it glided swiftly through the brine. Then, as the school detoured, the shadow in pursuit, Harris observed a green glint — a flicker from his hand. He looked to his ring finger. The jade signet glowed. His double *Columbincus* radiated to full brightness. *Hierarchus* flickered also, and *Tony* tugged from within the cane's hollow.

"What the fuck?" he muttered.

"*Oginali*," Yustichisqua said, having a similar experience with *gasohisgi*.

Suddenly, the lake smudged, green bile clouding its purity. The reflections muddied and miasma steamed from the surface. Cosawta dropped back, linking his arm into Harris'. Tomatly did the same with Little Bird.

"What's happening?" Harris asked.

"Shit if I know, Lord Belmundus," Cosawta replied. "It must be related to your *Columbincus* — the great double stab of power."

"*Yichiyusti*! *Yichiyusti*!" Tomatly exclaimed.

Cosawta glanced skyward.

"Ah! That too. He stirs."

The heavens changed to the green sky of *Yichiyusti*.

"Kuriakis," Harris gasped. "Is he here?"

"No," Cosawta replied. "But when the great muffin stirs, the air turns foul and nature reciprocates. *The Ama Udali* does not like *Yichiyusti* and, from what I observe, it does not like your array of power — ring, brooch and swords. You are a lightning rod, Lord Belmundus, I suppose. But what the fuck do I know?"

They were losing altitude fast as the fog thickened.

"What's wrong with my *zulus*?" Harris asked.

"I believe you have blown them out."

"What?"

"*Yichiyusti*! *Yichiyusti*!"

Tomatly tugged at Yustichisqua's arm, because Little Bird began to fall. Cosawta steadied Harris.

"Are we going for a swim?" Harris asked. "Because I saw one of those monster fish, and he looked hungry."

"*The torgentli* do not need hunger to bite your ass and chew your balls," Cosawta said, half laughing. "But I sense land ahead. Tomatly?"

Tomatly raised his *waddly wazzoo*, the lamp shooting a beacon through the mist. Harris watched it disappear, lost in the soup. Tomatly laughed like a hyena.

"*Tlugu*! *Tlugu*!"

"Trees, *oginali*. We no longer fly over water."

"We no longer fly," Cosawta said, grasping Harris fervently as they plummeted, the ground suddenly coming up.

Harris landed chest first — better than leg first. Still, it was not a gentle landfall. He groaned, spitting out clumps of mud — salty. The lake must still be nearby. He had lost touch with Cosawta and couldn't see much, the fog clinging to him like his sweaty *asano*. However, the various apparatus still glowed — ring, brooch, sword, and *Tony* danced inside the cane's hollow.

Harris sat up and took a quick inventory. His *waddly wazzoo* was still safely kindled on his belt. His *korinkle* stayed latched to his back. He tugged at *Tony's* hilt, sliding the sword out. It glowed. Then he heard the forest grumble — birds and toads and whatever slithered in this place.

"Old man," Harris called.

"I am here, *oginali*," came a disembodied voice from within the fog. "Stay still and I will find you."

"Are you hurt?"

"I am, but not injured."

Harris heard footsteps and suspected those were Little Bird's. But Cosawta appeared, stretching, and then cracking his neck.

"Welcome to *the Didadusi*, Lord Belmundus." He pulled Harris to his feet. "You fall hard, like a wounded dove from an amorous arrow."

"Go fuck yourself," Harris muttered.

"I have tried," Cosawta laughed. "But self-*gugu* requires a longer donger than even this Seneschal has."

"Longer donger! Longer donger!" came Tomatly's cry, emerging into the clear.

"Where's Yustichisqua?" Harris asked.

"I am here, *oginali. Torpeda.*"

"*Torpeda! Torpeda!*"

"Is he a fucking parrot?" Harris asked, brushing muck from his *asano*. He took an unsteady step, and then grabbed *Friend Tony* to keep him upright. "And what's wrong with *the zulus*?"

"I told you, they are blown out." Cosawta grasped Harris' shoulder. "*You* have blown them out."

"I can't see how. I didn't do anything."

"You are new to your special powers. Unusual things occur when Kuriakis stirs." He looked skyward as if he could see the green hue beyond the fog. "We will need to hike through *the Didadusi* forest and over the Nuckasee Hills."

"He cannot walk," Yustichisqua snapped.

"He must try."

"I will," Harris conceded. "But no guarantees."

Cosawta looked to Tomatly, and then plunged his hand into the buckskin pouch draped beside his *brantsgi* canteen. He pulled out a small black device, which Harris recognized immediately.

"A cell phone?" Harris exclaimed. "You have a cell phone?"

Cosawta held up the device.

"*A sillifoon*," he said.

"*Sillifoon! Sillifoon!*"

Cosawta peered at it, and then frowned.

"I fear it has been blown out too." He randomly pressed the buttons, and then shrugged. "As dead as our *zulus*."

Harris stood aghast. *A cell phone.* He had forgotten such devices had even been invented in this technologically backward corner of Farn. He reached for it.

"May I?"

Cossawta surrendered it. Harris scanned its face, Yustichisqua looking on with fascination.

"What does it do, *oginali*?"

"It allows the far speech," Cosawta replied.

"The far speech," Little Bird stammered, awestruck.

The keypad was oddly made, the numbers unintelligible to Harris, but he assumed there might be hidden features, if he could get the screen to illuminate.

"Where did you get this?" he asked Cosawta.

"Moe Culpeeper," Cosawta replied. "*The Fumarca* find use in such things. They insisted I have one, so they could . . . how did they put it: *ring me up*. I always forget to put it to bed, where *the aniniya* kisses it, renewing its life. They *ring me up* to say when they are coming to visit and to tell me of progress. Otherwise, it is a useless thing. It never worked in *the Kalugu*, because *the kowlinka* and the strange atmosphere during *Yichiyusti* dampen its operation."

"Amazing," Harris said.

He touched the keyboard and *the sillifoon* lit, flickering. He pressed a few keys randomly. Then the device buzzed, hummed and went dead.

"I thought we could . . . *ring them up* in Comastee," Cosawta explained. "Then they would know we needed assistance."

"Like calling triple A," Harris muttered. "Nice try, and good thinking."

"Glad you approve, Lord Belmundus, but it would be more helpful if you could walk through forests and climb hills."

"Go fuck yourself," Harris reiterated, grinning.

"I have tried."

Harris rolled his eyes, and returned *the sillifoon* to the Seneschal, before Tomatly reprised a chorus of *longer donger*.

"What now?"

"I suppose we should rest here for the night," Cosawta said.

"Is it night?"

"It could be, but . . ." he raised his palms as if checking for rain. "It might as well be night for us."

Harris looked to the sky, seeing tree boughs instead.

"The fog's clearing."

"Maybe. But we should gather around our *waddly wazzoos* and eat our provisions."

Harris glanced at Yustichisqua, who looked to the trees uneasily.

"They are watching us, *oginali*," Little Bird said.

"Who?"

"*The porgeedasqui.*"

Harris shuddered, but swung his lamp, joining the others. As they formed this campfire of sorts, Cosawta tucked *the sillifoon* in his pouch.

"Keep your double *Columbincus* glowing brightly, Lord Belmundus. The birds are not partial to the light." He grinned. "They are, however, partial to flesh."

"*To flesh! To flesh!*"

Chapter Eleven

The Treasures of the Yigoya

1

The ominous and hungry sounds in the trees kept Harris on edge. However, he kept his double *Columbincus* blazing, and both *Tony* and *Hierarchus* unsheathed at the ready. Yustichisqua held *gasohisgi* high as if to say *just try something, you nasty birds*. The *waddly wazzoos* shone brightly, creating an illuminated zone around the huddled travelers. Still, the birds hoped and watched. Other sounds — forest grumbles and ground tremors, promised other threats.

"*The Didadusi* holds many terrors, Lord Belmundus," Cosawta explained. "Our light keeps *the porgeedasqui* at bay, but there are things that favor darkness."

"*Zinbears! Zinbears!*" Tomatly chirped.

"*Zinbears?*" Yustichisqua gasped, holding *gasohisgi* higher, as if it made a difference.

"Not so," Cosawta reassured him. "*Zinbears* are solitary creatures of the pit. No. I think there might be a *gati-bati* roaming in these woods."

"*A gati-bati,*" Little Bird stammered.

Harris grasped Yustichisqua's arm, shaking it.

"What's that?" he asked.

"A dragon*, oginali* — one that walks on two legs and is higher than the trees."

The *porgeedasqui* stirred, obviously abandoning their perches, squawking to the night sky. Harris braced himself, glaring at Cosawta.

"What remedy have we for a *bati-gati?*"

"*A gati-bati,*" Cosawta replied. "I am afraid if such a beast shows up . . ." He glanced at the now silent boughs. "And something has scared the fucking *porgeedasqui* off . . . I would say we have no remedy."

The rumbling increased.

"*The lights. The lights.*" Tomatly said. "*Gati-bati* love the lights."

Yustichisqua sheathed *gasohisgi.*

"Good idea," Harris said, doing likewise with *Tony* and *Hierarchus.* "Dim our lamps."

Cosawta shrugged.

"Precaution is a thin wire walked by men with few choices, Lord Belmundus."

However, he dimmed his *waddly wazzoo.*

Harris draped his cape over his *Columbincus*. Suddenly, they sat in relative darkness, illumination peeking from shade and crevice. Harris listened intently. The rumbling subsided.

"Has it gone?" he asked.

"Hard to say," Cosawta replied. "I have never seen one and only know the legends."

"Then it could be anything. You could be wrong."

"I am often wrong, but I compensate for my shortcomings with rash actions. If a *gati-bati* came upon us, I would happily throw your *Taleenay* and my *steward* under its feet and help you escape."

"You're a bastard, you know."

Cosawta laughed.

"That is my pet *tludachi's* name. *The Fumarca* would have called me a shit head."

"That too." Harris listened. "Whatever it was, it's gone."

"I hear something, *oginali*," Yustichisqua whispered.

Harris listened again. He heard it now. A rattling, like the flapping of wings. *Wings?*

"Jesus H Christ," he stammered. "We'd better light up again. Those fucking attack birds are coming back."

"So they are," Cosawta said.

Harris quickly uncovered his *Columbincus*, unsheathing his *brashun* blades. The *waddly wazzoos* were fired up again. Yustichisqua raised *gasohisgi* above his head. They braced for a lumbering aerial attack, because *the porgeedasqui* had a momentum that would carry them beyond their distaste for light to the feast of flesh they loved so well.

"Hold tight, old man," Harris muttered.

But Little Bird had thrust himself from the circle and stood with his arms stretched wide, prepared to shield Harris from the onslaught.

"Lie low, *oginali.*"

"What are you doing?" Harris shouted, trying to pull Yustichisqua down.

Suddenly, the light increased, a wide circle forming above them, and hovering — a blinding light, which brought them into a huddle. Then, the illumination shifted to a spot just beyond the grove.

"What's going on?" Harris asked, rooting about on *Friend Tony.*

He turned to Yustichisqua.

"Are you nuts? You could've been killed."

"I am sorry to disappoint," Little Bird snapped. "I am expendable. You are not."

Harris felt like beating Little Bird to a pulp. When would Yustichisqua embrace his own worth? When? Harris turned to Cosawta, who grinned and pointed to the settling lights.

"We are saved, Lord Belmundus."

Harris squinted. Set in a clearing was a vehicle — a long version of *a Cabriolin*, but not quite. Hopping out were two rugged men, who marched toward the grove.

"What is it?"

"It is *a Loribringus*," Cosawta said. "A Culpeeper brothers special."

"*Loribringus! Loribringus!*"

"Hey, mates," came a voice through the shadows. Harris saw Moe Culpeeper standing before them, brother Larry directly behind. Moe held up *a sillifoon*. "Got your signal on me bog standard."

"It worked?" Harris asked.

"You bleedin' right it worked, friend Seppo," Larry replied. "I mean, it gave us a flash and a direction before it went shonky. But it was enough for a bearing. Your bleedin' *Columbinky* was ridgy-didge beyond that."

"We best get a move on," Moe said, shaking Cosawta's hand. "No time for pashing. You got a Gottibotti out tonight and we have no time for dancing in the *Never-Never* with a big boy opened for lunch."

Harris hadn't a clue what Moe said, but he knew what Moe meant and was happy to oblige him. He headed for *the Loribringus*, delighted it had come. Two other *mates* were at the driver's dashboard. They waved, and Harris returned the favor.

"They'd be Bettle and Bum," Moe said. "Now get in and hold tight. I canno' say good of these pikers' driving habits."

Cosawta leaped into *the Loribringus*, Tomatly bouncing at his side. Harris needed a hand-up, *Friend Tony* no aid on steps. Yustichisqua crawled aboard last. He appeared crestfallen. Harris felt guilty for having chastised him — for what? For protecting him?

"I'm sorry, old man, for snapping at you," he said. "You're always there for me and I'm missing in action when it comes to you."

"Not so, *oginali*."

"*Not so. Not so.*"

Harris looked to Tomatly, wondering if he could knock the little Cetrone off the truck. Cosawta settled him, and then turned to Yustichisqua.

"You show promise," he said.

"I am glad you think so, mighty lord of *the Asowisdi*."

Cosawta grinned, knowing sarcasm when he heard it.

"I think you will make *the chisqua* clan proud, son of Kittowa."

"He has already," Harris said.

"But I would become the pride of *the seegoniga*," Yustichisqua said. "I have earned a place there. All I need is to perform *Chewohe* and I shall change my *gollywi*."

Cosawta nodded his assent. *The Loribringus* took off, denying *the porgeedasqui* their dinner and *the gati-bati* its kill.

2

Harris was happy to see *the Didadusi* behind him. *The Loribringus* hovered above the trees, speeding at a good clip . . . for a truck. It wasn't fancy — more a flying flatbed, but he noticed the propulsion pads sloped into a coil, unlike *Cabriolins*. The drivers, Bettle and Bum, steered the vehicle with a fan-shaped navigational device. Power didn't appear to be sourced from anyone in this glorified buckboard, a fact which surprised Harris. He glanced over the side, expecting to see a wave of furious *porgeedasqui* or the wake of a massive *gati-bati*, but *the Loribringus* flew too fast for sightseeing. However, when they came to the ridgeline of the Nuckasee Hills, the trees fell away and a riot of fanciful roofs mushroomed between two notched peaks.

"Comastee," Cosawta said.

"*Comastee. Comastee.*"

The town, as large as Echota, was dominated by a long structure with an exotic covering — looking like thatch from a distance, but as they came nearer, Harris saw it was stone — highly textured stone. A barrel formed the roof's ridge, terminating at each end in two coils, reminding Harris of seafood — lobster for two, because these gargoyles were red lacquered.

"This structure is *the ganuhida ligolu*," Cosawta said.

"It means a long house, *oginali*," Yustichisqua noted.

"Good on you, mate," Moe said. "We're damned proud of the place."

"Especially the Yeegoya," Larry added

"*Yigoya. Yigoya.*"

"You're right to say it," Moe said. "All our best stuff's in the Yeegoya."

Harris shrugged. He couldn't see the building — this *Yigoya.*

"It is a place to show finished crafts, *oginali.*"

"A showroom."

"You got it, mate," Larry said, patting Harris' back.

"Good on you."

The merriment was infectious as *the Loribringus* descended through the trees, zooming over assorted dwellings — *ersatz* examples from the four corners of the outlands. Harris supposed *Fumarcans* lived here, but mostly he saw Cetrone in their various, but distinctive, clan couture. As the truck approached the Long House, Cosawta paced the planks in short strides, as if to leap off the contraption at the earliest possible moment, despite safety considerations. Harris would not join in the leap — dicky foot and all that.

The truck landed with a jolt, the drivers laughing it up and high-fiving it, as if the return to solid ground was never a sure thing.

"Out of the bucker," Moe announced, sliding over the side.

Yustichisqua aided Harris out, and then took care that *the korinkles* were adjusted and *brashun blades* were properly sorted.

"He's like your Mum, Lord Belmundus," Larry noted.

Harris nodded, embarrassed by the attention.

"Old habits are hard to break."

Yustichisqua turned away and walked behind Tomatly, who, *zululess*, plodded along, the ground being uncommon to him. Harris sighed. He didn't know why he should be annoyed with

Little Bird's attentions. Perhaps it highlighted the frailty of the foot injury and the dependence upon *Friend Tony*. Still, even the closest companions can get on each other's nerves.

Harris waved his hand toward the Long House, but Moe moved them across the plaza to another entrance.

"Come this way to *the Yeegoya*, where *the Coroboree* is the main show," Moe announced.

"The Long House is a Dingo's breakfast," Larry added, "if you know what I mean?"

Harris didn't, but followed them to the barrel portico of *the Yigoya*.

"Here be fair dinkum and ridgy-didge," Moe spouted.

"Knock your bloomers off," Larry crowed.

"Your fucking bloomers," Cosawta echoed.

"*Bloomers. Bloomers.*"

Yustichisqua turned and grinned at Harris, a sign his snit had passed. Harris winked as they crossed the threshold.

The showroom was elegantly appointed, as if the two Australian *Fumarcans* entertained prospective buyers here. But other than the local Seneschal, who else would buy? Three gentlemen dressed in lab coats emerged from behind a glass panel. They stood at attention. Harris expected another round of Aussie speak — a guessing game at comprehension. He would do better in Gurt.

"G'Day," Moe said.

The three men nodded.

"*Guten tag,*" they said in a collective chorus.

Harris twitched. *Germans?*

"Whatever," Larry said, turning to Harris. "Don't give their *sprechen* much mind, sir. They come from a part of *the Dodingdaten* somewhere east of Hamburg."

"*Heidelberg,*" one said (the tallest, who sported a pencil thin mustache).

"*Essen,*" said the second (short, stout and jittery).

"*Möchen-Gladbach,*" said the third (an older gentleman, with thinning blonde hair).

"*Ja wohl,*" Moe said. "Somewhere east of Hamburg, as I bloody well said." He came to Harris' ear. "They might go on with the liquid laugh as we peregrinate through the hall. But you give them no mind."

"Good eggs," Larry added. He looked at them. "Well, take us on in. *Zum zum.*"

The three men nodded again, and then turned toward the panel. Cosawta had already proceeded beyond them, but needed to wait at the unlocked door before springing into the place. He raised his *waddly wazzoo,* illuminating the wonders within — wonders which took Harris' breath away.

3

Harris now knew why it was called *the Yigoya,* because it was like a Mercedes-Benz dealership — shiny new vehicles standing in sexy poses, ringed by ambient lighting. He suspected the sticker prices were many *yedalas* steep. He shuffled behind Cosawta, who raised his arms and turned about as if he owned every one of these treasures. In fact, he did by dint of supplying power source materials and managing the wherewithal for the brothers Culpeeper's fertile genius.

Harris touched the handrail of a golden *Cabriolin* — a square one, which had a modified dashboard and a skirted bottom.

"Cool *Cabriolin,*" he said.

"Not *a Cabriolin,*" Cosawta said. "*A Seecoy.*"

"*Seecoy* model double-deuce A," Moe said.

"Top of the line," Larry added.

The Germans arrayed in Vanna White positions, touching the skirt, the dash and the rail respectively, while Cosawta announced each feature.

"Runs on *a chippo* married to *aniniya* and *Columbincus,* embedded in the chassis," he said. " No more manual driving. Hands free."

"Really," Harris noted, trying to climb aboard. Yustichisqua helped.

"And," Cosawta continued. "*A Seecoy* is faster — flies higher and banks better than *a Cabriolin.*"

"Better than the shoddy Gurt designs," Moe said. "I mean, their speckies were limited to the confines of Montjoy town."

"And the fookin' desert was never in their sketchable," Larry noted.

"So," Harris concluded. "Faster, higher and it can take on the desert."

Herr Heidelberg touched the skirt, rubbing its corrugated thrusters.

"The design is such," Cosawta said, "the wider truck line and the fluted intakes protect it from *the kowlinka. Seecoy double-deuce A* can cross the Forling in a blink."

Harris grinned, noting the showroom's other models.

"And those?" he asked. "Are those variations?"

"For every task we have a buggy," Larry said. "Do you need two men *Seecoys* or three men *Seecoys* — we got 'em. Need a cover from the rain or when the great one stirs the sky green as he does today . . ."

Mr. Möchen-Gladbach pressed a button and an awning flew over Harris as he stood mouth agape.

"*Jupsim* coated," Moe said. "With our special additive making it particularly resistant to *Stick* shot."

"It even repels *a Tippagore* fart if it opened up the lunch stand on ya," Larry laughed.

Yustichisqua bounced in and out of several models, while Tomatly played with an array of *gwasdi* and *Sticks*. Harris wandered between *the Seecoy,* noting their sleek design and distinct square shape compared with the rotund *Cabriolins*. He was no expert, but he could see that every precaution had been taken to make these vehicles ready for . . . ready for what? He knew, but feared to express it. Then the guessing dissipated, because Cosawta juggled several spherical objects.

"Observe, Lord Belmundus," he said. "*Wadi-wadi.*"

"*Wadi-wadi! Wadi-wadi!*"

"Take some heed with those, Lord Cosawta," Larry said.

The Germans appeared fearful.

"Those are fully charged," Moe noted, "and can blow the bush oyster out of you."

Harris crawled off *the Seecoy* and watched Cosawta continue the juggle. The Seneschal feigned to drop one every now and then, much to the Germans' chagrin and to the Culpeepers' nervous amusement.

"Are those some kind of bomb?" Harris asked.

He knew the answer, but still, if he was going to be blown up, he wanted to know in advance.

"*Wadi-wadi,*" Tomatly said.

"It means throw it and throw it damned fast, *oginali*," Yustichisqua explained.

"A hand grenade."

"We call them granaydos," Moe explained. "They come in a variety of sizes and punches."

"Various effects," Larry added.

"Perhaps, Lord Cosawta," Harris said, grinning. "Perhaps, you'd like to set those fucking things down. Your point's been made."

"Ah, Lord Belmundus shows fear."

"I'd rather shit my *asano* once than coat *the Yigoya*'s walls if you should miss your catch."

Cosawta laughed, threw *the wadi-wadi* high, and then caught them one after another ending his daredevil demonstration. The Germans sighed with relief.

"So they just blow up?" Harris asked.

"Is that not enough?" Cosawta replied, and then smiled. "But we cannot fool you, can we? Mighty Moe, give him a show."

Moe bowed, and then escorted Harris to a location at the far end of the showroom, where a stone plank was suspended on two wooden horses. Larry followed, carrying one of *the Sticks* Tomatly had found amusing. When they reached the plank, Moe turned to Yustichisqua.

"I require a volunteer from the audience," he announced, staring at Little Bird, who looked about for another candidate.

"There, brother," Larry said. "You have one there. No need to go to the Coathanger for one."

"Me?" Yustichisqua asked.

"You have all the makings of a volunteer," Moe replied, "Since this volunteer must be Cetrone, which only leaves two others and they know about this wee demo and it would spoil the effect."

"Go ahead, old man," Harris said. Then looking at *the Stick* had second thoughts. "You're not going to shoot him with that *Stick.*"

"No. And this is not a *Stick.*"

"It's *a Blundaboomer*," Moe explained. "It shoots . . . well, you'll see."

"I will do it," Yustichisqua announced. He stepped forward and closed his eyes. "Be quick."

"Open your fucking eyes," Cosawta said. "It is nothing to injure you unless . . ."

Yustichisqua opened his eyes, but didn't look any less fearful.

"Now, Mr. Yustee Cheeskwa," Moe said. "If you would be so kind as to touch this here rock we have suspended thusly."

Yustichisqua extended his hand and, after a pause, touched it, and then removed it quickly. Having not received a shock, he returned it securely, holding it there."

"That is quite good, sir," Moe continued. "You could do this as a profession. But what conclusions can we draw from your action."

"It is a rock."

"What kind of rock?"

Yustichisqua squinted, looking to the surface.

"*Phitron,*"

Larry applauded.

"Absolutely, ridgy-didge," he said.

"Now, let go of it, and everyone stand back." All complied. "My brother will now take aim at this here *phitron* rock with the aforesaid mentioned *Blundaboomer.*"

Larry raised *the Blundaboomer*, tapping its side. A red blast shot from the tip, striking *the phitron* squarely. It wasn't damaged, but it discolored.

"Good shot."

Moe applauded. Cosawta joined him infectiously.

"Now, Mr. Yustee Cheeskwa, if you would be so kind as to proffer your hand again to the stone."

Little Bird shrugged and reached. His hand struck the surface, but went through.

"*Kaybar,*" he exclaimed. "You have changed *phitron* into *kaybar.*"

Harris was amazed. He touched the stone himself. His hand was stopped, but when he latched onto Little Bird, he also passed through the rock.

"Amazing," he said.

"Withdraw it, please."

"Why?"

"Do it," Cosawta shouted.

Yustichisqua complied, as did Harris. Then, the stone changed.

"It is *phitron* again," Little Bird said.

"Alas, yes," Moe said, sadly. "The effect is temporary. Anyone using it in let's say . . ."

"Battle," Cosawta said.

"Yes . . . must take this wee drawback into consideration to assure their maximum safety and well being."

Harris looked squarely into the Seneschal's eye. He saw warfare spilling over the pupils and down his cheeks. He saw the vengeance of a thousand years percolating beneath the lids. Harris had his confirmation.

4

Here it was — the treasure of *the Yigoya*, fast cars and battlewagons. Grenades and grenade launchers (called *i-nu wadi* — far throwers) came in many varieties and the powerful red-smoke which changed *phitron* into *kaybar*, albeit temporarily, was called *Gigoo susti* — *smoking blood,* which the Culpeepers nicknamed *Gingergust*). There were ten different models of *Blundaboomer* and *gwasdi* which shot a caustic juice — a combination the Culpeepers named *Jellywhips*, after a lethal critter which lived in Australian waters. Harris didn't see the usual showroom stuff here — food blenders, toasters, improved *byudra* diggers, the latest model *korinkle* or even a line of *zulus* in fashionable shapes and colors. No — this was an arms laboratory. However, he was not horrified, nor surprised. He looked at Cosawta in a different light now.

"It is time, Lord Belmundus," the Seneschal announced.

"Is it?" Harris asked.

"Yes. You must visit the Long House."

Harris wasn't expecting this prosaic reply, having anticipated a deep discussion on the overall plan.

"Lead on," he said.

The Germans bowed clear, Harris thanking them in his best German, which was no German at all. The Culpeeper brothers seemed tagalongs now, the Seneschal leading the way out of *the Yigoya*, crossing the plaza to the Long House. The plaza buzzed with workers, both Cetrone and not, everyone with a specific task, little inclined to notice the visitors. Harris assumed Cosawta wasn't regarded as a visitor, but as an investor — perhaps the Chairman of the Board. Upon reaching the threshold, Cosawta halted and turned to Harris.

"Lord Belmundus," he said. "I will be frank."

"Franker than you always are, Cosawta?"

"Franker." No grin now. "What you shall see you must already know, but it is irrelevant to any future plan on Cetronia's part."

"Irrelevant?"

"Not irrelevant. Speculative. We are a divided people."

"Your father said as much."

"We are. But it is a universal understanding for all Cetrone, whether they seek the peace of isolation or the commitment to liberation, that *the Primordius Centrum* shall give us a sign when our division will no longer be tolerated and the forces of the liberation plan must commit." He drew in a deep and uncustomary sigh. He looked to Yustichisqua, and then to Tomatly. Finally, his eyes rested squarely on Lord Belmundus. "You, sir . . . you are that sign."

"The spark?"

"Doubt it not."

"But I thought the spark referred to a real spark, which now I know I have."

"Doubt it not."

"You refer to an abstract spark — a literary device."

"Doubt it fucking not, Lord Belmundus." He stood straight. "Now proceed."

5

Harris marched behind Lord Cosawta, Yustichisqua directly behind him. Tomatly took up the rear behind the Culpeeper brothers. Entering a foyer, Harris, confronted by a ramp, girded *Friend Tony* to ascend. He heard the rumbling of a hundred voices — nay, a thousand. When he reached the top, Cosawta ushered him onto a platform overlooking a vast room — a stadium-size warehouse.

"Holy crap," Harris muttered.

Stretched in long arrays were *Seecoys*, model *double-deuce A*, interspersed with vehicles he hadn't seen in *the Yigoya* — tank-like ships and long-ass transports. Cetrone and *Fumarcans* serviced this fleet, mightier than any to his knowledge outside *the Ryyve Aniniya*.

"A fighting force," Cosawta said, shaking his fist. "The liberators are waiting for one thing."

He turned to Harris.

"The spark."

"Doubt it fucking not, Lord Belmundus."

Harris surveyed the serried ranks assembled.

"What does it mean, *oginali*?" Yustichisqua asked. "Are the Cetrone mighty again?"

"It means nothing, old man," Harris said, drawing Cosawta's scornful glance. "You can cross the Forling and shoot the crap out of *phitron* walls, but if you are an uncoordinated rabble, it would mean nothing but food for *the porcorporians* and *noya tludachi.* "

"So you say," Cosawta snapped.

"*So you say! So you say!*"

Harris turned to Moe Culpeeper.

"Mr. Culpeeper," he said. "May I see your *sillifoon*?"

Moe appear confused, but thrust his hand in his pocket, producing the requested object.

"If you want to make a call," he said, "there is only one other beyond *the Didadusi*, and that one's a shitter case in Lord Cosawta's koriwrinkler. "

Harris seized it and pawed the buttons.

"How does it work?"

"Press the keys," Larry said.

"No. I mean, how . . . does . . . it . . . work."

"Oh, you mean the network. I see your point, sir. I was a dill not to see it." Moe took the phone and pressed two keys simultaneously. "We get a buzzer here, and then when it clicks . . . here we go . . . we have a network connection."

"Where's the network?"

"In Comastee," Larry said. "Strung hilly-gilly in *the branchy-wanchies*."

Harris grinned, and then turned to Cosawta, whose patience had frazzled to where he was about to throw his *waddly wazzoo* at something or someone.

"Cosawta, my friend and benefactor — a man who saved my life, it is my turn to make a contribution to your cause."

"How so?"

"*The sillifoons*, which you regard as useless pieces of crap."

"They have a use. To call here."

"They have a use," Harris replied. "To call from here to there." He pointed to *the Seecoy*. "And there." He pointed again. "And there and everywhere."

Cosawta shuffled, this time with delight.

"You have experience?"

"No. I've just been in the movies, sir. Mock though the battles may be, the audience still must be convinced. How can you coordinate an assault without communications — other than waving your hands or sending up a flare?" He grabbed *the sillifoon* from Moe. "With these you can be . . ."

"Invincible."

"Well, successful," Harris replied. He handed the phone to Yustichisqua, who turned it about mystified. "Start with successful and perhaps invincible might pay you a visit."

"Can you do what he says, Culpeepers?" Cosawta asked, demand in his voice.

The brothers looked to one another, and then nodded.

"We have already done it, sir," Larry said.

"Modifications. Modifications," Moe echoed as if he were Larry's Tomatly. "We can go beyond *the branchy-wanchies*."

"*Branchy-wanchies*," Harris mused. "I like that." He turned to Yustichisqua. "Are you game for this, old man?"

"I go where you go, *oginali*. I support what you support."

"I know that, but . . . are you game?"

Little Bird cocked his head, and then spoke.

"I would love to see . . . I would love to see Tarhippus' face when he sees *the Kalugu* fall down around his . . . his fucking head."

"Then you're game," Harris said, squeezing Little Bird's shoulders. He then turned to Cosawta, and bowed. "Name your poison, sir and this spark will subscribe to it."

"Truly?"

"Doubt it not Lord Cosawta. Doubt it fucking not."

And with those words Harris came to perform *Chewohe*.

Chapter Twelve

Chewohe

1

Although Kuriakis still stirred and *Yichiyusti* prevailed — the sky muddled green, the Cetrone gave no heed to it as they whispered that the spark prepared to perform *Chewohe*. Some were excited, the liberation at hand. Others wept openly, their isolated peace to be interrupted. However, none disputed the course as they lit their *waddly wazzoos* and prayed to Hedonacaria's spirit to bless the venture.

Harris returned to Echota in *the Loribringus* amidst fanfare and dancing. Although Cosawta carried the day with grand gestures, Harris sought the refuge of his *kaleezo*, hoping to see Littafulchee before he was subjected to the mysterious ritual. His hopes were dashed.

Yustichisqua braced Harris, assuring his comfort and confidence. However, the Echotans also treated Little Bird with honor, Cosawta telling the tale of Kittowa's son protecting Lord Belmundus from *the porgeedasqui* attack.

"Here has returned a pure *chisqua* specimen, proudly displaying a warrior's spirit," Cosawta crowed. "And he too shall embrace *Chewohe*."

Little Bird tolerated the attention, managing to slip away as soon as possible to *the kaleezo's* seclusion. There would be a time for grand display, but this was not it. This was the time to prepare — to meditate and to purify. This was the time for Nayowee.

The crone surprised Harris on his first night's return. She chanted on the threshold and burned a sickening sweet concoction, which almost made him give up his *selu gadu*. When Yustichisqua confronted her, she rapped him with her cane and hobbled after him in chase.

"Prepare yourself for pain, son of Kittowa," she groaned. "The passage to manhood is not a sweet dance or a gentle song."

"This I know," Little Bird said, deflecting her blows. "But you startled us with your cackle and stink."

Harris tried to intervene, but soon the old woman poked him with her stick.

"I can take two down at once, I can," she said. "Now be calm and listen." She raised a crooked finger to her nose, and then pointed at each in turn. "If you are men and not *snalligrogs*, you will listen and obey."

"Just stop beating us," Harris said. "Our journey's been long. We need our rest."

"Your journey has been nothing and rest is for those who sweep mats in *the Asowisdi*."

Harris raised his hands in surrender. Yustichisqua cowered, but then stood firm for one last blow, before turning aside.

"Listen and heed," Nayowee said. "You shall come to my *asi-asa* after two turns of *Solus* and *Dodecadatemus*. Then you shall be purified so you might step into *the Galoquodi gasoqualu.* Naked you shall come and naked you shall go." She poked at *Harris'* double *Columbincus*. "The children of *asusdu* do not wear such baubles."

"Take care, crone," Harris warned.

Nayowee laughed.

"You either listen or sleep, but if you sleep, you remain asleep for the measure of your days and waste no more of Nayowee's time. I do not purify second-guessers." She stared at Yustichisqua. "And that goes for you too, *Taleenay*."

She stepped aside. On the threshold stood Enitachopco, pipe in hand. Harris shuffled back, the Elector's imposing height inspiring reverence. Behind him clustered his brothers — Coweeshee, Elejoy and Tucharechee. Cosawta ushered them in, Tomatly at his side.

Harris, unsure of his next step, looked to Nayowee, who shrugged.

"In two turns come," she snapped, and then hobbled past the elders, leaving her sickly stench behind, replaced now by the tart smoke of Enitachopco's pipe.

Harris bowed. Yustichisqua knelt.

"Be upstanding, my children," Enitachopco said broadly. "I have come to witness our deliverance and to assure my brothers of the truth."

The clan heads gazed at the candidates, surveying them head to foot. Then Coweeshee cleared his throat.

"Has my nephew made undue promises to you?" he asked, dipping his pipe in Cosawta's direction.

"No promises have been made," Harris replied, sternly. "I assure you, I look forward to the enterprise."

Elejoy cocked his head.

"Have you been drawn by desire for my niece?" he croaked, winking.

Harris balked. A thornier question. He approached Elejoy, leaning on *Friend Tony.*

"That I desire Littafulchee it is true," he said softly. "That she desires me is also true. If this be a reason to perform *Chewohe,* I would gladly undertake it. But if it were the driving force, you would have heard my decision sooner rather than later. She's not a promise, my lord. Nor is she a condition. Our cloth has been woven by the hand of love and respect. It's beyond the matter, although you may dispute it."

"I shall dispute it not," Elejoy said.

Enitachopco grinned, nodding his approval. Tucharechee stepped forward, his craggy visage raised in challenge.

"You ring true, young lord," he snapped, "but I look to your companion." Yustichisqua cowered again. "He does not appear to be worthy of the rite."

Yustichisqua stood now, stepping directly into Tucharechee's path, his head coming up to *the tlugu* elder's hip. Looking up, Little Bird scowled.

"Who can be worthier than the son of Kittowa?" he asked. "I am your nephew, sir, and I would be *seegoniga.*" He pointed to his *gollywi* — the *chisqua* brand — a bird scarred blue into his upper right arm. "I would cut this *gollywi* from my being and take another."

Tucharechee drew a long knife.

"Shall I oblige you?" he asked, bringing the blade to Yustichisqua's skin.

Harris shuffled forward, but Yustichisqua raised his hand, halting him.

"I would welcome it, uncle."

"Then let it be so," Tucharechee blustered. He glanced to Cosawta. "Oblige him."

Cosawta grinned, and then grasped Little Bird's arm. Tomatly danced about and, taking a purple bandanna, wrapped it about Yustichisqua's upper arm, covering *the gollywi.* Little Bird appeared confused.

"Son of Kittowa," Enitachopco said. "You shall always be of *the chisqua*. But when you have performed *Chewohe*, you shall have a second mark — a distinction like no other. Then I shall call you *Ta-li Yu-do-we*, he of the two marks."

Yustichisqua bowed, and then reached for Enitachopco's hand. Instead, he received the pipe.

"Smoke, Yustichisqua. Smoke," the Elector said. "Then pass it to your brother."

Little Bird trembled, but brought the pipe to his mouth, inhaled, and closed his eyes. He then passed the pipe to Harris, who caressed it, embracing its smoke.

"I am satisfied," Tucharechee said. "If any in Cetronia doubt that the time has come, let them take their council with *the gati-bati*."

Enitachopco received the pipe from Harris, and then raised his arms in blessing.

"My children," he said. "You stand on the brink of promise — on the precipice of prophecy." He touched Harris' head. "Here the traveler comes from a different land. He carries the spark to transform us." He touched Yustichisqua's crown. "And from our blood flows this river branch. Doubt it not, son of Kittowa. No man walks alone."

Enitachopco's brothers came to attention, like tall pickets — a forest of lean buckskins. Together they mumbled until their words clarified:

"Naked shall you come and naked you shall go."

As they repeated this, Cosawta and Tomatly stripped Harris and Little Bird of their buckskins.

"Forgive me, Lord Belmundus," Cosawta said, as he released *the asano* and the loincloth. "I must also secure your *brashun blades* and take your *Columbincus*."

Harris grasped *Hierarchus,* and then his brooch.

"I will not part with them."

"Naked shall you come and naked you shall go," came the chant.

"I am sorry, my lord, but it is a fucking requirement."

Cosawta tugged at *Friend Tony*.

"But I need this to walk."

"You can walk without it," Cosawta remarked. "A little pitch here and tricky trip there, but you shall manage. I know you shall."

Harris gave *Friend Tony* up, but was more reluctant when it came to his *Columbincus*. In fact, it crossed his mind the Seneschal might keep the rare double brooch for his collection — put it in a cage like one of his rare birds. The jade ring was also difficult to surrender, especially since it glowed in protest.

"Come, come," Cosawta said. "I am to be your brother-in-law. Family breeds trust."

Suddenly, Yustichisqua relinquished *gasohisgi*. Harris relented, but removed *the Columbincus* himself, gently placing it in Cosawta's hands.

"Do not have a fucking worry," Cosawta said. "It favors you and not me. I shall return it unscathed. I do not mean to stuff it in a *wadi-wadi* and toss it at Montjoy's mighty walls."

Harris sighed, resisting no further. He stood naked before the elders. The evening breeze blew through his groin. He was embarrassed. However, he sensed Yustichisqua's comfort, so all was well.

"Go," Enitachopco said, pointing over the threshold. "Go to *the asi-asa.*"

"But we're not expected for two turns," Harris said.

"You cannot stay here."

"But she won't welcome us there."

"Go."

Harris shrugged. He stepped toward the threshold expecting his foot to snag him, but it worked fine now — a little stiff. The night breeze awaited him — he and his *Taleenay*. So into the murky *Yistiyuchi* night Lord Belmundus waded to stand outside Nayowee's *yehu* for two turns, a spectacle for the crone's night cackling and curious Echotan eyes for a short, but uneasy, interval.

2

Harris thought to chuck the ritual. Crossed his mind, it did, while standing naked in public — not his idea of a lofty act; although, as an actor, the public had seen less of him, but imagined more. He had never allowed a full-frontal nude scene in his work, but never ruled out the possibility. Time ticked on the option. Now he felt like a porn star or, at the outer margin, a calendar pin-up boy. If Yustichisqua had not acquiesced, Harris would have marched back (as best he could) to his *kaleezo*, retrieved his *asano* and his powerful bling and taken up a humbler occupation — *selu* picking came to mind. But what example would that set as his *Taleenay* quietly stood or sat or leaned while the clans filed passed, scrutinizing every ripple and crevice.

Harris sat more than stood, allowing his knees to rise, putting his nether parts in the shadows — a guessing distance for giggling children, who hunkered down to peek. He supposed this humiliation served a symbolic purpose within the ritual. Still, when the suns went down and the night breeze whipped, he shivered — no blanket or robe to keep him warm. Then Yustichisqua sidled coyly beside him, two warm bodies drawing heat for one. Then at dawn on the second turn, the cackling from *the asi-asa* ceased and Nayowee showed herself.

"You are here already?" she asked.

Harris stood, balling his fist.

"You've been snickering at us for two days, you bitch. You told us to show up and we have. Now I suggest you undertake the purification ritual so we can finish this business and take our rightful places."

Nayowee raised an eyebrow — the remains of one. She raised her cane, Yustichisqua cowering. She laughed.

"You have been marinating in the people's eyes for two turns, Lord Belmundus. You and your *Taleenay* have been purified enough."

"So that's it?"

"Unless, you would like another turn at it. It can be arranged."

"No. I'm purified." Harris grinned. "I feel as fresh as a daisy on a mountain meadow."

"You do?"

"I am fine also," Yustichisqua said.

Nayowee laughed, raising her arms skyward. There appeared *the Gananadana*, fully serviced and repaired, Cosawta steering the course, Tomatly dancing about the ropes. Inside the gondola, were two ladies. Harris sighed. Yustichisqua wept. It had begun.

The women of *the seegoniga* filed passed Harris and Yustichisqua, leading the way through the forest, chanting as they went:

> *Sacred Sittoquo, we come to take and share*
> *Your holy limbs to mark the way of light.*
> *Forgive us when we snap your core as we dare,*

To keep promise and prophecy through the night.
Come we, to the Asaylidodi
To make the Dulohu,
In your wondrous heart of gold,
Galoquodi gasoqualu.

Harris found the way hard, his foot kicking up after an hour of treading over roots and vines. Yustichisqua tried to help him, but Nayowee, surprisingly sprite and agile, whacked him with her cane each time he extended aid. Harris thought Little Bird would turn on the crone, provoking her to curse him, transforming him into some unpronounceable bug. Then from the sky ship came Cosawta's hoot and holler, littered with acquired street slang. It brightened Harris' heart. He realized *the Gananadana* scouted the path so the women would not lose their way. Harris' heart surged knowing Littafulchee watched him from the heights.

"My angel," he muttered. "Can any soul go wrong with such guidance?"

"Say you what?" Nayowee snapped.

"I said, old bitch, how can I go wrong with my lady aloft, my friend at my side and your cane at my back?"

"Purification suits you, Lord Belmundus," she cackled. "Just take care not to trip over your toes. I will not be mending you today."

"She is there, *oginali*," Yustichisqua said, glancing up to the gondola's underside, and Harris knew he did not mean Littafulchee.

"I hope it's worth it, old man."

"Not so old today."

The path never seemed to end. Uphill, downhill, over rivulets and through tangles until the green sky broadened through the leafless grove of *the Sittoquo* trees.

"I know this spot," Harris said.

"Hush," the crone snapped. "No man speaks here."

The women danced through the grove, emerging into *the Galoquodi gasoqualu — the sacred circle.* As the women chanted, they spun, drawing small knives.

Sacred Sittoquo, we come to take and share
Your holy limbs to mark the way of light.
Forgive us when we snap your core as we dare,

To keep promise and prophecy through the night.
Come we, to the Asaylidodi
To make the Dulohu,
In your wondrous heart of gold,
Galoquodi gasoqualu.

Several women surrounded the largest *Sittoquo,* knocking on its trunk lovingly. Then, standing on shoulders, they cut three short branches from the tree. With each cut, six women wept, lamenting the act, while six others performed *the alsagi,* a dance which Harris had learned in *the Deedaloquasdi,* where the children had laughed to see him muddle through it. As the branches were ceremoniously passed from woman to woman, each spat on them, drying them with their buckskin's hem, the blue dye staining the branches blue. Several other women built a small fire, kindled from their *waddly wazzoos.*

Nayowee corralled Harris and Yustichisqua near the fire, which raised Harris' anxiety. *Were they going to the stake?* Nayowee did not speak, so he dared not. Still, it was clear the ritual had begun.

The *Gananadana* hovered silently overhead. The women continued spitting and dying until the three branches glowed with an azure hue. Upon reaching Nayowee, she took the blue branches, raising them above her head, and then cradling them in her arms.

Yuyoyi atsilu,
Osda asusdu.
Galoquodi yuwanigalu
Asaylidodi soogasdi.

(Bad fire,
Good light.
Sacred branches
Oaths are smoked.)

She turned to Harris and Yustichisqua, nary a quip nor insult upon her lip.

"Dance, my children, out of respect for the sacred branches, and so the sweat may oil your hides for the cleansing."

Harris wasn't sure what she meant, but the women clapped and chanted rhythmically. Yustichisqua began to dance — shyly at first. Soon he muddled his way through his version of *the alsagi.*

Harris stared at his dickey foot and hoped it would serve this task. His toes cried out for rest and recuperation. Still, he managed it. Step-by-step, he twisted and twitched, finding the beat in the fire's glow.

"Faster," Nayowee said.

Harris turned with each clap, sweat beginning to flow.

"Faster," Nayowee commanded.

Harris tried, but his foot conspired against him. But before he could fall into the holy blaze, Yustichisqua grabbed his hands and twirled him around, the dance transformed into a whirling reel.

"Faster."

The women clapped, while the candidates performed a whiplash frenzy, pumping cascades of perspiration across their purified skins. Breathless, Harris halted, panting — reaping the wind, holding firmly to his knees. If he should plummet groundward, Yustichisqua assured they would do it as a single entity.

"Yes," Nayowee shouted, and then looked aloft.

She handed two branches to the women nearest the fire, while she stepped toward Harris, waving the longest and bluest. She tapped him on the head.

"Now?" he asked.

She gestured for silence, and then drew the branch across Harris' chest, sharp bramble thorns cutting his skin, perspiration blending with his blood. This stung, but he dared not cry out — no man permitted to speak in the grove. He tensed while Nayowee continued to streak his body with cuts — his belly, legs, arms and then his back now were striped with crimson. Little Bird whimpered as the assistants played the same ritual upon him. Nayowee hesitated when she reached Harris' injured foot.

"No," she said. "I will spare you that."

She turned, raised the branch and called skyward.

> *Galayidu gollywi seegoniga*
> *Yuyoyi atsilu sgi osda atsilu.*
> *Yuma ama udali quo*
> *Adatowetodi atsinonunu.*

(Brand of the seegoniga
Make bad fire good.
Then in the lake waters
Kiss the wounds to healing).

Before Harris could think further, a searing burn hit his left shoulder. He turned to cry out, but caught Nayowee's admonition. He trembled as he watched Yustichisqua receive the fiery brand also.

Cattle, he thought. *We are cattle now, marked for sale to the Primordius Centrum.*

He thought he'd pass out, but held fast, fearing to look at the mark. But he smelt his own flesh like a steakhouse special. He clenched his teeth. Yustichisqua was pushed into him. Harris clutched him as they moved out of the clearing and through the grove until they reached the lake's edge — *the Ama Udali.*

3

Abandoned on the bank, Yustichisqua wept.

"We must enter the water, *oginali.*"

"Truly?"

"Yes. It seals the wounds. We would die otherwise."

"Truly?"

Harris perused the lake — calm enough. He recalled evils in this lake — a predatory fish called *the atsadi* and snapping turtles — *terrapinsgi.* But one quick plunge and the rite would be over. How bad could it be?

He eased Yustichisqua off the bank, then, stepping with his bad foot first (being clear of cuts), he entered the glade. But the next step held truth, because this was a salt lake.

Harris winced.

Yustichisqua wept.

"It is painful, *oginali.*"

"I know. Hold tight, old man."

They clutched each other, moving deeper into the water, pain searing — a thousand firebrands worse than the one which had made its mark upon their shoulders. At waist level, Harris stopped.

"I don't know whether I can do this, Little Bird."

Tears streaked down his cheeks.

"I shall die, *oginali.*"

"No, old man. We'll live, but I think we must come closer to death before we come closer to life." Harris gripped Yustichisqua tightly. "Take a deep breath. It'll be over before you know it."

Harris counted to three, and then plunged, the lake covering his head. He took Little Bird with him. The pain whipped every wound, the salt biting chest and back — even assaulting eyes, where no cut had transgressed. The pain was so intense, if *an atsadi* threatened him, he'd tear it apart with his teeth. Let *the terrapinsgi* bite his ass. He'd beat its shell into *maracas.*

Harris pushed up from the bottom.

"Holy God," he shouted. "What did I do to merit this torture?"

He pushed toward the shore, but Yustichisqua had not reemerged. Harris panicked.

"Little Bird."

Bubbles only.

"Little Bird."

Harris frantically beat the surface, the pain replaced with terror. Tracking the bubbles, he dived under, searching through the murk. Then he saw him — his *Taleenay* near lifeless drifting in the brine. Harris tugged him, dredging him to the surface.

Yustichisqua bobbed, and then gasped, his eyes rolling back. Harris dragged him out, struggling to the bank. He tried to recall CPR lessons — mouth to mouth, but Yustichisqua suddenly came around, spitting gobs of lake water onto the bank, coughing like a consumptive. Harris embraced his shoulders, and then took him into his arms.

"Little Bird, Little Bird," he moaned. "Speak to me."

Yustichisqua gasped, trying to smile, but burbled more water.

"It still hurts," he choked. "Inside and outside, I hurt, *oginali.*"

"We hurt together," Harris said, rocking him, and looking to the sky. "We have not been defeated. We made it. Breathe. Breathe deeply."

Yustichisqua caught his breath, steadying with each gasp.

"*Oginali,*" he wept. "You almost lost me."

"Never," Harris said. "What would *the Didaniyisgi of the Yuyutlu* do without his *Taleenay?*"

"I *am* your *Taleenay.*"

"You are, old man. You are . . . what's the word? Tell me the word?"

"*Dinatli.*"

"Yes. *Dinatli — Brother.*"

They embraced as only brothers could, naked on the bank and as equals under the green sky in the shade of the sacred *Sittoquo.*

Chapter Thirteen

Husgi and Asgay

1

Harris awoke upon the lake's bank, aching and pained. His *gollywi* throbbed, but when he gazed at the scabbing mark of the blue holly, he grinned. He was now *seegoniga*, more than by the word of the Gurt *Ryyves*. As he gazed at the brand, he sighed, thinking of his *Danuwa*. Poor Melonius forced to the pits of Terrastrium. And how did Elypticus fare in the far-off islands with Garan?. Did Parnasus still live? Then Harris heard heavy breathing beside him. At least his *Taleenay* was at hand. More than *Taleenay* now. *A Dinatli* — a brother, who shared with him this painful ritual. How far Yustichisqua had come from a silent Trone in the shadow of his lord to this brave equal, sprawled on *the Ama Udali* bank.

Suddenly, a shadow blocked the sky — a silhouette casting a rose scent. Harris sat up. The person before him held open a buckskin, inviting him to embrace it — to cover his crimson stripes and his tender *gollywi* — to hide his nakedness from the world for the first time in three days. He tried to rise, but his foot was uncooperative. Then the robe-bearer hunkered down, wrapping him in suede.

"Lord Belmundus," she said.

"I know your scent. I long to dwell within it."

"You shall dwell in me as my *husgi*, and I as your *asgay*."

"*Husgi* and *asgay*," came another voice, a feminine charm — a second lady holding another buckskin, this one over Yustichisqua.

Harris looked at his lady and she, at him. She hugged him, and then lifted *Friend Tony*, *Hierarchus* and *the Columbincus* like presents given for the first time.

"With these, I shall array you — the honor and signs of the spark within you. The spark that shall be in me."

Harris grinned and embraced Littafulchee.

"My lord," the other said to Yustichisqua, covering him with the buckskin.

Little Bird stirred, and then, opening his eyes, sat up abruptly.

"Do I dream?" he stammered. "Did I dream that you called me *your lord*?"

Wanona kissed his forehead.

"You are my *husgi* for all times to come and all times to pass," she said, wrapping him. She held *gasohisgi*. "And to you I return your symbol of authority."

Yustichisqua grinned, taking the dagger, kissing it, and then kissing Wanona.

"I am a lucky old man," he said.

Harris covered Littafulchee in kisses. He reached for her breasts. She did not stop him. His *Columbincus* glowed as if in tune with his erection. But this was not the place for passion. He knew it could not cure his many pains. Coupled to recovery, passion would smack of consolation rather than love. Littafulchee must have sensed this also, because she gently pushed him away, and massaged his neck, causing his eyes to roll and his heart to race.

"We must be away from this sacred place," she whispered.

"We'll consecrate a new place more holy than this briny glade," he agreed.

She kissed him again.

Yustichisqua and Wanona were in the throes of passion. Harris didn't want to interrupt it; nor could he. He looked into Littafulchee's eyes. They danced wildly — smoldering and beckoning. However, as Lord and Lady of the Cetrone, they exercised restraint. They were not each other's reward. They were the destiny of the people. However, Little Bird was no such icon, so his passion roared as Wanona mounted him on the bank. He wailed like a young *tludachi* until they both collapsed into each other's arms. Harris grinned as if the climax had been his own. And who was to say it wasn't?

2

"*Husgi. Husgi. Asgay. Asgay.*"

The parrot of Tomatly's voice came from the rise above the bank. He hopped and danced, singing a merry and lascivious song. If Harris had a translation, he would have called downright pornographic. It made Wanona blush. Yustichisqua cropped his buckskins securely about his groin.

"*Dinatli*," he said to Harris. "*Dinatli,* I am very happy."

"For that I am happy too."

"And do you not shine for your own happiness?" Littafulchee asked, pouting.

"I'm over the moon," Harris said, grabbing her, dragging her to the ground, showering her with kisses, despite the pain. "I'm over all three moons."

Suddenly, a shower of stones — or nuts, something akin to acorns, pelted the couples.

"What the . . ."

Cosawta laughed beside Tomatly.

"Brother," Littafulchee called. "Is that necessary?"

Cosawta continued to throw the acorns, a few catching their targets. Harris tossed one back, but Littafulchee stopped him.

"It is for good luck," she said,

"And fertility," Cosawta added, throwing another fistful.

"I see," Harris said. "It's like throwing rice."

"If you say so, *husgi*, it is so. But it is an honorable tradition."

Harris managed to get to his feet, raising his arms, *Hierarchus* dangling from one hand and *Friend Tony* from the other.

"Then take your best shot, Lord Cosawta."

"We are brothers now," the Seneschal said. "I shall call you *Sisterfucker*."

"No you won't," Harris protested.

"And why not? It is a statement of truth and what else would I call my brother-in-law?" Then he raised an eyebrow. "I see. Well, we have not the time for it now, since you have exercised restraint. I certainly would not have."

"Brother," Littafulchee scolded.

Cosawta glanced at Yustichisqua, and then threw a fistful of acorns at him.

"I can see this one is a true Cetrone. No restraint here." He howled. "Good show. But *the Gananadana* waits."

"*Gananadana. Gananadana.*"

Wanona helped Yustichisqua up, brushing him off, adjusting his buckskin and fastening the dagger to the drawstrings. Littafulchee straightened *the Columbincus*, snapped *Tony* into it's cane sheath, and secured *Hierarchus* on a golden belt around Harris' waist. He kissed her again.

"I shall attend to your wounds," she said. "I have a balm from *Pajoquota* — from the edge of the sea, near *the Dodingdaten*. It promotes quick healing and is less noxious than Nayowee's lotions."

"I look forward to it," Harris said, then grinned again. "I look forward to your fingers plying over every . . ."

"I shall work my miracles upon you. Trust me."

Harris gazed at this woman — a beauty, who knew her own mind and might not always share his. But he didn't want a pliant wife. *Wife? Asgay.* Had he come so far so fast? He hadn't planned to marry until perhaps age thirty-five, when his career would be sagging or veering to a different set of roles — more Lear than Hamlet. Then it would be a big bang media affair — public not invited, but somehow they'd get a view. But didn't he just have such a wedding, with blue branches and salt water and most of Cetronia looking on? Then a thought stirred him.

"Where's my jade ring?"

Littafulchee frowned. She turned aside.

"You miss the glow of *the Ayelli?*"

"No. But it was a gift."

"It is a summoner," she said turning, holding it up in her right hand.

The ring glowed. Harris stared at it. It *did* summon him.

"She calls still," he muttered. "But it was given to me by Joella."

"As kind as the Memer of Montjoy might appear," Littafulchee replied, "she gave you this to bind you to her daughter. It was not the gift. You were so bound."

Littafulchee shook the ring, and then threw it toward the lake. Harris gasped, as if something was cut from his body. He watched the green glow turning in the breeze. It fell to the water, but before it hit, jaws emerged, breaking the surface, catching it — swallowing it, and then taking it under.

"*The atsadi,*" Harris said. "That fish has taken my ring."

"Let it," Littafulchee replied, holding his shoulders. "Let her call a monster from the deep to her bed. You are my *husgi.* I need no ring."

Harris glared at Littafulchee's crystal bauble, which danced from her headband. He thought it might be glowing — calling as strongly as the jade ring had. But then he realized, it did not. His draw to her was below his *Columbincus* and definitely further down. He embraced his new *asgay* with fervor.

"Come, now," Cosawta shouted. "*The Gananadana* waits."

"*Gananadana. Gananadana.*"

"*Oginali*," Yustichisqua said. "The sooner you come, the sooner you can be one with her."

Wanona tugged her man up the bank.

"There is much to do," she said.

"Yes," Harris said. "There is much to do."

He escorted his consort up the bank, his back turned on the lake, but in the ripples he thought he heard a fish . . . belch.

Part V

Mounting a Three Reeler

Chapter One

Much To Do

1

Harris enjoyed his new suite of rooms in *the seegoniga* clan house, especially since they contained his heart's joy. The clan house, a maze of halls and chambers, sprawled through a forest clearing, each court crowned by a high *kaleezo* roof. Harris had little time to explore, torn between preparations for the impending invasion and the attentions from his wife. As exciting as the former could be, the latter pinned him like a butterfly. He would rush about business — weapons training, invasion planning and the supply line, only to break off and disappear through the winding corridors of the clan house and into his *asgay's* arms. Here he forgot all promise and prophecy — all flash and pother. He would have clung to Littafulchee's breasts, engaging her with kisses and more, without interruption or disturbance, but for her urging him that there was *much to do*.

"Much to do?" he asked. "And I do it, freely and often."

She laughed, her breasts heaving for more of that doing. However, as unsated as Lord and Lady were, they knew time was not theirs to bid. She grasped him for one last embrace, and then gently pushed him aside. He rolled, his hand still seeking hers — their fingers entwined as only lovers can know.

"I shall stay here forever, and nothing you can do will force me from your side," he declared.

"You might think it, my lord," she replied. "But the plan will not do its own bidding. You lead us now."

This was true. Cosawta was departing for *the Kalugu, the Gananadana* outfitted for the long haul across the Forling. Two hurdles delayed the invasion. The continuance of *yichiyusti* and the completion of the new *sillifoons* and *the branchy-wanchie* system. The green sky was regarded as an ill omen and, as Enitachopco stated, *I shall not take advantage of Kuriakis while he stirs*. So it was decreed, the military mission would wait until the sky turned fair. There was still much to do — training, strategizing, amassing supplies, but also a need to reconnoiter Montjoy and, in particular, *the Kalugu*.

"I have been absent too long," Cosawta had announced at a planning meeting. "*The Yunockers of the mordanka* are accustomed to my contraband runs and will grow suspicious if I delay further. I fear their fucking curiosity might be piqued already, so long I have been gone."

Harris was not prepared for this. He assumed the invasion would be led by the Seneschal — Cetronia's natural leader, after the Elector. But Cosawta tinkered with the new vehicles and weaponry, ignoring Harris' entreaty to stay and lead.

"You are capable of the task, great *Sisterfucker*. You and your *Taleenay*."

Yustichisqua had been embraced by *the seegoniga* clan and had been counseled in new responsibilities. Little Bird threw caution to the wind and agreed to every task and mission bestowed on him. But he also complained, wanting to spend more time with Wanona. He also missed his constant commiseration with Lord Belmundus. Harris missed his companion, but this was the plan for Yustichisqua. Maturity. Reliance. Self-confidence and a married life — a different and more pleasant form of servitude. Still, Little Bird complained to his former overlord often.

"*Oginali*," he said. "I fear my squadrons will not follow me."

Harris scanned *the Taleenay*, who wore a new *asano*, a royal blue cape and a breastplate of *conontoroy* — a true martial figure. Who wouldn't follow this uniform?

"You were born to it, old man," Harris said.

"Maybe so, but I am more at ease fetching dinner from *the Scullery Dorgan*."

"Who wouldn't be?" Harris placed his arm around Yustichisqua's shoulder. "You're just untethered, that's all. You're not used to married life and having a household."

"I suppose you are correct, *Dinatli*." He grinned at the new term. "I am not a warrior, but I am true to my new clan. They say I must wield *gasohisgi* and lead the Cetrone into battle." He chuckled. "I wear two *gollywi* and must now have the bravery for two clans. Yet, I am just learning the ways of *blundaboomers* and *wadi-wadi*. I am unsure when I steer *a Seecoy*."

Everyone had a learning curve when it came to Culpeeper inventions. Harris took to it like a duck to minnows, but Yustichisqua preferred a close-in fight. Artillery and tricky strategems were hard for him to embrace. Still, he had more skill than the average Cetrone digger, weaver or baker, who needed to apply themselves to weaponry they scarcely could have imagined.

"You're doing fine," Harris said. "Besides, let *the Fumarca* do their jobs. We pay them enough."

True. As the hardware was delivered and assembled in Echota and, after the initial gawking and exploration of the new-fangled material by the citizenry, a contingent of *Fumarca* streamed in from *the Dodingdaten* and Comastee, their assignment to train *byudra* diggers and *adanadasga* workers to drive *Seecoys* and *Loribringus* — to fire *blundaboomers* and *i-nu wadi* and to operate *the sillifoons,* when on line. *The Fumarca* were a rowdy bunch amidst more settled folk and many Cetrone had to grow accustomed to discipline. Cosawta set the tone, moving amongst them, shouting orders and attending to their uniforms — drilling the squad leaders until they dropped and teaching them gruff orders dotted with colorful adjectives meant to shock new troops. By the time Cosawta neared departure, a cadre of cursing, barking, sneering sergeants and corporals littered the Cetronian training grounds.

As Harris wandered the halls of the *seegoniga* clan house, having left his wife's bed reluctantly, he mused on the one controversy this mobilization brought and, upon thinking about it, reached into his *asano* and pulled one out — *the sillifoon.*

2

Harris saw no point in Cosawta's journey to *the Kalugu* to spy unless he had a ready means of reporting his findings to Cetronia. Messages in a bottle were out. So a delaying point was the completion of useable, long-distance *sillifoons*. A working model had been presented to Harris within two weeks of his return from Comastee.

"Better range," Moe Culpeeper stated emphatically, popping a hood-like extension from the back of the device. "And when *the branchy-wanchie* is up, you can speak to the Queen 'neath London Bridge."

"You know . . ." Harris said, taking the device. He meant to say that London Bridge was in Arizona, but decided a discussion of its sale and removal would be a wasted tangent on an early twentieth-century Australian. So he weighed *the sillifoon* in his palm, and grinned with satisfaction. "This might be the ticket."

It would have been the ticket, except *for the branchy-wanchie*. *A Fumarcan* team of ten arrived from *the Dodingdaten*. They had been contracted to drape Echota in cable and antennae. The work began without problems, drawing only curiosity from every clan, and expected amusement from the children until Nayowee saw the work.

"Do not mar these sacred trees," she barked, waving her cane, and then beating ladders and hoists. "Never shall our city be marred by such damnation."

Although the workers continued, they found spectator's curiosity growing hostile, bands of detractors chanting beneath the project. Harris marched to the site, dispersing the crowd, but he was scant deterrent for Nayowee.

"You may conduct your aggression as you will, Lord Belmundus," Nayowee snapped. "But remember who healed you and who has the power to bring you down."

Harris bowed to the ranting woman, but drew *Hierarchus* and touched his *Columbincus*.

"This is not the business of *the asi-asa*, Nayowee. This is a necessary step to the Elector's plans and the Seneschal's mission."

Nayowee raised her cane as if to duel with her former patient. Yustichisqua arrived with a squad of newly minted *chisqua* and *tlugu* soldiers. He positioned them between Nayowee and Harris.

"Ah," Nayowee cackled. "The Little Bird has a new beak and will attempt to peck at his betters."

She laughed, but continued to threaten.

"Old woman," Yustichisqua said, his sternness never daunted. "You and I know each other, so do not try my anger. It is real when unsheathed."

"I suggest you unsheath your *gugubasgi* and rejoin your *asgay* in the nest," she snapped. "I am too much woman for you."

Yustichisqua drew *gasohisgi*. Harris came between Little Bird and the old healer — between *brashun blade* and *power cane*. The soldiers fidgeted, the extent of their training to date.

"Please," Harris said, touching the point of *gasohisgi* and the tip of the cane. "We prepare for the liberation. Don't either of you forget it."

Yustichisqua sheathed his dagger, and then bowed.

"I am sorry, *Dinatli*."

"I am not," Nayowee snapped, but lowered her cane.

"Is there . . ." Harris cocked his head, staring at the old woman. "Is there a way we can proceed and still preserve the sanctity of these groves?"

Nayowee snorted, but did not howl. She turned about, looking upward at the workers, who were frozen to their hoists and ladders.

"What need do you have of these bastards from the black shores?" She came close to Harris. "Their *conontoroy* and *yustunalla* will make the trees cry to the spirits and bring us dread and disaster. How can you succeed if you poison these groves?"

"Perhaps we could protect the boughs with . . . with one of your concoctions."

"I have no such thing."

"I do," came a voice in the crowd.

A swarthy Cetrone stepped forward, dressed in the Zecronisian robes of *the Wudayleegu*. Yustichisqua balked. Harris raised his arms in welcome.

"Garan," he stammered.

Garan *the Gucheeda* bowed, first to Harris and then to Nayowee.

"I can procure barrels of *jupsim*," he said. "It is made from the blood of these trees and will fare happily with their kin."

This was a lie and even Harris knew it. Even so, Nayowee pondered it.

"It might be so," she mused. She turned away, shaking her head, but retreating. "It might be so," she repeated until she was far from sight.

Garan bowed again to Harris.

"Lord Belmundus," he said. "You have become a great power in the land." He then acknowledged Yustichisqua. "And Captain, you cut a fine figure before your squadrons. If I were a Yunocker devil, I would crap my *asano* at your sight."

Yustichisqua chuckled nervously.

"You do me honor, sir."

"I am only *the Gucheeda*, come to make deals with these." He pointed into the trees at *the Fumarcans*, who resumed their work. "I am always ready with my hand extended for a fistful of *yedalas*."

"You wouldn't happen to have some *wisgi*, would you?" Harris asked.

"I might have a bottle or two at my disposal."

"Well, I can afford your price."

"Are you sure?"

3

Garan had come to *the Dodingdaten* by sea, in his grand caravel, *Ponsetossit,* moored in Brega Bay. When he heard *the Fumarcan* gossip about a great *Ayelli* lord who carried two *brashun blades* and *a double Columbincus,* he knew without doubt who had prospered in Cetronia. So he traveled inland to the border, and then to Comastee, where he witnessed the great stir of industry — weapons and vehicles on the move. He hitched a ride with his old trading partners, the Culpeeper brothers and had just arrived in Echota when Nayowee's diatribe reached its height.

"Good timing," he said, raising *a wisgi* flask, toasting Harris.

They had retreated with Yustichisqua to Harris' suite, where Littafulchee called for *selu gadu* and *segasti* cakes. However, she wasn't very hospitable. Harris wasn't sure if Garan presented a thorn in the clan's side. He was Cetrone and belonged nominally to *the alisoqua* clan. Still, he was as *Fumarcan* as could be. All Echota knew Garan, but few spoke well of him. Perhaps it was his ostentatious dress and his rugged manners.

"Tell me, friend," Harris asked. "How is Elypticus?"

"He is on *Borsa-pu,* the fifth island in the *Makronican Archipelago.*"

"He's settled then?"

"Hardly," Garan sighed. "He longs for Montjoy. He misses his companions and . . . and I believe he misses you, my lord."

"Me?"

"He is faithful."

"That he was."

"*Is* faithful, my lord." Garan poured more *wisgi,* even for Littafulchee, who had extended a clean cup forward. "If Elypticus could, he would have journeyed with me to *the Dodingdaten,* but he has a good head for business."

"That would have suited him then," Harris noted.

"It would, but . . ." Garan downed his liquor. "But the temptations of the port are more than he could resist. He is handy as my agent on *Borsa-pu.* I have tried to keep practicality alive in my enterprise."

"And what enterprise may that be, *Gucheeda*," Littafulchee snapped. "Any Thirdling would welcome the chance to romp in the bordellos of the outlanders."

"Just so, my lady."

Harris stared at his wife, puzzled by her aggression. Was it the *wisgi?* Could be.

"Forgive my *asgay*," he said to Garan. "She is not accustomed to . . ."

"To what, my lord?" Littafulchee asked, her eyes widening. "To men assessing a woman's disposition?"

Harris looked to Yustichisqua, who quickly drank up, and then glanced away.

"Perhaps, that's it," Harris said. "My lady is a treasure beyond all accounting, but like all models of perfection, is no such thing."

Littafulchee slammed the cup down, and leaned into the conversation.

"Forgive me, *Gucheeda*. My rudeness is perfect for my mood. My lord has been everything to me and is only now the source of annoyance, but . . ." She stood, turning away. Grief overcame her. "We must soon be parted," she stammered.

Harris stood, panic gripping him. *What did she mean?*

"We will never be parted."

He grasped her shoulders.

"Then you shall not go to war?"

"Of course, I go. But . . ."

"But I shall not."

"You can fight," he said. "I've seen you."

But did he want his treasure placed in harm's way? Of course, he didn't, but he knew better than to restrain her.

"I will not be at your side, *husgi*. I am forbidden."

"By whose command? Not the old woman?"

"She is not warm to it, but has no say in the matter. It is my father who decrees it."

Harris was aghast. The company departed quickly, with promises to meet again. Littafulchee drifted toward her bed, her anger waning to sorrow. Harris pondered the impending separation. He had assumed she would be beside him in his *Seecoy*, her own arsenal at the ready — *sillifoon* in hand, contradicting his commands and throwing her share of *wadi-wadi*.

"Why has your father commanded this?" he asked, sitting gently bedside. "I shall see him. Surely he can be persuaded. Surely *I* can persuade him."

"Why he has done so is . . . is for a mysterious purpose known to few."

"Tell me."

"I am not sure of it myself and so speculation would only divert you from your course."

Harris embraced her.

"Divert me, my love? I've been diverted since the first time I set eyes on you. How can I be expected to operate with you far from my side?"

"You must bear it, as I must."

"You're not bearing it well."

"I am sorry to have been rude to *the Gucheeda*, but he is not a person of favor in our midst."

"But he's been a great help. He planned my escape from *the Katorias.*"

"Cosawta planned that, my love. *The Gucheeda* was but a means, and paid well."

Harris rubbed her shoulders.

"Still, I regard him as *oginali.*"

"I cannot steer you from your true feelings, and will not. But we will be parted for a time, and . . ."

"Don't think of it further. Don't take it to the next level." He kissed her, and then drank in her eyes. "If time's not on our side now, then . . ."

She smiled for the first time. He was out of his *asano* in a flash and between her breasts even faster.

4

Lord Belmundus could have sailed in the perfumed sheets forever, but there was much to do. Reluctantly, he joined Yustichisqua and Garan beneath *the branchy-wanchie,* overseeing buckets of *jupsim* for coating the sacred boughs. The cost in *brantsgi* for the extra work would come dear, but *the Fumarcans* did not work free. The citizens of *the Dodingdaten* were not mercenaries and would not be racing across the Forling to fight in bloody battles. Although the defeat of Montjoy, whose leadership did not particularly favor *the Fumarcans* and the other outland denizens, would benefit from the business. There would always be shady deals and back alley barters among the various Farn constituencies. With that in mind, Harris headed to *the selu* field — one fallow by design — one designated for weapons training.

"Proving grounds," he told Yustichisqua.

"I am astonished, *oginali*."

"At what?"

"I am astonished the old woman has not complained about this place, which will most likely never sprout another stalk. Instead she raves over a few sacred boughs near the plaza."

"It is the difference between past and future," Garan explained. "The trees have stood unblemished since Cetrone arrival here. A fallow field beckons a future crop. The old healer does not look forward. She relies on the past for her power. The future can defend itself when and if it arrives."

"I had not thought of that," Yustichisqua said.

The Culpeeper brothers stood at the edge of the firing range, their field glasses peering at the results of the morning training initiative. A line of twelve *chisqua* clansmen stood, legs spread and anchored to a trench line. At the far end of the field, a cluster of *geetli* clansmen stood draped in *conontoroy* armor. Harris held his right hand high, *Hierarchus* sending up a beam.

"Hold your fire," he shouted, and then turned to Moe Culpeeper. "How's it going?"

"Their aim is a bit flippant, but with *gingergust*, it makes no never mind."

"And what's the rate down at the plate?" Harris asked Larry.

"They're shy still and might need an arse reamer."

"Can I assist in that?"

"You'll be the ticket, Lord Belmundus," Moe replied.

Both brothers shook their heads, encouraging Harris to take a stance. He looked to Garan.

"Warriors aren't born, my friend," Harris said. "I never expected farmers and basket weavers to master the art of war."

"Like actors do?" Garan quipped.

"Some acting is in order," he replied. "Yustichisqua."

"Yes, *oginali*."

"Let's give them a demonstration."

Harris approached a young *chisqua* soldier and snapped his *blundaboomer* from his hands.

"Easy now," Harris said. "You don't need precision in this game. You just need to discharge the stuff and be ready to fire again in eighty seconds. Can you do that?"

"I think I can, sir," the young man replied.

"Good. Yustichisqua! Run it down."

Yustichisqua ran toward the target — a wall of *phitron* thirty yards away. *The geetli* cleared aside. Harris shouldered *the blundaboomer*, and then turned as Yustichisqua approached the wall at a full gallop. Harris raised the weapon, locked his eye into the sights and pulled the trigger. A red powdery puff — *gingergust*, or as the Cetrone called it, *gigoo susti*, the red smoke, raced across the field, striking the wall, just as Yustichisqua reached it. Little Bird penetrated it when the *phitron* transformed into *kaybar.*

"Count it out," Moe shouted, and *the geetli* began to count.

When they reached eighty, Yustichisqua reemerged through the wall, turned and banged his fists on it.

"*Phitron* again," he shouted, and a great cheer went up.

Adadooski.

Arkmo.

Harris returned *the blundaboomer* to the young *chisqua.*

"Now that's the way we go at it. Eighty is the count for *the gigoo susti.* If you blast it or throw it in *wadi-wadi*, an eighty count is all you have. Do you fucking understand me . . . son?"

The young man shook his head eagerly.

"So do it."

Harris jumped aside quickly, as the dozen *chisqua* took aim and fired their *blundaboomers*, a thunderous wave of gingergust whipped across the field, striking the wall. *The geetli* hopped through it, their counting still heard, but muffled by preoccupation. At seventy-five, a few reemerged. At seventy-eight, the rest, except three, who popped through at the eighty mark, not quite clearing the transformation.

"Fry me arse," Larry shouted. "There's always one or two that need bleedin' extrication."

Yustichisqua was berating the stuckees, while Larry and Moe rushed toward the targets, yelling *if this were a bloody battle, you'd be as dead as me Aunt Tilde's brassier.* Harris shook his head, and then glanced at Garan.

"You should see them drive *Seecoys*. It's like bumper cars at Coney Island."

"I suppose that means they are inexpert at it?" Garan said.

"Suppose it not." Harris was suddenly demure. "But they have heart. They want to liberate their countrymen. They will die for it."

"At any rate," Garan noted, "I am not the Cetrone to speak to that. I will be on my ship braving sea serpents instead." Harris frowned. "Be not amazed, Lord Belmundus. There is a reason they call me *the Gucheeda*. I am no hero and have been shunned for my inaction."

"Yet you're here."

"I came to see you, my lord." Garan bowed. "I might be *a tludachi* turd for all Cetronia to spurn, but I care — even at a distance, I care."

Harris supposed Garan could keep his own counsel in all things. Lord Belmundus, newly indoctrinated, was not a proselytizer. Garan had done well by him. There was no need for him to go further. There were enough Cetrone patriots to die on the red sands of the Forling.

Within a day, *the branchy-wanchies* were functional. Harris inspected crates of *sillifoons* and set about distributing this first shipment to each clan. Cosawta held classes on the device's operation, code names and authetication. Soon the Cetrone were strutting about the streets talking to each other — walking into ditches and falling over drain covers. *Infectious*. Harris was amused, but knew the squadron leaders would need a strategy to communicate between the ranks. The casual glow of eased communication had to be reined and refined before the green sky mellowed — if it mellowed. However, with the *sillifoon* issue settled, Cosawta prepared *the Gananadana* to depart for Montjoy.

"I go to see what there is to see," Cosawta shouted in a grand speech from the gondola, Tomatly on the ropes.

"*To see! To see!*"

All Echota assembled to send the Seneschal off upon the great mission, including Enitachopco and his brothers. Only Littafulchee did not come and Harris wondered why. She had prepared to come, but was unusually sad by her brother's departure. Nayowee showed up, standing near the gondola, scowling.

"I go to see what there is to see," Cosawta announced, waving his *sillifoon* high. "And I will tell you of it using my *sillifoon* — God-speaker."

"God-speaker?" Nayowee shouted, and then turned to the crowd. "Believe it not," she croaked. "He will be speaking to the sacred trees and they will be speaking to you. But be on your best behavior, because if you anger the trees, they will swallow the words and be mute." She laughed. "The trees hold your destiny."

"*The trees! The trees!*"

"So be it," Cosawta said. "I can think of worse intercessors than these trees."

"So can I," Enitachopco said, raising his pipe.

His brothers did the same.

"The trees are friendly," Elejoy noted.

"The news will be favorable," Coweeshee added.

"Who cares about the trees?" Tucharechee snapped. He gazed down at Nayowee, who cowered. "I care more for the sky and Kuriakis' mood. Nephew," he shouted. "Knock on the Elector of Montjoy's silver door and tell him to wipe his ass and be about his normal business so we may blast away his walls and liberate our people."

A great cheer arose, drums beating and horns bleating.

Adadooski.

Arkmo.

"I shall do it," Cosawta shouted.

"*Do it! Do it!*"

Enitachopco blew three perfect smoke rings toward his son and raised his pipe again. The singing and the dancing commenced. *The Gananadana* started its journey to *the Kalugu.*

5

Littafulchee had taken to her quarters. She ate little and spoke less. Harris assumed she was still upset by her father's refusal to let her join the impending campaign. But there was no reason which Harris could fathom which would keep her from bidding her brother farewell. Still, Harris was cautious, not wishing to brook an argument. As dour as she had turned, she was still kind to her *husgi* and treated him with respect. He wanted more than respect, but chalked her mood up to the anomaly of womankind — an ignorant scapegoat of a reason handy for ignorant men — a convenience of an excuse — *women!*

Harris continued his inspection tours, supervising supply wagons — spacious *Loribringus* stacked high with armaments and foodstuffs. Other *Loribringus* were filled with precious metals (*aninya* in particular), woven goods, sacks of *selu* and . . . women. Yes, women, because this, along with *korinkle* upon *korinkle* of *yedalas* was payment for goods delivered and services rendered by *the Fumarcans*. Their work completed, they formed convoys to cross Mount Talasee and return to *the Dodingdaten* and Comastee.

Harris was loathed to see them go. He enjoyed sitting in their circles, hearing various stories and histories — how they fell through this hole or that into Farn. Some came through mountains, while others dropped in during sea tempests. A few came through the Bermuda Triangle, or at least that's how Harris deduced it. They came on all one-way journeys with never a guarantee they would find places in *the Dodingdaten*. For every outlander who blew about Aolium or hot-footed it through Volcanium, dozens were lost in the pits of Terrastrium or the mists of Magus.

Mostly Harris would miss Garan.

"I trust we shall meet again," *the Gucheeda* said on his parting evening.

"I would hope so, sir," Harris replied. "Battle might get me."

"Never you. Life in Farn is long and you are the consort to a Scepta."

"Two, perhaps."

"One," Garan said. "That other one has no claim on you now."

"I suppose," Harris said, thinking of Littafulchee's mood. "When you see my *Danuwa*, tell him that he is missed."

"Elypticus will hear those words. They will go directly to his heart. He is a noble spirit — much beyond my poor efforts. He has a place in Farn's story yet, if I am any judge of destiny."

"I sincerely hope you're right, and . . . I thank you again for the many kindnesses and services you've rendered me."

"I shall require payment someday."

"No doubt."

Garan bowed low, and joined the convoy.

Harris returned to the clan house with a heavy heart. He meant to divert his steps to Yustichisqua's place to discuss strategy and peruse maps. Little Bird had a fondness for cartography and had learned battle planning from Cosawta. It was all classroom stuff, but it might prove useful.

Suddenly, weariness overcame Lord Belmundus.

Much to do, he thought.

He had accomplished much already. Tomorrow would be soon enough for more. He found his way to his apartments — to his bedroom. Littafulchee was asleep. He gazed at her as she peacefully slept beneath cascades of silk sheets. He wanted to wake her and caress her and revel in her beauty, but she slept soundly and he was weary.

"I'd be too pooped to pop," he muttered, and then placed *Friend Tony* aside, unhitched his sash, *Hierarchus* falling to the floor. *The asano* and the brassets went next. He nuzzled into the bed with nothing but his *Columbincus* glowing. He was asleep in a flash, but he dreamed.

The dream — powerful as dreams could be to the weary, brought him back to Charminus' bed. Such images would stir stone to passion, but he embraced them with ardor. The Scepta was faceless — just a mass of breasts in a cloud of bedding, but he recalled the hours — the weeks imprisoned between her legs. As he trembled before the jade ring, he turned away. He was hanging aloft from *the Gananadana's* gondola, overlooking a red sea of *kowlinka*. *The porcorporians* snapped, trying their best to reach him, but the *Tippagore* charged. A battle ensued — a crimson tide with *gingergusts* and explosions — *wadi-wadi* flying aloft, exploding near black walls. *Cabriolins* buzzed overhead, as did *Seecoys*. The air was redolent with war — choking smoke and sweet blood pouring across the Forling. Then the stream turned clear and he saw Nayowee standing beneath *the Sittiquo* trees, her cane pointing at him. She cackled about something, but he couldn't hear her, so he popped open his *sillifoon*. So did she — remarkable that she had one. *Lord Belmundus*, she croaked. *Listen to the trees, because they have a tale. Your tale.* His lips quivered, meaning to ask her to tell him *his tale* quickly, but no need. She did. *The walls shall fall, but so shall many and you will see the hill of the Ayelli in a different light.*

Harris listened hard, but static clutched the message and distorted it. He shouted into the *sillifoon*.

Old woman, tell me now.

But he heard the trees — a chorus of *branchy-wanchies*, shaking their razor leaves and shouting *Adadooski. Arkmo. Hail Lord Belmundus, Boots of Montjoy*.

"Boots of Montjoy," he murmured in his sleep.

Then he awoke, reaching for Littafulchee. She wasn't there. He sat bolt upright, feeling the empty spot.

"Boots of Montjoy," he stammered. "What a dream. Where are you? Where are you, my love? I need you."

He glanced toward the light — toward the window. There his wife stood, draped in a starry nightgown. She wept.

"Littafulchee," he called. "You're crying. Why?"

She turned.

"We must be parted, *husgi*."

"Not yet. Not yet."

"Yes."

She stood aside, allowing the light to radiate across her breasts. She lifted her hand toward the window.

"Yes, my love, we must."

Harris stood, reaching for *Friend Tony*. He pushed toward the window, and then looked out.

"It's come," he said softly.

"Yes," she murmured. "Kuriakis no longer stirs."

Chapter Two

Like the Rolling Tide Across a Crimson Sea

1

Harris stared into the mirror, seeking the man who he had been — the frivolous actor, tethered to roles and junkets and scarce else. He saw him — the signature gap between his teeth. His hair had grown — shaggy even, and his stubble emerged on the warmest mornings. Still, the image looking back seemed different. Not older, nor wiser, if wisdom could be reflected. But his eyes were darker — redder, and his lips thicker.

"I'm a star," he muttered, and then chuckled, although on this morning he had nothing to amuse him.

He had to take it as it came, suspecting levity would be a pint low today. Suddenly, another face appeared in the mirror — an older face, which looked much younger, although gladder than his.

"A star," she said.

"Two stars," he replied, reaching for her hand and drawing it across his chest, as naked as the rest of him.

"Are you *Solus* or *Dodecadatamus*?" she asked.

"Which attracts which?"

"Who can tell when a lady is parted from her lord?"

She kissed his neck, and then wrapped her arms about his shoulders, pulling him into her breasts.

"I will miss you so," he muttered.

"Hush," she replied. "My father has declared a day of silence in your honor. I shall follow the fold and speak no more."

She pressed her fingers, first to her lips and then to his. She darted away. He stood, watching her while she arranged his undergarments. This task should not be her task. He had been dressing himself, having shed the private laziness of Yustichisqua.

Harris reached for his golden loin cloth, but Littafulchee wagged her finger. He sighed, and then assented. Her fingers prickled as she wrapped the garment about his waist and fastened the cloth about his crotch. He found it difficult to tame his baser nature. But she was quick about it. Soon she latched his *conontoroy* breastplate over his shoulders and shielded his chest. This was followed by his *asano* and cape. As she fastened the clasp about his collar, Harris grasped her wrists and drew her nearer. She allowed him one kiss before fetching his belt. On that circlet she hung *Hierarchus*, a *Stick* and a pouch containing his *sillifoon*. Then she lovingly affixed his *waddly* wazzoo to his *asano*, like a Scotsman wears his sporran. The brassets followed and a garter of *yustunalla*. He bowed his head as she crowned him with his helmet, a new tiara fashioned with three blue hollies — the crown of *the seegoniga* clan.

Harris lifted his feet in turn while Littafulchee clamped on *the zulus* — a special pair, bejeweled and fitted for comfort over his dickey foot. He would not go into battle hobbling on *Friend Tony*. Instead, the cane would be held like a baton — a symbol of leadership. Finally, she brought him the double *Columbincus*. This he took himself and fastened it as he had learned, allowing the brooch to catch the light. Once in place, Littafulchee caressed it, permitting one final, parting kiss.

Harris took her into his arms, his brass jangling for anyone who cared. He didn't. He had much to say now, but she stilled his lips with her fingers, running them to his chin, and then to his *Columbincus*. Tears rolled down her cheeks. If fingers failed to leave him speechless, her tears succeeded. He turned away to hide his own, fearing they might shake him from his course. But she would never allow him to stay, and he was hardened to the commitment. He felt her fingers on his back as she affixed the last element — *a korinkle* filled with *selu gadu* and other Cetrone delicacies. Gone were the days of hard tack and *mongerhide*, although he liked the sausage of *the Ayelli*. But that seemed so long ago.

His wife, the Scepta of Zacker, brushed her hands across his *zulus*, switching them on. He took flight, a gentle rise above the bedroom's butter pat tiles. He allowed himself to drift, turning as he did, watching her fade while the flying sandals transported him to the door and beyond.

2

Through the corridors of time, Harris Cartwright — Lord Belmundus drifted alone, pondering his departure, saddened at his loss. Yet, as he proceeded, he shook it off and focused on the task ahead; and such a task it was, with no guarantee for success, only the sureness of nature's force bashing against formidable rocks —

a rolling tide across a crimson sea — the red *kowlinka* of the Forling.

He had heard from Cosawta — *the sillifoons* proving useful. The Seneschal had reached *the Kalugu*, but was detained. Suspicions were rampant in *the mordanka* — Cosawta's absence prolonged and, by the tone of the interrogation, a spy, most likely from *the Dodingdaten*, had whispered of activity in the borderlands. That *a Fumarcan* would spill the beans could have been expected, these pirates self-serving to a high degree, but losing the element of surprise for an attack was a major blow, if it had indeed occurred. The Cetrone forces were comparatively few, under trained and reliant on superior ordinance, much of which they had barely mastered. If a large Yunocker force engaged them before they reached the gates of Montjoy, the campaign could be in jeopardy.

At least *the sillifoons* worked, and Cosawta had managed to bullshit his way out of custody, reminding his *mordanka* trading partners that he was nothing more than the ferryman — a dealer in contraband. Why would he return to *the Kalugu* if anything untoward percolated in *the Dodaloo* and beyond? He just wanted to get his *sqwallen* fix and dope out in the *sustiya.* Still, Harris was wary of the mission, especially if Tarhippus got wind of the plan and deployed his full might, nipping it in the bud. Although it was inconceivable that a Cetrone force could cross *the Forling*, the Yunockers might not be ignorant of the Culpeeper's *kowlinka*-proof hovercraft. They could put the pieces together, stupid as they were.

Harris reached the clan house's foyer. On the threshold hovered a young Cetrone warrior, fully geared and draped in a blue feathered cape. Harris thought he looked like a wild pheasant. The warrior blocked his path, and then, landing, went to one knee, raising his *blundaboomer* high — a sign of respect.

"Lord Belmundus."

Harris lifted the lad's chin.

"Who are you?"

"I am your new *Taleenay*, my lord."

"Ah, yes." Harris recalled that Yustichisqua, now a captain, chose a new adjutant for his lord. Was this he? So young, but who could tell with the Cetrone? He might have been seventy-five and not look a day over twenty. "What's your name?"

"Detonto, my lord."

Harris chuckled, but repressed a laugh.

"Detonto? Well, at least I can pronounce it, which goes to your favor. Be upstanding."

Detanto stood, and then drifted on his *zulus*, bowing again.

"They await you, my lord."

Harris didn't need to ask who. He knew. He had a new set of *Danuwa*, led by Little Bird. Detonto turned, and then preceded, Harris following him over the threshold and into the plaza. There the cadre hovered, bowing at once to their commander. Harris felt a pang of pride and fear. These men trusted him — his military judgment, of which he had none, and his battle experience, which amounted to a skirmish with a *porcorporian*. But he was an actor and act he would — as they expected. Any chink in the armor might prove fatal to *esprit de corps*.

Four *Danuwa* were present, each draped in their clan garb, armor light, but armed to the teeth. The headdresses were stunning. Harris wondered how the head gear would fare in battle. It might scare the enemy like a bunch of Hottentots on the warpath. But that was a good thing, wasn't it?

From *the alisoqua* clan was Oustestee, his chest hung with bear claws, his neck wrapped in a fur, despite the warm weather. From *the geetli* clan was Cheowie, a short man with a mongrel look, his face paint giving him a hang-dog expression. From *the chisqua clan* was Estatoie, a bony warrior with eagle feathers hung from an owl-eared headdress. Quite astonishing, especially the face paint, giving his eyes a hollow look. Finally, from *the tlugu* clan was Tosawa, his cape flaked with bark and twigs, branches bursting from his hair. Harris thought Birnam Wood might be on the march today.

The men settled to the ground at Harris' approached. They pounded their chests in a salute, and then shook their *waddly wazzoos*. Harris nodded to each in turn. He supposed a little speech was in order, something *a la Henry V*, but decided to cleave to the decree of silence. There was much he had to say, but mostly he had questions. There was plenty of time for a palaver once they got underway. He turned to Detonto.

"Is there much razzle-dazzle from the citizens?"

"Razzle-dazzle, my lord?"

"Partying? Celebration?"

"None," Detonto replied. "It has been decreed."

"Just so."

"Many stand and weep, my lord, but it is to be expected."

"Just so."

Suddenly, Harris heard hissing, and then spitting sounds. Across the plaza came the old woman. She pounded her cane furiously on the path.

"Here you stand while we wait," she croaked at Lord Belmundus.

"I see you're not observing the silence," Harris remarked.

"Why should I? I see a pile of danger sitting in my *selu* fields and I would see it gone. Yet you stand here with your *boobooyaks* dragging like *snaligrogs.*"

"You should be praying for our success and safety."

"I have, Lord Belmundus," she quipped, and then spit at him, the spray decorating his *Columbincus*. "There you have it. My blessing."

She turned to Detonto and spit at him. He bowed.

"I thank you," he said humbly.

Harris realized that this was truly the blessing and not one of Nayowee's insults. She faced and spit in turn at each *Danuwa*, who bowed his head in thanks. When she reached the end of the row, she turned to Harris.

"Yet, you are still here. Will you stand as rust for the ages, monuments to good intentions? Or will you take your *gugubasgi* from this place and do *the Primordius Centrum's* bidding?"

Harris wished he had *a blundaboomer* to blow the old hag away with one discharge of *gingergust* — turn her to stone perhaps. But he drew in his breath and nodded to his new *Taleenay.*

"Lead on."

As this Cetrone military leadership filtered through the lanes and groves, many Echotans stood vigil in silence, heads bowed and praying. Harris sensed their fears and sorrows, and yet he also felt their pride. He wondered what they expected from this mission. What was the endgame? He knew many wanted their enemies slaughtered at any cost, while some would just settle for a turning of the tables — an enslaved Yunocker nation under the command of *waddly wazzoo*-wielding Cetrone. In his heart Harris knew this could not be delivered — not with a ragtag contingent of *farmers-*

turned-warriors, despite the superior ordinance. The more Harris considered the mission, the more he dwelled on the desperation he had witnessed in *the Banetuckle*, the dying and starving souls awaiting *reaptide*. That was the key. *Liberation*. Still, the logistics of liberation was a battle unto itself. Secretly, he cursed his brother-in-law for rushing away to become the advanced guard, leaving him here to lead the charge. If Harris was writing a script, he would have crafted events differently.

"*Dinatli*."

Yustichisqua was there, hovering at the edge of the *selu* fields. He wore his grand blue cape; the one Harris had given him on the day of his first hunt. Unlike *the Danuwa*, Captain Yustichisqua wore a simple skull cap with one blue feather tucked in his headband. His breastplate was leather and both arms were bared to display his two *gollywi*, a point of pride and prestige. He was the son of Kittowa, after all, and was blood brother to Lord Belmundus. Aside his *waddly wazzoo*, *gasohisgi* was sheathed, but prominent. Harris grinned broadly upon seeing him, so proud was he.

"Old man," Harris said. "How many have we?"

"Eight-thousand and twenty-seven, assembled in double and triple *Seecoys*, *Fustigars* filled with forty each and *Loribringus* fully supplied and manned, *oginali*."

"Eight-thousand," Harris said proudly, although he knew this was not nearly enough.

"Eight-thousand and twenty-seven, *oginali*." Yustichisqua looked to Detonto. "Is your new *Taleenay* satisfactory?"

"I suppose so, old man. I've just met him and he's done nothing out of the ordinary yet. Seems young, but . . . I can never judge these things. Still, if he's your choice, I'm sure he'll work out."

"He is one of Lord Cosawta's many bastards, *oginali*."

"That doesn't surprise me."

"He is proud to be so," Yustichisqua said.

Detonto bowed, and moved closer, but Harris stopped him.

"Wait there, Detonto. I wish to confer with the captain."

Detonto bowed again, and then joined *the Danuwa*. Harris drifted beside Yustichisqua, voices lowered to a whisper.

"So, what do you think?"

"Think, *oginali*?"

"What's the plan of attack?"

"It is not for me to say."

"On the contrary."

Yustichisqua shrugged, and then slipped his hand into his left brasset and extracted a triangular device.

"*The navakawee* is working," he said, switching the pad on, a light blinking. He held it up. "The way is clear."

The Culpeeper brothers had developed a navigational system using *the branchy-wanchie*, which triangulated with a beacon attached to *the Gananadana*. Yustichisqua's love for maps made him a natural to assume the navigational duties.

"Is it, old man? Is the way clear?"

"Look and see, *oginali*."

Harris glanced at *the navakawee*, nodding.

"I'll leave those readings to you. Crossing the Forling this time will be a snap, but what do we do when we reach Montjoy?"

Yustichisqua frowned.

"We knock Tarhippus from his fiery *Cabriolin* and beat him with his own *gwasdis.* I long to see *the zugginaks* make him their dinner."

"Good goal," Harris said, sighing. "But we're only eight-thousand."

"Eight-thousand and twenty-seven."

Harris laughed.

"Yes, I see your point. Those extra twenty-seven make the difference."

"It is not in numbers that we are strong, *oginali.* It is in our souls. Every beating heart — every pulsing *waddly wazzoo* is set on the goal."

Harris read ardor on Little Bird's face and wished he could know what goal was set.

"You and I, old man — we have experienced *reaptide*. We have waded through *the Banetuckle*. No other in our band has seen it."

"They have been bred to it, *oginali.* They have been carefully taught to know of the suffering. They have waited for this day."

"So you've been told, not having been here yourself."

Yustichisqua shook his head.

"I must believe it or return to Wanona's bed and forget my life in *the Kalugu*."

"No," Harris chided. "We must stay the course, consider our limited forces and apply them to best effect. That may mean leaving Tarhippus to scratch his ass with a broken bottle."

Yustichisqua chuckled. Harris pointed to *the navakawee*.

"Set a course to the middle of the Forling. We'll cross in two stages. By the time we reach midcourse, I'll know and tell you my plan." He studied Little Bird's face. "Are you afraid, *Dinatli*?"

"Does it show?"

"No, and don't let it. But keep your fear at hand. You'll need it." He signaled to Detonto, who moved forward, *the Danuwa* in tow. "Gentlemen, let's do this thing."

3

Harris drifted into *the selu* field, where his *Seecoy* awaited him. He discharged Yustichisqua and *the Danuwa* to their posts, each commanding a squadron. Detonto revved *the Seecoy*, and then waited for Lord Belmundus to take his position.

"Take her up," Harris said softly, and Detonto skillfully worked the pedals and levers, raising *the Seecoy* above the heads of *selu*.

Harris was glad his new *Taleenay* could drive. Not every Cetrone could fly in a straight line, many *Seecoys* waffling more than flying. As he reached an altitude to survey the eight-thousand (and twenty-seven), Harris was floored by the panorama. Thousands of *Seecoys* were revved. With each squadron, were dozens of *Fustigars* manned with itching infantry and ready-to-explode ordinance. Additional supplies of food and weapons were packed into *Loribringus* — a convoy prepared to trail behind the fleet like a bridal train. Harris was moved. He felt downright Shakespearean and wished he could muster one of those *Henry V* speeches. He wouldn't even need a script writer. Had he not extemporaneously whipped out an impassioned recitation during the last moments of *Othellohito*? Still, there was nothing to aid him. He didn't have a *boomer-boomer*, one of those funnel thingies to amplify his voice.

"Detonto," he murmured.

"Yes, my lord."

"Isn't it grand?"

"In what way, my lord?"

Harris cocked his head, staring at his new *Taleenay*. This had to be Cosawta's son. Harris wondered, when acclimated, if Detonto would display his father's colorful vernacular.

"Where's your sense of grandeur, sir?" Harris asked. "Have you ever seen anything like this before?"

"No, my lord. I cannot say I have. But it is a means to an end."

"A means to an . . ."

Detonto was correct, but the moment was dashed. Harris was glad he didn't have a *boomer-boomer*. He might have clunked Detonto over the head with it.

Bing bong. Bing bong.

The *sillifoon* signaled — a ring-tone Harris created himself. He flipped it open, and raised the hood extender.

"Yes, old man," he said, and then corrected himself. "I mean, BeeDust here, who be?"

He heard Little Bird through the speaker — *lima-charlie*.

"2Gollies I be. Do *the tludachi* roar?"

Harris had not cared much for security over *the branchy-wanchie* system, considering the Yunockers were cellular mutes, but Moe Culpeeper insisted. *You never know who's got their flappers up and ready to blab to the moonbeams.* Harris took this to mean, you couldn't trust *a Fumarcan* as far as you could spit. So he assigned each *sillifoon* user a code name and devised a predetermined set of coded phrases. *Another language*, he thought, *and why the fuck not?*

"It roars to all points, 2Gollies," he responded. "Take two aspirins and call me in the morning."

"Swallowing, BeeDust. Look to *the selu* and you will see *the gadu* rise."

"Over."

"Over and ouch."

Bing bong. Bing bong.

Harris closed his *sillifoon* and looked to *the selu* to watch the rising of *the gadu*. The golden *Seecoys* slowly arose, a ballet in the making. *The Fustigars* waffled above the grain, the sheaves flattening in their wake. *The Loribringus* skirted the ground, and then spun upward like silvery fleas on a blond dog.

"Isn't it grand?" Harris murmured again as he watched his fleet arise and move forward under his *say so* — hundreds of *sillifoons bing-bonging* orders, rippling through *the branchy-wanchie* from

Yustichisqua's command. "Take the lead, Detonto," Harris said. "Take the lead."

Detonto throttled *the Seecoy* and overtook the fleet, reaching the base of Mount Talasee in short order. *Such speed. Such power.* Harris hoped the majority of drivers could master *Seecoys* as Detonto had, but hope was hope and not fact. Still, it was a good start. Harris glanced back at the fleet — Cosawta's fleet. How could he be pissed at the Seneschal? This logistical engineering feat was a colossal undertaking — a miracle of patience, something Cosawta often lacked.

"Isn't it grand?" he repeated, expecting Detonto to question him again. But *the Taleenay* was quiet, going about his duties. Harris tried to tear away from awestruck wonder and undertook the practical task of securing a store of *wadi-wadi.*

Bing bong. Bing bong.

"BeeDust here."

"2Gollies I be."

"Yes, 2Gollies, speak your mind."

"Isn't it grand, *oginali*?" came the voice.

"Yes, old man. All eight-thousand of them."

"Eight-thousand and twenty-seven."

Over and ouch.

Chapter Three

The Golden Eight

1

With *the Dodaloo* behind him, Harris scanned the crimson sea of *kowlinka*. To him the Forling was an ocean of blood — his blood running through memories of his last crossing. But there was a difference now. He was not alone. He had the eight-thousand at his back — and he began calling his force *the Golden Eight*, because their metallic brilliance shimmered beneath Farn's dual suns like a precious necklace drawn across a fiery lake. The other difference was speed. *Cabriolins* were remarkably slow compared with *Seecoys*, which had zoom-zoom in an overdrive, which Harris physically felt. *Seecoys* could also fly lower, the grillwork design impervious to *the kowlinka's* damaging effects. Although Harris did not believe in infallibility — *Seecoys* were machines, after all. However, *Cabriolins* would be sputtering at this point in the journey and this low to the dunes. Of course, flying low meant vigilance. A claw could snap up and pull a vehicle down. Therefore, constant *bing-bonging* was necessary between the flanks and the supply train, assuring lower altitudes were still higher than *a porcorporian's* reach or a *tludachi's* leap.

Heat was a factor. Harris believed *Cabriolins* handled the heat best. The humidity buckling from the dunes unsettled the *Seecoys*, making them waffle. He expected some fatalities from bad driving, but the expectation heightened when otherwise good drivers hung onto their levers like rodeo steer riders. He observed many near misses.

"*Sillifoon* ahead, Detonto, and tell Oustestee's squad to fly higher or we'll have a pile up for sure."

"Yes, my lord," Detonto replied, flipping his *sillifoon* open and coldly repeating the message, in code: *Off the griddle. Off the griddle. Flip those flap jacks.*

Harris watched as Oustestee's squad waffled higher, straightening. Soon after this correction, he issued another one to Tosawa's squad. This time the code was *Gadu cooking too close. Unstick. Unstick,* meaning, of course, your vehicles are too close together — separate.

Harris wished he could relax. Several checks with Yustichisqua told him the fleet was making steady progress and would be midcourse by nightfall; remarkable, considering his last crossing, which took the better part of two weeks. However, he didn't congratulate himself prematurely. He knew the desert heat would drop off at dusk and a freeze would make travel too cold for comfort. He wanted to be dug in and ready before the Forling creatures had a chance to penetrate *the Golden Eight's* vulnerabilities. He also wanted every swinging *waddly wazzoo* to be lit, and each warrior fed and energized — a good sleep, with one man on and one man off in a vigil. It was paramount to review the invasion plans with his *Danuwa*. Thus, his mind raced.

"Look there, my lord," Detonto said. "A mighty beast."

Harris raised his *gespocular* — a powerful spyglass fashioned by Larry Culpeeper in Lord Belmundus' honor (no charge — a gift). Harris grinned as he watched.

"That, Detonto, is *a Tippagore*."

"We had best run it down," Detonto replied.

"And why do you say that?"

"It might attack us or block the way."

"It's a harmless creature."

"It does not look harmless to me, my lord. I have never seen such a monster."

"Monster!" Harris was offended. He sat beside Detonto, blinking wildly. "You have no knowledge of the Forling. How can you be sure what is or isn't a monster?"

"I am sorry to offend you, my lord, but we are crossing on a mission and should not bypass possible threats undisturbed. The creature looks like a monster to me."

Harris shook his head.

"It's a *Tippagore* and the female has strong preservation instincts. She'll protect her babies and kill you, to be sure. But if left alone, she's as docile as *an awidena*."

"Bigger than any *awidena* I have ever seen, my lord."

"Well, you haven't seen much. You're a good driver and operate *the sillifoon* satisfactorily, but you must use more than your eyes when surveying the land."

Harris didn't know why he was taking his anxiety out on his new *Taleenay*. Perhaps he had become so accustomed to Yustichisqua's soft and supple touch, this new one's steely view of things unsettled him. This discussion could have continued, but Harris hobbled to the back rail, and then watched as they passed over *the Tippagore*.

"Mama," he said, taking another deep glance through *the gespocular*.

He saw the female stop, gazing at the vehicles overhead, her carpet train tightening over her brood. At a distance, the bull raised slightly to defend against the invaders. But as the fleet approached, they avoided his tusks and horns. Harris was glad for it. If one of these creatures were harmed, he couldn't bear it. He glanced again at Detonto. *Not a warm spot in his veins*, he thought. But not everyone was like Little Bird and, from a combat point of view, an unimpassioned companion might be best.

The red glow of the Forling turned amber at dusk. Harris became anxious. He could hear *the tludachi* roaring. He opened his *sillifoon*.

"BeeDust here."

"2Gollies I be," came the answer.

"Are we at checkmate by your charts?"

"Nearly so."

Harris sighed, and then tapped Detonto's shoulder.

"Bring her down on the other side of that bluff," he said, his *Taleenay* nodding and engaging levers. Harris raised the *sillifoon* again. "2Gollies, set the table for dinner and invite the guests for tea."

"Ringing the bell, BeeDust."

"When down, light the lanterns and serve the punch, and then gather the roosters in the henhouse to peck seed."

"Out at the plate, BeeDust. Over and ouch."

"Over and ouch."

Harris scanned the periphery, watching the flanks descend and land. One by one *the waddly wazzoos* lit. Detonto brought *the Seecoy* down gently. Soon a *Loribringus* parked beside them, its drivers anchoring into the dunes and pitching a gargantuan tent — the henhouse of the coded message. Detonto stood, nodded to Harris and waited orders. Harris, unaccustomed to taking the lead in *the Taleenay* business, Little Bird having taking the initiative automatically, paused.

"Good job, Detonto," Harris said.

"I am sorry, my lord. I shall do better tomorrow."

Harris was taken aback by this response. Was *good* not *good enough*? Apparently not. But Harris didn't want to change Detonto's perceptions. The *bastard* had been brought up in a menagerie, after all, where discipline was required to stay ahead of his father's *tludachi* pets.

"I'm sure of it," Harris stammered. "See to the henhouse. Make sure the table's set and the amenities prepared."

"Not too comfortable, my lord," Detonto suggested tartly. "We are roaming in the wild and should not delude our senses."

Detonto didn't wait for a response, but switched on his *zulus* and buzzed off *the Seecoy*, to attend to his duties.

Harris glanced at the sprawl of *the Golden Eight*, now a shadowy range of hills — tents pitched and *waddly wazzoos* displayed. He grabbed *Friend Tony* and kindled his own *waddly wazzoo*. Odd this lamp — comforting and symbolic, but as utilitarian as any lantern in the dark. However, the dark dispelled by this light was chased, retreating fast, but returning slowly as if its retreat was a conscious act. Harris activated his *zulus* and drifted across *the kowlinka*. *Zulus*, prone to outage, would be used sparingly in the Forling. Still, when Harris landed, he heard the distant howls of the desert denizens and raised his lamp high, expecting to see a tooth or a claw. Instead, he saw a welcomed face. His captain had arrived.

2

Yustichisqua munched on a large *selu gadu* chunk as he spun *the navakawee* at the center of the gathered *Danuwa*. They huddled beneath the henhouse tent, while Lord Belmundus made inquiries about the troops' temperament, the state of the vehicles and generally assessed *espirit de corps,* which he judge running high with a peppering of prebattle jitters, but no more. For all but a Cetrone handful, this was their first encounter with the Forling. A small band remembered an expedition many years ago — too long for most memories. They had seen the desert in the same way Harris had and recalled its brutality. The new way of engagement was an improvement, but still harbored fears. Harris acknowledged these sentiments, but preferred the fresh perspective of newly minted warriors.

Cheowie was one such veteran. He glanced over his shoulder with every distant *tludachi* howl.

"Gentlemen," Harris said, firmly. "So far, so good. If anyone has reservations, put them aside until they're warranted." He pointed to Cheowie. "*The alisoqua* have followed this course before, I know. But we're a new force in the land, and you're my *Danuwa* — a new warrior breed. You must know the plan in detail. So watch and listen."

Yustichisqua clapped and *the navakawee* shot a map projection across the floor. All present leaned forward to observe.

"Behold Montjoy and *the Kalugu*," Harris said. Suddenly, he and Yustichisqua were experts on the subject, few knowing things such as maps and terrain and walls and the refinements of wards. "You must etch this map in your mind to follow the plan."

"What are your orders, *oginali?*" Yustichisqua asked.

Harris drew *Friend Tony* from its cane-scabbard, amazing his *Danuwa* with *the brashun blade.* He struck its point at the gates of Montjoy.

"Montjoy — the home of your oppressor — a place where Cetrone work and die so the Yunockers can enjoy peace and pleasure."

"We shall destroy it," Estatoie shouted.

"The walls shall fall," Cheowie echoed.

"Let *the blundaboomers* blast every standing stone," Oustestee rumbled.

Tosawa remained silent, shaking his head.

"You have doubts, Tosawa?" Harris asked.

"They are high walls and strong," Tosawa said. "The enemy will not sit idle while we announce our welcome at the gates. When we blast them, they will return fire. They will pour onto the Forling and block our way. And if we should enter, they will be there at every step."

"How can you say such things, Tosawa?" Estatoie complained. "We are strong. We have *wadi-wadi.*"

"And when *the phitron* is restored after the eighty count?" Tosawa posed.

"We will throw more and more and again and again," Cheowie stated.

"*Gigoo susti* transforms walls, not men," Tosawa argued.

"Then we will trap them within their own defenses," Oustestee countered.

"That is true," Tosawa said. "But it does not strike me as a good application."

Estatoie's chest heaved, while his two companions pouted. Tosawa continued to shake his head.

"It is a most unlikely way of thinking," Yustichisqua said, drawing their attention from the gate.

Harris moved *Tony* to *the Kalugu*'s walls.

"*The Kalugu*," he said, tapping the projection poignantly. "While Montjoy is shame, *the Kalugu* is poison." He stared at his *Danuwa*, who seemed puzzled. "You're concentrating on the enemy and not the goal. The dark ward is sorrow's source. When *reaptide's* klaxon sounds, the Yunockers release *the zugginaks* to tear your countrymen's flesh. *The Banetuckle* is emptied into the mouths of hungry *tludachi*. Where blood doesn't flow, *the sqwallen* does, a hideous concoction snaring the Cetrone with dazed confusion — a dream state, compelling them to serve the overlords until they can't lift their *waddly wazzoos*. Then, they are stripped of *zulus* and thrown to the denizens."

Harris watched his *Danuwa's* eyes filling with horror and tears. Their mouths hung in disbelief, but they knew it to be true. The Seneschal had told them stories of *the Kalugu*, but Lord Belmundus' dagger tongue brought it home.

"I am a child of *reaptide*," Yustichisqua said. "I have tasted *the sqwallen* and watched my mother torn apart by *zugginaks*. I have served in *the kaleezos* of *the Yuganawu* and have climbed the hill to *the Ayelli*." Yustichisqua bowed to Harris, and then turned violently on the others. "Do not waste my time with foolish talk about attacking Montjoy and defeating the enemy until our people are free from *the Kalugu's* jaws. I am the son of Kittowa, but I was born a Trone. Then I met my *oginali*, who is now my commander and *Dinatli*. I tell you this. Until *the Kalugu* is free, we are Trones still. I mean to be a Trone no longer."

Little Bird raised *the navakawee* high and *the Kalugu* came into sharp focus. *The Danuwa* trained their attention on the black walls. The goal was clear — no glory in dominion. The plan was a glorified prison escape, and the logistics would be difficult.

"There you have it, gentlemen," Harris stated. "Our goal. The liberation of *the Kalugu*. Our left flank will do as Cheowie suggests — storm the gates of Montjoy, but as a feint. Its purpose is to keep the Yunockers thinking we lack a strategy — sure to lose, if that was our game. But this is *grusoker* of the highest order. While the flank keeps the enemy busy, our main force will skirt *the Kalugu* walls deploying wave after wave of *wadi-wadi*, penetrating *the phitron*. The walls are thick. I know, because I've passed through them — I and Yustichisqua. There will be casualties for those caught beyond the eighty count. Still, those sacrificed will get us through, tag-team fashion. Once we breech, each squadron is assigned a specific task and target."

Yustichisqua refocused *the navakawee*, bringing the interior of *the Kalugu* into sharper focus.

"Estatoie," Harris said. "You will liberate the clan houses. Lord Cosawta has prepared them for your arrival." Estatoie slapped his chest. "Good, but . . . many Cetrone will be drug addled and will resist you. Others will prove useless."

"I understand."

"Be sure you do." He turned to Oustestee. "The defeat of *the mordanka* falls to the *geetli*. You must fight hard — destroy the garrison and the kennels. Lives depend on it."

"Yes, my lord."

"Good. Cheowie, you shall split your squadron. Your best warriors will bring succor to *the Banetuckle*." He looked Cheowie square in the eye. "This will take courage. It will be hard. You must forewarn your warriors that what they'll witness will lie heavy on their hearts and minds. But the survivors of *the Banetuckle* must be rescued, carried to safety and caring."

"Yes, my lord. We will be strong, my lord." Cheowie nodded. "And the remainder of the squadron?"

"They will seize *the sustiya* — a stockpile of *aniniya* and other material. It'll prove essential, especially if we're besieged. Lord Cosawta's told me *the sustiya*'s guarded by trusted men, who will take up arms and join us."

"It shall be as you command, my lord," Cheowie replied.

"Tosawa."

"Yes, my lord."

"To you I entrust *the Kalugu*'s outer walls, and the bridge over *the Gulliwailit*. When the enemy realizes that our true goal is *the Kalugu*, they'll storm it. You must hold the walls at all costs until we secure the interior and evacuate the downtrodden."

Tosawa remained silent. Harris cocked his head.

"Is there a problem?"

"None, my lord. I am stunned by the honor you bestow upon me."

"It might be an honor, but it's also a death sentence."

"An honor to be so sacrificed," Tosawa said.

He reached for Harris' *asano* and kissed the hem.

"Don't embarrass me."

"I am sorry, but . . ."

"No need for sorrow. Five more like you and I could conquer Farn entirely."

The projection turned slowly, returning to the walls of Montjoy.

"And who shall lead the feint?" Cheowie asked.

Harris turned to Little Bird.

"I shall," Yustichisqua said. "I shall beat my head upon my enemy's walls and splatter my blood upon their gates."

He bowed. Harris choked back tears. He wanted his *Dinatli* by his side in this action — to have his *Noya Tludachi* at his back. But he knew it couldn't be. Yustichisqua had anger to vent.

"Just so," Harris murmured. "Those are the orders, gentlemen, and like most orders, they'll go awry. But if you cleave to your objectives, straight path or crooked, we're bound to make a difference and reach the final goal. We'll either succeed or die doing it. In any event, Montjoy will long remember the day — the day Cetronia struck back."

3

Shouts interrupted the palaver — shouts mingled with wails, followed by a chorus of *bing bongs*. Every *sillifoon* in the henhouse awoke.

"We are under attack," Cheowie announced after answering his.

Harris, whose *sillifoon* was the only quiet one, went for *Hierarchus*.

"How can the enemy strike so far from the city?" he asked.

However, hadn't a patrol attacked *the Gananadana* mid-Forling?

"Not the enemy," Yustichisqua said, closing his *sillifoon*. He pointed to the entrance to the henhouse. "There."

Creeping over the threshold, a sinister creature was poised to jump. Its eyes glared red, its long fangs set to strike.

"*Gasuntsgi*," Harris exclaimed.

His foot throbbed in remembrance, but he didn't loll about waiting for the vampire bunny to get the better of him again. He raised *Hierarchus* and shot a golden beam at the thing's head, splattering fur and blood across the tent flap. Several *gasuntsgi* followed in its wake, as if the example of one mattered not as long as the blood's fresh aroma egged them on.

"Quickly," Harris shouted. "Get your *boobooyaks* in gear. Shoot those fucking things back to the hell they came from."

Cheowie raised his *blundaboomer*, shooting a spiraling green flash of *aniniya*, blasting three *gasuntsgi*. Estatoie was still on his *sillifoon* shouting orders to his squadron to kill the invaders to the last rabbit's foot. Oustestee jumped through the tent flap, shouting at the monsters, blasting them left and right, sending them every which way to the *kowlinka*. Tosawa joined Detonto firing *Sticks*, and then batting the bastards, despite the creature's inclination to latch onto the weapon and attempt to suck *the aniniya* from the muzzle. A game of hockey ensued, pucking the greedy blood grubbers into the henhouse corners, where Harris and Yustichisqua mutilated them with *brashun blades.*

"Stay clear of their fangs, old man," Harris warned. "Even when dead, their fever can spread. We've left Nayowee and her *asi-asa* behind. I don't think our medics can cope with *gasuntsgi* bites."

Harris kicked a few carcasses aside, taking care where his foot landed, using *Friend Tony* to best advantage. He emerged from the tent. The roar of *blundaboomers* and *Sticks* enlivened the night, striking shadowy waves of hopping forms. The attack was met with fire power. Distinguishing blood on *the kowlinka* was difficult, but warren pits were evident.

"Holy crap," Harris said.

"I see it too, *oginali*."

"I think we pitched camp over their lair."

"It seems so," Yustichisqua replied. He lifted his *waddly wazzoo*, swinging it. "They are creatures of the night, *Dinatli*."

"What are you doing?"

"Making it daytime."

Harris kindled his lamp and swung it also. A brilliant light glowed above the ground — a burning mist. He grabbed his *sillifoon* and *bing bonged*.

"I am here, *oginali*. You need not call me."

"Shit. Wrong number." He fumbled again, still maintaining the lamp. "Damn." *Bing bong.* "That's better. Who be? Who be?" He waited. "BeeDust here. BeeDust here. Ah. BigDog. Listen to me and get the word in the air."

He glanced at Yustichisqua.

"Tell them to make it day," Little Bird said.

"Yes. Make it day. Make it day. Do you ken it? Do you? Good. Make it day."

Suddenly, the world of the Forling resounded with *bing bongs*, and then lit up as if *Solus* and *Dodecadatamus* had made an untimely appearance. *The kowlinka* shone bright in rabbit eyes — eyes stunned in the daylight.

"Kill them," Harris shouted. "Kill every last fucking devil."

Battle shouts, billows of *aniniya* and blasted bundles of devilment drizzled the dunes. Then, as *the gasuntsgi* bodies flew through the air, tumbling down sand mountains, claws arose to catch them. Lavender fur flew also, saber teeth clamping on rabbits — a natural clean-up for the spoils of war. *The porcorporian* and *the Tludachi* ate their fill, leaving *the Golden Eight* to thrive in the unnatural daylight until the battle line settled back into night's silence.

Chapter Four

Walls of Phitron

1

Morning brought aftermath's scene — scant remains, except the feast's stench, now that *the porcorporian* and *the tludachi* had had their fill. Harris stared as he stood on the henhouse threshold. He watched as *the Tippagore* lumbered passed, her knowing eyes glancing at Harris, as if she had come to assess a far-wandering child. She didn't stop — just trundled over the dunes like a giant caterpillar on a shifty crimson leaf.

"I can still take it down, my lord," Detonto said, suddenly at his side.

"For what purpose?"

"For meat, if for nothing else."

Harris shook his head and gave his *Taleenay* a side glance.

"We've had enough carnage for the moment. How did you fare in the attack?"

"I twisted my foot. The night was cold."

Harris grinned.

"You advised me not to make things too comfortable, Detonto. I try to oblige."

Detonto gave him a curt bow.

"At any rate, my lord, we have had target practice."

"Yes, but at what cost?" He opened *his sillifoon. Bing bong.* "BeeDust here."

"2Gollies I be," came the reply.

"Have you counted the beans, 2Gollies?"

"Counted, BeeDust. Eight still they be."

"Eight?" Harris laughed. "Full jar then? Full jar?"

"Eight and twenty-seven."

Harris glanced at Detonto.

"Looks like we came through unscathed." He returned to *the sillifoon.* "Find the mustard and pack the spoons. On a picnic we shall go. Do you ken it?"

"I ken it, BeeDust. Over and ouch."

"Over and . . ." Harris closed the device, and returned his gaze to the retreating *Tippagore*. "Goodbye, Mama," he murmured. "On a picnic we shall go."

<h1 style="text-align:center">2</h1>

They had survived the night — uncomfortable night, with no casualties except minor scrapes and a few weapon mishaps — dud blasts and jammed jimmies, but nothing to write home about. Harris still had his eight-thousand and twenty-seven golden warriors, who now had engaged an enemy — real targets with pointed ears and threatening fangs. They managed to blast them to kingdom come, or at least into the jaws of strange monstrosity allies, which waited on the periphery for dinner. Once sated, the more bestial threat retreated to sleep off their full bellies. The cold hardened the warriors and *the gasuntsgi* gave them target practice and enough adrenaline to chalk up a win for the home team. Harris was pleased.

He broke camp and soon *the Golden Eight* raced on their final stretch across the Forling. They were within a mile of Montjoy by late morning. The fleet stretched in a long chain across the height of the last dune. Harris looked left and right, watching for anomalies in the line. There were none. Had *the Golden Eight* straightened up to fly right? He awaited word.

Bing bong

Harris grabbed his *sillifoon*.

"BeeDust here."

"*Sisterfucker*, is that you?"

Harris nearly dropped the device, but recovering, he looked through *the gespocular*.

"I see you," he said, spying the top of *the Gananadana* rising from within *the Kalugu*.

"*O see yo, Sisterfucker*," came the generous reply. "*Tow hee joo.*"

"I'm here, you asshole, ain't I?"

"I never doubted you. But you should be *here*, where I stand. This is the moment in time."

Harris was glad to hear his brother-in-law's voice, but the apparent disregard for using code unsettled him, especially this close to Montjoy. The Cetrone phrases could go by undetected, and even *the Sisterfucker* address probably wouldn't register, but the last bit was clearly a clarion call to arms.

"Boatman1, watch the leaves in the wind. Do you ken it?"

"Just raise your *wadi-wadi* up and get your *boobooyak* here. *Do-no-du-ga-hu-yi*."

Cosawta's voice was gone, but *the Gananadana* was in full view now, the silvery glint of her *waddly wazzoo*s flashing across the desert. Harris grinned. The rules were made for all, but never for the Seneschal. Hadn't he insisted on the code words?

"I ken it," he muttered.

"My lord?" Detonto said. "Do we go?"

"We go, but first . . ." *The sillifoon* was open again, hood spread. *Bing bong.* "2Gollies."

"2Gollies I be," came the response.

"Front and center. *Solus* is high in the sky."

Before Harris could close the conversation, a squad of twenty-five Cetrone gleamed past him, like racers at NASCAR. Their *Seecoys* turned to face him. Then Yustichisqua zoomed to the fore, holding *gasohisgi* above his head. Harris closed his *sillifoon* without so much as an *over and ouch*.

"*Oginali*," Little Bird proclaimed, his voice booming. "We go to our fates in the name of Enitachopco and in memory of Hedonacaria." Then he raised his *waddly wazzoo*. "To Cetronia and all Cetrone."

His squadron lifted their blazing lamps high and repeated these words. It gave Harris chills. He waved Yustichisqua forward.

"Old man," Harris said, the words choking. "You have done me proud. I order you to live. Don't do anything foolish, like sacrifice yourself for me. I'm not worth it."

"*Dinatli*," Yustichisqua said. "Farn is upon your shoulders, but if you say you are worthless, then it is so. Know this, *oginali*, I will always be your Little Bird, serving you with heart and soul, because you lifted me from *the sqwallen* and showed me the son of Kittowa again. But if I can help it, I shall return to your side to serve another day. Do you ken it?"

"I ken it, *Dinatli*. I ken it well."

Harris bowed to Yustichisqua, who would have balked at such a gesture, but not this time. Not this time. He *ken it* well.

3

Detonto maneuvered *the Seecoy* from the left flank to the right flank, Lord Belmundus inspecting the fleet. As Harris passed each of his *Danuwa*, they saluted him. There was no need to bark commandments over *the sillifoons*. They had their orders. His assault would be the only signal they needed.

Harris assumed the commander's role, one he had played before — a junior commissioned officer in *The Battle of Fort Dixon*, but in that role the fort was a military academy and he was squashing a renegade uprising among students. This was a juicier role and . . . real. But the martial look was important to inspire the fleet to the steel force needed to penetrate *the phitron* walls — to blast them with *wadi-wadi* and briefly transform them into passable *kaybar*. With a wave of *Friend Tony*, the lead *Fustigars* drifted forward, preparing their approach to *the Kalugu*, warriors readied with *ino-wadi* launchers and *blundaboomers*. Their pounding would be the key to victory. They drifted forward, gaining momentum.

Suddenly, Harris heard violent explosions coming from the main gates of Montjoy. He grinned.

"Good job, old man," he muttered. "Detonto."

"Yes, my lord."

"Prepare for our run."

"Yes, my lord."

The fleet rushed forward, the disturbance at the main gate signaling the feint. A short interval was allowed the Yunockers to cluster to the Forling walls, and then *the Fustigars* landed, the gingergust warriors wielding the weapons, firing at *the Kalugu* walls. Others wielded *aniniya* blasters, because, as expected, the pounding of feet on the kowlinka (*zulus* impractical now), disturbed *the porcorporians*, their scaly bodies shifting to the surface for a meal. Still, amidst waving claws and streaks of *aniniya* firepower, *the wadi-wadi* troops managed the correct range to blast the walls.

Harris felt the rush of battle. Soon the Yunockers would wake up to the truth and deploy their forces to *the Kalugu*, but the window of opportunity was perfect. Only the count of eighty stood between his forces and their spectacular break in. He watched his *Danuwa* positioning their squadrons for their given tasks and was pleased.

"Detonto, get ready for the plunge."

"Yes, my lord. Secure yourself and be prepared to count."

"Got it," Harris said, strapping himself to *the Seecoy* seat, and taking a deep breath.

He prayed he was able to pass through the walls. This depended on tricky science now. The walls would transform for a time, allowing Detonto to pass through. This would permit passage for *the Seecoy* and its cargo and Harris was its cargo. But to better assure his chances, he leaned forward and placed his hands on Detonto's shoulders.

"We shall be fine, my lord. Count true."

The *Seecoy* surged forward, the world blurring. A *gingergust* blast preceded them, a cloud of red smoke, and then crimson and then . . . the wall transformed and they were inside it. *The kaybar* was thick — mucky and cold. Harris gasped, his breath hitching, but he remembered to count. "One," he muttered, as they struck. "Two," a second later, or he hoped it was a second and not a second and a half, or a millisecond. It mattered, although he had practiced the timing. He felt weak — dizzy. He was sure this distorted the count. He gripped tightly to Detonto's shoulders. Ahead was still murky and airless. He recalled the thickness of these walls and his passage through them with Yustichisqua. Harris never relished it, even when time wasn't an issue. Now the passage seemed interminable.

"Thirty-two," he gasped, and hoped it was truly thirty-two and not some number in advance of it.

Sleep. He felt like sleeping. He heard strange sounds, the creaking of stone and the melting of rock. He saw figures running in the muddle — figures tossing *granaydos* — *wadi-wadi* with the magic Culpeeper formula. Then he heard wailing. The walls were reverting, catching his warriors in their grip.

"Sixty-one," he yelped. "Faster, Detonto. Faster."

"We are at full speed."

"Then why are we slowing."

"The change is beginning."

"But we're only at sixty-five . . . I mean sixty-eight."

"Seventy-three, my lord. Seventy-four."

"Shit."

Harris had lost count. Now he hoped Detonto's backup count was accurate. Then he felt a mighty tug on his arm followed by a jolt. *The Seecoy* slowed to a near crawl.

"Eighty," Detonto gasped, choking.

But then, the air softened and the vehicle lurched forward, free of the walls. Estatoie's *Seecoy* was parked on the other side, his squadron firing *wadi-wadi* from the interior, freeing stuck *Seecoys* and allowing warriors to tumble into the clan house. There were many dead Cetrone in that tumble — sacrifices to the cause.

Harris patted Detonto's shoulders with renewed confidence.

"Are you okay, Detonto?"

"Dizzy and sore, my lord. Especially my shoulders."

Harris grinned, removing his hands.

"That was some fucking ride." He glanced up. "Estatoie. Remind me to give you a medal, when we come around to stamping one."

"Medal, my lord?"

"Don't sweat it."

Harris glanced about, trying to get his bearings. The place was familiar, and then he recognized a scrubby old Cetrone hovering near a passageway.

"Talqwah?"

The man gave a start, and then bowed.

"Lord Belmundus," the old spooner squawked. "The Seneschal has told us true. You have returned."

Estatoie approached Talqwah, his *Seecoy* having landed.

"Who are you, sir, to address our commander?"

Talqwah fell prostrate.

"It's okay, Estatoie," Harris said. "He is the spooner of *the sqwallen* house and the guardian of *the Yodanado*. He is also Yustichisqua's uncle."

"Welcome to *the chisqua* clan house," Talqwah muttered from his prone position.

Estatoie helped him up, brushing him off and daring to touch his *waddly wazzoo*, a new one Harris gauged it to be, since Harris sported the original. Harris approached the spooner, *Friend Tony* now much required, his foot not liking the trip through *the kaybar*.

"We don't have much time, Talqwah," Harris said. "Take me to *the siti*." He turned to Estatoie. "Enter *the sqwallen house*. Stir those you can, and muster all able-bodied Cetrone. The time is short. The clock is ticking."

Estatoie clapped his fist to his chest. He was surrounded by warriors. He then took off at a run in the direction of Harris' head nod.

"Detonto."

"Yes, my lord."

"See if you can find a few men willing to handle tough but precious cargo back through the walls and into *the Loribringus*."

"Yes, my lord. What is the cargo?"

"I'm fetching it. Just go." Harris turned to Talqwah. "Lead the way, uncle."

"I am not your uncle, Lord Belmundus. You do me too much honor."

"I'm Cetrone now." He displayed his *gollywi*, much to Talqwah's delight. "And Yustichisqua and I are blood brothers. So, that makes you my uncle. Besides, I inherited your *waddly wazzoo*."

"That, my lord, was not my doing. That was a gyration from *the Primordius Centrum*." Harris moved forward. Talqwah pointed. "You have an injury."

"It's a long story, uncle. Remind me to tell you if I survive this day."

Talqwah grinned, and then turned toward *the siti.*

4

Harris limped, choosing not to engage his *zulus*. As convenient as they were — in Nayowee's parlance, *a private laziness*, in *the Kalugu* they were the bane of the Cetrone, a sign of servitude. This didn't stop Talqwah from racing ahead on his.

In *the siti*, *the Yodanado* slept as they had on most days throughout the ages. The seven heads, resting on seven wigwam'd buckskin cloaks, looked like so many bowling balls (ancient bowling balls) perch and awaiting rental.

"They sleep, my lord," Talqwah said, raising his hand.

"Wake them."

"I dare not."

Harris raised *Friend Tony* and unsheathed *the brashun blade*. He aimed it at *the siti's* roof and let loose a thunderous blast.

"Euforsee," he shouted. "Wake and come."

Euforsee's eyes shot open, as did her sisters. Her mouth arched and a purplish tongue wagged over her lips.

"Lord Belmundus," she shouted back. "You have returned with a spark in hand and a fire in your heart. So my cousin has forewarned."

"Cousin, Euforsee?"

"Nayowee of *the asi-asa*."

This didn't surprise Harris, but he was not here to swap lineages or ancient legends. He sheathed *Tony* and raised his *waddly wazzoo.*

"Shall *the Yodanado* follow me to safety?"

"What do we know about safety?" Euforsee asked. "These are our children, who are not to be abandoned."

"They are not abandoned," Harris said. "They are protected."

"Or felled by the thousands."

"Mayhap they will, but those who die now die free, and not as enslaved Trones."

"Lord Belmundus," Talqwah muttered. "*The Yodanado* cannot move. They are . . . heads on lifeless bodies."

Harris feared as much. Was he suppose to grab Euforsee's skull as she jabbered, tuck it under his arm and collect the others in a brace held by hair roots. He bowed to the head.

"Lady," he said. "You cannot remain here. You are sacred. So are your sisters. But how shall I manage it?"

"Do not suppose we are without resources, Lord Belmundus," she replied. Her head twisted like a corkscrew, and then the buckskins fell — all seven. Harris gasped at what was revealed — seven doll-like bodies, wraithed and pruned, hung like peppers out to dry. "Sisters," Euforsee croaked. "Sisters, the time has come when the light is kindled and Zacker emerges from its weeping trail to hold the lamp high against the dark legacy. The time has come"

Euforsee closed her eyes, and then opened them again, her pupils golden — flashing like a firecracker. Then, *the siti* filled with crimson smoke. Harris knelt to avoid inhaling it. When it cleared, Euforsee stood before him — one woman, younger, and in one body with only one head.

"Lord Belmundus," she said. "We are not without resources, but you must hold to your course, because if you fail, all the worlds will darken and be extinguished in Zin's powerful darkness."

"Zin?"

Harris had no thoughts of Zin or darkness or any battle beyond liberating *the Kalugu*. He had no time to ponder this whisperer's warning.

"Talqwah, escort Lady Euforsee to the beachhead and get her through the walls."

Talqwah appeared hesitant, but Harris rattled *Hierarchus*. Soon, Lord Belmundus stood alone in *the siti*. He could hear the battle growing on the rooftops. The Yunocker defenders had come alive and would not sit still for this rebellion. Suddenly, the klaxon sounded.

Reaptide.

Chapter Five

The Mordanka

1

Harris rushed as best he could through *the siti* to the beachhead, where Detonto had readied *the Seecoy*.

"My lord," Detonto said. "There is an alarm sounded. The enemy knows we are here."

"That is *the reaptide* klaxon, Detonto."

Harris peered into Detonto's eyes, which didn't register this explanation.

"It is a call to arms, my lord."

"Trust me, Detonto. That alarm goes off automatically, although I wouldn't be surprised if we've been detected." He gazed up, witnessing *aniniya* beams shooting across the roof. "We'd better hightail it out of here." Detonto revved *the Seecoy*. "No *Seecoy*. We'll hoof it."

"Hoof it?"

"*The Seecoy* will prove useless in *the Kalugu*'s narrow lanes. It's better to run, dodge and jump." Then Harris felt a twinge in his foot. "Well, maybe not jump, but . . ." He switched on his *zulus*, rising to the occasion. "I hate to use these things here, but if I stood on ceremony, I'd never stand at all."

Detonto shrugged, gathered as much *wadi-wadi* as he could into *two korinkles* and swung one to Harris.

"Let's go then," Harris barked, and drifted into the clan house and through the dark corridors.

Reaching *the sqwallen* house, Harris met Estatoie, who was attempting to rouse cadaverous Cetrone, who pushed him away, returning to their addled slumber.

"Estatoie."

"Yes, my lord."

"They're useless. They'll die in the mayhem."

"Yes, my lord."

Harris turned to Detonto.

"Give each a good shake. If they open their eyes, pull them to their feet and tumble their beds over. We can't do more than that now."

Detonto quickly rattled twenty beds in turn. Only two Cetrone were drawn upward, their beds overturned. They watched helplessly from their stupor. Harris zoomed past Detonto, crossing the threshold and emerging onto the street, where dozens of Cetrone rushed by in panic. Overhead, the Yunockers did what Yunockers do at *reaptide.* They flashed *Sticks*, taking aim at poor innocents, who had not managed to find shelter before the klaxon's sound and *the reaptide* slaughter. *Zugginak* growls were heard nearby, but not one dog was in sight yet.

Harris saw Oustestee's *Seecoy* and his squadron zip by. They glided to the roofline, where they were open to Yunocker view. Harris hailed Estatoie.

"Yes, my lord."

"Get as many of these poor souls inside. Check the other clan houses. Secure them. Knock *the sqwallen* addled from their slumber, if you can. Enlist them to arms if possible, but be prepared for a shock, Estatoie. *The zugginaks* are coming."

"Yes, my lord."

"Detonto, with me."

Harris ascended to the rooftop, Detonto in tow. When Harris crested the eaves, he ducked out of view quickly. Oustestee was engaging a Yunocker patrol, *the aniniya* flying like fur. Harris managed to grip a rain gutter, hoisting himself up on the flattop. Then, he helped Detonto. The roof was thick with battle, Estatoie's squadrons coming to the Oustestee's aid.

"We outnumber the enemy, my lord," Detonto said. "We have the advantage."

"I wouldn't count on it," Harris muttered. "We've firepower, but *the regulati* are seasoned warriors. When their heads get in the game, we'll be shifting for our advantage." Harris point to a foreboding black dome. "*The mordanka.*"

He scurried along the flattop, *Friend Tony* his chief aid now. He kept his head low and his wits about him. *Cabriolins* and *Seecoys* were dog fighting directly above. If he could make a difference, he would try, but the action was intense. With one gauged shot, he could bring down *a Cabriolin.*

"Shall I try, my lord?" Detonto asked.

"I doubt *aniniya* would do the trick. It could go astray. Ricochet and catch us between the eyes."

Harris ran to a causeway between the clan house roof and *the mordanka's* dome.

"Oustestee must get inside and attack *the zugginak* kennels," he said. "If the dogs are released, we'll be in deep shit." Then he reflected. "Deeper shit."

The hellhounds may have already been released, but he hoped the klaxon's distraction drew *the mordanka* guards skyward, muddling normal *reaptide* procedures. But he had heard roaring. *The tludachi*, he thought. That was worse.

Suddenly, the sky battle came closer to the roofline, Oustestee's *Seecoy* pursued by three *Cabriolins*, peeling him away from his squadron. Detonto took aim at the lead Yunocker, but Harris pushed his *Taleenay's blundaboomer* aside, drawing *Hierarchus*. He aimed at the three *Cabriolins* and, touching his *Columbincus*, shot — fire ripping the air. The blast tore the undercarriages from all three vehicles. They waffled, spun, and then dropped from the sky like skeet plates.

"Yes, my lord," Detonto shouted.

"Now you can shoot. Blast their flank."

A five *Cabriolin* team raced at the squadron, but Detonto's pepper shot deterred them. They turned away, heading for the main gate.

"They'll get reinforcements and be back as sure as shit," Harris declared, patting Detonto's shoulder. "Good shooting."

"Thank you, my lord. My father taught me well."

Harris stood, taking aim at the dome, *Hierarchus* pouring steady fire at the ugly ribs. The structure trembled, cracked, and then the great *phitron* stonework dome came unglued, crashing into *the mordanka*.

"Let's go."

Oustestee's squadron zoomed into the gap just as Harris and Detonto reached the fissure. Harris had never seen *the mordanka* — *the Kalugu's* governing seat. He peered down, trying to discern the ground amidst smoke and rubble. *Regulati* rushed between the fallen stones. Despite injury, they attempted to rescue their comrades. Some Yunockers were beyond hope.

Harris shook his head, a gesture to compassion, but that was as far as it went.

Bing bong.

Harris held fast to the dome's ridge, fiddling for his *sillifoon.*

"BeeDust here."

"2Gollies I be."

"Little Bird," Harris said, anxiously. "Speak to me."

"It is hard, *oginali*," came the reply, dropping the code speak at the first mention of *Little Bird*. "The gate has been destroyed, but so have we."

"Where are you? You ken it?"

"I ken it, *oginali*. Much fire and smoke. Much destruction, but they know now that it was a trick."

Harris scratched his chin, shaking his head. The news wasn't a surprise, but the loss of his warriors weighed heavily on the heart.

"But you live, *Dinatli*."

"I do, but . . ."

"But what?"

"I am, as you say, pinned down and have no chance to . . ."

"To what?"

"To say . . ."

"To say what, *Dinatli*?" No response. Harris shook *the sillifoon*. "Stupid fucking thing. Never works when you need it." He raised it to his ear again. "Old man. Old Man. 2Gollies."

He sniffed, lowered the device and swallowed hard.

"Are they lost, my lord?"

"It's hard to say, Detonto. But if they are, it won't be for nothing." Anger swelled, and he pointed through the smoke and fire. "When I'm finished down there, the kennels'll be twisted *conontoroy* and I'll skin every fucking *zugginak* to make a coat for my lady."

Detonto grinned, gave a war whoop and descended. Harris sighed, shaking his head again. He would not weep — not yet. He was sure the Yunocker army was on the move now to *the Gulliwailit Bridge*. He touched his *Columbincus* and prepared to play dogcatcher.

2

The ground came up and Harris plunged toward the wreck of *the mordanka*. The quartermasters of *the Kalugu* were sprawled over fallen *phitron* and twisted furniture. Some stirred, but they were unlikely to challenge the invaders.

Harris landed hard, stumbling on his dickey foot.

"Steady, my lord," Detonto said.

Harris waved *Hierarchus* and positioned *Friend Tony* for perambulating around the zone. Oustestee and his crew zoomed through the place, striking anything that moved. Then a distinct barking sound roused Harris' attention.

"The kennel."

He waved to Oustestee to land, and then proceeded through an archway into a courtyard. There the building was intact. He spotted several Yunockers taking cover, positioned for a fight. He also saw the kennel gates — opened, *the zugginaks* released for the hunt.

"Hold steady," Harris shouted. "I'd hoped to get these bastards before they were let loose. Let's get'em before they get too far."

Detonto aimed his *blundaboomer* as the beasts rushed them.

"No time like now," Harris said, emulating his *Taleenay*, raising *Hierarchus*.

A blinding flash followed — *aniniya, Columbincus* and every promise from *a brashun blade.* But also in the mix were *Sticks* firing from behind a barricade normally meant to protect the Yunockers from stray *zugginaks.*

Harris ducked. Oustestee slipped ahead, firing blindly. Two members of his squad preceded him, only to find the hellhounds' fangs clamped on legs and arms, a feasting vise. Harris stood, disregarding the Yunockers. He rushed the dogs, beating one, and then the other with *Friend Tony*. He dared not fire and risk his men.

Detonto covered him, pulsing his *blundaboomer* at *the mordanka* defenders. The dogs snapped fiercely at Harris, and stupidly at *Hierarchus*, their teeth brutalized. Four other *zugginaks* ran in a circle around invader and defender alike. Harris heard screams from *regulati* behind their useless barricade.

"Detonto," he shouted.

"Kill them, my lord. They eat the very stones, they do."

"Retreat," Harris said, and then shouted it. "Retreat."

Before he could push back, his foot betrayed him. He stumbled. Oustestee was on the spot, but a hungry beast leaped on him, pushing him on top of Harris, pinning both to what could have been a dinner plate.

Harris shuddered. *The zugginak* mauled Oustestee, drooling as it assessed its quarry. Yellow canines were preparing a painful death. Harris tried to push Oustestee off, but his *Danuwa* was out cold. The combined weight of the Cetrone and *the zugginak* was too heavy to budge.

Harris tried to reach for *the brashun blades*, but they were beyond reach, his arms pinned. He couldn't even tap his *Columbincus*. Even if he could, he feared blowing Oustestee to *Kingdom Come*. Suddenly, the dog howled, lifting its head up, and then collapsed — dead. Then Harris felt the weight lifted.

"Oustestee," he said.

No answer from *the Danuwa*, who still breathed. Hands worked across Oustestee's shoulders, and then came the lift. Harris was free.

"Lord Belmundus," came the rescuer's voice.

Harris pushed up, and then gasped.

"Parnasus?"

"Yes, my lord. Are you injured?"

"I'll be fine. It's wonderful to see you."

"Your foot?"

"An old injury, lad. An old injury. I thought you were dead."

"So did I, but fortune has been kind to me. You are not the only *Ayelli* to break the treaty, as you can see."

Apparently, not.

Parnasus was shorn of his old *Danuwa* attire. He wore rags and a sloppy lopsided cap. Still, the sight of the Thirdling gave Harris reassurance and *korinkles* of joy.

"We are not safe yet," Parnasus muttered.

Harris looked about. Detonto and the remaining squad still battled the dogs, but were winning. Even down, *a zugginak* was dangerous, trying to kill with the last remnant of its strength. The Yunocker fire had ceased. Harris raised *Hierarchus* and rejoined the battle, his blasts effective, now that he wouldn't kill his own. He noticed one warrior wielding *a Stick*, shooting *aniniya* blast after *aniniya* blast with greater skill than ever a Cetrone could muster.

"That's no Cetrone," he muttered. "No clan garb."

In fact, it was a *Yunocker*. Perhaps one who had survived from the barricade, only to join in the kennel slaughter. When the last *zugginak* collapsed, Harris went to one knee, breathlessly. This was work, but they had lessened one *reaptide* horror. As he took this breather, the Yunocker turned.

"Buhippus?" Harris stammered, standing quickly. "You, here?"

"Yes, Lord Belmundus." He bowed. "You may ask how and why, but it is a story best left to the tavern."

"But your rank and station?"

"My fall from grace was sure and fraternally wrought," Buhippus replied, grasping Harris about the shoulders. "You are well met, my lord, even if by a *zugginak* shit-shoveler. My brother was thorough." Buhippus looked about, his *Stick* waving at the furry carcasses. "But I am thorough also. By my hands, they were fed. By my hands, they have died."

"Captain Buhippus has been a savior, my lord," Parnasus explained. "He rescued me from *the Yuganawu* gutters and I have helped him shovel shit until this wonderful day — the day these *Cabriolins* descended on *the mordanka.*"

"They are *Seecoys,* Parnasus."

"They are fast," Parnasus replied. "You must teach me to drive one."

Buhippus inspected Detonto's *blundaboomer*, *the Taleenay* resisting.

"Let him see it, Detonto," Harris intervened. "This man's an old friend."

"But he is a Yunocker, my lord."

"He's a friend. If there are Yunockers who show us half his compassion, I will call them *friend* also."

Detonto gave up the weapon, and nodded — still reluctantly.

"What does it shoot?" Buhippus asked.

"Do we have time for this, Captain?" Harris replied.

"I suppose we do not, and I am no longer a captain, even though Parnasus chooses to call me so."

Suddenly, a growl came from beneath the archway. Detonto snapped his *blundaboomer* back, and Harris raised *Hierarchus*, one hand on his *Columbincus*. Three *tludachi* crept toward them, drool spilling down their saber teeth, their lavender fur raised.

3

Oustestee awoke and, upon seeing *the tludachi*, nearly passed out again. His squadron clustered about him. Harris backed away, taking care not to trip on *zugginak* carcasses. The tension was intensified by the continued sound of *the klaxon* and the pandemonium beyond *the mordanka* walls. Harris knew a battle raged through the clan houses and into *the Banetuckle*, but here he was, his back to a wall, threatened by three hungry cats. He had slain a *noya tludachi — a sand tygger,* but he was aloft in *a Cabriolin* then with the Pod at his back. Despite the current company's firepower, it would take much to down three *tludachi* and still come through intact. The choice was clear. How many would die before the beasts fell? Who was the worthiest to survive?

"Lord Belmundus," Buhippus said. "We cannot fight these."

"I know."

"We could," Parnasus said, "but we would regret it."

"Would they be satisfied with dog meat, my lord?" Detonto asked.

Harris surveyed the carcasses. He remembered *the gasuntsgi* feast of the other night.

"These *tludachi* have been bred to avoid *zugginak* meat," Buhippus replied. "They will not touch it."

"They dine on Cetrone, my lord," Parnasus added. "They know the difference and will not bypass an opportunity."

"However," Buhippus said, "if we slowly back into the kennel, there is a way out on the other side." He shook keys hanging from his belt. "For once I do not regret my new position."

"They will not follow?" Detonto asked.

"Oh, they will," Buhippus replied. "Once in the courtyard, we shall be running for our lives, but at least we will have a place to run."

Harris backed up until he reached the kennel gate. He stepped in dog shit and grimaced.

"Lots of that in there," Parnasus said. "It shall be your new perfume."

As the group funneled through the gate, *the tludachi* approached.

"Just lock the gate, Buhippus," Harris suggested.

"That will slow them, but three can easily tear through it."

Once inside the kennel, Buhippus closed the gate and locked it. This was the signal for *the tludachi* to charge, ramming the gate, the fur flying. Paws poked between the bars. The hinges snapped. It would be a few minutes before they had the gate down.

Harris turned and ran, the others following in the dim, foul kennel. The smell alone could have killed them. At the other end was another gate. Buhippus fumbled with the keys. Harris pushed the bars open and rushed into the open courtyard. The others fought their way through the narrow exit just as the beasts raced through the kennel. Buhippus locked the gate and fell backwards, crabbing away from the swiping paws. The bellowing beasts, pissed and frustrated, crashed into this new obstacle.

"That won't hold them," Harris said. He looked about for a way out, but realized this courtyard was landlocked. "I thought you said we'd have a way out," Harris asked. Buhippus pointed up. "How the fuck do we manage that?" Harris grumbled.

Buhippus pointed to the walls — highly ornamental with plenty of foot and hand holds.

"We best be about it, my lord," Detonto said, heading for a ground-level mortise.

"No time," Parnasus said.

"They are coming," Oustestee muttered. "They are breaking through it."

The three marvelously vicious beasts — wonders of invention, had ripped the gate from its hinges and, using their teeth, pulled the bars into the kennel. Harris grasped Detonto, pulling him back.

"If we're going to die, let's go down in a blaze of fire and fur."

"Who said anything about dying?" came a shout from above.

The fugitives scattered as Lord Cosawta made his entrance in *the Gananadana.*

"Brother-in-law," Harris shouted, undisguised relief in his voice.

"*Sisterfucker*," the Seneschal said, and laughed.

"*Sisterfucker. Sisterfucker*," came the Tomatly echo.

Lord Cosawta jumped from the gondola before it touched down. He stared at the three *tludachi.* He raised his hand, grinning like Oz of old.

"*Zano zano, kalatifa. Kalatifa. Jaygo moti optipoop. Kalatifa. Kalatifa.* "

"*Kalatifa! Kalatifa!*"

The beasts sat, looking to each other, and then bowing to this lord of tyggers.

"How did he do that?" Buhippus asked.

"My father keeps them as pets," Detonto replied.

"And someday I will teach you to tame these fucking cats also," Cosawta said to his son. "Shame I cannot take these with me for the collection."

"You speak their language?" Parnasus asked.

"Nonsense, you *Ayelli* fool. *Tludachi* cannot speak. But there are many words to calm a host of wild things, and I have learned these well. There is no meaning in what I have spoken. They are mystified by it — fucking with their minds, I am. But it works every time."

"*Kalatifa! Kalatifa!*"

The beasts yawned.

"Where is Yustichisqua?" Cosawta asked Harris.

"I don't know. The main gate is down — the fighting tough. He might be . . ."

"No, no. That piker will survive and is probably on his way here to wipe your ass even as we speak." He glanced at Detonto. "How is this one behaving?"

"I have no complaints."

Cosawta stared at his son.

"You must try harder to piss off your lord. It is good for him. It will keep him humble, and he needs such pruning." Cosawta stared from *the tludachi* to Harris. "And still you are here? Get your asses into my ferry and I shall take you to the battle."

"Yes," Harris said, turning to the crew. "This campaign has just begun." He turned to Buhippus and Parnasus. "Will you fight with us?"

"Have we not been battling by your side?" Buhippus replied.

"I serve you in all things, my lord," Parnasus said.

Harris embraced them each, and then turned to Cosawta.

"Brother," Harris said. "You are full of surprises."

"As much as you are full of shit." Cosawta grinned, and then embraced Harris, patting his back hard. "What is that smell?"

"Dog shit."

"I might not want to pollute *the Gananadana.*"

"You?" Harris replied. "You who live in a house smelling like a stable?"

"A stable? I keep no horses inside. Here and there a *gufo*, but I assure you, I keep the horses outside." He laughed, and then turned to *the tludachi.* He bowed. "*Kabuma, sa zattipo. Fuyi, fuyi, oginali.*"

The beasts arose, bowed to Cosawta, and then turned, retreating into the kennel.

"What did you tell them?" Harris asked.

"I suggested they might find themselves a *zugginak* or two to whet their appetites. They will feast on Yunocker a little later." He hopped into the gondola. "Tomatly, bring this thing to *the Banetuckle.*"

"*To the Banetuckle! To the Banetuckle!*"

So up they went.

Chapter Six

The Kanaguda

1

Harris surveyed the situation from above *the Kalugu's* rooftops. *The Gananadana* wavered as the Yunockers tried to bring it down, but its skin was impervious to *aniniya* fire — *jupsim* coated and freshly so. Still, Cosawta maneuvered to avoid being boarded or losing one of his passengers, who were not shielded from *the regulati's Sticks*. Harris used his *gespocular* to assess the progress. He saw distant smoke and fire arising from Montjoy's gates. He also saw black specks approaching — the Yunocker army's full force. Below sprawled *the Banetuckle's* twisted streets and alleys. Much activity quaked there — Cheowie and his squadrons fighting one on one with Yunockers, who had turned out for a routine *reaptide*, now transformed into a bloodbath.

Bing bong.

Harris opened his *sillifoon*. The thing had been quiet for some time. He wondered if it ceased operating.

"BeeDust here."

"TossMe1," came the reply.

Tosawa.

Harris looked to the walls. He saw Tosawa's squadrons buzzing about the main gate and the parapets, dodging sharp spirals of *the Yuyenihi*. Yunockers fired at them, but *the Seecoys* were too fast and *the regulati* too stupid to see the full picture.

"I ken it, TossMe1."

"The geese are stealing the eggs, BeeDust."

"Get it in order and report back."

"I ken it. Over and . . ."

Static.

Harris turned to Cosawta.

"These things aren't worth a shit anymore."

"It is to be expected when not strolling in *the selu* fields," Cosawta replied. "Mine works fine when I fly high, but there are many variables between here and Cetronia. *The branchy-wanchie* is a fucking stopgap." He shrugged. "What did you expect, *Sisterfucker?*"

Harris shook his head. He didn't mind his brother-in-law's coarse language, but this new nickname denigrated Littafulchee. Harris thought to take Cosawta to task, but then recalled more important things. Harris raised his *sillifoon* again.

"2Gollies. 2Gollies. Do you ken it?"

No answer. He shut his eyes.

"2Gollies. Shit. Little Bird, come in."

No time now — no time for sorrow or regret. No time for mourning or worry. No time for speculation or remembrance. When war settles across the land, no time comes except the time to live or to die — considerations deferred to one or the other depending upon the outcome.

Harris scanned *the Kalugu*, and then pointed to the ground.

"Get us down, Cosawta," he snapped. "Get us to where we can finish this thing."

"Yes, my lord," Cosawta said, bowing. "Your death is my command." He laughed, and then looked to his bastard. "Detonto will watch your ass when your foot fails you. But remember: you must resist the temptation to die. If you see it coming, duck and run, because your spark is still needed . . . beyond the one you have already kindled."

What was the man talking about? Harris didn't have time for it. No time for idle chatter or Seneschal vanities or even death, when it came, if it came. No time to ponder the greater scheme. One step into the breach, and then another, and whatever flew here or there would be handled as it came — viscerally responding to the vagaries of war.

2

They landed with a thud, the warriors spilling out of the gondola and into *the Banetuckle's* pandemonium. Cosawta immediately ordered *the Gananadana* to ascend, because dozens of Cetrone rushed him, looking for an escape route. Harris blocked several desperate refugees from boarding. In this he was helped by Oustestee, Detonto and Parnasus, while Buhippus growled his best growl at the otherwise docile downtrodden.

"Stand aside," Harris shouted, pushing, and then wielding *Hierarchus*, but taking care not to harm the people.

Cries of terror and disappointment arose when *the Gananadana* cleared the jump zone, although some Cetrone tried to grasp the dangling ropes, but to no avail.

"Detonto," Harris said.

"Yes, my lord."

"See what we have here."

Detonto nodded, and then pushed through the crowd, catching buckskin after buckskin, looking into the eyes of the terrified and *the sqwallen*-addled alike. Oustestee formed a barrier with his squadron, preventing the crowd from fleeing. But beyond this stretch of *the Banetuckle*, Harris saw the shadow of souls peering from behind barrels and dung heaps. He witnessed an untold number of strewn bodies, piled in corners and tucked in nooks. Naked children with their ribs protruding and their bellies distended ran in aimless circles, seeking their mothers, who most likely were tossed in the gutters as waste. How foul the streets were. How detestable the crime of *the regulati*.

"It is terrible," Oustestee muttered.

Harris grasped his shoulder.

"Bear up," he said. "This is but a small taste of the place. It's the reason we've come."

Tears streamed down *the Danuwa's* cheek.

"I was told such tales," Oustestee said, "but did not believe them, my lord. I heard, but did not listen. An excuse for war and no more. Little did I know. Little did I know."

"Bear up," Harris snapped, although his own heart broke.

He saw Cheowie approaching over wreckage, a dozen warriors *zuluing* behind him.

"Cheowie."

"My lord," the warrior replied, bowing.

He had been weeping also, but swallowed his sorrow as best he could before his superior.

"You too?"

"It is disheartening, my lord, but we have no time to gather them up, because the Yunockers have attacked *the Kanaguda*. I fear they are rounding up the people."

"For *the Porias*, no doubt," Harris said.

"Prison would be an easy fate, my lord," Cheowie replied. "They go to *the Gonada Gigaha* — the place of execution."

Harris turned to Buhippus.

"Captain."

"I am no longer a captain."

"I don't give a fuck if you're the Princess of Mars," Harris snapped. "Tell me about this *Gonad Gogglehop.*"

"*Gonada Gigaha,*" Buhippus said. "It is a square near the western wall used to make examples of rebellious Cetrone."

"How far is it?"

"I am afraid *the regulati* have secured the place."

Harris gazed up at the rooftops. He saw *the Gananadana* drifting, playing cat and mouse with *Cabriolins.* He whipped out his *sillifoon.*

"Brother-in-law," he shouted into the receiver.

"Not using code, *Sisterfucker*?" came the reply.

"Can you get your ferry-ass over to a place called *the Gonada Gigashit*?"

"One might try."

"Might one be able to call the neighbors?"

"You mean Tosawa?"

"He's got the wall, doesn't he?"

"One might try."

Harris slammed *the sillifoon* shut.

"If he weren't the Goddamn Seneschal, I'd take aim at his *waddly wazzoo* and bring his ass down." He turned to Detonto, who still assessed the crowd. He then tapped Parnasus' shoulder. "Get Detonto's attention."

Harris strutted to the sidelines, requisitioning a stack of crates as a soapbox. He mounted them, and then shouted at the throng.

"Listen to me!"

This did little, but Buhippus corralled them. Cheowie and Oustestee followed suit, and soon the Cetrone squadrons brought ragtag order to the rabble.

"Listen to me," Harris shouted again. "We've come to set you free."

"Looks like you have," came an anonymous shout. "Many of the dead are free, indeed."

The crowd grumbled, shaking fists and *waddly wazzoos.*

"Many more will fall before we're done," Harris shouted.

The mob grew angrier, but Buhippus fired his *Stick* over their heads.

"Listen to Lord Belmundus," the rough and tumbled ex-cop proclaimed. "Consider yourselves dead already and you shall be better off for what comes next. *The regulati* are scourging *the Kanaguda. The Banetuckle* will be next, and then the clan houses — starting, no doubt, with *the chisqua yehu.* And where do they take your brothers and sisters, your children and parents. Where?" Tense silence. "To *the Gonada Gigaha.*"

Collective murmurs of horror grasped the crowd.

"But we shall not let it pass," Harris said over the mounting noise. "We shall move together. We shall drive them out. We shall save our people."

"With what?" came a solitary cry, followed by incredulous echoes.

"With these," Oustestee yelled, grasping Buhippus' *Stick,* raising it above his head. "With the enemy's weapons. We have *aniniya* for all."

A murmur of hope stirred. Harris looked to Oustestee

"You split your squadron?"

"Yes, my lord, as ordered. They are already in *the sustiya* gathering the necessary ordinance for distribution."

"They cannot shoot," Parnasus remarked. "It takes some skill to shoot."

"Quick lessons, and practical ones too, Parnasus. But I don't care if they shoot with them or crack the Yunockers over the head. They must liberate themselves. We're just keys in the lock." Parnasus appeared skeptical. "We didn't ram our heads into these walls so the people could climb back into their holes and wallow in bowls of *sqwallen.*" He turned to Oustestee. "Get these people armed. And that means with anything they have. Pitchforks and carpet bats will be fine if they can hit a Yunocker's head out of the ballpark."

"Yes, my lord."

"Cheowie."

"Yes, my lord."

"Find Estatoie and get him back here. I want the addled zombies trucked out."

"Yes, my lord."

"Gather them at the beachhead. Get your *wadi-wadi* working. If you can call the *Fustigars* drivers, get them to *gingergust* the outer walls. Pull these poor bastards to safety."

"Many cannot count to eighty."

"So be it, but many still can and will."

"Yes, my lord."

Harris turned to Buhippus, who stood amazed at Harris.

"What, captain?" Harris asked.

"I stand in awe of your fire, Lord Belmundus. You have come far."

"And I'll not stop here. Lead me to this *Kalligalli*."

"*The Kanaguda*,"

"Whatever."

Harris took a deep breath, gripped *Friend Tony*, and then kick-started his *zulus*. Detonto raced to his side. Buhippus led.

3

The stench of *the Banetuckle* appalled Harris. He could hear the stifled chokes of the patrol, which followed him into this stinking hell. They were all on *zulus* now, armed to the teeth, but, in the current situation, with only eighteen men against an angry enemy garrison, they could have used a Sherman tank. As they zipped through the narrow maze of alleys, a shadow cast over their path. Harris didn't need to look up to see *the Gananadana* drifting toward the place of execution. Cosawta wouldn't undertake the mission single-handedly — he and *Tomatly! Tomatly!* The Seneschal wouldn't relinquish the advantage of surprise either, although how one hides a *waddly wazzoo* powered zeppelin was beyond Harris' imagination. Still, Cosawta was resourceful, so Harris concentrated on his own mucky mission.

"Lord Belmundus," Buhippus said. "Ahead they lie in wait for us."

"An ambush? How do you know?"

"I was one of them. I know the drill."

Harris slowed, and then raised his hand, halting his crew. He landed, and then looked for cover. There was little here but rotting *kaleezos*, splintered rails and a full degree of rubble — a place fallen through neglect and ambivalence. He pointed to both sides of the street.

"Half there. The rest with me."

They scattered, Buhippus, Parnasus and Detonto cleaving to Harris.

"Now what?" he asked, to no one in particular.

In fact, he didn't expect an answer. He received none. Harris trained his eyes on the road bend ahead. Ominously quiet. The klaxon had ceased and only murmurs could be heard. They could have been in a windswept New Mexican ghost town. He expected tumbleweed. He turned to Buhippus.

"We can't dawdle here forever," he whispered. "What do you suggest?"

"Cover me," Buhippus replied.

Harris and Parnasus took aim — *Stick* and *brashun blade*, while Detonto raised his *blundaboomer.* Buhippus scurried around the corner, dodging to the next hide — an overturned barrel, which the Gurts called *a vargos.* Here he peered carefully over its girth, and then waved Harris forward. Parnasus covered Harris, who zipped to the hide on his *zulus.* There wasn't much room behind *the vargos,* so they needed to clear out before the others could move forward.

Buhippus rushed to the next hide — a woodpile, standing sentinel on a lopsided *yehu* porch. Harris zipped across the street to a pothole, large enough to envelop him, but just. Detonto rushed forward now, followed by Parnasus. The rest of the squadron dithered for as much cover as they could find. Still, relative quiet prevailed — ominous, and not to Harris' liking. Then he heard whimpering. He zipped to the remains of a *kaleezo,* flattening against a wall. Then carefully peeking around the corner, he spotted a dozen Cetrone corralled in the center of a square — the place known as *the Kanaguda* — the divide between *the Banetuckle* and the gate garrison. The Cetrone were tethered, locked in a circle, and quietly whimpering. Their fate was clear. However, they were lightly guarded.

Buhippus shook his head, trying to discourage Harris' next action. But Lord Belmundus couldn't leave these lightly guarded men shackled. He counted only three guards. *The regulati* were outnumbered. The advantage was too good to let pass. So Harris waved to his crew, despite Buhippus' warning.

The silence was broken, Harris howling like a banshee. The others joined in this war whoop and attacked.

The guards ran — an odd response for Yunockers, but Harris didn't waste time.

"Untie them," he told Detonto, who mustered the others to help.

"You must do this quickly," Buhippus said. "This is not what it seems."

"You still expect an ambush?"

"This *is* an ambush, but because we know it to be so, we will not be surprised when we die."

Harris' blood ran cold. He heard shuffling feet and barking. *The Kanaguda* was now alive with Yunockers appearing from the surrounding buildings, fully armed and *zugginak'd.* The prisoners had been freed, but what was the point?

"We won't go down easy," Harris shouted, touching his *Columbincus.*

The Yunockers released *the zugginaks* — only three, but three were three too many. Buhippus and Parnasus scattered, wielding their weapons in ways only a skilled dogcatcher could. Harris didn't have time to watch and learn. He pulled the prisoners to their feet.

"Out of here," he insisted. "Forget everything else."

"They say they were destined for *the Gonada Gigaha*, my lord," Detonto reported.

"I think we're all destined for that place, one way or the other."

Harris pushed his crew toward an archway, the only area not covered by Yunocker guards. However, it was draped with spirals of *Yuyenihi*, that dastard barbed wire bedeviling *the Kalugu.*

Buhippus managed to down one *zugginak,* while Parnasus was on the road to killing another. Harris raised *Hierarchus*, aiming it at the third.

Flash. Howl.

Direct hit, and the fur flew, not to mention a few Yunockers, who perhaps had second thoughts about confronting *an Ayelli* lord. But after the blood had been drained from the pooch, a barrage of *aniniya* rolled across *the Kanaguda.*

Harris sought cover again. *None.* Even the road back to *the Banetuckle* was blocked by *the regulati.*

"Sorry I doubted you," Harris said to Buhippus.

"Sorry you did also, but if it did not happen here, it would have happened elsewhere."

Harris suddenly registered this thought — the hopelessness of the situation. His gut clenched with thoughts of never seeing Littafulchee or Yustichisqua again. When had he forgotten Santa Monica and the red carpet? Still, he wasn't prepared to die. He was only nineteen, after all, and as good a cause as this might be, it was an adaptation at best.

Harris raised *Hierarchus* again, and then unsheathed *Tony*. Two *brashun blades* are better than one. He clenched his ass cheeks and spit. He felt a rush from his dickey foot to his feathery crown. A wave of *Columbincus* poured from the swords, joining above Yunocker heads.

"Duck," he screamed, and his crew hit the ground to avoid the weapon's might.

The *yehu* and *kaleezos* shook, windows breaking and roof tiles avalanching onto walkways and porches. Yunockers flew in all directions. When the dust cleared, their numbers were thinned, but not enough to assure a victory.

Harris was drained. He staggered.

"Do not fall, my lord," Detonto said. "If you fall, so shall we."

"I don't think I've another bolt like that up my ass — not any time soon."

Buhippus and Parnasus led the squad, firing at the now-charging guards. The end had come. Prisoner and rescuer would fall with honor, but they would fall. Then an amazing thing happened — one of those things Harris had read in many passed over scripts. He would have never believed it. The Yunockers were distracted — turning and watching their rears. Cetrone rushed at them — armed Cetrone — some skilled, others swinging bats and clubs, but their numbers were such, it took Harris' breath away.

"Oustestee," he muttered.

"And Cheowie," Detonto added. "Maybe Estatoie too, my lord."

Suddenly, the Yunockers were pushed off their feet, beaten and clubbed. *Blundaboomers* shot and *Sticks* did their best to find targets, which were easy now with so many targets.

"This amazes me," Buhippus said. "I never thought I should see the day when *the Kalugu* raised its hands to give my brethren their due."

The quiet of *the Kanaguda* became a thing of legend: how the Yunockers meant to capture Lord Belmundus and bind him to *the Gonada Gigaha*. Generations would tell the tale of a thousand clubs bashing enemy heads, and how, after the savaging had passed, the former Trones knelt to their leader — *an Ayelli* Lord now of *the seegoniga* clan, the consort of Scepta Littafulchee. This

Lord had come into their midst and showed them how to be free again using the fabled blades called *Tony* and *Hierarchus*, and the sheer force of his magnitude, because he was a spark and a luminary — a new star in Farn's vast firmament.

Chapter Seven

The Gonada Gigaha

1

The way to *the Gonada Gigaha* was blocked by *yuyenihi* — thick, sharp and spiraled. *A Seecoy* could hop over the wall, but *the Kanaguda* was a vehicular void. *Zulus* might take a glide over, but most in the Cetrone throng were *zululess*, having shed them in protest. There were too few warriors to fight the next battle alone. The mob's thrust was needed. Harris thought to use *brashun blades* to cut through, but that would only accommodate a single file and at great risk. He pondered the barbed-wire with his back to the crowd.

"I wonder, my lord," Detonto said, toying with his *blundaboomer.*

"Any thoughts you have, Detonto, would be better than any I've got now."

"I wonder whether *wadi-wadi* would work here."

"That's for transforming *phitron*. This barrier looks like *conontoroy* or *yustunalla*."

"Still."

Detonto raised his weapon, a *gingergust* canister weighted to one side. Before Harris could speculate further, Detonto fired, startling the assembly. He shrugged, and then raced forward.

"Wait," Harris shouted. "Just because you hit it, doesn't mean it worked."

"Only one way to find out," Detonto replied, approaching the twisted blade work.

"Stop."

Detonto ignored him.

"Start counting, my lord."

Detonto crashed into *the yuyenihi*. The coils shook, but swallowed *the Taleenay*, his voice vaguely counting.

"It worked," Harris mused.

"What worked?" Buhippus asked.

"Hard to explain, captain. But watch, and perhaps it'll be self-evident."

Harris held his breath and mentally counted. He was beyond eighty, but that didn't matter. He was never precise at it anyway. Then, Detonto emerged unscathed, but breathless.

"Ninety-seven," he shouted.

"Excellent," Oustestee yelped. "Here and back again."

Harris opened his arms, embracing Detonto, who tried to regain steady breathing. He resisted the hug, but nodded profusely.

"It appears *wadi-wadi* will transform other elements, my lord."

"Astounding," Parnasus said.

"Yes," Harris exclaimed. "It's a remarkable invention." He turned to his *Danuwa*. "Remind me to erect on this exact spot a statue of the Culpeeper Brothers. On the plaque it will read — dedicated to the faith of a brave Cetrone named Detonto, son of Lord Cosawta, Seneschal of Zacker."

"Bastard son," Detonto corrected.

"I believe all your father's sons are bastards, so what's the point?"

"Zacker?" Buhippus asked.

Harris grinned. The world was behind the times when it came to Cetronia's secrets.

"You have much catching up, captain."

"It would appear so."

Harris looked to his *Danuwa*.

"Oustestee. Cheowie. Estatoie. Get *the wadi-wadi* going," The lieutenants immediately prepared to blast *the yuyenihi*. "Detonto, are you up for pulling a chain of *kaybar*-challenged people through the blade work?"

"I am honored to do it, my lord."

Buhippus and Parnasus appeared puzzled, but Harris latched onto them, while Detonto caught Parnasus' hand.

"Do we need to count?" Harris asked.

"We do not even need to shoot, my lord," Detonto said. "The change appears permanent."

Harris caught Parnasus' hip as this train left the station. Unlike passing through *phitron* walls, *the yuyenihi* was opened on three sides. But the blades were worrisome. They didn't cut, but Harris' flesh swallowed them nonetheless. No cuts, but thoughts of being sliced like bologna gave him pause.

"Strange journey," Buhippus muttered as they reemerged into another courtyard, one bounded by a high wall — an assailable *phitron* obstacle, easily penetrated when time and plan was settled.

"The gang's all here," Harris said, watching the Cetrone squeamishly engage the *wadi-wadi* passage, red puffs continuously blasting through the archway.

"How does it work?" Parnasus asked.

"Beats me," Harris replied. "I mean, I thought I knew when it worked its witchy-woo on plain old fucking *phitron*. This effect on *conontoroy* and *yustunalla* is a new twist — one I don't think the inventers even realize."

"They might, my lord," Detonto said. "My father often told of experimentation. That is why I made the attempt."

"You've saved the day."

"Perhaps, my lord." He gazed up at the next wall. "Perhaps not. But might I make a suggestion?"

"Absolutely."

"Since the count is no longer relevant, the incessant *wadi-wadi* blasting is not necessary."

"You're right. We're wasting *gingergust*."

Buhippus stared at Harris, bewildered by the new term, but Harris signaled his *Danuwa* to assemble.

"I need to see what there is to see," he said, gazing up at the wall's top. "Buhippus and Parnasus will come with me."

"My lord," Detonto said. "If you mean to rise to this occasion, the enemy will pick you off before your crown clears the *yuyenihi*."

Harris grasped his *Taleenay*'s shoulder.

"Don't worry. I'm not in a sacrificial mood today."

"Just suicidal," Detonto quipped.

Harris grinned, and then looked to Buhippus.

"Are you with me?"

"I agree we must know and not guess."

"Is that *a yes*?"

Buhippus nodded his assent.

"Parnasus?"

"Always, my lord."

"Watch for my signal, Detonto. I'll send you one *bing bong* on my *sillifoon*, if the fucking thing works. If not, I'll drop it on your head." He laughed. "Then I want a concentrated force of *wadi-wadi* on this wall and an all out assault on whatever's on the other side."

"Why not blindly charge now, my lord," Oustestee asked.

"Timing," Harris said. "If they're waiting beyond *the phitron*, *Sticks* aimed to welcome us, we will not do it. I want their pants down and their asses exposed. Many will fall, but we shall not be slaughtered. If anyone is the butcher boy today, it's me." He looked to his companions. "Ready for this?"

Buhippus grunted. Parnasus grinned. Together, on *zulus*, they arose, like cream to the top.

2

Harris faced the wall as he ascended, thinking of a time when he rode an outside elevator at the Hotel Concordia. But that had been a different experience — a glass capsule facing the brilliant, moonlit (single moon) night with the endless carpet of Los Angeles' lights spread before him. This was a solid wall of black *phitron*, featureless until the top, when the ominous blades of *yuyenihi* forced him and his companions to push away, floating precariously above the courtyard.

"I shall look first," Parnasus said.

"That task falls to me," Buhippus replied.

"No," Harris said. "Together. Rise steady and be prepared to be blown off your perch."

Harris gradually arose to the barbed wire, Parnasus and Buhippus keeping abreast. Harris clenched his hand on *Friend Tony*, anticipating a pounding. But as his eyes cleared the wall, he observed the Yunockers preoccupied with their revenge — the execution of the Trones — slaves who dared to raise hands against their masters.

"Not a sound," he whispered.

He stared toward the outer walls and the gates. He spotted Tosawa's squadron taking the sentinels out, one by one — stealthily as if scripted in a castle invasion flick. He also saw the Montjoy *regulati* approaching in force. Soon this invasion of *the Kalugu* would be a siege, but when it came to that, every Yunocker inside now must either be dead or dying. Mercy was not an option for survival. Harris could also see the top of *the Gananadana*, still submerged in a distant skywell, hidden from ground sight.

The great square known as *the Gonada Gigaha* — *the Place of Execution* was living up to its name. In a pit, the executed Cetrone were layered to be either burned or turned into *tludachi* food. He noticed, even from this height, victims still alive, squirming to the trench's edge, using their dead brothers and sisters as cover. Still living were huddling Cetrone, struggling under their tethers, beaten into submission by Yunocker guards. A line of *regulati* stood in an ordered array, their *Sticks* at their side, while a tall Yunocker conducted the drill. Twenty or so Cetrone were segmented from the main group and pushed forward to the wall. They still struggled to be free — men, women, and children, clinging to each other with the knowledge that, in this last clutch, they would pay for freedom's audacity. Free they would be, but not liberated to rule the day or even *the sqwallen* bowls.

Harris trembled as *the regulati* raised their *Sticks.* He reached into his *korinkle* and withdrew his *sillifoon.* One button press and, far below, he heard the ubiquitous *bing bong*. Soon, many *sillifoons* were *bing bonging* — like small church bells calling the faithful to prayer. He nodded to Buhippus, and then to Parnasus. With a flourish, Lord Belmundus raised his *waddly wazzoo* to cheers from below. It was two quick maneuvers to the top of his *Columbincus,* and then he fired *Hierarchus* at the chief Yunocker, sprawling him at the firing squad's feet.

"That got their attention," Harris barked.

"This will get it even more," Buhippus shouted, firing his *Stick* at the executioners.

Harris felt the wall vibrate as *the inu-wadis* blasted the surface and hundreds of Cetrone leaped through the narrow barrier. With a wave of fierce vengeance running and zipping and trundling across *the Gonada Gigaha*, Harris swept down into the fray. *Sticks* fired wildly, a good thing, which surprise could only muster. If planning had kicked in, the Yunockers would have formed battle arrays and systematically picked off the intruders. But surprise inspired random warfare, a tactic giving better odds for a mob of club-wielding patriots.

Harris lost all notions of form. He plunged into the execution grounds, wielding *Hierarchus.* He watched as his crew battered the reckless *regulati* forces. He aimed his dickey foot in the direction of the pinioned prisoners, who still feebly tried to loose their bonds. He raised *Hierarchus*, and then, after sweeping the field of all comers, he snapped the bonds fettering a Cetrone woman, who wept from fear and thanks.

"Do your best to earn your freedom," he said to her.

She nodded, and rushed into battle. He continued cutting the bonds.

"Earn your freedom."

Children, men, both clear-eyed and *sqwallen*-addled, heard the same message.

"Join your brethren. Do your best to earn your freedom."

Then Harris was confronted by a fierce warrior — a Yunocker set on ending this liberation. The man was a foot taller than Lord Belmundus and, unlike the others, armed with a battering staff, one with an array of vicious spikes at its tip.

"*Ayelli* intruder," the warrior barked. "I am Pupissicus, *the tludachi* tamer. This is my taming stick. Beware it, because it is your doom."

Harris was unnerved by the man, hesitating as the staff lashed downward, missing him by a single happy hop to the right. Harris unleashed *Hierarchus*, but the flash rebounded against the wall and downed combatants both behind and to Pupissicus' side. The staff came down swiftly again and Harris prepared to be struck. Damage, it would do. But before the spikes did their worse, Pupissicus was pushed into the wall by three Cetrone. The warrior grunted, but before he could regroup, another three Cetrone pushed him to his knees. A child kicked him in the face. Harris stood dumbfounded. The prisoners he had freed were earning their freedom or, at any rate, his freedom. He left them to slaughter the giant. They beat him to pudding with his own *tludachi* taming staff.

When Harris turned, he was further amazed. Yunockers fell into blood pools beside their Cetrone assailants. There was no victory dance — just a slug fest, *Sticks* firing and *blundaboomers* blasting — smoke and death everywhere. He looked to the walls, where Tosawa's squadron pushed over Yunocker bodies, securing the parapet, an absolute necessity with the Montjoy garrisons assembling on the other side of *the Gulliwailit*.

Harris sought familiar faces — his *Danuwa*, his *Taleenay*, Parnasus or Buhippus, but in the chaos, all men were anonymous. What if they had fallen? He couldn't bear that. So he raised *Hierarchus*, switched on his *zulus* and buzzed across the battleground. He confronted a Yunocker who had gained the upper hand in a bout with an old Cetrone man, who was armed with a *bubrapti* — a club used to pound *quillerfoil*. The old man was on his back, growling and fiercely protecting his *waddly wazzoo*. The Yunocker pinned his chest with his *Stick*. Harris drew his attention, but didn't succeed ending the threat, until *Hierarchus* glowed blue and the enemy's head was relieved from its body in one, steady stroke. A fountain of blood spouted from the falling torso, covering the old man, who shot to his feet and danced in the puddle. The sight both gladdened and sickened Harris. He wasn't cut out for this shit, but conceded that *the Gonada Gigaha* had been appropriately named.

Then a terrible rumbling shattered the far wall, the one between *the tludachi* pit and the main gate. He heard ominous growls through the smoke. The ground glowed, and then fire shot across the field, taking many Cetrone and Yunocker alike by surprise. The flames whipped into a storm, the smoke drawn aside, revealing a fiery *Cabriolin*, flanked by two massive *zugginaks*, harnessed to the master *regulati* himself — General Tarhippus.

3

Harris had no time to admire this entrance, because Tarhippus moved swiftly, his glowing *gwasdis* snapping Cetrone after Cetrone as he gained prominence in *the Gonada Gigaha*. Harris raised *Hierarchus* and slapped his *Columbincus*. He shot his most powerful blast, knowing it would leave him drained, if not dead, but it was now or never. The flash whipped across the battleground, knocking combatants left and right, but on target for Tarhippus' *Cabriolin*. But suddenly, it dispersed, ricocheting off the vehicle, the full force striking the parapet, downing a dozen warriors in Tosawa's squadron.

"Shit."

Tarhippus roared, satanic to the toe.

"Lord Belmundus," he shouted, still laughing. "You cannot hurt me. This vehicle has been crafted to shield me from such *Ayelli* tricks."

Harris watched as *the zugginaks* raced toward him. He wondered whether they were coated in *jupsim* or trained to deflect *Ayelli tricks.* He staggered, the last blast draining him, but he wasn't about to end his life as dog chow. He fumbled for *Friend Tony*, drawing it from its cane-sheath. He slapped his double *Columbincus*, fully expecting it to play fart sounds or *Stars and Stripes Forever* — anything but a responsive defense to two big-ass, maddened *zugginaks*. But it flashed his signature sapphire-blue and *Friend Tony* woke up forming a forked spear of lightning, catching both killer dogs between the eyes, simultaneously. A CGI artist couldn't have done it better. Lord Belmundus crashed to his ass. He didn't think he could get up again. It was his last hurrah.

Tarhippus' laugh diminished. In fact, it turned to rage, evidently unhappy with the death of his two favorite pets. His *Cabriolin* raced toward Harris with one undeniable aim, *gwasdis* snapping the ground and downing any warrior deterrent in its way. The electric green whips came close to Harris' *zulus*. He crabbed back, his *asano* riding up his ass, and then he turned over, protecting his *waddly wazzoo*. When he did this, the lamp shone brightly, blinding Tarhippus temporarily, and affecting aim. His *Cabriolin* overshot its mark, Harris watching the undercarriage pass overhead.

Quickly, Harris got to his feet. He couldn't feel his feet, but that didn't mean he was ignorant of his one opportunity to thwart *death-by-gwasdis*. He ran a few steps before realizing this wasn't going to work. He swiped his hands to his *zulus*, switching them on, soon finding the ground gone and the wall-gap approaching. He knew the way out, but to where? He would be over *the tludachi* pit, but he had the presence of mind to recall the pride of *tludachi* Cosawta had tamed. They were probably these pit tyggers. Still, beyond that, there was the gate, which, if Tosawa was still negotiating the issue, could be manned with *a regulati* gate garrison. Then there was the bridge — exposed over *the Gulliwailit* and, at the other end, the whole fucking Montjoy army waiting for one speck of *an Ayelli* renegade to burst through the portcullis and declare himself a victor. Still, did Harris have a choice, with Tarhippus on his heels?

No.

Harris was correct in his assessment of the pit. It was open and empty and he was on *zulus*, so he didn't need to tip-toe through the tulips and over the planks. He also was happy to see the gate unguarded, although the bodies heaped along the portcullis were Cetrone, victims of Tarhippus' rude entry. Beyond he saw the army, but it was engaged.

"God bless you, Tosawa. I'll mint that medal yet."

The parapets were returning fire, keeping *the regulati* at bay. Harris assumed they had orders to stay put until Tarhippus could prove he had the biggest balls in Montjoy. Harris zoomed over the pit and through the gate, *gwasdis* coming close as he escaped. He slowed as he came over the bridge. He sensed entrapment, so he landed and turned.

Tarhippus was under the portcullis, laughing again.

"You have thoroughly pissed me off, Lord Belmundus."

"I hope so," Harris replied, the moment for negotiations long past.

"Those pups were my children."

"They looked like you."

"I should hope so, but where are my manners? Let me introduce you to your death. You have been abandoned by the Elector and I am no longer constrained to capture and bring you to judgment."

"Looks like I'm a goner, Tarhippus," Harris said, pointing to the army at his back. "But if you haven't noticed, *the Kalugu* is free of you. Thousands of Yunockers drip blood in their favorite haunt, blood drawn by the people — my people — a down payment on their liberation."

"Down payment?" Tarhippus said, still laughing.

"Yes." He turned to the army. "Hear me, foolish followers of this mindless turd. *The Kalugu* is open for business, and that business is Yunocker-killing. Come across and join the bloodbath."

Many murmurs met this assessment, and Tarhippus no longer laughed.

"Enough of this," he growled, moving toward Lord Belmundus, who raised *Hierarchus* knowing he had barely enough energy in his system to make a decorative flower display, even if it couldn't penetrate Tarhippus' shield.

Tarhippus' *gwasdis* were at the ready, a double whip to slice Lord Belmundus asunder. But then *the Cabriolin* rattled and hemorrhaged. A fire display disrupted its undercarriage. When the thing landed, Harris looked beyond. There, in the portcullis, stood Detonto, his *blundaboomer* streaming *wadi-wadi*, experimenting evidently with the Culpeeper's invention on yet another metal.

Tarhippus twirled about, *the gwasdis* having a new target. The whip aimed at the *blundaboomer* and succeeded in snapping it out of Detonto's hands. The other *gwasdi* latched onto *the Taleenay's* ankle, pulling him down. However, *an aniniya blast*, fired from the bridge's edge, caught Tarhippus on the shoulder. He wailed and dropped one of his *gwasdis.*

"Yustichisqua," Harris murmured, watching Little Bird rise on his *Seecoy* from beneath the bridge.

"*Oginali*, 2Gollies I be."

"Evidently," Harris said, tears welling.

He rushed to the bridge's edge, just as Tarhippus caught Little Bird about the waist with *the gwasdis. The Seecoy* dropped into the moat, Yustichisqua dangling from the bridge.

"*Dinatli*," Harris shouted. "Hold on."

"It burns, *oginali.* It burns."

"Just hold on."

Harris tried to touch the whip, but Tarhippus was reeling Little Bird in, laughing the whole time. Harris gripped the strand tightly, but the burning was horrible. He could smell his flesh baking. He turned and looked Tarhippus in the eyes — those devilishly crimson pupils filled with distilled hatred. His laugh exposed sharp, pointed teeth — a monster's grin. Then, the eyes rolled back, and the shoulders were pinched. Tarhippus let loose his grip on *the gwasdis*. Harris watched as the handle slipped and, with it, Yustichisqua.

"Hold on, old man."

He also saw the reason for Tarhippus' lapse. A man was in *the Cabriolin*, beating him about the head.

"Buhippus?"

The slugfest ensued, Tarhippus wearing a surprised look, while Buhippus pounded away. But after the initial surprise, the devil of Montjoy renewed his aggressive spirit and pushed back. The brothers wrestled about *the Cabriolin* until the vehicle overturned and they both tumbled into the drink. *The gwasdi* failed, slipping more, Yustichisqua screaming in pain and now about to spill into *the Gulliwailit*. But before he could drop, a whistle came from above, and then a shout.

"*We are here! We are here!*"

The gondola swept beneath Little Bird as he dropped, catching him in *Tomatly*'s lap. *The Gananadana* had descended dangerously low, but just in time. In fact, Cosawta waved Harris to jump also, but the gap was too wide to assure a safe landing.

With Tarhippus' fall and *the Gananadana's* rescue effort, the Montjoy army's orders to stay on their side of the bridge were cancelled. They moved forward, shooting at *the Gananadana*. Despite *jupsim*, two *waddly wazzoos* were damaged, making any ascent over *the Kalugu's* walls precarious, if not impossible.

"Go," Harris shouted.

"We will be smashed to death, *Sisterfucker.*"

"No, go," came another shout.

It was Parnasus, who raised *the blundaboomer*, and aimed it at the wall.

"*Wadi-wadi! Wadi-wadi!*"

Blast.

"Start your counting," Parnasus shouted.

Cosawta steered *the Gananadana* directly toward the transformed wall, a barrage of *Stick* fire peppering the gondola and bouncing off the canopy. Harris held his breath as the gondola passed through *the phitron*. The canopy was caught up on *the yuyenihi* temporarily, but finally pulled through — battle scars and all.

"Thank you, Parnasus, my loyal *Danuwa.*"

Parnasus turned to bow, but stopped, frozen to the spot. Harris shrugged, but also turned. He was struck by a green flash — a mesmerizing glow from a hand he knew too well.

"My lady," Parnasus said, now bowing.

"Charminus?" Harris muttered, kissing the jade ring.

She stood beside a pure white steed, a foal of the great beast *Nightmare*. She was dressed in black denim and wore the look which had drawn Harris into this world.

"Harris Cartwright," she said. "You have gone astray. I am here to put you right."

Harris felt weaker than he had all day, even after the massive blast from *Hierarchus*. He grasped his *waddly wazzoo* and trembled.

"Parnasus," he muttered weakly. "Return to *the Gonada Gigaha*. Tend to Detonto and Yustichisqua. Assure that an *Ayelli* continues to break the treaty, because I am done for."

He heard Parnasus scurry away, and then was lifted onto the Scepta's steed and flown away from the battle.

Chapter Eight

The Temple

1

Harris recalled Tarhippus' words — *you have been abandoned by the Elector and I am no longer constrained to capture and bring you to judgment.* So why was Harris slung across the white steed's back like road kill, while Charminus drove hard up the hill, over the *Zinbear's* lair, across the invisible gate and into the gardens. When Harris had passed over the great riff — boundary to Montjoy and *Ayelli*, he thought to push off the horse's rump, voluntarily falling into *the Zinbear's* jaws. He had been saved from the Yunocker assault, but it felt like desertion to him. He didn't deserve to be saved. Worse, he no longer craved the luxuries of *the Ayelli*, if he had ever craved them. He was no longer Charminus' to command, but evidently the jade ring still kept its hold on him — magic, pure and complicated.

Harris, weak and bruised, smelling worse than *a Zinbear*, caught the scent of the Roses of Scaladar and thought of his lady-wife, now separated from him by the Forling and the clutches of this Scepta, who claimed him once again. But did she? Why would she? He was useless to her. He hadn't kindled her. He was sure another could be drawn from some outland — perhaps *Oz* or *Wonderland* or *the Way of the Mountains and Seas.* Any Mad Hatter would do. Yes, a push off from the horse's ass would solve Harris' heartbreak. He would fall into darkness, a fate he deserved for deserting his friends in *the Kalugu.* He worried now for Yustichisqua and Parnasus and Detonto. Did *the Gananadana* safely land in *the Gonada Gigaha?* What of Captain Buhippus? For a man to assault his own brother to save the man who had caused his fall was a mighty demonstration of loyalty.

As Harris drifted, the warm breezes of *the Ayelli* wafting across his cheeks, he found himself lost in a jade cloud — his thoughts unsettled — paranoid and depressed. He lost all sense of being and direction. Where was he? Did he care? Everything dear to him had been lost. What more could Farn take?

Jolt.

The white steed landed, and Harris was suddenly aware again. He was at the reflecting pool, approaching the portico of the temple — the Temple of Greary Gree. The horse slowed, and then halted at Charminus' command. She dismounted, holding the ring steady, controlling her former consort as if it were necessary. Harris was weary and, even if the opportunity came, he could barely muster a dickey walk. A *run-for-it* was out of the question. Besides, where would he go? He slipped from the steed, landing as cautiously as he could, and then turned to the Scepta. She cocked her head.

"Harris Cartwright," she said, lowering the ring. "You shall no longer see me. But before I consign you to your fate, I shall show you the truth."

Harris, puzzled by this speech, winced. He stepped toward her, *Friend Tony* propping him. He nodded to her, reverentially, but not a full lordly bow. Then she grinned, and in that grin he saw a visage beyond the goth-girl and the denim. Her face was deeply lined, arroyos forming beneath her eye sockets. A wrinkled staff dotted with pockmarks decorating her forehead. Her crimson lips were black. Her jowls hung in leathery folds like a turkey's wattle. Her breasts hung like pawn balls from her black denim jacket. He balked. Had this been the creature who had drawn him into this world? Is this the succubus from Grimm and Zohar — Lilith the enchantress, tempting him beyond his limits?

"Charminus?" he stammered.

Although appalled, he wasn't repulsed. That he had shared himself with this creature was undeniable, but the façade, which magic accorded, to make her and her sisters alluring to the eye and male passions, was gone, lost in a halo, clinging to her like an outer garment briefly raised for his sight only.

"You were good," she said, her voice a rasping saw. "You are a beauty and a wonderful performer on all stages, including mine. I would take you back from that she-witch, who tempted you from my side. I could keep you for an eternity, but know this, Harris Cartwright. Farn's troubles go beyond you and me and even the petty squabble between Trone and Yunocker. So my wishes for your destiny cannot be taken into consideration."

Harris trembled. This was honesty from a woman who had been dishonest in most things. It took the shedding of her radiant form to bring her to truth's light. He was suddenly endeared to this hag, who stood gauntly, but proud, yet humbled before him. It was a rude awakening, but not for him.

Charminus raised her ring, and Harris' mind clogged with lies again. She transformed into the Scepta, the darkly divine object of desire she had always been. Yet, her allure was nothing to him now.

"I release you, Harris Cartwright."

She pointed to the temple's portal. It opened, revealing a somber light. When it did, his *waddly wazzoo* began to glow. Sadness overcame him. He didn't hate this woman, but pitied her. She was more entrapped than ever he had been. He bowed to her.

"My lady," he said. "Lord Belmundus will remember you always."

"Would that you could forget me, Harris Cartwright. Would that you could forget."

2

The vestibule, dim and foreboding, afforded Harris little comfort. However, in an array and their full regalia, stood his fellow consorts as sentinels. Silence prevailed. Harris thought to rush them, embracing each. But what could he say? Could he ask their forgiveness for crimes he didn't commit? He had left their company and no more. Except Tappiolus, he had bonded with them. They had borne him no grudge. But here they stood like the palace guard — alabaster statues, demure and patrician.

Harris approached them, hobbling and battle worn, his eyes squinting, trying to catch glimmers of encouragement. None came. The consorts stepped aside when he reached the archway, which separated the vestibule from the Temple's rotunda. Here he paused, scanning each face. As his eyes met each, they turned their faces away. He noted an expression of disgust on Agrimentikos' lips, as if the chief consort meant to deliver a chastisement, but put it aside in favor of one more fervent. Arquebus pouted.

"Sir John," Harris said.

Arquebus shook his head, and then looked down. Posan and Hasamun bit lips and twitched noses. Only Tappiolus made a menacing gesture.

"Boots," he quipped. "I see you have become a barbarian." He swept his hand noting Harris' battle scarred *asano*. He then tapped *the waddly wazzoo*. "Totally native," Tappiolus said, spitting.

"Totally," Harris replied, displaying his *gollywi*.

"I should demand you as my Trone," Tappiolus snapped, pulling Harris toward him by his *Columbincus*.

Harris pulled his nemesis even closer.

"You would never sleep again," he growled, and then pushed back.

Tappiolus desisted, catching a glance from Agrimentikos.

"Lord Belmundus," Agrimentikos said, softly. "You are wanted within."

"Am I still Lord Belmundus?" Harris asked.

"That remains to be seen, but you shall not fall by these hands or by any of our race."

Harris nodded to Agrimentikos and scowled at Tappiolus. He proceeded under the archway into the rotunda. He had been here before in dreams and visions from *the Cartisforium*. He knew the Temple held Cetronia's deepest secrets — dark ones. He gazed along the walls scarcely noting the ornate carvings and statuary. That Kuriakis the Provost of the Arts had attempted to enliven the place was clear. The attempts failed, at least in Harris' opinion. A mortuary it was and would always be. Through a thin veil at the opposite side he spotted Joella sitting on a grey stone throne. At first he thought it was just another statue, but her rosy cheeks gave her away. Still, she was silent and immobile.

At the rotunda's center, a platform held a sarcophagus. Harris knew this tomb. It belonged to Hedonacaria, Littafulchee's mother. The spot was sacred — revered by all Cetrone, and yet they never approached it closer than climbing the hill on Brunting Day. Harris bowed his head, and then approached the resting place. He gazed at the effigy of the holy woman. A tear welled, knowing this remnant was his mother-in-law — a pawn in the politics of Farn. He sighed, and then raised his *waddly wazzoo* over the clasped hands of the effigy.

"Mother of the nation," he chanted. "Mother to my wife and wife to my father, see me here before you. I have been unworthy of the task set for me, great mother of Zacker and daughter of Zin."

He heard a stir, and turned.

"Father?"

Kuriakis approached.

3

"You call me father, Boots," the Elector said, softly. "Yet you evoke another father beside great Greary Gree."

Harris swallowed hard, and then bowed.

"You're still my father."

"Am I, Boots?"

Kuriakis looked toward Joella, who cast her eyes down. Harris wondered what the man would do. He was a giant and could crush him with one blow to the head. One kick in the balls would send Harris to *Kingdom Come*. But the Elector just encircled the tomb, staring at Lord Belmundus, taking in his full measure.

"You look like a Protractan bug," Kuriakis snorted. "I see you have been in battle. You limp and wield two *brashun blades* and have doubled your *Columbincus*. Normally that would please me, Boots. But you also sport a Cetrone lamp and the brand of the Blue Holly clan. Clearly your allegiance has changed."

"I am the consort to Scepta Littafulchee of Zacker."

"Zacker!" Kuriakis exploded. "Zacker does not exist. It is kept in check. It is my mandate to do so — anointed by *the Primordius Centrum* to keep the balance of light and dark, to never allow the conflict to arise again. Never!"

Kuriakis turned. Harris wasn't sure of his next course. Should he humble himself at the Elector's feet, apologizing for embracing the peoples of *the Dodaloo* — for making *Chewohe* and falling in love with a maid who, unlike Kuriakis' daughter, wasn't a hideous hag cloaked in a halo of lust?

"Boots," Kuriakis said, more kindly. "You have disappointed me." He turned. "I favored you."

"And I thank you, father."

"Even when you were misguided by elevating that Trone to a position he could not handle, I supported your actions as novel and liberating. Little did I know you would become intoxicated by these small concessions."

Harris stood tall now, sucked in his breath and raised a single, poignant finger.

"I've acted according to my conscience, father. I can't stand by and watch one people enslave another."

"So now we stand by and watch both peoples destroy each other." Kuriakis grimaced. "I have not intervened in the little war you have started because it will come to terms when the last of each tribe fall into a sea of their own blood. I have a greater threat at hand — a shadow streaming from the barren lands of Zin — a shadow which takes advantage of the instability you have caused."

"I did not . . ."

"How could you? Why could you? I kept you entertained with tasks, which pleased you so you would kindle my daughter and provide *the Ayelli* with Thirdlings by the dozens — chances to fulfill the promise and the prophecy. But instead you blindly challenged the equilibrium of Farn."

Harris looked toward Joella, who covered her face with a veil. He then glanced toward Hedonacaria's tomb. It shimmered, as if the war for balance was fought beneath its lid.

"I am to die," Harris said. "Like Hierarchus."

"I did not kill Hierarchus," Kuriakis replied. "He was never suited for Farn. He stole from me. He sought escape, but not with his soul and skin intact. He sought to tote treasures back to the outlands, which would enrich a life he had forfeited. He fled to Cetronia to fleece the Trones of their patrimony. That he is dead is no surprise and that you found his *brashun blade* is even less so." Kuriakis clenched his fists. "I shall not kill you, Boots. You shall not die, but you shall be punished."

Harris knelt.

"Death would answer my soul's call, father. I've wronged you, but I've abandoned my people and my wife and my friends. How I can live beyond that, I can't know."

"Then life is your punishment, Boots. You shall be returned to your *place and when* in the outlands, at the precise time of your drawing."

Harris glanced up, not believing what he heard.

"Truly?"

"Truly. But do not think this is a reward or a gift. I must rid Farn of you and restore the balance. But hear me. You will keep your memories of this place — of the events and the people. Of your beloved Littafulchee and the Cetrone you have abandoned. You will live with the memory constantly and in a place where no one will believe you. I suspect you shall go mad. I suspect it, truly."

Harris grasped his *Columbincus* and glanced toward Joella. She was gone. The prospect of returning home was exhilarating, yet the thought of never seeing Littafulchee again or knowing the fate of *the Kalugu*, wrecked the prospects. It would be different if he were returned as a blank slate — on his way to MTV Studios for a Q&A. But how does one just drop one paragraph and go on to the next, still knowing the lost paragraph existed — details complete? How?

"Death might be preferable," Harris murmured.

"You are honorable, Boots. Nothing has changed you in that respect. But my judgment is final. You shall be returned with memories intact. As for me, I will stir as a sign of agony for you. The sky shall turn green and all will endure *Yichiyusti*."

Harris could say no more. Arquebus stood beside him now, helping him to his feet.

"Sir John?"

"Lord Belmundus," Arquebus said. "I am to conduct you to *Mortis House* and beyond."

Harris grinned.

"I'm glad it's you."

Kuriakis stirred.

Chapter Nine

The Outlands

1

Harris' old quarters in *Mortis House* had been neglected — dimly lit and cobweb gray. Arquebus escorted Harris by *Cabriolin* to the portico, and then led him through the museum that represented the career of Lord Belmundus. Here his gifts, enshrouded in dusty displays, gave no pleasure or assurance now. Harris was miserable, where he should be on the pinnacle of joy. He had reached his goal, after all — escape, although Farn called it exile.

"I suppose I must leave everything behind," he murmured to Arquebus, reviewing the many appreciations encased in glass.

"You may take whatever you wish, Lord Belmundus," Arquebus replied. "It matters little. Relics are different in the outer lands."

"You call me *lord* still," Harris said.

"Of course. In Farn a name is not extinguished, nor its heritage. Honor and shame live on in tandem. You shall always be Lord Belmundus."

Harris touched his *Columbincus*.

"And this?"

"It is still yours, but it is nothing more than a pretty thing, and might be considered gaudy in some circles."

Harris managed a fretful grin.

"You say this to a man from Hollywood, where starlets parade with the Hope Diamond and men pierce their nipples with Tutankhamen's scarabs. A gaudy double brooch would scarcely be noticed." He raised *Friend Tony*. "And this?"

"You will need that to support your battle wound, which you shall also take with you."

"Battle wound? I wish it were so, Sir John, but my foot suffers of complications from a *gasuntsgi* bite. Attacked by the fucking Easter bunny, how d'ya like that?"

"I am sorry for your pain, Lord Belmundus — brother. Truly I am. But you once told me you would escape at all costs and it appears your schilling is up, dear boy."

Harris smiled. A Trone entered carrying a stack of linen. Harris, startled, momentarily hoped Yustichisqua had returned. He'd take him in any form now, and if he truly belonged to him in true Farn manner, he would take Little Bird to the outer lands. But this wasn't his faithful friend. Instead, the Trone placed the stack on the platform bed, bowed reverentially and departed.

"Respectable attire," Arquebus said, pawing through the pile. "Not much — sturdy cloth, but it will help in the return to your where and when. It is best to be less conspicuously dressed."

"I thank you," Harris said.

"And there is a wet rag to wash away the battle dust. I am afraid we do not have time for the full blast for your skin, but this should serve."

Harris removed his *Columbincus*, *Hierarchus* and the torn *asano*. His cape fell to the floor. It was in tatters. He deposited his crown, a bent circlet of *conontoroy*, on the platform bed. He set aside his *waddly wazzoo*. Finding the wet cloth, he caressed it, pushing his face into the lemony scent, one particular to *Mortis House* and one he would miss. The cloth felt good on his forehead and cheeks, but even better across his chest and groin.

He noticed Sir John watching him intently. Then Arquebus touched *the gollywi*.

"You were serious in this," Arquebus muttered. "To have your flesh seared with one of their marks is dedication, I must say."

"It's more than dedication, Sir John. I have a family here with the Cetrone."

"It is beautiful. It must have been painful."

"Nothing worthwhile is painless. I've learned that and now continue my education." He sniffed, and then inspected the trousers and the shirt provided. "These are unusual."

"They are mine, Lord Belmundus."

Harris suppressed a grin because, although the trousers were a bit old-fashioned with eyelets to hook on suspenders, the shirt was a lacy affair, with puff sleeves. Captain Hook couldn't have done better. Still, it would rouse less attention than a battle worn warrior in cape and kilt ambling through New York like Long John Silver. Now he would have only the piratical shirt, some gaudy bling, his cane and a strange swag lamp, which could proclaim him more priest than buccaneer.

He found the suspenders and thought perhaps a bow tie might be hiding in the stack, but no. He reattached his *Columbincus*, gripped *Friend Tony* and latched his *waddly wazzoo* precariously from a button hook. He abandoned his cape and crown, but then lifted *Hierarchus*.

"Here," he said. "A gift."

"I cannot take this."

"Not a gift for you, my friend, but for another friend, who I had hoped to see once more before I left this world."

Arquebus cocked his head, and then shrugged.

"For Elypticus," Harris said, emotion choking him. He glanced away, hiding a spontaneous tear. "I shall miss them all, you know."

"Be better cheered," Arquebus replied, taking *Hierarchus*. "My son will prize such a sword — *a brashun blade* from Lord Belmundus. He honored you."

"He was the pride of my *Danuwa*, Sir John, and now he grows like wild grass in *the Makronicans*. *The Gucheeda* has made him worldly and wise, I'm sure. He'll prove a great asset to you when he returns."

Arquebus held the sword to his forehead, and then bowed.

"The time is upon us, Lord Belmundus."

Harris sighed, and then gazed about his quarters, a thousand memories rushing him — memories which would crush him in the outlands and deliver Kuriakis' promised madness. This room would stalk him to the grave.

"I once asked you about the exit — the portal which would release me. You said you didn't know. Now I see you . . . you had a memory lapse."

Arquebus led his charge out.

"No lapse, my dear boy. No lapse." He stopped, and then turned, staring into Lord Belmundus' deep blue eyes. "Portals there are many, but free passage there is none. Only Sceptas and Seneschals can go freely between the worlds. Only Sceptas and Seneschals can grant us free passage in their wake."

2

As they strolled the corridors, Sir John continued his explanation.

"Think of *Mortis House* as a glove with many fingers," he said. "The palm is secure in *the Ayelli*, but the digits stretch and transform as they pass through the many outlands. I have known this, but knowledge and utility do not equate. In escorting you to your where and when, I am also a passenger in *Mortis House's* tentacles."

"But I know people — *Fumarcans*, to be precise, who have slipped into Farn accidentally."

"This is true, but it is not free passage. It is a trip over a stone and a fall off a cliff. Like all things under the suns, portals have flaws and every rule has exceptions."

They had entered *the Scullery Dorgan's* corridor, Harris smelling the cooking aromas. He hadn't eaten in a day and was suddenly alive to it. But Sir John rushed him along, babbling about how the Sceptas stood sentinel over the portals. To keep them waiting would be disrespectful. But Harris longed for *terrerbyrd in cream sauce*.

Suddenly, through the walls came Trones — arms stretched toward Harris, heads bowed, *waddly wazzoos* shimmering. Some held flowers, while others grasped parcels of food. Harris was touched.

"They like you, Lord Belmundus," Arquebus noted. "You have made an impression."

As Harris passed them, his heart hitched. He saw the sadness in their faces — swollen eyes and drawn lips. Then one began to sing, a doleful tune, heavy on both heart and ear:

> *Ya meni kay-ya,*
> *Datamon wazzoo besqua tlugagi.*
> *Spasatosdi misgahu?*
> *Wazzoo popo fatstahu?*

Soon the hallways hummed with this chanting. Arquebus picked up the pace. However, as they approached the doorway beyond *the Scullery Dorgan*, an old Cetrone woman impeded the way. She bowed her head and offered a buckskin-wrapped gift to Harris. Trembling, he took it, carefully unwrapping it. He whimpered when he saw it.

"*Selu gadu,*" he murmured.

"*Torii sgi na patli kani,*" the woman replied.

"What did she say?"

"She brings me corn bread, prepared and baked by her own hand, Sir John — a rare gift and an extraordinary effort."

Harris touched *the gadu* to his lips, and then kissed the woman's forehead. She smiled, and then bowed, stepping aside. The others took up the chant again.

> *Ya meni kay-ya,*
> *Datamon wazzoo besqua tlugagi.*
> *Spasatosdi misgahu?*
> *Wazzoo popo fatstahu?*

Harris rushed now, clutching the precious bread in his fist. He limped through the open door and into a small waiting room. Here he found a hard seat and collapsed. He let loose a flood of tears.

"I do not deserve it," he wept. "Their kindness is without limits."

"It is only bread, my dear boy. You are too affected by the gesture."

"I am undeserving of their hymns."

"They are a musical people and sing all the time. What did they chant? Did you understand it?"

Harris pushed Arquebus away.

"Of course, I understood it." He gasped, and then moistened his lips.

> *"Oh, spark of the world,*
> *A great lamp is extinguished by your going,*
> *Who shall save us?*
> *Who shall lift us to the light?"*

He shook his head, unconsoled.

"I don't deserve it. I've left *the Kalugu* in the lurch. I may have started this thing, but I won't see it through." He set the bread aside. "They put much trust in me. I'm a nineteen-year old actor, for shit's sake, who's lost his way through the looking glass. I'll be as mad as any hatter."

Arquebus stood imperiously, staring at his charge. He then pointed to another door — the way out.

"Through there, Lord Belmundus. They wait for us on the other side."

3

Harris wasn't surprised to see the Sceptas Soffira and Miracola standing sentinel by the portal — a round moon door ablaze with crimson light, like a laser oven. He was surprised by Charminus' absence, but he guessed when she divorced him (if that term could be applied) it was final. He bowed first to the lovely Soffira, she of the flaxen hair and Sir John's mistress. She grinned, and then pointed to the open portal. Harris looked to Arquebus, who had shut his eyes. So Harris turned to Miracola, she of ample flesh, who didn't grin, but waved her hand impatiently for him to enter. So he took a bracing breath, grasped *Friend Tony* and stepped over the threshold.

"Sir John?" he murmured.

"I am here, dear boy. Never fear. You will experience . . ."

No need to tell him because he felt giddy as the floor stretched like putty through a tunnel. He didn't move. He just rode the wave, trying to keep his balance as the fingers of *Mortis House* did their thing. A blinding light struck him and he could only think he was dead and this was the famous light which housed God. But it flickered to dim blue, and then subsided. He took a step and didn't fall — a good sign.

"Sir John?"

"I am still here. Move forward to the first door on your left."

Harris stepped cautiously to a plain door, which could have been a door in this world or any other. He pushed in and entered a sitting room. Sir John joined him.

"Sit and watch the lights."

Lights. Yes, the room streaked with lights, like a train passing through communities and cities and day and night and eternity. The pulsing mesmerized Harris and he sat by what may have been a window, except he couldn't see through it. He suspected he would see the outlands — fragments of other worlds — Plageris, perhaps, with its serpentine inhabitants or maybe the Red Queen's palace or the Bridge to Terabithia. The light lulled him to slumber. In this state he was beyond fantasy. He could see Littafulchee sitting in *the Kaleezo*, weeping for her loss. He watched as Detonto bound up Yustichisqua's wounds. He saw Joella's veil lift, her eyes tearing at her loss. But central to it all, he saw Hedonacaria, sitting in her casket, dark and dreary, speaking in whispers. *He is gone*, she said. *He is gone, but I shall tell you where he is.* He sighed and awoke to see Sir John staring at him, puzzlement on his face.

"I shall miss you, you know," Arquebus said. "We have not had anyone of your caliber through these gates in many ages."

"Cheer up," Harris replied. "The next one through might be Justin Bieber."

"Who?"

"Never mind. You're not making this any easier, you know."

"I am sorry for that."

Harris reached out, touching Arquebus' hand.

"I didn't mean that. You have always looked after my interests."

"I underestimated you," Sir John said. "I thought you would be a cock-up from the silver screen — much like Jack Batemore."

"Jack Batemore?"

"I mean, Lord Hierarchus."

Harris gasped. He remembered when Jack Batemore went missing. He recalled the headlines. He wondered if he had a headline like that, but he would never know, because he was *en route* to his own when. He might even arrive early and miss the glamorous Bo Peep at *Happy Pings*.

"I could have been as reckless," Harris said.

"But you have something that others see — something I did not see until Elypticus drew my attention to it."

"The Cetrone call it the spark," Harris replied. "According to *the Whisperers* of the *chisqua siti*, all consorts have it. Therefore you have it too. The Sceptas are drawn to it like a moth to a flame."

"It goes beyond that, dear boy. You have managed to shake loose the bounds of their magic. You have seen the truth of Farn. You have brought your own magic to the place."

"And I take it away with me." He glanced to the flickering wall, the pulse lessening. "I'm a thief in the night. I raised their hopes and then, through my vanity, I placed that hope in jeopardy. Now the outcome is nothing more than a game of *grusoker*.

Arquebus touched Harris' hand.

"We have arrived, Lord Belmundus."

"Truly?"

"Truly."

4

Harris opened the door, hesitating to watch if Sir John followed him. He did not.

"Why not jump ship?" he suggested to Arquebus.

"I cannot."

"You'd be free of Farn. Didn't you wish that also?"

"Once I did. I deserted a wife and two sons when Soffira drew me across the threshold. They are a distant memory now. I would be lost in this when, even with your guidance, I could not do it. Soffira has been good to me and I have Thirdlings. They still need their father's keen attention. If you had a Thirdling you would not be so quick to depart."

"I have no choice, Sir John, Thirdlings or not."

"True." Sir John raised his hand and gave the sign of peace. "Whatever the book of life has written for your course, think of me and Elypticus whenever you find your mind slipping into the abyss. Remember us fondly, even when your body begins to age and your career sinks into the sea. There is a place where decay is banished and that place holds the memory of your deeds high — an example for all, long after your beautiful head rests in the quiet earth."

He bowed. Harris fought back tears, quickly opening the door and emerging into the Victorian corridor he had once known. The creaky old staircase was there with its gargoyle ornaments. He remembered how he had first seen Littafulchee here, floating on her *zulus* fetching *Corzanthe* for her mistress. Such thoughts weren't helping him now.

Slowly, he descended. When he reached the foyer, the door opened, the grey light filtering across his dickey foot. He emerged onto the porch of 13-13 MacDonald Avenue and stood in Washington Cemetery.

"My goodness," he said, sighing. "I can't believe I'm back, but . . ."

He trundled down the porch stairs to the rows of grave stones, the prayer rocks still sentinel since the day Harris left. He saw the rusting gate beyond, opened as if to kick him out for trespassing.

Bing bong. Bing bong.

He gasped.

"2Gollies I be," he muttered, before realizing the signal came from the doors of the elevated train line. "Oh, God."

Harris turned around. *Mortis House* was gone. He trembled.

"2Gollies I be," he muttered, unable to keep his footing, even with *Friend Tony's* aid.

Harris Cartwright huddled beside the grave markers, bawling for all the wrong reasons.

Chapter Ten

The Prisoner

1

Harris hobbled into the SoHo Grand still dazed that he had landed back where he had started like some faulty Parcheesi piece on an insane game board. He had made the trip back from Brooklyn without a hitch and without being recognized. Perhaps his fame had disappeared in the few minutes he had been gone from the scene. He doubted it. There were a few fish-eyes aimed at his puffy shirt and weird brooch, but this was New York, after all, and the average citizen was inured to the bizarre and the unnatural.

When he entered the Grand, he supposed Tony was still waiting for him for breakfast and the ride up to MTV Studios for the Q&A. All Harris wanted was his bed, but he peeked into the restaurant anyway. There Tony sat tapping his fingers and feet, looking back to the door. He spotted Harris and stood.

"Where ya been, chary boy? Your *wavos rancheros* is cold now."

Harris raised his hand for silence, and then entered the restaurant, a waiter nodding to him. Harris indicated he already had a place at the table.

"I was detained," Harris said, looking at the mess of eggs on a fancy white-on-white china plate. "Couldn't be helped."

Tony cocked his head and surveyed him.

"You're different, mate."

"You just saw me. How am I different?"

"You've lost weight, and you're limping like a 'orny gay ostrich lookin' for a date."

Harris chuckled.

"I twisted my ankle."

"That was some bird you 'ad last night, but where d'ya get the fancy cane and that God awful bling." He sniffed. "And, I 'ate to say it, but you're not perky fresh in the aroma department."

"What? I showered."

That was a lie, but he did wash the battle scum off and hoped the scent of Farnian lemon lingered. Evidently, not.

"Well, your eggs are all fridgy. So you'll 'ave a short stack of something and be 'appy with it. Sit and eat. We gotta move."

The waiter came, pad poised and ready.

"I'll have . . . just *kawee* with *selu gadu*."

The waiter shrugged.

"Coffee and toast with butter," Tony chimed in. When the waiter withdrew, Tony pulled Harris into the chair and leaned forward. "What's with you, mate? What the bleedin' fook is a kawee and the Sadie gateaux. Some fancy cake? We don't 'ave time for it."

Harris stared at him. Then he remembered he had a pocket full of *selu gadu* and hungered for it, but he didn't dare take it out here. He didn't know how to answer Tony. *You're right, mate. I'm different. Oh, so different. Since you last saw me, twenty minutes ago, I've been shacked up with Goth Girl, hunted for Tippagore, acted in a Japanese-Shakespearean play, ruled the marketplace, almost died in the desert, got married and led a rebellion. Sorry I'm late.*

"Say something," Tony said.

Harris dipped his head to his chin and struck his *Columbincus*. Of course, nothing happened, but the gesture was weird enough to make Tony shudder.

"I'm sorry," Harris muttered. "I can't do this?"

"What? Breakies? MTV? Life in general, you sodden dick pussy?"

Harris pushed up from the table, grabbing *Friend Tony*. There was nothing more to say. His heart was breaking and he needed his bed — perhaps forever. He turned and trundled out, Tony's protests falling on deaf ears.

2

The room was miraculously clean — the bed made and fresh towels on the rack. This wasn't its state when he left, but at these prices, housekeeping kept an eye when the room stood vacant. Suddenly, he imagined a dozen invisible Trones rushing in, making the bed, vacuuming, tidying the wardrobe, folding the towels and polishing the mirror. He shook his head, trying to release these thoughts.

"It's beginning," he muttered. "The madness."

He knew it had begun earlier in the portal, but now Sir John wasn't here to help him through it. No one was here. He also imagined going to MTV for the Q&A and, when asked a routine question about his career, answering in Cetrone and other Farn gibberish. That would be one for the record — on tape and on YouTube within an hour. *Young star speaks in tongues unknown on this planet or on any other.* It could double as a publicity stunt for *The Magic Planet*, but it wouldn't fool the cast and crew. McCann would have his balls. He'd never work in Hollywood again.

"I'm not going," he stammered, and then bounced at the bed's edge.

His foot ached and he was hungry, not for *wavos rancheros*, but for his gift — the sacred food of the Cetrone. He edged his hand into his pocket and pulled out the buckskin packet. Lovingly opening it, his lips trembled. When this bit of bread was gone, he would never taste *selu gadu* again. Oh, there was old-fashioned corn bread, but not this. They ate *sqwallen* in *Mortis House*. This bread was a rarity and baked with absolute love and devotion. Each bite would caress him. He chipped off a piece. Raising it to his lips, his tongue caught the first morsels. *Divine.* In the sweet moist texture came Littafulchee's kiss, with its tart afterglow. In the buttery warmth, dwelled Yustichisqua's devotion, attending to his *oginali's* every whim and want. In each swallow lived Cosawta's feigned cursing, Elypticus' moral fiber, Melonius' growth, Parnasus' bravery and Buhippus' sacrifice. It was too much for him. Harris swallowed hard and wept.

Then he realized also in his pocket was his cell phone — *the sillifoon*, dead in this world beyond the *branchy-wanchies*. He slipped it out, studying its dead keypad. Then he glanced to the bed stand where a real phone sat. He grabbed the receiver and dialed. He was surprised he remembered the number, but his fingers did, despite the veil his memory had taken. He waited as it rang.

"Hello," he whispered, anxiety in his voice. "Mom. Is that you? Yes . . . Yes, it's me. Oh, I didn't realize what time it was. Sorry, but . . . but, I wanted to hear your voice. I wanted to say . . . Yes, I know. I know. Nothing's wrong. I'm doing okay, you know. Q&A, carpets, press, lights, just . . . flying about and seeing stuff and learning stuff and . . . and you know." He sniffed, and then wiped his nose. "No, nothing's wrong. I know it's early, but I'll be busy in the next few days and might not catch up with you. Is Sarah there? Oh. Hope she has fun. I'll catch her later." He pawed *the selu gadu*. "You know, Mom, I had the most wonderful corn bread the other day and . . . Corn bread. No, I didn't call you to tell you about corn bread. I just wanted to say . . . Well, we haven't said much to each other lately — you seeing Thad — and me being all over creation." He put the receiver to his *Columbincus* and stifled a tear. "I'm back. You didn't know I was gone? Well, just for a moment, you know. It only takes a moment. No, I'm okay. Hanging out with the Bentley-Jones guy and . . . No we're keeping out of trouble. Anyway, just called to say I love you and . . . goodbye."

He listened for a moment, and then hung up the receiver. He took another bite of *selu gadu*, and then grabbed *the sillifoon*. He turned, staring at the mirror — that constant reminder of his mortality. He shook his fist at it, and then hurled *the sillifoon*. The glass cracked.

"Shit," he said, tripping over *Friend Tony* to retrieve *the sillifoon*. "I'll pay for that one."

He stared into the glass. There were two Harris' now — two stars and, to his current apprehension, both were in decline. He clenched his fists, slamming them onto the dressing table. The two images were cracked in different places, much like his soul. Kuriakis was right. This would be his punishment — to remember it all until he could no longer live with his fellow creatures.

Harris Cartwright stood erect, and then touched his *Columbincus*. It was a dead thing, but it still inspired him to action. He glanced back at the phone, the real one which had connected him to the other coast. He would not go to MTV today.

Chapter Eleven

The Portal

The rusty gate was still ajar, the wind rattling the lock. Harris hung on the slats looking to the patch of ground where *Mortis House* had stood, briefly and twice to his memory. It would never appear there again. But somehow this felt more like home than anywhere else. He gazed at the line of tombstones — the Jewish Cemetery named for an American president.

"Ghosts," he muttered, and then pushed the gate opened and trundled to the first line of stones.

He had read these before. This time, among the Vernicks, Finckelsteins, Sterns, Zuckerbergs and Rothbergs, he might find a ghost — a lingering spirit to show him the way. If not, he was resolved to bury his madness here. He wouldn't share it with this world. It was better to let his memories consume him until some mourner reported seeing a strange drifter talking to the trees and peeing in the open graves. Then the men in white uniforms would collect him — gratefully, and he'd sleep forever taking *the sqwallen* dutifully, by the bowlful — glassy-eyed and addled until old age devoured him or some loved-one corralled him from public view.

He knelt before Zuckerberg's grave — a polished marble monument, with several prayer stones stacked at the corner. He wondered if he could pray and, if he did, whether God would hear him. It was lust which had brought him here the first time and madness the second, so why would prayer help him now? Hypocrisy. Still, he supposed praying for the long-lost and rested J. Zuckerberg, whom he had never known, couldn't disturb the universe. So he clasped his hands, bowed his head and mumbled *The Lord's Prayer*.

"*Oginali.*"

He started. Madness would not leave his prayers alone, he guessed. He shook his head and began again.

"*Oginali.*"

He looked up and nearly collapsed.

"Little Bird?"

Before him stood the ghost of Yustichisqua — had to be. But then the specter touched him.

"*Oginali.* 2Gollies I be."

Harris bolted up, grabbing the figure, pressing him into his arms.

"It can't be you, old man."

"It is, *Dinatli.* I am here."

"But how?"

Yustichisqua turned Harris around, facing the spot where *Mortis House* had stood. There, in full canopy, was *the Gananadana.*

"Good day, *Sisterfucker,*" Cosawta called.

"*Good day! Good day!*" came the Tomatly echo.

Harris also spotted Detonto in the gondola.

"It can't be." His excitement was boundless. "How?"

"Portals there are many," Cosawta said. "Free passage there is none. But I am a Seneschal and control the portals of the worlds. My mother, Hedonacaria, appreciated your prayers and listened well. She has told me where to find you."

Yustichisqua pulled Harris along.

"*Oginali,* I understand you will not want to leave your outland world, because you always wanted to return here. But just as 2Gollies I be, you have two homes too. I am sure you can come back here when you are homesick. But . . ."

"But we need you now, Lord Belmundus," Cosawta crowed. "You have kindled my sister and my niece will not be a bastard like my sons."

Detonto bowed.

Harris was stunned. He didn't know what to say.

"I'm to be a father?"

"It will be a daughter, if Nayowee is correct, and that bitch is never wrong." Cosawta laughed. "Get your ass aboard before the winds change and the portal shifts. I would not want to land in fucking Terrastrium."

Harris came aboard. He hugged Detonto, who broke it off quickly. Harris waved to Tomatly, who took the *waddly wazzoo* and added it to the others for propulsion.

"Second thoughts, Lord Belmundus?" Cosawta asked.

Harris grinned.

"None whatsoever."

"A father you shall be, *oginali,*" Little Bird said. "And I shall be an uncle."

"Yes. Yes. I can't think of anyone better."

"I might qualify," Cosawta said, not unkindly. "Bring us up, Tomatly."

"*Up. Up.*"

Harris gazed into Yustichisqua's eyes. Questions hung there. "What?"

"Nothing, *oginali*. I only wonder who has dressed you? We must certainly attend to that before the battle is rejoined."

"I missed you too, old man. I missed you too."

And so the spark returned to Farn to save the world entire.

Afterword

And so the spark returned to Farn to save the world entire; and in the next book, **Boots of Montjoy,** the tale will continue with many promises and prophecies — battles and endearments. The balance in Montjoy has changed — and thus it has in *Farn*. The realms are restless and the pit is stirring. Settlements are made, but will diplomacy succeed? Much for us to ponder as Lord Belmundus drifts in *the Gananadana* through the elusive portal to the foot of *the Gulliwailit Bridge*. Until then . . .

Glossary

Adadooski	Hallelujah
adanadasga	bakery
adatowetodi	kiss
adesegua	a pig
Agrimentikos	Consort, Krypto Melos
alisoqua	the bear clan
alsagi	Cetrone waddly wazzoo dance
Altacantris	a councilor
Ama Udali	Salt Lake
Amaykwohi Sea	the great lake of Farn
A-ni-lo-li-ga	thank you in Cetrone
aniniya	a power gem
Aolium	Realm of Air
Aquilium	Realm of Water
Arkmo	Amen
Arquebus	Consort, John Briarcliff –
asano	a skirt (or kilt)
asaylidodi	an oath
asdoyuwi	sausage
Asgay	wife
asi-asa	a healing place
asinoki	a jackass
asorba	pine
Asowisdi	The House of Light
Asses-assis	asi-asa
assinoki	jack-ass
asusdu	light
Atliyidee	stringed instruments
atsadi	predatory river fish
atsilu	darkness
atsinonunu	wound
Augustii	Zecronisian free agents
awidena	a lavender sheep
awi-eeni	deer
Ayelli	The conquerors of Montjoy
Banetuckle	the Place of Desperation
banibara	a granite building block
bed sit	bedroom
bettlebuds	mites
blundaboomer	a new fangled gun
Boboli Dikano Geesti	big bellied guitar
bobyfysmagu	hooray
bolingara	a cheap wine
bollinganga	a constrictor snake
boobooyaks	asses (backsides)

Book of Adjustments	the Tariff list
boomer-boomer	megaphone
borabas	phitron boots
borripsuns	a flashlight
Borsa-pu	the fifth island in the Makronican archipelago
branchy-wanchies	the internet
brantsgi	a better class of wine
brashun blade	an alloy of Columbincus and aniniya
Brega Bay	the port of *Dodingdaten*
Brisvegas	Brisbane
bronskers	aniniya lamps
Brunting Day	a sacred holiday
bucker	buckboard
buggeroo	byudra digging tool
Buhippus	captain of the Yunocker guard
bull catonin	the pancreas of the meadow ox
bupka	a kind of bread
bush oyster	snot
busker	a flip-flam man
Byllymycky	the Chief three of the Zocor council
byudra	beets
Byybykyyip	the open market
Cabriolin	a flying vehicle
caliseegee	sugar
cayna	beef
Charminus	Scepta of Montjoy
charpgris	tyyger piss
Chewohe	rite of passage
chippo	a computerize circuit board
chisqua	the bird clan
chumwhat	barley used in a porridge
chunder	vomit
Church of the Pontifraxian Orbitum	an orthodox religion
Coathanger	Sydney Harbor
Comastee	a mountain town
conontoroy	a metal used in zulus
Corn Eater	Southern Australian
Coroboree	an aborigine market festival
Corzanthe	an intoxicant
Cosawta	Littafulchee's brother
Coweeshee	alisoqua clan head
Cyprytop	a Gurt archon
Danuwa	a marshal
deedaloquasdi	a school
Deegosgi	an official Arbitrator
deetsaneeli	a crossing place

delfins	seagulls
Didadusi	the Nuckasee Hills
Didaniyisgi	a Provost
digali sodi alasulo	zulus
Digsa Gonana	The Weeping Road
Dikano Geesti	percussion instruments
dill	a dope
diluwopeen	a female bear, whose milk makes a dandy cheese
dinatli	brother
Dingo's breakfast	common and ordinary
Dodaloo	The Spice Mountains
Dodecadatamus	smaller of two suns of Farn
Dodingdaten	the colony of the outlanders (Fumarcans)
DoDingoDatenus	the Dodingdaten
dollywaggle	a low pull cart
donger	penis
Doonedin	the open market in Yunocker
dragget	a hunting dog
drongo	stupid person
dulohu	the act of cutting, particularly the skin
dunny	swamp
dunny budgie	swamp fly
Echota	capital of Cetronia
Elejoy	geetli clan head
Elohim al Fazir Galafindrus	the deity of all
Elypticus	a Thirdling in service
Enitachopco	Littafulchee's father
Equa Agatoli	The Eye
Euforsee	The chief Yodanado
fair dinkum	true to tell
fairy floss	cotton candy
fantin	jailers at the Katorias
figjam	people who hold a high opinion of themselves
Finistrians	the Pearl divers of the Makronican Islands
Forling	The desert
fossick	prospect for gold
fregallen	spinach leaves
fuggipantis	night soil
Fumarca	pirate
Fungimus	a mushroom
fustigars	troop carriers
fuveratski	a banana
Fyndicapus	a patrol leader
Fytzyfu	a Gurt steward

gadu	bread
galayidu	burn
Galoquodi gasoqualu	the sacred circle
Gananadana	the balloon ferry
ganuggle	crocheted vestments
ganuhida ligolu	the great Long House
Garan the Gucheeda	a piratical trader and official
gasohisgi	Yustichisqua's
gasuntsgi	vampire rabbit
gati-bati	a dragon akin to a predatory dinosaur
geetli	the dog clan
gespocular	spyglass
gigoo susti	the red smoke
gingergust	the red smoke
glassifon	clear, quartz-like stone
gobsmacked	dumbfounded
gollywi	a clan tattoo
Gonada Gigaha	the place of execution
gondercoils	hand restraints
googani	a giant spider
gorettle	center of the grusoker board.
gorsatsgi	baking paddle
gosaka gaheeni	a silly goose
granaydos	grenades
Greary Gree	the spirit of the Temple
griffies	stevedores
grumperian	a rat
grusoker	a gambling card game
Gucheeda	an outlaw
gudi	to weave
gufa	an elephant-like creature
gufawpup	a way bill or invoice
gugu	to have sex
gugubasgi	penis
gukpeckyns	a duck
Gulliwailit	a river separating the Yuganawu from the Kalugu
gwasdi	a whip
Gypysyp	a Ryyvty of the Ryyve Aniniya
Harandu	freebooter
Hasamun	Consort, Yorisaki Musahito
hawiya yukayosu	bacon
Hedonacaria	the Memer of Zacker
Hierarchus	a former consort
hilly gilly	every which way
hiloseegi	a sour fruit
Husgi	husband
hyryod	a tariff

i-nu wadi	grenade launchers
Itsayusi Yuweya	The Green River
Jamabispa	a Corsair
jellywhips	lethal gwasdi whips
jipjipjiptipu	yippee
Joella	The Memer of Montjoy
jomar	wheat
jupsim	a proofing material
kaleezo	servants quarters
Kalugu	The Cetrone ghetto
Kanaguda	The Meeting Square of the Kalugu
kanuwudi	recovery period
kaseegee	a native beer
Katorias	the new kaybar prison
kawee	coffee
Kaybar	penetrable building material
Keowee	a Cetrone enclave
Kero	kerosene
kibanaquo	extinct Cetrone clan
Kittowa	chisqua clan head
Korinkle	a knapsack
Kowlinka	red sand used in making ceramics
larrikin	a harmless prankster
Lily of Murrow	a sacred herb
liquid laugh	diarrhea of the mouth
Littafulchee	Cetrone maiden
little naughty	to have sex
London to a brick	exactly as expected
Lord Cheelum	Elector of Volcanium
Lord Dunaliski	Elector of Magus
Lord Grimakadarian	Elector of Zin
Lord Kuriakis	The Elector of Montjoy
Lord Lododi	Elector of Pontifrax
Lord Sestanum	Elector of Protractus
Lord Yama	Elector of Aquilium
Lord Yehohi	Elector of Terrastrium
Lord Yunoli	Elector of Aolium
Loribringus	a transport vehicle
lyricadim	gemstone denoting Cetrone royalty
lys	a light
Lyspykyn	the pavilion of light
Magus	Realm of Magic
majorin	business Yunocker class
Makronican Islands	a chain in the Amaykwola(y) Sea
mellowbeer	a drink made from mollicops
Melonius	a Thirdling in service
mikaruni	a bedroom
minorin	the trader Yunocker class

Miracola	Scepta of Montjoy
misancorpus	a sea serpent
mollicops	raisins
mongerhide	a tart sausage stick
Montjoy	Realm of Art
mopyn	an elastic building material
mordanka	Kalugu quartermaster warehouse
morggus	cockroaches
Mount Talasee	highest mountain in the Dodaloo
Mumpfredis	a councilor
Myrkpykyn	the Gurt courthouse
Naperonus	a dish cloth
navakawee	a navigational device
Nayowee	the Medicine woman
Nikodemos	Zecronisian elder
noya	sand
Noya Tludachi	dune tygger
Nuckasee	a Cetrone enclave
nunehi	a path
nuwodi	drugs or medicine
odala tludachi	a Mountain Tygger
old Fella	penis
open for lunch	farting in public
opening up a lunch stand	farting
osda	good
O-see-yo	hello, how do you feel?
Pajoquota	a town on the border between Cetronia and the Dodingdaten
Parnasus	a Thirdling in service
pashing	a hug and a kiss
perpadranum	a basket
pertupa stew	a pottage of ground lake crabs
phitron	building material
piece of piss	easy task
pikers	malingerers
pilocarpinus	antidote for sqwallen overdose
pimpsqua	a type of chair
Plageris	an island in the Bottleblue Sea
plonk	cheap wine (brantsgi)
pogo-pogo	a pig
pokiepen	a paddy wagon
Ponsetossit	Garan's ship
Pontifrax	Realm of Ritual
porcorporian	sand crustacean
porgeedasqui	deadly scarlet tanagers
Porias	the old phitron prison
Posan	Consort, Chang Wen
praeters	noble Yunocker class

Primordial Centrum	the great unknown
protastitorium	potatoes
Protractus	Realm of Science
prysyst	a poppy like seed
pukas midaskoos	a root of the midas herb
Pulveris stream	the legendary last river for Thirdlings
pulverkempin	healing herb
pupernisgi	a variety of hanging blossom akin to fuchsia
pykyn	a Gurt house
quillerfoil	barley
reaptide	a time of disposal of the dead or dying
regulati	the warrior Yunocker class
Ricktus Morphinus	Augustii spinctus of the Ryyve Aniniya
ridgy-didge	genuine
Ringus Mordancus	an Ayelli Month – April
rip-snorter	inventor (engineer)
road train	truck rig
Roses of Scaladar	flower of the Ayelli Hill
Rypchypy	a Ryyvyty of the Ryyve Aniniya
ryyve	a Gurt guild
Ryyve Aniniya	the Power guild
Ryyve Bomertoss	the Baker's guild
Ryyve Gudi	the Weaver's guild
Ryyve Pykyn	the Building guild
Ryyve Sulasgi	the Pottery guild
Ryyvyty	a Gurt selling agent
Sakwoladi	the Danuwa in Gurt
scratchy	scratch-off lottery ticket
Scullery Dorgan	the kitchen zone
Seecoy	an improved Cabriolin
seegoniga	the blue holly clan
selu	corn
selu gadu	corn bread
Seppo	an American
Sheepshagger	a New Zealander
shitter case	broken
shlombrera	umbrella
shonky	in disrepair
siti	the whisperer's place
Sittiquo	a sacred tree
sketchable	blueprints
snalligrogs	snails
Soffira	Scepta of Montjoy
Solus	larger of two suns of Farn
soogasdi	smoke
Spasatorium	The promised Savior
speckies	specifications

sqwallen	drugged porridge
sqwallen yehu	a drug den
stewganasti	muffin
Sulasgi	pots
sustiya	the old shelter
suweechi	omelet
Swede	a rutabaga
Taleenay	a provost's second
Ta-li Yu-do-we	He who has two marks
Tappiolus	Consort, Giovanni Muti
Tarhippus	General and city chief of Montjoy
Tassie	Tasmanian
terrapinsgi	tortoise
Terrastrium	Realm of Metallurgy
terrerbyrd	a pterodactyl
threadnickery	silkworm
Tippagore	a desert denizen
tludachi	tiger
tlugu	the tree clan
Toe-hee-ju	I am fine — how are you
Tomatly	assistant to the Ferryman
Toqua	a Cetrone enclave
torpeda	damn it to hell
Treaty of Parazell	Restrictive laws governing entrance into the Kalugu
Trelaw	ancient textile center
Tricentee	a Cetrone enclave
Tucharechee	tlugu clan head
Usquanigo	the Mystery Valley
Usti	baby
vargos	water pots
Villamorticus	Warder of the gate at the Kalugu
Volcanium	Realm of Fire
vyrjyt	an assigned workplace
waddly wazzoo	a rope lamp
wadi-wadi	hand grenades
Watoge	a Cetrone enclave
Whacker	Western Australian
wisgi	whiskey
Wudayleegu	the Zecronisian ward
Xyftys	a Gurt tailor
yahuli	a horn
yarrow tarrow	a sweet herb used in tea
yedalas	currency (money)
Yeholo	the three moons of Farn
yehu	house
yichiyusti	green sky conditions
Yigoya	the showroom

Yinaga	The Forling desert
yiyutli	measurement — 1.3 miles
Yodanado	the whisperers
Yudolayda Asdodi	the secret door into the Kalugu
Yu-do-we	a tattoo
Yuganawu	The Yunocker ward central Montjoy
yunogolada	rainbow
Yustichisqua	Harris' Trone
yustunalla	a metal used in Cabriolins
Yutumi Dikano Geesti	harpsichord
yuyenihi	barbed wire
yuyona	a drum
yuyoyi	bad
Yuyuli	trail of tears (weeping road)
Yuyutlu	the Gurt ward and marketplace
Zacker	Realm of Light
Zin	Realm of Darkness
Zinbear	a mythic 12 headed monster
Zocor council	the Zecronisian high command
Zocorpykyn	the Wudayleegu customs house
zugginak	an attack dog
zulus	flying sandals

Also Available

No Irish Need Apply **ISBN 1434893952**
Cutting the Cheese **ISBN 1434893847**
Bobby's Trace **ISBN 1434893960**
The Closet Clandestine: a queer steps out **ISBN 1438220502**
Come, Wewoka & Diary of Medicine Flower **ISBN 1438227639**
Surviving an American Gulag **ISBN 1438247230**
Turning Idolater **ISBN 1440422109**
Look Away Silence **ISBN 1448651921**
The Road to Grafenwöhr **ISBN 1460973860**
Are You Still Submitting Your Work to a Traditional Publisher? **ISBN 1441407383**
A Reader's Guide to Author's Jargon and Other Ravings from the Blogosphere **ISBN 1468071432**
Oh Dainty Triolet **ISBN 1451535376**
The Academician - Southern Swallow Book I, **ISBN 144149975X**
The Nan Tu - Southern Swallow Book II, **ISBN 1449994202**
Swan Cloud – Southern Swallow Book III **ISBN 1466499591**
The Jade Owl **ISBN 1440447977**
The Third Peregrination **ISBN 1441456724**
The Dragon's Pool **ISBN 1442170999**
The People's Treasure **ISBN 1453850813**
In the Shadow of Her Hem **ISBN 1478203064**

Edward C. Patterson has been writing novels, short fiction, poetry and drama his entire life, always seeking the emotional core of any story he tells. With his eighth novel, The Jade Owl, he combines an imaginative touch with his life long devotion to China and its history. He has earned an MA in Chinese History from Brooklyn College with further postgraduate work at Columbia University. A native of Brooklyn, NY, he has spent four decades as a soldier in the corporate world gaining insight into the human condition. He won the 2000 New Jersey Minority Achievement Award for his work in corporate diversity. Blending world travel experiences with a passion for story telling, his adventures continue as he works to permeate his reader's souls from an indelible wellspring.

His novel *No Irish Need Apply* was named Book of the Month for June 2009 by Booz Allen Hamilton's Diversity Reading Organization. His Novel *The Jade Owl* was a finalist for The 2009 Rainbow Awards.

Published Novels by Edward C. Patterson include *No Irish Need Apply, Bobby's Trace, Cutting the Cheese, Surviving an American Gulag, Turning Idolater, Look Away Silence, Oh, Dainty Triolet, The Road to Grafenwöhr, The Jade Owl* (Jade Owl Legacy Series Book I), *The Third Peregrination* (Jade Owl Legacy Series Book II), *The Dragon's Pool* (Jade Owl Legacy Series Book III), *The People's Treasure* (Jade Owl Legacy Series Book IV), *In the Shadow of Her Hem* (Jade Owl Legacy Series Book V), the Southern Swallow Series (Book I – *The Academician*, Book II – *The Nan Tu*, Book III – *Swan Cloud*), and The Farn Trilogy (Book I – *Belmundus*).

Coming soon: The Southern Swallow Series (Book IV – *The House of Green Waters*; Book V — *Vagrants Hollow*), The Farn Trilogy (Book II – *Boots of Montjoy* and Book III – *The Adumbration of Zin*), and *Green Folly*.

Look also for Dearest *Flower of My Heart — Mail Call from Two Generations, Plum Flower Journey* and *Nicholas Firestone – China Hand Series*.

Poetry books available are *The Closet Clandestine: a queer steps out* and *Come, Wewoka & Diary of Medicine Flower*. Coming soon: *Pacific Crimson — Forget Me Not*

Also – Non-fiction: *Are You Still Submitting Your Work to a Traditional Publisher?* and A *Reader's Guide to Author's Jargon and Other Ravings from the Blogosphere.*

Dancaster Creative <u>www.dancaster.com</u>

From my mind to your imagination . . .

Printed in Great Britain
by Amazon